OTHE RWOR LDST HANT HESE

LUKE BRAM / LEY

José,
thank you so much for
your support! Any (other!)
typos, please let me know
Luke _LB_

PublishDrive

Published by PublishDrive Inc.
541 Jefferson Ave Ste. 100, CA 94063
Redwood City, California 94063

Publication date: January 1st 2022

ISBN 978-1-7398109-3-1

Author: Luke Bramley
Email: lukehollinbramley@gmail.com
Address: 272, St Helen's Road, Hastings, TN342NF
Website: www.otherworldsthanthese.uk

Please direct all enquiries to the author.

PART ONE

"It is the secret of the world that all things subsist and do not die, but retire a little from sight and afterwards return again."

—RALPH WALDO EMERSON

Chapter 1.

The Accident

AFTER DREAMS AND BEFORE waking came a drifting feeling that for a few moments felt like hope. Groping for it with sly fingers, Will sensed it melting away just before he could grasp it. A thin pattering of rain on the window. He opened his eyes to see birds on a poster, the dangling tendrils of a spider plant, its leaves stirring in the heat from the radiator. The wintry half-light glowing behind the curtains made everything in the room seem both heavier and more diffuse.

Feeling only half there, he tried to coax his waking form back towards the netherworld, unwilling yet to inhabit the life that had taken on acts and forms other than his choosing and beyond his control. But opening his eyes had been a mistake. Though he closed them now, he'd already seen too much—the toy car he'd found in a drawer, the damask wallpaper his thirteen year old self had picked out to reflect his burgeoning maturity, that silly poster—all of which were only too eager to remind him of who and where he was and who and where he wasn't.

So many times as a boy, he'd woken in that very same bed and lain there gauging the light, the sounds of the house, the feelings in his body, trying to guess the time. Wind or rain or sunshine at his window gave him a clue to the weather. Sliding a foot outside the duvet told him something of the temperature. Harmless childhood games. Now waking in a bedroom that was no longer his felt like waking up in clothes that no longer fit.

He'd thrown his mobile phone aside in his usual, half-drunken manner and had to feel around on the floor for it. Finding it under the bed, he checked his messages. Several missed calls—all from Lorenzo. Nothing from his wife. Knowing that tomorrow— Christmas Eve, no less—was the start of Ruth's maternity leave, he dashed off a quick text: *Missing you. It must feel good knowing tomorrow's your last day. Would love to come over x*—sure that, as with all previous efforts, it would go unanswered, before groping for his dressing gown.

Following the smell of burnt toast down into the sunroom, he found his parents bickering about something, though the moment he walked in, they both looked up, his father, a short, olive-skinned Albanian with shrewd brown eyes, pressing his lips together, his mother smiling, her plump, English face creasing into its usual lines, her blue eyes sparkling as she spoke.

"Will, darling, we have a surprise for you."

His father had been eating a boiled egg. His teaspoon, which he placed now beside his plate, was smeared with yolk. He glanced at his wife, then spoke in his usual, thickly fermented accent. "We've noticed you've not been going out. We thought you might get out more if you had your own car."

Will felt a momentary excitement—a brief opening of vistas, followed by the suspicion that his father was goading him. You're twenty-six, he seemed to be saying, you should be able to afford your own car.

Perhaps sensing his thoughts, his mother hastened to reassure him. "It's a Christmas present, darling. Nothing expensive, just a little run around."

"I've called Piotr," his father said, as if this were the most important point. "He has something in mind."

A qualified engineer, Will's father had arrived in the UK to find that his credentials were not recognised. Undaunted, the man had found work at a garage just outside of Ashling and when given the chance had bought the place. Soon, nearly everyone in the village was taking their vehicles to Avni's, Will's father being known for his expertise and for his good humour—and also for the bright-eyed boy who, every Saturday, accompanied him to work.

Will used to get up to all sorts of mischief there, opening anything and everything he could get his hands on, pots of paint, boxes of nails, drawers full of toxic substances and tools that might have doubled as torture devices. To him, the forecourt and the workshop and the yard behind it were places of flux, to be shaped by whatever whimsy entered his head.

Perhaps that was why, when Avni finally sold the place, claiming that he wanted to spend more of his time writing (though he'd also been suffering from arthritis), Will had experienced an unexpected sense of loss. It had been years since he'd thought of the place and yet the idea that he might never return there, though he hadn't, even for a minute, imagined doing so, felt as if he were losing some vital piece of a puzzle he'd not known existed until that moment.

Except that his father's announcement that morning meant that he was going to go back after all, if only for one last time—and in the same beat-up old Saab he'd been driving all of Will's life. A lesser man would have scrapped the thing years ago but Will's father was a stubborn old goat and not once since he'd sold the garage had he let anyone else so much as touch the 900. The only thing he couldn't do was sign off the MOT. Instead he had to take the car back to the garage that had once been his and watch while Piotr Wójcik, the Pole who'd bought the place, pored over the car's every inch with what Avni described as an unseemly relish.

"As if I can't sign my own papers," he grumbled as they got into the car that day, their mission having reminded him of this particular indignity. "Can't a priest hear his own confession, a doctor heal his own wounds?"

In fact a priest couldn't hear his, or *her*, own confession but Will knew better than to mention it. Best to let the tic run its course. Instead he listened to the familiar drone of the exhaust and stared out at the town, feeling as if, with the simpler days of childhood gone and both of them having grown apart, he and his father were two strangers sharing the same time machine.

They found Piotr in the workshop, his head under a car bonnet, the insect-like buzz of a ratchet vying with the tinny music springing from the little black radio propped on the vehicle's carburettor. After one last twist, Piotr wiped his fingers on a rag and turned to shake both of their hands with a firm grip. He was wearing his usual outfit, a grubby blue vest and overalls. He gave them the usual smile too, a

9

wry, grey-stubbled pursing of the lips. It was a smile that welcomed company, if only so its owner could gripe about the state of the world.

"Goddam government," Piotr said cheerfully as Avni pumped his hand, "got me over a goddam barrel."

After slapping each other's backs, the two men strolled out onto the forecourt, leaving Will to admire his old playground in peace. Inhaling the scents of oil and rubber, he experienced a surfeit of pleasure. The car Piotr had been working on was parked over the grease pit. Another lay jacked up on its side. The shelves were crammed with grimy-looking rags and tubs of Swarfega. Chests of drawers stood open, revealing hundreds of tools, wrenches and ratchets and socket sets, many of them layered in grease. Just like the forecourt, everything looked exactly as his father had left it, a fact that filled him with a strange sense of relief.

The two men had walked over to a three-door Vauxhall Chevette, its red paintwork flashing in the afternoon light. As Will joined them, his father was peering under one of the wheel arches.

"Needs new tyres," he said. "I wish for at least six months tax too."

"Well I wish for new liver and quiet wife," Piotr said, winking at Will. "But we can't always get what we want."

Invited to do so, Will climbed into the car. His father had lifted the bonnet and he could hear the two men talking about the tyres again but when he slammed the door, all was peaceful. He breathed in the comforting scent of pine. Everything was tidy, the red leather seats worn and comfortable, the dials and the radio antique looking. He liked it all. He ran his hand along the dash, then leaned forwards to check out the glove compartment, only to spy the top half of his face in the rear-view mirror. A forehead crisscrossed with dark hairs, staring, denim eyes, the protuberance at the top of his nose. But no mouth. Without it he lacked something vital. Emotion. Depth. Something.

For some reason, the sight filled him with a disturbing premonition: His father must not buy the car. He'd never been so sure of anything in his life. But even as he reached for the door handle, his phone started buzzing and he found himself scrabbling with the flap on his coat pocket, trying to extricate the thing before it stopped ringing. Fishing it out just in time, he thumbed the answer button and said hello without knowing who it was.

He heard a distant, rushing sound, like a car going past a window, its resonance contorted by the amp—saw abstract shapes move just below the upright bonnet in front of him that may or may not have been the two men—and then the person on the other end of the line said his name. "William?"

Only rarely did Ruth call him William. They might be lying in bed, her leg draped over his, her eyes as clear as a cat's, her voice playful as she said something like, 'Why, William, you do look handsome tonight.'

Now though, her voice, stripped of any playfulness, sounded only reserved and slight and more than a little stiff. Unsure what to say, he asked if she was calling from work.

After a Ruth-like sniff, she said, "I was going to call you later but I figured I'd be too tired, so . . ."

She sounded tired already but he resisted saying so. Instead he asked after the baby. The subject brought the blessed hint of a smile to her voice. "Always kicking. It's like she wants to come early."

Such intimacy must have proved too much, though, for a moment later, Ruth called the meeting to order. "You got a letter," she said with a brisk sniff. "From the school. I wasn't going to open it but then Lorenzo called. He's been trying to get hold of you. He said you'd moved back in with your parents, that you've not left the house. It got me worried, so I opened the letter." A clink of gold as she shook her head. "Will, it says you've been suspended. What happened? Are you in some kind of trouble?"

So this was why she'd phoned, she was worried. And there was him hoping all was forgiven. The raised bonnet swam in a red haze. How could he even begin to tell her what had happened?

"I just . . . I'm out with Dad right now. Believe it or not, he's buying me a car." He actually laughed, the sound wet with emotion. "When we're done, I could drive over. We could talk face to face."

"I don't know." Another silence, in which he waited with bated breath, followed by slow, hesitant words. "The truth is, I've been worried that if I saw you again, that if I even spoke to you . . ." He heard her breathe in, then sigh. "But when I got your message, you remembering that tomorrow's my last day? It sounds silly but it felt nice. As soon as I got it, I just wanted to call and tell you that I miss you." She sniffed again and he wondered if she'd been crying. "That's all. I miss you."

The haze fell apart and tears rolled down Will's cheeks. Finally he managed to say something, the words bubbling in his throat. He heard her say something too and then they both ended the call. Afterwards, he sat there, aware of a weight in his chest, a sort of simmering gold that rose up and up until, finally, it burst out of him, leaving him feeling cleansed. He had not, until that moment, realised quite how much pain he had been in.

He heard a clang as his dad dropped the bonnet into its housing. A decision had obviously been made, for Piotr was making his way along the side of the car, a set of keys dangling from his middle finger. The old Pole was smiling and didn't seem to notice that Will had been crying.

"Starts first time," he said as Will took the keys.

And he was right.

ii.

BACK AT THE HOUSE, his mother was making tea. "Don't drive home tonight," she said, offering him a cup.

"That obvious?" he asked.

"A little." Her voice hinted at a smile. "It's just, I think once Ruth's had the baby, she's going to want you around. But I'd wait until she asks."

He didn't want to tell her Ruth had called. It was too precious, too close. He'd hoarded secrets ever since boyhood, when he used to carry a jotter around with him and make notes of things he saw and heard. Swear words, both in English and in Albanian, the filthier the better, though he preferred the Albanian, words like *lesh* and *mallkoj*, which sounded to him both more barbed and more barbarous. He'd once dedicated the top shelf of his wardrobe to secret things, dead beetles with hooks for feet, a jay's wing with its luminescent patch of blue, broken bottles and pots dug up from the garden. Too often, when one told a secret, it became tarnished. When his mother found his secret stash, she'd forced him to throw everything away.

"Birds are covered in lice!" she'd said. "And beetles, what do you want with dead beetles? You're not a wizard."

He drank the tea in the Chevette, fiddled with the radio, found a few stations, then switched it off. Inspecting the car's gleaming red body, his pleasure deepened. Piotr had said he'd change the tyres after Christmas but they looked fine. Hearing the front door, he turned to see his father standing on the doorstep, his gnarled hands thrust into the pockets of his cords.

"It wasn't my idea to get you a car," he said, as if Will needed telling. "Actually, I was making you something. It's not quite finished but if you've got a moment, I'd like to show you."

In the hallway, Will was caught by the faint hint of lavender and of the lemon oil his mother used on the furniture, which never failed to bring back memories he only recalled in their presence.

Upstairs, another surprise awaited him. All his life his father had kept his study in an orderly fashion. Now though, the room looked as if it had been ransacked. Both the tallboy and the bookshelves were groaning with papers and books. The walls were stacked with boxes, sometimes three or four high. Even the table on the far side of the room, normally kept conspicuously uncluttered, was all but hidden by several Airfix models and a number of tubs of grease containing what looked like engine parts.

"The very day I told your mother I'd stopped writing, she happened to have one of her brainwaves." Avni was moving some of the rolls from a box so Will could sit down. "Apparently she wanted to revamp the house." He turned and brandished a roll of brightly-printed cloth. "But so far not a single cushion!"

He'd stopped writing. Will had been too wrapped up to notice. Not hearing—or *imag*ining—the thud of his father's fingers, it felt as if the house's heart had suddenly stopped. He asked why but his father had already moved on.

"This is what I wanted to show you," he said, revealing a triangular arrangement. "You remember you wanted to build a kite?"

Will vaguely recalled his Teto Karrina buying him a kite making kit when he was younger, only for his father to 'accidentally' snap one of the spars, before claiming that it was obviously made from inferior material.

"As soon as she's done, we'll take her out," the man was saying, "see if we can't get a few cartwheels out of her . . ."

Yet beneath his enthusiasm, Will sensed something else.

Finally the man said, "I'm not very good at helping, Will, that's my problem. Not with this kind of thing."

The study door was still open and Will glanced at it but Avni was quicker. "Please," he said, pushing it to, "sit. *Sit.* I don't wish to interrogate, I just, I'd like to help if I can."

Will did as he was told, if only to avoid his father's watchful gaze, for though the man's brown eyes were opaque in nature, the clear splash of green in his left pupil had always given him a hint of the clairvoyant.

"Had I been better," Avni began, "more open, maybe . . ."

"This isn't your mess, Dad."

"No but . . ."

"But Mum asked you to try."

"Maybe. Listen, let us have a drink." Avni opened a drawer and removed two glasses and a bottle, its label adorned with a double-headed eagle. "Did I ever tell you your grandmother once beat me for stealing a shishe just like this?"

He brandished the bottle before leaning forwards and gripping Will's knee. "But I was so drunk I didn't feel a thing!"

As the Raki slid down Will's throat, the brief, intense heat felt good, as if he were celebrating some minor triumph.

"Ruth rang," he said, the slipperiness on his lips allowing this precious secret to slip out. "I think it's going to be all right."

"I knew she'd come round," his father said, refilling his glass. "And the baby?"

"Kicking like a mule, apparently."

"Fighting spirit," Avni said, turning and raising his glass to the map on the wall. "After all, she is *Shqiptar*. Sad to think she might never see the country of her origins."

Will had only been to Albania once, when he was young, and recalled no more than a few fleeting impressions. Wide, dusty squares, wizened old women, dozens of mangy-looking cats and a kind old man who'd given them tickets to some sort of show. Much clearer, he saw the Albania described in his father's stories: tall scarps and narrow gulleys, horses skittering among rocks, wide, sweeping valleys lush with meadow flowers, mountain passes guarded by hard men with well-oiled rifles. Yet at the same time he was aware of another Albania, a superimposed ghost that had been stretched into a kind of howl.

"Perhaps we could go together," Will said, taking another shot. The words and the sweet burning sensation that followed them felt good, as if intention and sensation were momentarily one.

Avni's eyes were like wrinkled fingertips pinching at his tears. He said it would make him very happy.

Will shrugged. "It's all I've ever wanted."

"And all you've ever done," Avni said enthusiastically. "Listen, I raised the best read boy in England. "Let me tell you something, a *se*cret. All those books I put by your bedside. You'd pretend not to read them but I knew!" He wagged a finger. "Why do you think I kept replacing them?"

When Will blushed, his father gave his hand a rueful little pat. "Your obstinacy will never be a match for my cunning. Those books did not come cheap," he said, reaching for the bottle. "I mean, second-hand, sure, but you got through so many."

Will looked at his father. The man was a good writer. He'd had several stories published, most of them set during Enver Hoxha's dictatorship and each one torn like a cancer from his brain. Yet, Will thought, the world was already forgetting its monsters. Or too busy making new ones.

"All this though," Avni said, waving his hand, "you're managing okay?"

Will tried to smile. "I think the problem is I don't know who I am anymore."

"Who you are?" his father said gently. "You are my son. No," he said when Will went to speak, "you are my son, a proud young man of whom I am proud. And you come from a long line of proud people, all of them making mistakes because of this flaw of theirs, this pride. It's like a fault line running through the Zifla gene. Our people have been overrun for a thousand years, driven up into the mountains, across the seas. But have the invaders ever defeated us where it matters, in here?" He patted his chest. "No! Perhaps if we were better at taking the slings and arrows that have beset us over the years, we would not fight. But we are fighters, Will, it is in our blood."

The man's eyes had filled up and he was nodding. They sat like that for a little while, neither of them speaking and then, as if talking about himself, Avni said, "This is who you are. Our mistakes do not define us, only what we do with them."

He nodded again and then said perhaps it was time for bed. "But we will go together one day," he said, eyeing the map one last time. "I like that."

As Will stood up, his father pulled him into a hug. With the man's hand cupping the back of his head, Will found himself staring down at the kite. "It looks like an eagle," he said.

"Then it is an eagle," his father said. "When are we going to let her fly?"

Will looked at him. "When you start writing again."

"Easier said than done." Avni seemed to think for a moment and then raised an emphatic finger. "Writers must give their imaginations free rein, yet at the same time, they must rein them in." He shook his finger. "They must let go even as they hold on. It is this paradox we must nurture if we wish to write. But not long before you came home, I found I'd been holding something very tightly and when I looked down, I saw I'd crushed it. That is why I stopped writing." He wrinkled his nose. "I lost the knack."

"But not forever," Will told him. "You must finish your novel."

"And Ruth," Avni said warmly, "you must trust her."

But there was in his look and in his touch, something else, as if he wished to say more but though Will saw it, he said nothing.

iii.

THE NEXT MORNING, Will called Lorenzo and they agreed to meet at the pub. Wandering through to the living room, he found his mother sitting on the sofa, a shoebox on her lap. She was wearing what she called her Rousseau shirt, a blouse patterned with a jungle scene that she only ever wore it when she was in a good mood.

"I'm meeting Lorenzo at the Dog and Duck," he said.

She met this announcement with a look of amazement. "You're going out?"

"I'm not a nun, Mum," he said patiently. "I am allowed out."

"Yes, of course," she said. "Oh, but I think it's wonderful that you two talked."

He wrinkled his nose. "Actually," he said, "Lorenzo and I tend to grunt."

"You know what I mean," she said happily. "Your father came to bed last night smelling like a brewery. He said you'd like to go to Albania. Then this morning, I remembered you asking about Sazan Island, so I decided to dig out the photos. Nobody's allowed to visit the place at the moment but your father knew someone, so we were given a pass. We spent the whole day swimming in the caves there. They're thinking of turning the island into a nature reserve."

While she spoke, he looked at the photographs. Sazan Island lay off the coast of Albania and was made up of dramatic cliffs, vaulting caves and slanting bays, their slopes covered in ash and oak. In one photo he could just make out the tip of a lighthouse. Of all the stories his father told him when he was a boy, his tales of his time on Sazan

17

were the most exciting. But when Will had asked him about it more recently, Avni had told him different stories, how the place was riddled with tunnels and bunkers designed to survive a nuclear strike. Those odd pillboxes, he said, that Hoxha had built all over the country to remind his countrymen that an enemy attack was imminent.

"The Soviets had a chemical weapons plant and a submarine base there. It was actually pretty scary. When I fled Albania, I was running away from that place too."

Apparently now, though, they were thinking of turning the place into a nature reserve. A paradise made in hell. His mother showed him photos of vine-choked buildings, glassless windows, piles of abandoned gas masks. "It was like two worlds, one laid on the other. Rather like this box," she said with a smile. "I went looking for photos of our holiday and underneath, I found these."

In the photo she passed him, he and his father were both holding fishing rods. Avni was staring at the camera, the green flash in his eye particularly bright-looking. Will, who must have been seven or eight at the time, was wearing a hat that obviously belonged to his father.

His mum tapped the photo. "Remember when we used to call you Whim, because you couldn't say your own name?"

He hadn't heard the nickname in so long, he'd forgotten about it. The truth was it had always annoyed him.

His mother showed him another photograph, an early colour print. A woman wearing a white dress in an open top car, half-turning, smiling back at the photographer, one hand holding down a wide-brimmed hat, a blue scarf billowing beneath her chin. Behind her, a rocky landscape fell into a deep valley.

"You?" he asked.

"Yes," she said.

He told her she looked beautiful and she blushed but then nodded and they laughed. He picked another photo from the box, a black and white.

"You too?" he said. The woman in the photograph looked the spitting image of Elizabeth. The man beside her wore a dark suit, his hands clasped behind his back. He had pale, bruised-looking eyes and a strong chin.

"No," his mum said. "Your grandparents, my parents."

"Nana Constance? I can see where you got your looks."

His mum laid a hand on his cheek, her eyes sparkling. "Thank you for last night. I know Avni can be difficult." He tried to protest but she shushed him. "I know," she said. "But when he does unravel himself, it's usually worth the wait."

The saloon at the Dog and Duck was as Will remembered it, long and dark and smelling of wood smoke. Seeing Will, Lorenzo jumped up from his seat and gave him a hug. He was heavier than Will remembered, his cocoa-coloured skin darker, his hair shorter. Will touched it and Lorenzo laughed.

"My auntie cut it," he said, his voice as mellifluous as ever. "In Trinidad. We just got back. Mum insisted we get a little winter sun."

Between sips of beer, Will talked about Ruth, relieved to be able to unburden himself to someone he trusted. Lorenzo couldn't believe that she'd kicked him out. Just, as he said, because he'd kissed another woman.

"I mean, it's diabolical," he said, not without humour. "But a kiss? Surely grounds for counselling, not eviction?"

"It was a little more than that," Will said. "She found my journal. I'd written some things that were hurtful to her." He shrugged. "The important thing is that she called me yesterday. Thanks to you, apparently."

It was Lorenzo's turn to shrug. "I was worried about you. You weren't answering any of my calls, so I phoned her instead. I'm sorry, I didn't know what else to do. I'm surprised you didn't call Eric," he added unexpectedly. "As her brother, he probably knows her better than you do."

"How do you know I haven't called him?" But then Will shook his head. "It's true, though, I haven't. Maybe I should have."

"The guy's pretty dope," Lorenzo said. "Ruth mentioned an article he wrote recently. I looked it up. It was very interesting."

Surprised, Will asked, "What article?"

"He called it 'Fractured Dimensions'. I thought you'd know about it. It was published in *Nature* so I figured it must have some scientific grounding."

Will couldn't believe his ears. "Scientific grounding? When have you ever cared about science? At school you were about as interested in science as you were in watching paint dry."

"Of course!" Lorenzo said. "Nearly everything on the syllabus was boring. But that doesn't mean science is boring."

"So you call Ruth," Will said, his tone growing cooler, "because you're worried about me and you end up having a nice cosy chat about Eric?"

Lorenzo was drinking while Will spoke. When he finally put his glass down, his eyes had a stormy look about them. "Listen, Will, we've been friends since the first year of primary school. The first day, practically. I will always have your back. So whatever weird thing you're suggesting, may I suggest you *un*suggest it?"

Realising he was right, Will said he was sorry and then tried to gloss over his error by asking about the article. It was a double-edged move, for though this gave Lorenzo the space to dutifully lay out the article's hypothesis, something about how, converse to popular thinking, creating certain limits under certain circumstances might expand one's imagination in such a way that one was literally able to create another world, it also meant that Will was forced to just sit there, not really listening, wondering what kind of a person he'd become.

"Anyway," Lorenzo said, his grin already reigniting, "the article got me thinking. What if we could all have that kind of power? To create new worlds? To follow a path that avoids all pitfalls?"

His beautiful eyes shone with a dreamy look now. "First I'd get the body, then the tattoos—a blazing phoenix right across my back." He laughed at Will's expression, the sound finally free from impediment. "You should come to Trinidad. We could go together, work with our hands, feel the sun on our backs, drink rum." He leaned in. "Spend our nights roving dark alleyways."

Will shook his head as if disappointed. "You haven't changed. Still as perverted. What about Karen? What does she think of your plans?"

Lorenzo winked at him. "I'll just have to make sure she doesn't find my journal, won't I?"

iv.

WILL TOLD LORENZO he was going home but as he stood there in the pub car park watching his friend drive off, he decided to go and see Ruth's mother instead. He didn't like how things had gone with Lorenzo and needed a little flagellation and there was no one better for that particular job than Veronica Fairweather.

By the time he reached Montrose Avenue, it was almost dark. Ruth's mother stood squinting in the doorway as if she hadn't been out in days, then sat him in the kitchen while she hunted out the kettle. He watched her search through piles of clothes, her cardigan hanging round her shoulders like dried seaweed.

Needing something to say, Will asked about Eric's article. "Have you read it?"

Veronica peered round at him. "You want me to call him?"

Will wondered if she was teasing him. He hadn't spoken to Ruth's brother in months. Yet he couldn't help feeling sorry for her. After his father had died, Will had heard that Eric had started working on one of his dad's old trawlers. If so, it must have driven his mother to despair.

"Actually, I came here to apologise. For what happened."

Veronica set two mugs on the plinth and sat down. With her dyed black hair and dark cardigan, all Will could really see of her was her face. Everything in it looked screwed down like she was waiting for a storm.

"What you did is inexcusable," she said. "And while she was pregnant too. What were you were thinking?"

When he didn't answer, she said, "Ruth's very proud. Once she gets scuttled up, it's hard to get her out." This last comment though seemed to set her on a different track. "Then again, I also believe you shouldn't throw stones in glass houses." She got up, fetched a bottle from the pantry, added a few drops to her coffee, before sipping at it. "Truth is, there are those who'd never stray and she's one of them. But then again, there are those with their noses so close to their navels, why would they?"

She peered at Will as if she only had one good eye. "Do you remember the time she came back to Ashling? You'd been married, what, less than a year?" She tapped the plinth. "She called her father that weekend. Bad weather'd brought his boat in and she phoned him to ask his advice. Not a thought about how worried he'd be. And when he said *no*, when he said she should think of *you*, she did it anyway."

"Did what?" Will said, confused.

Veronica leaned forwards and he could see in her face the breath she was holding, as if she could feel the poison in her words. "Had an abortion." Her words rattled in her gullet. "She got pregnant but decided not to tell you. Said it wasn't your decision. Then blow me if a year later she only wants another one."

Will's first thought was that Veronica was lying. That she was being spiteful towards Ruth for some reason. Towards him. Yet it didn't feel like a lie.

He floated down the hall, opened the door to the blue-orange glow of evening. "You had to know," Veronica said from somewhere behind him. "All I'm trying to say is, she's no right passing judgement."

v.

NIGEL'S WAS STILL OPEN. Will bought a quart of vodka and settled in the churchyard. Silhouetted stones stood around him, their writing erased. An old hawthorn tree spiked the darkness. He wanted to write out his feelings but it was too dark. Besides, he didn't have a pen. When the pain clamped down, writing was like cutting, the ink as good as blood. Only drinking provided a comparative relief. Raising the bottle, he toasted his 'not-first-born' with the first sip.

Back home, he found his father's study door open and peered blearily across the threshold, again recalling how tidy it used to be. Not that he went in there much as a kid, especially if his father was typing, but there had been a time when he'd regularly crept across the threshold.

He'd known his father wrote stories but hadn't read any of them. So one day he'd asked his father to read him what he was writing. Avni had looked at him as if sizing up his soul and then, with a rather sorrowful shake of his head, had said no. They're horror stories, he'd said. Maybe when you're older.

A few weekends later, Will had pretended to be ill. Then, after waiting until his father had left for work, he'd crept into his study and turned on his computer. The desktop had not been password protected. Even so, despite searching every file, he'd found nothing. Giving up, he'd searched Avni's wastepaper bin instead, there to discover several screwed up pieces of paper, the contents of which provided exactly the kind of insight he'd been hoping for, passages his father had obviously been dissatisfied with but that were nevertheless at once thrilling and horrifying to the boy: one about a man who went for an interview, only to find that it was being conducted by the secret police, another about a woman pregnant with twins who had died in a car crash. Will had read each one with great avidity and had even kept a few. Stepping into the room that night then, he felt an all too familiar sense of trespass.

The kite was leaning across the Airfix models as if protecting a brood. His father had pinned an Albanian flag to the wall, a large rectangle of red cloth emblazoned with a black, double-headed eagle. Not for the first time, Will wondered why it had two heads. Was it a matter of the past and the future? He'd been shown a glimpse of his own past that afternoon and didn't like it. Another world broken off, another path untrodden. And of his future? Ruth was going to call him again tonight and he wondered now what he would say to her.

It was in this mood that he realised he'd nudged the mouse. His father's unfinished book blazed on the screen. Sliding down into the seat, he read the first line, something about a man lost at sea . . .

A while later, he heard shoes being scrubbed on the mat and was filled with a sudden alarm. If his father caught him—but this was different. He wasn't a child anymore. What he'd been doing need not remain a secret. He would go down and tell his father he'd been reading his book and that he must finish it.

The living room lamp cast angled light across the walls. Avni was sitting in a chair near the fire wearing a wax jacket and a white shirt with a button-down collar. He was sifting through his fishing box but looked up as Will walked in.

"Not one fish," he said, as if that had been his intention.

Will opened his mouth to tell him about the book but for some reason blurted something else. "Dad, what would you write about if you hadn't been through what you went through?"

"Something else," Avni said, still sifting through the tray. Realising that this was not enough, he nodded to himself for a moment. "William, there are some things so painful, most people cannot look at them. But those who want to write *have* to look at them—right into the heart of the flames. They have to embrace the pain. I watched my whole family torn apart. This you know. I told you last night that I'd stopped writing because I'd lost the knack. That wasn't entirely true. The truth is, I grew sick of looking into those flames. I'm in there too, you know? Burning away." He turned slightly in his chair and glanced at his son with an oddly bashful expression. "I didn't lose the knack, I lost the *nerve*."

Will couldn't help feeling as if his father were trying to tell him something else but before he could ask him what, the phone rang. Straightaway he thought of Ruth. A few seconds after it rang off, his mother shouted them from the kitchen.

She was dressed in a flour-dusted apron, the sleeves of her Rousseau shirt rolled up to reveal plump, braceleted wrists. It took her several attempts to replace the receiver and Will realised she was upset. When she turned to look at them, her eyes were very round.

"The baby's coming," she said.

"But it's too early."

"She was on a flight to Manhattan. The plane had to return to Gatwick. An ambulance is taking her to Crawley. It's the nearest hospital. She gave them our number. She wants you there."

When he didn't move, his father said, "She needs you, Will. Go grab your coat."

The feeling that had dogged him all day settled over him, dark and billowing and full of vague fires. When his father picked up the phone, Will asked who he was calling.

"Eric," Avni said. "He's her brother. He needs to know."

Upstairs, Will jerked open a drawer, causing its contents to spill forwards. He was looking for his keys but saw instead Eric's cassette recorder. He pulled it out, then dug through the piles of pens and abandoned CDs until he found the book of poetry Eric had given him. If Eric was going to be at the hospital, he might as well return them to him. The thought enabled him to move.

Downstairs, his father was pulling on his boots. "Eric's in Portsmouth," he said. "He's got to fix a bulb in one of his headlamps. He should reach the hospital about the same time we do."

"We?" Will said, when his parents went to follow him. "It's my mess. I need to sort it."

"You're upset, William," his mother said. "You need us there."

He shrugged bitterly. "If you guys want to come, fine. Just don't go telling me everything's going to be okay."

He pulled the seat forwards before stepping aside to let his parents climb into the back. After juddering along the lane, he took a right, was aware of the road into town only as a series of lights. He switched on the radio. Snowstorm voices came and went before he found a piano piece, its notes as clear as crystal.

"Moonlight Sonata," his father said promptly, "Wilhelm Kempff."

It was the first any of them had spoken.

Will watched his parents' faces glow and fade in the rear-view mirror. One after the other, drops of water began to break across the windscreen and soon they were driving through a downpour, the rain so loud on the roof, the noise all but drowned out the radio. His mother made an amused noise and then said something about God's little stage notes. Her timing was perfect and just like that the tension evaporated. Will said he was sorry.

"What was that?" His father was leaning forwards.

Will spoke up. "I'm *sorry*. I'm just worried."

His father's voice was full of a glib irony. "Well you shouldn't be. Worry is a misuse of imagination."

Will smiled at his mum in the mirror, saw her smile back and recalled the photograph. Everything would be fine. Doctors worked miracles these days and none so regularly as childbirth. The baby was only four weeks early and Crawley was a large town. It stood to reason it would have a good hospital. That was when he smelt the alcohol on his breath. In all the excitement, he'd forgotten he'd been drinking. It was such a shock, he nearly hit the brakes and imagined the car sloughing across the road.

Thankfully, the M25 was fairly clear and they were soon off it, though by the time the Chevette's tyres crossed the M23 slipway, if anything the rain had increased. Just as he took the turn for Crawley, his father pointed out a brook to their right. Will caught a glimpse of it through the trees, its surface like boiling oil.

"It's been quite a year for floods," Avni said loudly.

The road wound away from the brook and they passed a petrol station. Streetlamps floated by like Chinese lanterns. Everywhere crashed with rain. Will slowed down, worried he'd miss the sign for the hospital but then the headlights lit up a red sign with a white H on it and his mother shouted from the back. "It said a mile and a half!"

Surprised by the sudden appearance of a roundabout, Will hit the brakes and before he knew it, the car had almost collided with the central reservation.

"Steer *in*to the skid!" his father shouted.

Recalling what Avni had said about Eric, Will asked why he was driving with only one headlamp.

Still speaking loudly, his father said, "This thing with Ruth caught us all by surprise, it's no one's fault."

The next stretch of road ran parallel to the brook again, which flashed at them from beneath the roadside barrier. They crossed another roundabout and then the road went over a bridge so that the brook ran to their left. To their right lay a small housing estate, bordering a school and playing fields, rugby posts rising out of a mournful marsh. They saw a second sign for the hospital, the road straightened out and Will sped up. After that, they could have been anywhere, some black planet where it rains forever.

For some reason, Will was thinking about what Lorenzo had said about Eric's article, how limiting one's senses could increase one's imagination. He and Eric had discussed such ideas before, he realised.

"Ayrs' Der Todtenvogel," Avni said as another song came on the radio. "Your mother used to play this when she was pregnant with you." Will sensed him leaning forwards to read the clock on the dash. "One minute past. We make good time."

The rain was thundering on the car, erasing the world. Will glanced at the rear-view mirror. "This is the song?"

When his mother spoke, he thought she was answering. "I think we missed the turning."

After that everything happened in slow motion. Feeling his mother's hand, Will glanced over his shoulder, unaware that he was pulling on the steering wheel. When he turned back, he saw a bright light in the opposite lane. At first he thought it was a motorbike but then realised it was a car, its driver's side headlamp broken.

Too late, he pulled on the wheel.

As if all their hearts had stopped at once, there was a moment of stillness and then a bang as the wing mirrors collided, followed by a bright flurry of sparks and a noise like a knife being drawn through steel. With a final flurry, the other car vanished into the rear-view mirror. It was all over in little more than a second and had Will not hit the brakes, things may have been all right. But he did.

As if flicked, the Chevette spun end-to-end on the wet tarmac, scribing a perfect halo of light. The steering wheel was useless. They were moving very quickly, yet everything felt very slow and very peaceful. The music was a single note drawn in a circle and then they hit the barrier and all became very, very violent.

As Will found out later, the railing at the edge of the road had fallen into disrepair so that when the car hit it, it acted more like a seesaw than a barrier. He heard a crumpling sound and then the car was rolling up and over the barrier and sliding down the embankment towards the brook.

After a long, tortured scream and a grinding of sparks, the car hit the water with a thumping crash, jerking Will against his seatbelt so hard that he smacked his head on the wheel. Dazed, he fell back to see the windscreen splintered, the rear-view mirror askew. In it a wave rose down and water crashed up and he realised that the car was on its roof. He saw his mother's hair hanging in long, wispy curls, her jacket bagging around her shoulders, his father's eyes like diamonds set in knuckles of flesh. Both of them were struggling with their seatbelts. And everywhere water hissing through the seals.

He closed his eyes. When he opened them, he saw a black sheet rising inside the car, water, much deeper in the back than in the front. He reached for his seatbelt, aware of his weight on the belt, knowing that if he pressed the button he would fall but pressing it anyway. He did not fall. He looked down to see that he was pinned to his seat by the steering column. He heard gasps, his parents trying to keep their heads above water.

His mother called his name and he tried to turn. He kept thinking, what have I done? He had a sick feeling in his stomach, as if he'd seen something he couldn't unsee and then on all sides there rose a host of red flecks, each one shooting upwards and then falling down. And with each one he heard a voice inside his head say, Të kam shpirt, të kam zemër, eja dritën e hënës, eja shiun, më lash dhimbjen. I have a soul, I have a heart, I have a soul, I have a . . .

And the words were fire and the fire was cloud and the cloud was bursting and then the throbbing in his thigh became so intense he blacked out.

2

RUTH REACHED THE AMBULANCE just as it began to rain. While one paramedic closed the doors, the other asked her to change, then checked her cervix. Ruth stared at the ceiling, only dimly aware of the woman's probing scrutiny and of the gurney's cold padding through the gown. The baby—*Fay*—had been underweight the whole pregnancy and now she was coming four weeks early. Rain drum-drummed on the roof.

They put her in a windowless room decorated with NHS posters and a jar of plastic flowers. The midwife, a rounded, red-cheeked woman, kept asking if she wanted gas and air and if she'd brought any music and if she'd settled on a name. Ruth didn't care. All she could think was that her little girl was early.

She asked after Will.

The nurse was fiddling with her pillows. "I'm sure they'll do their best to get here."

Feeling the start of another contraction, Ruth said, "He's only coming from Kent. What's that, fifty miles?"

The nurse said, "I think they had car trouble."

Next came a tiny woman with a red dot on her forehead and a firmly serene air, who asked Ruth a hundred questions, none of which related to Will. "Baby is fine," she said finally. "If all goes well, you'll be home in a few days."

Recalling the midwife's words, Ruth asked if her husband and his parents had arrived. The two women exchanged glances and Ruth knew she'd scored. Will wasn't travelling alone.

The registrar, obviously the mother of several children, told her not to worry. "Baby come first."

Except that what actually came first was a night and a day of labour, battles in which Ruth bore down and breathed in, sucked at the gas and then bore down some more. She couldn't describe that time. She didn't remember most of it. What she did recall was the midwife's glassy smile, as if Ruth had given her a disappointing gift, her tone as she told her the baby's heartbeat had dropped, that she'd have to have a caesarean. To wage war for that long, it was a kick in the teeth.

Just over an hour after being given the epidural, an exhausted little bundle was placed in her arms. It was only for a minute but it was still precious. Ruth felt numb, as if she were hovering somewhere else. She imagined herself looking down as if at the survivors of some battle. At Imperial, she and her girlfriends often crawled in around that time, the streets filled with a grainy light, their makeup smeared around their eyes. For Fay and her, this was their first night on the tiles.

Ruth woke with something like a hot wire across her abdomen. She lay staring at Fay's crumpled skin, her tufted hair, the bluish slinks each time she squinted. Careful to move her midriff as little as possible, Ruth lifted her out of her cot, sank her nose into her hair, sniffed like an addict at her damp, kittenish head. Someone had dressed her in an oversized bodysuit, placed socks over her hands. For Ruth, life had always been a tightrope of carefully placed choices. But now she was no longer walking that rope alone.

They'd wheeled her onto the ward in the near-dark. Now though it was morning and she could get her bearings. Her bed was in a corner of the ward next to a window welded shut. There were two other new mothers there, one four beds down, the other in the opposite corner, as if the nurses wanted to keep them apart. Ruth kept glancing at the entrance, hoping to see Will come striding onto the ward. She wondered if he was downstairs buying chocolate. Somehow though she doubted it. The tightrope quivered and she stood very still.

Only after Fay's feeding time did they come. Only after the baby had coughed herself into a red rage did two orderlies and a nurse line up at the foot of the bed. The doctor was young, with red hair. He had a bulging forehead, the limbs and torso of a runner. Ruth wondered which was crueller. First God giveth red hair, then He taketh it away.

Dr Needlemire, as his badge declared, was not one to beat around the bush. He told her Will's car had been in a collision and had crashed off the road into a stream. He hugged at his clipboard as if it were bulletproof. "I'm afraid Will's parents were trapped in the back." He had the decency to clear his throat. "Unfortunately, the car filled with water and they both drowned."

Ruth was staring at Needlemire. She felt as if she were seeing things, as if, were she able to rub her eyes, he might disappear.

"Your husband received a blow to the head," he said. "The steering column punctured his abdomen. There was a lot of internal bleeding. Someone called the emergency services but what really saved his life was the angle of the embankment."

Ruth breathed in the sweet smell of colostrum. How painful, she thought. A mire of needles. "He's in a coma?" she said distantly.

"Yes." Needlemire was nodding like one of those toy dogs that sit on the parcel shelf. "But that's not all. Your brother was in the other car. It hit a tree. His injuries are more severe." He squeezed his clipboard. "He suffered massive head trauma. Recovery is unlikely."

"Unlikely?" she said.

The orderlies tensed. Needlemire rubbed his forehead.

"Yes. But your husband's prognosis is more favourable. In fact," he said, squinting *un*favourably, "by our prognosis, he should be awake."

ii.

LIKE MANY SUCH INSTITUTIONS, Crawley Hospital was one of those rambling, much-added-to buildings that's always being improved and yet is never done. Everywhere Ruth went, she saw long, white corridors dotted with insipid prints and the kind of doors that whisper as they close, yet if she listened closely enough, she could also hear the whine of drills and the flap of plastic.

Will's room overlooked the car park and was decorated with cream-coloured curtains and a grey carpet. Someone had left a Bible on the bedside table, and Ruth had to resist the urge to place her hand on it. Nor was this the only sign of life. Beside it sat a pair of glasses that obviously did not belong to Will, on the nearest chair, a print of the hospital's fortnightly menu and a December edition of Hello! magazine, its cover graced by a celebrity couple she did not recognise. Will lay as if asleep, his forehead taped up, his left leg elevated and heavily bandaged, his foot swollen and waxy. The sheet hid his crotch and Ruth left it that way. Between the bed and the far wall stood an ECG machine and an unused ventilator. Needlemire had said Eric's coma had been caused by severe blood loss and hypoxia. Will's was different.

Ruth touched his arm but his skin felt strange, cool and slightly clammy. She tried to talk, to tell him about the birth, how beautiful Fay was, how much stronger she was already. Yet she kept picturing Elizabeth's eyes, so like Will's, so like Fay's, their blue faded as if by the water in which she drowned.

Her own eyes filled with sudden, exhausted tears. "Don't you drown too." She struck the bed with surprising force. "Don't *you* drown too."

Eric was in the next room along. Visiting him was also difficult, though for different reasons. Unlike Will's, her brother's room was like a still life, a place out of time. No half-eaten apples or half-drunk cartons, no clothes tossed on a chair, no books laid open at a certain page. Just Eric propped on pillows, a camera either side of him, a large, unlit monitor on his right, seven or eight on his left, white and blue and clear tubes everywhere. Eric's lip was taped and an oxygen mask lay against his cheek, though most of the time he breathed unaided. The first time Needlemire had taken Ruth to see him, she'd found herself staring at the heart monitor, convinced that if she looked away that little line would stop jumping and Eric would die.

She used to feel the same about aeroplanes. That if she didn't watch them all the way across the sky, they'd come crashing down. She knew it was nonsense but it became a habit. When she was just five, her mother had told her that the Fairweather gene was flawed by ill-luck and suicidal impulse. It wasn't just Veronica's usual hysteria either. Ruth's grandfather had died young and one of her uncles had killed himself. Eric was born with the umbilical cord round his neck and their mother once suggested that it wasn't by accident. They'd been in a caravan somewhere and their father was out and Veronica had woken Ruth up stinking of cider and cigarettes and made her sit with her in the little back bedroom while she smoked and talked in the dark. "Watch this space," the woman had said, as if urging Ruth to contemplate an empty coffin.

She'd always thought that was the reason she started watching the sky. Looking for a way out. Yet at the same time she could never leave Eric. That was why she found visiting him so hard, knowing she'd failed.

iii.
———

WHEN NEEDLEMIRE NEXT visited, Ruth noticed he seemed wary of the nurses. He said he wanted to speak to her but before he could say more, a nurse rustled over to say it was Fay's lunchtime. The doctor grinned and turned away. As if afraid lunch was already being served, he glanced back, asked if he could speak to her later. "I've got something I need to show you."

On his return, he talked for maybe five minutes. Afterwards, Ruth sat staring out of the suicide-proof window, then began dressing Fay. She was allowed to take her for short walks as long as she dressed her warmly. Ten minutes later she found herself on a swing in the park behind the hospital. It was very cold and she nestled into Fay's neck, drawing the smell of regurgitated milk into her lungs and swinging back and forth until a leaden calm crept into her limbs.

Needlemire had told her two things. With Fay gaining weight, they were being discharged. She thought about Will and Eric. The idea of leaving them behind felt strange. She hadn't even taken Fay to meet Will yet. But when the doctor told her his second piece of news, Will suddenly became the last person she wanted to see.

33

Back inside, she asked one of the other new mothers to watch Fay and took the lift to the second floor. Will's face glowed like ivory in the low winter light. Surprised by a sudden pining, she reached out, her hand hovering in mid-air, arrested by the image of Needlemire clutching the toxicology report, one ginger-knuckled finger resting just below the figure stating Will's blood alcohol concentration level. "More than three times the limit," he'd said, in case she hadn't understood.

"More than three times," she said, her words blood-thick in her ears.

When the man behind her spoke, she jumped as if she'd been doing something wrong.

"You can only blame yourself."

She turned to see an oldish-looking man, his skin grey, his balding head skull-like in its dips and curves, a worn white coat hanging from his stooped shoulders.

He seemed familiar but she couldn't place him. "Sorry?"

The doctor spoke in a shrill, off-key voice. "I said you shouldn't blame yourself." He loped forwards, held out his hand. "Sorry, we haven't met. My name is Dr Keep."

His hand felt dry, like cardboard, and she let go of it as soon as she could.

He told her he'd been looking for her. "Right now this young man is going through quite a battle. But," he piped, "the good news is his vital signs are in fact quite lively."

The man was quite a talker which was actually a relief after Needlemire's taciturnity. He suggested she sit in the far chair.

"It came as quite a shock to us all," he said, settling in the chair nearer the door. "In truth, he should be awake. I suggested to my colleagues that maybe his condition's somehow self-induced. I believe that in order to help him, Ruth—sorry, may I call you Ruth?" When she nodded, he said, "I believe we must be honest with him, Ruth. He needs to know his parents are dead."

Having guessed what he was going to say, she was already shaking her head. "I can't."

"Of course you can," he said shrilly. "He can't face what he's done. We need to set him free."

Ruth looked at the doctor's stained white coat, the blunt pencil and round glasses poking out of his breast pocket. "But isn't that your job?"

"You'd like me to tell him?" Keep didn't even try to disguise the disappointment in his voice. But after a resigned cough, he nodded. "So be it. He's running away. Soon he may have gone too far. Someone must tell him what he's running away from." He shook his glasses from his pocket, pushed them onto his nose, picked up the clipboard at the end of Will's bed. Replacing it, he cleared his throat and leant forwards.

"Hello, William. My name is Dr Keep. I would like you to listen to me." He paused as if gathering energy. "I'm afraid, young man, you've been in a car accident. You are in a coma. I believe you could wake up but that you don't want to."

Ruth got up, walked to the window. Her temples were throbbing, an underwater sound punctuated by the checkout beep of Will's heart monitor. The wind was combing the trees at the edge of the car park and she tried to imagine herself caught on the updraught, drifting up and over the houses . . .

"You knocked your head against the wheel," Keep was saying, "but that doesn't explain your state. Your scans show nothing alarming. We can only conclude that your condition is self-induced, that you don't want to face what you've done."

The words reached Ruth through a low roar. Even so, she wondered if the bleeps were getting faster. She felt the tightrope beneath her feet sway and knew she ought to look down but couldn't take her eyes off the trees.

"William, your car came off the road. It landed in a stream, boot-first. Your parents were in the back."

Ruth watched her reflection stare through her, heard the roar in her ears as if it were the wind.

"You were fine. The slope of the embankment saved you. But your parents, your mother and father, it seems they couldn't undo their seatbelts. Their belts jammed and they drowned. Water would have dashed in from every side. They wouldn't have stood a chance."

"Stop." It was too much, too real and at the same time too unreal. Yet even as she spoke, she realised she'd been right, the heart monitor was definitely bleeping faster. She turned to the doctor, her own heart swelling with hope. "Is he—?"

But even as she spoke, an alarm started beeping.

Keep clambered up. "Sit, *sit.*" he said. "Just a precaution. I'll get a team in here right away."

He marched out. A moment later, Ruth followed. She heard voices, turned to see Needlemire and several other members of staff hurrying towards her. He told her to wait outside before rushing into the room.

iv.

RUTH SPENT THE NEXT two hours in a waiting room adjacent to the maternity ward trying very hard not to think about what had happened. There was nothing she could do and being this powerless was not something she was used to. She'd just finished writing a difficult message to her mother when Needlemire appeared and began pacing back and forth, his tone reminiscent of a law student friend of hers who used her to practise his orations.

"Will suffered a relapse," he said. He was holding a ballpoint pen and kept clicking it on and off. "We managed to stabilise him. His brain's unusually active. Normally, a coma is the body's way of rejuvenating itself, a kind of hibernation. Nearly all functions slow down or are suspended. But if anything, Will's brain has done the opposite." He stopped pacing. "But why were you in there, I mean, besides the obvious. What did you say to him?"

She thought about it, almost told him, then said, "I'm not feeling too well. I haven't been sleeping. I was hoping you might prescribe something."

"It's complicated when you're breastfeeding. But come and see me before you go," he said. "I'll see what I can do."

She didn't go. She thought about it but the idea of contaminating the breastmilk put her off. Before they left, however, she did take Fay to meet her father. It was the right thing to do. Placing the baby on his chest, she watched her paw at his gown and neck, tears pricking her eyes. Yet at the same time, as if her tears had released her, she saw her hand, seemingly disconnected amid the glimmer, settle on Will's head. Touching Fay too, she felt a kind of electricity pass between them.

In Eric's room, she forced herself to look at her brother's face. Less than ten percent. That's what Needlemire had said. Less than ten percent of such cases ever wake up. And only a few of those who do make a good recovery. He'd suggested all Ruth need do was sign a few forms and it could all be over. The thought filled her with a sickening jolt each time she recalled it.

The ride home was dreadful. She kept her arm across Fay the whole way so that by the time the taxi drew up, her arm was numb. As she got out, the house seemed to radiate an alien energy. Not that there was anything overt. The whole street was full of similar-looking Victorian terraces. It was just that she'd already spent several weeks alone in the house. The thought of being there with a new-born was almost too much.

Except that such was not to be the case, for as she stepped up onto the kerb, she saw that someone—her mother—was sitting on the low redbrick wall in front of the house. She was holding a present, something for the baby by the wrapping. Ruth was so surprised to see her, she almost dropped her keys. Veronica had only visited twice since her husband's funeral. In fact, she left Ashling less and less. The last time Ruth had seen her, she'd seemed washed-out. Now though, dressed in a long grey skirt, lamb's wool cardigan, ivory-coloured blouse and red-beaded necklace, she looked almost glamorous.

They sat on the sofa while Ruth opened the present. Wooden building blocks. Somehow, the gift seemed appropriate. After that Ruth told her mother what she knew. Veronica wanted to hear about

Will but only in a distracted way. She was much more focussed while Ruth was talking about Eric.

"But he'll live?" her mother said.

Ruth had been told that when they brought Eric in, he'd had intracranial damage and wasn't expected to last. The doctors had fought for two hours to stabilise him. They'd performed an emergency tracheotomy, put him on a ventilator and taken him to theatre where a surgeon had managed to relieve the haematoma. They'd immobilised his neck and taken a spinal x-ray but the results were inconclusive. Measures were taken to clear the cervical spine but the true extent of the damage could only be assessed if he regained consciousness. And right now, Needlemire had said, it's a big if. On the Glasgow Coma Scale he's a three, completely unresponsive.

Ruth told her mother about his face. He'd broken several bones, including those around his left eye, his left cheekbone and his jaw. She said the doctors didn't want to perform reformative surgery until he regained consciousness.

"The extent of the damage is hard to tell until he wakes up. But he's a fighter," she said, trying to muster a lighter note.

Hunting the hope in her voice, Veronica said, "He is, though, isn't he?"

Ruth nodded. "He just needs the right cause."

"Well now he's got it," her mother said, as if sealing the deal.

3
———

THE DAY OF ELIZABETH and Avni's funeral was cold and windy. People kept spilling into the church and blinking at the candles. Ruth waited while her mother dipped her hand in the stoop and then followed her to the front. The only person on the front row was Grandma Constance, her frail body swathed in a black taffeta dress and scarf. Apparently the woman had once threatened Elizabeth with disinheritance if she married Avni. The thought had always hardened Ruth against her. Yet the sight of her now swept all that away. Ruth knew Constance's last stroke had left her face paralysed on one side, yet she wasn't quite prepared for the sight of her. Her skin drooped, as if her cheek had partially melted. She looked confused when Ruth greeted her but when she finally recognised her, her face lit up.

"Ruth!" she said, loud enough to ring the bells. "And who's this?"

Risking the wrath of the funeral gods, Ruth lifted Fay from the pram and handed her over. As she pulled Fay inwards, Constance was nodding.

"Got her father's eyes," she said.

"And yours," Ruth told her.

After the service, Father Michael led the congregation out into the cemetery. Will's parents had reserved a plot at the back of the church under an old hawthorn tree. That part of the cemetery was raised and Ruth glanced back at the church to see a stained glass Christ looking as if he might stroll out of the window and cross the grass. A liquid somewhere between rain and snow hovered in the air, soaking into their hair and clothing. The priest's voice, the sight of the two boxes, the dark earth, the grass and trees made greener by the rain, all were so similar and yet so different to the summer's day they'd buried Ruth's father's empty coffin, it was as if she'd stepped into a parallel universe.

During the wake, Fay was treated with even more reverence than other new-borns, perhaps due to her being born so close to her grandparents' death. Before Constance was taken home, she sought Ruth out. "Take Fay to him," she said, her face puckering like a wave. "Her light will bring him home."

Ruth knew she ought to check on the Zifla house. It would have been easy while she was in Ashling but she couldn't face it. Instead, she asked her mother if she'd like to visit Eric. She didn't feel up to that either but Constance's words kept ringing those bells.

When Veronica saw Eric's face, her face crumpled into a teary mess. Ruth watched her approach him, almost touch him, then touch him. "Oh, my boy," she kept saying.

Murmuring something about going to see Will, Ruth picked up Fay's car seat and slipped out of the room. The corridor was so bright that the light seemed one with the reek of ammonia. Breathing it in with her usual reticence, Ruth marched the sixteen steps that separated her brother's room from her husband's before pausing. Will was not alone. Through the observation window she could see, sitting on the far side of his bed, a large man, with long, greying hair pulled back into a ponytail, some sort of brochure clutched in one of his meaty looking hands, his lips moving as if he were reading out loud.

When she pushed at the door, the man was so startled, he leapt up, a smile trembling on his lips like someone trying and failing to blow up a balloon. "I'm so sorry! I shouldn't be . . . I should've . . ."

He offered his hand, before just as quickly retracting it. Flapping the brochure in his hand, he said, "I'm Graham, Graham Bull. The hospital chef. I, I just . . . sometimes between shifts I like to visit one or two of the patients. I figured, just because your husband's in a coma, why should he miss out on the culinary delights on offer?"

He presented her with the brochure, which she realised was a menu of sorts.

The smile blew up and stayed for a moment, further crinkling the man's small green eyes. "I just reckon if he knew what he was missing, he'd spring out of bed." He grinned now with all his teeth. *"Loose Belts Sink Hips'*, that's my motto—No, I'm only joking, though I quite like that one. What I'm really thinking is," and here he drew his hand through the air as if describing a vision, *"Eager Patients on a Meagre Budget'."*

As Ruth placed Fay's car seat on the carpet, she noticed her watching the chef with the same attention she gave the television. "But isn't it cruel?" she said, feeling a little cruel herself. "I mean, if he can hear you, isn't it like talking to a thirsty man about water?"

The chef shuffled along the side of the bed and stepped towards Ruth, treating her to a waft of body odour.

"Please, take it," he said, offering the menu again. "Plenty more where that came from." The man's guilt was almost charming.

"Hospital food gets a bad rap. The budgets are cut to the bone and most of the chefs are just counting the seconds down to their next day off. But if you're going to do something, you might as well do it right, right?" The man obviously took Ruth's smile as acquiescence because his enthusiasm all but bubbled over now. "I grow herbs in the hospital gardens, get everything shipped in from the local area: Spuds from Shipley Bridge, greens from Pease Pottage. This week it's been all about my fish stew."

"So where'd you catch the fish?" Ruth asked, her smile widening.

"Well, *mostly* local," the chef grinned.

Nor was that the last Ruth saw of the man. Two days later, she'd just returned to her car in the hospital car park when someone rapped on the roof. Whoever it was, was standing so close to the car, all Ruth could see was the side of a stained white tunic. She wound down the window to be greeted by a familiar grin.

"So what brings you to this grey and pleasant car park?" the chef said, before reddening. "To see, ah, yes, of course." As usual though, the man's smile was not so easily defeated. "One of the porters here has a boat moored up at the Brighton Marina. We're going down there tomorrow to do some fishing. When I saw you, I wondered if you might like to come?"

Thinking of her mother, Ruth shook her head. "Thank you though. Another time, perhaps."

"I hope so," Graham said, the look of chagrin that flitted across his face belied by the rather jaunty way he patted the sill.

ii.

OVER THE NEXT FEW NIGHTS, the baby woke Ruth so often, she didn't know if she was coming or going. Sometimes the child was just hungry, at others, Ruth couldn't work out what was wrong with her and spent hours walking her round and round her bedroom with the lights off, her hand patting the baby's back, her mind drifting in a kind of grey fog.

Her mother was oblivious. She didn't emerge until midmorning and rarely spoke until lunchtime, preferring instead to smoke in the backyard or watch TV in her dressing gown. She did take Fay out most afternoons though, leaving Ruth to clean in peace.

It was on one of those afternoons that she saw a man standing in the hallway, his head haloed by the light coming in through the panes in the front door. Her heart jumping in her chest, she pulled a knife from the knife block but when she turned back, the vision had gone.

She phoned the hospital. Someone there said Needlemire was unavailable, that he'd call her back but though she waited in all afternoon, no one phoned. She needed pills, she needed sleep, yet her pride wouldn't allow her to call the hospital again. Screw the hospital. Screw Needlemire. The fact that she didn't think of ringing her GP was testament to just how strung out she was.

Several times she came home from visiting Will and Eric to find the fridge empty and half-a-dozen empty bottles in the outside bin. The pattern was dully familiar. On the first day her mother cooked and cleaned. On the second she cooked. On the third she drank.

The problem reached critical mass a week after the funeral. Despite agreeing to go shopping, on the day, Veronica said it was too windy. She'd gotten dressed up in a red jacket and a rather ugly black cloche that made her look like she was collecting for The Salvation Army. She said she was worried that the wind would blow her hat off and it was only when Ruth offered to pin the thing up that her mother finally agreed to go out.

In town they had a coffee at a little café with steamed up windows and orange counters before being blown up North Street towards the Clock Tower. There in the Oxfam window, Ruth spotted a snow globe, a rather hefty looking ornament containing a miniature Brighton: the austere, stuccoed houses on Regency Square, the towers and minarets of the Royal Pavilion, a brightly painted Pier. Veronica used to collect the things and as a child Ruth had liked nothing more than to drag a chair over to her mother's cabinet, there to shake each one, the game being to see if she could get all of them whirling with snow at once. Smiling at the memory, she turned to her mother, intending to mention the object, only to see that Veronica had been distracted by a feather.

"For luck," the woman said, picking the thing up and sticking it in the band of her now unpinned hat. Only then did she see what Ruth was pointing at. "I love it!" she exclaimed, before insisting they go in and look at it.

But of course they did no such thing, for the wind chose that very moment to nudge at Veronica's hat as if testing its resolve, before snatching it from her head and lifting it into the air. Horrified, the two women watched the hat tremble along the concrete overhang above their heads, then spin out into the road and plaster itself onto the windscreen of an oncoming bus.

Ruth might have laughed had the bus's wipers not caught the hat and crushed the feather. Even as the vehicle ground to a halt a few yards down the road, Veronica began to jump about in front of it. The hat, however, lay just out of reach and the driver, perhaps taking umbrage at the way Ruth's mother started banging on the door, folded his arms and refused to open up.

As Ruth approached the bus she saw that a crowd had gathered, students and vagrants and shop workers on their lunchbreak. She was just wondering if things could get any worse when a teenager wearing a diagonal ribbon beating the words All You Can Eat across his chest, stepped into the road, extended an impossibly thin arm and seized the hat. Ruth wanted to shout at him but it would have done no good. This was her fate. As the youth grabbed the hat, the feather caught under the wiper. Enraged, Ruth's mother snatched at the hat and swung it at the boy, who raised a handful of leaflets in defence. A moment later the air was shimmering with luminescent sheets.

Mortified, Ruth seized her mother's wrist and began to push the pram up the hill, old resentments whirling inside her. Teeth gritted, she said, "I've been waiting for something like this. Can't you see how close I am? All you had to do was open your eyes. Why are you even here, Mum?"

She looked back at her mother. "What do you want?"

Veronica was trying to swallow. When she finally managed it, she raised her wrist and told Ruth that she was hurting her.

Back at the house, Ruth paced the living room while her mother packed. Finally, they met by the front door and stood staring at each other while the hallway pulsed with light.

"You need me here, Ruth," Veronica said.

Ruth gave a strangled laugh. "What've you ever done for me, Mum? I mean, really?"

Veronica's eyes blazed. "Have you ever thought that this might be your fault, Ruth? Nothing's been right since you got rid of that baby. I told you not to. Your father told you not to. But Ruth always knows best. Your father's dead. You put that on him and he died."

Ruth was incandescent. "He died long before he got on that boat." Fay was whining at her chest but she didn't care. "Who did that to him, Mum, do you suppose?"

Her words wormed at Veronica's skin. "I told him," she said, her voice stone-cold. "I told Will what you did, *your* husband. He came to see me that afternoon and I told him the truth. Lies, Ruth, isn't that why you kicked him out?"

Ruth's head was throbbing. "You told him?"

Veronica straightened her jacket and raised her chin. She was obviously preparing some final motion but before she could deliver it, the buzzer sounded and Ruth opened the door.

Outside, the first streetlamp glowed red against a fading sky. With her mother's bags stowed, the taxi driver jumped back in the car and pulled away in a crunch of stones. As her mother passed, Ruth saw her cheeks were wet with tears.

iii.

———

THE TAXI TURNED the corner and the street was empty. Ruth closed her eyes, saw dark houses, a leaf-green sky dotted with stars. A very hot bath, that's where she wanted to be. Little dripping splashes echoing against ceramic. A glass of very cold vodka on the soap dish. She laid her cheek on the baby's head, smelt her mother's perfume. Veronica had told Will about the abortion, she'd told him and he'd gotten drunk. The crowd in her head was baying for blood but she couldn't give them her mother's. Nor could she blame Will. Not anymore.

"Mrs Zifla?"

She opened her eyes to see someone walking up the street, a vague presence getting closer. Yet even though he'd used her name, she was still surprised when the man turned in at the gate. A square, clean-cut jaw, deep-set, tawny-coloured eyes. He was wearing navy chinos, a white cotton shirt, the top two buttons undone. A gold St Christopher glinted in the twilight.

"I'm sorry," he said in a not-quite-English accent, a hint of a smile showing the edges of very straight, very white teeth. "I would have called but I don't have your number. I'm a friend of Will's. From work," he added, as if Will had friends everywhere. "I just wanted to pop round and see how you were doing." When still she hesitated, he said, "We were squash buddies."

"Oh," she said. "You must be Frank."

Before the separation, Will had come home from work almost every day with some wild tale about the new History teacher. How he'd scared a kid so much, the kid had truanted for a week. How just about every woman at the school was madly in love with him.

She showed him through to the living room, switched on the lamp and headed for the kitchen where she prised Fay loose and put her in the pram by the back door. When she stood up again, she could see Frank's reflection in the glass, distorted, eyeless.

"I just wondered if I could help," he said gently.

After fetching the milk and stirring the tea, he carried the cups into the living room and placed them on the coffee table. "Nice house," he said, perching himself in the armchair nearest the window. Then, in an almost embarrassed tone, "I still can't believe he's in a coma."

He was rubbing his hands together, the sound, dry, not unpleasant, the gesture emphasising the size of his shoulders and chest. "He stayed with me. After you two split up. I hope you don't mind."

Ruth picked up her tea. "He involved you, not the other way round." Then, a little more softly, she added, "But it was kind of you to take him in."

He shrugged. "I feel bad. Like I shouldn't be here. I just wanted to see if I could help in some way." He fixed her with a brief, penetrating stare, his eyes hazel in the lamplight. "Maybe helping Will out wasn't for the best. I just figured the two of you would sort it out and in the meantime . . . I mean, he told me what happened. It must've been difficult for you . . ."

"But it's not like he slept with her?" Everything came welling to the surface and she was powerless to hold it down. She felt herself gripping her cup too tightly. "What else did he tell you? Like how I found the two of them together? Like how I was seven months pregnant? Did he tell you her name?"

Frank's head was bowed, his shoulders hunched. "I'm sorry. I'm just making things worse."

"Well, he told me. Shelley Givens. It's been spinning round my head ever since. They used to be friends, childhood friends, hadn't seen each other in years. But then just like that, up she pops. What kind of a coincidence is that?"

Seeing the look on his face, Ruth took a deep breath, caught herself.

For a few moments neither of them spoke and then she apologised. "No," she said before he could speak. "You've been nothing but a good friend. The truth is, I've had no one to talk to about all this. It's been driving me round the bend."

In the end, Frank was very attentive and it'd been a long time since Ruth had received that kind of attention. When he said he should get going, she told him she could put Fay to bed. "Bring us a glass of wine?"

"I'm driving . . ." he said. "Maybe half a glass?"

Ruth poured him a full one but he hardly touched it. He asked after her brother, told her the details had been in the papers. She told him it was too early to say. He asked her what it was like having to drive all the way to Crawley and back. She told him the doctors seemed competent enough, though both were lacking in the bedside manners department.

After Frank left, Ruth realised she was pretty drunk. She picked up the phone, thinking, vaguely, of her mother. But after their last scene, she couldn't imagine where to begin. She thought of Alison, a friend from her university days, but they hadn't spoken in months. She called her anyway, sat on the sofa with her feet up, her wineglass resting on her lap. She'd always considered Alison a good friend, a better person, kinder, more dependable. Or as another friend put it, the type one can't help deploring slightly. But no one picked up.

In need of an amulet, Ruth began to grope around in the cupboard under the stairs.

She carried the box she'd been looking for into the living room. It contained things from the accident, personal effects from Will's car the police no longer needed. She picked up Avni's glasses, lifted out compact discs with corrugated covers, smudged papers, warped envelopes, an old ice-scraper and a green leather glove, its fingers flat and stiff. She pulled the glove into shape and put it on. With her gloveless hand she drew out a book. On the inside cover, in her brother's handwriting, she read: *Eric, 1992*. She burred the pages. To her surprise, they were unmarked and she only conclude that Will must have been carrying the book in one of his pockets.

Nor was that the box's last treasure. Underneath a swollen A-Z of London, she found a small, black cassette recorder. Like the book, it was undamaged. It was the type of device she associated with old-school journalists, buttons on the side, black tape wound round tiny spools. She pressed rewind and put it to her ear, listening as the tape spun from spool to spool. As it neared the start, the machine began to whine before clattering to a halt.

Taking a sip of Frank's wine, she pressed play.

iv.
—

THE NEXT MORNING, Ruth found the two glasses still sitting on the coffee table. The box, though, was gone, as was the cassette recorder, though this last item would not cross her mind for several weeks.

Intending to spend the morning seeing to various work-related chores, she made a pot of coffee and started going through the files. As a safety specialist for a major airline, it was vital that the paperwork was kept up to date. In truth, however, it often grew into an unmanageable pile and in the past she'd been forced to play catch up over the weekend. Now though that she was on maternity leave she had the chance to get on top of things.

Yet despite the coffee, she could barely keep her eyes open. Fay was in her playpen on the floor and the first time Ruth jerked awake, she found the child staring up at her, her hand in her mouth, her chin covered in drool. Pouring herself another coffee, Ruth started going through her emails, only to wake up at the keyboard to find that she'd leant on random keys while she dozed. It was just lucky that she hadn't accidentally hit the send button or Andrew from Licensing would have received an email that read—*There were three examples of failxxxrehffffffrehyjrp###*—not, she told herself with some amusement, the type of message that would have instilled faith in her had Andrew opened and read it.

Finally, she decided to ring the hospital. She didn't want to take sleeping pills if she could help it but Needlemire had told her to come and see him. Maybe there was something he could do. The first time she called, no one picked up, the second, she left a message with a bored-sounding woman, but though she stayed in for the rest of the day, no one called back. It wasn't until the next day, having just put a wash on and laid Fay down to change her nappy that the phone finally rang. The woman on the other end of the line started speaking straightaway, her accent such that Ruth wondered if she'd had elocution lessons.

"Mrs Zifla? Yes, hello, this is Penny Spence calling from the hospital. Dr Keep asked me to give you a call. Can you come in at one? He would like to see you."

Only as she was about to leave did Ruth remember the washing. Having previously decided to hang it out, she searched in vain for the backdoor key, acutely aware that if she wasted too much time she would be late for her appointment. She normally left the thing in the keyhole but sometimes she dropped it into one of the little pots on the windowsill but though she searched high and low, it was nowhere to be found.

Not that this surprised her. The truth was, ever since having the baby, nothing in the house seemed to stay still, nothing was where she last put it. Pressed for time, she threw the clothes in the dryer, strapped Fay into her car seat and set off for the hospital.

On the way, she thought about what she wanted to say to the doctor, to *both* doctors. Will had gotten drunk the night of the accident, that much they all knew. But only she and her mother knew why. Perhaps if she shared this information with Dr Keep, if they both shared it with Will, it might help. She also wanted to speak to Needlemire about getting something to help her sleep. With such thoughts flitting through her mind, she traversed the hospital's blazing corridors as if in a trance.

Penny turned out to be a nurse. She caught up with Ruth as she stepped out of the lift and introduced herself with a firm shake of the hand. "You must be Mrs Zifla," she said.

Ruth took in the other woman's short, slim stature and light blue dress with its dark blue trim and the rather austere way she'd tied her long, caramel-coloured hair up in a neat bun, all in a numb, rather bemused silence.

"I've just come from your husband's room," the nurse added, her accent as neatly arranged as her appearance. "I'll walk you down there if you like."

While they walked, the nurse with neat, quick steps and Ruth swaying a little to counter the weight of Fay's car seat, Penny asked Ruth if she was coping.

"All this must be putting a great strain on you," she said.

Ruth stopped for a moment and almost laughed. The question reached down into her core, deep enough to stir up the truth. "We're taking it a day at a time," she said finally.

"Maybe," Penny said kindly, "you could try reading to him. Dr Keep said it might help. The Bible in your husband's room is mine. I hope you don't mind." Stopping outside Will's door, she said, "Dr Keep's in there now if you want to go in."

When Ruth pushed open the door, Keep, who was standing by the window, turned in an agitated way, as if waiting for her had put a strain on his nerves. He was holding a small tape-recorder and held it aloft, not noticing, it seemed, the exhausted way she clutched at the handle of Fay's car seat as if it were the only thing keeping her upright.

"Good news," he said, his voice piping with excitement. "Your husband has been *speaking*."

Glancing back at the observation window, Ruth saw that Penny was watching them through the glass, aware perhaps of the doctor's odd news, though as soon as Ruth looked at her, the woman gave a strange smile and walked away.

When Ruth turned to look at her husband's closed eyes and serene expression, Keep said: "Please don't misinterpret what I'm saying, he's not awake. But it does suggest a level of consciousness even more animated than we suspected." He jiggled the tape-recorder. "I keep this on me at all times. I managed to record most of what he said, though what he was talking about, I've no idea. I was hoping you might know."

Placing Fay's car seat on the carpet, Ruth sat down in her usual chair and then looked up at the doctor, before finally nodding.

He looked at her tellingly. "You need to prepare yourself, Ruth."

Only when she nodded again did he press play.

The recording lasted no more than a minute. The first thing she heard was a scrabbling sound, followed, a few seconds later, by a voice, Will's, she supposed, though it was gruffer than usual. He was mumbling, something about a wedding, his brother's, which made no sense, about how they (whoever *they* were) were carrying his brother and his wife through a garden. It was all very strange. He said he found his brother's arm, something about a watch. Then he started muttering about bombs and fire, deserts and death. What shocked her most though was his talk concerning a young girl he called Amena. Keep stopped the recording.

"What does it mean?" she said. "He doesn't have a brother." Tears trembled in her throat. "And who is Amena? He said his little girl is dead. Does that mean . . . does he think . . ?"

But Will hadn't spoken his last. As if summoned by her voice, he began to move under the sheet, only slightly at first but then in a more agitated fashion. Ruth had seen him move before, both on his own and due to the bed, which occasionally hummed and rolled beneath him to ensure he didn't get bedsores. This though was altogether different. It was like watching someone suffering a nightmare. Noises came from his throat, a kind of growling, followed by a shallow, doglike panting.

Ruth stopped speaking and stared at her husband's face. Will's sheet was tucked in very tightly across his body and round his bed so that when his arms moved, they stood out against the cloth.

Keep stepped forwards. "*Speak!*" he said, his already shrill voice coming out almost as a squeak.

Will's head slipped first one way and then the other. He was groaning and sweat broke out on his brow. It looked as if someone were pressing his head into the pillow.

"*Rs*ing," he said in the same rough tone Ruth had heard on the tape.

With his neck twisted to the side, his voice was restricted. His eyes were moving back and forth under his eyelids and he kept taking quick, gasping breaths.

"I, I can hardly see. I am a wall of water, my body . . . my arms. But there's light, the surface, I can see the surface."

Keep's excitement was almost unseemly. "Look at him, *look*, Ruth! He's sensing consciousness. He's so close to us."

Ruth tried to loosen the sheet but it was too securely wrapped. Taking hold of her husband's shoulders instead, she began to shake him. "Come back to us. *Please* come back to us."

Keep was talking too. "Return," he cried. "Return!"

51

Feeling Will's whole body stiffen, Ruth thought they'd done it but then, just as suddenly, he slumped into the mattress, his breath shallow, his skin flushed and sweaty.

"You said he was close," she insisted. "You've got to call someone. Someone needs to *do* something."

Keep looked up from checking Will's pulse. "I'm sorry, it may seem otherwise but he's still very much unconscious." He reached over but she moved her hand. "This is how he was before, Ruth. Believe me, whatever's going on is very unusual."

"But is that it?" she said. "Surely we can do more?"

Keep said he had to call a meeting, that he must consult with his colleagues. When he took off his glasses, she saw that his hand was trembling. "But in the meantime, Ruth, I need you here every day. Will needs you here. You are the key. Isn't it obvious? He needs to hear your voice."

Chapter 2.

The House of Visions

1

COLD WATER, A CEASELESS roaring, a vast, eddying flow that dragged at his arms until he thought they might break. Lit by a brief burst of light—black and white—he glimpsed a wooden wheel, his arms spread-eagled, his wrists bound to the outer edge. It was this wheel that kept drawing him to the surface but also this that kept him from the air, for he was caught beneath it.

He heard a violent fizzling, deep undernotes growing longer, then louder. Again the wheel broke the surface. Screaming wind, white rain all around. Kicking and pulling, he managed to reach his lips between the spokes: "Hel—!"

A watery avalanche, a shuddering violence that tore at his shoulders as the wheel was driven under. Lungs screaming for air. Yet through the pain and panic, he saw something, two people, both wrestling with odd-looking belts. Again he sensed a break in the darkness, air, a choking lie that drove him downwards.

He twisted his hands, blindly searching for the wheel's rim, sensed the wheel sitting in the surface of a wave. When the wave began to tumble, he lashed out with his feet, felt a moment of triumph, only to lose his grip. *Patience!* Kick too early and he wasted valuable energy, too late and he was thrown across the wheel. Several times already this had happened. He felt the wheel rise, the ropes tighten, experienced a sudden lifting and thought—Kick, *kick* and then, *plant your boot.* Even as he thrust his toe between the spokes, the wave disintegrated, driving the wheel under. Yet as the debris cleared, he was uppermost at last.

Howling winds, rain shooting up through his body, a sky full of mutated swellings. One moment the sea roiled as if with eels, the next it broke into wide, white swathes. But despite the brutal world in which he found himself, he was filled with joy, for every breath was a step away from the abyss.

He'd been with his parents. Realising this, he called for them. He saw his mother pulling at something, her shoulders trembling, his father stretching his head, his lips contorted. He lay on the wheel, felt the waves pull it upwards, almost tip it, leant with his body, pressed with his hands, steered with his boots. One moment he was between slopes, the next atop lightning-lit hills. Wind harried, waves roared, clouds pressed as if just above his head and then became marbled beasts, flashing for miles around. He was icy cold and shivering so hard it was a wonder he didn't fall apart.

A light, coming and going. A lamp, he thought. They're looking for me. But no one came. Slashing, slapping, rising, falling, the waves bullying, teasing. Several times, he saw himself from above, a dim furnace in a listing scape.

A desperate battle ensued. Rope sawed at his skin. Blistered, raw, bloody, numb, his head to one side, his neck stiff, his eyes red, he fought on. Shift, lean, pull. Do everything to remain on top. He may have slept and in his sleep obeyed the crafty voice that told him to keep on fighting. Eventually though, the wind fell and he saw that the light was actually a star. He was shivering so badly he wondered if it was this that had loosened the ropes. He tried to lift his legs but they were numb. He was sodden, weak, his head heavy, his eyes sore. Sleep was an intoxicating siren. He told himself he would drown but his mind worked against him. You'll be fine, it said. Your body will know what to do, you need only catch a few moments.

Startling awake, he found his head on one side, water suckling his ear. It had not been this though that had woken him, but rather a voice, a soft, troubled whisper—*Don't you drown too.* Yet despite its gentleness, it seemed to be, even now in its absence, as pervasive as the air itself. Certainly it had been powerful enough to wake him and in so doing, save his life, for both his wrists were now untied. One of the ropes had already snaked into the depths, the other drooped between the spokes.

But how long had he slept? Only now, as the wheel crested a wave, did he see the stars, an endless field of cold white embers. The storm had passed and though the waters were still choppy, they were much less so. He could actually see the waves now, their jellied flesh swelling with white blood. Both his legs and the lower half of his torso lay in the water, their weight dragging at his arms. He could no longer feel any part of his body, yet he was too weak to pull himself up. He tried and failed to curl his fingers around the wood.

For how long he clung there he did not know. He may or may not have fallen asleep again. What he did recall was the moment the craft turned, causing his breastbone to drop. As he slithered from the wheel, he felt only an exhausted relief.

At the same time, he heard a cry, saw a light made green by the water, a finlike shadow and a slippery shape dip under the surface and seize his arms.

ii.

HE'D NEARLY DROWNED, that's what they told him, the two who fished him from the sea. He'd stopped breathing and they had to revive him. He remembered none of this, only the cold stones of the shore, the unforgiving wind, his unending shiver. Those first few moments, they could have cut off his limbs and he wouldn't have known it.

Someone had set a lamp on the shingle. By it he saw the contours of a vast cave, its sides piled with rocks, its centre strewn with sand. A large, red-faced man was dragging the boat towards the rocks. Nearer to, an older man with a bald pate and sunken cheeks was rummaging through a canvas bag, his rough brown smock riding up almost to his knees, revealing thin, veiny legs. He shouted to his companion, his voice shrill and whining: "I told you to pack *blan*kets, Gribble, if this man dies—!"

Seeing him stir, the old man turned and spoke to him, his voice thinly querulous. "What were you doing out there? Only a lunatic would have gone out in such a storm. Were you trying to reach Sazani?" He peered down with watery green eyes. "What is your name, son?"

But though he searched his mind, it was like shining a torch into the dark. The shivering was so bad, every sight, every sound, every thought, was fragmented. Again he flicked the torch. Something was there—a wriggling germ—but his tongue was frozen. Stretching out a trembling finger, he wrote several letters in the sand.

Picking up the lamp, the old man stepped forward to read what he'd written, before issuing a vinegary laugh. "What kind of a name is *Li*am?"

He tried to focus. Four letters glowed in the light, preceded by the old man's sandal.

After securing the boat, the one called Gribble clambered across the shingle and heaved him to his feet. Clamping a hand under his arm, he began to drag him up and over the rocks.

The cave seemed too big for echoes but occasionally a slithering noise came skittering across the stone as if from some snake-filled crevice. In this way, climbing over barnacle-covered rocks and slipping down into wet crannies, they made their way across the floor of the cave to a narrower opening, a dark cleft that led into a maze of passages, their dimensions blown like molten glass by the light. The scrape of boots on gravel filled their ears. This way and that the passageways led, each one tending upwards until finally the trio came out from under a rocky lip to find themselves on a narrow path overlooking tufted cliffs and a shallow bay, its edges decorated with seething ribbons.

Here the wind and the wet, gravelly path made the way even more treacherous. Shadows writhed together in a mad dance as the old man swung the lamp to and fro. When they finally crested the cliff, they were confronted, far up the slope, by a black tower topped by a revolving beam of light. No longer afforded the protection of the rock-face, the wind seemed determined to sweep them back into the sea. This constantly opposing force made the final stretch of their journey exhausting and when the three men at last staggered through the tower's heavily-joisted doorway, their breaths were as ragged as dogs on heat. Gribble proceeded to drag the stranger down what appeared to be a long, windowless passageway and out into a chamber hissing with light. Laying him on the floor, the red-faced man all but collapsed, his breath pawing at the walls.

The space was surrounded by deep niches, each one containing a variety of lamps, their light casting the seats encircling the chamber and the staircase at its centre in an obscure pattern of shadow and radiance. It was to the staircase though that the stranger's eyes were drawn. This impressive structure spiralled on wrought iron steps, both up into the ceiling and down into the floor and seemed, each time his eyes fluttered open, to raise a chastising finger.

It was the older man who helped him up the stairs, for the way was narrow and it was difficult, even for their slim frames, to fit side-by-side. In this manner, they began to lurch upwards, causing the ill-secured staircase to quake, its nuts and bolts to creak.

Reaching the first landing, the old man handed over his guest, retrieved a box of matches and lit a candle, bringing to life a low ceiling, bare stonewalls and two wooden doors. But this was not to be their destination. Beyond the landing lay more stairs, their rough stone surface and the curling, coarsely rendered brickwork above them wavering as the old man led the way to a second landing identical to the first. Here he unlocked the right-hand door, before ordering Gribble in the same shrill, piercing voice, to carry their catch into a white-walled room with darkly gleaming floors.

The man laid him on a narrow bed to the left of the doorway and began to pull at his clothes. He heard the creak of hinges and then felt a blanket settle over his body. It was as the breath of God. He clawed it about his shoulders. As if through water, he heard something about coffee, saw Gribble shake his head.

"It's barely daybreak," the man said. "I'll go."

The old man spoke sharply. "Is Penumbra's sleep more important than this man's life?"

Gribble was leaning on his knees, his scalp glistening with sweat, his thick neck crimson in the candlelight. He seemed to be considering something but then nodded and lurched away, causing the candle to waver as he reeled past.

After checking that the door was closed, the old man dragged an ancient-looking chair across to the bed, before lowering himself into it with a loud sigh and a creak of wicker. "Got to get you warm," he said as he exhaled.

So saying, he began to rub at the stranger's torso and limbs, his words coming and going with his efforts. "A miracle you found us. Was that your intention, to come to the island of Sazani?" Nodding to himself, he said, "It's an empty world without friendly faces, is it not? This here's a lighthouse, the House of Visions, I call it, and I its keeper. You perhaps saw its light, though little good that did you. And you? Are we really to call you Liam? I mean, I don't mind either way but the islanders are an ignorant lot and if they hear a stranger's washed up here, one not even certain of his own name, they may see it as a bad omen. And round here, bad omens are likely to get their throats cut."

Despite the iron swords resting against his skin, the stranger was listening. "I don't *know*," he managed. "I can't re*mem*ber *any*thing."

The Keeper shook his head. "You've not heard of Sazani, nor even of this house?" A kind of whistling laughter issued from his nostrils. "Well if you remember nothing, Liam it will have to be. But you must show a little more certainty."

With the heat at last trickling back into him, he curled his body around the warmth, drawing in his knees and clenching his hands and screwing up his eyes. He had to protect that puny flame. Yet even as he hunkered down in that drawn in darkness, that name, those two soft syllables, *Li-am*, became as one with the ember he was so carefully nurturing, so that the warmer he grew, the more he warmed to it. At the same time, though, a little voice inside kept nagging at him, a doubt like a stone in a shoe that wouldn't leave him alone.

The candle guttered and he opened his eyes to see a woman placing a lantern on the chest of drawers opposite the bed. A savoury aroma filled the room and he saw that she was also carrying a silver pot. Taking a blanket from the pile in Gribble's arms, she shook it over him.

"Good to get a man out of his wet things," she tutted. "But why not get him dressed again?"

After tying her long hair up in a bun and pulling up the sleeves of her dress to reveal blue-veined wrists, she dragged a woollen sweater from the chest and began to tug it over his head. Next came a mugful of coffee, though he'd barely had a sip before she was taking it from him so she could inspect his forehead.

"A nasty cut," she said, running a thumb over his brow and squeezing his cheek when he winced. "Clean though, at least. Salt's made a new moon of it. What's your name, lad?"

The Keeper hobbled closer. "His name is Liam," he insisted. "And Liam's troubles obviously run far deeper than that cut. He remembers almost nothing. But from such a piffling wound? It is my belief that just as the Flood cleansed the world, so has Liam's mind been wiped of dead works. That he has been delivered to us, a clean vessel as it were, for some divine purpose. Not," he said, rounding on his guest, "that we and thee are yet on trusting terms. Make no mistake, Penumbra will be at your service while you convalesce but both she and Gribble will be keeping a close eye on you."

iii.

LIAM WOKE TO DISTANT thunder. Waves, he realised, crashing against the cliff. A shuttered, deep-set window cast faint bands of light across the room. He heard clattering plates and more than once, a low, huffing bark.

His head throbbing with loneliness, he got up and began to search the chest and then the trunk. Both contained only clothes. Apart from a small brass cross above the door, the walls were unadorned. Finally finding the coffeepot under the bed, he peered into its curved surface, hoping to recognise something. Dark, untidy hair, light blue eyes fazed slightly by the warped surface. The cut on his forehead. He turned his head, bared his teeth, stuck out his tongue, frowned and pouted, yet felt as if he might have been watching a mimic.

At the window, he opened the shutters and breathed in the cold air. Leaning out, he felt a whirling sensation. He was only on the second storey but the ground seemed far away. Shelves of land, each quivering with vegetation, declined into a diffused glow. A path of beaten earth dropped down between dark rocks towards the cliff-edge. The bay beyond looked relatively calm, especially compared to the wilder sea beyond, its dark green surges fringed with foam. The sun was setting, the sky along the horizon a pure, pale orange. To the right, a sparse wood surrounded a number of stone dwellings. Several men were making their way up from a distant point on the cliff, nets slung over their shoulders, their forms made indistinct by the light and distance. Further out, atop a steep hill, he saw what looked like a curved stone mound.

Just then the tower's light came on and he leaned out, though much more carefully this time. The glinted darkly in the sun. Its zenith looked no bigger than a thumbnail. The beam returned, sweeping across the sea. He wondered why he hadn't seen it during the storm but then realised he had. Just before Gribble pulled him from the water, the light had swept past, momentarily silhouetting the wheel.

"I always think it must be lonely."

He turned to see Penumbra placing a large wooden tray on the bed. "The light," she smiled. "All it ever does is leave."

She lit a candle before sitting him down and passing him a bowl of soup. "Round here we eat a lot of fish," she said. "Eat up, it's good."

And it was, the fish soft, the broth deep and rich. He ate it in great mouthfuls, glancing at her over his spoon from time to time.

"Was I the only one found?" he said finally.

The housekeeper was rearranging his drawers and peered back at him with a queer look in her eye. "You saying otherwise?"

"I think . . ." He gave her a quick smile. "There were others. I can see them in a, in something like a mirror. I think maybe they're my parents."

"Ask the Keeper," Penumbra said, closing the drawers. "He's the one found you."

"If he knows something," Liam said, feigning disinterest, "I'm sure he'll tell me in his own time."

"You can trust the Keeper," Penumbra said rather stiffly. "He saved your life, didn't he?"

And with that, she swept from the room and locked the door.

Still exhausted from his ordeal, Liam drifted off, only to find Gribble looming over the bed. The man's face looked particularly ruddy in the setting sun. His hair, which was pulled back into a ponytail, gleamed silver, as did the cleaver in his belt, a pitted instrument that rode up as he placed one foot on the bed, his elbows on his thigh. "Thought I'd come see if you liked the stew."

Liam struggled up into a seated position and then nodded.

"I like to think we do all right, despite a meagre budget." But though the man was smiling, his eyes were cold. "Trouble is we can't feed every mouth wants it. Folks wash up here all the time with some story for the old man. Before you know it, they're robbing us blind. Last man tried anything left here minus a few fingers.

"So what I'm saying is," he said, giving the cleaver a squeeze, "are you fish or eel, honest or slippery?"

"You know as much as I do. We were in a storm—"

"We?" the chef said lightly. "And who's this 'we'?"

Feeling his face redden, Liam got up and walked to the window. "I can't remember. All I know is, I wasn't alone."

Just then a rattling growl rose up out of the night, causing him to start.

"The generator," Gribble said, smiling again. "Keeper must be working on something. And that's it, you 'member nothing more?"

When Liam shook his head, the chef made an odd clucking sound. "Well, the way I see it, a man with no past has no regrets. And its regret that makes us human."

His final visitor of the night was the Keeper. With the generator now silent, Liam heard footsteps, the scrape of a key. "We're going to my chamber," the man said, ushering him out. Stay close, the stairs can be unpredictable."

Liam tried to count the number of floors they passed but found the task difficult. The steps were so irregular and the old man's candle so unreliable that he arrived at the Keeper's chambers with both knees the worse for wear. Waiting for them on the final floor was the chef, his features florid in the candlelight.

The Keeper's room was small and tidy. One wall was lined with closets, another with shelves, each one filled with neatly arranged books. At the centre of the room stood a low wooden table, around which were arranged three wooden chairs, though by the look of it the Keeper did most of his work over by the window, where stood, in a little nook, a leather-topped writing desk stacked with books and papers. Liam's eyes settled last on a narrow bed, beneath which he saw two glimmering lights. Even as he realised they were actually eyes, the bed took a terrific leap into the air and an animal bristling with teeth and fur, leapt at him.

"Down, Bloodhorn!"

The Keeper's voice was savage in the enclosed space. The dog, a powerful-looking beast with an enormous head and long, thick tail, collapsed and began to back away, its brown furred haunches rolling. Reaching the bed again, it lay down and proceeded to stare at Liam with heavy-lidded, golden eyes.

Rubbing his balding pate, the Keeper sat down and invited Liam to do the same. "Don't mind Bloodhorn," he said, "he's not used to strangers." He gave a watery smile. "Now, Gribble here tells me you've remembered something."

Moved by the dog's golden gaze, Liam said, "I was tied to a wheel."

"But there was no wheel when we found you." The Keeper waited but Liam said nothing. "And who tied you to this wheel?"

Liam shrugged. "Obviously not myself."

"You've no idea?"

"There were others." Liam paused. "I think maybe . . ." He looked at Gribble but the man was staring at the ceiling. "Maybe my parents."

The Keeper shut his eyes while the light fluttered and the dog stared and then he nodded. "You *were* on a boat, a *sail* boat to be precise."

When Liam started to speak, Bloodhorn growled at the change in his voice. "You knew?" he said again.

"I have no reason to trust you. What I decide to share with you is at my discretion."

"But you saw me!" Seeing the dog's ears prick again, he took a deep breath. "Please tell me what you saw."

The Keeper glanced at Gribble. "Your boat was listing, waves smashing over the side. By my glass I saw someone at the wheel. Whoever it was, was trying to turn the bow but the boat kept being swept broadside. There were others there but with the rain and the dark . . ." He shrugged.

Recalling the struggling forms that had haunted his dreams, Liam felt a dreadful hope. "I remember my father telling me to steer into the wave."

The Keeper's gaze was cold and steady. "Your craft was too far out for me to make out much. When it was finally overwhelmed, it sank like a stone. By the time Gribble and I got out there, there was only one person in that water. You."

Liam felt his eyes grow hot with tears. "So they're dead?"

"Water would have dashed in from every side. They wouldn't have stood a chance."

"But . . ." Liam faltered. "If this is a lighthouse, why didn't I see the light?"

"It was on," the Keeper said calmly. "I light it at sundown. It was by its light I first saw your boat. I imagine in all that roaring water and darkness you were confused but let me assure you, the light was on."

2
—

THE NEXT DAY, PENUMBRA found Liam lying in the space between his bed and the outer wall, a plate of eggs congealing on the table above his head. He'd been there all day, all night probably and did not look at her when she touched him, nor answer when she spoke. "They were in a mirror." It was all he said. "Why a mirror?"

The pain was too much. He felt as if he were being crushed by an unbearable force, as if everything inside of him, his flesh, his bones, his organs, all were being squeezed into a single, immovable mass.

Even in sleep were his movements restricted, for in his dreams, again and again, he found himself in a room from which there was no escape. All was black. Hands extended, he would shuffle forwards before finally touching a wall. Concrete. Icy cold. Groping sideways, his bare feet scraping across the concrete floor, he would find another wall. But nothing in-between, no furniture, no windows, no doors—just a concrete box full of darkness.

On the third morning after the Keeper's revelation, Liam clawed his way out of sleep with a word caught in his mouth. "*Ligi.*"

His heart a-clatter, he looked about him as if to see who had put it there. Blades of sunlight streaked the floor. Under his bed, where the bed's stout brown legs met the wall, he saw a coiled black body with yellow stripes uncoiling, a muscular distension slowly feeding itself into a hole in the wall.

Repulsed, he pushed himself against the wall. "What was that?"

Penumbra was sitting in the chair on the other side of his bed, two knitting needles clacking away. Only when she'd completed a final turn did she look up. "What was what?"

He pointed. "Something went into that hole."

She beckoned him to his feet and began to pull the garment over his head. "Did this something have a forked tongue?" she asked when his head reappeared. When he nodded, she said, "Then that'll be Gilgamesh. Hard to tell now but these rooms used to hold all manner of beast. At one time you couldn't hear yourself think for the growling and chattering that used to go on round here. All gone now, 'cept the rats and they get fewer by the day thanks to Gilgamesh."

Holding his wrists, she stepped back to admire him. "I spun the wool myself," she said, smiling and then nodding. "I knew blue would be your colour."

After eating, he allowed the housekeeper to guide him down the stairs and out of the house. A bright grey light hung over the sea. The air smelt of smoke.

In this way, Penumbra began to rehabilitate him. Often they wouldn't go further than the gardens, where she would sit him down and read him what she called her poems. "Where shall the word be found, where will the word resound? Not here, there is not enough silence, not on the sea or on the islands . . ." At others they would pick their way along the cliffs, causing the birds there to rise up in shrieking clouds. Liam rarely spoke during these walks but Penumbra didn't seem to notice, talk enough as she did for the both of them.

The makeshift gardens were built on slanting tiers, the furthest of which was bordered by a swathe of bracken so dense that it hid the cliff-edge beyond. Penumbra always stayed close during these walks, not yet trusting his frame of mind and she was right to do so, for one afternoon, when she let go of his arm to pick a flower, he waded into the ferns, senseless to the brambles snatching at his trousers.

He found himself standing on a crumbling edge, the wind chopping at his hair, his eyes full of distant breakers, white froth followed by soft thunder.

Penumbra stood nearby, her body as shiveringly erect as a hare's. "Go on then," she said. "Take the weakling's way out."

"Better short and sharp," he said, "than long and slow."

Penumbra wrapped the edges of her cardigan about her. "You think you're the only one grieving?"

"I killed them," he said. He felt the wind snatch at his hair. "It's all I know. Nothing but grief." It was true. The loneliness in his head was like a glass wall, everything beyond it unknowable and loathsome in its unknowability.

"It's not grief, it's guilt." She shook her head. "Yes, you're grieving but clinging to this inclination is a weakness. What would they want?"

She spoke quietly, kindly, treading the bracken between them with each word. Then, without warning, she pounced. He was tall and strong and much recovered from his ordeal and could have jumped, taking her with him, but a moment later she was pulling him back and they were falling among the ferns.

"What would *they* want?" she said again.

As they walked back to the house, Liam listened to the wind plough through the grass, watched the trees bow and ripple.

Everything was distant and cool. Penumbra was pointing to a line that ran round the tower's upper limits, above which the building was darker. She told him the sea was never this high. "But once it was even higher."

She took his arm. "The flood took everything, my mother, my father, my brothers." She turned him and pointed towards the bay. "Our village was down there. Before he started building the lighthouse, the Keeper used to preach in the village square. Most of them laughed." She shook her head. "Not my father. He got me a job up here, cleaning, tending the gardens. Whenever I made the Keeper his supper, he'd invite me to join him. He was always talking about God's grieving. I asked him, what was he grieving *for*? It was He told me to build the tower, he said, and cover it with tar. To build it four hundred and fifty feet high but make only one door.

"When the flood came, water spouted from everywhere. You couldn't see for the rain. Waves smashed against the cliffs, engulfing the town. It went on for weeks. When the waters finally retreated, everything was gone. There used to be lights everywhere—down there, across the sea—all along the sky. But soon even those began to wink out and the lighthouse was the only one left."

Her grip on his arm tightened. "Starvation and disease got most of those who survived. Ships came through here full of unspeakable sights. Fewer and fewer as the months went by. We took in as many as we could, craftfolk, dreamers, workers . . . there are very few islands left and only three inhabited, or so I'm told. The Island of T'heel, the Island of Hats and here."

The housekeeper sighed. "What I'm trying to say is that this thing for which you feel responsible, it's not your doing. It's not you but the sea that took them. And He who bids the sea."

He stared at the glittering beyond the cliffs.

"What's a dreamer?" he said at last.

"What do you *think*?" she said, half-mockingly. "Once several of their kind lived under this roof. Now though, they're rare as red glass. All we've left is Gale."

"Who's Gale. Does she live here too?"

Pen laughed her soft chuckle. "Indeed she does. Matter of fact, she resides in the room above yours."

ii.

WHEN PENUMBRA NEXT brought supper, Liam's impatience was such that the woman had barely unloaded the tray before he'd blurted out his question. "What is it that Gale does exactly?"

"Eat up," she said, "and I just might tell you."

Only when he'd begun to tuck into the smoked fish and thickly buttered bread, did the housekeeper scoop up her skirts and sit down in the wicker chair as if to say that this was a very serious subject. "As I mentioned," she began, "Gale is a dreamer. The last as far as we know—"

"But what does that mean?" he interrupted.

"What does it mean?" Pen's laughter danced somewhere between doubt and delight. "They say dreamers can build kingdoms, castles that float in the air . . ."

"But can't everyone?"

She shook her head as if at a naive child. "Gosh, no. Our heads were washed clean of such fancies. But Gale's special. When she goes to sleep, she finds herself elsewhere, in many elsewheres, fanciful, beautiful, *terrifying* places. The kind of places where you don't want to be but where you don't want to leave . . ."

Seeing something in his expression, she asked if he knew what she was talking about. "I can tell. You too have escaped this room despite lock and key."

"Escaped? I'm not so sure. But elsewhere, certainly. That's a good name for it."

"I thought so," she said, an envious glint in her eye. "What's it like?"

"Like a darkness full of knowledge," he said, half-glibly. "The kind of place you don't want to turn the light on, in case you don't like what you find. Yet the whole time, all you're doing is searching for a switch."

69

After the housekeeper had gone, he stood at the window, breathing in the damp evening air. Rainclouds trailed curling plumes along the horizon. Nearer to, an ivory light dappled the sea. He thought about the dark room. It was totally unfamiliar to him and yet, in the way its dimensions shimmered inside his head long after he'd woken, its shapes defined solely by hearing, touch and emotion, it felt as if it had always been inside of him, just as he was inside of it.

Hearing a familiar click, he turned to see the Keeper standing in the doorway, his face lit by a peculiar smile.

"I come bearing gifts," the man said, holding up a big black book. "Penumbra's been singing your praises, young man."

So saying, he closed the door and shuffled across the room, before lowering himself into the chair with a slight groan. "Apparently, you've made something of a revival," he said. "I told her, the young are too impatient for grief but she suggested maybe it's faith that's changed your mind."

Not in the mood for the old man's riddles, Liam turned back to the view beyond the window. "What can I believe in when I remember nothing?"

"In life? In dreams, perhaps?"

"But what use are dreams when I've lost the memories that give them meaning?"

"They may return. You've more hope than some."

Liam tutted. "Such as my parents, you mean?"

He heard the Keeper place the book on the floor. "It seems my words vex you," he said. "I want you to know, I can live with that. I'm not here to make you feel good, only to test your worth. But before all that, we need to get past any misplaced feelings."

Liam saw that the rain had reached the bay. Where it touched the sea, it looked like mist. "I won't be trapped by words," he said quietly.

The Keeper's words came from just behind him. "I don't wish to disregard your sensitivities but I can't feed you lies. You've spent days in your room in silence. This is not because you grieve. How can we grieve what we do not remember? It's because you feel responsible. Two people bear you, raise you. But when you were called upon, not for a lifetime but for a moment, you failed."

Though the man's words filled him with a dark fire, Liam didn't quite dare to face him.

"Perhaps," the Keeper said lightly, "you don't believe in dreams because your sleep is dreamless?"

"And if it is?"

The Keeper spoke gentle words. "Then be ready to leave."

Liam heard the rattle of matches, sensed light, turned to watch the old man place a candle on his side of the bed.

"What must I do?"

"Dream," the Keeper said, retreating to his chair. "No more, no less."

Stepping over to the light, Liam stared down at the pool of wax forming around the base of the wick. "But why me?"

As if this were the very question he'd been waiting for, the old man leaned forwards. "Because I believe your coming has been prophesised." He patted the bed. "Come, *sit.*" The wicker creaked as he bent down. "I've marked the page, let me read it to you."

Opening the book, he cleared his throat, flashed Liam a look and then began to read, his high voice full of a quavering authority. "'When he passes through the seas, he will not drown, when he passes through the rivers, they will not sweep over him. When he walks through the fire, he will not be burned. Blessed with visions, the oracle will rise from the sea and the people who walk in darkness will see a great light. Those who live in a dark land, the oracle's light will shine upon them. Those whose eyes are milky with blindness will have their sight returned.'" His own eyes moist, the Keeper said, "I believe it refers to you, to your coming."

The man clapped the book to, slapped a hand on its cover. "Don't o'er think! There are only the use*ful* and the use*less.* Before we were brought low, there was a time when confusion was a beautiful thing. But these are *sim*ple times. I believe you are the one, come to give the world your gift. Then was a time full of dreamers and no one paying much mind to what was real. Now is a time too real, direly in need of a dream, a dream to wake us from our slumber. What you remember of your life amounts to nothing, *worse* than nothing. I'm offering you a chance to change that.

"Take some time," the Keeper sighed. He placed the book on the table. "Read, if you will. But before I go, perhaps you'd like to ask me a question."

Liam hesitated. "What did we do that was so terrible that God felt the need to drown all the world?"

"Yes," the old man cried. "For doesn't that go right to the heart of the matter? This," he said, touching the book once more, "is a *war* story, the war between darkness and light. Yet in the period before the Flood, belief in its truths waned. And all because of a trick. You'll find none such in this house but they are called *mirrors*. We surrounded ourselves with our own reflections, put them in every room. They lined every street, twinkled like stars in the sky. We even carried them round in our pockets. Everywhere we turned, we saw ourselves endlessly repeated. Mirrors called film wrapped us up. Others called webs ensnared us. But what were we hoping to catch in that glass? Some said we were looking for the truth, a single divine theory that unified everything. But the only truth we found was the knowledge that at the centre of everything, where we hoped, finally, to find ourselves, lay only emptiness. It became like a madness. After all our cleverness, to know that what we are is *nothing*, it was as if the void had been poured into our very souls. And the mad are easily enslaved, for they know not what they do.

"The Flood," the Keeper sighed, "was not a testament of wrath but of grief. But even beneath God's glare, life has a way of crawling out. This then is our second chance. Now the light upon the sill draws our eye. We have the chance to look outwards again. But not everyone has been so gifted. It is they we must reach."

The man's voice became querulously persuasive. "I believe you've been sent to dream for us, a dream to light up the dark. And just in time! The final battle looms, yet there are those out there who don't even know it, those who will be swallowed up when the dark tide cometh.

"But I've said enough. You look tired—and I," the old man said, gripping the wicker by its arms, "am no spring herring." Exhaling a quick, nostrilly breath, he stood up. "As a gesture of good faith, I shall leave the door unlocked. The house is yours lest locks keep you out. Some rooms hold delicate things. Go out, explore. As for this . . ." He held up the book. "Read it at your leisure. And in the meantime, get plenty of sleep. Important choices are best weighed with a rested mind. And, of course," he said, stepping close enough for Liam to smell the tainted scent of his breath, "the more you sleep, the more you'll dream and the more you dream, the *more* you'll *see*."

iii.

SOMEONE WAS TAPPING at Liam's door. Now that it was no longer locked, it seemed he was afforded this courtesy. Yet as Penumbra tutted her way into his room, followed by the scent of seared mullet, he realised that that was where such civilities ended.

"So you've agreed to help the Keeper," she said, setting down the usual tray in such a manner that the items on it jumped and rattled.

He waited for her to break into a smile but such was not to be. Instead, the housekeeper began to pick up his clothes, again with an unnecessary gusto, before sweeping from the room without another glance in his direction.

He brooded over Penumbra's rather odd behaviour for exactly as long as it took him to eat his breakfast. But with sunlight on his sill and a sweet breeze blowing past his window, he was also aware of the fact that his door was unlocked and he was free to explore. Polishing off the last of the buttered fish, he decided that it might be nice to go upstairs and say hello to his neighbour.

Yet after stepping out onto the landing, he felt less certain. He imagined the house filled with animals, all buzzing and screeching and slithering about. Now though it was almost completely silent and filled only with the light seeping in from the windows above and below his floor.

Gale's door was similar to his own, a series of panels secured with horizontal slats and cast iron hinges. Knocking on it was of course a simple enough task but as he raised his fist he found himself hesitating. *Some rooms hold delicate things.* Nor was it just the Keeper's words that made him hesitate. One of his own also raised its prickly head. "*Ligj . . .*"

His voice in that gloomy space sounded trapped somehow, weak, alone. The word was a question, the answer to which he was not yet ready to hear, and before he knew what he was doing, he had turned and was running back down the stairs, each step away from the room above his own filling him with more and more relief.

When he reached the circular reception chamber, however, he decided, again on a whim, to continue down the stairway and into the basement. The ante-chamber in which he found himself was cluttered with broken chairs, an old drop leaf table, an even older typewriter and a wooden bird cage that stood almost as high as the ceiling, all of which made the door in the opposite wall appear overly grand. Formed from six vertical strips of dark wood, each of which bore a letter made from what might have been ivory, the door seemed very different to the others he'd so far come across. The impression it made on him, combine as it did with the word itself—

LIBRARY

—stirred in him a sudden and subversive delight. He imagined books in all shapes and sizes, saw himself blowing dust and poring over sleeves, heard spines cracking, felt the paper warm and dry beneath his fingertips and it was almost without thinking that he reached out and tried the door. The handle turned but to no avail. It was locked.

Disappointed, he returned to the chamber and strode across it to the outer door, where he was presented with the passageway Gribble had carried him down that first night, a dark, roughly-hewn tunnel that stank of damp clay. This brick-paved shaft led to a door many times thicker than those inside the house, an ironclad wedge that, despite its obvious weight, opened with ease, revealing a familiar view of stunted slopes and well-trodden paths. Far down the right-hand slope, a man squinted up at him, his body diffused by light. Behind him and beyond the cliff-edge, the sea and sky were a sparkling blur.

"What you up to, lad?" the man shouted up.

"Just looking," he shouted back.

The man disappeared, only to return with others, their silhouettes glittering as they made their way up the cliff. As before, they turned and headed towards the buildings Liam had spied from his window.

Forgotten, he stepped out and looked about him. The thin grasses and brown rocks reminded him of the Keeper's skull. Though many of the trees were leafless, the air was edged with warmth. Everywhere new buds strained towards the light. Deciding to head for higher ground, Liam followed the path round the lighthouse, to find, in a shallow gully edged by orange turf, a shed, its door secured by a rusty padlock. Through wooden slats he could see a large, grey machine. The generator. Behind the shed lay a tall, rocky bluff that appeared impassable but was in fact cut with gulleys, scored perhaps by wind and rain and rooted with grasses that provided secure enough handhold.

At the top of the bluff, a series of ridges rose through dense patches of grass and briars. A blue-throated lizard perched on the side of a rock, its head twisted as if listening. Determined to reach the island's highest point, Liam began to scramble up one ravine after another, exhilarated by the combination of fresh air and sunshine and movement.

Finally, from a high plateau, he could see, far down on one side, a waterfall crashing into dark green brush, slanting patches of green dotted with early spring flowers, long groves of trees and in the distance, sloping cliffs. He turned and gaped at the view. From what he could see, the island was small, just a few miles across, the lighthouse and the few simple buildings beyond it, its only structures apart from a series of strangely domed shapes that dotted the higher portions of the island and pointed seaward as if searching for invaders. But it was the sea itself that took his breath away. Inside the harbour, the water was grey but as it reached the ocean proper it became a deeper, greener shade. This green circle surrounded him on all sides. Distant rocks appeared and disappeared in a series of delicate, white rings and though he could see water fanning into the air, each collision came to him as no more than a sigh. If the lighthouse were a spindle, the sea was a record playing the same endless tune. Had he come from somewhere beyond all that water, he couldn't believe he'd ever get back.

And then he experienced the strangest sensation. His eyes were closed and yet they were open. The world didn't know he was looking and all was still. Not grew but was. The world might have been a painting so perfectly rendered it appeared to have dimensions. He reached out, felt the surface heat up as if his fingertips were red hot and then the world rippled once more.

Looking down past the waterfall, he saw the silhouette of a creature, its antlers taller than the trees. As he stared, it tore a great mouthful of grass and flowers from the meadow at its feet and stood there, its jaws churning. He held up his hand but could barely make out the lines on his palm. He'd set out just after breakfast, yet the light was already dim. Hours had passed. Shadows filled the ridges. Pink sunlight gossamered the leaves, crystallising in the glass atop the lighthouse. And then the last rays vanished and everywhere was dewy. Without thinking, he went to move, set his foot among wet grasses, slipped and fell, catching his hip on a rock. Pain flashed through his side. The cold, rather than dampen the feeling, only magnified it. He was lying amid a spray of green-winged orchids but though the plants were soft, he felt only the deep cold radiating up through the rock. Eyes slitted, he moved the sea with his breath.

"This is becoming a habit."

A faint moon and the cold shatter of light on the sea carved the Keeper's shape against the air. White hairs danced in the wind. The old man stooped to help him.

"Let's get you up."

Liam felt a sickness in his stomach, a kind of lurching hunger that made him want to throw up. "I hurt myself."

"I can see that," the old man said. "Come, we need to get you home."

OVER THE NEXT WEEK, the Keeper showed a new warmth. Liam had taken a chill and this, coupled with the knock to his hip, made him feverish. But the man's patience was barely tested. Only once, when Liam woke moaning, did he speak harshly.

"You must slough the sorrow from your skin. Let it go, oracle, move forwards, be free . . ."

Liam was glad of the man's company. He saw many confusing things, visions that seemed too plain to be dreams. Birds drifting over fields, their eyes earthward, lambs jumping one after the other, rabbits darting from holes to feed on the grass. During one such vision, he saw a vast circle of water dotted with bodies.

"In a mirror . . ." he said.

He went through periods of icy cold and boiling heat, pulled the blankets round him, then threw them aside, only to go through the same cycle an hour later. Meanwhile the Keeper read to him from the book, first from the passage concerning the oracle and then from others. Burning villages and freezing mountains, plagues and pestilence, drought and flood, all filled his dreams.

Then one morning he woke to hear himself say, "You will fall three times."

The Keeper stared groggily at his ward before feeling around for the water jug. "Bad dreams?" he said, pouring Liam a cup.

The younger man took a mouthful, coughed and then sipped again. "I feel better," he managed. "Better than I did."

The Keeper went to say something but seemed to change his mind. "You must save your strength."

Liam cleared his throat. "No, it's true. I feel better."

As if to prove it, he sat up, rested his shoulders against the stone. Breathing in and out, he felt a heaviness spread through him, as if someone were treading snow into his guts. His nervous disposition had fled with his illness and in its place he felt instead a cold serenity. There had been a flood, he believed that now. He'd seen proof of it and had heard of it from someone he trusted. And during his illness, he'd seen visions of a beleaguered land. But it was the Keeper's kindness that convinced him more than anything else.

"I saw a creature out there." He nodded towards his window. "Enormous . . ."

The Keeper chuckled. "You mean Abraham? Believe it or not, this whole house was once a menagerie, top to bottom. Abraham's one of the last. After the Flood, we penned him up outside but he was soon off. Moose they used to call him. Biggest creature on God's green earth. In the end we let all the creatures go. This house was only meant as a temporary sanctuary. But it was wrong to do it," he said, pursing his mouth. "Letting them out, I mean."

He looked very tired and spoke in a querulous voice. "A few years ago, I noticed certain creatures were going missing, the larger, slower kind. Five nights I kept watch and then, at last, I saw them. Half-a-dozen shapes moving across the sea. Upon reaching the island, two swooped over the far pasture. I saw them lift one of the boars, a vast brute so fat he could barely move, clean into the air, there to tear it in two. Within months, all we had to keep us company were the rats. That and Ol' Abraham. I guess he was too old or too tough."

"And what are they?"

The Keeper peered at him. "When I spoke to you before of mirrors, I neglected to mention who gave them to us. The testament tells of winged seraphim sent to watch over us. Except that they did more than watch. Lusting after our women, they took them for wives and created offspring known as Nephilim, half-blood, bastard children that were a demented fusion of human and divine. For this they were cast down."

Taking up the book, he fingered through the pages, before finding what he was looking for: "'And the angels who did not keep their positions of authority but abandoned their proper dwelling—these he has kept in darkness, bound with everlasting chains for judgment on the great Day.'"

He closed the book in his usual manner. "Envious of our blessed place in the universe, the Nephilim set out to destroy us. In God's image we were made and it was that very image they used against us. Their gift of mirrors blinded us. Oh, the many cruelties men are willing to inflict on one other! It is no wonder God was forced to flood the world. If you were to find a vipers' nest, you too would want to flush it clean. Yet God's plan did not bode well for us. Today there are as many of these creatures as there are of us. Our very survival lies in the balance. The Nephilim's gestation period is only a matter of weeks. They mature in just a few years. If given the chance to spawn, we will be overrun. Yet most of our kind do not know of the battle that looms."

He pierced Liam with his gaze. "But now we have you, the man who survived the waters, born to fill men's hearts with a brightness even the blindest will see." He raised his hand. "This is more than just a lighthouse, Liam. It is a transmitter. With it we can beam the truth into every man's heart."

The old man pressed his advantage. "You are a dreamer, I've seen you in their thrall. Of what do you dream?"

Liam hesitated. "Of a room, a rustling in the dark . . ."

"As of wings?"

"I reach down and something grasps my finger . . ."

"You dream of wings? Of being pulled down?" The Keeper's voice simmered with excitement. "And below you, what there? But of course," he said, answering his own question. "There lieth the embers of hell, seven leagues deep. Then this *proves* it. You lost two souls but you can save thousands more. If you're afraid, do it for them."

Seeing his doubt, the man leaned forward and said in a high, breathless whisper, "What if I told you I had a Nephilim child here in the library?" He took hold of Liam's arm, his eyes burning with a gravid intensity. "If you're not too weak, I could show you."

Liam recalled trying the library door and imagined what might have happened had it not been locked. Still he nodded, an affirmation that caused the Keeper to all but spring to his feet.

"Get dressed," he said. "Wear something warm. We need you well again."

As they descended the stair, the man's words were very loud in the enclosed space. "The Nephilim grow to enormous sizes. I've heard they're even partial to human flesh. This particular specimen came to us three years ago when a boat drifted ashore, its sail slack, its deck empty. What I found in that cabin will haunt me forever."

They followed the staircase down past the ground floor, their boots clanging the metal.

"After descending the cliff with my men, I climbed onto the deck alone and made my way down into a small galley kitchen. There, on narrow seats either side, lay the bodies of two men, their eyes and mouths crawling with flies. Everywhere was covered in blood. At the back, there lay a cabin, its door open, the doorway framing a bed. On the bed, lying on her back, was a pregnant woman, her belly so big it rose almost to the ceiling. She was staring at me. Upside down, her eyes looked almost completely white. I nearly retched at the stench but this poor, distorted woman . . ."

Nimbly traversing the cluttered antechamber, the Keeper thrust a key into a hole hidden at the base of the letter Y, before turning once more to his audience. "What could I do? The woman begged me to save the child and though I'd little knowledge of childbirth, I was still the most qualified midwife in the house. My men carried the woman up the cliff and laid her up there." He pointed towards the ground floor.

"She began to writhe so violently, they had to pin her down. Meanwhile, I administered to the lower end. The baby's head was enormous and covered in a thick mound of hair. Its *eyes*, Liam. Black as oil. The woman screamed again and the child slid out, causing me to catch it before it slithered to the floor. It seemed that half the woman's innards followed with it and soon after she died. That was three years ago. Of course, I did not know what to do with the child. I couldn't kill it but nor could I set it free. Oh, but the way it has grown in only three years! I daren't think what could happen when it comes of age."

With that the Keeper turned the key and pushed open the door, revealing a set of wide stone steps leading down into a huge, vault-like room. From above, the meandering wooden stacks that made up the majority of the library's structure were not unlike a maze built to test a rat, except that this maze was lined with hundreds of book-filled shelves and various nooks and crannies lit by lamps, each one casting a green shaft of light towards the rocky ceiling. After descending the steps and entering first one and then another of these narrow, greenlit corridors, the impression of a labyrinth only increased. Marvelling at the tomes passing either side of him, Liam longed to pull this one or that from the shelves and may even have done so had his contemplation not been interrupted by a low, barking cough.

The old man stopped and listened, then turned and whispered the rest of his story. "Not wanting to alarm the staff, I made the men swear a vow of silence and together we built a cage. The creature's been down here ever since." He held up his hand. "But I must warn you. Fear is nourishment for its kind. I fear but I show it not. If I am to gain anything from this curse, it is to know mine enemy."

The Keeper gripped Liam's shoulder. "Come. Let me show you why dreams must once more rouse mankind."

Liam followed the man along a shadowy corridor, its various cross-sections interspersed with greenlit reading areas. At the far end lay a space that may have once housed a large table. Here wooden stakes had been driven into the stone in a semi-circle that backed onto the wall, their tips touching the ceiling. At the rear of this makeshift cage, where the light barely reached, stirred what looked like a pile of rags. Working a key into the lock binding the branches that made up the door to the stake beside it, the Keeper pushed the door inwards and stepped inside. He beckoned the young man to follow.

The bare, twenty-foot square space reeked of urine and excrement. As they entered, the pile of rags stirred and then rose up, causing a faint band of light to pass across a dark hood, the tip of a nose, a large lower lip. Liam had barely registered the fact that the thing was actually hovering before it launched itself at him, a high-pitched shriek on its lips. With a cry, the Keeper caught hold of him.

"Show no fear! Trust in the Lord!"

At the last moment, the creature snapped to a halt, its fingers inches from Liam's throat, previously unseen chains whining behind it. Its lips were drawn back, exposing sharp little teeth. Finally, it slumped to the ground and shuffled back the way it had come.

The Keeper's eyes were moist. He gave Liam's arm an almost painful squeeze. "Now you see why we must warn our brothers and sisters. These creatures spawn in their thousands. Their hunger is insatiable."

After locking the gate, the man led the way back into the labyrinth, found a table and sat down. "I want to hate it but I can't. It cannot help its fate. But we can stop its kind from spreading once more. You were sent here for a reason. Let not our past become our future. Dream for us," he said, giving Liam's arm another squeeze. "Dream of the wave that swallowed the earth—of the giants that drove us to madness—and I shall shine those visions into the darkest corners and in the morning our brethren will wake and know their enemy. We will arm them with knowledge and they will keep their young closer and their fires brighter."

Liam recalled the creature's eyes. In them he'd glimpsed burning fires, dark shapes, vast bellies opening like obscene flowers. He'd seen himself aboard a ship, lashed to a wheel, about him, a violent storm, behind him, his parents and there, up through the rain, moonlit wings. He glanced behind him. "Only three years old, you say?"

"And every day stronger."

"Then we must begin."

"Not," the Keeper rapped his knuckles on the table with decisive force, "until you're strong enough."

"I'm ready now," Liam insisted.

The Keeper shook his head. "No. Powerful dreams require powerful energy. We will wait."

THE KEEPER HAD NEGLECTED to mention how he was going to extricate Liam's dreams. Over the next few days, the thought had begun to alarm him. This then was why, on the day in question, Penumbra found him pacing his room. To his surprise she addressed him as if her previous truculence had never happened.

"You're very brave," she said, passing him a tall glass of tea. "Agreeing to help the Keeper, I mean."

She sat him down and then sat beside him. Her brown eyes searched his as if shepherding a nervous lamb.

"I can see you're anxious," she said. "To tell the truth, I've been anxious *for* you. That's why I've been so irritable of late. It's not an easy task, giving up your dreams. But it is a noble one."

"But how does he do it?"

Penumbra lowered her eyes. "Such things are beyond me. It is not my place to enquire."

"Then maybe I could ask Gale."

The housekeeper seemed to consider this for a moment, before nodding. "I'll see what I can do. But only if you eat up. You'll need your strength."

The Keeper was due just after sunset. Liam had hoped Penumbra might return before then. If he could only meet Gale, what she had to tell him might put his mind at ease. Yet when his door finally opened, it was the old man and not the housekeeper who greeted him.

"An auspicious evening," the Keeper said gravely.

He was carrying a little black box and a silver tray, upon which glittered a long, glass instrument. Placing both on the bedside table, he turned to the bed and pulled back the sheet. After Liam had climbed in, the man began to tuck the sides of the sheet under the mattress so firmly that the edges were as taught as drum skin. Finally, he picked up the black box and sat down in his usual chair.

"I trust you're feeling better?" he said, taking out Liam's hand as he spoke.

"Much." Liam nodded at the black box. "What's that?"

The Keeper smiled thinly. "Let's just say it records your essence, your, your . . . unconscious vibrations." The man's voice was calming and his hand, rather than cause discomfort, only served to soothe Liam. "Now, please, close your eyes."

Doing so, Liam heard a click, after which the Keeper's tone took on a soft, lilting quality.

"There came a time when man was freed from hardship. The need to work, illness, old age, all receded. And such freedoms might have been liberating, were it not for the envious worms in our midst. One by one, their mirrors began to call to us: How clever you are! How beautiful! How divine! But in turn, they taught us to doubt those whose reflections looked other than our own. We retreated into ourselves. Anger became the prevailing emotion. We were encouraged to misunderstand, to become ever more insular. Such were the right conditions for war, the state the Nephilim desired above all others. Only if they could drive us against each other, could they triumph.

"It is to one side of this many-sided reckoning I wish to take you now. I need you to imagine a land sheathed in yellow ribbons, a place of deserts, one of the few places God's name was still spoken with any conviction. I want you to imagine darker faces than yours or mine, faces incensed by visions, I want you to hear their cries, hear their belief ringing in your ears . . ."

Though he was drifting into sleep, Liam sensed the Keeper reach over the bed, remove the glass instrument from the tray and slide its tip behind his ear before depressing the piston. The man replaced the instrument, wiped a drop of fluid from the pillow and eased back into his chair, all without letting go of Liam's hand.

"Tell me what you see."

As if testing his confinement, Liam arched his back but the sheet remained firmly tucked. His eyes moved faster beneath his lids. Frowns flickered across his face. His head turned one way and then

the other. When at last he spoke, it was in a thick voice. "This watch
. . ." He tried to raise his arm. "My brother's." Mumbled word, then
more clearly, "I gave it to him for a wedding present. We carried him
and his bride through the gardens on a table. Such a day, such a
*ha*ppy day."

But he did not sound happy. "I found something in the road. After
all the bombs, everywhere was in ruins. This thing, it might have been
a piece of pipe, a branch. But then I saw the watch and realised it
was my brother's arm."

His voice grew furious. "How many more must die? They have set
fire to the night. What is one more body?"

Tears formed beneath his lids and his next words sounded broken.
"Amena, my love, my only daughter." He smiled and saliva shone in
his mouth. "I can still see you springing out at me, laughing, making
me jump."

The smile shrivelled, became nothing. "We dug for days. Among
all that rubble, Amena was just one more lump, all that energy
drained into the dust. My little girl choked to death, alone, in the
dark. I kissed the dust from her skin." Like something trying to walk
again, he said, "Is it too much to want her body here, to want to show
her that she was wrong. *This* is how Allah treats our enemies. But
look!" His head was tipped back as if he were seeing something.
"Look—*see*." He began to wrestle beneath the sheet. "*Takbir*! They
know our position. Allah, protect us. They have fired on us!"

iii.
———

LIAM WOKE TO A ROVING darkness, the candle flame
drowning in its own wax. He tried to pour the liquid away, only to
spill hot wax across his fingers. For a moment he felt bathed in fire
and recalled, as if in a flash, giants hovering above the ground,
seraphim turning like vultures overhead, fire melting sand into glass.
He was so tired, he could barely keep his eyes open, yet the idea of
sleep was abhorrent. Only after what felt like hours of tossing and
turning did he drift into a troubled slumber.

The next night, the Keeper came again. Again he brought the black box and the glass instrument.

"I've brought your supper myself," he said, presenting slabs of cheese on thick brown bread topped with an evil-looking chutney. "I didn't want you distracted."

Though he didn't feel hungry, Liam took a small bite. "When I woke, you were gone," he said.

"You were exhausted. I let you sleep. Tonight will not be so tasking, I think. Tonight I want you only to watch."

Liam settled his limbs and slowed his breathing, willing his body to comfort. Directed by the Keeper, he closed his eyes and counted his breaths.

The man's words were as pumice. "You've dreamt for me of the final fire. Tonight, I want you to see the aftermath, the brick-choked streets, the living crawling among the dead. Oh, the cries for mercy! The things men will do when God is blinded by smoke. Now rise up—rise *up*—see the carnage below you, see how it dwindles into nothing the higher you climb, how abstract it all becomes. Now you are one with the heavens, the world below you no more than a burning ember in the enormity of space. All you need do is command the seas to overwhelm the earth and all that pain can be washed away. Look, see the waters rise. There, Liam, the Flood! Watch it *rise.*"

The previous evening, the Keeper's words had calmed him but tonight something in him fought the man's visions. At first, he did indeed see the world from afar but though the sight of its scorched hills and valleys was painful, it was too distant to seem real. Godlike he sat among the stars, observing the flames flicker across the planet. But he wanted nothing of this absence and his face began to tighten. Again he sensed the Keeper slip the syringe behind his ear and press the piston.

"Now, Liam, witness. The Lord has commanded the waters to rise, watch and tell me what you see." The man's words hissed into the ear behind which he had pushed the needle. "*Speak!*"

But he was no longer in space, he was falling through an iridescent emptiness, down and down, faster and faster, the planet beneath him unfurling like a blue flower, his body roaring as it punctured the stratosphere, his skin bubbling, his hair ablaze. Smoke spun in the air and he breathed his own burning. Flames whistled in his ears and then he was tumbling towards an ocean, its surface rising towards him at a terrific rate. He saw a meteor reflected in the waves and then the water was all around him, replacing the sound of rushing air with a hissing reminiscent of white hot iron thrust into a bucket. He opened his eyes, stared into blanketing depths, saw steam coalesce about him, capture him, extend his body in all directions until he could no longer see his extremities. As he sank, the winking sunlight weakened, the water darkened, the fish darting from his plummeting form grew less distinct until finally he settled, a giant in the darkness of his own imagination. He wondered if he might drown but drowning was not to be, for he was rising again, slowly and then faster until he was ascending at such a rate that the water pressed at his eyes and dragged at his hands.

"*Rising*." His skin was taut against his skull. He kept gasping as if he couldn't get enough oxygen. "I am a wall of water, my body—" His head slipped sideways—"my arms . . . but there's light, the surface, I can see the surface." Tears ran from his eyes. "I am rising, the waves are mountains, high enough to tear down the sky. And each wave a wing."

For a moment, Liam was inside the boat that had carried the foetal Nephilim to the island. Wall, floor and ceiling soaked in blood. Before him, a woman on a bed, her chin jutting, her eyes staring. Then her stomach blossomed, its crown opening like a flower.

The Keeper's words sounded far away. "Rise, Liam, see it below you. See with *God's* eyes."

He was at the crest of a towering wave, his body spread across its peak. He could see land now, a burning shore, a river mouth, a city of lights. "*Run*," he cried.

But though those below him sought cover, tumbling through doorways, alleyways, along streets, it was no use. He saw one woman very clearly. She was standing in the middle of a green-treed park, a child in her arms. She was staring upwards and though her lips did not move, her voice was very clear.

"Please come back to us," it said.

And then the four states became one. Thundering downwards, he made splinters of boats, shards of trees, coils of bridges, skeletons of buildings, turned earth into bedrock, tunnels into trenches, streets into gulleys, while all around him swirled with mud, rubble, grit and among it, bodies and parts of bodies.

"Return." Someone was shaking him.

He felt an irresistible tug, a great sucking and then he was being drawn back at a tremendous rate, pulling everything he had destroyed with him, rising once more into the sky.

"Return!"

Liam felt himself thrashing on the bed, his feet drumming, his teeth grinding and then a slap, once, twice, and he woke with a gasp. His hands were still trapped, his nails pushed into his skin. Meanwhile, the Keeper was arranging his robe as if having just finished some unseemly business. He was panting, his chest heaving.

Liam pulled his hands free, saw blood-smeared palms. "What have I done?" he croaked.

The tray shook slightly in the Keeper's hands. "You have saved us," he said, his eyes not quite meeting Liam's. "Mark my words, this day will be remembered forever."

And with that he opened the door and was gone.

Chapter 3.

The Man in the Kitchen

1

THE SUMMER WILL MET Eric, his second at the university, Birmingham was so hot, it resembled a refracted maze of glass and light and sky. On campus, students sunbathed on the library steps or lounged in the shadows, their usual enthusiasms stymied by the heat. The University Square, surrounded by the library and the English block, the refectory and the Great Hall with its clock tower—the tallest in the world and one which Will had climbed only once, for the height did not agree with him—was as hot as a furnace, its grassy expanse populated only where the trees afforded shadow.

Will was heading across the Square, intent on getting the majority of the books on his summer reading list from the library. Most were sold in the university bookshop but they were always overpriced and he'd already used up his overdraft. Had he decided otherwise, had he even approached the library along a different path, he would have marched up the library steps, sighed with relief as he stepped into the building's cool interior, then spent half an hour looking for the desired material before realising that all but one of the tomes had been checked out already by students who were a little faster on the draw. But as it was, he did none of these things, for the path he chose that day took him within hearing distance of a conversation between a boy and a girl sitting in the shade of a lime tree, their limbs and faces laced with light-green shadows, their discussion heated enough that when the boy said something about 'Ashling', it was clearly audible. It was also rather surreal. No one in Birmingham had ever heard of Ashling, so for Will to hear that word there on that sun-blasted lawn was enough to stop him in his tracks.

"Ashling in Kent?" he said, disbelievingly.

The girl was eating an apple and glanced up at him, an unfriendly look in her eye. The boy was wearing a long leather coat that made Will break out in sweat just looking at it, his hair tied back in a ponytail, his temples surrounded by loose red curls, his skin blotchy with freckles. He had been leaning back but he bent forwards now and looked at his palms as if to inspect the grass lines there.

"Don't tell me you're from Ashling?" he said, his eyes narrowed in the light, his irises two mint green glints as he frowned upwards. When Will nodded, the boy added, "I was just telling Ezzy here, nary a more soulless place exists. I mean, pretty but pretty soulless, right?"

Yet even as he spoke, he was inspecting Will's face, his head cocked, one eye closed in a squint. "Where do I know you from? You didn't go to Aldham, did you?"

Aldham was Ashling's one and only private school. Will's parents would have liked to send him there but they couldn't afford it.

"No," he said. But then he too saw something in the other. Take away the long hair, the leather coat. "Were you in that poetry thing by any chance?" he said, recalling a pale-cheeked, flame-haired youth sitting up against a wall between two stacks of chairs.

The poetry competition was an annual event put on by the Ashling Borough Council. It was quite a big deal in the town. Most of the parents went and children spent weeks memorising and practising their lines.

"Yes! That's right, didn't you . . ?"

"Total brain freeze," Will said. "I could only remember one line and I kept saying it over and over . . ."

The girl was looking at him now like he was slow.

He gritted up a little smile. "Didn't you take first prize?"

"Lucky me," the boy said drolly. "The winner of a tatty little book of poems."

"Keats, of course," Will said.

The boy introduced his friend as the Unseasonable Esther, himself as Eric the Eveready. "Just remember Assault and Battery," he said in the same droll tone that Will would soon find typical of the boy. "Are you hungry by any chance?"

They ate in the refectory, sitting by a window overlooking the Square. Eric and Esther were studying Astrophysics. Like Will, they were just finishing their second year. Before they parted, Eric scribbled down his address.

"Come over," he said, "we'll do lunch."

Catching the train a week later, Will found himself reassessing Ashling. Passing the old bathhouses, the most notable candidate when looking for the town's soul, he decided that any such spirit had fled the moment the spring dried up. The buildings had since been used for a variety of misbegotten schemes, none of which had revived the town's former glories. Yet despite Eric's rather dismal appraisal, when Will finally stepped out onto Ashling's single platform and took in the dandelion-and-ragwort-choked sidings and listened to the magazine racks twist rustily in the wind, he quite liked the effect. It made the town seem both quainter and more sheltering, as if the tentacles taking hold of the world would never bother with such backwater haunts. No virtual adverts for us, the fading, flapping posters said, no gastro pubs, no multiscreen cinemas, no bowling mazes. Just a butcher's, a baker's and a place that sold scented candles.

Will was bored within a week. In August, with Lorenzo gone, it got even worse, especially since employment in Ashling was so limited. As for his parents, his mother had become obsessed with gardening and his father rarely graced the ground floor.

It was in this mood then that Will found Eric's address turning blue in his back pocket. He recognised it as one of Ashling's nicer areas. Certain Eric didn't really want to become buddies, Will looked up his number anyway and called it several times. No one answered. The last time he let it ring a dozen times before a girl picked up and said, "Hell?"

He waited for the 'o' before asking for Eric. The voice said, "No, it's not. Hold on."

Eric took an age to come to the phone and if Will hadn't been feeling stubborn, he might have hung up. When Eric did finally pick up, he seemed neither surprised nor put out. He asked if Will had had lunch and then told him to come over.

His house certainly was in a nice area. Montrose Avenue, set on the opposite hill to Will's parents', was part of an exclusive little development built in the fifties. The house itself, though not gated, was a double fronted villa with a line of cherry trees either side of a wide drive.

A wiry, dark-haired woman answered the door and peered past Will as if he might be leading a mob. The inside of the house was dark but she didn't switch on any of the lights as she led him down the hallway and through an archway into the kitchen. After she left, he sat there listening to the clock clack above the backdoor. When a girl walked in, he knew straightaway she must be Eric's sister. She was dark like her mother, though with hair a little straighter and eyes a little browner. She and Eric shared an unmistakeable confidence. Will's presence seemed to surprise her about as much as might a loose button. Will, on the other hand, felt like he'd taken a shortcut at the zoo, only to find himself on the wrong side of the bars.

The girl asked if Will was the boy on the telephone, then, when he nodded, held out her hand.

"Ruby," she said, a wicked glimmer in her eye, "Ruby Moon, at your service."

Noting how cool her fingers felt in his hot, damp palm, Will nevertheless managed to rise to the occasion. "No, please," he said, "Billy Blake, at *your* service."

As they shook, the gesture long and languid and self-mocking, something passed between them, an understanding neither would ever put into words but that both would remember long after that day.

"Billy Blake," she laughed. "Come to save my brother."

"From what?" he asked.

"From himself, of course."

It was an obvious challenge but Will had no time to pursue it, for just then Eric came in, got two Cokes from the fridge and told Will to follow him. Will glanced at Eric's sister as they left but she was stirring her tea and didn't look up.

ERIC AND WILL SAW a lot of each other that summer but to Will's frustration, Eric's sister did not reappear. Her real name was Ruth and she'd just completed her third year at Imperial College but beyond that, Eric told him very little. He seemed uninterested. He did, however, look rather keenly at Will when he asked what Ruth was studying. They were lounging in the grass bordering Stour Pond, the remains of a bottle of cider festering in the weeds between them. Cream and copper clouds crowded out the light, piling slowly upwards into a rose-tinted sky.

"It's going to rain," Will predicted. He readjusted the grass in his hand so that the blade was trapped more tightly between his thumbs but when he blew on it, the noise was still feeble. A flopping sound reached them from the pond.

"My sister's an over-achiever," Eric offered unexpectedly. "I'm not sure she's your type. I could see you with some chirpy checkout girl, one of those happy little bubbles who always ask if you want help with your packing." He rose up onto his elbows. "You're a fun-loving guy. Ruth's dead against the stuff. If I were you I'd stay away. Take it as a friendly warning."

His words heralded the first drops of rain and they jumped up and followed the curve of the pond until its southernmost edge disappeared into a patch of mud. Rather than take the path towards town, Eric led Will in a different direction.

Beyond the pond lay a smaller pool, bordered, on the far side, by a slanting shelf of rock, its surface darkening in the rain, its uppermost edge hidden by a thick canopy of leaves. Eric leapt across the edge of the pool and began to climb the rock towards the treeline. Determined to beat him, Will ran up the steep, sloping rock, before ducking beneath the overhanging leaves that shrouded the top of the bluff. Too late, he realised that the rock ended very suddenly. Amid a confusion of leaves, he lost his footing and went over the edge, only just managing to catch himself. As he tried to find a foothold, he felt his foot paw at some sort of opening and then Eric was pulling him up and they were collapsing together onto the rocky lip, the branches and the dark green leaves above them dripping with rain.

Eric's eyes were catlike in the gloom. He was panting but managed to catch his breath long enough to say, "I guess that means I saved your life."

When Will told him about the opening, they pushed their heads through the foliage to take a look. The slab of rock ended as abruptly as if cut with a cleaver. From the hollow thirty feet below, seven or eight alders fought upwards, creating the canopy above their heads. They craned their necks and saw a jagged opening in the surface below them. Before Will could stop him, Eric began to lower himself off the edge, before securing a foothold and vanishing.

Gripping the edge of the rock, Will leaned out but Eric was nowhere to be seen. From where he lay, he could see that the rock beneath him was split in two. At the top of this divide lay a wide, tear-shaped fissure that closed a few feet below him. He was just contemplating what might have caused such a violent division when Eric reappeared, his howling head filling Will's vision. It was obviously meant as a joke but Will was so startled that he jerked sideways, hit a patch of wet leaves and slid over the edge. He managed to get a handhold but only for a moment. The rock was wet and he slipped.

As he fell, Eric tried to grab him, only to lose balance himself, so that a moment later, both boys were tumbling down into the hollow. Branches flashed by, thrashing twigs and leaves, flickering stems. Will's feet struck a branch, shooting his knees up into his stomach. He snatched at a trunk, wrenched his shoulder and then crashed between two alders, sinking into a bed of leaves. He heard birds, raucous and fading, as if cry and host had been parted. He felt a blissful moment of numbness, then sharp lines of pain flaring across his back, his stomach, his fingers. His ears sang and for a moment his lungs refused to fill. Remarkably, though, that was all.

Eric, who had landed a few feet away, lay there for a few moments, laughing and coughing, before pulling himself up. "Fuck me," he wheezed. "We live to fight another day."

"What were you thinking, jumping out like that?" Hardly able to contain his angry, Will dashed at the leaves on his clothes before standing up and lurching away.

Eric shouted after him, "It's deep up there, you know? Don't you at least want to see it?"

Will suspected that Eric had known about the cave all along. If so, then he should have warned him about the drop. As he marched home, he kept mulling over Eric's advice concerning Ruth. Despite saying otherwise, it had not sounded friendly. He swore then, if he saw her again, he would take a chance.

That chance came a week later. Needing to get out of the house, he biked down to the newsagents, left his absurdly undersized Raleigh Grifter propped up outside and went into the shop. As he walked along the nearest aisle of overstocked shelves, he heard the door chimes jangle as another customer came into the shop. Picking up a packet of Jaffa cakes, he made his way to the counter, where Nigel stood blinking at him from behind the same spectacles he'd been wearing ever since Will's paper-round days. Will nodded and waited for Nigel to recognise him but Nigel just licked his fingers and took the box.

Will almost said nice to see you too, Mr Jacobsen, but bit his lip. The man was clearly not the sentimental type. Instead, he asked for a bottle of vodka. Mumbling something about the hour, the old man turned to scan the shelf behind him. That was when Ruth appeared.

"Well, if it isn't Billy Blake. A little early for vodka, isn't it?"

"Actually . . ." Will said but Ruth just laughed.

"I know," she said. "It's William Zifla. I believe William Blake was more of an ale man."

Will left the bike outside the shop in the hope that some kid might nick it and they walked up Market Street and out towards the old sewage plant. The day was hot and the settling tanks filled the air with a sweet, faecal scent. When he mentioned it, Ruth said that it reminded her of where she came from.

"Soon you'll hardly notice. It's like Ashling. Proof that you can get used to anything."

Someone had thrown a red leather car seat over the fence. "Austin Allegro," Will said, squinting through the chain-link. "Why would someone go to all the effort of throwing it over?"

Ruth wasn't interested in why, only that it was there. She'd obviously visited the place before and knew exactly where the hole in the fence was. They stooped through the chain-link and threw themselves down on the chair. Will opened the vodka and stared at the wheat field beyond the furthest wall, catching little snatches of Ruth's face and body each time he passed the bottle. She was wearing a thin blouse, the top buttons undone. Her eyes were tawny in the sunlight. Will's head was crawling with thoughts and every now and again, much to Ruth's amusement, he leapt up and marched about. He told her Eric had warned him away, he couldn't help it. He asked if Eric was always so over-protective.

Ruth raised her eyebrows as if to suggest surprise. "You were asking about me?"

Throwing himself back down, Will glanced at her. "I just like to know what kind of trouble I'm getting into."

"More than you can handle, Billy," she grinned. "More than you can handle."

It felt as if the heat were pushing them together. They drank some more, closed their eyes, listened to the insects.

Ruth said something about Eric needing a friend.

Still with his eyes closed, Will said, "I didn't think the two of you were that close."

"He doesn't get close to anyone," she said. "But he likes you."

"I'm a likeable guy," Will said, opening his eyes finally.

"That's what I thought."

They were sitting very close together so that when Ruth lifted her chin, kissing her was natural. Will felt lightheaded, as if they were sitting at the centre of a spinning top, its rushing surface decorated with sunlight and trees and birds.

iii.
—

BACK AT UNIVERSITY, he decided not to speak to Eric for a while. It was a childish impulse but he was worried that Ruth, out of some sibling spite, might have told him about their day together. But then Eric called Will. It was a Saturday and he was supposed to be going to a party but the moment he heard Eric's voice, he forgot all about it. Eric said he was at the OVT. Will could hear *By the Way* pounding out of the jukebox.

"Someone here wants to see you!" Eric shouted.

Will's digs were a mile from the Old Varsity Tavern. He made it in half-an-hour, walked into an uproar. Jostling students were shouting and laughing at each other over the sound of *Out of Space*, its thumping, jangling rhythms causing everything from the stained floor to the cluttered bar to the bottles and glasses behind it to rattle and hum.

Will found Eric and five others arranged along a wall seat in the back bar. Ruth was sitting the furthest away, her hair shorter, her mascara darker, her eyes full of violet hints. Eric jumped up, threw an arm round Will and began pointing with a lit cigarette at each of his friends, all of whom were sedate by comparison.

"Last but not least," he said, "there's my little Rook."

Eric peered sideways at Will, a special kind of knowledge in his eyes. "But I believe you two are already acquainted. As for *mon bel ami* here," he said, clapping a hand on Will's shoulder, "be careful, he's a writer!"

He planted a kiss on Will's cheek and headed for the bar. Will felt Ruth's eyes watching him as he said hi to everyone.

"What a coincidence," she said when it was her turn.

Will just shook his head. "It's odd seeing you outside of Ashling."

"Yet that's exactly where I like to be," she said, creating a space between herself and Haddam, a moustachioed boy from Jerusalem.

99

"Rook?" Will said, sitting down. "What's that all about?"

Ruth made a long-suffering face. "When I was a kid, I had a thing for pickled eggs. Eric thinks they're disgusting. He says they look like eyeballs. He read somewhere that rooks like to land on sheep's heads and peck out their eyeballs, hence his delightful nickname."

Eric reappeared, asked if Ruth had any change. When he'd gone again, Will asked why Ruth was in Birmingham.

"I was at a loose end," she said lightly. "It's reading week at Impy. I went to Spain for a few days but then I thought, why not visit my baby brother?"

"I'm meant to be going to a party," Will said. "I thought maybe you'd like to . . . I mean, Eric could come too," he finished lamely.

Even as he spoke, the man himself appeared, three drinks caught between his long, pale fingers. "Come where?"

When Will told him, he said, "Christ, man! Griffin Close may as well be on Mars."

"I'm not allergic to buses," Will said defensively. "Besides, I'll be living closer next year."

Eric snorted. "How do you know you'll even *be* here next year?"

At the same time Will heard Ruth say, "Sounds cool."

She was leaning on him, he could smell her perfume. Where their bodies touched, he kept feeling little shocks.

"The party," she said when he looked confused. "I'd love to come. Who needs Eric, anyway? If you ask me, he can be a little over-protective."

Eric didn't appear to be listening but he must have been because he reached into his pocket and threw something at Will, or rather two things, one of which he caught, the other he missed. As he bent to pick it up, he realised it was a condom.

"You can never be *too* over-protective," Eric said, grinning at Will as he sat back up.

The party was a disaster. Neither he nor Ruth had thought to bring drinks and all they found in the kitchen was a flat bottle of cola and a few cans of Carling. They fought their way from room to room, found someone throwing up in the bath and then Will asked if Ruth wanted to see his flat.

The thought of sex filled him with a sudden, lurching dread. It wasn't that he didn't want to, he'd certainly imagined it, it was just that the vibe was wrong. At the same time a voice kept asking him what he was waiting for.

Ruth followed him into the flat and shut the door. With the windows steamed up, the kitchen felt claustrophobic. Ruth's reflection ghosted through the glass before settling in the rented television. Five storeys up, they could still hear the party. Will turned on a lamp and searched the fridge, found only sour milk and stale bread. Finally he discovered an out-of-date bottle of Baileys hidden in a box of Rice Crispies. He filled an eggcup and Ruth sipped at it while it was still in his fingers.

She was looking at him. "Why do you write?" she said.

The question surprised him. No one had ever asked him it before. "Because," he said, thinking about it, "I want someone to know I was here. I want to write a great novel and until I do, I won't give up."

Not trusting the way she was looking at him, he tried to think of a question of his own. "Eric told me you're an over-achiever. What did he mean by that?"

Ruth carried on looking at him, then looked away and smiled. "If you're going to do something, I just think, do it properly, otherwise what's the point?"

Seeing her smile, as if she were hiding some secret, he thought how lovely she was. "Why Ruby Moon?" he said.

Ruth laughed. "It's the name of a play. Ruby never really appears. I liked it, it was really screwed up."

He was nodding. "I thought it was something like that. Billy Blake is probably one of my favourite writers." He looked up, remembering. "I was angry with my friend: I told my wrath, my wrath did end."

"I was angry with my foe . . ." Ruth said slowly, but she couldn't remember the rest.

"I told it not, my wrath did grow," Will finished for her.

They looked at each other anew and then Ruth reached out and smoothed down the logo on his t-shirt.

"Tell me something more about yourself."

He thought about it for a moment. "You know the little auto-garage just outside of Ashling? It used to be my dad's. It's where he met my mum. He said a pretty girl walked in one day and he just had to see her again. When she came back for her car, he'd replaced half the engine, the tyres, even the radio. Mum was so impressed, she couldn't say no when he asked her to take him for a spin."

"Interesting," Ruth said. "I ask you to tell me something about yourself and you tell me something about your parents." She laughed. "I'm only joking. It was a lovely story. Mine is not so . . . more Baileys, please."

While Will poured, she told him about her parents, that her mum used to work for the Fisheries Commission, that after having her and her brother, she'd suffered from depression.

"Dad comes from a big fishing family. They used to own a large fleet up north. But after his parents died, he and his brother sold up and Dad bought a couple of trawlers in Portsmouth. That's where I was born. But then Mum got sick and the doctor suggested she might do better in familiar surroundings, so we moved to Ashling, her home town. Dad kept the fleet on but Mum didn't like him being away. My Uncle Philip bought a lobster boat and Dad started going up to see him in Yorkshire and got really hooked. I think he did anything to stay away. That's when Mum started going a little mad. Whenever Dad brought a lobster home, she'd have to go out. She couldn't bear to hear it scrabbling round in the pan. So Dad went back on the boats and Mum went back on the bottle."

They were both quiet for a moment and then Ruth said, "Have I told you that I'm taking a voluntary course in Spanish?"

Will laughed. "Who takes voluntary courses?"

She squinted at him, then shook her head. "The point is, you remind me of someone, a writer. A friend from the course lent me a book of short stories by Roberto Bolaño. Do you know him? He's from Chile but he's dying in Spain somewhere. When I read his

102

stories, I fell in love. Just like that. Anyway, you remind me of him, of his writing. Something. I've been translating the title story, *Putas Asesinas*, in my spare time. Perhaps you'd like to read it sometime?"

"In your spare time?" Will grinned then nodded. "Yes. I'd like that. Roberto Bolaño . . . never heard of him. A great name for a revolutionary. Or a writer, of course."

Ruth shrugged. "I'd read stories written by William Zifla."

They kissed, their lips slippery with Baileys. Yet when she led him to the bedroom, he knew they weren't going to have sex. They'd been intimate but there was still some obstacle. The room was in shadow, the curtains a faint, quivering orange. They got undressed and slipped under the duvet in their underwear. Ruth lay her head on his chest so that her hair gathered under his chin in a green-apple-and-smoke scented mass.

He lay there as lost as a lamb in the forest, drawing in her scent, feeling the swell and creak of her bra against his chest. Finally she asked what he was going to do after he graduated. "Even writers need to pay bills," she said. He felt her fingers slide across his skin. "You'd make a good teacher. You've got the right vibe. Earnest, you know?"

Though she hadn't drunk much, she seemed tipsy. "I think," she said, yawning, "I might be falling for you . . . But, *but*," she said, tapping his chest, "I mustn't." Her finger slowed, finally settling over his breastbone. "I'd only break your heart."

iv.

THE NEXT MORNING, WILL felt oddly relaxed, as if the Baileys were still curdling in his stomach. Ruth ordered a taxi and they waited out on the kerb, her leaning on him, one hand around his arm. They said very little and he found himself mulling over her words from the night before. He wanted to share with her his conclusion. That maybe broken hearts aren't so bad. That muscles must be torn before they can grow.

In the end, though, he said nothing. He didn't even ask for her number and only thought of it as the taxi pulled away. Of course, he

103

had her home number and knew where she lived but this point proved a frustrating one, the problem being that for the next few months, whenever he called, she wasn't in. She did leave something behind though. After seeing her off, he went up to his room to find several printed sheets of paper sitting on his desk. It was the story she'd mentioned, *Putas Asesinas*.

In the meantime, Eric and he started skipping lectures to play pool, blocking up the pockets of the table in the OVT and eking out a couple of pints while they shot balls round the baize. It was there, watching the balls bounce round the table, that Eric laid out the thesis upon which he had based his dissertation. It had something to do with what he called 'entanglement', the mystery as to why the quantum world of the microscopic behaved so differently to the classical world.

"When two objects, protons, for example," he said, lining up a shot, "are entangled, even when they're billions of miles apart, if you affect one, it instantaneously causes a reaction in the other."

He smacked the white ball, splitting two reds so that one bounced off the cushion and the other rolled down it to nudge against the paper he'd wadded into the pocket. "But what I want to know," he said, lining up another shot with the same thoughtful nonchalance, "what I'm working on, in fact, is a theory of why we can't see these effects in our everyday lives."

It was the last he spoke of it until that Christmas, when the two boys, having returned to Ashling for the holidays, started meeting up nearly every day. The Dog and Duck was their preferred rendezvous point, though sometimes they just met at one or the other of their houses, there to play Canasta and drink beer. Always when he was at Eric's, Will hoped to see Ruth but according to her brother she was in London getting paid to wrap presents in some fancy department store. Still, the ghost of her resided and each time he caught a certain scent as he passed her room, or spied one of her blouses lying on the floor, he was visited by a strange thrill.

As for his own dissertation, he'd already been docked a whole grade because he was so late handing it in. The subject, the Romantic poets, had seemed a gift but after penning what he thought was a decent introduction, he'd only succeeded in writing himself into a series of dead-ends. Out of desperation, he turned to Eric, whose knowledge of the subject stretched much further than the poem he'd memorised all those years ago. He may have been a Science major but he could just as easily have done his bachelors in literature.

"I've got until the end of the holiday," Will told him. "If I don't hand it in then, Gobby's going to throw me off the course."

The two boys were sitting in Will's bedroom, Will on the bed, Eric in a chair by the window, a copy of Will's introduction in his hand. Will had described his tutor, Professor Grobesby, as a kind seeming gentleman whose threats were nevertheless to be taken seriously. Rumour had it that several students had already been forced to repeat the year due to his influence.

Eric was reading Will's introduction with a great deal of concentration and did not respond to Will's lamentations, a fact that made Will rather nervous. He did not relish Eric's appraisal, for he could be quite critical, and waited until he was absolutely sure that Eric had finished his deliberations before asking him what he thought.

"This line here," Eric said, returning his gaze to the paper, *"The romantic poets believed imagination to be a force that could be used to both transcend and transform the world . . .* where did you get it?"

The question caused Will to blush. "I read it somewhere," he said. "Not exactly in those words, of course, but . . ."

While he spoke, Eric rose from his chair to survey the back garden, his face so close to the window, his breath created brief blooms on the glass as he shared his thoughts. "Does it not remind you of my own thoughts? The talk is always of *consciousness*," he said, as if to himself. "But such is not exclusive to the human race. Imagination, however,"—and here he held up the paper without turning around—"that is ours and ours alone. The problem, as laid out in my own dissertation, is that in the quantum world everything is little more than possibility. But then in the classical world, when observed, that possibility collapses and become particles."

Will couldn't quite grasp what Eric was talking about, nor what it had to do with his dissertation. Still, in the hope that the two might be connected, he tried his best to listen.

"But what's interesting," Eric went on, "is that, with one of the theories I've been dallying with, the wave function doesn't necessarily need to collapse, not," he said, breathing on the glass and drawing two lines in the condensation, "if what actually happens is that both wave and particle go their separate ways. In other words, when a quantum event occurs, this *decoherence* causes another you to branch away from the original and move off into a kind of parallel world."

No. Will was definitely lost. "Are you trying to suggest that my dissertation might be one of these quantum events?"

"A quantum event," Eric said, with mock patience, "is any event that does not obey the rules of classical physics. At the moment, your dissertation most definitely lies within the classical realm."

"Well, *half* of it," Will said, in the hope that he might nudge things in the right direction.

"What I'm trying to say is, all previous postulations on such events hypothesise the new world as being identical to our own, at least at the moment of branching. But what if that's not true? What if those with a powerful enough imagination were able to influence the quantum world? I mean, it says it right here," he said, shaking the paper. "The romantics believed imagination to be a force that could be used to both trans*cend* and trans*form* the world. Meaning to go beyond, to *change*. But how can we do that with only our imaginations? Unless," he said, turning around and fixing Will with a rather smug grin, "imagination can affect matter. Which of course it can. It is, after all, a form of *en*ergy. If matter can become imagination then obviously imagination can become matter. Ergo, e = mc2. Energy equals mass and vice-versa."

Will had lain back against the wall and was looking up at the shelf above him as if to ground himself in the material. "This is just a theory, Eric, a *thought experiment.* Having to get my dissertation onto Grobesby's desk by January 12th is a *fact.*"

106

"*Just* a theory?" Eric said, whirling and throwing Will's papers at him so that they scattered across the room. "*Just* a thought experiment? First of all, applying the word 'just' to anything scientific is a misplaced modifier if ever I've heard one. And secondly, I'll have you know that the many-worlds interpretation is not just a thought experiment. There is a lot of evidence to suggest that all matter springs out of consciousness, not the other way round. I'm talking about your poets, here. What if imagination is the driving force behind everything? What if the romantic poets *didn't* all die young? What if they found the secret to the universe, of the *multi*verse, and sauntered off to pastures new? I mean, they were into all sorts of drugs, opium, laudanum, *God* knows what else. Imagine giving minds like that a trip! It's holy-fucking-Catherine-wheel time, isn't it?"

Finally beaten, Will told Eric that he was going to get them both a drink and went downstairs, only for Eric to follow him.

"What do you think, Mr Zifla?" he said to Will's father who was in the kitchen, spooning coffee into a cup while the kettle boiled.

"About what?" the man said good-humouredly.

Ever since Will had introduced Eric to his parents, both parties had gotten on surprisingly well. In fact, whenever Will came home with him, his parents had gotten into the habit of dragging both boys into the kitchen for glasses of G&T and the kind of conversations that drove Will up the wall. And Eric seemed to enjoy his parents' company too, returning Elizabeth's covertly flirtatious banter with much laughter and the occasional wink and providing Avni with what he craved most, someone to argue with.

"So are you suggesting," Avni said, after Eric had explained his hypothesis, "that Keats and the rest tried to bring about one of these quantum events in order to create a branch? That they actually set out to kill themselves? Sorry, Eric," he said, "but that is the most ridiculous theory I've ever heard."

Eric was not to be dissuaded. "But you have to admit," he said, "that they put themselves in harm's way. Byron, Shelley and Keats all died young and all of their deaths unusual." He counted on his fingers. "Byron caught a fever while fighting in the Greek War of Independence, Shelley drowned during a boating incident and though Keats officially died of tuberculosis, apparently he was giving himself massive doses of mercury to 'cure' another ailment." Eric held up his fingers. "What if they learned the secret, the ability to choose which path they followed? It would be like stepping off a sinking ship. What if we too could follow the one path that led us to happiness, to triumph, to truth?"

Will raised his eyes to the ceiling, his patience finally at an end. "Not that any of this is helping me with my dissertation."

It was a thoughtless comment, for his parents had no idea how behind he was with his work. If they found out, he would be grounded on the spot. But as it was, his father was laughing at something Eric was saying and missed the comment.

v.
———

ON NEW YEAR'S EVE, Elizabeth invited Eric to eat lunch with them. He'd already eaten but Will's mother insisted he stay for seconds and served roast turkey with roasted onions and carrots followed by homemade trifle stuffed with rum-soaked gurabija, an Albanian biscuit she was particularly good at baking. Afterwards, they all sat watching the snow, which had begun to drift past the windows in thicker and thicker flakes. Will knew that New Year's Eve was a difficult time for his father, who always shut himself in his study and wouldn't come out until the new year had officially arrived. They'd never had a party or even watched the fireworks on TV. He didn't know why. That evening, though, bolstered by Eric's presence, Will insisted his father come out to the pub with them.

"You too, Mum," he said, though he didn't really mean it. "Let's get sloshed together."

Elizabeth said, "Your father doesn't want to go out."

"I do like getting sloshed," Avni said, smiling. "But I don't think I'll be going out tonight. You two go though. And you, Lizzy, if you wish?" His smile became something else for his wife.

108

"Or," Elizabeth said, "maybe it might do Will some good, them both, perhaps, to know what this evening means to you?"

Avni looked troubled. But even as he stared down at his empty bowl, he started nodding. "Maybe we could take a drink in my study. Yes, you're right, maybe we could do that."

Upstairs, he opened a drawer and rescued a heavy-sounding bottle as it rolled to the back. "Skanderbeg, three star," he said, filling their glasses and raising his own in a toast. "*Gëzuar.*"

Yet though they clinked glasses and drank, the two boys could see that Avni was troubled. He was still nodding and, uncharacteristically, avoided their eyes. Eventually though he looked at them both and when he did, it was as if he had made a decision.

"This is a very special evening for me," he began. "I would like to tell you why. This very night, nearly thirty-eight years ago—to be precise, on the 1st of January 1964—my sister Karrina and I fled Albania. What you'll see out there tonight was once forbidden in Albania. Too bourgeois," he smiled.

"At the time, I was working on Sazan Island, an important Soviet military base. Enver Hoxha was courting the Chinese and we were due to be visited by the Chinese Premier. Because of this, in a typically hypocritical move, festivities were planned, traditional folk dancing, fireworks and so on. I'd asked for a special pass for my sister, so she could join me for the celebrations. However, we had very different plans for the evening."

Avni took a sip of brandy, his eyes on Will. "Your grandfather promised Karrina's hand in marriage to someone who turned out to be very dangerous, someone, who, after the war, became close to Hoxha. Unfortunately, your grandfather died before he could discover the man's true nature. Your grandmother too. It was up to me to get Karrina away. I hoped the festivities would provide cover, that we could get away during the furore, which is what we did. A friend at the base knew an Italian who could come across on a boat and pick us up. I knew the plan must not fail. Like Ceauşescu, Tito and so on, Hoxha had ordered the deaths of hundreds of thousands of his fellow citizens. You didn't try to escape. You either escaped or you died.

"The way the so-called father of our country treated those who defied him, I witnessed first-hand. I was very young when my father died. I have few memories of him. But I do remember my mother mourning his death, ripping her clothes, cutting her hair. It left a deep impression on me. Their marriage was arranged but they were fortunate enough to fall in love. By all accounts, my father was a good man, funny, handsome. They had six children altogether, with Karrina the youngest and myself, second youngest. But my mother coped, she had to and all may have been fine but for the fact that a few years after my father's death, we were visited by my Uncle Sopi.

"I was five at the time and remember him in very simple terms. He came to Kukës on a pony, a big man on a small horse, more muscle than fat, apart from his face, very round, heavily bearded. My mother and he greeted each other with much love, kissing each other's cheeks, slapping each other's backs. We had a big house with a large open area downstairs for the animals. A sheep was killed, goat's cheese and milk served. I watched my uncle with a kind of awe. He left Kukës a few years before the war to help the King build his roads and had only returned half-a-dozen times. He came to tell us that Hoxha was rooting out all royalists, that unless we got away, they would find us. My mother suggested they hide in the mountains but Sopi insisted we'd be safer in the city.

"We were never to return," Avni said soberly, "though of course we weren't to know that then. Kukës has since become a den of thieves but for me it was beautiful. The day we left, we forded the river and worked our way up through the meadows, towards the mountains. When we finally looked back, all I could see of the town were a few roofs, a line of smoke, the rivers like two twisting snakes.

"I was asleep as we entered the city and woke to see trees and buildings rising out of an incredible dust. I heard the creak of wheels, barking dogs, shouts and cries, though not always their source. Carriages and horses, streaming with dust, would leap out, almost on top of us and then plunge away. Women, their heads piled with bundles, limbless, toothless beggars and stooping peasants surrounded by yapping dogs and wide-eyed children, all wove to and fro like ghosts. Used to clean mountain air, it felt as if someone had tied a sack around my neck.

"But I soon forgot all that, visited as I was by a phantom of the future, a slab of obsidian that came out of the haze, its chrome and glass and rims sparkling as if possessing some inner power. My first car. That vision was to follow me as we made our way through the centre and out into a series of tree-lined streets bordered by two storey dwellings with well-tended gardens. When we reached Sopi's street, he pointed out a large villa with orange walls and narrow windows. But my attention was taken by the Bentley Sedanca de Ville parked outside. Worth a fortune today. I found out later it'd been stolen from the King's stables. In that moment I knew only an unadulterated love. That beautiful machine proved to me that human beings are capable of greatness."

Avni watched his audience, his eyes old in the wintry light. "Inside the house," he said, "the secret police were drinking tea. They showed no emotion, no sense of triumph, not even surprise. They simply replaced their cups, stood up, put their hats on and arrested my mother. An enemy of the people, they said." He smiled.

"I didn't see her for six years. When Samir, my eldest brother, tried to stop them, they kicked him unconscious. Didn't even off take their hats." He shrugged. "Always they wear hats. Wolves in waistcoats. Sopi had led us away from the mountains, where we could have fought for months like Skanderbeg himself—" Avni held up his glass—"and taken us to Tirana in exchange for his son and wife. It wasn't Sopi's car parked outside. When the communists came to power, anyone connected with Zog was arrested. Many were tortured. Many executed. The police had stolen the car from the King's stables. Sopi had been starved and beaten, as had his eldest son and wife, both of whom were still in prison. In order to save them, he'd agreed to bring my mother to the city. My father was a cousin to the king and even though he was dead by then, my family were still seen as a threat."

The evening was upon them. The liquid in their glasses, three glints in the gloom. Avni finished the story in a calm, wistful tone.

"After my mother was arrested, no one was able to tell us if she was alive or dead. By the time she was released in '63, Samir had been shot, apparently resisting arrest and my elder sister raped and killed. Karrina, my brothers and I were living in an apartment without running water or reliable electricity. Sopi was also dead, or so his widow, my aunt, told us when she found us. Somehow she'd heard my mother was still alive and was being released. They'd imprisoned her in Shkodër.

"She'd been bound hand and foot and made to stand for days without food or water. One time they electrocuted her and her hair and teeth fell out. She was tried and sentenced to death but a year later they rescinded her conviction and released her."

Avni hadn't taken a sip for a long time but now he threw back the rest of his drink and swallowed with a sound like cracking bones. "Before that, she was sent to the *dhoma e territ*, the dark room, where she stayed for days with only the light through the keyhole. She did not recognise me when I found her, or the street I carried her to. She was as light as a sparrow. And her smell, I cannot describe it. Karrina tried to bathe her but she was so starved, the soap blistered her skin. A few months later, my last two brothers were shot and my mother died of a broken heart."

Avni took a heavy breath. "So you see why we had to get away. Too many good Albanians were driven mad. And, of course," he said with a weary shrug, "I am grateful we escaped their fate. But the truth is I cannot celebrate. After we left, the man your aunt was engaged to marry, he made sure they found my friend, he who put us in contact with the Italian boat driver. I was told the story years later, how they took out his eyes and sewed his eyelids shut but only after they'd filled his sockets with insects. It drove him mad and in the end he took his life."

Afterwards, they sat in silence, the light in the glasses slowly dimming. Eventually, Avni stood up and, bidding them watch their eyes, flicked on the light.

AN ACQUAINTANCE FROM school had invited Will to a New Year's Eve party but after leaving the house, Eric and he headed over to the railway track instead. After taking a short cut, they climbed the spiked fence there before clambering up the embankment onto the track. Moonlight graced the rails. On the slopes either side, snow lay in brief, isolated patches. Twigs glittered with frost. They sat opposite each other, the iron freezing, the line curving in each direction and uncorked the bottle Avni had given them before they left the house.

Eric asked about the party. Will shook his head. "Andrew Bennett's a wanker. My only real friend from school is Lorenzo." He passed Eric the bottle. "How's Ruth?"

Eric waved his cigarette as if making a circle around things. "Off being responsible somewhere."

Will accepted the bottle and tipped it back until his throat blazed. Eric said he'd been reading.

"Did you know that Byron was a great admirer of the Albanians? Made of iron, he said, as hard as the rocks they inhabit. Which makes you superhuman." He looked at Will, the rings under his eyes blazing in the odd light.

That's when he mentioned the pact. "They have a custom in Albania," he said. "Friends become brothers. You have to prick one of your fingers and soak a lump of sugar in blood. We should do it."

"So we're friends?" Will asked.

Eric ruffled his hair. "Don't be an idiot. I mean it. I've brought some sugar. Let's swear brotherhood." His eyes were mad in the moonlight. "Afterwards we have to give presents and have dinner at each other's houses. Your family becomes mine and vice versa."

Will could tell he was drunk. There was an ease about him normally absent. "Blood?" he said, feeling merry himself.

Eric had a drawstring on his hood. Using a flint from the railway track, he cut the string, pulled it out and cut it in two. Soon the tips of their little fingers were tied so tight, they shone. Eric took out two sugar cubes. He flashed his eyes at Will, raised the flint. Gripping his hand, he scored his finger. The pain came and went like light through a keyhole. Will winced and then laughed. Eric squeezed his finger and the sugar grew darker. Then it was his turn.

"To brotherhood," Will said, touching his cube to Eric's.

Eric's eyes glittered. "May our pain and our joy become one."

They washed the sugar down with brandy, then rose up, their arms round each other, their faces to the dark, breezy sky. Will's parents had bought him a gold watch for his birthday and he held it up so they could see the time. "It's almost *miiidniiight.*" he sang.

Eric smiled. "To cease upon the midnight with no pain, while thou art pouring forth thy soul abroad in such an ecstasy."

They counted down the seconds, hugged each other, pushed each other over and sprinted down the track.

"Presents," Eric panted when they finally stopped. "We've got to give presents."

On other streets, fireworks spat at the stars but not on Montrose Avenue. Eric's Dad was fishing somewhere in the Atlantic, his Mum was in bed. They made their way down the side of the house, stumbled over several garden chairs. The back door was unlocked and Eric guided Will into the kitchen and sat him down.

He lit a candle. "There is not enough darkness in all the world," he said, "to put out the light of even one candle."

He told Will to wait before creeping out of the room.

Just as Will was wondering if Eric were going to jump out at him, he came back holding a bottle of whisky. He poured them both a glass and then held up a book.

"I want you to have it," he said.

Only after opening the book, did Will realise what it was. "But it's yours," he said, pointing out Eric's name inside the cover.

"Not anymore."

Will remembered Eric calling it tatty but actually, the book was quite beautiful, its red cover gilded, the various tree-shaped swirls surrounding the title— *The Complete Works of John Keats*—dotted

114

with tiny white flowers. "I can't." He tried to give it back. "I was useless."

"Well. Now you can learn it again," Eric said. "I've marked the page."

Will tried to thank him but couldn't speak. His watch glinted in the candlelight and he slipped it off. "I insist," he said, handing it to Eric.

After putting it on, Eric looked at it. He went to take it off but Will gripped his wrist. "No, I mean it."

"I'll never take it off," Eric said finally.

They were being so serious but then they both sighed at the same time and it was as if the kitchen were full of vapours. One moment they were sitting still, the next they were falling off their stools, their hands clasping at their mouths, laughter bursting from their noses and clouding their eyes.

vii.
—

WILL WOKE UP ON the floor, saw wooden legs, half-open drawers, a dangling hand, the nearest finger marked with a cut.

He crept downstairs and out the front door. It was New Year's Day and there wasn't a shred of snow in sight. The air smelt of smoke and mouldering leaves.

That Sunday, Avni drove them back to Birmingham. On the way, they stopped at Burger King and Avni and Eric started discussing Afghanistan. When Will came back with the food, his father was saying something about historical precedent.

"Unless you count economic history," Eric said, popping a handful of fries into his mouth. "Your great white American contractor will never be an endangered species, not in our lifetime at least."

That was when Avni asked about the watch. Eric glanced at Will and then tried to take it off but Will wouldn't let him. He told his father that they'd taken an oath, that Eric had given him a book. His father was surprisingly accepting.

"Just don't tell your mother. She wouldn't understand."

115

In Birmingham, Will resolved to write more but found the experience frustrating. The alchemist's art of making satire by mixing humour and anger escaped him. Anger on its own was just ugly. Nor did he even know what he was angry about. Had he known, perhaps he would have been less angry. Better still, perhaps he would have had something to write about.

That was one of the reasons he was drawn to Eric—Eric bore enough anger for the both of them. Being around him calmed Will down. When Eric started raving or punching walls, Will pulled him away from himself, got him moving again. He asked him once why he got like that. Eric just said it was in the air—that it was a millennial thing. All the good ideas had been dismantled. What was there left for anyone to believe in?

Whatever Will did manage to write, he bottled up in his Documents file, as if, like good wine, it might improve with age. In contrast, Eric wrote and published (in several respected journals) a number of articles and then stopped writing altogether. It was as if he were trying to solve something, his anger issues perhaps. He would get very excited while he was working and keep Will up late into the night explaining his theses, most of which went over Will's head. But the moment he finished whatever he'd been working on, he almost didn't want to publish it. He lost interest. He had an agent for a while and this was the only reason anything got published at all.

It was round that time they started doing silly stuff. Getting drunk and hanging from bridges, throwing bins into rivers, stealing bottles of milk from people's doorsteps, sloshing round in freezing-cold golf ponds looking for balls. They were supposed to be revising for their finals but whenever Will reminded Eric of this, he just laughed. They had a favourite spot on the railway track between Selly Oak and Selly Park where they used to lie so close to the track that when the train rushed by, the whoosh of air made their cigarettes glow.

"There is," Eric said on one of those nights, the chirp of early summer crickets and the smell of hawthorn in the air, "just as much of a chance that we will do good things, *great* things, if we don't qualify. Education is no substitute for experience."

Will found himself nodding. "Not a single great writer ever took a creative writing course."

Eric laughed. "And if they did, that'd be the end of them."

There wasn't a shop in town they hadn't shoplifted from, sometimes on several occasions. That was until the day Will got caught. He stepped out of House of Fraser wearing a stolen pair of shorts under his jeans, only for several store detectives to melt out of the crowd and pin him to a wall. He was let off with a caution but for a while he thought he'd blown everything, that he'd be kicked out of university, that he'd have a record for life. Eric, on the other hand, was never caught.

And then in the summer term, Will was waiting for Eric under the redbrick arches outside the School of Physics and Astronomy, reading a copy of *Pincher Martin* for his class in Modern Fiction with Professor Grobesby, when the Unseasonable Esther came out and told him that Eric hadn't been to lectures all week. Will hadn't seen her for months and it seemed as if something had happened in the meantime because she was actually quite friendly with him. They both walked back to the Vale with Esther talking most of the way. She was worried about Eric, though she kept saying that she wasn't: "It's not like he can't look after himself," she said. "He's more grown up than most grownups."

Will wondered which Eric she was talking about. The one who'd lost his keys and had to climb through his own bathroom window for two weeks or the one who liked to go skinny-dipping in the lake when he was so drunk he couldn't even remember his own name. After getting someone to let him into Eric's building, Will found him curled up beside an ashtray full of cigarette butts, his coat and hair smelling as if he'd been out all night. His room, which lay in a fetid, curtained gloom, was a minefield of papers and books, old pizza boxes and CD covers. Will started stacking relevant materials together, refilling Eric's bookshelf, the whole time with Eric staring at the ceiling. Only when Will went to touch one particular pile of papers did he respond.

"Read it," he said, touching the printout topping the pile.

It was a copy of a newspaper article. Will was surprised to see that it was about an Albanian man who'd accidentally shot his best friend and was in turn killed by the brother and the cousin of the deceased.

"It's known as an honour killing." Eric pushed himself up onto one elbow and lit a cigarette, his red-rimmed eyes full of a laconic nostalgia.

Will picked up the next story from the pile. It was about a police officer who'd shot nine men in revenge for the killing of his brother, one for each of the bullets found in his brother's body. Will went into the kitchen and heated up a slice of leftover pizza, then made Eric eat it.

"There are rules," Eric said, licking his fingers and taking another mouthful. "A book called the Canon of Lek Dukagjini." He pointed at his bookshelf. "I've got a copy of that too somewhere. These feuds, they're never forgotten. Revenge is passed from father to son like an heirloom until the job's done. You're only safe in your home. That is the law." He pointed the slice of pizza at Will. "Apparently some Albanians haven't left their houses in years."

Will shook his head. "What is this, Eric?"

He tried to get him to his feet but Eric pulled him down, the move quick, violent. He seized the collar of Will's coat.

"But isn't it right?" he said, his eyes searching Will's. "To take blood, to defend your honour? What are we without souls?" He wiped his nose, gave the wall behind him a jab with his elbow. "I've had enough, Will. I'm leaving. I've got to do something. I can't take this shit anymore."

Will couldn't believe what he was hearing. "But finals are so close! Let's at least go for a drink first. Talk it over."

The OVT was packed. England was beating Paraguay in the World Cup and there were a few locals among the crowd. Round by the pool table, Eric slapped a ten pound note on the head-rail and challenged a pair of lads in paint-spattered overalls to a game of doubles. The lads were winning until one of them potted the black and the white at the same time. He immediately accused Eric of trying to distract him. If Will hadn't bought both of them a pint, there would have been a fight.

The air along the Bristol Road smelt of coriander and capsicum. It was one of those English summer nights that drop cold and sharp at the end of a warm day. Eric though was hot, his normally pale cheeks flushed. He would have forgotten his coat if Will hadn't picked it up. Eric insisted Will put it on.

"You feel the cold," he said.

Will told him to come back to his but Eric said it was miles. Will had moved to Selly Park by then. Eric kept walking up and down. "I could have had them, you know?"

Will smiled. "A couple of months, that's all you've got left."

"Time is irrelevant!" Eric turned to leave before letting his friend steer him up Dawlish Road. "I need to get out there, start preaching. All the arseholes need do these days is keep feeding us until we burst. Too much information *para*lyses. Instead of darkness we get a light so bright we're blinded!"

He carried on in this vein all the way back to Will's flat so that by the time they got there, Will felt half-sober. Eric seemed drunker than ever. He kept saying, "Wherever I go, wherever I go . . ."

Will tried to steer Eric towards his room but he stumbled into the lounge and collapsed on the couch. "If there's one thing we're guilty of," he mumbled, "it's feeling guilty. And I'm sick of it." He put his hand on Will's cheek. "But you love me, don't you?"

Will brought him a blanket but Eric was asleep.

Will went through to his own room and lay down, only to realise that he was still wearing Eric's coat. He tried to wriggle out of it but the thing was so long and heavy, it was almost impossible. By the time he'd succeeded, he was joined on the bed by keys, a wallet, a number of coins and a small black box. The keys and the wallet were easy to identify in the dark but it took him a moment to realise that the box was a mini-cassette recorder. Opening the housing, he found a tape and a slip of paper inside. There was a little moonlight coming through the blinds and he was able to angle the paper in such a way that he could see some kind of message written on it. He peered closer. *This is my pain.* It was penned in Eric's usual scribble. Will was immediately reminded of the words of their pact. Maybe, he thought, Eric had made the tape for him. Maybe he wanted him to listen to it.

Will lay on the bed, the recorder rising and falling on his chest. He was tired, drunker than he'd realised. Perhaps, before he listened to it, he would shut his eyes. Just for a moment, he thought. He could feel the little black box on his chest, its weight growing heavier and heavier. Finally it slid off and he fell into a drunken sleep.

The next morning, he woke to the sensation that he was very much alone. Ambling through to the living room, he realised he was right. Eric was gone, as were his coat and its contents.

A week later, Will came out of Grobesby's office to find Esther waiting for him. She had on a pair of round glasses with dark blue frames that made her grey eyes look very pretty. As soon as she saw him, they filled with tears.

"He quit the course," she said. "He's gone."

Will ran round to the Vale. This time Eric's room was empty. Two days later, he rang Veronica. When she finally answered, she said Eric was in Paris. He asked her why.

"How should I know?" she said. "Maybe because children can't see anything beyond the ends of their own noses."

2

IN JULY, WILL QUALIFIED with upper second class honours, a better result than he'd expected, especially as he'd come to believe in Eric's doctrine regarding the value of education. Nor was the last exam followed by the expected euphoria. He was tired and even a little ill and all he really wanted to do was sleep.

Ashling was going at the usual two miles an hour, which suited him just fine. He spent a month reading pulp fiction and getting drunk with Lorenzo and only twice walked round to Montrose Avenue. Knowing he'd have to face Veronica, he couldn't ring the bell.

Perhaps that was why he started applying for teacher training courses. Though Ruth was out of the picture, her moment of sleepy clairvoyance kept returning to him. Did he want to impress her? Probably not. But he did want to have something to say to her, something that might release them from the deadlock they were in. When he told his parents his decision, their response was typically pragmatic. If he was going to study in Canterbury, he might as well stay with his aunt.

Teto Karrina's husband had died several years before, after a long battle with cancer. It had left his aunt a little unhinged, though his parents only saw fit to tell him this the day he moved.

He insisted on catching the train and turned up at Karrina's alone, a decision he regretted the moment he got out of the taxi and stood before the overgrown rhododendron bushes fronting her property. In a village like Shatterling, loiterers were probably shot, or so he thought to himself as he gathered his nerve and knocked on the door with the tentative rap of someone who's just been told the person on the other side is mildly deranged.

He hadn't seen Auntie Karrina for years but apart from the fact that her long, thick hair had since turned grey, she looked exactly the same. A barrel of a woman with tattooed wrists, a furry upper lip and bright, full eyes, her neck weighed down with so many scarves it was as if she were trying to bury herself. She made them herself, what she called her story scarves, each one printed on silk, their various scenes depicting some aspect of Albanian folklore, whirling patterns scattered with birds and lizards and bright budded trees. She was quite a sight to behold then as she peered at him, not from the front door, but from round a corner to his left. "The front door doesn't work," she said. "Come."

He followed her through a latticed archway to a door hosted by pink geraniums. Once inside, she pressed a key into his palm. "Yours," she said, her eyes fluttering up at him as she spoke. "I have my own."

Looking round the kitchen, he realised that unhinged meant untidy. It wasn't a trait he remembered in his aunt. Books lay open on every surface, several of them sealed to the side with grease. Dishes may have needed doing but it was hard to tell in the traffic surrounding the sink. His aunt pulled out two cigars, offered one to him and then began to smoke the other one. She bade him follow her and they walked to the top of her rather overrun back garden where she began to scatter seeds in every direction. "Everyone gets fed," she said.

It was a hard year but rewarding. Between all the assignments he had to complete and bringing home friends to meet his mad aunt, time flew by. Karrina loved company and pottered around serving up wedges of three-milk cake and refilling glasses with homemade sloe gin and it wasn't long before Will fell into the kind of routine that's almost instantly forgettable and yet contains much of what is good about life. In years to come only two events would return to him absolutely intact.

The morning of his twenty-second birthday, he came downstairs to find Karrina standing on a stool in the kitchen, the ends of her scarves held up in the air. "Don't kill them," she said shrilly. "But please, get them out."

Overnight, ants had built a nest behind the fridge. Will could see them scurrying back and forth across the linoleum, the vacuum cleaner abandoned on the tiles. Normally, Karrina was a real St Francis and would feed anything that came nosing into her garden. She couldn't even kill a wasp. That morning, though, she told him that ants were the exception.

"They just seem so mindless and yet so mindful at the same time. They make me feel as if the universe is busy building itself without us. Like we're one big anomaly," she said with a sad smile. "Due for a catastrophic readjustment."

Following her instructions, Will moved the fridge and began to vacuum them up, getting the hose into every corner, watching, not without a twinge or two of his own, as the little creatures scattered this way and that before succumbing to the probing nozzle. His aunt told him where to empty the machine and watched, cigar in hand, as he shook the ants over a compost heap at the bottom of the garden.

After he'd finished his studies, Karrina had planned to surprise him. Not being very good with surprises, however, she spilled the beans long before the promised date. She wanted to take him on holiday with her. They were sitting in her rather forlorn-looking front room, its many shelves and sideboards cluttered with little china knickknacks, their dusty surfaces cast the colour of old bandages by the net curtains which cut the light in half and reminded Will of a funeral parlour. His aunt was fond of travelling, that he already knew. She had, on occasion, left him in the house for weeks at a time, not to go on holiday but to visit various fairs where she sold her scarves both wholesale and directly to customers. Of all the places she visited, she told him that day, her favourite, by far, was the little pine island of Ibiza. "I have someone there who I like to see," she confided. "A good friend. You will love it," she went on. "The people are so friendly."

To go on holiday with his aunt, to Ibiza of all places, seemed an odd idea, yet over the days and weeks that followed, Will grew more and more excited about it. But as it happened, they never went, for the second event, which occurred just before they were due to go, threw such a dark shadow over everything, such innocent ideas were instantly unthinkable.

Having handed in his last assignment, Will had been out celebrating and had gone to bed drunk, only to be woken in the early hours by the sound of raised voices. Creeping downstairs, he peered in the direction of the kitchen which lay at the other end of the hall. Karrina was standing near the doorway talking to an older man, who was pacing back and forth so that he kept appearing and disappearing. He sounded very angry. Each time he marched into view, he would jab his finger in Karrina's direction. *Ju*, he kept saying, meaning you. Though Will didn't understand Karrina's response— *si thatë se nuk ju dëgjova*—he could tell she was apologising.

And then the man slapped her. Without thinking, Will ran down the hall and took hold of him. The smell of alcohol and sweat struck him like a blow. The corners of the man's mouth were balled with spit. He leapt against Will and then away, his anger so potent Will could feel it boiling from his skin and yet that same emotion seemed also to weaken him, for though he pushed at Will's chest, he hardly felt it. He heard his aunt cry out and then, as if holding something hot, he let go of the man who fell to the floor. Will heard the leaves of the table clatter against the legs, saw the man grab the back of a chair, saw the chair topple over and then found himself standing over him.

The man was lying on the lino hissing up at Will. He sounded out of breath and Will could only make out one word. "Ligj!" the man said, his breath rattling inwards between each effort. "Ligj!"

Will stood there feeling naked, his aunt crying beside him, the old man writhing on the floor, two chairs nudging this way and that. The man oozed that word one more time and then stopped, his mouth contorted, his eyes white beneath half-shut lids.

Will retreated to his coat, found his mobile and called his father.

When Avni came into the kitchen, he stood there staring at the dead man, then at Karrina. He told Will to take his aunt back to Ashling. He said Elizabeth was expecting them and gave Will his car keys. Even as Avni rang the police, he was pushing Karrina and Will out of the house. Will heard him say that there'd been an accident. Avni stood by the front door, the phone to his ear, watching as Will backed out of the drive. The old man, whoever he was, had parked his car up on the kerb. Will looked at it as he drove away, then back at the house but his father had already gone inside.

The next morning, he woke feeling numb. He'd dreamt he was lying in a grave. Someone was throwing earth onto his chest. Downstairs the family sat round the breakfast table, sharing a loaded silence. Elizabeth drank several cups of tea and kept glancing at Will over the rim of her cup. Karrina had phoned a friend and was going to stay with her for a few days. She squeezed Will's hand before she left. "Speak to your father," she said.

When he went up to see him, Avni sat looking out of his study window. Finally he told Will that the old man had been a friend of Karrina's, that their reminiscing had stirred up unpleasant memories. Will asked about the word the man had used and his father told him it meant law. Avni looked older, his skin more dimpled, his eyes redder.

As if to himself, Avni said, "*Ligj e paligjshëm*, law and unlaw. To some it is as natural as breathing, the law that governs both falcon and dove. To me it is only barbaric."

He told Will the police had requested a statement. "You need to write it while your memory's freshest," he said.

Something about the way his father refused to meet his gaze left Will feeling dissatisfied. It was all too simple. Yet he was too afraid to ask.

It was another week before he returned to his aunt's. He was still angry with his father but knew this was only because he was frightened. He kept imagining himself walking into Canterbury Police Station. All week he'd been expecting Avni to say they wanted to see him. In that moment, as the old man lay wracked on the floor, he'd seen blood. It came and went as the man moved his head but though Will had not looked too closely, he'd known it was there.

Avni tried to say he didn't need to go to Karrina's, that he'd collect Will's belongings for him. In the end they went together. On the way over, Will thought about his statement. It had taken him a long time to write. He kept trying to recall the exact details. He remembered grabbing the old man, pulling him away. He remembered expecting him to weigh more. But after that his memory grew unreliable. Maybe his anger had made him stronger. Maybe he'd thrown the man to the floor. He didn't know how to phrase such things. In the end, whenever he was doubtful about a particular detail, he said so. But still it wasn't enough.

But then it all came to an unexpected end. The day before they returned to Canterbury, Will answered the door to find a man standing on the doorstep wearing a peaked cap and epaulettes. He introduced himself as PC Lesinski. "I've come to talk about the incident," he said without smiling.

They sat in the dining room. Lesinski said no to coffee. He had a copy of Will's statement and went over particular details with him. He also took a statement from Will's father and said he'd talk to

Will's aunt when she got back. When he left, he said Will might need to come down the station but that he'd let them know.

Karrina was still away. Will put a bag of scraps and a note on the kitchen side: FOR THE FOX. The chairs were back in place, the linoleum clean. Upstairs, he found a note inside his suitcase, signed with a spidery K.

> *I'm so sorry. Thank you for trying to help.*
> *To forget or not to forget, both are a*
> *challenge. But whatever happens, I hope*
> *you remember our year together. A warm*
> *wind has blown through this old house.*

As his father drove away, he remembered Karrina's words when he first arrived and looked back, wondering when the front door had last been used.

ii.

ELIZABETH RESPONDED TO the 'terrible affair', as she called it, by contacting a teacher friend of hers, a piece of chicanery that only came to light when Will found a letter propped up against the toast rack. It was an invitation from his old school to 'come in for a chat'. Suspecting her of meddling, he waved the thing under her nose, only for her to place her newspaper on the table and launch into a surprisingly heated lecture on the healing powers of employment, the whole time with Tony Blair's sharp little fangs grinning up at him from between her fingers.

The next day, he found a copy of the Times Educational Supplement by his bed, several job adverts encircled, followed, the day after, by a Southern Rail timetable. He got the message. Walk to work or spend hours commuting. When he continued to resist, his mother was forced to use drastic measures. Avni tried not to get involved in his wife's causes but sometimes she gave him no choice. The first Will knew of it, his father called him into the living room to help sort his tackle box, saying he couldn't find his glasses. When Will was down on his knees, Avni asked if he was all right. It was a

126

decidedly undadish question. Busy placing swivels with swivels and hooks with hooks, Will said he was fine.

"But what about your future?" Avni said.

Will stopped and looked at him. "Okay," he said. "If I do this and I don't like it, I need you to support me, Dad."

"If you do what?" he said, frowning.

That evening Will told his mother he would go to the interview and the next day he contacted the school. This time Elizabeth's response was typical. She laid out his graduation suit, having had it dry-cleaned the week before and presented him with a new tie. "For luck," she said, barely able to contain her triumph.

However, all seemed for nought. During the interview, as if his subconscious were still resisting his mother's machinations, he kept seeing the old man's face, the sheen in his eyes as he writhed on Karrina's kitchen floor so that, though he tried to teach an amusing lesson to first years concerning the perils of misplaced punctuation and spoke to a panel of interrogators about the joys of differentiation and the importance of positive behavioural management, he did so in a complete daze and left the school certain he'd failed.

There was good news waiting at home though. Even as he dusted his shoes on the mat, Avni waved a letter entitled *Coroner's Inquest Report* under his nose and was so excited that he snatched it back before Will had chance to read it. He turned it so they could read it together. "See—" Avni said, pointing to a passage—"*heart attack.* What did I say?"

It was as if someone had removed a stone from Will's chest. Suddenly he could breathe again. When his mother got home, she hugged them both, ordered pizza and they drank beer. And then the phone rang and a Mr Harding, whom Will vaguely remembered as the only member of the school panel to smile at him, was telling him that the board thought he was eminently suitable etc. etc.

When he told his mum he'd been offered the job, she started hugging him again. "But did you say yes?" she said, holding his chin so he couldn't look away. When he nodded she laughed. Tears rolled down her cheeks. "Then you must stay here, at least until you get on your feet. Please say yes."

He said yes.

Yet as it happened, the ominous twinge he'd experienced upon hearing Mr Harding's good news turned out to be genuine intuition. The first sign of trouble came just a few weeks after he began work. His Head of Department told him a parent had complained. Apparently he'd called a boy arrogant. The fact that Will had actually critiqued the boy's attitude didn't matter. There was no trial. He was simply told that such was unacceptable—if the parents went to the papers, as they'd threatened, there could be trouble. As a kid, just a mention of his parents brought Will into line. Now he was being threatened with parents again. It felt as if the whole world had been turned upside down, yet he hadn't moved an inch.

And it wasn't just work that started getting to him. Before long he couldn't shake the feeling that there was little point growing up if he just ended up back in the same house, attending the same school, as friendless and as loveless as when he was fifteen years old. Not to mention the fact that his mother carried on pruning the garden as if it were her own personal Forth Bridge and his father was still calling down for coffee, his bellow deadened by the curtains and carpets so that it sounded as if some ruminant were trapped in an upstairs room.

Close to his wits' end, one evening, he came in to hear his dad shouting, "Ma? *Ma*, kafe!" and decided to take him up a cup. He'd had a bad day and was looking for a little sympathy but when he placed the cup on his father's desk, served in his favourite mug just the way he liked it, the man barely looked up. Halfway across the room, Will turned and said, "This place is driving me up the wall."

He realised his father was glaring at him, not maliciously but with an uncustomary intensity. "Things may have changed since I was a young man," he said, placing each word as precisely as if he were laying bricks, "but I used to find that a girl usually did the trick."

Will stalked away and threw himself onto his bed. A girl, as if it were that simple.

EXCEPT, OF COURSE, it was, for that Sunday he answered the door to find Ruth standing on the doorstep, her breath smoking in the wintry air. She was wearing a long black coat and had her hair up in a bun. She could have been delivering a subpoena. Caught between wanting to kiss her face and wanting to slam the door in it, he stood there with his fists in his pockets.

She had tears in her eyes. "It's Eric," she said. "He's missing."

He shrugged. "I haven't spoken to him. Not for months. What makes you think I'll know where he is?"

"Because he's your friend," she said.

Apparently Eric had returned from France the month before. Veronica had called to say he'd been missing for several days. "Dad's away on the boat," Ruth said. "I called everyone I could think of. I don't know what to do."

Will told himself not to get involved, yet a place came to mind and though he couldn't imagine Eric being down there for two days, he could imagine him being down there.

"If this is about us," Ruth said, "I'm sorry. I just didn't want to hurt you."

"Am I so fragile?"

She looked at him, her face pale in the clear, grey light and then he went to fetch rope from the garage and they drove along Foxglove Lane, neither of them talking.

It was February and many of the ponds along the Stour had flooded into a single expanse. Silver birch stood in the water like broken bristles. Wind flurried the surface, drawing a brackish smell into the air. The sloping rock was further underwater but was still reachable, though they both got their feet wet. At the top, the alders stretched nakedly towards a sullen sky.

Ruth looked over the edge and called Eric's name. When there was no response, Will tied one end of the rope to a tree trunk, knelt down and peered over. The cave was easy to see now the trees had died back. He curled the rope round his middle, leaned into it, found footholds in the cliff and eased himself downwards. He kept expecting Eric to leap out but he didn't.

Finding a foothold, Will pulled himself into the gap, his buttons scraping on the rock. The cave was crescent-shaped and he had to bend down before wedging himself with one arm. Silver light cast a staggered crescent on a rocky interior wall twenty feet away. Keeping his head inclined, he released the rope and began to feel his way into the gloom. The cave smelt of wet moss and sandstone. Water dripped everywhere, flashing as it passed through the light. As he reached the point where the cave began to open out slightly, a voice said, "I guess now it's your turn to hide."

Will slipped and must have cried out because Ruth shouted from above. He could make out a shoulder, the edge of a hood. Eric was sat on a rock.

"You're alive then?" he said.

The hood moved slightly, an eye glinted. "I've water." Eric tossed a pebble. Water plinked.

"You've been in here two days?"

"I thought I told you to stay away from her."

"She came to me. She was worried."

"That's what I was trying to get away from." Eric leaned forwards. The stubble on his chin shone orange. "You ought to thank God you're an only child." He nodded upwards. "She's not my keeper."

Will looked around. There were no food cartons, no bottles.

"You know," Eric said, leaning forward again. "I already knew about this cave. I only pretended to find it with you."

Will nodded. "I guessed as much."

"And yet you came to find me," Eric said almost gently. "I found it when I was a kid. Used to hide in here for hours." He spoke from inside the darkness of his hood. "I wanted to fade far away, dissolve and quite forget . . ."

"Why are you here, Eric?"

"Just trying to crawl back into the womb."

"Is it something to do with that tape?"

130

He shook his head. "That was a mistake. I knew you hadn't listened to it. I'm glad. Pain is a solitary ritual." He nodded upwards. "You might think I'm trying to torture her but I'm not. You want to play the hero, fine. I'll come out with my hands up. But my advice remains the same."

Back at the house, Ruth took Eric upstairs. When she came down, she smiled and it was as if her whole body were being pulled by invisible strings. Then she took Will to Brighton.

iv.
———

ON THE WAY, HE ASKED if she wasn't worried about leaving Eric on his own. She said there was no point watching over him. "He'd only wait until we were asleep."

"What is it with him?" Will said. "He said I wanted to play the hero."

"He's jealous," she said. "You don't know why?"

He felt her glance at him and was happy for an excuse to look into her eyes. "No, why?"

She smiled and looked away. "Because he's in love with you."

Will shook his head in disbelief.

Ruth's smile was almost wistful. "Isn't it obvious? That's why I left you alone for so long. After all, he met you first."

Will thought about Eric warning him away from Ruth, their pact, the tape-recorder. *Pain is a solitary ritual.*

"He told me he's hidden in there before."

Ruth had stopped at a junction. Cars began to queue up behind her but she didn't move. She appeared to be thinking.

"He went missing one time. When he was ten. Mum and Dad were very worried. Me too." Finally, a car beeped. Ruth glanced in the rear-view mirror. "We looked everywhere," she said, pulling out. "Maybe that's where he went."

They were on a dual carriageway, frost-dusted fields either side. Will stared at a hill in the distance, waiting for Ruth to speak. He could tell she wanted to tell him about it.

She kept squeezing the steering wheel, her driving gloves creaking each time she tightened her fists. "He used to be really wild, you know?" The wistful smile again. "I was always worrying about him. All he wanted to do was goof off and get into trouble. The day he disappeared, we'd gone out together. He had a dog back then, a puppy, really. If anyone ever said anything to him about Mum, we always knew about it because Eric would come back covered in bruises. That's why Dad got him the dog. He came home one day with a black eye and Dad went straight out and bought him a little Collie pup. I guess he hoped a dog might make the other boys think twice before saying anything. Eric fell in love with the thing the moment he saw it. I've got a photo somewhere of the two of them that first day, both of them with one black eye, it was very funny. He was doing a project on Egypt and decided to call him Tutankhamen. He wanted something cool to shout out in the park." She smiled and shook her head. "We just called him Toot most of the time."

They both watched traffic traverse a roundabout for a while, before Ruth finally pulled out. "Mum hated the dog," she said as they came off the roundabout. "She was very house proud but Toot was a nightmare. That summer, we spent most days out of the house. Mum preferred it that way. Sometimes we walked for miles and didn't get in until evening. That day we'd planned to go up to Paul Farrington's farm. Eric had heard there was an old well on the property. He said Farrington had thrown his wife in there." Ruth smiled again, though more to herself this time. "All I wanted to do was swim in the river. Even though Eric's younger than me, most of the time he still got his way. I told him I'd only go up to the farm if we could go paddling first. He agreed but on the way he started saying if little Rook wants to paddle, little Rook must paddle."

Ruth's smile had dwindled into something small and vulnerable. "I was so wound up by the time we reached the river, I challenged him to a race and ran off. First one in the water. There was a platform where you could jump past the reeds. We were wearing shorts, so all we had to do was kick off our shoes but Eric's laces were knotted and I was wearing slip-ons. I've always wondered how things might

132

have turned out if he'd been quicker getting his shoes off or if I'd jumped a little to the left or to the right. But as it was, it was me who jumped in first and me who landed on a rusty can and sliced my foot open.

"I started hopping about, which of course Eric thought was hilarious. In the end I tried crawling back to the bank. It was only when I slipped and fell face first into the water that Eric realised I was hurt. He jumped in and dragged me out and I showed him where I'd been cut. He tried to say it looked all right but then it started oozing blood and he went white. He said he could run up to the Granger's to get help. Apparently he'd done it before when his friend Jez was hurt. He told me Mr Granger had carried Jez all the way back to the Grangers' house.

"Toot kept jumping around and Eric was even worse. The last time they'd done it, he said, Mrs Granger had given him and Jez loads of biscuits. I realised then that the biscuits were all he was interested in but I couldn't help thinking it might be a good idea. At least someone would take a look at my foot."

Will saw a sign for Brighton. Nine miles. "So what happened?" he said.

"Eric said it would look better if I lay down. I remember hearing him and the dog run off and then everything becoming very peaceful. The sky was really blue. The ground smelt dusty and old. We were on the edge of a wheat field and I could see several crickets clinging to stalks. I could hear them all around. I was feeling weird though, you know? Like something wasn't right. Maybe it's just the way I remember it, because I know what happened afterwards. The river smelled like something had died. And the sound of the crickets just seemed to get louder and louder. So I decided just to shut my eyes and count. The Granger house was maybe half a mile away. I figured at five miles an hour, it would take Eric six minutes to get there. That he'd run back as well, only slower because Mr Granger would be with him. I figured it would take him twenty minutes in all."

She shook her head as if slightly embarrassed. "I remember counting really slowly and then, when I'd nearly reached twelve hundred, slowing down even more. But even so, when I finally finished, Eric still wasn't back. All I could hear were the crickets. When I opened my eyes, I could see the path up the valley. Eric was nowhere. I leaned on my elbows, looked up the valley again, saw the Granger's roof and upstairs' windows.

"My first instinct was to go up there but after standing up, I started having doubts. Eric probably hadn't even gone up there with Jez. Or if he had, this time he was playing a trick. Or even if he had run up there, he'd probably found Mr and Mrs Granger out and run home instead." She shrugged. "Anything rather than be burdened with a whining sister. I was certain that he was punishing me for spoiling his fun, for beating him to the river, for not going up to Farrington's farm. Or maybe he was just up there filling his face and hadn't even mentioned me. Either way, I was sure Eric was playing a trick. So I just picked up my shoes and began to hobble home."

They had reached the outskirts of Brighton. Midmorning traffic, roundabouts and dog walkers, a lone jogger. In slow intervals, a long, green park slid by behind regularly planted trees. Expensive houses on their right.

"Back home," Ruth said, "I knew I'd be in trouble for returning without Eric but I didn't care. Even so, when Mum shouted me, I jumped. I told her I had a head, that I was going to my room. It was the sort of thing she might say. Mum's hand was on my forehead before I could take another step. I heard her going through the cupboards and then she was pushing me upstairs and sitting me on her bed. She put a thermometer under my tongue and told me not to bite it. I was fine, of course. That was when she asked about Eric. We'd told her we were going to the park and she asked if that was where he was. I tried to stop myself from talking, before saying that that was what *he'd* said. Mum said so where did you go then? I told her we were going up to Farrington's farm but had stopped to play in the river. Mum said, And? I told her, And I cut my foot."

"That was when she realised I was barefoot. She fetched a bowl of water and a tube of Savlon. She asked me again what had happened. I didn't know what to say. I didn't want to tell her where Eric had gone. He'd never forgive me and I'd be in trouble too. In the end I told her part of the truth, that he'd gone to get help but hadn't come back, that I'd got worried and come home. That I didn't know where he was. In truth, I'd expected him to be grinning at me from the living room window or skipping round the garden saying, You took your time, but he wasn't. I thought maybe he'd realised how angry I'd be and had decided to stay away until I cooled down. I certainly hoped so. Mum asked if I knew what day it was. Dad used to go to sea for four or five days at a time. He was due back that day. She said he'd be tired when he got home. The last thing he needed was Eric missing.

"Downstairs, I heard her rifling through the bureau. She was looking for the phone directory. I leaned over the banister and watched her. Finally she pulled a thick yellow book from under the bureau and then picked up the phone. She was phoning Paul Farrington. I heard her say his name. She asked if he'd seen Eric, told him that he was missing. I could hear his voice but not what he said but I could by the way Mum sort of slumped that he hadn't seen him."

Ruth glanced at Will, then back at the windscreen. "When Mum put the phone down, I remember her looking up at me and saying: What we gonna do now, Ruthie? It was awful. The way she said it was like she believed the worst.

"When Dad finally came home, I heard him drop his bag and walk down the hall. We were in the kitchen. I was sitting at the back door, my feet outside. Mum was sitting at the plinth. Then he was standing in the doorway. The moment Mum looked at him, he asked after Eric. I told him Eric had gone, then wished I hadn't spoken. Dad's always been the fun parent. We used to play cards for hours, or lie in the back garden naming the stars. But when he gets riled, he's different. He rocks back and forth like he's still on the boat. He's got this scar running down across one eye where he was hit by a boom. When he gets angry, his face gets really red and his scar shines white. Mum told him what I'd said, that we'd gone out, how I'd hurt my foot and Eric had gone for help. She said we'd been everywhere, phoned everyone, that the police had said we had to wait. Dad was staring at me the whole time. He asked me where Eric had gone to get help. I looked at Mum and then just came out with it. I told him Eric had gone up to the Granger's. Mum was looking at me and I didn't dare look back. Dad asked if I meant the old French teacher and when I nodded, he asked when. I told him I'd cut my foot but he was unmoved. I said Eric never came back, that I'd come home angry, sure he must've been playing a trick. Mum started shouting about how we'd run all over town when the whole time Eric was up at the Granger's. I tried to say I was worried about getting in trouble but Mum was crying and calling me a liar. That was when the kitchen door moved.

"We heard steps in the hall. When Eric pushed open the door, he looked terrible, his clothes muddy, his lips white. He was holding the door handle like he was exhausted. He wouldn't look at any of us. Dad asked where he'd been. Mum said we'd been sick with worry. Finally, Eric said, Nowhere. It was the wrong answer. Dad started shouting and Mum was crying."

Ruth stopped speaking for a moment and Will could see that her eyes were wet. "And then, just like that," she said, "he turned and ran. Dad ran after him. Eric pulled the door to, which caught Dad across the arm, then turned towards the front door. I heard it open before immediately slamming shut again, followed by a sharp cry. On the few occasions Dad ever hit Eric, Eric never cried out. This time, he sounded like a frightened animal. I heard Dad dragging him upstairs, both grunting as they went up. Eric was obviously struggling and I didn't understand that either. He never resisted when he was going to be punished.

"When Dad came back down, he told us Eric was staying in his room. Then he sent me to mine. It was only then that I wondered where the dog was."

WHEN THEY ARRIVED IN Brighton, Ruth drove along the seafront to show Will the beach. Rust-coloured shale was divided up into green-rimmed diamonds by a long iron fence. The sea beyond lay like a strip of oxidised copper. Behind them the pier flashed and whirled. On their right balconied terraces formed squares and crescents in shades of white and pink, their salted fronts, backdrops to any number of potted plants put outside to enjoy the winter sun.

So Eric had known about the cave for years. Perhaps he found it the day he went missing, perhaps before. Whatever the truth, the story of it almost definitely lay on that tape. If Will had listened to it, Ruth's worries might be over. Eric had suggested Will wanted to play the hero. Maybe it was true. If he'd listened to the tape, he might have been the one to slay Ruth's demons. Even so, being this close to her made him feel high. The rosy lightness of her perfume, the sight of her white, slightly crooked teeth, the circles of pale flesh where her gloves were cut away at the wrist, each made his nerves tingle.

He arrived at the house on Rutland Road already half in love. It was very near Poet's Corner, an appropriate place for the beginning of such things.

After closing the door, they hardly went out for a week. Instead they ordered takeaway and watched old movies in their underwear. One night, after a few drinks, he asked her to read her translation of *Putas Asesinas* to him. He'd read it a few times but still couldn't work it out. In Ruth's mouth it became lyrical, as if it were an old love letter written by a mad woman. That was the only time Will showed Ruth some of his writing. It was a short story about a man who loses his hat. It was a little absurd and he thought she would find it funny but when she finished it, all she said was that it was nice. Hungry for affirmation, he asked her what she meant.

"I like it," she said, giving him a kiss. "It's very you."

He rang work and told them he'd caught some kind of bug while Ruth rested her chin on his thigh and laughed so hard he got a hard on. That queasy, electrifying word—*love*—was similarly hard to keep down. He wasn't sure whether to be dismayed or delighted.

Ruth drove him home the following Saturday. He invited her in but they only got as far as the garden. His mum was weeding the flowerbeds and didn't turn round but he could still tell she'd been crying. When he asked her what was wrong, she turned, smiled waterily at Ruth and then told him his Aunt Karrina had died. Apparently she'd left the gas on. She was found with a cigar stub between what was left of her fingers.

"Thank God you weren't living there anymore," she said.

Will walked Ruth to her car. They hugged and kissed and then he watched her drive off down the lane, his mind already following her out to the motorway. The world didn't feel upside down anymore, he'd fallen into step with it. At the same time, he imagined Karrina's burning body. Taking a deep breath, he held it as long as he could and then breathed out again.

3
——

OF THEIR WEDDING DAY, Ruth remembered little. Her veil billowing around her in the unseasonably cold wind, the church gazing over her head, the car idling behind her as if waiting for her to step back into it. For a moment she was not of this world. The organist's fingers hovered over the keys, the guests checked their watches with ever less furtive glances, Will stared forever at the church's open doors. And then she moved and the organ's first few, robustly merry notes sprang into the air, announcing, even as the guests turned to look, the advent of two more fools willing to place their hearts into uncertain hands.

She remembered Will taking her hand. Just like that, time became infused with feelings, of confusion, of love, of joy and before she knew it, a taxi was driving them down to the lodge and they were walking into a room full of candles and rose petals and Will was snoring in his shirtsleeves.

Two days later they flew to Ibiza. It had been Will's choice. She got to arrange the wedding, he got to choose the honeymoon. She remembered him resting his forearms on the curved, glass-plated desk at reception, his chin on his shoulder. There were orange trees at the entrance, straggly plants lining the lobby, ochre and mustard floor tiles. The lift made an odd, grinding sound. He told her he'd chosen the hotel because of the name—*Paradiso*. "If we get up to anything kinky," he said, "you think they'll kick us out?"

They came down the next day to find the hotel and beach heaving with the kind of mindlessness that set Ruth's teeth on edge. It was just the spur they needed. Ibiza was like a jewel. If you looked where everyone else was looking, you found only glaring surfaces. But turn it and you saw sparkling depths.

They hired a car from a shop on the *Calla de Sant Rafael*, a dusty street just behind their hotel, and drove all over the island, stopping at pine-scented bays and tiny white chapels full of blue Madonnas and flickering candles. For Ruth, with all the build-up to the wedding, it was like running through woods, being snatched at by brambles and branches and suddenly stumbling out onto a beautiful, sun-drenched beach. The whole three weeks she had no desires beyond the moment. Never before had she felt such contentment.

Most evenings they sat on the beach watching the sun set fire to the sea, before wandering along to a bar to play cards and drink San Miguel. Often they were joined by other couples from the hotel, though in their last week, most of them left and they were on their own. Before Karrina's funeral, Will had made some enquiries and found that his aunt's 'good friend' was called Tomas Ribas, also known as Tommy the Rib after the bar he owned that claimed to sell the best ribs on the island. After telling Ruth the story, how his aunt had been planning to take him on holiday, it was she who suggested they try and find the bar. And so they drove their hire car from place to place until eventually they were directed to S'Escalinata in Ibiza

Town where they found the bar on a dusty street decorated with mosaicked plaques and colourful streamers.

The bar was part of an old nightclub that had once been popular but had since fallen out of fashion and into disrepair. Tommy's Bar, its narrow saloon, dark and cool, the games area at the back full of pool tables and pinball machines, was therefore the only jewel in a dead crown. But it was the beer garden, an enclosed space shaded by tall dusty cherry trees, that made it so popular. With the smell of slow-cooked barbecue ribs blowing over its wrought iron chairs and tables, each one inlaid with the mosaic of a laughing fish and occupied by laughing, smoking, barely dressed locals, nearly all of them sporting glowing suntans and long hair and cheap jewellery, the place seemed a symbol of love and possibility.

Tomas was a big man with a belly so huge he could balance his cup on it. When Will and Ruth walked in, he was sitting at the end of the bar scolding his staff and sipping tea from an old Bovril mug. The moment they told him who they were and why they'd come, he broke down in tears. Will had not been able to find an email address or a phone number for the man and had posted a letter telling him of Karrina's death and the date of her funeral but had heard nothing back. Tomas said he never got it.

"Or if I did, one of these *idiotes* probably misplaced it," he said, grabbing his teenage niece and nephew by the neck and kissing one and then the other of their heads so that their long hairs stuck to his wet cheeks.

After opening a bottle of local wine for the honeymooners, which he said he wouldn't dream of letting them pay for, he told them he had something he wanted to show them. From behind the bar he pulled a square cardboard box and lifted the lid to reveal a scarf. Will could see straightaway it had been made by his aunt. Its silken surface was decorated with a geometric pattern of lizards and leaves, each one a slightly different colour to the last, their radiating, criss-crossing parade set against a light blue background and bordered by tiny pinecones.

"She was an artist, you know?" the man said, his tears still falling. "If you look at the pattern, what do you notice?"

But though Will and Ruth stared at the swirl of tiny lizards and leaves, they couldn't see it. Finally Tomas told them to follow him. Beyond the beer garden lay another part of the house with narrow rooms cluttered with old furniture and open windows filled with the smell of barbecue smoke and the whine of mosquitoes. Deeper into the labyrinth, Tomas unlocked a padlock and pulled open a reinforced door to reveal a long concrete room filled with tall plants. The room was windowless and the long spiky leaves of the plants drooped in a kind of regal stillness, their green surfaces tinted a pinky orange by the lights blazing down on them from above. A sweet, woody scent filled the room.

Will couldn't believe his eyes. "This is . . ?"

At the same time, Ruth said, "Is this . . ?"

"Look at the scarf," Tomas said and they did, if only to tear their gaze away from the hundreds of marijuana plants.

"See," Tomas said, "here, the spikes? The leaves and the lizards are one."

Will could see it too. His aunt had designed the lizards in a radiating pattern that suggested many marijuana leaves laid one atop the other. It was very clever and very surprising.

"I never knew . . ." he said.

"Before Karrina's husband died, she started growing plants in her greenhouse. It helped him with the pain. After she told me that, I showed her my own little greenhouse here. We used to smoke together in the garden after the customers had gone. She was a very generous lover. Very generous too with her imagination." Tomas raised the scarf to his nose and inhaled.

They visited the bar every night after that and more than once sampled Tomas's *màgia botànica* as he called it. It was magical indeed. Tomas was a big Bolaño fan and he and Ruth would talk about the man's books for hours while Will played pool with the niece or nephew or put money in the jukebox. He said Tomas reminded him of his aunt. Ruth had only seen photos of the woman but she had to admit, there was something similar about them. Both of them, she decided one night, smiled with their eyes. A little high and a little giggly, she asked Tomas his secret. Sunshine, he said without a moment's hesitation. We Ibicencos have more than our share of joy because we are born with sunshine in our bones. Our mothers work in the fields, in the gardens, they swim in the sea, they walk everywhere. They live in the light.

ii.

IT WAS IRONIC THEN to find that it was drizzling when they landed at Gatwick. Ruth woke with a jolt just as the wheels touched the runway to see rain sweeping like smoke across the tarmac and knew that the honeymoon was most definitely over. At the same time she heard a voice so cold and clear it might have been the rain itself speaking. Stop hiding. I know who you really are. This isn't happiness.

The house smelt of old coffee grounds and damp tissues. Ruth scooped up the mail and made her way down the hall to the dining room. Will made them both a cup of tea and they sat at the little fold down table with a kind of cabin pressure building between them. Finally he kissed her and said he was going to bed. Alone, Ruth noticed all that was wrong with the dining room. The peeling sill, the cheap laminate. But she didn't know what was wrong with *her*. She told herself it was to be expected. Post-holiday blues. But she couldn't help thinking of Will and of foreverness, of weight, of irreversibility.

Later on, she kept thinking, I'm not unhappy. It was a strange thought, something akin to making the sign of the cross, a warding off of malign spirits. Yet after they came back from their honeymoon, after that first evening at least, things couldn't have gone better. Will was kind and attentive, Ruth receptive and patient. They had lots of wine-soaked evenings and lazy Sunday afternoons and became very adept at tiptoeing round each other. Their differences, those that hadn't yet shown through the weave, were a long time surfacing.

There were other distractions too. Eric visited regularly, always half-cut before he'd even rung the doorbell. And Alison with her kids, Lorenzo and Karen too. Sometimes all of them together.

Ruth often thought her fear of what it meant to be a mother started there. The kids would run amok and Will would chase them, throw one under each arm. Her role was that of relief worker following in the wake of some disaster, righting furniture, clearing up spillages. And always at those parties, the same question: When are you going to start a family? She became a master of deflection. They had to get the house sorted first. They needed to look into nurseries. It might help if they lived nearer to family. But each time she spoke (wine in hand, laughter on lips), she felt something cold and irredeemable crawl across her soul. Her feet were already set in concrete, all someone had to do was push her off the edge.

It was about that time that she found the first hairs on her pillow. A few months later, she glanced in a shop mirror and hardly recognised herself. The doctor recommended she change her birth control pills so she did and then stopped taking them altogether. Even work began to cause issues. The stress, something she had always rather enjoyed, began to reveal itself in unexpected ways. She grew irritable, forgot people's birthdays, found herself forgetting smaller things too.

She expected Will to do more at the weekend. Most Saturdays she had to go into work but found very little done when she came home. Will always quoted his writing. Yet he never showed her anything. When she suggested they replace the built-in wardrobe in their bedroom, he said he'd do it but ended up cracking one of the mirrors. Then when they ordered a new one, instead of replacing it, he left it leaning against their bedroom wall for months. It came to symbolise many things for Ruth.

The weekend she became more or less certain she was pregnant, they caught the bus into town and she visited the pharmacy. Will said he was going to have a look round Snoopers' Paradise.

Ruth found him at the tills buying a tin plane.

"It's for you," he said.

They walked through the crowds along Kensington Gardens, surrounded by the usual hubbub. Ruth asked when she was going to get her present and Will held out the bag before snatching hers. "Night cream?" he said, taking out a little pink jar. "My mum uses night cream."

Ruth fretted all the way home, then locked herself in the bathroom. She'd secreted her other purchase in an inside pocket. She kept thinking, I can't be pregnant.

Afterwards, she sat there picturing those two blue lines reaching into an uncertain future. I'm not unhappy! the voice said with particular force. She kept seeing Will pinning Alison's kids under his arms. The thought filled her with a nauseous kind of love, an uneasy sickness she tried to shrug off as she flushed the toilet. A hollow sound, of rushing water, of rushing blood. You've made promises, the voice said. And it was true, not only to work but to herself, vows made as she witnessed her mother filling her father's absences with her own kind of leaving. This she only recalled now. What if she were like Veronica? Someone who thought she was a good mother just because that's what she told herself? The voice kept asking if Will was ready. Even if he says so, the voice said, will he mean it? Ruth knew if she told him, it would be too late. The cat would be out of the bag. This last was the most persuasive. To give her body into his hands, to hand him her future. But wasn't that what love was supposed to be, a belief in the future, in the impossible?

A week later she had to go to a conference and asked Will to sort out the wardrobe while she was gone. He promised to do it, so she decided to wait. If he'd replaced the mirror by the time she got back, she would tell him she was pregnant. If not, well, then she wouldn't.

The conference was exhausting. She caught the train from Hertford to London and from London to Brighton, half asleep. Yet from Brighton to Hove she was wide-awake. She walked back from the station very slowly, unsure what she would find, what she *wanted* to find, closed the front door and stood there listening to the house. It seemed to hum with unmet demands. She made her way along the hall, poured herself a glass of water and went upstairs. Will was in the spare room. As she walked in, he looked over his shoulder and they both smiled. He'd been working on something but Ruth saw that he'd minimised it. Feeling like Judas, she kissed him and then walked into their bedroom. The mirror was still leaning against the wall.

iii.

WHEN RUTH SAID SHE had to visit her mother, Will was pleased. He'd have the house to himself for a few days. He caught up with her in the hall the morning she left and gave her a hug. Lorenzo was in town, he said. He'd call her when he got back in. When he pulled away, she was crying.

"I mean, I don't have to call you," he said. If anything, her tears increased. "I will call you," he said. "I won't stop calling you. And if you don't pick up, I'll leave a hundred messages, all of them drunken and soppy."

Encouraged by her quick, glittery smile, he laughed and said, "Or you could always phone your mum and tell her whatever it is can wait. Stay here instead. We'll have a lazy night in, order Thai food, watch *Dr Zhivago* again, the Sam Neill version . . ."

Perhaps he'd been too sentimental. He watched her eyes grow clearer.

"No, I'd better go," she said with one last sniff. "I'm just going to miss you, that's all. I'm being silly."

Those were the words he recalled after she'd gone, if only because Ruth was never silly. They created a sense of dissonance, a tremor in the air that returned a few days later when Veronica called in floods of tears to tell him the terrible news.

Lorenzo and he had a great night. He was tempted to call Eric but they hadn't been as close since Ruth told him of Eric's feelings for him. He didn't know what it was, him or Eric but there was an awkwardness between them neither were willing to address.

For some reason, he also read Ruth's translation of the Bolaño story again. At times there was something about Ruth, a distance that

145

made him feel uneasy and at the same time, made the closeness they occasionally shared a far sweeter experience. The story reminded him of both Ruths, the one who was out of reach and the one who had, at times, lowered her drawbridge and allowed him into her inner chambers. He knew the story was a challenge, that Ruth had laid down a gauntlet and had given him time to think about it. What that challenge was, he still couldn't say. That if he was to try, he mustn't fail. That he must listen to her when she whispered of the underground streets. Certainly the trial was not without both its warning and its promise of reward. He sensed that this was the key to the labyrinth, Ruth's quiet call reflecting his own secret soul.

It was also this that inspired him to start writing again. Even though he'd reread his story about the man who'd lost his hat several times, he couldn't find what was wrong with it. In many ways, though, this only drew him to Ruth more. He was determined to write something that she would fall in love with, just as she had with the stories of Roberto Bolaño.

But the problem was, he believed so ardently in his own abilities that he did not realise that it was this very belief that got in his way.

iv.

FOR RUTH, THE DRIVE to Ashling was a blur, the roads and cars, fields and houses, all smears that she might erase were she to turn on the wipers. She kept wondering what was wrong with her. She'd been so close to confessing. But then Will had spoilt it. She'd told him she was going back to Ashling because her mother was worried about her drinking, that she wanted to talk to Ruth about it. It was a despicable lie and one she knew Will would never try to catch her out on. The subject was far too intimate. But in fact he'd forgotten it. His suggestion that she could phone her mum and tell her 'whatever it is can wait' had touched a raw nerve. Her lie had gone in one ear and out the other.

This absurdity, that it was a lie that had pushed her in one direction rather than another, had not escaped her. But in reality she was running away from something else, her own weakness, things of which she was mortally afraid. The truth was, she wanted to be free. She wanted to be her*self,* whatever that was. Becoming a mother was not an option. All of this she found out only after she became pregnant.

She parked the car and walked to the surgery, sat in a small, ugly waiting room where the décor might have been purposefully chosen with the theme 'despair' in mind. The coffee table was scattered with lifestyle magazines, the covers of which embraced a single narrative: Eat-very-little-and-smile-a-lot-and-one-day-you-too-may-get-a-house-as-big-as-mine.

Ruth wanted to tear the lot to shreds.

She could have seen a doctor in Hove but had decided she'd rather deal with a familiar face. The moment she saw Dr McNamara though, she realised her mistake. The man began by asking about the wedding. It wasn't until he realised why she was there that he finally shut up. Still, he kept his dismay as neat and tidy as his office. They discussed her reasons, he gave her a check-up, took a blood sample, doled out literature and offered an ultrasound. Ruth said no. He worked out the date of conception to be around mid-November. She was eligible for a medical abortion, which, he said, came in two stages. On her next visit she would take mifepristone to block the hormones that encouraged the pregnancy. On the last she would be given prostaglandin, a hormone that would make her womb expel the pregnancy, usually within a few hours. All this he related in a level tone. He said she needed to have a chat with a second doctor in order to confirm . . .

Ruth recalled listening to him explain to her mother about the tetanus injection, watching as he inspected the cut on her sole. She glanced at the wall beside the door, imagined Eric leaning against it, dull-eyed. A few weeks later it was his turn, her leaning against the wall while Veronica explained that Eric had gone missing, that he wasn't eating. The doctor peered into his eyes and ears, felt his stomach, checked under his arms, Eric the whole time like a mannequin. A week later, he'd seemed a little brighter and she'd plucked up the courage to ask him what had happened. Eric became dead-eyed. When she pushed him, he snapped at her—Where*ev*er I go, *there* I am. It was all she could get out of him.

Ruth thanked McNamara and promised to relay his regards to her parents. "I know you'll have thought about it, Ruth," he said, holding the door open. "You've always been sensible. Just know that I'm here if you want to talk."

The next day, she saw the second doctor who confirmed that she was sound of mind, then swallowed the mifepristone in the car, aware that the deal wasn't done until she took the second dose. Back at the house on Montrose Avenue, she found her mother sat in the kitchen wearing a cyan wrap. Ruth felt dowdy in comparison and wondered if that was the point.

Veronica was in a contemplative mood. "Whatever Will says, the decision's yours, Ruthie. You don't have to do this if you don't want to."

Ruth had told her mother why she was there. She'd sworn she wouldn't but the moment she saw Veronica, it just spilled out. The woman had neither tutted nor interrupted. Now Ruth knew why. She thought Will knew, that they both wanted the same thing. Ruth told her it wasn't Will's fault, that it was her decision.

"I know you, Ruthie," Veronica said. "We haven't always seen eye to eye but you're a sensible girl." There was that word again. "If he were a real man," she said, "he'd be here."

Telling her mother the truth was like sicking up a fur ball.

Veronica was horrified. She insisted that Ruth tell him. You can't make this decision on your own, she said.

Ruth went to bed wishing her father was home. He had three more days at sea but she couldn't stay that long. Her mother had cleared out most of her old room. All that was left was a framed picture of a Boeing 747-100. Almost her whole childhood she'd wanted to fly away somewhere but they'd never gone further than the coast. She used to love watching the huge airbuses passing over her and blazing into the distance.

It wasn't that though that started her dreaming. It was something she saw on TV. Just after her seventh birthday, she found her mum sleeping in the lounge. The TV was on. A reporter was saying that a plane had crashed in Scotland. Pan Am Flight 103, *Clipper Maid of the Seas*, had blown apart over a town called Lockerbie. All of its crew and passengers were dead, as well as eleven people on the ground. When an expert came on the screen, Ruth felt as if the woman was speaking directly to her. She said the suddenness of the aircraft's descent and the pattern of debris suggested a bomb but until the black box was found, other theories had to be explored.

Over the next few days, Ruth crept after the story, knowing that her mother wouldn't approve. She found out that the bomb had been planted by terrorists (the first she'd ever heard the word) but it was not this, nor the fact that everyone had died that fascinated her, it was the way they'd died. The bomb didn't kill everyone outright. A hundred and forty-seven passengers showed no signs of injury from the blast or the depressurisation. Some of the dead were even found holding hands or clutching crucifixes, all still belted into their seats and driven into the ground like some failed fairground attraction. All Ruth heard as she listened to the reports were those two words: Black box. No one knew what had happened, they needed the black boxes.

And then two boys driving a tractor discovered both flight recorders in a field near their home. Ruth knew in that moment who she wanted to be. She wanted to be the person who opened that box, the person who picked through it and solved the riddle.

Staring at that old picture, she knew she was close to that ambition. She had a good degree and more than six years' experience as a chartered member of an engineering institute. Working for BA Engineering had given her knowledge and experience of modern avionics. Before going on honeymoon, she'd asked for an application form. It was on the doormat when they returned.

She thought about ringing Will, stared at her screen for several minutes and then rang her father, before remembering that mobiles didn't work in the Atlantic. She slid the phone shut, imagined her father dealing cards in the cabin, out on deck, shouting into the spray. She was still picturing his face when he called her back.

His accent reached out with warm hands. "Sorry 'bout the noise, Ruthie. Ya' call for anything particular?"

She heard cheering, music. He told her the boat had come in due to bad weather, that he was having a few 'wi' the lads'. "What's on your mind, chuck?"

She tucked the duvet under her chin. She didn't want to come out with it straightaway but she had to, before she clammed up. "I'm pregnant." Crying a little, she began to tell him how confused she was but he soon shushed her.

"Slow down, take breath. Ya've had tests, I s'pose?"

She told him everything, heard him thinking, heard the pub clamour around him. He told her to wait. "You're married now. You need to tell Will. At least wait till I get home. Just a few days, Ruthie. If it still feels right, I'll go wi' ya."

In the bar of light beneath her door Ruth saw two blue lines. She thanked her dad, said she had to go. As she shut her mobile, Veronica opened the door. "Well, what did he say?"

Ruth was caught in a box of light, the question speckling in the brightness between them. Veronica repeated the question and then the landline rang. As she disappeared, Ruth slipped out, peered over the banister. Her mother's head, a mass of greying hair, twitched as she spoke. After replacing the receiver, she went into the kitchen. Ruth heard the fridge door open.

Veronica came back up smelling of sour apples. "He's blaming me. As if I've ever been able to stop you doing anything. He'll be home in three days. Why couldn't you have waited?"

Ruth thought about work, about Will, about her future. "I needed him to say everything would be okay."

"Oh, of course. Ruth worrying about Ruth again. What is it you always say? I've been caught up? I always imagine you on barbed wire." She snorted. "So why worry about motherhood? Surely one trap's as good as another? But your dad, can you imagine how worried he'll be now? Why put that on him when he's got work to do?"

The next morning, Ruth attended her second appointment, took the prostaglandin. Back home, she packed, almost left without saying goodbye, before pushing her mother's door open at the last moment. Veronica was sitting up in bed, the television on. There was a riot somewhere, silent people throwing silent projectiles. Ruth was surprised to see that her mother had been crying. Dewy mascara clung to her eyelashes.

She raised the remote control like a wand. "I'm such a bad mother, Ruthie. I drove Eric away and now you."

"You're not driving me away, Mum, I've got work." When Veronica struggled to get up, Ruth said, "It's done now, Mum. I'll give you a call when I get home, let you know I'm safe."

Though the M20 was unusually clear, Ruth drove slowly, afraid Will would read her mind the moment she walked in. She felt sick. She spent an hour in a roadside café sipping coffee and thinking about her father, about what her mother had said. She was wrong, Ruth was sure of it. She remembered her father making lobster chowder in the kitchen. The recipe had been in his family for generations. Whenever he made it, Veronica went out. If her dad could do that, defy her mum like that, he could handle a phone call from his daughter.

Even so, as Ruth turned onto Rutland Road, her fear turned with her. She imagined Will playing his favourite video game, building bridges over water or fire, lemmings trapped somewhere waiting to be sent home. He'd shown her how to play it but she'd been useless. Whatever she did, the critters either drowned or burned to death.

She found a spot close to the house and pulled up. This thing she'd done would stand between them for a long time, perhaps forever. She closed her eyes. Opening them again, she took a deep breath, grabbed her bag and got out of the car. Her hand was shaking but the key went in easily enough. She practised a smile and opened the door.

Will was in the kitchen, the tap running, water splashing into something she couldn't see. She slammed the door but he didn't turn his head. Mum's phoned, she thought. He knows. She felt a disconcerting wave of relief. Whenever she looked back on that moment, she thought about how lucky she'd been until then, about how her luck had come to an end and she didn't even know it.

Finally Will looked over his shoulder. "I couldn't get you on your mobile."

Ruth was still standing by the door. For a moment she almost walked out but instead, put her bag down and walked down the hall. "I forgot my charger," she said.

He switched the tap off. "Your mother called," he said. "She tried to get hold of you but . . ."

"When was this? What did she want?"

That was when he told her. "Your mum got a call about an hour ago. It's your dad. He's had an accident." Will paused, took a deep breath. "He was dragged overboard by a towing chain."

Palsy-like, something was shaking her head. "No, that can't, no." She walked across the room and leant on the sink. Numbly marvelling at her ability to do so. "I called him." It was all she could say. "I called him."

"Call your mum, she needs you," he said.

The yard was dark, yet there lay a well of gold against the back wall. It was the mirror from the built-in wardrobe, its cracked surface catching the last of the sun.

v.

FREDERICK'S BODY WAS NEVER found. In its place, Veronica asked family and friends to put something personal in the coffin, which was why, over the next few days, Ruth began to turn the house upside-down, agonising over what to choose. Will had been asked to say a few words and was trying to write an appropriate eulogy when Ruth came in holding an old fifty pence coin.

"When I lost my first tooth . . ." She stopped, nodded, the look on her face new. It wasn't just her puffy eyes, there was something else, or a lack of something, a delay before she spoke, an inability to focus so unlike her, it made Will start each time he saw it. "Mum told me there was no such thing as fairies but I put, I put the . . ."

"Tooth?"

Ruth looked at him. ". . . under my pillow anyway and in the morning . . ." She held up the coin. "Dad."

"It's perfect," he said.

"I never spent it . . ."

He showed her a shark hook Frederick and he had found on Folkestone beach. "He told me perhaps one day we'd make use of it."

The day of the funeral, St Augustine's was packed with mourners, including more than a dozen fishing families. Veronica had asked the organist to play Frederick's favourite song—*Rolling Home*—and stood listening with tears streaming down her face while everyone sang: *"Up aloft amid the rigging, blows the loud exulting gale, strong as springtime in the blossoms, filling out each blooming sail. And the wild waves cleft behind us, seem to murmur as they flow, there are loving hearts that wait you, in the land to which ye go."*

After the hymns, she asked those who wished to place something in the coffin to do so one at a time and then turned and laid a ring on the white satin at the bottom of the coffin. Ruth went next, followed by Eric. When it was Will's turn, he walked up the aisle, staring at the redwood coffin with its arrangement of lilies as he went. Inside the coffin he saw Veronica's white gold wedding band, the coin, several photographs, a toy boat, a black box and several other, smaller items. The essence of a man. He placed the hook on the satin and walked back to his seat, his heart thundering in his ears. Why he did it, he didn't know. The secret sang to him and he had to answer.

Afterwards, as he sat and listened and prayed, he tried not to look around him. Still, as they left the church and Ruth turned to talk to Eric, he couldn't help glancing at his erstwhile friend. He looked thin and pale. If he felt Will's eyes on him, he did not show it and so Will continued out into the day, before following the wall as far as the gates. He stopped beneath the branches of an old yew tree. Only then did he remove the box that he had taken from the coffin.

"What's that?"

His father had followed him and was standing by his elbow. Will pushed the recorder back into his pocket and stared up at the tiny pinecones clustering the branches above him.

Instead of repeating his enquiry, Avni asked if Will had spoken to Eric. "It's a terrible thing to lose a parent."

"I thought you were looking after Eric these days?" Will said, a little too peevishly.

His father fixed him with a look. "I needed someone to go fishing with. Eric's part of your story, not mine. An essential character, I would say. And one who needs looking after." He stared up the path. "They both do."

That night, Will waited until Ruth was asleep before tiptoeing through to the spare room. He wanted to listen to the tape straightaway. At the same time he wondered why. Partly he figured if he didn't do it now, he might never do it. Partly he was excited. He wanted to know the secret, not for Eric's sake, or even for Ruth's, though she did feature in his calculations, but mostly because the gulf between himself and those closest to him was so wide at times it frightened him. There was no way of crossing it without a bridge. The recording might well be that bridge. First though he needed to type something, another kind of eulogy.

Placing the device by his keyboard, he opened his journal and typed: *I have the box—Pandora? E thinks it's buried. If R knew . . .* He stopped, before adding: *There's a story here that can never be written. So why take it?*

The answer was that it had been as irresistible as it had been reprehensible. He could feel his heart beating a sloshing, hollow rhythm, like some wet thing trying to escape. His usual room was right next door to their bedroom. If Ruth woke up she might catch him red-handed. He went through to the third bedroom, closed the door and slid down the wall. He listened to the house, his thumb resting on the button. Only when he was sure all was quiet did he press play.

He heard a sniff, a pause, then Eric begin to speak. As Will listened, he realised there was nothing in his friend's voice of the disdain he had grown so used to. Eric described the day he ran up to the Granger house, what he found there, the girl in the greenhouse, right up until his last words, Now, wherever I go, there I am, all in the same monotonous drone. Yet rather than being dulled by that tone, the poignancy of his story was only sharpened by it.

Will recalled how he'd seen Eric. Confident, nonchalant, full of a certain, seductive cynicism. Traits Will himself perhaps desired. But after listening to the tape, he realised that Eric's personality was a trick. If he were confident, fewer people questioned him. If he were nonchalant, fewer people cared. His cynicism, which charmed certain people, spurring them on to try and prove him wrong, was, Will suspected, closest to the truth but it was still camouflage.

Desperate to share what he knew, Will swayed to his feet, convinced that it was in Ruth's best interests. Yet when he reached their bedroom doorway and saw her sleeping form, he couldn't do it. He'd taken the box from her father's coffin. A secret like that might break them. Besides, Eric was right, pain was a solitary ritual. What was Ruth's burden of ignorance compared to the knowledge he now carried? By listening to the tape, he'd not shouldered Eric's troubles, he'd only increased his own. To give Ruth the recording would be a terrible gift. The best thing to do was to destroy it.

155

Chapter 4.

The House of Love

1

LIAM WOKE TO FIND the darkness accented by moonlit lines, bright bands that stretched across the sill and up the wall. Far off, he heard a birdlike screech, its cry long and mournful. And then he smelt the fumes in the air and saw what looked like part of the door move closer and realised that he was not alone.

Before he had time to react, whoever it was had placed a hand over his mouth.

"The walls have ears," a voice hissed. "Hush up."

It was the chef, drunk by the smell of him.

The man spoke in quick, hissing whispers. "I'm not here to hurt you. I just want to talk. Things are not as they seem." The bed creaked as he leaned in. "The Keeper's been telling you all sorts of tales and I've had to stand there and listen to 'em. Tonight though, I'm going to do something about it and I wanted to speak to you before I did."

Perhaps sensing Liam's doubt, Gribble muttered, "I'm guessing he told you of the flood, how God was all teary eyed and wringing His hands?" When Liam nodded, the man leaned in. "Well, that's all a load of horseshit. It wasn't God caused the flood, it was *him*."

The chef breathed this last word so persuasively, the alcohol on his breath was all but palpable. "Now if you'll listen without crying out, I'll let you go, understand?"

Again Liam nodded, more fervently this time, and then took a deep breath as Gribble removed his hand.

"You're no doubt wondering," the man murmured, "how someone could change the world in such a manner? Well, the Keeper was once a member of a group calling themselves the New Adventists, a religious sect who were fond of telling anyone who'd listen that the end of the world was coming. 'Cept that the Adventists weren't the patient types who go knocking on doors and handing out leaflets. Unwilling to wait on God's sweet time, they began to dream up ways of causing the flood themselves. This world once contained an island called Antarctica, a white and towering realm made up of so much ice, no man or woman had ever crossed it alone. Can you imagine what would happen if all that ice melted? Well that was exactly what these Adventists started to wonder. So they invested in a shiny new laboratory.

"People used to have a deeper understanding of the world back then. Like how to look at things the eye can't see. And how to mess around with 'em. Apparently, everywhere, even in the coldest and most inhospitable places, lived things called bacterium. It was one of these the Keeper messed with in his nice new lab, a feisty little fellow that liked nothing more than to feed on certain nutrients found in frost.

"After it was released, no one was more surprised than the Adventists themselves how fast all that ice melted. Water levels rose at an unprecedented rate. This world and everything on it was dashed to pieces. We were not afflicted by one flood but by *many*."

This story was so preposterous, Liam wondered if perhaps he'd become intoxicated by the man's breath. The Keeper's version was more believable.

"Nor do the man's lies stop there," the chef said. "You must keep quiet while I tell you this." Liam saw the man's jaw ripple and then open just wide enough to murmur, *"Your parents were not with you on that boat."*

"They're alive?" Liam cried, his voice electrifying the quiet.

The chef clamped Liam's mouth. "The walls have *ears*," he hissed, his voice painfully loud. "Just *lis*ten. The night we found you, I went to bed with that storm raging outside. Woken by the alarm, I made my way as quickly as I could into the kitchen. The window there looks out over the bay and I could see your boat straightaway. It was hard to make out in all that rain but I could tell it was in trouble. When I fetched my glass, I saw a figure on the quarterdeck *but no one else*."

Liam shook the chef's hand away. "But I re*mem*ber."

Gribble's expression clouded over. "I can only tell you what I saw. You need to understand who you're dealing with. The Keeper is a very dangerous man. Two days ago, Pen went to fetch Bloodhorn from his room and saw a parchment on his desk, an anatomical study of hulking proportions. Drawn inside it were hundreds of compartments, most of them filled with runes. There were only two empty boxes, one in its head and one in its heart. Now what do you suppose was meant to go in those boxes?" Gribble's grizzled brow was raised. "That's right," he said, seeing Liam's expression change, "the dreams you gave him. *But*," he said with a shrug, "what's done is done. What we have to work out now is what we're going to do about it. Trust me, whatever the man's up to, he's up to it in the basement."

Liam nodded. "Yes, I saw it. The creature in the cage."

The chef's lips hinted at a smile. "No, lad, the girl in the cage is harmless. I talk of something be*low* the library."

Liam was certain the fumes had finally gotten the better of him. "What do you mean, girl?"

Gribble spoke very slowly. "Listen. There're men and women in this world that look like us, 'cept they're not. I've seen 'em. She's one of 'em. Though I believe she's a woman where it counts." His lips twitched. "It's not her I'm worried about, it's what's be*low*. That's why I'm going down there tonight. I think the Keeper's up to some evil and I need to find out what. But I wanted to speak to you first. Just in case."

"In case of what?"

The chef shrugged. "Just remember, don't trust a word that man says." His voice wavered for a moment, then came out in a fierce whisper. "If something does happen to me, it'll be a pity—you'd've loved my apple pie."

ii.
———

WHEN PENUMBRA BUSTLED into his room the next morning, she seemed agitated but at least she was still speaking to him. "Bloodhorn needs a run," she said. "Come on, you look like you need a little exercise yourself."

161

Outside, they'd barely reached the runner beans before she was clutching his arm. "Gribble's gone."

Liam shook his head. "But he can't be."

"He's gone," she repeated.

Beyond the vegetable patch, the dog was lolloping across a field littered with rocks and rabbit holes.

"It was the Keeper told me. I checked his room. Gribble didn't have much but what he had is missing. And his room's all tidy like he knew he wasn't coming back."

Liam felt gripped by a familiar illness. "Gribble thinks my parents might still be alive." He dipped his head, then looked her in the eye. "He came to see me last night. When he told me, I cried out. Maybe the Keeper overheard and told Gribble to leave."

Penumbra stared at him. "So you think the Keeper's lying to me?" She stared across the rutted land, loose hairs snaking in front of her face. "When he said he wanted to build a lighthouse up here, the people in the village thought him mad. They were laughing right up until the day the flood came and washed them clean off the face of this earth."

"But how could he know it was coming?"

"Because God told him," Penumbra said fiercely.

"Or because he caused it?"

Pen tutted. "The point is, you're not the first to doubt him and you won't be the last. But I'm telling you, everything he's foreseen has come true. Which is why," she said, drawing a slip of paper from her pocket, "I can't believe I'm doing this."

She shoved the note into his hand, watched him frown over the spidery letters written there.

Dreamer, meet me in the library after
all are abed. Your own, Gale

"I'm sorry," Penumbra sniffed, "but I've already read it. I was worried about Gribble. And I thought maybe I could help. You wanted to meet Gale and she's obviously willing, though why she wants to meet you in the library is anyone's guess." She took out a key. "You won't get in there without this. The Keeper thinks he has the only copy but I cut this myself."

"But how will Gale . . ?"

"She has her ways," Penumbra said mysteriously. "One thing more," she added. "I've a friend who trades among the islands. Last I heard, he was heading to the Island of T'heel. If you like, I could send one of the birds in the aerie, see if there's any news concerning your parents."

Her offer and Gale's note, come as they did together, felt fateful, as if he were finally beginning the journey his feet were made for. "I can hardly wait," he said, closing his fist around the key.

"Then do something else instead."

That said, Penumbra didn't leave him alone all afternoon. As soon as he'd finished peeling the mound of potatoes she put before him, she had him polishing the brass and mopping the floors, before finishing off by wiping down the sides. Only after he'd removed several trays of roast potatoes from the oven and served a plateful for Penumbra and himself, was he allowed to go to his room.

The housekeeper had told him to go down to the library only when he could no longer hear the generator and he listened to it whine with some apprehension. It was strange to think that the Keeper was toiling away somewhere, for only he needed electricity at that time of night. Liam also wondered why Gale wanted to meet him in the library. Why couldn't he just go upstairs and knock on her door? But the chef's departure was enough to curb such thoughts. No matter what Penumbra believed, Liam was certain the Keeper was behind the man's disappearance. The housekeeper must doubt him too. Why else would she insist they go outside to speak that morning? Thinking such thoughts, he nodded off.

He was surrounded by a cold, still silence. Realising that he was awake and that he could no longer hear the generator, he jumped up and crept to the door. Pandora too must once have gripped the lid of her jar in the same way he was now gripping the door handle. But what happened when she removed that lid? He opened the door to a yawning darkness, its density only accentuated by the flickering candle in his hand.

The stairs afforded him little shelter and he might well have been caught had anyone been coming the other way. Yet in his rush to escape the dark, he didn't think of this until he was standing in the cluttered antechamber. Only then, with Pen's key jammed in the lock, did the moment seem to roar with ill-intent. The pins aligned and the door creaked inwards, revealing a familiar subterranean glow. Aware as he descended of the hidden presence at the far end of the room, he picked his way down the steps as quietly as possible. Not knowing where Gale meant him to wait, he decided to take the same route the Keeper had chosen, his ears pricked for any strange sound. Again the books called to him but when he plucked a few at random, he was disappointed, their subject matter being almost always religious in nature. Deeper into the catacomb, the library was less well tended, the books more haphazardly shelved, their covers dusty. There he found books on ornithology and island lore and another on the life cycle of the hawkmoth, each stage illustrated by sketches. Distracting himself thus, however, meant that he was soon lost. He felt time creaking on and was growing ever more agitated when he turned a corner to discover a solitary trail of footprints. His own, or so he thought. But when he looked closer, he realised these prints were fronted by little oval shapes. Whoever had left them was barefoot. The trail ended at a reading area near the back of the library. A dusty message had been scrawled across the boards in the same spidery hand as Gale's note:

The ode world meets the new
Rub me out to find what's true

Rubbing at the words, Liam watched with growing delight as the dust accumulated in two previously-hidden cracks that appeared to form the edges of a trap door. There seemed no way of lifting it but when he moved the nearest table, he found a finger-sized groove. Expecting the door to be heavy, he slipped his finger into the hollow and heaved it upwards, only to find that it lifted with ease, revealing a series of steps.

Seizing the nearest lamp, he dragged its cable round the table legs and thrust the globe down into the hole. The way was narrow, the steps steep. *Whatever the Keeper's up to, he's up to it in the basement.* He walked down the first few stairs, pulled the cable after him, lowered the door and then continued his descent until the door closed above him. It was like standing in a greenlit, diagonal box. As he resumed his journey, his breathing panted back at him, as if he were accompanied by some animal.

Just as the last coil fell from the top step, the light swelled, picking out the confines of a low-ceilinged room filled with more books. The place smelt of contraction, of desiccation, of empty husks and dead skin. The books were stacked almost to the ceiling with hardly enough room to walk between. Liam placed the lamp on the floor and picked up the nearest volume, a little hardback, its cover worn, its title—*Thc Ccmp ctc Vcrks cf Jc n Kcats*—barely discernible. When he opened it, he found it was a book of poetry. Inside the front board, in small, precise print, were the words *Erin, 1992.* Neither name nor number meant anything to him. More curiously, when he turned to the middle of the book, he found several pages missing, though a scrap still remained, a stubborn fragment adorned with some ten lines of poetry, the reading of which created in him a strangely pleasing sense of dislocation:

> *My heart aches, and a drowsy numbness pains*
> *My sense, as though of hemlock I had drunk,*
> *Or emptied some dull opiate to the drains*
> *One minute past, and Lethe-wards had sunk . . .*

He heard birdsong, its call like a hammer. These words had once meant something to him. He did not know the poem's title, nor what came next but he knew the poem nonetheless. He wondered if Gale had intended him to find it. If so, why didn't she just come out of hiding and tell him so? Thus thinking, he turned to leave, only to spy two book-clogged archways either side of the stairwell. Clearing the nearest, he realised they came together behind the well to form a single passageway. He held up the lamp. Books vanished into the dark like so many green-fringed scales. He imagined Gribble setting off along the tunnel and never returning.

Abandoning the lamp on a pile of books, he began to inch his way along the passage, his shadow stretching ever-longer and ever-fainter before him. The further he went, the more books blocked his way and occasionally he had to burrow like a mole. The walls too closed in, their protrusions reminiscent of ribs. In that blinding darkness only his heart seemed real. Yet though he became convinced that the chef couldn't possibly have come this way, not once did he think of turning back. When the books finally began to peter out, they did so almost all at once, so that within a few minutes, he was walking again. Turning a corner, he saw a light ahead.

The tunnel ended in a cavern, a vast space shaped as if some titan had ripped a giant peach stone from the hillside. All of a sudden the ceiling was far above him. The light, darting and strobing from the far end of the cave, flashed against the cavern walls, which oozed in places, highlighting several dozen rigs, their wooden structures drilled into the stone. Each was filled with what looked like corpses, their size diminutive compared to the furthest figure, a tall, loose-limbed shape more than twice the size of the others. It was from this apparition that the lights sprang.

Blue light spilled from its head, forming, when they caught the red shafts pulsing from its chest, purples and violets that danced among the dead bodies along the wall, sporadically delineating their soft, puffy features. Nearer to, Liam saw various instruments had been fused into the creature's torso and limbs. Its shrivelled complexion and straight black lips formed a horrid contrast with its deep blue eye and ear sockets.

He was horrified. A dream to light up the dark indeed but with what? Crossing the cavern floor, he saw that the creature's torso and head contained hundreds of compartments, all sunk in a gelatinous goo and bound in a transparent exoskeleton. The thing was shaped like a man but at the same time sexless, a translucent worm in its glowing, neatly-segmented trunk but with strongly masculine face, hands and feet. A smell as of burnt plastic filled the air.

He was standing very close to the thing when it breathed hard as if sensing his presence and a convulsive motion agitated its limbs.

"Firethefire . . ."

It was an odd refrain and Liam stepped closer in, trying to catch its meaning. Only then did the creature's eyes flutter open and its arm jerk upwards, seizing his hair. Terrified, Liam stumbled backwards, caught his heel on something and sprawled to the floor. He saw strands of hair in the creature's fist. Its wide blue eyes drilled into him and when it opened its mouth, its scream engulfed him.

"Firethefirethefirtherfartherfather!"

As blue wings sprang from behind its back, Liam tried to push himself away, only to find himself face-to-face with the object he'd tripped over. Gribble's overcoat and tunic were dark with blood. His eyes stared. Where his chest had been, a hole gaped. The creature was heaving at the air, a whistling sound forcing its way in and out of its nostrils but already the sounds were dimming and Liam looked up to see the thing's eyelids drooping, its wings slowly folding, its mouth closing—but not before one last word slipped from between its teeth: "*Fa*ther."

As Liam fled, he kept expecting to be dragged back into the chamber. What kind of animal does a thing like that? What kind of animal? When he finally stumbled into the room at the bottom of the stairs, he fell among the books and lay there, his lungs like bellows. A moment later he was up again and charging the stairs, lamp in hand, his head low.

Shoving at the underside of the trapdoor, he lurched back into the library, causing the door to clatter to, the sound echoing around the room like a shot. Discarding the lamp, he scrambled backwards to collapse in a heap, his breath sawing in and out of his mouth.

But there was no time to gather himself. In his panic he'd backed into the bars of the Nephilim's cage and before he knew it, fingers were grasping at his neck. He tried to throw himself forwards but the Nephilim's grip only tightened. Blood pounded at his temples. At the same time, he heard the thing breathe what might have been a word.

"*Li*am," it said again.

He felt the creature's fingers loosen, heard its chains clinking to the floor as it retreated. Turning, he saw the thing crouching in a dark, odorous pool.

He tried to swallow. "You can speak. You know my name."

The creature's eyes glowered beneath its hood.

Waves of weakness and anger coursed through him. "Speak, or I'll go. If he finds me here . . ."

Its voice was rusty from lack of use. "*He* spoke it."

"The Keeper?"

"*Him.*"

Liam squinted through the bars. "What are you? He said you're a monster."

The creature pulled at its hood, revealing long, greasy hair, limpid brown eyes, sharp cheekbones. Through a tear in its tunic he glimpsed the side of a small soft breast.

"Do I look like a monster?" it croaked.

He flushed. The chef had been right. "You're a woman."

"He told me not to speak," she said. "That I'd wither away behind these bars if I did. They found me at sea, chained me here. I don't know who I am. *Rooo*," she said softly. "It's all I remember. He calls me Rook."

Liam frowned. They'd both been found at sea—the same night? And neither of them able to remember anything. Had the Keeper given them something? Certainly, the man had needed something from them both. That was why he'd caged Rook here, threatened her. "Our stories are so similar. Except," he said with a half-smile, "you can fly."

Rook raised her chains. "Not in these."

Liam shook his head. "We're not the only ones trapped in this house. There's someone in the room above mine, a dreamer called Gale. It's because of her I came down here tonight. Perhaps she wanted us to meet. We're obviously all prisoners here but Gale's been here the longest. Maybe she can help."

168

Just then they both heard a noise. It may just have been one of the books he's replaced but the sound reminded him that he had already tarried too long.

"I must go," he said. Seeing her stricken expression, he reached through the bars and squeezed her hand. "If he catches me here, it'll do neither of us any good. But I will come back for you. I promise." And with that he turned and fled.

Yet the moment he left the library, he was almost caught. He couldn't find the key and had just decided that he must have lost it on his travels when the stairs began to ring out above his head. Someone was descending. Pulling his pockets inside out, he located the key, threw it into the keyhole, locked the door, hid the thing under the birdcage and ran up into the chamber. He'd just managed to throw himself across one of the couches there when the Keeper rounded the last bend, a benign expression on his face.

"There you are," he said, his tone almost jocular. "I was getting worried."

Liam pushed himself up, blinking and peering around him. He asked where he was.

"Surely you've not been sleepwalking?" the Keeper asked, his tone gently mocking. "If only we'd kept you under lock and key. Come, let's get you back to your room."

Liam kept expecting Bloodhorn round every bend, its eyes bleary with hunger but when they reached his landing, the only thing to startle him was the Keeper's chuckle.

"Your room key," the man said, holding the thing up for inspection. "As luck would have it, I keep it right here in my pocket. No," he said firmly when Liam tried to protest, "we *must* keep you where you belong and more importantly *safe*. What if you were to walk off a cliff in the middle of the night?"

Hearing the man lock the door, Liam had to stop himself from pounding at the wood. He needed to be careful, for Rook's sake now as well as his own. Throwing himself onto the bed, he remembered the book and pulled it from his trousers. 'Thou, light-winged Dryad of the trees,' he read again, 'in some melodious plot of beechen green . . .' Once more, the bird's lilting call filled his head with trees and darkness and sweet summer air. Yet though the words and the music they conjured were just as charming, he still had no idea why.

iii.

THE NEXT MORNING, he opened his door to find a leprous-looking man standing on the landing.

"Not walked off a cliff yet then?" the man sneered, before pulling the door to and locking it.

By the time Pen came with food and a chamber pot, Liam was all but climbing the walls. "He's keeping me locked up like an animal," he hissed as the housekeeper closed the door.

She pushed him towards the windowsill and only when they were both leaning out into the wind, did she speak.

"A bird came back," she said quietly, "from *T'heel.* A trader I know sent a message. A man and a woman matching the description you gave me have been spotted on the island. The message said you're to speak to someone called Erin."

The name went through him like a kick of electricity. "Erin?" he asked, sure he'd misheard. He'd only just come into possession of the book and here was the housekeeper mentioning the name in the inscription.

"Yes," she confirmed. "But before you can do any such thing, you need to escape."

"But how," he said, "when I'm guarded?"

Here Penumbra's eyes narrowed above a complicit smile. "There's more than one way to skin a fish," she said, leaning out the window and pointing.

Following her finger, Liam saw a long, green rope running up the side of the house from a hoop at the base of the tower to the aerie above. It passed within a few feet of his window.

"Gribble was worried about fire. He strung it himself. With the right equipment you could use it to escape."

170

If they could all escape, if that were something he could participate in, then maybe, or such was his sudden and secret hope, his memories might be returned to him by some kind of divine osmosis. "Not just me," he said. He told her about Rook. "And you and Gale too. It's too dangerous for you here."

Penumbra looked stricken. "Not Gale. If the Keeper knows I've freed the dreamer . . . I might be able to make it look as if Rook freed herself but Gale's safest here."

"The Keeper lied." Already regretting the pain he was about to cause her, he reached out. "Gribble didn't leave . . . he's dead. I found his body in a room beneath the library. There's a creature down there chained to the wall. Gribble must have gotten too close. Whatever it is ripped out his heart."

A sound like two striking rocks sprang from Penumbra's mouth. Her thin face became wracked with sorrow.

"Whatever it is that man's planning, you've *got* to come with us," he insisted.

"And leave Grib's body down there?" The woman's breath rattled in her throat. "If what you say is true, the Keeper's day is coming and I'll be here when it does." She tipped her head back, sniffed. "You must get off this island tonight. Use the boat in the cave. I'll speak to Rook. If she is what you say, she can help. As for you, I'll explain what you need to do when I next bring food." She nodded towards the door. "In the meantime, try not to do anything daft."

Liam reached out to her. "Be careful."

The housekeeper patted his hand. "That's all I *am* full of." She cupped his cheek and looked into his eyes as if reading his soul. "Eggs," she said at last. "That's what you need."

He spent the rest of the day reading and his evening standing by the window watching the spring darkness close over the sea. As good as her word, Penumbra brought him an enormous plate of eggs and several rounds of black-crusted bread, before watching him wolf down the lot.

She gave him a thick canvas bag but only allowed him to open it after he'd eaten. Inside he found ham sandwiches, a flagon of water and several pieces of equipment. While he read the note, Penumbra indicated the piece to which each paragraph related. He read the note again, then took hold of the harness, and let the housekeeper show him how to put it on, how to connect the figure-eight-shaped device to the rope and how to clip it to the harness.

After reading the final section, he whispered, "Will it work?"

"It has to," she mouthed back.

Aware of the ordeal to come, Liam tried to get some sleep but it was no use. Lighting a candle, he read again the inscription inside the book. *Erin, 1992.* Nothing. Yet the housekeeper's message had lit up something inside of him and he waited with a mounting impatience, his imagination turning her absence into ever more horrid possibilities. It didn't help that his shutters had begun to rattle, or that the sky was filling with darker and darker clouds.

Finally a key turned in the lock and he started forwards, only to see the Keeper, his face all hollows and ridges in the candlelight. The man was looking for Penumbra.

Liam ground his teeth. "I saw her walking Bloodhorn," he said, as Penumbra had planned. "Why?"

"She's supposed to be preparing supper."

"Well, perhaps if you took the dog out yourself," he said, trying not to grit his teeth, "Pen might be able to perform her latest duties in a more timely fashion."

"Don't worry," the Keeper said, his smile enhancing the darkness under his eyes. "I'll be giving Bloodhorn exercise soon enough."

It was another hour before Penumbra arrived. When she did, she looked exhausted. "I can't stay," she said. "I just came to say goodnight."

"The Keeper came," he said. "I told him you were out with Bloodhorn."

Undercover of this last word, Pen leaned in and said, "'Tis done . . ." before adding in a clearer voice, "Chasing Bloodhorn through this blasted weather's got me all but beat."

"Well," he said, knowing that they were to be parted and wanting to say more, "pleasant dreams."

"You forget," she said, pressing a quick kiss to his cheek, "I leave that to those better equipped."

iv.

AS MIDNIGHT APPROACHED, Liam's panic grew. Rain sprayed the shutters and he was worried he might not hear the knock. He kept imagining a rapping, only to find it was the wind between the slats. Finally he sat on the sill to watch the waves and the rain cast into luminous, white rags by the sweeping light, their forms black and crawling as the light swept by. Many times the light lit up the clifftop, the waves, the clouds beyond, until he was mesmerised and then something was there, a darting, slipping form, momentarily far out, then closer. Rook was blown off-course several times before she managed to grip the window frame. He leant out, felt the wind like a wet comb across his face, touched her fingers and then her arm. Rook grasped at the sill, before slipping but he was just able to seize her wrist. As if trying to restrain some sleek black dog, he felt his grip tested, leant back, heaved and then they were falling into the room.

At the same time, the shutters clapped one after the other against the sconces. A moment later, despite the wailing wind, Liam heard a key scrape in the lock and saw a familiar head peer in, its pockmarked skin made craterous by the flame beneath it. Aquamarine eyes observed the room.

"The shutters," Liam said, getting up from his bed as he spoke. "The wind." Even as he said it, one of the shutters banged open again and he slammed it shut.

The man swept the candle in a silent semi-circle, gave Liam a mildly murderous look and then closed the door with enough force to suggest that he wished some part of Liam's anatomy were in the way.

"Next time," Liam whispered, peering under the bed, "why not try the door?" All he could see of Rook were her eyes. They shone like a cat's. He could smell her well enough though, a pleasant scent of

173

pumice and straw that reached for him even as he spoke. "You met Penumbra then?"

Rook nodded, her eyes blinking on and off. "Where are we going?"

"To find my parents. Penumbra thinks they may be on an island by the name of T'heel."

"Then let's go."

His legs shook. He located the harness and clips, shoved the book and Pen's note into the bag she'd given him and began to pull the harness up round his waist. At the window, he opened the shutters, being careful not to let them bang. The wind rifled the room, flapping Rook's clothing as she edged onto the sill. Clinging to the frame, she slid forwards and leaned out. The wind made a black flame of her and then she was gone.

Seconds later she was back, every part of her clothing alive. She had the rope but a sudden gust shoved her aside and she almost lost her grip. Liam sensed the drop before him, the steep path to the cliff-edge, the spuming sea beyond. The pull of it terrified him. Surely he must fall. He spread his knees and tensed his arm, before reaching out and seizing the rope. He felt a tremendous tug. With his knees jammed, he attached the figure-eight device to the line. Then he grabbed the clip at his groin and connected it to the device in his other hand, securing the connection with several quick turns. He was now attached to the fire escape.

He shut his eyes for a moment, tensed his stomach muscles and then let go of the rope. Resisting the force that seemed to pull ever harder at his middle, he stepped to the edge and braced himself against the stone. The wind was deafening. Seeing him hesitate, Rook darted in. *"This s'it. Now or never!"*

He looked down, saw glittering rocks and groaning trees and then Rook was pulling him loose and they were swinging through the air. They struck the wall, Rook fell away and Liam sprang in the other direction, his shoulder and head clattering against stone. Air screamed in his ears. Dazed, he managed to right himself, began to feed the rope through his hands, steady himself with his feet. His clothing kept whipping at his face, his feet slipping on the streaming rock. His hands were instantly numb. Yet the lower he got, the less the rope swayed and the quicker he was able to descend. At last the ground leapt dark and slippery beneath him and he fell to his knees and kissed the rock. "Thank God!" he said, over and over.

As if thrown there by a wave, Rook appeared beside him and began pulling at him. "We'll freeze! Get up!"

He unclipped himself and they staggered away. Buffeted back and forth, they finally reached a crevice in the cliff and began to pick their way down a path slick with rain and overgrown with weeds. The scent of vetch and wet clay was overpowering. The lighthouse's beam vanished and the way grew dark. Here the difference between land and air was negotiable. Slipping on loose rocks and walking with their hands as much as with their feet, they followed the trail until they reached a fork. With the wind harrying their clothes and the rain stinging their faces, they stared in each direction. The path veered left and right between crumbling slopes and a steep edge. They may have stood there much longer had they not seen the snake. It was weaving between the rocks like so many stripes in the dark and straightaway Liam felt as if it were calling to him.

He shouted, "Gilgamesh!" but Rook was already following the snake's dim little stripes and he quickly fell in behind her. Beyond the left-hand fork lay a slope running with rain and beyond that, an overhanging rock, its inner wall dark. The snake was gone but they found, by shuffling under the overhang, that it was the beginnings of a cave. Inside, the space seemed very narrow, though it was so dark, they were only able to navigate using their hands. Slowly, awkwardly, they inched their way forwards, following the nearside wall until finally they heard a deep, low rushing and then a sound like thunder. A vague, grey light, broken at first into grains but becoming more and more whole, grew upon the gloom until they could see that they were in a much larger cave. Again they heard a long, whooshing roar followed by a crashing boom and Liam saw waves, much higher than he remembered, rushing into the cave with all the heedlessness of startled horses.

He found the boat jammed between two rocks and began to wrestle it free. At the cave mouth the noise was tremendous. The rocky funnel caught the wind and echoed the sea even as the water frothed in crevices and cast silken sheets into the air. If they didn't time it right, the boat would be dragged back into the cave and smashed on the rocks. Yet it was too loud for him to be able to communicate his fears. It seemed though that Rook already understood, for she watched the waves and jumped into the boat even as he shouted for her to do so.

Shoving the craft at the breakers, he sank into the water, breasting the waves until they broke over his shoulders. Shingle slipped beneath his feet, the craft bucked in his hands. With an almighty kick, he clambered over the side, rocking the boat. Rook had already slung the oars into the locks and he took hold of them now and began to row away from the cave. Water broke over the boat but he dug in.

The tide had obviously turned and with each wave crested, the mouth of the bay grew nearer. There conditions were much worse. Where the natural harbour had afforded some shelter, out in the open, the storm's power was uninterrupted. Rain swept across them like arrows. Waves rose and fell at a terrific rate. Golden-throated kingdoms glowed over the water. The boat yawed beneath them and they were forced to jam themselves beneath the thwarts. Not once did they think of what they were leaving behind and only when the boat almost tipped bow to stern, did they look back at the lighthouse, to see that already its light seemed no bigger than a pinhole.

2

LIAM WOKE TO THE SLAP and trickle of water, a tilting creak that lifted and laid low, a glop-glip of liquid and a gust of wind, which blew across his face, causing him to squint against the light. There, overhead, crouched a figure, its form made indistinct by the sky.

Alarmed, he scrabbled from beneath the seat, causing the boat to lurch and Rook, who had, until then, been perched above him, to spring into the air. The sky looked washed out, the shifting horizon an uncertain promise in every direction. The sudden sight of so much water only increased his distress. Sapped by that vast and endless unmaking, he had to look away and stared instead at the grit at the bottom of the boat.

Meanwhile, Rook was rifling through the bag. She took out a sandwich and Pen's instructions and sat reading while they ate.

"In order to reach the island," she said, "we need to keep the White Rock to port and head into the setting sun."

Liam glanced at the horizon. "But there's nothing there. What if we can't find this White Rock?"

"*You* might not be able to," Rook said. "*I* on the other hand . . ." And with that she darted upwards, her speed such that she was back before the boat had stopped rocking. "It's that way," she said, barely out of breath and pointing towards a seemingly arbitrary spot.

"Of course it is," Liam said, his spirits already reviving.

"The sun's too high right now but if we plot its course, we can work out where it will set. That way is west."

And so it wasn't until the day began to leave a blueberry haze about the boat that they set the oars and started rowing towards the bonfire of cloud and sunlight illuming the western horizon. Neither did they stop when the sun finally sank into the sea, plunging them into a star-smashed darkness.

Rook pointed out a cluster of stars shaped like a ladle. "If you follow the two stars that make up the ladle's pouring edge, you'll see the North Star." She pointed to a vague-looking speck. "Pen said the North Star stays at all times above the North Pole. Orion, on the other hand," she said, pointing at another collection of stars, "rises to the east and sets in the west. Between them we can work out which way we need to go."

They took turns rowing and seemed to make good progress. The sea stayed calm, the skies clear and the boat travelled at quite a clip. The task, though, was doubly arduous, first due to the aches and pains that began to spring up all over their bodies, second due to a growing sense of futility, for it seemed as if the stars and sea were moving faster than the boat.

They fell asleep just before dawn and woke with the sun directly overhead, their skin pink. Both were thirsty but with their water supply already low, they had to satisfy themselves with only a few sips. They decided rowing during the daytime was dangerous. It would be better to try and stay cool. With this in mind, they jumped into the sea and swam about the boat, their hands occasionally grazing each other's bodies, before clambering over the gunwale and creating a makeshift tent using the oars and several items of clothing.

"I prefer this den," Liam said, "to all that water out there. It makes it hard to imagine who I am."

Rook's lips twitched in the green light. "And is that how we make ourselves, through imagination?"

He thought about it. "It's either that or let others do it for us."

"They do anyway," Rook snorted. "Look what happened with the Keeper. To them we're just the stories they tell about us. That's all they want us to be."

By nightfall a mist had settled about the boat above which Rook had to rise in order to read the stars. Meanwhile, Liam slung the oars and began turning the boat this way and that, testing various grips to see if he could avoid his blisters. The longer Rook was away, the more oppressed he felt. The dull chop and drip of the oars and the cloying mist made it seem as if he were floating on some underground river. At last Rook landed on the prow behind him. She was panting and frightened. She asked where he'd been.

"Right here," he said. "Why were you so long?"

"I couldn't find the boat. I kept thinking I was going to drop into the sea and drown."

The next day, they ate the last of the bread and drank the remaining water as if participating in some final ritual. Knowing they were in need of distraction, Liam showed Rook the book of poems. "There's a secret here," he said, tapping the torn pages. "Something I think I was meant to find."

Rook barely glanced at it. She'd been irritable ever since her return the night before. "But what use is only one verse?"

They'd hoped to row again that night but by evening huge clouds began to appear and by nightfall the sky was completely covered. They huddled under the centre thwart and watched the sky—the motion of the boat and their nagging thirst making it more and more difficult to keep their eyes open.

They woke to tumult. Lightning fractured the clouds, columns of sound fell in protracted exclamations. The boat heaved like a matchstick on a lake of fire, pinning the pair to its boards. They prayed for rain, thinking they might be able to slake their thirst, but when it came, it drilled into their skin and soon they were praying for it to stop.

Just when Liam thought it could get no worse, lightning struck nearby, rocking the boat and causing him to slip and hit his head. The air was suddenly full of moving objects. Bright balls bouncing around a table. Words came to him, '. . . Reminds me of our honeymoon . . .' in the same voice that had told him not to drown, the same voice, he realised, that said, 'Please come back to us.' Before he focussed on them, the balls were waves whizzing across the darkness, dividing again and again. But looked at directly, they were crystals of light.

Only in one place was there nothing. Honeymoon, he thought. Reaching out, he pushed at the place and it became a moon. At the same time, the radiances receded, became stars, bright droplets along a wave. He found himself standing up, the boat still, the craft at an angle. Around him the world was frozen, waves at the point of breaking, unbroken, white spraylets lying in the air like ragged handkerchiefs. He drank raindrops from the air. Stepping from the boat, he scooped handfuls until his body was purged of drought.

Rook was lying under the central thwart, her eyes closed but before he could investigate, something moved, a fluttering form that tinkled downwards through the frozen rain to settle somewhere behind him. Turning, he saw a man standing a few yards beyond the boat's prow, his slim body darkly clothed, his hair wet.

"How fitting, *djali im*," the man called. "You lived for your dreams and now they live for you." His smile caused the splash of green in his eye to sparkle. "You've outdone King Canute himself."

"Who are you?" Liam slipped and then steadied himself. "How did you find me?"

The man tipped his head back and smelt at the air, his hair twinkling in the moonlight. "I followed the lightning. I came to bring you this." He withdrew a scrap of paper. "It's from your father."

Liam recognised it straightaway. Still he frowned. "But why didn't he come himself?"

Removing the book, he saw that the strip fitted perfectly beneath the first verse. He pored over this new portion, again feeling as if something were calling him.

> *O, for a draught of vintage! that hath been*
> *Cool'd a long age in the deep-delved earth,*
> *Tasting of Flora and the country green,*
> *Dance and Provençal song and sunburnt mirth!*

"Words, dreamer." The man shook his head from side to side, his smile widening. "They're tap-tapping. But wither shall they lead? To happiness, triumph and truth, perhaps? Or perhaps simply round in a circle, back into the arms of the man who makes chase."

Liam looked up from the book. "You mean the Keeper? You know him?"

"I know *of* him."

Recalling the chef's words, Liam said, "He's planning some great evil."

The man chuckled. "For tribes as old as ours, such concepts are meaningless. Unfortunately for us there is only *ligj e paligjshëm*."

"Ligj?" Liam tried to swallow but the word caught like a hook in his mouth.

"*Ligj e paligjshëm*, law and unlaw. The triumph of tradition over reason."

The night was eerily quiet, the darkness, a shimmering net.

"You said this verse is from my father. I am looking for him. When did you see him last?"

"You will meet him soon enough," the man said. "Besides, you have others to think of now."

Even as he spoke these last few words, the silence was disturbed by a high, drifting howl.

"We have company," the man said, glancing up. He reached the crest of a wave in a single bound. "Yes," he said, focussing on the scene behind them. "I believe it is your friend. He's far off. Still, you should get going." He glanced down at Liam, warmth in his eyes. "The man is an idealist of the worst kind, a hev'n hoaxer. And jealous? Oh, ho. He's greener than the tinkle in my eye. Why do you think they call him the Keeper?"

"And what do they call you?" Liam yelled as the man rose into the air.

Words drifted down, each one fainter than the last: "They-call-me-Eagle."

It was as if the maze of moonlit raindrops had swallowed him whole, yet when Eagle's last few words drifted down, they trembled among the raindrops as clear as tiny bells: "We're-birds-of-a-feather, you-and-I. Never-fear, we-shall-meet-again. *Listen-for-my-cry.*"

Rook's lips were slightly parted, her eyelids blue, the tips of her small white teeth glowing as if with an inner light. He wondered that he'd ever thought her a monster.

"The Keeper's coming," he said, shaking her awake.

She stared at the mountainous landscape around them, asked in a sleepy, wondering voice what he had done. Liam scooped water from the air and held it out. Even as she drank, another howl drifted across the wasteland.

"He's getting closer," Liam said. "We need to know which way to go."

Rook chased raindrops into the air before darting upwards. Throwing the bag onto his back, Liam ran at the nearest wave but miscalculated the height and fell flat on his face before slithering back down the steep surface. Finally though, he managed to get his fingers over the edge. It burned cold against his skin. He pulled himself up and looked about him. Mountains rode in every direction, their tops cast yellow by several bright trees that he realised were lightning bolts.

Rook flew down and pointed. "We need to go that way."

Most waves were passable. Some had shallow inclines that were easy to traverse. Others had been caught in the middle of their own destruction and were full of odd sproutings and pitfalls that were difficult, though not impossible, to cross. Even those whose concave walls loomed over him, eventually sloped into narrow ravines that he could slip through without too much trouble. Several waves later, he slid down into a light-filled dip. Shielding his eyes, he looked about him. A bright yellow trunk descended into the depths and rose into the heavens. The hollow was dotted with dark shapes, their forms half hidden by steam. When he pulled one from the air, he realised it was a fish, cooked by lightning.

With Rook pushing at him whenever he faltered, he struggled onwards but his efforts became more and more laboured. The scape around them was so quiet, the quick, predatory sound of their own breaths was startling. Occasionally they heard their pursuers too, their rough songs and barking dogs spurring them on. Finally giving in to exhaustion, Liam pulled the fish out of his bag and they began to devour the flesh, Rook looking at him as if he were some kind of magician. Only when she glanced up was she distracted.

"Look," she said, pointing.

Following her finger, Liam saw that the Keeper's tenacity was not due to good guesswork. Their path lay behind them, carved through the raindrops like a dark tunnel.

"We might as well have left breadcrumbs," Rook said.

From the top of a tall wave, Liam saw dogs pulling boats, a number of men pushing them, others cutting through the ice with axes. The Keeper stood in the prow of the lead boat urging the dogs on with a great fury and a long whip that he cracked between each exhortation.

Spying another lightning fork, Liam headed towards it, an idea forming in his mind. When he finally slipped down into the light-blasted hollow, he approached the huge shaft, wary of the heat emanating from its core. Placing his hand inside his bag, he reached out and touched the nearest branch. By slipping first one hand then the other into the bag, he was able to work at the branch until it broke loose. He raised the thing into the air and grinned at Rook as she flew down.

"And then there was light!"

But though this made his passage easier, it also made their whereabouts clearer. Cries drifted across the wilds. "There! There! Follow the light!" Nor was it the only light now, for though the waves were still frozen, the sky had taken on a violet hue.

Finally, Rook settled beside him. "The Island of T'heel," she panted. "We're almost there."

He looked to where she was pointing and could make out a narrow headland, a bay sweeping to his left. At its edge, a necklace of sand glowed palely in the surfacing light. It was very close. So too were the boats.

It seemed like an age later that they finally collapsed onto the beach's crystalline surface, their lungs and limbs burning. Yet, despite his exhaustion, Liam knew there was one more task to perform. Pushing himself up, he tried to remember how he'd stopped the sea. The moon. It still glowed in the sky, though it was lower now. He reached out a tired finger and made as if to press it.

Loose sand whipped at his ankles. Waves broke as if struck by hammers. A roaring filled his ears. Staring out to sea, he saw its twisted surface heave and watched as tragedy struck those caught upon it. Men struggled in the sudden spume. Dogs who managed to stay afloat were dragged down by their harnesses. A boat was broadsided by a wave.

The Keeper's boat had vanished but then it reappeared half full of water, its starboard edge listing, the Keeper heaving on an oar. Dogs were tied to the prow. Liam watched as the man cut at the ropes, before hauling on the last harness and dragging the body of a dog over the side. Throwing out a second oar, he turned the boat into the waves, his body almost horizontal.

The shaft of lightning lay on the sand. The magic had not entirely melted. Instinctively, Liam picked it up and held it in both hands, creating a circuit, a supercharged revolution that ran up his arm, across his chest, through his heart and down his other arm. Here was the power of dreams, here was fire and water. The Keeper had used him direly, as he had others. He thought of Rook exhausted at his feet, of Gale trapped in her room. He thought of the chef, his heart torn out. He felt the lightning grow hotter and pointed it at the craft. In a moment of doubt, he relaxed his grip but it was too late. The lightning electrified his teeth and streaked across the water, striking the boat's hull and causing wood and iron to explode into the air. Even as the splinters settled on the foaming waves, the Keeper's boat was gone.

ii.
—

WATER RUSHED IN, petered out. Rook lay asleep, her hand touching his. He watched the flutter at her neck. A polished sky shone above them. He looked around but the sea was empty, the beach deserted. T'heel's shoreline was edged by steep dunes. Sharp, blue rocks, scattered with flowering grasses, rode into the sea. The sand had blown inland, across broken walls, half-covering what might have once been buildings. Beyond this, stunted palms fingered the sky. Behind, far to his right, he saw a steep, slanted roof.

"We're safe," he said as Rook stirred. "He's gone."

She rubbed at her eyes. "Where?"

Approaching the house with the slanted roof, they realised what had looked like dunes were actually burst sandbags scattered in front of a series of low, broken walls. Though the central building was the least damaged, its roof was half-shorn of tiles, its timbers and much of its upper floors exposed. On the ground floor, wooden steps led up to a veranda, beyond which lay double doors. A few feet from the doors, a figure, half-shaded from the sun by the broken boards above it, stood with its hands resting on the railing. For a moment, whoever it was remained motionless and then began walking down the steps towards them. The morning haze made the figure shift and flicker and not until it grew nearer did it solidify into the shape of a woman wearing a green dress, the cut of its collar exposing a slim green pendant. The moment Will saw her eyes—like grey pools, he thought—he shivered. Words came to him then so whole and clear, he almost spoke them aloud: *Her eyes are pools, grey pools into which one might slip.* He realised she was speaking.

"... couldn't believe my eyes. Where on earth have you two come from?" The woman took in at their damp, sandy clothing and hair. "What on earth has happened to you?"

Still feeling lost, Will said, "We came here looking for—"

"Help," Rook interjected. "We lost our boat. In the storm."

The woman seemed to consider this. She was looking from one to the other of them, her hands circling each other as if washing themselves.

"This is Billy," Rook said, introducing him before he could speak. "And I'm Ruby."

The woman smiled. "And I am the Giver." She indicated the shore. "'Tis a treacherous coast. But fate has brought you to the right place. We always help those in need."

As they followed her, Rook touched Liam's arm and warned him to be careful, her quiet voice at one with the peep-peep of the birds darting across the dunes.

They walked up the wooden steps, past potted orange trees and into a wide hallway laid with ochre and mustard tiles and dotted with at least half-a-dozen doorways. A variety of plants lay on either side, their greenery stirring in the breeze. The place smelt of warm dust and dead flies.

"Welcome to the House of Love," the Giver said.

As they passed the first room, they glimpsed a long, heavily-jousted table, large, white sinks, several plinths and an untidy scattering of chairs. The other doors were closed, including two doors opposite each other that their host called 'the circle'.

"It takes you right round the house," she explained.

Double doors at the other end of the hallway led out into a walled courtyard awash with sunshine. Lemon trees stooped above lush undergrowth. Honeysuckle and jasmine framed dark windows. At the centre of a large lawn lay a blackened fire-pit, its ashen piles surrounded by a number of youngsters, some with their eyes closed, their faces warm with sunshine, others, lounging, one upon another, their gaze fixed upon the strangers' faces, their lips twitching with curious smiles.

In the shade of an old olive tree, someone had arranged several wrought iron chairs around a small table inlaid with the mosaic of a laughing blue fish and it was here they settled.

"My children," the Giver said, pointing to the youngsters, "like to think of this place as their little piece of paradise. I hope you will too. But you must be thirsty."

She clicked her fingers and a few moments later a girl with dyed red hair came out and served them ice-cold water.

"This is Lisa," the Giver said. "My second born."

With barely a nod, the girl turned and left.

"Have you come far?" the Giver asked.

Liam gulped at the water. "Yes," he said. "We came because . . ." He glanced at Rook. "We're looking for a couple."

The woman observed him with renewed interest. "Well, there are several here that might suit. What is your preference?"

But when Liam described his parents, she wrinkled her nose.

"We've no one of that age, I'm afraid. But you're welcome to look. And in the meantime you will stay with us, I won't take no for an answer." She laughed at this, as if at a joke and then breathed in so that the tops of her breasts became golden in the sunlight. "So, tell me, what is it you do? We're always looking for new blood."

"He dreams," Rook offered.

"Oh, how de*light*ful! To visit new realms, to defy nature, to be anything and everything your heart desires . . ." She looked at Rook. "And you?"

Rook smiled. "I don't sleep long enough to dream."

The Giver trilled at the youngsters and a moment later the pair were surrounded by kisses and laughter. None of them looked older than eighteen and all of them acted even younger than they looked, tickling and pinching each other and hugging Liam and Rook as if they were old friends. Two girls, one with red hair and a blonde with glittering eyes, came last, each pecking at Liam's cheeks, their giggles half-deafening.

The redhead asked if they'd like to swim but the Giver said they needed to rest. She smiled at Liam.

"Perhaps we could talk some more this evening?"

3

LIAM WOKE TO FIND the aching in his muscles punctuated by a pulsing sound that came and went through the windows in dry, throbbing waves. The room's white-tiled walls and candle-filled alcoves were laced with shadows. Mirrors and tables glinted in the gloom. Stretching his sore muscles, he got up and made his way outside.

"Cicadas," the Giver said when he asked her about the throbbing sound. "I love to listen to them. Like blood pulsing in your ears after you've done something particularly vigorous."

She was sitting on a lawn chair, her legs crossed, her eyes closed, her head tipped back to catch the last of the sun. Several youngsters, still sandy from the beach, were lazing on the lawn but as Liam sat down, the Giver clicked her fingers, causing those nearest to stir. Under her instructions, some went in to lay the table, while others went to get changed. Lights sprang on inside the house, highlighting the shrubs that bordered the ground floor and the arches complementing the first floor balcony.

Rook was already up. Liam could see her helping a young woman distribute candles around the garden. As he watched, the woman stopped to apply a flame to the bowl of a long, white pipe. She drew at the pipe and blew smoke even as she smiled at something Rook was saying. He found himself wishing he'd told the Giver exactly who he was looking for. She'd shown them nothing but kindness. He felt annoyed at Rook's lack of trust. He asked the Giver if he should help.

"Only yourself," she said, indicating the red-haired girl from yesterday who had arrived with wine and was pouring it into glasses. "Lisa will serve you well." Their eyes met and Liam thought he understood but the Giver was quick to move on. "Last year we were plagued by storms," she said. "Half the vines were destroyed. This vintage is quite precious."

As Liam accepted a glass, he recalled the words of the second verse. *O, for a draught of vintage!* He took a sip, aware that the Giver was watching him. A crimson richness fumed in his throat and his head filled as if with warm evenings and simmering afternoons. Rook was also watching him but for a moment he could not place her. He swallowed and the feeling vanished. "Delicious."

The Giver smiled. "I've named the vintage *Vin de T'heel.*"

The mouthful placated the butterflies in his belly. The possibility that his parents might be at hand seemed less important, as did the significance of the second verse. Briefly, though, as if the quiet dusk descending on his mind had thrown it to the surface even as other details were subdued, he recalled the name inside the book. It could do no harm to ask if the Giver knew of anyone called Erin. But then he took another sip and the feeling of disassociation deepened. Rook was frowning at him but he couldn't think why. He'd been about to ask the Giver something but didn't have time to work out what, for just then Lisa re-entered the garden to announce that dinner was ready.

Hearing Lisa's announcement, Rook, who was by then standing beside him, turned as if to go inside, only to knock into him, tumbling the glass from his hand. She immediately bent to pick it up, apologising as she did so, though he was sure he saw her glance at the Giver as she spoke.

The Giver's look was coolly withering. "Worry not. There'll be more wine with dinner."

As they filed in to eat, Rook took his elbow, her hiss so fierce she didn't need to repeat it. "Whatever you do, drink no more wine."

Dinner was a raucous affair. By the time it was over, the table and floor looked almost as well-fed as the diners. Glutinous dribbles stained the beading, beans lay mashed into the wood, bones scattered the table in miniature graveyards. Liam was uncomfortably full. He was also exceedingly sober, Rook having made a point of looking at him each time he was offered wine.

The Giver hardly noticed. She spent most of the meal scolding her children, who seemed oblivious to her attention, their raucous laughter and horseplay all but drowning out her indignant cries. Liam felt there was something theatrical about it all but when he told Rook he was rather enjoying it, she gave him a look that suggested he was stupid. That was when she raised her voice above the din and said they were going to bed.

"It's been a long day and we're very tired."

"To bed so early?" a dark-haired girl called, causing the room to ripple with laughter.

"I'm afraid so," Liam said, though actually he could have stayed longer.

A plump faced boy jabbed his fork. "Being afraid don't make no difference!"

A howl of merriment rose from the crowd, a wolfish cry that hunted the pair even as they made their way down the corridor.

As they reached her room, Rook turned to him, a troubled look in her eyes. "Doesn't it all seem a little strange to you?"

He shrugged. "Everyone seems perfectly friendly."

After closing his door, he fell onto his bed. With his eyes barely open, the room's soft sheets and shimmering fabrics were an agreeable blur. His limbs felt like fallen tree trunks and when he closed his eyes, the candlelight shone warm and orange through his lids.

He was woken by a rap at his door and mumbled a welcome, before raising his head. Expecting Rook, he was surprised to see the Giver, her eyes sparkling greyly in the low light.

"I've come to see if you need anything," she said, pushing the door to.

"Actually, I was almost asleep," he said, struggling to sit up.

"Yes," she said, perching beside him on the bed, "you must be so tired. I just wanted to make sure you were enjoying yourself."

"You've been very generous." He nodded at the bolster as if to mean more. "You have a lovely house."

"Thank you. But the way you left the table, I thought maybe you were displeased with something."

Liam heard himself blustering. "No, it was wonderful."

"The children can be rogues sometimes but they mean well." The Giver reached out and stroked his face. "But your eyes are drooping. Perhaps there is something I can give you after all." Before he could respond, she moved her hand to his shoulder, slid in behind him and began to work her fingers into his shoulder muscles. "Giving and taking are equally necessary," she said, purring the words beside his ear. "Are you sure there is nothing I can give you?"

"Thank you," he said, twisting gently away. "Not unless . . ." Pressed into asking for something, he said, "Unless you know someone here called Erin?"

"Erin?" she said, frowning. "How odd that you might know him."

"I don't," he said, worried at her tone. "I found a book with his name in it, that's all."

"Well, if it's the same Erin, we had to lock him up. I'm afraid he's completely mad."

ii.

THE NEXT MORNING, Liam found Rook and the Giver talking in the garden.

Rook addressed him as he crossed the grass. "Apparently there's a market here."

He hadn't slept well. He'd dreamt of the dark room again but this time he was lying on his front and someone he couldn't see was astride him, their fingers kneading at his muscles.

"I've arranged a guide," the Giver said, a half-smile on her lips. "He works on one of the stalls. But first you must get out of those shipwreck clothes."

In Liam's room, Rook pulled aside a curtain to reveal shirts, trousers, jackets, waistcoats, even suits. There were shelves of shoes and a drawer filled with boxes of watches and jewellery.

"Apparently clothes get washed up here all the time," Rook said as if she didn't believe a word of it.

Liam realised she was wearing a yellow dress decorated with white polka dots. "I didn't, you look . . ."

"Yes, well," she said, pressing the garment to her. "The early bird catches the pretty yellow frock, I guess."

Liam pulled on a shirt and jacket and Rook showed him to a mirror. Half-shocked, he saw a young man with dark beard and burnt skin staring back at him.

"She was waiting out there this morning," Rook said quietly. "She asked about us. I said we were friends." Liam saw her grimace in the mirror. "Let's just say she seemed pleased. She told me this house used to be an old dance hall. She renamed it after the flood, just as she did the island."

Rook laid a hand on his shoulder and met his eye in the mirror. "She said T'heel stands for 'the heel', as in, 'those of the heel will inherit the earth'. I think the suggestion is that those who have other forms of transport at their disposal are not welcome. In other words, if she finds out who I am, she'll have my guts for garters."

"Guts for garters?" he said, turning and looking at his profile. "What are garters?"

They cut across the garden, through an alleyway and out into a dusty, windblown area full of shops and tavernas. A youthful crowd jostled between several dozen market stalls. Caged birds shrieked and flustered behind bamboo bars, lizards padded in the dust, twisting thick, calloused necks inside metal collars, crackling roasts flavoured the air. Drifting screens of smoke opened to reveal brightly coloured clothing, woodcarvings, bronze, pewter and silver utensils and, towering over the stalls, palm trees, their leaves slowly rattling in the wind.

They stopped at a stall selling large, pink-knuckled shellfish. The creatures were deep-fried and crunched when bitten into but the flavour was sharp and sweet. The next stall was lined with bottles of sloe gin and packed with boxes containing dried herbs and fungi. Rook read the labels, before inspecting one of the boxes more closely. "The secret ingredient for any party," she read, "good for cooking." She winked at Liam. "Maybe we should do a little baking. You remember the girl I was talking to last night? Her name is Joan. She hinted that there's more to this place than meets the eye. Maybe if we can loosen her tongue . . ."

The stallholder was a short man with a thinly haired top lip and a belly so big it peeked between the buttons of his cardigan. He grinned at them from round the edges of a much-chewed cigar.

"The girl of my dreams," he said removing the cigar for a moment. "And who might you be?"

"Ruby," Rook said with a half-curtsey. "And this is Billy."

The man beamed. "Then you'd be the guests the Giver wants me to show round. I am Karrin," he said, beckoning to them, "Come, let me make you a brew."

The top of the stall was decorated with handwoven bags and red and yellow scarves patterned with tiny lizards, all of them a slightly different colour. The pair had to duck to get round the side of the bench. After settling them both on a crate, Karrin boiled an old iron kettle and then set about making tea using lemon-scented herbs.

Finally, after much small talk, he said, "You dream too, I hear."

"You also?" Liam asked.

"Yes." Karrin blushed. "Though only the one. And really it's more of a nightmare." He took a pensive sip. "Perhaps I could tell you, a burden shared, as they say? I'd be grateful for your opinion." Seeing him nod, Karrin's eyes swelled. He passed them each a cup and then began his tale.

"It's like this," he said. "I'm walking home but as I get there, I see the front stoop crawling with ants. I can't go another step." He held up a pair of plate-sized hands. "I don't like killing things but I find insects so unnerving. Ants are the worst. Always busy about some mysterious business. So I grab a handful of dead rhododendron heads from the border and crumble them over the ants. As soon as

I do though, I realise my mistake, for the little monsters start streaming over the dead petals and it looks like some creature quivering on the doorstep. I jump over them and retreat indoors but there are more ants inside and I can't escape. I have a machine and start sucking them up but it soon gets full and eventually starts spewing ants everywhere. Worse still, many of them now have wings."

He'd been rubbing his hands together but stopped now and looked at them both to say he'd finished. Liam began to drum his fingers. He felt oddly relaxed now he's finished his tea.

"The ants are people. They rush around you, a mystery."

Karrin nodded eagerly.

"The flowers," said Liam, warming to the task, "are your hopes. But they're dead. Alive, they might have helped but dead, they're a poison. You scatter your dead hopes over the ants but the two become indivisible. Inside the house, you should be safe but you're not, you've been invaded and must defend yourself. But you cannot touch the ants, so you turn to a machine. You try and contain them but there are too many and, in fact, they become more threatening: they grow wings. But if the ants are actually people, it's not their individuality you fear, it's their collectiveness. For you, it is this that makes them so alien, their ability to move as one, seemingly mindless force . . ."

Karrin waited before realising Liam was done. "Food for thought," he said, rubbing his belly. "And you can tell I've had a fair few thoughts. Thank you. A great gift indeed. Dead hopes? The Devil certainly does make thoughts for idle heads." He nodded again. "If you'll give me a few minutes to pack up, I'll take you on that tour."

"If it's no trouble," Rook said.

"Not for a smile like that," he said, with a grin. "Besides, it won't take me long to get my stock under cover, my house is only over there." He pointed across the market. "See? The one with the small front yard."

"And the rhododendron bushes," Rook said lightly.

Karrin gave her a small bag. "As a thank you," he said.

As they squeezed round to the front of the stall, Rook's eyes glinted playfully. "So you're useful after all, even if it is to talk nonsense. What was all that about?"

"I don't know. It was like I didn't have to think. Like I'd done all my thinking beforehand."

Karrin reappeared, startling them both.

"I know," he said, chuckling. "Built like a house, moves like a ghost. Now where'd you like to go? Nowhere's too much trouble for the gift you've given."

"How about the prisoners?" Liam hadn't meant to say it. He and Rook hadn't even spoken about it yet but still he persisted. "Can you take us to the prisoners?"

Karrin sighed. "Prisoners of love are off limits. They're infectious."

Yet Liam sensed a crack. "I'm looking for my parents." He glanced again at Rook. "I believe there's someone who might know where they are but he's a prisoner. If you could point the way at least?"

Karrin's brow lowered and his eyes seemed to turn inwards but eventually he nodded. "All right. But incognito. Folk my age have to keep their noses clean."

He gave them scarves and they headed towards the palm trees on the other side of the market.

"It's best," he said, "to go around the houses as they say. That way you will have something to tell the Giver if she asks where you've been."

On the way he entertained them with the names of the streets they were walking through. "The *Calla de Sant Rafael*," he said, "where her Excellency, the Catless Queen of Valero resided for almost two hundred years." Further on they turned into the *Calla Ramón y Cajal* upon which the Baby Squire of Ramón had taken his first and last steps. Here the flood had caused great devastation and there had been little restoration. Walls jutted like broken teeth. Dead trees leaned on piles of rubble as if giants had abandoned their brooms. From all sides came the throb of cicadas.

Karrin led them out to the beach road, the *Calla Balanzat*, barely discernible beneath the sand, so that they approached the House of

Love from the south. Soon they turned into a side street where several buildings leaned together. An even narrower alleyway finally opened into a third passage. Removing his scarf, Karrin announced that the wall in front of them was the south side of the House of Love. Liam looked up. On the third floor were five barred windows.

"Only one room is occupied," Karrin said. "He's guarded, so be careful." He rubbed his face and then looked at the pair of them wide-eyed. "I lost someone dear to me too. My husband, bless his soul. Kindest man ever swam the sea. This must be our secret. To the grave," he said, kissing his fingertips.

"You've our word," Rook said. "And if we don't see you, good luck with the ants."

Karrin gave them both an affectionate squeeze before sidling back the way they'd come.

The moment he was out of earshot, Rook rounded on Liam, her eyes flashing. "You said you'd be careful! Then you go spilling your guts to the first person who's grateful to you? This man owes his loyalty to her, not you. How do you know he can be trusted?"

Liam felt cowed. "He didn't have to help us."

"Who is this prisoner?"

"Before I left Sazani, Penumbra told me to look for someone called Erin, that he might know where my parents are. It's the same name as the one inside the book. So last night I asked the Giver if she recognised it." Seeing her face, he said, "I didn't tell her I was looking for my parents, only this Erin. I mentioned him on the off chance. She said she knew him but that I couldn't see him."

"But when? You two weren't alone last night."

Liam took a deep breath. "She came to my room after dinner. To see if I wanted anything."

"And did you?"

Liam stared at her. "Only to know where my parents are. Whether they're dead or alive. My soul rests on the answer to that question. I'm sorry but if we wait too long, my parents, if they're here at all, might be gone."

Rook was staring at him, unblinking. But then she nodded.

"Okay. But there can be no more secrets."

Liam thought about Eagle but then shook his head. "No more secrets," he agreed.

Rook gazed up at the windows. "Why did the Giver say you couldn't see this man?"

"She said he was infectious."

"Well, we'll just have to see about that, won't we?" she said, her word trailing after her as she rose into the air.

Why hadn't he told her about Eagle? He was sure he could trust her, yet something had stopped him. He knew it was something to do with the man's words—ligj . . . law and unlaw. In his mind, they'd ground into a pearl of possibility he was unwilling to relinquish. Eagle had said they would meet again. Until then, he wanted to keep that pearl to himself.

Rook was hovering in front of the last window, her hands against the glass. The stone, reflecting the sunlight, cast her face in bronze. She appeared frozen, the only movement, the flap of her clothes in the hot, lazy breeze.

"Rook?" he called, his words whispering against the stone. He waited and then spoke her name again, a little louder this time. Still she remained entranced.

Aware of where they were, he decided to whistle. It would be more discrete. But when he pursed his lips and blew, he was surprised by the piercing note that escaped them.

"Screritttt!"

Rook started and then fell. Skittering down the wall, she hit the dirt, balls of dust puffing into the air. "What are you doing?" she asked, her words a furious whisper.

He apologised. "I thought whistling might be better."

"Than what, a foghorn?"

He shrugged. "Did you see him?"

"He was there," she tutted.

"Then what's wrong?"

"Did I say anything was wrong?" She glanced at him, then looked away with an angry sigh. "Okay, I know him, that's what's wrong. We

196

couldn't hear each other, the glass was too thick. So he wrote me a note."

"What did he write?" Liam had wrapped Karrin's scarf around his hand and found himself twisting it now.

Rook was nodding her head in a slow, dazed-seeming way. "His exact words were: I am your brother."

"I am your brother?" Liam said.

"Yes. And he's right."

He gave the scarf another twist. "How do you know? If you don't remember anything, how do you know he's telling the truth?"

"I just do." She threw up her hands. "I can feel it like I can feel myself breathing." Golden brown eyes ticked back and forth. "He's being guarded. We have to get past that guard."

iii.

THE HOUSE WAS EMPTY when they got back. Rook suggested they do a little baking and started searching the cupboards for ingredients. She lit the stove and began to melt butter, before crumbling Karrin's dried leaves into the gently bubbling liquid. She set him to stirring it.

"Keep the heat low."

She loaded a bowl with baking powder, cocoa, flour and salt, scattered sugar across the melted butter, blended eggs and vanilla, took the butter off the heat and added both the eggs and the contents of the bowl. Finally, with Liam looking on in amazement, she filled several trays with paper cases and poured the mixture into each.

"I know," she said, when she'd placed the last tray in the oven. "It must be like riding a bike."

Half an hour later, she removed the trays and gave him a cake. "As the Giver's honoured guest, you must be the first."

As he broke it open, the cake's contents oozed, wafting the smell of chocolate and vanilla across his nostrils. He ate it and then took another. "Delicious," he mumbled.

Just as Rook was finishing her first cake, Liam decided that everything was suddenly very amusing.

"Are you all right?" Rook said, humorous twitches flitting across her face.

"Let's see," he said, counting on his fingers. "I don't know who I am, I don't know if my parents are dead or alive and I don't know who to trust."

Rook laid a hand across one eye and tittered. "I know but the only way is up when you hit rock bottom."

For some reason the words 'rock bottom' struck them both as being hilarious and they worked themselves up into a fit of giggles.

"Well you have all the answers," Liam said. "You tell me."

"How should I know? I'm as empty headed as you are."

This had them laughing even harder. Finishing a third cake in two bites, Liam said, "So what's it like being a bird?"

"I'm not a bird," Rook said, narrowing her eyes.

"Really?"

"No. Our difference is all in the mind."

"That's right," Liam said, "you're bird-brained and I'm not."

Rook darted at him with a rolling pin. Too late, he dodged away, rubbing furiously at his elbow.

"I am not bird-brained!"

Rook leapt at him again catching his heel. Hopping away, he grabbed a stool before turning and defending himself.

"Get back, fiend!" he cried, fighting off the pin with the legs of the chair but the moment he spoke, Rook dropped her arms. The mirth fell from her face.

"I am not . . ." she said, shaking her head.

"Oh." Liam put the stool down. "I'm sorry. I didn't . . ."

"You will be!" Rook said, springing to life and smacking him in the ribs.

"That's it," he yelped. "I'm going to beat the life out of you!"

He chased her round the central plinth, through the door and across the hall into the dining room. Chairs were knocked over, an impasse was reached across the table and then Rook darted for the door, almost gliding as she ran. They only stopped when she ducked into his room and leapt onto the bed.

Heaving at the cover so that she fell over, he pulled her to him, one hand at a time, though he was laughing so hard it took all his effort. Rook, also giggling, tried to get up but he blocked her way, his knees landing either side of her hips, his arms either side of her head. "Fly your way out of that one," he said, smiling down at her.

"I could if I wanted to," she said.

"And yet here you are."

"I'm sorry for getting angry," she said, suddenly relaxing beneath him and staring up into his eyes.

And then she was lifting her head and he was lowering his and they were kissing. When she pulled away, she looked as if she might say more. "I'm starving," she said finally.

He said he felt rather peckish himself, giggled, tried to stop and finally had to cover his mouth. "But no more cakes," he said, tears running down his face.

"I have another idea," Rook said.

Slipping from under him, she disappeared out the door, only to return holding a large jar. "I saw these when we were baking." Setting the jar on the floor, she unscrewed the lid, dipped her hand into brown liquid. Liam watched her fingers swim through the fluid, chasing what looked like eyeballs. When she handed him one, he realised it was an egg.

The thing was tastier than it looked. The white sliced between his teeth in wet slivers, the yolk crumbling on his tongue. He was reminded of drinking the wine but only because this sensation was its antithesis. The flavour of the egg did not dull his curiosity, it sharpened it. It made him sensitive to possibility. He swallowed, watched Rook do the same and then, as if there were no time to waste, began to kiss at her lips and neck, gently at first and then more and more hungrily, while she, with an equal ardency, began to pull at his clothing.

Chapter 5.

The Centre Cannot Hold

RUTH HAD TOLD MCNAMARA she didn't want to know the baby's sex but even so, after having the abortion, she'd decided that it had been a boy and had even given it a name. Eli. The day Eli would have been celebrating his first birthday then (or rather, the day she had appointed), she got in the car as normal but instead of going to work, she drove along the seafront to the Palace Pier roundabout, headed down to the arches and parked outside an art shop. It was a cold winter's day. Easels quivered in the wind. Paintings of animals, seagulls, cows with enormous nostrils. She crossed the railway track and crunched over the stones.

Just as the shingle dipped down to the water, the wind dropped a little and she decided that that was where she would sit. Only one other individual was down there that early, an oldish-looking man wearing a pair of black Speedos. She watched him dive into a wave, waited until he reappeared, realised what she'd thought was a mop of black hair was actually a cap. Pale sunlight glinted off it each time he resurfaced.

She sat down, picked up a few stones, dropped them one-by-one until she was left holding a brown, egg-shaped pebble. *'E's a good egg, Farrington, always gets a round in.* Appropriate to remember her father on Eli's birthday. She slipped the stone into a pocket, recalling at the same time a line she'd written for her father's funeral. She'd not used it in the end. She raised her chin and spoke to the clouds.

"If we forsake one love, is not all love forsaken?"

"But if you give away your heart, how can it be taken?"

The voice came from up the slope. She looked up to see the man with the swimming cap, a towel round his shoulders, his elbows keeping balance as he skittered among the stones.

He worked at his hair with the towel. "From a poem?"

She felt embarrassed. "I was quoting myself actually."

"It's a nice line."

She noticed his hair was as dark as she'd imagined it. He had an athletic body and a lined face. She grated a handful of stones.

"So where did the second line come from if I wrote the first?"

He waved a hand. "It's what I do. Put a cap on the pavement and spit bars." He grinned mawkishly. "You throw a line at me, I come back with one of my own. None of it's written down, none of it's ever said again. It's like those mandalas monks like to make except a lot less skilful. I was making my way back to my palace," he pointed towards one of the beach huts, "when I heard you and couldn't resist."

Ruth shook her head.

"I'm Alfie."

After only a moment's hesitation, Ruth said her own name. They squinted at each other for a moment.

"So why the long face? You're dressed for work but you're not going. Surely cause for celebration?"

She picked up another handful of stones. "I've made some pretty shitty decisions of late."

"And now you're feeling irate?"

She peered sideways at him. "I'm not irate."

"Not even a little hate?"

"Is this what you do?"

"Let's focus on you."

"A free session of street poetry from Grey Master Flash?"

"Now let's not go calling it anything rash."

Ruth raised her eyebrows.

He grinned. "Sorry."

She wrinkled her nose. "I hate myself, mostly. Today . . . today is my boy's birthday. Eli."

"Where is he?"

She shrugged. "He was never born. I had an abortion."

Alfie looked at his feet. "I'm sorry."

"Me too."

"You shouldn't be." He looked up. "You look like a sensible woman."

As Ruth stood up, slowly but with an air of off-kilter finality, he added, "You could always try again, I mean, if you've changed your mind." He held a hand out as if towards a frightened dog. "Sorry if I spoke out of turn."

Ruth looked at him. She wanted to tell him not to apologise. "It's not you." Stray hairs lifted across her eyes. "Some bridges can't be rebuilt. And no amount of poetry can change that."

"Certainly not mine." He smiled. "Your own, perhaps?"

He said nothing more and when she looked back, he was walking up the beach towards the huts.

That Sunday, Will suggested they take a walk along Beachy Head. While he drove, Ruth sat in the passenger seat thinking about Alfie's words. *You could always try again.* As if it were that simple. Nobody gets to start again.

Will parked the car and they followed the path down towards the cliff-edge. The view was breathtaking: grassy slopes, a few clumps of gorse and broom and then white cliffs, sudden and sheer, preceding an iron-blue sea. Ruth used to volunteer for the National Lifeboat Institute. Beachy Head was very familiar to her. RNLI staff were sent there more than any other location. Suicides, mainly. Sometimes a lost dog. So for her the place was full of ghosts. It was nice being there for a different reason though, other than bringing up the dead.

At the pub afterwards, they talked about work. Will said he was much happier at Hellerbys, the international school just outside of Brighton he'd been teaching at for the last three years, that it was nothing like his old school in Ashling.

"Everyone's from somewhere else so all the students know what it's like to be different. It's the first time I've felt like it's an advantage to have a mixed heritage."

"Heritage?" She smiled at him.

When he asked her how things were going at BA, she shook her head, unwilling, suddenly, to broach the subject she'd wanted to broach for weeks now. She didn't deserve it. He didn't deserve it— not unless it began with the truth. He knew how much she'd always wanted to work for the Bureau. As if to hear herself say it though, she said, "If I applied now to be a Flight Recorder Inspector, I think I'd have a good chance of getting in." Despite telling herself not to, she reached out and took his hand. She wondered if he could feel the way her pulse was racing. "The problem is, lately I've been wondering if that's what I really want. If I start all that, it's going to take years and, of course, we'd have to move to Hampshire and we both like it in Hove, don't we?"

She watched him take a tentative sip of beer. He knew she had something else on her mind. She looked him in the eyes.

"What I'm trying to say is . . ." She felt her tongue pause between her lips. "Maybe we could try for a baby first?"

After gulping a bigger mouthful than perhaps he'd intended, Will broke into a smile. "Yeah, why the hell not?"

Just like that. Ruth felt such a rush of love for him, she wanted to run out to the car and start trying straightaway. Yet at the same time she felt a contrasting rush, a sense of disgrace that hollowed out her smile even as it grew on her face.

It was a feeling that was to stay with her for a long time. Fay was conceived in guilt, that's how it felt. She thought about how people spent their lives trying to avoid pain, trying to protect themselves against guilt. That was the real reason she wanted to protect Eric, she wanted to protect herself. Or so she thought. She had turned a corner and caught a reflection and not known herself. She was proud of her intelligence, of her independence, these were her strengths. But they were also her weaknesses.

It was a while though before those particular birds came home to roost. Even though she took everything into consideration, her ovulation cycle, the positions they should use, what they should be eating and drinking, even the music they listened to while making love, one month and then two went by without her getting pregnant. Will thought it all hilarious. I wouldn't want it being *too* cultish, he said to her one day before dragging her out to Lewes to buy knitted booties and blankets and Tupperware and a beautiful silver rattle, after which they drove home at top speed, their passion such that they didn't quite make it to the bedroom.

In the third month, Ruth felt different. She waited until Will had gone out before slipping the test out of its white paper bag. The bathroom was cold. A crack in the window frame let in just enough air to waft the shower curtain. Her goose bumps weren't just due to the cold though. Afterwards she lay on the couch and stared at the applicator, remembering a similar looking device, two blue lines. The pills that had cut them in half. She felt stupid, selfish. But also happy. She thought of her mother carrying Eric, of her frayed nerves, her bitten nails.

A while later, the door went and she heard Will wrestle shopping bags into the kitchen, then walk back down the hall. When he walked in, he must have seen something on her face because he asked her what was wrong. He crouched down and placed his hand on her head.

"Are you okay?"

She tried to smile, almost told him about the abortion. She stared at him, breathing in the faded, comforting scent of his aftershave. Dad's dead, she thought. Because of me.

"I'm pregnant," she said.

"But that's good, right?"

She was shaking her head. "The odds of me not screwing it up . . ."

"Well, we'll screw it up together," he said cheerfully. "They'll be enough blame to go around. And love." He was smiling. "Los Putas Asesinas," he said in a terrible accent, "and Panchito Pistoles."

"La puta asesina," she said gently.

"Besides," he said, "Fay will have a very forgiving nature."

It was the first time he'd mentioned the name.

"Fay," Ruth said, resting her forehead on his. "I could get used to that."

That was just before Easter. Normally they went away during the holidays, even if it was just for a weekend break, but they both agreed that they had a lot to do and that there was no time like the present. Or rather that's what Ruth suggested and Will agreed with. The holidays were spent attending antenatal classes, decorating the spare room and building a cot. In the meantime, Will drank lots of wine and found himself nodding to lots of things he only half listened to. If he were to describe that time, he'd probably have used the word bewildering. He'd always imagined being a father but now that possibility was becoming reality, he found himself feeling slightly at odds with the situation. In contrast, Ruth all but glittered. She knew exactly what she wanted and never showed a moment of doubt. It was easy then going along with whatever she said. They painted the nursery a colour called Cookies 'n' Cream which Will said was beige by any other name and Ruth all but singlehandedly put up the cot. Lists started to appear, usually on the fridge but sometimes on Will's desk and late night telly watching took a slide in favour of discussions regarding diet and nurseries. It was in this mood of mild bewilderment then, as if he'd allowed some benign force to take control of his brain, that Will met Frank Stine.

ii.
——

THE PREVIOUS HISTORY teacher had left the post under a rather odd cloud. Something about an inappropriate text message. That was just before Easter. Normally it took the school a month or two to find a replacement, yet when the teachers returned in April, a replacement had already been found, a rather dishy one if the dinner ladies were to be believed. It was after overhearing them discuss the topic at the top of their not inconsiderable lungs, that Will walked into the staffroom to see the man in question sitting in one of the Holy Armchairs. The chairs were placed in a U shape at the far end of the room and were reserved, by unwritten decree, for the P.E. department, which by some strange power, dominated many aspects of school life. Yet there sat the new History teacher, talking rather loudly, his wide hands cupping the back of his head.

Will was watching the kettle boil when he sensed a looming presence and turned to see Frank grinning at him, his arms folded, his chest muscles shifting beneath his shirt.

"Thought I'd introduce myself. Frank Štěpán," he said, taking Will's hand in a firm grip. "Though Štěpán's a bit of a mouthful—for the kids, at least—so I asked Simmons to put me down as Stine." He was still grinning. "Your name is Zifla, right? Albanian, if I'm not mistaken."

Will nodded. "Half," he said.

"Half not mistaken?" Frank said.

They didn't speak again until the Friday morning meeting when Frank sat next to Will and asked if he had any gossip. When the Head introduced Frank, the man stood up amid a smattering of applause and said, "I thought a nice way to get to know people would be to start a staff football team. I think a few of us round here could do with losing a few pounds. Not that I'm suggesting anything," he said, grinning at Simmons.

Will didn't like football, so when Frank asked him if he wanted to play squash instead, he felt obliged to say yes.

They met at the leisure centre. Even warming up, Will could tell Frank wasn't taking any prisoners.

Smashing the ball along the wall, the man shouted, "For me squash is the closest sport to boxing." He lobbed the ball and Will chased after it, returning it awkwardly.

"The dance of domination and submission," Frank said, belting it straight down the line. "The violence done to the body as you slam into the wall, into your opponent." He gave Will a friendly shove. "The battle for centre ring. The trick," he said, after killing the ball in a corner, "is to tire out your opponent and only then move in for the kill."

Though Will chased every point, Frank dominated the T, effortlessly scooping up the ball. "A knock out," he said after the last ball died on the board. "And now a drink. As commiseration."

Red-faced and out of breath, Will tried to say it was just a game.

"That's right," Frank grinned. "And I'm just a winner."

Frank was unlike any other teacher Will had ever met. When he shouted at a kid, you didn't want to be that kid. But it was more than that. For Will, the man possessed the kind of glamour that spoke of treasures. He could tell that the other teachers found him brash but Frank simply didn't care. He spoke his mind and no one opposed him. For Will, however, he reserved a special kind of warmth, a ray that broke loose whenever Will stepped into the room. One moment he'd be walking down a crowded corridor and the next Frank would be bellowing over the heads of all those around him: "Česká-Republika-Albánie!"

Having struggled with his roots, especially at school where most differences were a cause of friction, Will suddenly found himself rather proud of his unusual name. Frank had that kind of power in him.

They played squash every Saturday after that, almost always followed by a visit to the pub. It was there Will told Frank about Hellerbys' various factions, its molehills and turrets, its soapboxes and closets. And also, after several pints, about Ruth's pregnancy.

They were lounging on a sofa, music and laughter flowing around them. Still warm from the match, Frank's eyes shone hazel in his reddened face.

"You seem too young for fatherhood," he said. "But then again my father had me when he was in his forties and it didn't make any difference. He was still a bastard."

He gave a vicious grin and then raised his pint. "I'm sure you'll be a great dad. And a great writer too," he added with a wink. "I read your stories."

As soon as Frank had heard Will was a writer, he'd asked to read something. When Will had protested, the man had said, "If you can't show me, what's the point?"

The point was Will should have shown Ruth. He felt guilty giving his stories to someone else. But though he was confident, something made him hesitate. He wanted to be absolutely sure before he showed Ruth anything else.

"I liked the story about the girl," Frank said. "I think maybe you had a little crush on her. The ending though? What was that all about?"

210

The story Frank was talking about was the one of which Will was proudest. He'd recently gone home to see his parents, only for the trip to stir up certain memories. The girl's name was Shelley Givens. As kids, the two of them had shared a brief but intense relationship. Their mothers had been friends, though the two families had never hung out, which was why it had been such a surprise when Elizabeth had invited Shelley round to play on the first day of the summer holidays. Will had been ten at the time and remembered being particularly excited. His father and he had just finished building a go-kart and he couldn't wait for Lorenzo to try it out. Unaware of his mother's plans, he'd heard the doorbell and run downstairs, expecting it to be his best friend. It was quite a shock then when he opened the door to find a feral-looking girl on the doorstep, her hands pressed into the doorjambs, her flip-flopped foot kicking at the boot scraper. Grey eyes smouldered at him through several strands of lank blonde hair. Will's immediate instinct was to slam the door in the girl's face. He knew her, though only vaguely. The two of them went to the same school but were in different classes and had never spoken which was exactly how Will wanted to keep it, for Shelley had a reputation for being rather wild.

The previous summer, Will's parents had bought him an upright swimming pool. The day before Shelley's visit, Will's mother had cleaned the pool and filled it with fresh water. Realising that Shelley was wearing a swimming costume, Will suddenly understood why and was seized by an immediate and terrible dread. After watching his mother shoo Shelley through the house, he turned to her with his best hangdog expression and told her he wasn't well, that maybe he had a cold coming on. The last thing he should be doing was swimming.

Elizabeth had stood with her arms folded, a dusting of flour on her nose, looking nonetheless formidable. She told him that the Givenses had helped them move in, that they'd had a hard time, that Shelley's father was in jail (for fraud, she said, rolling her eyes) and that, if he didn't want to get changed, she could always do it for him.

Stepping outside in only his trunks, Will was suddenly aware of how skinny he was, of his concave chest, of the thin bright curve of his ribs. Shelley was already in the pool, her arms resting on the pool's plastic edge, her eyes like glass splinters in the sunlight. It wasn't until he'd climbed into the water though that she asked him the one question that seemed chosen especially to nettle him. With a spiteful sunniness in her voice, she asked him why the other kids called him Sniffler. The question caught him off guard. Perhaps they called him Sniffler because he used to cry a lot (though he couldn't remember doing so) or perhaps just because it rhymed with his surname, but the truth was he didn't know.

"My name is William," he'd said pointedly.

"Well I think I'll call you, Sniffler," Shelley had said before drawing her hands through the water and splashing him.

Will had done all he could after that to avoid the girl. Getting up early the next morning, he'd left his mother a note—*Out with Lorenzo*—and then ridden his bike down into the village. That first day he and Lorenzo had played Monopoly in Lorenzo's room, after which Lorenzo's father had insisted on making them lunch. Will and Lorenzo had then crept through the paddock at the back of Will's house to the old sycamore tree at the far end of the property. The tree grew in a clearing just beyond the paddock wall and was bordered, on the far side of the property, by an abandoned building site. Searching the site, the boys found pallets and nails and even an old hammer, which they used to start building a treehouse. Every day after that they would pack a lunch and meet at the sycamore tree, there to carry on with their rather shoddily conceived construction. Most days were sunny and there was nothing like sitting up in the tree, eating their sandwiches with their feet dangling among the leaves.

This may have gone on all summer had Lorenzo's family not been from Trinidad but from Trinidad they were and to Trinidad they went, despite August being one of the island's rainiest months. Lorenzo had reminded his friend of this pending disruption on

212

several occasions, yet to Will it still felt like a betrayal when it actually happened.

On the last day of July then, having said goodbye at the top of the lane, Will watched his friend bike down the hill, a familiar dread swilling in his stomach and went to bed that night feeling only marginally better. The next morning, he woke to the sound of the doorbell. Called by his mother to answer it, he trudged down the stairs and pulled open the door, to be confronted by the one person he wanted most to avoid, her eyes brimming with malice. In later years he came to suspect that Shelley had no more relished their enforced companionship than he had, that in fact she didn't hate him but only resented the way in which his company had been foisted upon her. At the time though, all he could think was that she got a kick out of torturing him.

That first day, she took him into the woods and then abandoned him the moment she thought he wouldn't know the way home. In the fields, she enjoyed pushing him into bramble patches or throwing stones at him. At Sunday school, which his mother thought would do them both good, she often tried to stamp on his foot while they were lining up along the pews. Her favourite trick though was to invent guessing games he had no hope of winning and then to pinch him when he got the answer wrong. She'd known just where to pinch him, too, right under the arm where the flesh was softest.

And so it may have gone on for the rest of the holidays had something not happened that changed their relationship. Some days, Shelley wouldn't call for him until mid-morning and when she did, he noticed an unusual smell about her. He'd wanted to ask her about it but was worried she might take it the wrong way, which she was very good at doing. But then one day, feeling, for some reason, rather distracted and more than a little fey, he asked her anyway. For a second he thought she was going to hit him but then her face changed and she held out one of her hands. This is witch hazel, she said as he gave her fingers a quick sniff. Holding out her other hand, she said, And this is cedarwood. Put them together and you get this. With that, she opened the top pocket of her denim jacket and removed an ivory-coloured bar. When he smelt it, it was as if he were smelling her. Inspired once more by his rather odd mood, which may, or so he suggested in his story, have been the beginnings of some kind of intuition, he asked her if he could keep it and to his surprise, she said yes.

Not long after that, she stopped calling him Sniffler. She also started being nicer to him in other ways. One time she took him to her shed and showed him her soaps. They melted lye together (though only after, upon Shelley's insistence, they'd both put on goggles and gloves) and sniffed at all the little phials of oil Shelley kept in a kind of test tube rack. When it was sunny though, she loved nothing more than to race around the paddock. She was very fast and almost always won. Soon after showing him the soap though, it was Will who reached the wall first, only for Shelley to run up and give him a kiss. It was an odd sensation, dry and quick and not particularly agreeable but it proved another turning point. This then became the new rule, the winner received a kiss, something Will became increasingly good at, especially after he discovered the trick of licking his lips just before they did it.

What really prompted him to write the story though was their last day together. Looking back on it, he'd become convinced that Shelley had wanted to tell him something. The moment he opened the front door that day, he could tell she was in a strange mood. In all their time together, she'd not once suggested they play in the treehouse, perhaps aware of the bond he and Lorenzo had formed in its creation. That day though, she took him by the hand and marched him straight through the paddock to the breach in the wall that preceded the clearing. Standing in the shadow of the treehouse, she pointed at the slats he and Lorenzo had nailed into the trunk and told him to climb up. Feeling a little traitorous then, Will had scooted up the makeshift ladder and, as instructed, sat himself in the old armchair the two boys had reclaimed from the outhouse in which Will's father kept any unwanted pieces of furniture.

Almost immediately, Shelley had begun kissing him. Nor did she allow him to kiss her back. "Juste moi," she said firmly, a look in her eye like she might start crying. "We have been together a month," she said, kissing his ear. "*Un mois.*" He watched her strawberry-pink lips kiss his bicep, the crook of his arm, his wrist. He felt the platform sway, heard the leaves murmur and wondered if he were dreaming. Then, so quietly he almost missed it, she whispered, "I have a secret." Her grey eyes glanced up at him through the strands of her hair. "Puis-je te croire?"

It was as if a series of doors had been opened and he could see straight into her soul. He knew not a word of French but there must have been some magic in the air that day for he understood. *Can I trust you?*

Yet even as he reached for her hand, a voice clapped above them with all the terror of ground zero thunder. "Shame on you, you filthy creature!"

His father had climbed up the slats and was peering at them through the leaves. It was as if the giant had climbed into the clouds and caught Jack caressing the golden harp. The man leaned forwards and seized Will by his collar, trapping the hairs at the nape of his neck, before yanking him out of the chair, across the floor and down the ladder. Will had barely gained his feet before he was being dragged out of the clearing and into the brightly lit paddock.

"I never saw her again," Will said.

Frank wanted more. "This ending, it is unfinished, unfinished business." He was staring at Will and seemed exasperated by the expression on his face. "Bah! This is why I don't read anymore. Because of writers like you."

This said, he stomped off to the bar to buy another round.

"I want to know what happened," he said, upon his return. "Let me put it another way. Writing is pain, it is sacrifice. To capture it truly, first you must feel pain, you must sacrifice something, something as dear to you as life itself. You wrote this story," he said, rooting around in his bag and then shaking a few printed sheets under Will's nose, "because this girl means something to you. It is unfinished business."

All Will knew was that just after the incident in the treehouse, Shelley had called round for him several times but every time, he'd refused to see her. After that she'd left town. Maybe his father had called her mother. Still, that wouldn't have been reason enough to pack up and leave. The only other thing he'd heard was that Shelley's father had gotten out of jail around the time she left.

He shrugged. "What can I say? I never saw her again, that's it."

"And her name," Frank said, "is that real? If so, you'll have to change it if you want to publish the story."

In the end, Will changed the subject. He didn't really feel like talking about it. Maybe some writers enjoyed sparring sessions with their readers but, he decided, such was not for him. He'd written what he saw, what he felt, what he thought was the truth. Why would he change it? Nor was he inspired to show Ruth the story, even though he was sure it was his best.

Besides, the writing had caused him to rethink the events of that day. For years he'd believed that his father's words—*Shame on you, you filthy creature!*—had been meant for him. Now though he was not so sure. This was not, however, a revelation that brought any relief. The truth was that during all the years since, that is what he had believed and (or so he concluded) it is too often with such false beliefs that youthful foundations are laid.

It was several months before Shelley's name came up again. In the meantime, the weekly squash games continued, hardly letting up even during the summer holidays, though it wasn't until they'd returned to Hellerbys that Will finally won a match, after which he insisted on buying Frank a pint.

The pub was so busy, Will had to push his way to the bar, where the crowd seemed disinclined to make room for him. Placing his shoulder between a woman wearing a kaftan and an overweight student in a rugby shirt, he thought about the game. He'd bewitched the ball, causing it to whip and glide and curve through the air, to bounce with incredible force or to die with barely a whisper, all at his whim. Not so much a boxing match as a good kicking, he'd said on the way to the pub. Frank had barely grunted. He seemed in a bad mood, though sometimes it was difficult to tell.

While Will jostled at the bar, Frank managed to find them a table, after which he became engrossed in his phone. Only when Will finally put a pint in front of him did he crack open his usual grin.

"Here he is, the champ," he said, raising his pint and proposing a toast. "To flukes!" He took several large gulps, then wiped his mouth. "What would you say," he said, squinting an eye at Will, "if I told you that that girl, the one in your story . . . what if I told you she doesn't live too far from here?"

Will couldn't believe his ears. "What? How do you know?"

Frank was scratching his jaw, causing his smile to spread crocodile-like across his chin. "To be honest, I was curious. Besides, I think there's more to the story. A good writer should always do his research, you know?"

It sounded pleasantly strange. Still flushed with triumph from the game, it was easy for Will to accept Frank's rather glib reasoning. "So where does she live?"

"You really wanna know?" Frank said, taking another swig of beer. He seemed to think about it for a moment, then reached into a jacket pocket and took out a piece of paper. "I wrote down her address and phone number. Don't take it," he said, holding onto it for a moment. "Unless . . . but, hey, it's up to you."

iii.

THE IDEA OF BEING pregnant, of being intimately connected to another life, that everything she did and said and felt might somehow alter the little human being inside of her, was so terrifying that Ruth would sometimes sit for hours, a book on her lap, staring into space, trying to formulate thoughts as one might try to build rafts or bridges.

This then was why she wrote lists. Such were essential in her job. Without them, things got forgotten. And when you were in charge of airline safety, forgotten meant potentially endangering lives. At home, too, lists were a lifesaver. Inside her, the items swilled liked detritus after a plane crash at sea, visible yet unnameable. On paper they were ordered, seeable, doable.

She had learned that lists were also of benefit when it came to Will. Perhaps it was the writer in him but when he was presented with written proof of her desires, those desires often became reality. It was on one such list, jotted down on the back of a supermarket receipt, that she found the little slip of poetry that set in motion all of the events to come. Normally very guarded when it came to his writing, it was a surprise when Ruth found the list (all but the last item crossed off), with three lines of poetry scribbled along the outer edge:

> *Her eyes are pools, grey pools into which one*
> *might slip, smooth grey rocks, a shallow seeming lip*
> *and then a plunge, a laughing sudden plunge.*

Half expecting Will to ask after it, she put the list in her purse and promptly forgot about it.

Only on the following Saturday, when Will went out to play squash, did she recall it again and only then because of a thought that occurred to her while she was cleaning the kitchen. Her parents had bought them both a set of Scandi knives as a wedding present, a beautiful set of six blades in a wooden block that ever since she'd cleaned by hand so as not to bleach the handles. Having used the carving knife that day, she was drying it when she caught sight of her eyes in the blade. Brown eyes, she thought. Then, Not grey. Why she thought this, she didn't know, nor why she then sought out her purse. Only when she came across the scrap of paper upon which Will had scribbled those three lines of poetry, did she realise. The woman, whoever she was, had grey eyes. The poem didn't say so directly but her 'eyes' were 'grey pools'. Her eyes were grey.

Upstairs, she went to empty the bin under Will's computer desk, only to find it full of screwed-up paper. On one crumpled surface she saw the word '*her*' and opened it to read: *She had thought to touch her own face*—then, after some crossing out—*but her hand passed through the mirror as if into water. There, while the house burned down around her, she stayed, her hand cool, her mind on fire.*

218

She opened other sheets, found more lines, fragments of what might have been dreams. On one scrap she found a code, CINNMFLQDV. Lit by some inner-clairvoyance, she sat down, switched on Will's laptop and typed in his username. They'd shared several passwords over the years and she tried them all now. Nothing worked. She thought of him playing Lemmings, his favourite game, what he called his guilty secret. She'd seen the start-up screen enough times to remember its four levels: Fun. Tricky. Taxing. Mayhem. The first password she tried, Fun82, was politely rejected, as were Tricky82, Taxing82 and Mayhem82. She was about to give up when she rattled out the code CINNMFLQDV and pressed Enter. Just like that the stone rolled away. The password screen vanished and she was presented with Will's desktop.

The file she was looking for was sitting right in the middle of the screen. MY JOURNAL. She only knew of its existence because she'd seen it on the taskbar, minimised there, or so she suspected, whenever she walked into the room. As she hovered the cursor over it, she told herself she'd just scan it.

When she finally stopped reading, the sounds of the day returned one-by-one. She copied and pasted a passage, pressed print, watched the printer spray a few words and then sat back.

It seemed like only minutes after that that she heard the front door. A creak on the stair later and Will was leaning in the doorway. She kept expecting him to ask why she was sitting in his chair but instead he told her the kitchen was full of smoke.

"Dinner is charcoal."

And just like that she could smell it.

"I was cleaning." She looked over her shoulder but not at him. "I remembered that game you like to play." She sounded so calm. She thought about the poem. One thing at a time. "So I turned on your laptop. I wanted to read your journal."

Outside, a gull landed on the fence, its wings clumsily flapping. Ruth held up the sheet. On it was a passage, short but damning.

I have the box—Pandora? E thinks it's buried. If R knew . . . There's a story here that can never be written. So why take it?

219

She felt as if she were walking up a muddy track. With each step, the mud grew thicker. "I'm sorry. I need to know. What's in the box?"

He took the paper. "Just thoughts." Then, "It's not right."

She'd been feeling calm but suddenly she was furious. She turned in the chair. "You want to talk about right and wrong? You can't think up your own story, so you have to use mine, my *family's*? I mean, how many stories have you got on here about Eric? And the way you've described him, it's like you don't know him at all."

He said, "Dad told me Eric's a part of my story . . ." Even as he said, he heard how lame it sounded.

She rose, a noxious fume rising with her. "Why do you always blame your father?"

He was trapped in the doorway. "Because he gave me the idea, I didn't mean any harm."

"That's just it," Ruth said, "you don't mean it but it happens."

When he tried to say they were just notes, she asked who E and R were. "Is that your idea of a code?"

Downstairs, she opened a window to let the smoke out, rolled up her sleeves and began attacking the washing up. "What's this story that can't be written? What's it got to do with Eric and me?" She looked back at him. "It's disgusting. You have to delete it, all of it."

He was staring at the paper. "Why?"

"What's in the box?"

A story you don't want to hear, he thought. "Eric and I buried a few things," he lied. "The book he gave me. My watch." He shrugged. "But then I dug them up again."

Ruth kept her hands busy. "The book and the watch?"

"Yes."

She placed a bowl on the draining board and turned around. "Except that I Skyped Eric, a few days ago. He was wearing the watch, I'm sure of it. But I could call him?"

Will's jaw was clamped, his lips pursed. "I haven't done anything wrong."

"If you'd just asked, Will, taken the risk. If you want to write about us, don't you think we have a right to know? Why do you need to keep everything a secret?"

When he spoke, Ruth could see that his teeth were clenched. "I'm going out."

She watched him turn and march away. He grabbed his coat, jerked open the door, stepped through it and then slammed it so hard, the letterbox clanged.

The noise made her jump. All her anger drained away in an instant and she wondered what had been so important that she'd thought it necessary to violate his trust. And why, when it was those few lines of poetry that had driven her to do what she'd done, the vision of those grey eyes, hadn't she mentioned them.

iv.
―――

WILL THOUGHT OF GOING to Frank's but Frank didn't need to hear what he had to say. He kept hearing those words: *You have to delete it.* Righteousness blazed through murkier emotions. Writing about Eric was Will's way of figuring him out. Ruth had shut him down, tamed his tides. She judged him by her own standards, as if they were the only worthwhile criteria. He marched along Western Road until he was out of breath, then down towards the beach.

The sea was quiet. The Palace Pier shone red and green above the pillars yet barely glinted in the water below. The West Pier lay blackly on the sea. He leant on the railing, recalling videos of it burning, pigeons amassing on the pavilion even as the flames consumed it. By the time he dug out his phone, the sky was dark. He scrolled down to Eric's number and then stood there staring at it. He remembered their last scene together. Eric had come round to the house with a bulimic blonde by the name of Melody, his girlfriend, perhaps, though neither of them had said as much. They'd certainly been very touchy-feely with each other. But then at some point Melody had stormed out and when Eric went after her, Ruth had asked Will to go check on him. He'd found him sitting on the front wall staring at his palms, which were scraped raw. Apparently Melody had pushed him over. Will had just opened a bottle of Bud and they sat there together, sharing the beer, neither of them saying very much. Finally Eric had asked if he was happy. It was such a simple question, yet it took Will by surprise. He'd said yes he was, even looking Eric in the eye as he said it. He wondered now though, recalling the brief flicker of pain in Eric's eye, if it had been true.

He called the number Frank had given him three times before someone picked up. The woman on the other end of the line sounded husky, as if she'd been asleep.

"Who is this?"

He almost hung up. Finally he said, "An old friend."

They met at a pub in Kemp Town, ordered two glasses of wine and sat at the back. The only other customer was an old man leaning on the bar, a plastic bag round his wrist. They sipped their wine and stared at each other. Shelley was wearing a suit and blouse. Her eyes were as he remembered, clear, bright, grey, her face longer, her cheekbones, forehead and chin accentuated by the fact that she'd pulled her long, blonde hair back into a ponytail. Her ears, pale, pink, prominent, stood out against the loose strands of hair tucked behind them.

"Sorry," she said, looking down at herself. "I'm doing agency work at the moment. I didn't have time to put on a fresh outfit."

"You look nice," he said.

"Do I?" Her eyes smiled at him. "You haven't changed."

"Maybe a little," he said. "But I mean it, you look really nice."

She told him she'd been married but that they'd separated. She was much happier now. She had her own house and had joined an art class. She had a boyfriend.

When he got home, he switched on his laptop, deleted his journal and crawled into bed. He had a copy at work anyway. Ruth was lying on the opposite edge, either sleeping or pretending to. He turned his back and tried to relax but couldn't. In the bar, Shelley had touched his hand and then, as they left, he'd briefly placed his hand on her hip. The curve of it still burned on his fingertips. He couldn't remember the last time he'd touched Ruth like that.

He went to sleep thinking about what Ruth had said about him needing to keep everything a secret. He didn't know what she was talking about but then he began to wonder if it was true.

Perhaps it was this thought that troubled his sleep. He was woken by Ruth calling his name. Downstairs, he saw her through the panes in the kitchen door. She was lying on the floor, the frosted glass revealing her body in shifting sections, one knee up past her ear, the other near her elbow. And then he was in the room, kneeling down and staring at the island between her legs, the huge pink shell of her belly rising up from it like a manmade mountain. The cleft swelled as if some mole were burrowing through a spinney. She was panting and reaching out and when he looked up, he saw that her belly was now made of glass, a huge crystal hill through which he could see the child suspended among amber-filled tubes:

And then, from out of the darkness, someone was swinging a hammer.

On the Monday, he told his first class to read and then began typing. Only as he finished writing up the details of the dream did he remember the rest. The way the blood pooled around his knees, the wardrobe of innards, dark, intestinal scarves, red, bejewelled necklaces, thick, corded belts, all slithering to the floor. And there among the wreckage, their child, its dark eyes glittering.

After school, he found the caretaker replacing a pane of glass at the far end of the corridor linking Literature to History. All Will knew about the man was that his name was Lenny.

"Third one this week," Lenny said, rubbing his baldhead so vigorously, it jiggled his thick white eyebrows.

Realising the man wanted to talk, Will walked along the corridor. The glass-walled passageway ended in double doors, both framing large panes of reinforced glass, one of which was cracked from top to bottom. Lenny was kneeling down, his blue dungarees and white t-shirt hugging his short, sturdy frame, his quick, brown hands digging a putty knife into the edge of the window frame as he spoke.

"I wouldn't mind, except the poor bugger who did this actually hurt himself." After laying the knife in an odd-looking box, he pulled the broken pane free, picked up the undamaged sheet of glass leaning against the wall behind him and began to putty it into place. "He ran away but they followed the trail of blood all the way back to his house." He blinked and smiled at the same time, causing his eyebrows to bristle together. "And in the meantime, we get to put the pieces back together again."

Will was nodding. "Nice box by the way."

Lenny rubbed his nose with the side of his finger. "My daughter gave it me. She found it in a second-hand shop. Ivory," he said, tapping the pattern laid into the lid. "I don't like to think some giant died just so I could own this pretty little thing but I guess we can't resurrect the dead. Did Mr Stine find you, by the way?"

"No, why?"

"He came looking for you." Lenny's blue eyes were peering up at him as if from beneath a snowdrift. "What's he like, by the way? You chaps seem close."

Will shrugged. "Pretty decent, I guess. Why?"

As if by way of explanation, Lenny pointed at the wall. "Buggers can't even spell," he said.

In black marker ink, someone had scrawled *Fiskin can get notted.*

Will shook his head and grinned. "I blame the teachers, myself."

v.

THAT EVENING, HE TOLD Ruth about the broken window, how it was like a metaphor within a metaphor but she was hardly listening. She told him she'd forgotten to pay the house insurance, that it'd been up for renewal but that she'd cancelled it to avoid . . .

But Will wasn't really listening either. Instead, he was thinking about a conversation he'd had with Roger Fiskin, the Deputy Head. Will had been on duty outside the main house when Fiskin, a big man, who preferred rugby shirts and jogging bottoms to suits, had come running across the rugby field.

"We've got to get you on that coach, Zifla," the man had said, a little out of breath. He was referring to the upcoming trip to Stratford. "We need someone there who knows the Bard better than old Carreras."

Old Carreras was a pain in Fiskin's backside, or so he was fond of saying.

Will had made a long-suffering face, the devil of an idea slowly raising its head. "I would," he'd said, "but Ruth's been having a hard time. With the pregnancy, I mean. Definitely put me down for the next one though."

That idea surfaced again now, red horns rising from the murk. They were watching the ten o'clock news but Will didn't have a clue what the broadcaster was talking about. What if he told Ruth he was going on the trip but then . . ?

Even though they'd both apologised, things were still strained between them. He'd been angry, the stuff bubbling inside him like black oil. Meanwhile, the way Shelley had touched him kept returning, the way the curve of her hip had felt beneath his fingertips. Then, just as Ruth was saying something about a better deal with such and such, he just blurted it out:

"Fiskin spoke to me today." He stopped, told himself to look at her. "He wants me to go on the Stratford trip. I don't want to," he said, "what with . . . but I've said no too many times."

To his surprise, Ruth said it was fine. "It's good to go the extra mile."

The morning of the trip, however, Ruth looked particularly tired. When he shouted from the hallway that he was off and she all but waddled down the stairs, he almost blurted out the truth. The baby was right there. All he need do was reach out and touch her.

Ruth smiled wanly and he said, "I don't have to—"

But then the phone rang and she went to pick it up. He drifted after her, watched her listening, obeyed when she waved him away.

Frank had been right, Shelley didn't live far, just eight miles away, in fact, in Peacehaven. Her boyfriend was elsewhere but Shelley had told Will to meet her on the beach. She said he'd get lost trying to find the house. To ensure no one from work called home, Will had told his Head of Department he was going to his parents' for the weekend.

As the bus shuddered down North Street, he made his way to the back, his stomach churning. Alighting in Peacehaven, he walked across the road and looked down the cliff to the sea. Shelley was wearing a black skirt patterned with white roses and a dark blouse. She was sitting down but by the time he reached the beach, she must have seen him because she was walking towards him.

She stopped and squinted at him. "You came then?"

Behind them, a group of children chased each other onto the beach. He shaded his face against the glare and looked at her, the thought of their long-ago summer surfacing once more. He sat down and watched gulls wheel through the sky, heard the children run past, trailing laughter, felt Shelley staring at him, waiting for him to divulge his own mystery.

They ate at a café and then Shelley took him back to hers. The houses on her road overlooked long fields, beyond which lay the bungalows of Saltdean. They stopped outside a small, detached house and she smiled at him over her shoulder.

"The kids are out." She went in and shouted hello. "Yep. Definitely out."

The front door opened into a long hallway. He glimpsed a living room with well-worn sofas, a brown carpet. A round glass table lay to the left of the kitchen door. Two windows punctuated a bank of units on the opposite wall. He sat down and watched Shelley glug yellow wine into two glasses.

He'd got her a gift, yet each time he felt his pocket, he wondered why he'd bought it. Perhaps he just wanted to detract from the sordid nature of their assignation. Wanting to be rid of the thing, he took it out and gave it to her.

"It's beautiful," she said, lifting the jade-green pendant from the box. She undid the clasp and put it on. He told her it was hollow. She touched it and stared at him, before raising her glass. "To school reunions."

He'd only had a light lunch and the wine made his jaw tingle.

She asked him why he was there, her eyes on his even as she topped up his glass. "Perhaps you're writing a kiss-and-tell."

She laughed at his expression. "You were always scribbling away when we were kids." Despite her laughter, there was a fragile quality in her voice.

He went to say something but just then a key sounded in the front door and Shelley shouted that they were in the kitchen. There came a shuffling noise, the door opened and a girl walked in. She'd recently dyed her hair an auburn colour but Will still recognised her. It felt as if someone had plunged his body in ice.

"This is Mel," Shelley said, "my daughter."

Mel had her mother's height and eyes but was narrower in the hips. She raised the bags she was carrying slightly. "Hi, Mr Zifla."

Shelley looked surprised. "You two know each other?"

"I teach Melissa," Will said. He'd not talked about Ruth in class but there was his wedding ring. He watched the girl throw her keys on the side. Everything about her suggested nothing in the world could surprise her.

Shelley clicked her fingers. "Mel mentioned a dishy English teacher. I should have put two and two together. Is he any good?"

"You tell me," Melissa answered. "Anything to eat?"

Shelley shook her head as if scandalised. "Check the fridge."

Melissa grabbed a bag of crisps and helped herself to wine. Shelley opened a bottle of red and asked if they should take it upstairs. Without waiting for an answer, she stood up and Will followed her through the living room and up the stairs.

They settled in a bedroom to the left of the landing. A poster of a crop-topped girl sucking a red lollipop was tacked to the wall. Will could just make out the words '*grand thef*' in one corner. Shelley turned on a lamp and sat on the bed before reaching for his glass.

"My son's room," she said. "Wes. I thought it would be more neutral." She poured wine, glancing at him as she spoke. "Fancy us living so close to each other all this time."

As he sat down, he felt the space between them shrink.

"I still haven't worked out why you're here," she said, offering him the glass. "Are you angry with Ruth?"

Hearing her use Ruth's name, he spoke a little more coldly than he'd intended. "Maybe I'm just here because I'm trying to work out what happened that summer."

"I was right the first time," Shelley said, withdrawing her legs and leaning forwards. "You want to know what happened to me so you can turn it into one of your seedy little stories." She leaned forwards as if inspecting him. "Yes," she said, inspection done. "You want to turn poor little Shelley into a nice little metaphor."

"I promise you," he said, "that is not true."

"So Ruth knows you're here?"

She was using Ruth's name on purpose now, he was sure of it. "No, of course not."

"Maybe we should call her," Shelley said. "If what we're doing here is real, we should build it on honest ground." She came forwards on her knees, her wine tipping in her glass, then stopped and looked at him. "Will, I can't have any lies in my life. I don't think you realise what you meant to me back then, how important our time was together. It kept me sane. I can't afford to spoil that." She smiled and he almost relaxed but then she said, her voice a high singsong, "Wisdom cries from the high places, 'Whoso is simple, eat of my bread and drink of my wine.' But the foolish woman says, 'Whoso is simple, stolen waters are sweet and bread eaten in secret is pleasant.'"

She took hold of his knee. "It's about you, Will. You came here because you heard a whisper. You've come to finish the feast." Even as he shook his head, she leaned closer. "But do you want to know what happens to the man who listens to Folly? '*Et ignoravit quod gigantes ibi sint et in profundis inferni convivae eius.*' 'And he did not know that giants are here and that her guests are in the depths of hell.'"

While at university, Will had worked as a silver service waiter. One time, between gigs, he'd gone back to another waiter's house to have a smoke. The guy had gone upstairs to change and Will had gone

228

into the backyard to pet the dog. The animal, a big Alsatian, had seemed perfectly friendly in the living room. In the yard though, it was completely different. The dog was inside a small hut, hidden behind a curtain. Will couldn't see it but he could hear it. It was growling deep and low in its throat. It was an eerie sound and just like that the day changed. That was how it felt in the bedroom now, as if he'd stepped into the wrong world.

Shelley had placed her wine on the nightstand. He went to do the same but then felt her hands on his belt.

"Forget your silly stories," she said softly. He took hold of her hands but she'd hooked them inside his belt. "Admit why you're really here," she insisted, her eyes seeking his. "You came looking for love."

"This isn't about love," he said, trying with his free hand to push her away. "I felt . . . something but we were so young. You wanted to tell me something. . ?"

"The way you used to look at me," Shelley said, her eyes full of a beseeching intensity. "You made me feel visible. Why does it have to be about more than that? You don't want to hear about fun and games in the greenhouse . . ." She was softer for a moment, more real. She still had hold of his trousers but her grip had slackened. "My father went to prison, I'm sure you heard. When he got out, someone told him what happened to me and it finished him off. A few months later he hung himself." Her smile was heart-breaking. "I blamed myself, of course. If only I'd not told anyone . . . But I did and look what happened. So you see, Will, no one likes a sad story. Unless, unless . . ." She freed a hand and held it to his cheek. "You *are* here to save me. But, but . . . my big, grown-up hero, you can only save *one* of us. That's the way these stories work, right? So who's it going to be? Me or Ruth?"

His back was against the wall so that when she leaned in, he couldn't stop her. He'd imagined them kissing again, two consenting adults, but not like this. When they were children she'd been in charge. She was in charge now. But they weren't children anymore, he couldn't surrender himself to her. Too much had changed, there was no going back.

She kissed his neck. "It doesn't matter if you deny it," she said, her mouth so close to his ear, her words were almost painful. "This *is* about love, the most perfect love of all, *first* love. What we did," she breathed, "who we were, was not so awful, I think. And that's what matters. That other stuff, you need to forget about it. I know I have."

Will felt her perfume and the wine rolling together, her hand pushing inside his waistline, her fingers touching him, her other hand draw his to her breast.

"Forget about the pain and all you have is the pleasure."

It was into this darkness that Ruth's voice came, a blade of light, quick and sharp. "Will?"

She was standing in the doorway, her body in silhouette, her belly a black melon. He thought he was hallucinating, imagined himself on the edge of some waterfall, thundering white masses dropping straight down into hell.

"Will," she said again, her face rippling with emotion, "what are you doing here?"

He was so frightened, he couldn't breathe. Nor feel the words on his lips. "I don't know."

He had one foot on the floor, his other leg bent beneath him, Shelley sitting astride his thigh.

She leaned forwards and crooned in his ear, "Forget her. For*get* her."

"Well you know where your parents live," Ruth said, her voice wavering then catching. "Your bags will be there."

Too late, he scrambled off the bed and rushed down the stairs. The front door was open, the sky beyond the houses sulphurous. He stood on the doorstep, looked left and right. There was no one. He couldn't think how to use his phone. Somehow he found her number and called it. He ran along the pavement, peering into cars, images washing over him like out-of-body-experiences. He got Ruth's answerphone but what could he say? A car pulled out ahead but he couldn't tell if it was hers. Blood roared in his ears.

When he finally returned, he found Shelley sitting on the front step, the roses on her skirt seeming to float in her lap.

"You're afraid," she said, holding out her hand. "Don't be."

Two people appeared in the doorway behind her, Melissa and a teenage boy with pockmarked skin.

Will dug his hands into his pockets, stretched his arms until the shaking subsided. "Was it you?"

Shelley laughed tipsily. "This is not my work. God is not always so mysterious."

"Then how did she find me?"

Shelley stood up. "Come inside, you're shaking."

He heard scrubbing feet, a glare of kitchen cupboards, Shelley making drinks. Mugs being placed, water poured. Melissa sat down, her hands wrapped round a cup. The boy, Wes, slid a can of beer from a plastic ring, cracked it, leaned against the side. In the phosphorescent light his acne blazed across his cheeks. As if to detract from this, he'd had the letters WGL tattooed on the side of his neck. In contrast, Melissa's skin was flawless. She tutted and looked about her, then stood up. Shelley asked where she was going.

"To my room."

"Nowhere else," Shelley ordered. "I'll call you down for dinner."

Melissa trailed an upraised palm.

Will heard chopping, the click of a hob, the roar of flames. When Shelley sat down, she spread her hands on the table, stilling a nervous tremor in her fingers. "You know I'm actually glad this has happened."

"What can I do?" Will was pressing the sides of his head.

"Stay?" She saw his expression. "For dinner, I mean." She reached for his hand but he pulled it away. "It's for the best," she said.

He felt like he'd woken in a strange room, turned his head to look at the door. The hall light was off. Shelley touched the pendant at her neck and he wondered who had given it her. She stood up and opened a drawer.

"I'd like to give you something too." She was holding out a book. "It has given me strength."

231

He read the cover: *The Book of Jubilees.* Shelley was looking at him as if she expected him to start reading it straightaway but then Wes asked about dinner and she smiled.

"It's pork," she said. She looked at Will. "You will stay, won't you?"

He slid the book into a coat pocket. "Can I use the toilet?"

"Wes will show you," she said. "Watch him though."

Will shook his head. "I don't need watching."

"I was talking to you," she said, smiling. "When Wes gets anxious, he can't help himself." She rolled up both her sleeves. Her slim arms were scarred with bite marks.

The living room glittered with streetlight. Will glanced at the front door, caught the outline of a Yale lock. When Wes peered back at him, Will asked if he knew what had happened.

"Mum's happy. It's all I need to know," the boy said.

When they reached the upstairs landing, Wes pointed. "Straight ahead. I'll be waiting."

The window was painted shut. Will imagined smashing the glass, shouting for help. Did he need help? As he stood there trying to pee, he recalled Wes's poster, pictured him looting imaginary shops, screwing imaginary prostitutes. It made him so sad, he started laughing and pissing at the same time.

Wes was waiting on the landing. Will followed him down the stairs, wondering if he could bring himself to punch him. "World's greatest lover?" he said, nodding at the boy's tattoo.

"World Gamer Live," Wes said without looking back.

In the kitchen someone had switched off the main light. Candles burned on the table and two of the hobs were hissing, the pans above them bubbling. Shelley moved through the air like emerald glitter. Somehow she'd found the time to change. She loaded the table with dishes while Melissa laid out the cutlery. The children sat down and Shelley said a prayer. She poured herself a Bacardi, served wine, then sat opposite Will, her wineglass twirling in her fingertips.

Will could hear Wes's teeth crunching on a mouthful. He picked up the saltshaker but the lid was loose. Grains skittered across the glass. The memory of going mussel picking floated upwards like a hand rising through water. He'd been five or six. He distinctly recalled the rough, sandy rasp as he tore the mussels from their mooring, the gloop of waves in a nearby crevice, the crumbling path along the cliff, how the shingle slithered and scraped beneath him. They started a fire and his father asked him to blow on the flames. They'd been out on a trawler earlier that afternoon and caught mackerel. He remembered the way the skin stuck to the foil, the slosh of the mussels as his mother poured them into a bucket and placed it over the fire.

"It's good to have you here," Shelley said, "in your rightful seat."

Wes looked at him, his lips greasy with fat, said, "Man, I *love* crackling."

It was too much. Will got up so hard, his chair clattered to the floor. Something moved to his right and then Wes was biting down on his hand. He lashed out, struck Wes's ear, looked up in time to see Shelley's plate flying through the air. It smashed on the wall behind him, followed by the wine bottle, which hit him in the stomach. He doubled up, seized the tablecloth, saw the candle topple over, flames ripple across a napkin. Wes screamed and threw Shelley's drink, causing a yellow fire to scatter across the table and up his arm. At the same time, Will heard a voice in the hall and shouted for help.

Before he could wonder who it was, something seized his ankle and he went from dim recognition to excruciating agony. He stamped at the darkness beyond the edge of the tablecloth, dislodging his attacker even as he heard the sound of splintering wood and saw torchlight lance into the kitchen. There were shouts and then several men burst through the door. He heard Wes wailing, saw him waving his smouldering arm, looked down to see Shelley's eyes flashing at him from under the table, her face covered in blood. "You have no idea what is coming," she said, her voice thick with fury. "No idea!"

HE WOKE IN A CONCRETE cell slightly hungover. Streetlight glowed through a window high above the bed. They'd taken his phone along with his belt and shoelaces. When a breezeblock of a man brought him a cup of tea, he asked if he could make a phone call.

"I need to talk to my wife."

The man said she already knew.

The interview room was blue and white with cheap furniture and a window made of glazed glass blocks. The police officer sitting opposite Will had dark hair and grey sideburns. He wore a navy blue jumper with a star on each epaulette. On the table between them sat a large tape recorder.

"Your wife reported a fire," the officer said. "Said there might be drugs on the property. As it turned out, both were true." He sucked at the gap between his incisors. "So now all we need to know is why you were there."

As far as Will was concerned, he hadn't been, just as he wasn't now at Brighton Police Station. The police officer said he wasn't under arrest but that he still had some explaining to do. When Will nodded, the man pressed a button on the recorder and relayed the necessary details, after which Will proceeded to tell all.

After clearing up a few points, the man sucked his teeth again, then loosened his tie. Leaning over laced fingers, he fixed Will with an unforgiving eye. "Right now they're not pressing charges. No, listen," he said, "they could. Mrs Givens and her son have both had to receive medical attention. It would be your word against theirs. But as I say, they're not, which means you're free to go." He allowed himself a wry smile. "Just don't go leaving the country."

As soon as Will got his phone back, he called Ruth but it went to answerphone again. He thought about ringing his parents but rang Frank instead.

"What happened?" Frank said as he climbed into the car.

Will watched the police station disappear in the wing mirror. He thought about the Alsatian, the one in the waiter's backyard. It had sprung through that curtain so fast he could barely grab its neck before it was biting him. It wasn't its bite that was so bad though. When it jumped up at him, it hit him so hard, its nose knocked out one of his teeth. He had a false one now, held in by a bridge.

"Come on, Zifla. You drag me out here in the middle of the night and you won't say why?"

While they drove along the seafront towards Kemptown, Will made his second confession of the evening. By the time he'd finished, Frank was reversing into a parking spot. The two of them sat there staring out at the buildings. Apart from the shops, almost every door was lined with buzzers.

"I live just down there," Frank said. "St James's Place. My island in a sea of apartments."

Will saw a narrow alleyway he'd not noticed before. They got out and approached a Victorian terrace in the middle of a row. Behind a low flint wall, a short path led to a fanlight doorway. The hallway was laid with oak and contained a telephone table and a coat stand, the former devoid of telephones and the latter of coats. Stairs led up and down. In the next room Will glimpsed a flint-pebbled wall and tall windows. The sitting room next door was empty except for a large couch and a coffee table.

He followed Frank down into a big kitchen with exposed beams and black and white tiles. The room smelt of clean clothes and coffee. At the far end, four chairs were arranged around a circular table. On a television suspended from the ceiling, a group of men were crouching down behind The History Channel logo, silently shooting at another group of men.

Frank took two beers from the fridge, sat down at the table, pushed one over, asked how he was.

Will stared at the beer and then shook his head. "I just need to go to bed."

Frank said, "Of course. We'll sort this out in the morning."

235

As Will made his way upstairs, he felt on the edge of some vast herd, people moving in the dark, none of whom knew him, or cared to. At least tomorrow was Sunday. No work. Small mercies. He would find Ruth in the morning and try to explain.

His bedroom was on the first floor, next to the bathroom, which lay opposite Frank's room. The room was simply done with a double bed, bedside table, sea grass flooring, a chest of drawers and French doors leading out to a small terrace with wrought iron railings. The bathroom was next door but it was locked. Before he could slink back to his room, a toilet flush and the door opened. As the light flashed off, he saw a woman wearing pink. He stepped aside but she didn't move and for a moment he thought she was going to scream. He felt like some ugly insect in the dark, sensed her reaching into her dressing gown and heard the click of a lighter.

"I know who you are," she said when he tried to apologise. She blew smoke. "I'm CJ, from . . ." She gestured at the ceiling and moved past him.

The bathroom had a claw-foot bath and natural stone tiles. He locked the door, moved towards the sink but ended up on his knees. His brain was like a toy train, running through events, recalling every decision before going round the houses all over again.

Frank's voice buzzed at the wood. "You okay, buddy?"

"Nearly done." He climbed to his feet, felt the bathroom swim back into focus.

"I'll see you in the morning then."

He stared at himself in the mirror. "Goodnight, Frank."

The next day, when he returned to Hove, his key no longer worked. He couldn't believe it. Surely Ruth couldn't have got in a locksmith at such short notice. He walked down a side alley and climbed over into the yard, catching the mirror with his heel as he did so. The back door was locked, all the windows closed.

The bus back to Brighton sighed at every stop. He called Ruth's office twice. Both times her assistant took a message. A minute after leaving the second message, his mobile rang and he thumbed the answer button. It was his mother.

"Why didn't you call?"

A lady in front of him with red dreadlocks was listening to an iPod. To his left, a couple wearing white tracksuits appeared to have locked antlers.

He spoke quietly. "I screwed up, Mum."

"We all do," she said. "It doesn't mean you can't call me." She told him to come home. "Whatever it is, we'll work it out."

He let himself into Frank's with a key. He'd risen that morning to find the man frying black pudding in the kitchen. He'd asked if he could do anything. Will said he needed to borrow a computer. Frank said he could stay as long as he wanted but he betted Ruth would have him back before the end of the week. After eating, Frank had got out a kitesurf bag, thrown Will a key and gone to the beach.

Will pushed the front door open, shouted but no one answered. Frank's bedroom had its own sink and a king-sized bed draped in a damson-coloured duvet. The computer sat on a desk between two sash windows. Will opened his emails, wrote Ruth a long, rambling message, almost deleted it, then sent it. For the millionth time, he wondered how she'd found him. When he was done, he turned off the computer to see CJ's reflection in the screen. Her bathrobe looked dirtier in daylight. Turning round, he saw something he'd missed the previous night. Her lower lip was decorated with a big gold ring. Bars and studs lined her ears and nose. Even her cheeks were pierced.

"I asked," he said, pointing at the computer.

"I know." She pulled a crumpled packet and a lighter from her dressing gown pocket and lit a cigarette. "I don't care." She blew smoke out the corner of her mouth. "I just wanna know why you're here. Frank doesn't usually have friends over."

"He's helping me out."

"He's not normally the helpful type."

"You know him well then?" Will said.

"Not as well as you apparently. My dad's Lenny Southgate? Caretaker at your school? I needed a room and he asked around. Frank offered and Dad spoke to someone he trusted, an English

237

teacher." She pointed, disturbing the line of smoke rising from her cigarette. "You. So how well *do* you know him?"

"Well enough."

"Well enough to know his real name?"

The stairs creaked and Frank grinned into the room. "And there's me thinking my ears were burning because of the wind."

CJ wafted a hand as if warding off evil spirits.

Frank was wearing a black wet suit with yellow stripes. "The beach was great," he said. "You should've come. But Jane's up!" he said with a grin. "We must celebrate. Why not run along and mix us some cocktails?"

"Mix this," she said, raising a finger as she padded out.

Frank unzipped his suit. "What an honour. Crazy Jane up at this time. Normally, she's a creature of the night."

"She said her dad's Lenny Southgate."

"Yeah. He heard I had a room. Good man to get to know. The school would sink without him."

Down in the kitchen, Frank poured drinks, drank his off and then suggested they go out.

To Will, the idea of going out seemed repugnant and yet the only sane option. Frank was rolling a cigarette. He looked at Will as he licked it.

"She'll come round," he said.

They drank in a couple of places before stopping at The Lion and Lobster. The place was teeming. In one corner, three bankers still wearing work shirts had obviously not been home yet. Only one was still wearing his tie, its knot pulled down, his plump neck pushing at his collar as he spoke.

Will and Frank ordered beers and carried them to a table occupied by a young man wearing a t-shirt with *Brighton Rocks* printed across it. Frank asked if the chairs were taken. The man picked up several glasses. "Help yourself," he said, standing up.

As they sat down, Frank asked if Will had a plan.

"I've got to let Ruth know nothing happened," he said.

"But is that only because she broke up the party?"

"How did she even get into the house?" Will said.

A girl approached the table before glancing at the bar.

Frank broke into a wolfish grin. "Why if it isn't Emily Pritchard."

The girl gave a half-smile, not uninviting. "Oh, hi, Mr Stine. You remember me then."

"How could I forget? You took my class two weeks, then decided History wasn't for you. You said the past is gone, we can't change it, what's the point?"

Emily looked distracted. She waved to *Brighton Rocks* who was at the bar. "Yeah, something like that," she said.

"I was covering the Crusades," Frank said to Will. "Nothing to learn there, right? When they captured Jerusalem and thousands of Jews and Muslims, men, women, children, were cut open, dismembered, burned alive, I guess it's simply too long ago to count." He leaned in and spoke as if in confidence. "There was so much blood shed that it literally flowed through the streets, yet Christian historians called it God's just and wonderful judgement. So today, when our Eastern brothers liken our current forays into Arab lands to crusades, we should tell them to stop bleating on about history. The past is gone, we can't do anything about it. What's the point?"

Emily was nodding. "Oh, I'm sorry, this is Duncan."

Brighton Rocks was approaching the table, two glasses of wine in his hands. He smiled at Will and Frank, sat down next to Emily.

"This is Mr Stine," Emily said, "and . . ."

"Will," Will said awkwardly.

He had no idea what mischief Frank was up to. Nor would he find out, for just then a hand reached over and grasped Frank's shirt.

It was the banker with the loose tie and the plump neck. He was close enough for Will to smell the sour stench of sweat.

"She left 'cause of you," he said.

Will saw his fist. Even as he decided the man wasn't going to use it, he felt it shoot past him and thump into Frank's jaw.

He stood up just in time. The table shook, chairs tumbled, his drink was knocked from his hand. Both men crashed into the next table, upending it and sending glasses to the floor. Frank was on top, the man's tie in his fist, his elbow across the banker's neck. Then two doormen were pinning them to the floor, forcing their arms up their backs and dragging them to the door.

Frank laughed all the way home. "That fat fuck's nearly fifty," he said. He clapped Will on the back, then hooked an arm round his neck. "He marries a Czech girl half his age. It's prostitution. Tell me, am I right? I offered her money to leave, then told her, if she didn't take it and go back to Czechia, I'd tell her husband I slept with her. She didn't go so I told him. It was a lie but, who cares? She's gone now. Hey, listen, it was a favour. For them both."

Will was laughing too. Not because it was funny but because he was nervous. By the time the bouncers had managed to pull Frank and the banker apart, Frank's mouth was covered in blood and the banker's earlobe was hanging off like a broken earring. To see another man so casually and completely ignore the rules was difficult to digest.

Nor did the surprises end there. As the half-term holiday approached, he began to wonder who he was living with. Strange people came to the door at all hours. Once he crept down to the kitchen to be greeted by a cloud of smoke and half-a-dozen girls playing strip poker. Whenever he answered the door, whoever was standing on the doorstep would ask to talk to Frank. The wording never wavered, it was obviously some sort of code. But Will knew not to interfere. Frank had been kind to him. And it wasn't too difficult to picture that ear.

Ruth still wasn't taking his calls. The following Saturday, having hung round Portland Road for more than an hour without seeing her, Will headed back to St James's Place through cold streets and let himself into the house. Finding no beers in the fridge, he helped himself to one from the cupboard and looked in the freezer for ice. At the back he found a plastic bag packed with what looked like marijuana. Next to it was a bag of pills. He heard Frank come in and closed the freezer door.

"No," Frank said jovially, "take a look." He opened the door again. "The curious cat must know."

"I only wanted some ice."

"Ah," Frank said pleasantly, "ice I have less. But I always keep a little for special occasions." He pulled out a small bag of yellow powder. "This stuff'll keep you going all day. I never sell it, though. Meth users are a pain in the ass. But I can recommend it for parties. There's no taboos with this stuff." He shut the freezer door. "Hey, listen," he said, "let's throw a party. Trust me, Ruth'll be the last thing on your mind."

Frank took the bottle from Will's hand, grabbed some ice, poured them both a drink. "There you go again with your mouth open," he said. "All these late night callers asking to talk to Frank? It's my little joke, like the advert. How do you think I paid for all this? We don't all have parents with deep pockets. Hell, we don't all have parents."

"But you're a teacher."

For the first time Frank looked annoyed and Will was reminded of the curious cat. Of what Frank had done to that ear. "So what?" he said, "We walk the halls and hang our heads. They can't even *spell* respect. I say, look after number one. As for the drugs, the scumbags come to me, it's their decision. If it's not me, it's someone else, simple as that. It's not about supply. They run out, they don't take up fucking yoga. They make do with something else till their usual *sraček's* back on the street. You wanna sort out problems like that, you've got to make sure only people with their shit together have kids and that's a little too totalitarian for most people."

Will told him he wasn't judging. He wasn't talking about morals, just the risk. "You'd lose your job, go to prison."

"Only if I'm caught. And that's not going to happen, is it?"

"But they come to your home?"

Frank glanced up from the text he was writing. "What's life without a little risk?" After pressing a few more buttons, he said, "It's done. Watch the lice crawl out of the woodwork now."

THE FIRST CALLERS came at nine. Frank told Will to get the door. When he opened it, a young man and woman, both with very short hair, bent to one side and said in unison, "Talk to Frank?"

"Bingo." Will stood aside. As they moved past him, the woman touched his chest and smiled, the fake diamond on her tooth glinting. More people came. Three youths with baseball caps grunted the code and stepped in without further invitation. Next came four girls who Will recognised as ex-students, their age disguised by makeup and dresses that swished just below their buttocks.

After that the trickle became a flood and by the time he headed back downstairs, the hall and living room were busy, the kitchen vibrant with music and laughter. Halfway to the fridge, he saw Frank muscling through the crowd. He pressed a beer into Will's hand. "Well, what d'ya think?" he said. "Enough hotties for you?"

He put his forehead to Will's. Will felt sweat grease the point where their heads touched. "It's all for you, Sniffler. Treat every day as your last, right?" Frank's voice was loud, despite the music.

Someone touched Frank's elbow, spoke in his ear. He winked at Will. "Business calls. Enjoy the party."

Jane was cutting up lines of powder on a glass table in the sitting room. Velvet curtains were drawn against the night. People sprawled on the sofa or on the carpet, docking spliffs in blue-glass ashtrays. Jane was wearing leather trousers and a long denim jacket with a fur-lined collar.

Will sat down next to her. "It's like a storm blew in."

"Yeah, a shit storm," she said.

She rolled up a ten-pound note, placed it between her nostril and a line, snorted half and then switched nostrils. "For balance," she said, snorting the other half. She rubbed residue into her gums, then offered Will the note. He declined. "Why are you still here?"

"My wife kicked me out. Frank said I could stay."

"I told you, Frank isn't the kindness-of-your-heart kind of guy. You must have somewhere else you can go." She gripped Will's fingers for a moment. "Let me do your cards." Her trousers creaked faintly. "Then we'll know."

"Know what?" he said.

"Why you're here. Where you're going. That kind of shit."

As they made their way upstairs, the music grew fainter. Jane's room was a large, untidy incense-smelling space with slanted walls and black beams. Two skylights looked out over St James's Place. Red and orange shawls obscured the ceiling. Cupboards and bookshelves stuffed with magazines and books crowded a large chimneybreast. A single bed covered with blankets and fake fur lay in a corner. Cushions and beanbags and ashtrays scattered the floor. At the centre of the room stood a device Will recognised as a bong. There were three lamps set on the floor, their light dimmed by green shawls.

Jane offered him a cushion. He took off his jacket and joined her on the floor, finally cracking open the beer Frank had given him. Jane reached over, removed several items from a drawer. "Before we do your cards, we need to worship at Henry's phallus. Meet Henry." She picked up the bong and touched Will on both shoulders as if she were the Queen.

He watched her clean a small, silver sieve and pour water and rum into the bowl. She loaded the sieve with herb, screwed it into place. Removing a lighter, she put her mouth over the top of the bong, lit the bowl and inhaled deeply. The liquid bubbled. Will smelt rum and marijuana. She repeated the process before passing the bong to him.

He copied her, breathing in from the top as he lit the bowl. Halfway through, he began coughing so hard he saw red. Smoke jerked from his mouth with each convulsion. The hit was instantaneous. It was like being dropped into water. Everything became slower, more fluid and then clearer.

Crazy Jane peered at him. "Better?" She removed a large pack of cards from a box. Their backs were detailed with a linear design that

243

radiated outwards from a central point. "Tarot is not a precise art, nor a definite answer," she intoned theatrically. "The cards do not hold the answers to the future, they only suggest a likely path based on past and present." She squinted. "Even so, I hope you'll learn something."

Despite the setting and the premise, Crazy Jane didn't seem so crazy anymore. Will was neither expectant nor nervous. He floated in a rum-flavoured bubble.

"First you must ask a question. Each card I lay out relates to an aspect of the answer. Be as specific or as general as you like."

He thought nothing would come but then something did and though it was a little naff, he was just stoned enough to say it. "Will I ever find happiness?"

CJ shuffled the deck and asked him to cut it.

"The first card represents you."

They sat on a red rug decorated with fleur-de-lis. Where the rug ran between Will's feet, Crazy Jane laid a card, facing him. On it was the figure of a youth, his eyes looking towards a sun. He carried a staff and a bag. A small dog barked nearby. At his feet lay a vast drop. Will tried not to laugh. It felt like a set-up.

Jane frowned. "Busy dreaming of what may be and ignoring what is, the fool has no idea where he's going or what he's going to do. He's heading towards a new beginning, perhaps a second chance but he must watch his step. Someone close to him barks a warning. Your happiness is inside that bag, all you need do is stop and unpack but you can't see what's just over your shoulder."

She slid another card from the deck, laid it at the centre of the rug facing herself. A full moon, twin pillars, a wolf howling, a stream running to an ocean, something emerging from the water. "This represents your present situation: the Moon Reversed. The moon's energy is chaos but reversed, its power is blocked. You are restricted somehow? You're afraid of going through a door, stepping outside? Or inside, perhaps . . ?"

She laid another card. "The nine of swords." On it was depicted a man on a bed, nine swords on a wall above him. "This indicates your obstacle. You are afraid of the dream you have just been having, a dream of night. You are not sure if you are awake yet, if it's safe to open your eyes."

She placed the next card below the cross made by the first two. On it was a red heart, thrice pierced. Behind it, a growing storm. "The three of swords. You will fall three times before you rise again." Jane looked at him. "Your wife threw you out because you were unfaithful?"

He nodded.

"You locked up something poisonous inside." She spoke as a doctor might, firm, distracted. "Now, though, the heart has been pierced and the poison is coming out."

The fourth card, laid to the left of the cross was difficult to discern, blending as it did with the rug. On it was a winged devil, a black pedestal, a naked man and woman, an inverted pentagram. "This card indicates something from your recent past and its influence on you now. The Devil is king of obsession. Most cards urge balance and unity. Not this. It is wholly masculine, it revels in extremity. If you are to succeed in finding happiness, you must first defeat the Devil."

With the next card, Crazy Jane actually smiled, crinkling the crow's feet round her eyes. It was of a skeletal figure on horseback, wearing armour. In its hand it held a flag featuring a white rose on a black field. Behind it climbed a pale sun. At the skeleton's feet lay a small child. "I'm smiling because of your expression."

Will realised she was looking at him.

"Death *can* be a card of hope." She pointed at the child. "Do you have children?"

He shrugged. "Soon."

Crazy Jane was unfazed. "Or maybe the child represents you. Death naturally mirrors its opposite. Perhaps your inner child must be reborn again? It also represents transformation: from scorpion, to serpent, to eagle. Maybe you'll be brought low despite the warnings of others."

How ironic that the first good card he'd been laid was Death. Her mention of the eagle reminded him of his father. He looked at the card, imagined his unborn child beneath the horse's hooves.

"So we come to the near future, the short-term answer to your question." Jane turned a fifth card and grimaced. A man lay on his front, his back impaled by many swords.

Will counted. "I got the nine of swords, what's one more, right?"

"The ten of swords is not good. It suggests the worst is yet to come. One more sword will strike a terrible blow. There is light here, though. Simply put, when you reach this time, things won't get any worse." She rubbed her nose. "Remember, the journey is not ended, this is only your near future."

She'd placed this last card in its own line to the right of the cross. Now she placed another above it. A winged figure stood with one foot in a brook, the other on a rock. It appeared to be pouring fire from one flask into another containing water.

"Ah!" Jane said, with some satisfaction. "And then there is Temperance. Someone in your life holds your happiness dear. She or he seems capable of the impossible, harmonising extreme opposites, fire and water, man and woman."

She laid another card. "Yes, this is you on your journey, after the worst has happened." She pointed at the details. "A man and a woman in a boat. They are going somewhere and they are together. This is good, the six of swords is also about finding a solution."

The penultimate card faced Will. A woman in a garden.

"Normally the nine of pentacles is good. The woman, though she's retreated from the world, resides in a pleasure garden. But like the Moon, this card is reversed. It indicates that there's nothing pleasurable here. Instead of comfortable solitude, there is only loneliness for her." She smiled at Will.

He felt as if he'd been moving for a long time, as if he'd only just stopped. There was one card left. "So how does the story end?"

Jane dealt the final card. A tower on a rocky outcrop, lightning, two figures falling, waves below. They both laughed. Jane breathed in deeply, shut her eyes, opened them again and looked down.

"The Tower represents the war between lies and truth. In the original story of The Fool's Errand, the fool returns to where it all began: the monument he built to himself at the start of his journey, the tower. Inside, arrogant men still live. Seeing the tower again, the fool feels as if lightning has flashed across his mind. He thought he'd left that old self behind when he began his journey but realises now that he has not. He's been seeing himself, like the tower, as alone and singular, superior, when in fact, he is no such thing. Captured by this insight, he opens his mouth and shouts. To his astonishment, as if the shout has taken form, a bolt of lightning strikes the tower. In a moment it is rubble. The fool experiences grief and fear but also, clarity. Here and now, he's done what was hardest, destroyed the lies he held about himself. What's left is the absolute truth. On this he can rebuild his soul."

"The End," Will said, not without feeling. Through the window he noticed a light come on in one of the roofs opposite. He got up. "I'm going to make tea if you want one."

As he descended, he decided to take a piss. The bathroom next to his room was dark and he left it that way. The door was ajar and he kept his eye on it while he tried to pee. Maybe it was the weed but he felt as if everything was rushing past him, like he was clinging to a rock during a flood.

It was a long time before he could pee. Just as he was finishing, a voice floated up the stairs.

"The ribbons on Miss Givens . . ."

Wondering if Frank had said 'misgivings', Will stepped closer to the door.

Another voice said, "But you promised!"

Through the crack, Will saw Frank's head bob into view. He was looking behind him. "The ribbons on Miss Givens were all she ever wore . . ."

Two well-coifed heads of hair appeared at once, one blonde, the other, a coppery red. Frank unlocked his bedroom door, pushed it open and the girls went inside, sipping at glasses of wine.

Instead of following, Frank looked back down the stairs. "I'll tell you the rest but you mustn't get angry."

"*Out* with it then." A third head appeared. From the darkness of the bathroom, the scene was vivid. Her dyed red hair, the pink of her lips, the curve of her hand, all were unmistakeable. It was Melissa Givens, Shelley's daughter.

Frank held out his hand and she took it. "The ribbons on Miss Givens were all she ever wore. But though I call her angel," Frank spun her round, "the world still calls her . . ."

He leaned in and whispered in her ear. Even as Melissa slapped his arm, a whinnying laughter sprang from her lips.

The other girls had kicked off their shoes and were on Frank's bed, their legs curled beneath them. Melissa wobbled into the room, her laughter wobbling with her. Frank followed her, then turned and shut the door. But not before he winked.

Will wondered if he'd imagined it. Or if it were a tic. But, no. Frank had definitely turned to push the door to and then, just before it closed, leaned forwards and winked. He knew where Will was. He knew Will was watching. Will stood there in the dark, thinking, He can't know I'm here.

Melissa was only fifteen. He imagined barging in there but was sure they'd only laugh at him. He thought about phoning the police, before remembering that he was in a house full of teenagers. Drugs were being sold in the basement and consumed on every floor. He could call anonymously. Get out of the house and call from a pay phone. No one would know.

He recalled that wink. Frank would know.

3
—

HE WENT UPSTAIRS to fetch his coat, the music draining from his feet as he climbed. Green light swam at him. The rum-bubble quivered and surrounded him again. Jane's face was attached to the bong, her eyes watching him. His coat was on the rug next to the cards but when he reached for it, he misjudged the distance and fell over.

Jane placed her hand over the top of the bong. Smoke pulsed from her mouth as she spoke. "We out of teabags?"

He tried to remember. "Oh, yeah, right. But, no. I need some air."

"One for the road?" She held the bong out a moment too long and he took it. "Dutch courage," she said, smiling.

He lit the chillum. As he inhaled, he saw himself from above, his back hunched over his legs. He saw the chillum burn, the bong fill with smoke, Jane's hand reach out. She spoke as if from a distance.

"I thought you'd gone home. That's where you belong, y'know?"

He wanted to write but he couldn't. There was some impediment.

"Every man needs a dream," Jane said. He realised he'd spoken aloud. "That's Frank's problem," she said. "Without dreams, men go mad." Her voice grew clearer. "Perhaps I could come? For a walk?"

Silk mushroomed over his head. Thoughts broke apart on the ceiling. He needed to go alone. He couldn't even get up. He needed to make a phone call. He needed someone to tell him he was doing the right thing. He needed Eric.

Downstairs, someone was playing *Walking on the Moon*.

"The Police," he said.

"You've got good ears," Jane said.

He couldn't move. There must have been something in the smoke. The ceiling seemed lower, its angles threatening. Despite all our grand structures, he thought, nature is always at hand.

Jane was talking. ". . . at least Dad gave me that, even got Sting to sign my t-shirt." She'd been docking her cigarette forever. "I slept in it for nearly a week." And then her face, or rather, some grainy facsimile of her face, rose up, crossed the room and loomed over him. "Hey? *Hey*, you all right? Whoa!" He felt her hand on his shoulder. "You idiot, you're pulling a whitey!"

He knew if he moved, he would puke. Jane left him, came back. He sensed others nearby, laughter. Finally, he moved and vomited into a bucket. Then he curled up and slept.

SOMEONE HAD COVERED him with a blanket. He woke to see Jane lying on the bed behind a young man. Apart from a sour taste in his mouth and a dead arm, he felt all right. Recalling Melissa's face, he got up, picked up his coat. He needed to talk to Ruth. Frank's door was open, his bed empty. The house was silent.

Outside, the dawn felt tumescent. As he walked up St James's Place and onto St James's Street, it grew paler, making the frills all the more stark. The air smelt of chips and mildew.

In Hove, he rang the doorbell several times. No one answered. The bedroom curtains were pulled. The house felt empty. He threw stones at the window, before giving up finally. Only as he turned to go did the curtains stir. Looking up, he saw Ruth, her body and face half hidden by the light on the glass.

He beckoned for her to open the window, put his hands together, saw her reach forwards. With a great trundling sound, the window rose halfway, then got stuck. She knelt down and peered at him. The rings under her eyes looked darker, her lips thinner. They were so close together, connected by damp air and a thin whining sound that neither grew nor faded. She wanted to speak, he could see that, or was it his imagination? Encouraged, he began to talk about Shelley, how they'd known each other as kids, how the whole thing had happened so quickly, how he didn't know it would get so screwed up.

Ruth stood up and he thought she was going to shut the window but instead she turned and walked away. He thought she might open the front door but then she reappeared, knelt down again and threw something, a memory stick he realised as he caught it. Someone had written 'RUTH' on it in red ink. He stared at it, trying to work out if this was benediction or damnation.

He asked what it was but Ruth just stared at him. He asked if he could use his laptop and finally she spoke.

"It's at your parents." He tried to say it was his house too but she just shook her head. "I pay the mortgage," she said, "So technically it's not."

Then, quick as a trap, she shut the window.

Back at St James's Place, he inserted the stick into Frank's computer. A few seconds later the E: drive screen appeared. The stick contained only one item, a Word file entitled *MustRead*. He opened it. It was his dream of Ruth giving birth, his description of her death. It was dated 24th November. She would have known he'd written it after she read his journal. Nowhere on it did it say it was a dream. As far as she knew, he'd argued with her, written a story in which she'd died and then had an affair.

He ejected the stick and went upstairs. Jane wasn't there but he found the bottle of rum. The Fool smiled up at him, his foot hovering over the precipice. "Take a running jump."

Back in his room, Will paced the floor, slugging at the bottle. He'd eaten no breakfast and was soon very drunk. Twice he found himself outside, the second time in a neon-lit corner shop. He played Patience and drank for hours. Whoever had sent Ruth the file obviously wanted to wreck his marriage. He thought about Eric. They hadn't spoken in months, years really. He'd come to the wedding, of course. Lorenzo had been best man and Eric had acted as usher. That night he'd given a rather drunken speech laced with his usual dark humour. *Because he's in love with you.* That's what Ruth had said. Certainly when he and Eric had spoken in the cave, he'd seemed jealous. But jealous enough to try and destroy his marriage?

Recalling what CJ had said concerning Frank's name, he crossed the landing to check Frank's room. The door was ajar, the room empty. His drawers contained only clothes. Logging onto his computer, Will searched for some kind of online presence but found nothing. No Facebook page, no Twitter account. He also found no evidence of a teaching qualification. The Teachers Register was only accessible by schools or local authorities but Will had a friend from Canterbury, now deputy head of a school in Faversham, who owed him a favour. As a young man, he'd gotten particularly drunk at Will's aunt's one night and would have had to go home in the morning with vomit-stained clothes had Karrina not seen to him. After a little gentle persuasion the man was able to confirm that Frank did not have QTS status. He couldn't say whether or not he had qualifications from elsewhere.

When it grew dark, Will switched on a lamp. By its light, he saw that one of the panes in the French doors was cracked. *Did Mr Stine find you, by the way?* The caretaker, Lenny. He'd been replacing a pane of glass. Will had wondered how Frank had missed him but then he recalled going to the staffroom to make a coffee. He'd been out of the room just long enough for Frank to copy his documents. Will sat down, added a two of diamonds to the ace by his knee, counted three cards, turned the third. The ten of diamonds. *The curious cat must know.*

The dark smelt of lavender wax and dust. He was standing in front of Frank's door, the empty bottle in his hand.

The door spilled light and Frank's head appeared. "Come to brain me?" he said.

Will realised he was holding the bottle by the neck. "No, Frank." He was feeling cold, rational, triumphant even. "I came to ask you who you are." He waited, half-expecting Frank just to come out with it. "I looked you up," he said. "Nothing. You're not on the Teacher Register. No QTS, no CRB. It's as if Frank Štěpán doesn't exist."

"Well you know why, don't you?" Frank said, leaning a sulphurous smile his way. "Because that is not my name." And with that he shut the door in Will's face.

Will went out, bought another bottle of rum, found himself on the floor of his room, cards scattered around him. He smelt Jane's perfume, felt someone pull a duvet over him, heard Frank whispering Ruth's name, but when he lashed out, no one was there.

If Frank had sent Ruth the file, Will wanted to be as far away from him as possible. But what was his motive? To sleep with Ruth? He'd never even met her. Besides, anyone could have gone into Will's room and made a copy of his work. He wasn't overly popular. Yet even if it was someone else who'd copied the file, that didn't excuse what had happened on Saturday night.

iii.

ON MONDAY MORNING, Will woke feeling exhausted. Frank had taken him in, listened to him, given him a key to his house and now Will was thinking of betraying him. It seemed wrong and yet it had to be done. Frank was working at the school under false pretences. He sold his students drugs. More abhorrent was the idea that he slept with them. If one more sword was going to strike, so be it. Better that, Will thought, than my soul.

He hadn't done any laundry. He chose the least pungent shirt and crept downstairs. Frank was nowhere to be seen. After helping himself to cereal, Will stared at the bowl, his spoon suspended, then got up and checked the freezer. It was filled with white. He pushed goods aside, saw a wedge of green but it was only a bag of frozen peas. There was nothing more suspicious than an overly frosted choc-ice. Frank had moved his stash. Will shut the freezer door, put on his jacket and left the house.

'Twere well it were done quickly. It was all he could think. It was all he could think so that he didn't have to think. He checked inside his jacket for the key. If things went as he imagined, Frank would be arrested and Will would be sent home. If that happened, he had to get back to St James's Place as quickly as possible to pack. He didn't want to be in Brighton when Frank got out, which, Will guessed, he would.

He'd decided to arrive before the Head and wait for him. He kept going over what he was going to say but each time it sounded different.

Getting off the bus, he felt the wind pick at his hair. Rain fell in tentative drops. He sniffed at his jacket. Coitus? Had someone used his bed? He could definitely smell marijuana but when he checked his pockets they were empty. The Head's Renault was already there. Will turned into the waiting room beside the main office, looked up through the window separating the two. Rebecca, the Head's assistant was sitting at her desk. She saw him but didn't wave. He opened the office door, felt a wave of warm air. Rebecca wasn't there. A moment later she walked back in holding a file. Trying to sound relaxed, he asked if John was in.

She was nodding. "He asked if you can see him in his office."

Will grinned blankly. "How does he know I'm here?"

"Because I told him," Rebecca said. "He was expecting you. I just let him know."

The Head's door was open. From the corridor, Will could see the man's desk, the easy chairs where he liked to entertain. Stepping into the room, he saw more chairs to the left of the doorway, three of which were occupied by John Simmons, Melissa Givens and Frank.

Simmons actually blushed. He said, rather too loudly, "Thank you for joining us, Mr Zifla."

Will stood in the doorway imagining himself, his look, his smell. "I'm not doing this," he said.

John was holding a file. He told him to sit down.

"This is bullshit, John. Whatever he's said." Will pointed at Frank. "Tell him, Melissa. I know you're probably frightened but for God's sake."

She just said, "It's all true. It's your fault, Mr Zifla."

Simmons told Will he'd better sit down.

Will stepped forwards. "I came in this morning to tell you that Frank had a party Saturday night. Melissa was there."

Simmons was nodding. "I know, Melissa's already told us."

Melissa was looking at Will. "You told me where you were staying. That there was a party. I decided to gate crash. But then . . ."

Simmons said, "Despite my advice, Melissa doesn't want to press charges. The police have not yet been called. I told her, a clean breast, it'll all come out in the wash. But it's not my choice. Know this though, there will be an investigation."

Frank sat with his legs crossed, a look of universal concern on his face. When his eyes met Will's, his expression remained unchanged.

"*Call* the Police," Will said. "Do it. She doesn't want to press charges because it's not true. It won't stick."

"She says the two of you were alone together," John said. "It's enough. When you leave, please don't go up to your room. Your computer has been confiscated."

Will looked at each of their faces, settled on Melissa's last. "Where's your sense of decency?"

Tears shone in her eyes. "You chose this," she said.

Outside, the weather had worsened. Rain plastered Will's hair. At one point, he actually thought he was walking to school, not away from it. Only the memory of Mr Simmons's last words stopped him from turning around.

Frank's house was full of slow ticks. Will had been suspended and that was exactly how he felt. He squelched upstairs to the attic. It was empty. He walked back down to his room, changed into dry clothes, the whole time thinking about Jane and her stupid cards. He'd decided to rat on Frank but Frank had proved the bigger rat. He'd left Will to stew in his own juices, then got up, shaved, showered and beaten him to the punch. Will put his things in a bag along with the mini-recorder. He hadn't listened to Simmons. He'd gone straight up to his room—the man was right, the computer was gone. But Will's filing cabinet was still locked, his things still in it.

Cards lay scattered on the floor. Rain rattled the panes. Will drew a deep breath and then rang his mother.

iv.
—

IT WAS HIS FATHER WHO picked him up. They drove all the way back to Ashling barely exchanging a word. As they turned onto Foxglove Lane, Will saw smoke drifting in loose lines across the fields. Despite the rain, someone had lit a fire. He wound down the window, breathed in the scent of decay. There, set back along a narrow, laurel-lined drive, was Shelley's old house, its windows dark, its staggered corners dripping.

Elizabeth was on wildfire watch. California was still burning. An odd thought with winter settling in outside. The moment she looked at him, Will felt his own fires spring up. "Poor boy," she said, cupping his cheek. She told Avni to put the kettle on.

Will kept it brief. He had to tell them something. While he spoke, his mother looked into her cup as if reading whatever was written there. His father stared out of the window. Will wondered if the man remembered Shelley. When Will had finished speaking, Avni cleared his throat, as he often did before delivering asinine advice. Let it be known, that sound said, Avni Zifla is a straight talker.

"If," Avni said, harrumphing again, "you'd taken better care of Ruth and Eric, none of this would have happened."

Will felt as if his last drop of blood were pooling in his heart. Before he could let it freeze, he squeezed the cup in his hand, then threw it. The dull, wet sound it made as it struck the wall reminded him of bones breaking beneath skin. It was a pathetic act, yet all he had left. Breathing heavily, he jumped up and stalked away.

Upstairs, a copy of *The Blind Assassin* stared upwards from his bedside table. He threw himself onto his bed, glared at the poster on the opposite wall. Below the title—*Birds of the British Isles*—were dozens of pictures. To each he'd added notes, feeding habits, preferred nesting sites. His favourite bird as a child was the peregrine falcon. Below its picture he'd written: *drops on its prey at nearly 200 miles p/h. Watch out pigeons!*

He heard a knock and looked up. His mother peered round the door. "Alright if I come in?"

He glared at her. "How do you put up with him?"

She hesitated. "We put up with each other, William."

"Well, I'd have left him years ago," he said.

"And it's often to your detriment that you run away from things," she said. "If you're not careful you'll find yourself with nowhere left to run."

Catching herself, she raised her head, breathed in a half-sniff, then softened. "I don't want to fight," she said. "Your father doesn't always say the right thing but he loves you very much."

Will apologised about the cup.

Elizabeth stepped into the room. "In Japan," she said, "when they break something precious, sometimes they stick it back together with gold lacquer. They don't try and hide the lines, they show them."

She sat down beside him and asked about Ruth. He told her she wouldn't even let him in the house.

"Things are rarely as bad as they seem." She smiled and her eyes filled with tears. "Sometimes it's hard to see how but God has a plan."

He told her Shelley had said something similar.

"I remember the two of you being close." His mother's face wrinkled with concern. "But why go to her house? I'd promised myself I wouldn't ask. But if you can bear to tell me . . ." He felt her arm and almost shrugged it off. "Don't, if it's too much." She pulled him to her. "You're a good boy, you know? Misguided occasionally but good."

"I thought I was losing myself." He shrugged. "Instead, I've lost everything else."

After she'd gone, he crept downstairs and retrieved his bag. He uncorked the bottle of rum and stood at his window. Dusk glimmered on the pool. He followed the line of the fence separating the garden from the paddock, imagined the sycamore still wet from the day's rain.

Later, after his parents had gone to bed, he phoned Shelley. A girl answered and then lowered the receiver. Someone asked who it was and there was a scrabbling sound as the phone exchanged hands.

It was Shelley. "What do you want?" Even as he began to protest his innocence, he heard her laugh. "Just kidding," she said. "Didn't the coincidence ring any bells? Frank with Melissa? I said my boyfriend was out of town, I just didn't say how far."

Will stared at the ghost of his reflection in the window. "So Frank and Melissa weren't . . ?"

"Oh, I wouldn't go that far. I've always believed in sharing."

"But she's underage."

"What and we were babies?" He heard her blow smoke. "Listen, I wanted to see you again. After Frank found me online, after we started dating, he said he had a house in Peacehaven if I wanted it. That's why I live so close, that's why Melissa goes to your school. Then one day, I mentioned your name and Frank couldn't believe it. I mean, it's not like there are too many William Ziflas in this world."

Will asked if the way she'd used Melissa, the way she and Frank had split up his marriage, was right.

Shelley's voice hardened. "Melissa's a big girl. And you're supposed to be a grown up."

"But what was all that 'depths of hell' crap?" he said.

"Well, now you are," Shelley said and cut the line.

The next day, Will rang the school. Rebecca told him Mr Simmons was in a meeting. He asked her to get him to call him but she said Mr Simmons could have no contact. Not until after the investigation.

Finally, he called Frank. The man sounded sleepy but his tone soon changed when he realised who it was.

"I wondered when you'd work up the guts to call, Sniffler."

Will breathed in, held his breath. "Why, Frank?"

Frank's voice pooled like acid in his ear. "I just did unto you before you did unto me. I can read you like a book, Sniffler, the one you'll never write. And why is that, do you suppose? Is your heart of darkness simply too light? Maybe now you're starting to get some real material together. Thanks to Uncle Frank."

Will said that he'd spoken to Shelley, that he knew they'd cooked the whole thing up between them. Frank was laughing.

"And I suppose you got that in writing? But if you really want to know why," he said, his voice all but bubbling. "I'll tell you. You broke the law."

Will gripped the phone. "For Christ's sake, Frank, what the hell are you talking about?"

"Christ?" Frank said. "A good Catholic boy like you, using the Lord's name in vain? Though you could look to worse examples," he said, his voice growing intimate. "Did you know that on the cross, Jesus only cried out once? Not when they hammered those thick carpenter nails through his wrists and ankles. Not when he had to raise himself up on those nails in order to breathe. Only when he thought his father had abandoned him did he cry out, '*Eli, Eli, lama sabachthani?*' 'My God, my God, why have you forsaken me?' Isn't that the question you've been asking it your whole life? The reason you write all that drivel, to try and impress a father who would laugh at you were you man enough to show him what you'd written?"

Will's words felt as thick as blood. "That's it, Frank. This is war."

Frank didn't hesitate. " *You?*" he roared. "You haven't the *stomach* for war. Why do you think you went crawling back to Mummy and Daddy? Even though you're an embarrassment to them, a fu—"

Will ended the call. He was shaking so hard he had to clamp his hands under his arms. He found his father's whisky and sat by the fire, breathing in dead coals while he slugged at the bottle.

Frank had reminded him of all of those Sunday sermons, his mind full of sunshine, his backside fidgeting, a body and spirit unsuited to catechisms and homilies. Seeking some kind of anti-venom, he dug out Shelley's book, only to find that it was not what he expected. It was a retelling of the story of Cain and Abel, the one murdered, the other a murderer and of their brother, Seth, who took his sister for a wife, a woman who gave birth to daughters who coupled with angels. It was a difficult read and he wondered how Shelley found comfort in such things.

The next day, Elizabeth suggested he dig out his old duffel coat and though the thing was musty, he was glad of the warmth. It was late afternoon by the time he got to Nigel's and almost dark by the time he reached Ruth's old car seat. Despite a layer of mulch, it was still comfortable. A new more efficient sewage plant had been built on the other side of town. The old plant, with its concrete walls and hard-pressed earth, reminded him of Sazan, or of his mum's photographs of it at least. There were plans to build three hundred houses in its stead. Lego as far as the eye couldn't see.

It was a cold evening but between the coat and the vodka, he was warm enough. He listened to the birds twitter in the gloom and watched the light degrade until it lay only here and there, on a branch, in a web. It was a moment he should have cherished. His parents were still alive, his future open to interpretation.

But such was not to be for much longer.

Chapter 6.

The Feast

1

LIAM WAS DREAMING. Smooth sand. Two mounds. Waves rushed and withdrew, revealing a foot. At the opposite end, sand collapsed, an eye blinked, a mouth spat grit. "Bloodhorn."

Another shape suggested itself, lifted at one end, heaved at the sand. Eyes opened above a muzzle, a tail rose and fell.

"Bloodhorn. Up."

This second shape gathered its legs and pushed before finally swaying to its feet. Then, having mustered enough strength, it began to dig.

Liam woke with the sound of claws in wet sand ringing in his ears to find the shoulder he'd been sleeping against gone. Several of Rook's hairs curled across her pillow and he plucked one of them up now and began winding it round his finger, the task briefly easing the sense of premonition tingling across his skin. If the Keeper was still alive, he and Rook needed to get off the island. But where was she? Maybe, he thought, with a smile, she was peckish again. Yet the longer he waited, the less likely this seemed. Finally, he recalled her determination to get to Erin.

Shadows stretched across the room. The afternoon light was almost gone. Feeling uneasy, he got up and started pulling on his trousers, wondering, as he did so, if Rook had lain with him simply to get him out of the way. Was that the real reason she'd made the cakes? She'd certainly seemed agitated enough. Except that even as he thought this, he heard someone push at the door and turned with a smile on his face.

The Giver was wearing a white gown dotted with tiny holes, the neckline plunging, the seamed sleeves and body revealing flashes of sunburnt skin as she stepped into the room. Her hair was in braids, exposing rather protuberant ears. She stood there with her hands behind her back, watching him pull on his trousers, a waggish, smiling expression on her face. He heard a crystal sound and realised she was holding three glasses and a bottle of red wine. As she held them up, her smile widening, he read the label: *Vin de T'heel.*

"I thought we might celebrate," she said. "But sadly your friend's not here. But no matter. It's you I want to talk to."

He imagined Rook talking to the guard. "Where is she?"

The Giver glanced at the bed. "I don't think she trusts me enough to tell me such things."

"Of course she does." He looked for his shirt before offering a smile. "You've been nothing but kind."

"Humour me then," the Giver said, laying the glasses and the bottle on the bed. "I've been thinking about the prisoner. I was too hasty, I think." After lighting several of the candles, she told him to sit, then picked up the bottle and glasses and sat down beside him, her dress flowering around her as she did so. "Friends drink together do they not?"

The Giver filled his glass and waited until he'd taken a sip before speaking again. "Am I to assume you would like to meet this Erin?"

When he nodded, she fixed him with a serious expression. "Then first I must tell you who you're dealing with. His arrival here was very mysterious. He said he came by boat but that his craft had capsized. Yet we found no evidence of wreckage as there was for the two of you."

Liam realised they must have found the remains of the Keeper's boat. The thought reminded him of his dream and the need to find Rook buzzed at his skull.

"Drink," the Giver said, pushing his glass to his lips.

As before, the moment he took a sip his anxiety lessened.

"Like Rook," she said, "Erin refused the wine. I asked him why but he refused to tell me. Then I found this."

From a hidden pocket she drew a black box similar to the one used by the Keeper. "It contains a story I think you need to hear." So saying, she pressed a button on the side of the machine and he heard a voice, Erin's, he assumed.

The story he told was an odd one. Apparently, before the flood, Erin's father had been a fisherman and spent his days dredging up lobster pots and selling his catch along the coast. Erin said his mother stayed in her room and left him and his sister to run wild. Theirs was a small fishing community with everyone's yards full of old nets and rotting lobster pots and Erin's mother hated the smell. She used to burn incense and lie in bed all day. Then one day, a boy insulted the woman and he and Erin got into a fight. When Erin's father saw his son's bruises, he asked what had happened. Erin told him what the boy had said, that his mother was a lush who drank all day and threw the bottles under the bed and though his father tutted, he told him he'd done the right thing.

Having just sold a good catch, Erin's father decided to buy his son a gift. The neighbour's dog had just given birth to a litter of some half-dozen pups which he was selling for a good price. Erin's sister, normally jealous of her brother's acquaintances, immediately fell in love with the pup and begged to sleep with him, though most nights the dog would not be parted from Erin. Sometimes, though, Erin would sleep in his sister's room, just so the dog would stay with her. In this way, the animal cemented their relationship and the three of them became inseparable. That was until the day Erin's sister got hurt.

The siblings' favourite game was to collect those pots too broken to bother patching up, borrow their father's needle and thread and try to patch them up anyway. They would make buoys out of milk cartons, row the pots around a narrow headland and sink them in a hidden cove. Unfortunately though their handiwork was no match for a lobster's claws. Also the lathes were often too rotten or the cord looping the netting too loose, not to mention the fact that the cove was too shallow to attract many lobsters. They did catch other things, crabs and catfish and so on, each of which they cooked and ate. Only very rarely would they haul up the pots to find a lobster in the trap.

Such occasions were full of a mad revelry in which brother and sister would leap about in a frenzy, unmindful of the way the boat rocked beneath them. Their father never brought lobsters home for the table. This perhaps was why they were so set on catching and eating one. Yet, whether due to their mother's abhorrence of the creatures or their father's warning that the smaller lobsters needed to be thrown back or simply the way the dog barked each time they drew one out into the light, they never cooked even a single one.

Instead they would row the boat out to a suitable spot and release them. It was this habit that got them into trouble. Their favoured spot was by a glass-bottomed boat, an old tub moored out there for years, for they imagined it to be host to an underwater world of likeminded critters. But like the pots, their boat had seen better days. They'd tried patching it up but on the day in question, the moment Erin pulled in the oars and took hold of the trap containing their rather small lobster, he noticed the runnels at the bottom of the boat flowing with water and knew they'd sprung a leak. So while the dog leapt up onto the rear thwart and started barking, the two children started bailing.

Rook (though Erin, whose voice droned from the machine with a monotonous reluctance, never once called her such) was the first to say that they should swim for shore. They were away from the usual fishing lanes and, she said, if they carried on bailing they might be too tired to swim. Erin disagreed. He didn't want to leave the pots behind. There were several on board, each one representing many hours of work. Besides, he argued, the dog was too young to make it. Erin's sister was watching the bags of bait, fish heads, mealworms, spools and eyelets swirl up from the bottom of the boat. No, she insisted, we mustn't wait until it's too late.

That was when events took another turn for the worse, for having decided to remove her shoes, ready for the swim back to shore, the girl placed her bare foot back into the detritus swilling round her ankles, only to tread on a fishhook. The thing bit into the soft flesh between her toes, causing her to scream and jerk her foot from the water. Hopping sideways, she caught her legs against the cleat and half-stumbled, half-fell overboard, dragging the coil of rope that had snagged itself around her legs and the lobsterpot it was attached to with her.

Stunned by the sudden turn of events, Erin only leapt for the end of the rope as it slithered over the transom. He could see that his sister's feet were entangled and knew that if he let go of the rope, the pot, which was full of rocks, would drag her into the depths. Reaching into the water, he seized her wrist and leant back as far as he could, allowing Rook to get her fingers over the gunnel. Despite the rope still wound round her leg, she then managed to crawl, hand over fist, back into the boat, there to lie gasping and groaning, her leg at an odd angle. Knowing he had to be quick, Erin reached forwards and cut the line, allowing the pot to sink into the depths.

The more Liam drank, the harder it was to focus on the story, though he kept telling himself to do so. The Giver was leaning back, her legs crossed, her flesh gleaming through the pinholes in her dress. Trying to focus on something else, Liam stared at the bottle's label. *Vin de T'heel.* The name struck a chord, though he didn't know why. But then as he took another sip, the letters swam, first becoming *Vin de Lethe* and then *Devil in Thee.*

"It was then," the recorded voice said, "that I remembered the abandoned boat."

Again, Erin described the old glass-hulled tub moored up nearby. He reckoned if he could reach it, they could wait there for rescue. By then his boat was waterlogged, making rowing difficult. His sister's leg was twisted, her foot bleeding. He doubted she could swim. But matters were taken out of his hands. As if reading his mind, the dog started yapping, turned about the transom a few times, then leapt into the water and started swimming towards the other boat. Without thinking, Erin put the mooring rope between his teeth and jumped in after it. Pulling and swimming at the same time was awkward. Each time he looked back, the boat seemed lower in the water. He said that by the time they reached their destination, his sister looked like she was floating on the surface of the sea.

Up close, the glass-hulled boat was very rundown, the kind of tourist tub, Erin said, that used to run up and down the coast in the days before the flood. The glass was covered in algae but when he swam closer, he could see inside. It was full of plants. Nor was that all. There was a girl in there, a man bent over her. Erin looked about him, hoping to find a ladder. So doing, he did not see the man move until he was towering above him.

A purple-faced monster. Those were Erin's words. The man was brandishing a boat hook and Erin thought he was going to attack him with it but then he realised he was wrong. Instead, the man reached down, hooked the dog out of the water and started shaking it. He shouted at Erin, threatened him, said the vilest things. That, according to the voice on the recording, was the last thing Erin remembered.

The Giver pressed another button and then slumped against Liam's arm, her cheeks and neck flushed, as if, in her own words, she had been doing something particularly vigorous. "He lost his sister, the dog, everything. That's all he knows. I saw it in him the moment he arrived. Such terrible pain. But though I offered to relieve him of his burden, he refused to drink."

Liam felt her hand on his chest and realised anew that he was half-naked. He felt giddy, smelt incense, iris, musk. Again the label swam. *Devil in Thee . . . Vin de Lethe.*

"I sense your pain too," the woman said.

"But why?" he managed. "Why refuse?"

"When I told him I'd listened to the tape, he grew very angry. Still, he answered my question. He said that he didn't want to forget the pain. To remove it would be like cutting out his heart." As she spoke this last, she kissed him. "But you," she murmured, "you're different, you came looking for love in stolen waters. And here it is," she said, placing his hand on her breast. "Feel it beating."

With his eyes closed, he felt as if he were in some underwater lair and it was in this murky place that the unfamiliar name found him.

"*Liam?*"

"Billy," he mumbled. Breaking away, he turned to see a strange girl standing in the doorway. Whoever it was, she looked slightly ridiculous. She was swaying slightly, her hand gripping the doorframe, her eyes burning with a feverish light.

Finally she said, "What are you doing here?"

268

He knew he was meant to respond but didn't know how. "I don't know," he said at last.

"Forget her," the Giver said, turning his head until her eyes filled his vision. "For*get* her."

The girl said something more, lingered a moment longer, her expression full of feverish flashes, then turned and fled.

"Let me deal with her," the Giver said softly. "Erin too."

But despite the pleasure elicited by her hand, the name Erin troubled him.

"If I could dream," the Giver was saying, "I would dream of your hands touching me. To my children, I am nothing but a wet nurse, worse, a *gnaw*ing post." She held up her forearm which he saw was covered in bite marks. "But to you, I am visible, de*sir*able. In this moment, I transcend flesh . . ."

But Liam was only half-listening. Several candles had blown out. His mind was similarly dimmed. Yet he was bothered by something the girl had said. Something about his parents . . .

"Get drunk with me," the Giver whispered.

He mumbled something. "Transcend . . ." shook his head, then spoke words that surprised them both: "O, for a draft of vintage."

"Yes," the Giver said smiling and nodding.

"No." He was shaking his head again. "It's a *po*em."

"You want to recite a poem?"

"No. I *have* a poem." But when he reached into his pocket, the book was gone. It had been there but . . . he'd removed his trousers. Why had he done that?

For some reason, as if he could hear the book calling to him, he began groping under the bed, certain that that was where it was, only to find the Giver's caramel legs either side of his head, the edge of her dress like a canopy across her thighs. As if something had crawled out and seized him, he felt her fingers in his hair. He raised the book.

"Found it," he said, pushing himself away and landing on his backside. He felt a silly grin on his face. "You reminded me of . . . but I can't . . . ah, yes." He opened the book. "Erin, see? But that's not, it's . . ." He began to rifle through the pages. "Here." He read aloud. "That I might drink and leave the world unseen and with thee fade away into the forest dim." He looked up. "It's just . . ." He tried to think through the fog. "You and the poet share seem to similar desires . . ."

The Giver's fiery glance faltered suddenly. "Fade . . ?" After casting an eye over the words, she turned to stare at him as if he'd just performed a wondrous trick. Her voice too trembled with wonder. "The same word begins the psalm that has informed my whole life. Listen." And just like that she began to recite from memory. "Fade far away, dissolve and quite forget what thou amongst the leaves hast never known, the weariness, the fever and the fret . . . but," she said, tutting, "you must read it for yourself." So saying, she lifted the pendant at her neck, unscrewed a cap attached to its base and removed a slip of paper. "Here." She placed her cheek against his and read it to him. "Where men sit and hear each other groan, where palsy shakes a few sad, last grey hairs, where youth grows pale and spectre-thin and dies, where but to think is to be full of sorrow and leaden-eyed despairs, where Beauty cannot keep her lustrous eyes, or new love pine at them beyond tomorrow.

"Beyond tomorrow," she said again. "Don't you see? What are the odds of uniting two such fragments? Read the verses again. Can't you hear their meaning? Sentimentality is the enemy of desire. How can we love with all our hearts, if we're always looking behind us? Memories are liars. But not in the House of Love. Here we drink and eat and know the price."

Liam was confused. The Giver's ardent tone, her trembling body, her flushed skin, all were so different from the hollow lust of only moments before. Yet he sensed her passions grew from dark soil. "What price?"

She kissed him, her eyes soft with laughter. "We have a feast tonight in your honour. There you will see."

"And the girl?" he said, still trying to recall her name.

"She'll be there," the woman said, returning his glass. "But not as a guest. But let us drink and forget this nonsense. And," she said, taking the book from his hand, "this silly book."

ii.
___

A WHILE LATER, LIAM found himself in a room with long, tiled plinths. He'd woken with the Giver sleeping beside him and had crept out of bed, hoping to find something to eat. Someone had been baking but he was craving salt. Discovering a jar full of eggs, he unscrewed the lid, thrust his hand into the vinegary liquid, lifted one out and raised it to his mouth.

"What are you doing?" The Giver was silhouetted in the doorway.

"I'm hungry."

"Then have a cake." She pointed. "Someone's been baking."

"But I want an egg," he said.

She took a step into the room. "You mustn't."

"What harm can it do?" Liam popped it into his mouth.

The Giver wailed, her face crimson in the candlelight. But by the time she had hold of him, it was too late. The egg had sprouted like a root in his stomach, uncurled branches in his head.

He glanced at his hand, saw a curling ring of hair around his middle finger. "Where is she?" he said quietly.

The Giver's voice was as flat as a blade. "Safe."

"How do you know?"

"This is my island. I know everything that goes on here."

"Such as?"

"Such as where Karrin took you today. And where Rook went after the two of you fornicated." She laughed, the sound of it coldly mocking.

It was true, they had lain together. But Rook had returned to find him with the Giver.

He understood other things too. "One minute past," he said, "and Lethe-wards had sunk. Lethe is a place . . ."

"The river where the dead drink to forget," the Giver said, her tone calmer now. She was even smiling.

"This poison you've been feeding me, its real name is Vin de Lethe, isn't it? What did you do with my book?"

"I have it," the Giver said. "I will give it to you. But first I need something in return. You must play a little game with me."

"I have done too much already," he said, taking an angry step forwards.

But the Giver was prepared. With just a click her fingers, her children came, from out of the cupboards, from under the plinths, from the darkness of the hallway, their limbs stiff from hiding. With them came the stench of wine. Several of them lurched Liam's way and pinned him to the floor.

The Giver's face appeared, her eyes blazing. "You thought you could just take what you wanted? To think we were to hold the feast in your honour. But you shall attend. And you shall eat and know the cost."

She told her two tallest children to escort him to one of the cells. "But not with the prisoner. We don't want them discussing his parents." She laughed at the look in his eye. "As I said, I know everything. Including who you're looking for."

He was dragged from the kitchen, down the corridor and out into the night. In the garden, people were putting out chairs and stacking dishes and cutlery. Heads turned as he passed, eyes stared. His captors hauled him through one of the archways, behind which lay the alleyway where Karrin had pointed out the prison windows.

Halfway down the inner wall, a set of steps led up to a broad balcony that swept all the way round the garden. This curved gallery was framed by a wall inset with dozens of doors and, on the garden-side, by as many pillars, their squared columns breaking the courtyard into a series of rectangles. Lounging against the wall was a youth, his bony head and blotchy face suggestive of a shaving accident, his neck marked by three letters.

"World's Greatest Lover," he said, seeing Liam's eyes linger on his tattoo. He stroked the letters and grinned. "You still looking to talk to the prisoner?"

"Erin?" Liam asked uncertainly.

"The very same," Loverboy said, knocking on the second door. "His Highness to see you," he said, before turning and laughing. "Just kidding. Our Lady of Gifts would have my nuts if I let you in there. I'm in enough trouble as it is."

Liam was shoved into the room next door, a narrow space with a stained mattress in the corner. Hearing the all too familiar sound of a key in the lock, he listened at the wall separating his cell from Erin's, then slumped onto the mattress, dark thoughts flashing like raindrops. Why were his instincts always wrong? Even Rook had let him down. And he her. If Rook had stayed, the Giver could never have taken advantage of him. Or if he'd avoided the wine. Livid with frustration, he jumped up and banged on the wall. "Where is she?"

After a moment's silence, a voice said, "Will?"

"Will *what*?" he said. Then louder still, " *Where is she*?"

Nothing.

A while later, he woke to a commotion. Rook panting, swearing. So she hadn't yet left the island. He thought the sounds were coming from next door but when he crossed the room, he found they were coming from the balcony. He heard more panting followed by a groan. Someone shouted and then several footsteps shuffled past his door and down the stairs. A few minutes later he heard footsteps going the other way, Erin's door being opened, another brief scuffle.

Finally, they came for him, the same two youths who had accosted him in the kitchen, both swarthy looking despite their age. One of them lashed a fist into his gut, the other tied his feet with a few inches of rope between each ankle.

The courtyard was lit by a huge conflagration, flames leaping and whirling into the sky. Around it a crowd jostled and laughed, their shadows thrown into distorted shapes by the firelight. A band of musicians clutching various instruments, each one decorated with delicately carved motifs, were attempting to play an up-tempo piece,

273

their ill-tuned, ill-timed noise vying with the sound of the dancers around them who were all clapping and hooting.

"Everyone's come for the feast." Liam's captor was chewing on his beard as if it were an appetiser. "It's been a while."

Once among the crowd, the pair lowered their hands to Liam's wrists. He appeared thus to walk freely towards the fire. Orange-lit faces turned to watch his entrance. Groping hands reached out and touched him. Lisa was there. She stood near the fire, her skin pricked with perspiration, her eyes alive with flames. "Remember," she said loudly as he passed, "you chose this."

He found himself on the edge of the circle surrounding the fire. Feeling its heat play across his skin, he wondered how those faces nearest it weren't blistered. Broken tables and chairs and chunks of driftwood blackened beneath the blaze. Either side, two 'Y' shaped stakes had been driven into the ground. The Giver was clothed in green, her face sparkling with glitter. She was sitting on one of two raised thrones. Propelled towards the second throne, Liam was urged up the steps surrounding the two seats.

The festive banter continued for some moments more and then the Giver raised her hand and the various noises slowly died. As the last instrument squawked to a stop, the night, as if in answer, rose around them, an insect hum that filled Liam's ears to an almost painful pitch.

The Giver raked the crowd with her voice. "We are gathered here this evening to celebrate our love for each other. This is what I give to you and what you in turn pass on. In this way our love flows ever onwards." She swept a magnanimous hand in Liam's direction. "With this in mind, let us first extend our love to our honoured guest this evening. It's good to have you here, dreamer," she said, her voice slow and intimate, "in your rightful seat." As she turned her smile back to the crowd though, its sequins fell away.

"But before we begin our feast, we must reflect on a most heinous crime. It is an indictment of the times when we take guests to our bosom, only to find our generosity spurned. But I will not have it said that we are not fair. With that in mind," she said, sweeping those before her with a magisterial look and giving her fingers a sudden, decisive snap, "let the trial be*gin!*"

iii.
—

NOISE ERUPTED AROUND the enclosure. The band sprang up and all around, people started banging knives on plates. Only then did Liam see Rook and Erin. They lay together on the far side of the fire, their feet tied, their mouths taped. The crackling flames distorted his vision but he knew it was them. They were both staring at him and he could only imagine what he looked like enthroned beside the Giver.

The woman raised a hand and the din abated. "I call the first defendant," she said. "Wesley G. Lobe, you stand accused of conspiracy. You may step forward and plead your case."

Loverboy stepped out of the crowd accompanied by several cheers. Hands hanging out of his pockets, he turned to the Giver's chair and spoke with a calm confidence, the marks on his face flickering red and black in the firelight.

"Everyone knows me here. Some," he said, smirking at Rook, "better than others. So you'll know I'm the first to admit, I'm not perfect." He flexed a little as if he couldn't quite believe his own words. "It's alleged I helped our visitor here meet up with her lover." He pointed at the pair on the ground. Those around Rook and Erin parted so the crowd could see them. "And I suppose, on the face of it, I did."

The crowd gasped. Some booed.

"But only 'cause I'm too trusting." He pointed at Erin, then Rook. "I was guarding the prisoner when this one comes up and says she'd like to speak to him. She says her Ladyship's given it her seal of approval. Well, as you can imagine, I was in a quandary. If I go and check out her story, I have to abandon my post. If I don't, how do I know she's telling the truth? Then she only goes and pulls out a cake.

Must be hungry work, she says and when she says the word *hungry*, it's like it means more than hungry, if you know what I mean?

"Now, like I says, I'm not perfect. You lot know I've a sweet tooth. And there was her, standing so close to me, whispering that word up at me and smelling just about as delicious as that cake." He peered round, savouring the punchline. "What can I say? I'm only human. Only *flesh* and *blood*."

Whistles slashed at the air. Forks flashed as if in salute.

"Well that's what did me. I took that cake and I let her in. I know I done bad and I understand why I've been accused." Loverboy clasped his hands. "But I swear, I'm only guilty of trust. That," he said, giving those nearest him a wink, "and having a sweet tooth."

The crowd broke into spontaneous applause. Jeering children, red-faced lovers, drunken dancers, all began to cheer and stomp their feet. "*Not* guilty! *Not* guilty! *Not* guilty!"

The Giver had appeared to give his story her full attention and only when the crowd reached fever pitch did she raise her hand. "Wesley G. Lobe," she said, her voice carrying to every part of the garden, "you stand accused of the crime of conspiracy." Her hand still raised, she waited until the noise had completely subsided. "Having heard the evidence and knowing your trusting nature . . . I pronounce you *not guilty*."

Hats, drinks, even cutlery, were thrown into the air. The sound of cheering shook the walls. Loverboy smirked and rolled his shoulders as if he'd just won a fight. He worked his way round the circle, shaking hands and slapping palms.

Liam looked through the flames. Rook was slumped on the ground, her face hidden. Erin was also still. He wondered if he could work on the knots tying his feet without being noticed by the meathead skulking nearby.

The Giver waited for the mob to settle again before saying, "And now, we call to the circle our next defendant, Karrin Goodbody."

Karrin was shoved before the throne. He fell to his knees, his hands, which were bound in front of him, hitting the ground only moments before his face. He was stripped to the waist. Rolls of skin glowed in the firelight. He was blubbering, his chin gooey with saliva.

"Karrin Goodbody, you stand accused of the crime of conspiracy. You may plead your case but be brief, we are hungry!"

Several in the crowd were laughing so hard they had to grab their groins. As Liam observed the differences between how the accused were treated, he felt a prickle of dread. Every inch of Karrin's flesh was shaking. He was trembling so much, it was difficult to focus on what he was saying.

". . . as I left them," he was saying, "I heard them arguing and looked back down the alleyway. Until then," he said, "I didn't see what harm it could do."

The Giver laughed. "Harm? It is the law! Prisoners of Love are placed in solitary for a reason. They are toxic and you knowingly led them to him." She looked down at the quivering man. "How am I to preserve our purity with sneak-thieves such as you among us?"

"He told me he was looking for his parents!" Karrin said.

The Giver spun in her chair and stared at Liam. "You came in search of your parents?"

Thrown into the spotlight, he did not react to this trick. The Giver knew the truth already.

Still looking at him, the woman said with obvious relish, "But come to think of it, they did mention a son."

Stung into retorting, he said, "So you did know them?"

"What I know," she replied coolly, "is that truth is not a kind mistress."

"Tell me where they are," he insisted. "Are they still here?"

"Not anymore," the woman said, turning to the crowd with an expectant look. "Except, of course, in an excremental fashion."

It took a moment for the horror of this statement to sink in. When it did, Liam choked. He tried to rise, only for the meathead below him to thrust at him with a sharp pole, pinning him to the chair. A moment later, his lap felt as if it were on fire and when he looked down, he saw that the tip of the pole had pierced his thigh before sinking into the side of the throne.

A wild, red-skinned applause, wolf whistles and more banging rippled round the garden, drowning out his moans and quietening only when the Giver shouted, "I will deliver the verdict!"

She pointed a finger at Karrin. "Karrin Goodbody, for the crime of conspiracy, I pronounce you *guilty as charged*. Your example will be a warning to all would-be traitors. Break the law, suffer the consequences. Go. Prepare him!"

These words were like fireworks to the crowd, whose hollering reached new heights, above which could be heard snatches from the band. Liam's stomach heaved. He refused to accept the evidence staring him in the face, the stakes either side of the fire, the pole that had been used to trap him but proof was soon to follow.

"The trial is over. Prepare the others." The Giver flashed a hand towards Rook and Erin who were hauled to their feet.

Liam could only watch. Rook kicked out as she was picked up but Erin rose gracefully, his eyes marking Liam as he did so.

Karrin sobbed and pleaded, using his considerable weight to keep himself on the ground. He was so slick with sweat, Loverboy and the two men helping him kept losing their grip. "I have more! Please, I have more!"

The Giver seemed to hesitate and then slowly raised her hand. "Speak, worm. What do you have to say?"

Karrin, his face contorted with terror, raised his hands and pointed at Rook. Whether it was the look on his face or something else that caused her captors to let her go, Liam did not know. What he did know was that doing so was a mistake, for even as Karrin screamed, "She can fly!" Rook darted upwards, leaving her captors' grasping at nothing. As shrieks swept outwards from the place Rook had so recently departed, many in the crowd threw themselves to the ground.

"What!" The Giver was on her feet. "You knew and yet you kept quiet?"

Liam stared into the embered sky but Rook was gone. He looked at the Giver, saw her nod. Loverboy stepped forwards, placed a knife against Karrin's throat, gashed a cut in it deep enough to puncture his windpipe. Choking, the man pawed at the wound but it was futile. His front was quickly soaked and within seconds he'd settled in a crescent of his own blood, his rump raised at an obscene angle by his enormous belly. There were half-cheers but too many of the crowd were still watching the skies.

The Giver was feverish with fury. "I'll rip out her gizzard, I'll rip it out and nail it to the wall! Quick, *quick*," she said, clicking her fingers at those nearest her, "prepare the carcass." She glanced darkly at Liam. "A meal for our guest. Even bait needs feeding."

Liam wondered if the Giver was hoping Rook would return for him. While two men pinned his arms, Loverboy, his hands still wet with Karrin's blood, began to tug at the pole. With one last, vicious twist, eliciting a groan that travelled all the way up from Liam's bowels, the pole sprang free and he watched through blunted eyes while the men bound his arms to the throne.

Karrin's trousers and underwear were pulled down. His buttocks gleamed like moons in the firelight. Loverboy was now standing some way behind the upended corpse, the pole raised as if he were about to try and jump over the man's back. Gripped by a horrid fascination, Liam stared. Only when Loverboy began to run towards Karrin's corpse did he look away. He did not see pole and body connect but the sound was enough, a wet, tearing followed by muffled slurps. The youth panted as he pushed, jerking the spike through. Unable to cover his ears, Liam was forced to listen. When it was done, he heard a twang as the pole was settled on the stakes, followed by a sizzling sound as the man's hair and fat began to burn.

Loverboy's voice rang out with an almost sentimental enthusiasm. "Man, I *love* crackling!"

Liam retched again, sputtering the steps with bile, only opening his eyes when he was sure he would not see what was directly in front of him. With his head back, he was greeted instead by a sight so unexpected, his jaw fell open. Rook was hovering to one side of the fire, a large bundle of what looked like dry compost in her hands. Seeing his eyes elsewhere, the Giver also looked up but it was too late. Even as she howled a warning, the bundle broke across Karrin's body and dropped into the flames beneath, where it blazed thick and yellow. Smoke mushroomed into the wind and travelled in ragged sheets, catching those on the opposite side of the fire first.

The revellers there were already out of breath. As the smoke struck, their deep gasps drew the stuff quickly into their lungs and soon they were in fits of laughter. Others smelt the wind and actually stumbled forwards, inhaling it as deeply as possible. But they'd not reckoned on the potency of the smoke and soon they were staggering about. After that, from what Liam could see between each flurry, stoned panic broke out. The wind drove the stuff in circles, finally billowing a waft of it in his direction. He saw Erin. The young man had begun to shuffle away and had already reached the far side of the fire.

And then the Giver was slapping Liam so hard, his vision reeled. Her eyes were red. "That bird-bitch will not get away with this. You have no idea what is coming!" She gagged as another cloud passed, slapped at him again and then began to back away. At the same time, a central section of the fire collapsed and a log rolled out of the inferno, striking one of the stakes. The wood tipped to one side, spilling Karrin's body into the fire. Sparks whirled into the night. The smell of cooking meat intensified. "Drink of me," the woman screeched, phlegm quivering in her mouth, "*for this is my blood.* Eat of me, *for this is my flesh.* What you have done here is sacrilege!" She began to weave across the garden, her last words echoing around the walls. "You have no idea what is coming!"

Liam felt a giggle whistle in his nose and weaken his chest. He tried to raise his hands before remembering that they were tied. Instead he shouted at the night, "Ignorance is *bliss!*"

Caught in a yellow swirl, he slumped forwards and it was sometime before he managed to open his eyes again. When he did o, he saw two flaming mouths, two burning ribcages, two shadows fall from the sky. The shadows coalesced into Rook, her skin black from the smoke. He smiled with all his teeth and tried to speak. His tongue felt as if it had been stung.

280

Rook was struggling with the ropes tying his arms. He saw her jaw grind and then her chestnut eyes flash at him out of her darkened face. "This isn't over. You must find Erin."

He grinned. "And you?"

"I must leave." She parted two ropes, pulled one through the gap, began to work on the last knot.

He swallowed. "Where?"

Rook used her teeth, shook the knot.

Despite the fumes, Liam thought he understood. Tears smeared his eyes. "Is it Erin?"

Rook shook her head. "Not the way you think."

As the last knot fell away, he saw her intent and reached out but she was already gone. He looked up. All he could see were cinders and stars. As he rose to his feet, colours seared his vision. Rook must have broken into Karrin's house. That was the bundle she'd thrown on the fire. As a result, he was alive, he was *free*. So thinking, he took a step forwards and sprawled down the steps, remembering, too late, that his feet were still tied. This close to the fire, the heat sizzled his hair. Still, it took a great effort to roll away.

He lay there breathing hard, trying to ignore the smells, the sounds. All he could think was, she's safe. The bait is off the hook. A night wind was busy dispersing the fumes. The drugs crashed in his brain. All around, bodies lolled, a few groaning and giggling. One girl continued to laugh even as her arm set on fire. Too weak to stand, Liam began to crawl towards the outer wall. The border came to him slowly, a serrated wooden edge, a curving mound of soil, plants pushing up towards the windows. He turned and propped his back against a vine-covered trellis and looked around. The Giver was nowhere to be seen. Loverboy had reached the double doors before his legs had failed him. He lay on top of a young boy. Liam's grin creaked in his ears and then he heard a *crack* just above his head and felt hands slip under his arms. A moment later he was being dragged up the wall and in through a window.

2

LIAM SAW A BRASS cornered trunk, the foot of a bed, a porcelain washbasin, seaglass eyes. Erin was kneeling by the footboard, his left arm resting on his thigh, his wrist encircled by a gold watch, something that looked a lot like Loverboy's knife in his hand. His eyes were little more than glints in the dark and then Liam sensed movement and felt the other's breath on his face. A thumb pulled at his lids and he saw peering eyes, radials, tiger orange, aquamarine.

"You're as high a kite."

Erin's grin crinkled the soot-besmirched skin around his eyes. "You know, when I woke up on this island, I was lying on a beach. Didn't know how long I'd been there. Sand had piled up . . . I thought maybe I was in some kind of . . ." He made a quick, abortive sound that might have been amusement. "I mean, I'd been in an accident, I should've been in hospital. But instead . . ."

He shrugged a shoulder. "The boys who found me took me to the Giver and she was more than welcoming. Even then, I was still sure that all this might only be . . . but that just didn't add up. I mean, look, *look . . .*"

He glanced around the room before lifting the lid of the trunk. Pushing aside several papers, he pulled out a large picture book. Opening it, he found a passage and began to read: "'*The duck-billed platypus, with its duck-like bill and beaver-like tail, is a most curious creature . . .*'"

He looked up from the book. "Odd words," he said, "but forget all that. No, it's the fact that I can *read* them. If this were a dream, they'd be a blur. You can read them too, right?" He turned the book but Liam just shook his head.

"Though, actually, you probably can't." Erin laughed. "You're too smashed. But take my word for it. Look . . ."

He lifted the knife and thunked into the trunk's wooden top. Twisting it, he tore out a chunk and held it in front of Liam's face.

"See?" He forced Liam to touch it. "It's real. And you know what that means? It means I was right, the wave function doesn't collapse. Of course, it also means I might be dead but there's nothing I can do about that. What I still don't understand is how this world, the world of things, can be born out of quanta. Our imaginations, certainly mine, are too unstable . . . it wasn't something I reckoned on before but now that I'm here, in the field, as it were, it's obvious."

Liam tried to speak, before managing, "Wha' you say to Rook?" He tutted. "Who *are* you?"

Erin reached down and began to saw at the knots binding Liam's legs. "Who are *you*?" he said, glancing up. "Isn't that the real question?"

"I don' 'member." Liam squinted. "You know me?"

"Of course I do . . ." Erin said, refracted firelight glowing in his eyes. "But you don't know me, do you? My sister, she thinks her name is Rook. Rook!" he laughed. "And I am Erin—and she said your name is Liam. New names, old faces. So the name Will means nothing to you?"

Liam shook his head. "I have to find Rook," he said. "But first, first my *book*." He cast a wild eye at the window, then swallowed. "The Giver, she's . . . but wait, *wait*." He tapped his temple, then pointed at Erin, a sly note in his voice. "Yes, of course, you must know it, it has your name in it."

Erin raised a quizzical eyebrow. "A book? What book?"

Liam's face was knotted with concentration. "Written inside, *Erin, 1992*, it must have been yours."

Erin laughed, as if at a good joke. "Okay, yes, I might have owned a book like that once."

"And the poem? My heart aches and a drowsy numbness pains my, my *sense*?"

"As though of hemlock I had drunk . . ."

"So you *do* know it!"

Erin was nodding. "But why is it important to you?"

Liam told him how he'd been found at sea. "I was with my parents. We were going somewhere . . ." He shook his head. "Beyond that,

283

nothing, no memories . . . not until I found that book. It was like it was calling me. If I find the missing verses, I might find my parents. And if I find *them* . . ."

Erin began to walk Liam back and forth, past the end of the bed to a velvet chair at the far end of the room and then back towards the door again, his words no more than a whisper. "Why this world? Why *this* world?"

Finally though, Liam stopped shivering and could walk on his own.

"Have some food," Erin said, pulling out what looked like a strip of dried meat. "They gave it to me in the cell. You must eat."

But Liam just pushed it away. The thought repulsed him.

"Either way," Erin said firmly, "if you want to find this book, we have to go now. If this is my world, I am quite happy to indulge an old friend. But if we don't hurry up, I've got a feeling that when that lot out there wake up, someone's gonna wanna relight the barbecue."

ii.

PULLING OPEN THE DOOR, he beckoned for Liam to follow and was gone. Liam trailed after, one hand shading his eyes. The corridor was impossibly bright. All was hot pink flashes, orange streaks, yellow fantails.

Beyond the door leading out into the central hallway, Liam could see bodies strewn across the tiles. Heaving at some obstruction blocking the way, Erin stepped out. A mountainous figure with false eyelashes, their curls burnt down to little plastic nubs, was lying passed out on the other side, though as Erin stepped over her, her eyes fluttered open. Without a moment's hesitation, he leaned over, held the girl's nose and mouth until her eyes closed again, then winked at Liam.

"May her dreams be full of exceedingly large lovers."

The way to the garden was open, bringing with it the smell of burnt flesh and charred wood.

"Which way?"

Liam shrugged helplessly but even as he did so, he felt a tug, as if someone were pulling a rope wrapped round his middle. The house was twice dissected, once by the hallway in which they now stood and once by the circular corridor. However, the pull came from neither of these places. It came from below. Picking his way between the bodies, he pushed open the door into the other half of the circular corridor, to be greeted by a similar view. He opened the first door on the right. Stone steps curved down and away, each lit by candles. Urging Liam onto the first step, Erin shut the door behind them. A faint beat, as of drums, rose up the stairs.

"Is that why you came this way? Drums?" Erin asked.

Liam stared at Erin's blackened face. "Something else," he said. "The poem. It's down there somewhere."

As they descended, the drums grew louder. After rounding a final corner, the passage opened up into a large underground area ringing with music and voices. Red and yellow bulbs waxed and waned, their lights bouncing off hundreds of mirrors, each one cemented into the walls at odd angles. Spaces appeared and disappeared, shining ribs and black holes, cages barred and barless. The place was tiered three times around a wide, open shaft. Seating areas led off from each tier, all of them filled with people. Long-limbed creatures wearing grasses, flowers, claws, strode from one wavering space to the next, or sat lounging in seats, while others stood with only their eyes or lips moving, talking or drawing on cigarettes, the smoke from their mouths growing in faltering bursts. All of it, floors, walls, people, shook to the sound of the drum. It was an insane balm after the horrors above.

Erin made his way past a group of swaying youths and leaned over the railing skirting the inner circle. As Liam joined him, he spied his own reflection and realised why no one had reacted to his presence. His face was as black as Erin's. He looked down through the pulsing light and smoke. Three storeys below, people were swaying on a dance floor.

He had to shout to make himself heard. "I don't like it!"

"I know," Erin yelled. "Give me Motörhead any day!"

Liam waited until he felt another pull before leading Erin down a staircase to the next tier, coloured cheekbones and fluorescent eyelashes tracing bright lines across his vision. He stepped onto the dance floor and looked up. In the ceiling high above them, between an interlacing system of horizontal beams and diagonal columns, he saw a thick circle of glass and the underbelly of the grate that sat at the centre of the garden. The fire was still burning. He imagined the dancers down here listening to the drums and watching as Karrin's body was heaved over the flames.

The musicians were arranged in a circle on a low podium, their drums and keyboards complementing the singer who stood in their midst. It was the same woman Liam had seen Rook talking to the previous evening. She was smoking a rollup, the tip of which was in the habit of shedding, so that as she sang and swayed, the fur of her long white coat kept sending up little smoke signals.

"Keep sniffing," Erin said, digging him in the ribs.

Liam concentrated. The tug came from just beyond the dancefloor, where he could see, beneath the steel and concrete of the tier above, a high, doorless archway, the sandy floor and uneven walls beyond it lit by a line of bulbs. A bulbous-eyed man was standing in the tunnel entrance, his tattooed arms folded, his eyes scanning the dancers.

With a stoned confidence, Liam strode straight up to him. "The girl has returned," he said. "We must tell our Lady of Gifts."

The man squinted an eye. "Did something happen at the feast?"

Wanting to test a suspicion, Liam said, "The girl who came yesterday, she is Nephilim."

The man's eye danced as if threatened by an ember. "I knew there was something wrong with that one."

Catching on, it was Erin's turn to frown. "You knew?" Louder still, he said, "You *knew* and yet you said nothing?"

"Please, *no*," the man said, hushing him. "I suspected, I sus*pec*ted."

Erin leaned closer. "But still. A man your age needs to keep his nose clean. I know another who spoke too late and now look at him."

They both looked up between the girders. The circle of glass glowed like a harvest moon.

"We shall say nothing," Erin said, his eyes still on the grate. "But I suggest you guard this entrance with your life. No one must get by. We need to talk to Our Lady alone."

The man seized his arm. "Wait. Is it true? Are they coming? The seraphim, I mean?"

Erin shook him off and he and Liam entered the tunnel, Erin chuckling to himself. "I could get to enjoy this."

The air in the tunnel smelt damp and salty. A number of alcoves had been carved into the grey rock, though for what purpose was unclear. The yellow sand under their feet deadened their footsteps but the walls gave back a faint echo. The way led gently upwards and was interspersed by unlit sections. Trickles of water wrinkled the rock. After a while they reached a particularly flat spot and were presented with a door set into the right-hand wall, guarded by two men.

"This should be easy," Erin said, holding his hands wide. "Gentlemen!" He strode forwards, seized their shoulders as if to hug them and then clouted their heads together. The sound, as if someone had smacked a clay jar against the side of the tunnel, echoed dully around the rock. The two crumpled at Erin's feet.

The tug was continual now and Liam felt as if he needed to plant his feet to avoid being dragged through the door. He pointed at it and Erin gestured for him to go first. Reminded of the Giver's verse concerning thinking, Liam decided that the answer was not to.

He opened the door as quietly as possible, before placing an eye at the crack. At the same time, he felt Erin's head push in below him. They were looking at a low-ceilinged, windowless space bereft of all but a bed and two dozen candles, their wicks smoking as they burnt. The Giver was bent over the bed, whispering to the bed's sole occupant.

"Call it, my love. You must call it."

Liam couldn't see who the Giver was talking to but he did recognise the shaggy head resting just beyond the foot of the bed.

Bloodhorn was lying on the floor, its head on its paws, its thickly haired brow drooping over its eyes. And then the dog was lifting its head and looking at him, its eyes lit by pinpricks of light. Looking down, Liam saw that Erin was holding the strip of dried meat.

The Giver was still speaking and the Keeper, for it was surely he, was murmuring something in response. Unnoticed by either of them, the dog licked its chops, rose and padded towards the door. Erin whispered for Liam to wait and only when the dog was close enough did the two step back into the tunnel with the dog following. Interested only in its prize, Bloodhorn settled on the floor, the strip of meat trapped beneath its front paws.

"Okay," Erin said, taking a quick, excited breath, "let's go get your book."

And with that, he turned and launched himself into the room, leaving Liam in the corridor with the dog, a fact that was encouragement enough for him to follow. Though it had only been a few seconds, Erin had already pinned the Giver to the floor, their grunts seeming almost carnal in nature. The Keeper had pushed himself up and was shouting for Bloodhorn but Liam was quick to close the door.

He heard Erin hiss and realised that the Giver had bitten him. The woman was trapped under Erin's leg but her left arm was free. Even as Liam looked at the pair of them, he saw her reach for the knife in Erin's belt. He stepped forwards but he wasn't fast enough. The knife flashed upwards and this time when Erin cried out, his face drained of colour. Being close to him, the Giver had been forced to thrust the knife at an awkward angle and had jabbed it into the flesh under his arm.

Wasting no time, she turned and hissed: "Speak, Adam. *Call* it!"

Liam's skin prickled with dread. For some reason, the woman's meaning was immediately clear. Yet though he scrambled over the bed, he was too slow. He heard the Keeper mumble a word that sounded like 'Ma'kin' and then say, in a much clearer voice, "Come to your father."

Erin must have struck the Giver's hand on the floor, for the knife clattered away but Liam barely heard it. His head was full of a roaring wind, a tempest strewn with red-hot embers.

"Better run, rabbit," the old man smiled. "Or soon you'll be joining your dead father."

Liam was leaning over the old man's body. Without thinking, he lifted his head and drove it into the man's face. Snap! He pulled away to see that one of the Keeper's incisors had been shorn off at the gum. As if tasting something delicious, the old man licked his lips, smearing blood through the hairs there.

Erin had pinned the Giver to the floor and was shouting him. Dazed, Liam followed the other's orders, tore the bedsheet into strips, bound the Giver and the Keeper, even as a great violence coursed through his bones. He seized the Giver's jaw so that she couldn't bite him and then began to search her dress.

"The hooked fish has but one solace," she said, staring up at him. "It gets to gobble the bait."

You have no idea what is coming. Those had been her words. And she was right. They'd used him as bait for a far bigger bird than Rook. Liam could hear Erin breathing through his pain. At the same time, he saw the book. It had been slipped under the mattress, its hiding place revealed by the commotion. Kneeling down, he checked its contents and then turned to the Giver. When he reached for her neck, she tried to bite him but he still managed to yank the necklace from her throat.

"Death's coming," she said, her grey eyes glowing in the candlelight. "He'll see you wherever you run. Words won't help you now."

Erin's shirt was red with blood, his eyes glassy. Liam caught him under his good arm and led him across the room. The dog had finished its snack and was staring at the unconscious guards. Liam pulled the door to and lowered Erin against the tunnel wall, his eye on the dog.

"Beautiful dog," Erin winced. "Hey! Here, doggy."

Horrified, Liam tried to stop him. "What are you *do*ing?"

Erin laid his head back on the stone and raised his hand, which was covered in his own blood. "*Here*, doggy!"

Releasing a low yip, Bloodhorn stood up. It shook itself and then padded past the door towards them. Offering a red palm, Erin began to talk to the dog as if to a baby. His words were nonsense but they seemed to work. Bloodhorn sniffed, nuzzled and finally licked his fingers. Liam waited, his body tense, while Erin tousled Bloodhorn's fur and kissed its mouth.

Rubbing his chin through the fur at the back of the dog's neck, he glanced back down the tunnel. "It's quiet," he said. "What happened in there? Who did he call?"

Liam was listening too. "The drums, they've stopped."

He could hear Bloodhorn's tongue sandpapering Erin's palm and then the bulbs stuttered, once, twice—their flashing semaphore a reminder that he was still high—then went out. Ghost bulbs blazed on his retina before slowly fading. They listened in the darkness, heard their own breathing, then a scream. Even as it echoed against the stone, the lights flickered back on again. Liam saw coloured trails, Erin crumpled against the wall, Bloodhorn's head against his chest.

"I can't leave," Liam said finally.

Erin winced. "How did I know you were going to say that?"

Liam stared back down the tunnel. "The night I found the poem, I also found something else. A creature chained to a wall. *That's* what he called. I've got to go back. It's my fault."

"Then take this," Erin said, holding up the knife. "Just in case."

The tunnel entrance was thronged with people, angry, wild-eyed youths whom the bulbous-eyed man was struggling to restrain. He yelled something to Liam but Liam ignored him and ran on. Ahead of him he could see the dancefloor, several people looking up, their mouths agape, Joan, the singer, among them. The tiers above were even busier, the top tier particularly, which all but overflowed with people, a number of whom he recognised from the garden.

Loverboy was standing at the edge of the highest tier, debris and dust falling around him, his hands on the railing, his eyes bugging. "They're coming!" he shouted. "The seraphim are coming!"

Looking into the shadows beyond the highest struts, Liam saw that the fire at the centre of the garden had been scattered, the glass disc beneath it thrown aside. Now, instead of a fire, something else glowed in the hole, a bright blue head on a thick, sinuous neck.

Ma'kin, Liam thought, was that its name? If so, then perhaps he too could control it—but just then, the creature opened its jaws and released a scream far exceeding its effort in the cave beneath the lighthouse, a discharge that rose in both hertz and decibels until one by one glasses and bulbs and even mirrors began to explode. Liam covered his head, felt shards spray against his hands, saw people drop to their knees and raise their eyes in dumb alarm as Ma'kin forced its shoulders and then its torso through the hole. Dust and masonry rained on all sides, bouncing from struts and clanging against railings, covering those below it in a fine grit.

Like some kind of supple salamander, Ma'kin proceeded to walk down to the highest tier, before dropping onto the balcony and taking hold of the railing. From where Liam stood, it looked like a fairground gargoyle, its head flashing purple-green, purple-green in the strobe light. When it spoke, however, its voice was surprisingly human: *"Where is he?"*

It was staring at Loverboy who was still gripping the opposite railing, the look on his face one of absolute terror.

Joan had stepped forwards and was observing the scene above them, though Liam only realised this when she spoke. "Why are you still here?"

He turned to see her picking a shred of tobacco from her tongue. "That thing's looking for you, isn't it?" she said. "And I'm guessing it's not the kindness-of-your-heart kind of creature."

"No," Liam murmured, "more the rip-your-heart-out kind."

"Then you need to get out of here." She looked at him, her eyes troubled. "I want you to know, I like your girlfriend. What she did up there, that was something else. Which is why I've decided to help you. If you live long enough, there's a boat at the end of the black pier. They should give you passage."

"To where?"

"To the Island of Hats. That's where you'll find her." Joan's coat had deep pockets and it took her a few moments to find what she was looking for. "It's from her," she said, holding out what looked like a child's toy.

Above them, Loverboy still hadn't moved. But then someone on the podium accidentally kicked over a drum and the noise it made as it bounced down the steps—*boum, boum, boum*—acted like a starter gun.

Ma'kin sprang into space. Gliding on blue wings, it fell among the crowd opposite, causing everyone there to burst into a screaming panic. Surging left and right, scantily dressed men and women began to thunder down the stairs, treading the smaller among them underfoot, crushing them against walls, pushing them over balconies. Yet only when Loverboy was thrown over the railing, his head lolling, his neck broken, could Liam tear his gaze away.

It was only for a moment though, for just then the air blazed once more and he looked up to see Ma'kin falling towards the dancefloor, its wings unfurled. As it landed, its claws skittering across the wood, a melted plastic stink whooshing from its lungs, people scattered left and right. Rising to its full height, twice that of the tallest person around it, it turned this way and that, its body casting curlicues of light across the floor, its deep-set eyes clicking from one face to the next, its wide, leonine nostrils breathing in quick, rough gasps. A long, dark tongue played in its wide, sharp-toothed mouth, while its long, sharp-tipped fingers rippled in a kind of gentle urgency.

Everywhere around it, people cowered. As the creature looked their way, those few still standing fell to their knees. Only Liam remained rooted to the spot. With nothing else to place between himself and the monster, he raised the toy in his hand, only to realise that it was a silver rattle. But though it seemed only a trifle, Ma'kin's interest in it was clearly writ, for it strode towards him now with surprisingly graceful movements.

"How fitting," it said, "to bring a gift for your firstborn."

"Firstborn?" The creature's blazing eyes made it difficult to meet its gaze. "What do you mean?"

292

Ma'kin's voice became colder. "Why did you leave me all alone, father? All alone in that dark, wet cave?" It peered at him, a curious frown creasing its features. "Perhaps my appearance displeases you? Is that why you left me, father?"

Liam could barely breathe. He felt a hands patting his clothes and realised it was his own. He hoped to find Loverboy's knife but must have dropped it somewhere. Still, he felt a reckless anger burning in his heart. "I am *not* your father."

"Here and here," Ma'kin said, touching its chest, its head, "this boiling heart, these drowning thoughts, your dreams, your gifts. But you came here with another. *That*," it said, pointing at the rattle, "might suffice. For now at least."

But Joan was having none of it. Liam saw her stoop to the floor and then rise up, a glittering point at the end of a fur-wrapped arm.

"Why are you cowering?" she shouted, pointing Loverboy's knife at those around her. "Get up, get up. Can't you see? This is no seraphim, it's a ma*chine*. And what has been built can be taken apart."

A few of those around them looked up but no one rose to join Joan. Nor was it the creature that was to be taken apart. With a catlike grace, Ma'kin crouched and leapt, its blazing body knocking her to the floor. As if showing off a trick, so quick it was almost invisible, the creature splayed its fingers and, one-by-one, pinned Joan's ears and cheeks.

"My *gift*," the creature insisted, before extending its other arm.

Liam watched the creature pluck the rattle from his palm. With a look of great concentration, it raised the thing to its ear and shook it, the gesture macabrely delicate. Nothing. The rattle was silent. It shook it again, more urgently this time, before throwing Liam a murderous look. The toy might have been made of paper. Ma'kin crushed it and threw it down, the fingers of its other hand dallying in Joan's skin as it did so.

Even as Liam stared, slack jawed, he saw Joan flick her eyes. Following her gaze, he saw the rattle. Where the toy lay crushed on the boards, a scrap of paper protruded from the tear. This then was why it had made no noise, it had something inside it, something that began to sing to him even as he reached for it. Kneeling down, he freed the piece of paper, before wobbling to his feet. The words swam in front of his eyes.

"Away," he said glancing at the paper and then at Joan. When she blinked in acquiescence, he looked down at the paper again. "Away! Away!" he said, more loudly this time. "For I will fly to thee, not charioted by Bacchus and his 'pards but on the viewless wings of Poesy, though the dull brain perplexes and retards—"

Ma'kin jerked its claws free, causing Joan to double up where she lay. Her bleeding cheeks, both of which had been twice punctured, looked as if they'd been bitten.

"If you think you can undo me with poetry—" Ma'kin's heart flared with mirth—"it is you who are retarded."

"Already with thee," Liam said, his voice shaking with disbelief. Yet he needn't have doubted.

As he read the rest of the line—"tender is the night"—something marvellous happened. The lights paled, shadows joined hands across the tiers, faces grew vague, the monster's head glowed aquamarine in the dark, its heart, the red of a wind-blown fire. "And haply the Queen-Moon is on her throne," Liam said, more loudly still, "clustered around by all her starry Fays." An ivory glow sprang up between the columns, shapes crept across the floor. "But here there is no light, save what from heaven is with the breezes blown."

As if the dancefloor had been shrouded in velvet, a profound darkness fell all about, in the midst of which Ma'kin seemed like a glowing tower of light. People could be heard stumbling for the stairs, scuttling for the corners. Several of them fell against Liam before he managed to gain his feet. Ma'kin was nearby but moving in the wrong direction. A series of flashes from the podium, screams. Liam stumbled and looked down to see Joan on her hands and knees.

"Get up!" he said, taking hold of her arm. In the flashes of light, the blood on her face looked black.

She shook him off and handed him the knife. "Take this. This too." He felt her push something into his pocket and then she was pulling him down, her breath hot in his ear. "You will fall three times 'fore you rise again." She held him so that he had to look her in the eye. "Find the pier. Be on that boat."

He looked back once. Joan was on her feet and was lighting her pipe. A match flared and the bowl of her pipe glowed. Only as the plume of smoke rising from the bowl flashed purple did he think to look away.

iii.

LIAM SHOULDERED HIS WAY through the crowd until he sensed the tunnel. The route was in complete darkness and he tripped over several times before stumbling into Erin's hunched form. Bloodhorn gave a quick, high yelp. Erin's face floated before him, a pale moth in the dark.

"Kicked over the beehive, did you?"

Trying to get his breath, Liam managed, "We've got to go."

From behind him came a series of interrupted screams, followed by a change in the airflow as if something were blocking the tunnel. Liam pulled Erin to his feet, slid a hand under his arm and began to hobble up the shallow incline, his other hand in front of him in case he fell. Their footfall was all but silent, blanketed by a drifting carpet of sand. Feeling his way along the tunnel wall, he found himself having stoop and realised the sand beneath their feet was rising. At the same time, he felt a salty breeze. He heard muffled exclamations that seemed nearer then further away.

Finally, the tunnel turned unexpectedly and the two fell to their knees. The stone ahead was lit by a faint glow. Daylight. At the same time, violet rays threw shadows across the walls behind them. A delicate clacking reached their ears. Lurching upwards, they lumbered on, sand grinding beneath their feet. And then the clacking grew louder and Liam turned to see Ma'kin's undulating light reaching around the bend behind them. Next came a bulbous outcrop that forced them to get down and crawl on their hands and knees.

"The dog," Erin panted.

Somehow Bloodhorn was ahead of them, watching them struggle up from beneath the overhang. It whined and ducked its head and Liam glanced at his shoulder. To his shock, he saw that Ma'kin was right behind them, its body lodged beneath the overhanging rock, its long arm and skeletal fingers groping ahead of it. Had Erin not lifted his foot, it would have seized it. Crawling forwards, Liam heard a great racket and turned to see Ma'kin trying to free itself, a cloud of shale bursting around it shoulders.

Ahead of them, through the sulphurous curtain hanging in the air, Liam could see a circle of light and began to pull himself towards it. The ceiling was so low he kept scraping his head and had to inch forwards, all the time waiting to be seized, knowing that this time he would not escape.

With scree scattering in yellow clouds from its head and wings, Ma'kin had wormed its way into the next section, the light in its chest susurrating in anticipation. Bloodhorn was first to reach the cave-mouth and wriggled out into the dawn, Erin close behind. Looking back, Liam saw Ma'kin's neck and head straining forwards, its tendons taut around its neck. And then its teeth snapped forwards. Had Erin not seized him and dragged him backwards, he would have lost his leg. Maddened, the creature opened its mouth and screamed.

Deaf, half-blind, Liam jerked himself from the tunnel, felt his legs buckle, sprawled into soft sand. A quarter of a mile away, the House of Love glowed red in the pale light. Dawn birds swooped along the tide line. Nearer to, the strata of lithified dunes above the tunnel shuddered as Ma'kin threw itself forwards, its head a blue egg in a dark cervix.

Finally it lay still, its nostrils blowing furrows in the sand, its eyes pouring a furious despair. Its voice was choked with rage. "I promise you, this is not the last. And when we meet again, you, Rook, your unborn. All will be torn asunder."

Only then did it begin to reverse its course. The dark hole shook with dust, the egg retreated, the light receded and, slowly, slowly, the tunnel grew dim.

3

ERIN LAY WITH HIS ARM half-buried in sand, Liam cradling his head. Remembering Joan pushing something into his pocket, Liam took it out now and stared at it. It was a card depicting a black tower, two figures falling towards a stormy sea. The tower he knew. As for the figures, they could have belonged to anyone but he saw only two.

Finally Erin asked him what had happened and he explained how the Keeper had created the creature (though he resisted divulging Ma'kin's secret name) using what the man had called his essence.

"But why is it so angry if you gave it life?"

"My dreams were full of fire and death. I think such has driven it mad."

When at last they could rise, Liam led Erin along the high tide line, aware, even as his eyes searched the beach ahead, of the dog dancing in and out of the waves. They followed the beach to the next bay where a rocky promontory forced them up and over pitted rocks proliferated by odd, oval-shaped pools, their waters full of darting fish and fat red anemones.

It was only here that the roar caused by Ma'kin's final cry began to give way to the roar of the sea. Still Liam continued to look behind them. Seeing a flock of birds burst through a stand of pine, he craned his neck, wondering what had startled them. Erin however did not seem to share his concern and even stripped off his shirt and lowered himself into one of the deeper rock pools, saying he had to clean himself.

"We must be quick then," Liam said, his gaze returning to the horizon behind them.

Soon though, he was working at his skin and clothes with a quick, teeth-chattering efficiency. Erin was not so quick. The wound was a puckering welt and it was obviously painful for him just to move his arm. He managed to take his shirt off and even to scrub at the dog's fur but cleaning himself proved difficult. Finally Liam offered to help. Up close, Erin's skin, which was matted with patches of sweat and sand, exuded a sour scent that somehow worked in harmony with the salty tang in the air. Liam cupped water and trickled it along Erin's shoulders and down his back before working his hands in sandy circles, scouring Erin's skin of stink and leaving behind a fresh mineral scent.

Erin was obviously in pain but he was also smiling. "Indeed," he murmured, "I could get used to this."

Half an hour later, they rounded a tall bluff to see the end of a pier, its wooden columns just visible beyond a short plateau. Following the waterline, they traversed a curving strip of sand until the pier once more crept into view, its blackened boards and thick struts carving the water beyond it into a green and blue mosaic. Where the structure ended was only a burnt husk. The boat, anchored on the far side, rose and fell in the gently undulating tide.

"We need to go up there," Liam said, pointing to where the pier began.

But Erin was frowning. "Not so fast. I've got a bad feeling about this. I know that boat."

"What do you mean, you know it?"

Erin only shook his head. "What if we did something else? What if we stowed away, instead?"

"But Joan suggested that we're expected."

"And if we're not?"

Crouching low, they began to make their way towards the pier, Bloodhorn following suit. The pockmarked iron columns that made up the base of the structure, were bearded with seaweed and barnacles, as were the cross-struts between them. The sun was not long up, the shadows long, their forms stirring as the waves surged past to break on the sandy beach in a series of glassy sighs. The top of the pier was thirty feet above their heads, its boards intact for a longer distance than that. The boat was moored to one of the last posts, a blackened stump that stood out against the morning sky like a portent.

Erin waded out. After placing the card and the necklace inside the book and the book between his teeth, Liam followed suit. Halfway out, Erin, seeming to change his mind, turned and swam back to the dog, before engaging in what appeared to be a whispered conversation, culminating in a final yip from Bloodhorn. The dog then began to paddle back to shore.

Looking up through the blackened slats, Liam could see the boat's orange hull and a plaque emblazoned with its name: *The Sixer.* Erin had returned and was already clambering up the diagonal struts, leaving Liam to scurry after him.

The pair paused just below the pier's patched boardwalk, their clothes dripping. The sea sucked and eased beneath them. Triangles of light danced across the wood. Liam heard the clatter of nails. Bloodhorn was walking along the pier. He waited for the screams to begin, for the dog to start wrapping its jaws around legs and heads but all remained silent. Then he heard a cry.

"Hey, Enzo, see waa wav ear! Sir dawg!"

Erin tapped Liam on the head and then stepped out between the pier and the back of the boat. The cabin there had half a dozen portholes. Erin was careful to climb up past the last one before checking the short deck at the aft of the boat. He hooked a leg over the boat's railing and got a foot on the deck, one eye to the bow. Liam waited, also watching the front of the boat. Bloodhorn stood on the gangplank, which lay between the boat and the boards, its legs straight, its ears back. Despite the tension in its stance, it was allowing itself to be stroked by a wiry, dark-skinned man. The man knelt on the boat's edge, his sinewy fingers smoothing the fur on the dog's back and scrunching the thick ruff about its neck, his face only inches from Bloodhorn's teeth.

Liam waited but nothing happened. A second sailor joined the first, a tall black man with a muscly, tattooed body, the many colourful birds on his skin glowing like an overshadowed aviary. Erin tapped Liam on the shoulder.

"Perry! Your mama's arrived!" the second man shouted just as Liam reached out his leg.

"I ere dat!" Wiry chuckled, the two men's laughter causing Bloodhorn to growl nervously.

A third man appeared and asked what they were laughing at. Then he saw the dog. "What a beaut! A good omen, surely . . ." The rest was muted as Liam stepped over and knelt beside Erin who was working at one of the windows. Through grimy glass he could see a cabin with berths and doors at the far end.

He gave Erin the knife and soon they were squeezing through the aperture. What Liam had taken for berths were actually seats, arranged either side of a low table. Opposite lay two sets of stairs, each with five steps, one leading up to a closed door, the other leading down.

At that moment, the closed door opened and a deep voice shouted, "Lest you want your toes for bait!" The man appeared to be addressing someone in the cabin above. Even as Erin and Liam slipped down the left-hand stairwell, the man slammed the door and stepped down into the cabin. Liam heard the rasp of a match and caught a charcoal whiff before Erin was dragging him along a narrow, metal-plated corridor scented so strongly with fish, his stomach was all but heaving.

Erin looked to be struggling with something. He smiled through gritted teeth. "Did you see him?" His voice was a glitter of emotions. "I mean, did you get a good look?"

"No, why?"

Erin placed his hand on Liam's shoulder, then said, "It doesn't matter. Listen, I'm going to need you soon. We have to get this tub moving. But if I go up there alone, he might rush me."

"But you said we were going to stow away."

"How long do you think it will take that thing to find us? We don't have time to wait around."

"But Joan said they'd give us passage."

"And if they don't? That man up there, he's . . . my guess is, he won't be the sort who takes kindly to demands. Besides, as I said, we haven't got time for a debate."

From the top of the stairs they could see, sprawled across one of the seats, a big man wearing loose trousers and tunic and a faded blue cap with a short peak. His eyes were closed above a cratered nose and sagging cheeks. A long scar ran down through one eyebrow. His lips pulled on a thin cigarette, causing the tip to glow cherry-red.

Casting Liam a final look, Erin crept up the steps and across the room. Liam was aware of the boat gently tipping back and forth, creaking against its mooring, metal clanging against metal and then Erin had the man's beard in his hand, the blade at his throat.

"*One word.*"

The cigarette rolled to the floor.

"Tell your men we're leaving."

The man opened green eyes and nodded, the hairs in Erin's hand straining as he did so.

"Let's go." Erin pulled him up, kept the blade in place.

The man gave Liam an unsettling smile, the movement creasing the scar across his eye.

Erin pushed him up the steps. "Tell them. And no tricks."

The captain cleared his throat. "Listen up! We're movin' out!"

There were cries of disbelief, even a yip from Bloodhorn.

"Tell them you're tired, you don't want to be disturbed."

"I'm gettin' some shuteye. Hoist sail. I wanna be halfway to the White Rock before I wake."

Liam heard scurrying feet, the drawing of the gangplank.

But then Erin's expression became alarmed. He pulled the captain back down into the cabin. "Door!"

A second later, the door was thrust open by a young man with a meat cleaver. More from fear than anything else, Liam shoved at the door, striking the man in the face and knocking him backwards. When the door opened again, the man with the tattoos filled its frame, surveying the situation.

Erin thrust the knife at the captain's neck. "Get her moving."

The captain nodded and the man backed slowly away.

Erin gave a grim smile. "He told them to hoist sail, yet there's not enough wind. This one," he glanced at the captain, "is not afraid to die. And who can blame him? We've just pissed all over his pride. So I think he deserves a chance to get even. Shut the hatch. If we can't see out, they can't see in."

Erin sat the captain down, the knife tip steady. From below them came a loud, ugly rattle and then the roar of an engine, jerking the boat on its moorings. They heard footsteps along the side, ropes being slung on board, the anchor slowly cranking up into its housing. Finally, with a frothy roar, the boat began to pull away.

Only then did Erin throw the knife to Liam and pick up the discarded roll-up. It was still burning, scenting the room with a dark, oily aroma. Drawing deeply, he spoke through the smoke. "If I lose, you kill me, that much we've established. But if I win?" He looked down at the captain. "We want safe passage."

Erin spat into his palm. The captain glared at him, the scar across his eye glowing.

Even as they shook, the man struck Erin with his free hand, slapping a mark across his face. However, as it connected, Erin twisted away, lessening the blow. At the same time, he stretched out his free hand, spread his fingers on the floor and kicked upwards with his feet. Before the captain knew what was happening, Erin's ankles were locked behind his neck and twisting him to the floor.

The captain's hand grappled with Erin's neck, his fingers trying to close around his windpipe. Erin took the man's hand, pulled his fingers back along his palm, eliciting a grunt of pain. With one hand incapacitated, Erin had only to worry about the other, which was going for his groin. Moving himself in towards the other's body, Erin reached out his free hand, pulling the captain's searching fingers upwards until his teeth were able to clamp down on the captain's thumb, a short, thick digit black with grease.

"Huh?" Erin held his free hand in front of the captain's face before pointing his middle and index fingers towards the man's eyes. His message was clear. Finding a point on the man's wrist that sent his hand limp, he pulled the thumb from his mouth. "I don't want to fight," he panted. "But we're desperate. There's something coming you don't want to meet. The Devil himself. We need to get to sea. This thing, I believe it can smell our friend here, like seabirds smell fish. If we can get some salt between us, we might stand a chance."

Erin relaxed his ankles. Islands of white appeared across the captain's features. His voice was a rasping snarl.

"You win. In a cowardly way but beat is beat. But if I take you where you want to go, I want another chance."

Erin rolled to one side, grasped his opponent's forearm and pulled him up. He asked Liam for the knife and gave it to the captain. "As a sign of faith. It's our only weapon."

The captain rubbed his neck. "Ya've others besides. Perhaps when we're done, I'll take those too."

Only when Erin finally turned to Liam, did he see that the redhead was close to fainting. His shirt had a rose-sized stain on it and he was unsteady on his feet. Yet still he insisted on climbing up to the foredeck unassisted.

ii.
———

BY THE TIME CAPTAIN Fredrickson introduced the pair of would-be-stowaways to his crew, the island had disappeared. The men sat on the deck and stared at the intruders, their eyes the kind of coals that burn all night. Enzo, the man with the tattoos, had been waiting at the hatch when Fredrickson finally stepped up top but the captain told him to stand down, saying he'd given his word. Enzo had sworn in a language Liam did not know. The wiry man crouched nearby, stroking Bloodhorn and glancing at the pair of them as if they were possessed. When Bloodhorn looked at him, Erin closed his eyes for a moment and the dog stayed put. The third man, whom Liam thought was called Perry, stared down from the cockpit, his face framed by long, dark hair.

They sat in a circle, surrounded by coils of rope, broken nets, rusting chains, while Fredrickson explained his promise to his men in a voice stretched by an obviously uncharacteristic restraint. Erin, already much recovered it seemed, introduced himself and then Liam.

Only the wiry man, whose actual name was Wires, showed any interest. "A dreema? Neva thunk I'd seen such."

Liam remained silent.

"He can also interpret," Erin said. "We've started this journey rudely so if you have dreams you'd like answers to, just ask. As for myself, I know boats. Anything you need."

Just then, the young man with the cleaver appeared, rubbing his skull. He looked to be no older than seventeen. Fredrickson introduced him as Chilli.

To Erin, he said, "If you can flavour food with anythin' other than heat, you could try a turn in the galley. Chilli's better on the nets than cookin' what comes out of 'em. Get some seawater on that, boy," he barked, in answer to Chilli's stare. "'Fore it grows into an egg I might have to crack. As for the rest of you, back to work."

While the men grumbled and spat their way aft, Liam looked around him. Everything, even the red and white flag snapping on the mast, appeared to have been eaten by salt and bleached by sunlight. Flakes of rust were peeling from the boat's gunnels, the boards beneath, orange where it had been trodden into the wood. Perry glowered down from the main cabin. Behind this, invisible from where Liam sat, was the deck he and Erin had climbed onto when first boarding the boat. At the opposite end, the bow was raised and hemmed by a railing. A makeshift metallic mast and two diagonal poles sprouted from the beginning of the bow, the two poles joining at a height just below the crow's nest. Hanging from the point where the poles met was a long chain and a hook.

"'Tis true?" the captain said. He and Erin had been talking.

Liam looked at Erin.

"About Joan."

A flush of guilt coloured his cheeks. Still, as he began his account of the events leading up to his last sighting of Joan—he saw again that flash of purple, lilac claws slicing through the air—he left nothing out.

Fredrickson listened with obvious emotion. "She used to be part of my crew," he said. "One of the original six. The gutsiest gutter ever manned a cutter. But then one day, out of the blue, she asked us to leave her on T'heel."

"It was her who told me to find your boat," Liam said.

Fredrickson was nodding. "Well, then, that sheds a different light on things. But you'll understand," he said, looking at Erin, "when we reach the Island of Hats, I'm still owed."

Erin smiled. "I only hope it won't come to that."

The captain eyed Liam coldly. "As for you, Joan died on your account. I only hope her faith was well placed. An' if this seraphim of yours does find us, don't stand in my way."

iii.

———

OVER THE NEXT FEW days, Erin worked the nets and began to cook more and more of the meals and though the men barely spoke to him, it was clear they liked his cooking. Bloodhorn took to lying on the deck close to wherever Erin was working, though not so close that the others might suspect their bond. After mealtimes, Erin started giving Wires certain choice scraps for the dog and Liam, who watched all this with some amusement, noticed how the dog would glance in Erin's direction as it devoured the food.

At night Liam and Erin shared a space on the lower deck shielded by a tarpaulin stiff with sea salt. But though this gave Liam opportunity to question his companion, Erin refused to be drawn. He seemed distracted and Liam often caught him mumbling under his breath. He'd also taken to scribbling on an old canvas sheet with the stub of a pencil he'd borrowed from Perry, though whenever Liam tried to look at what he was doing, Erin would fold the canvas

305

in two and stow it in his pocket. Only when Liam asked about his parents did the redhead finally stir.

"How many times do I have to tell you?" he said. "I told Rook nothing. There is nothing to tell. But I'm sure they'll turn up eventually. Everybody else seems too. Speaking of which, the captain, do you know him? I mean, do you recognise him?" When Liam shook his head, Erin added, "Don't say anything but I've got to tell someone. I've been trying to work out the rules, you know? But it's impossible."

"Got to tell someone what?"

Erin leaned in, his eyes sparkling. "Captain Fredrickson is my father."

The pair were lying almost shoulder to shoulder, their heads propped on old nets, their bodies rocked by the movement of the boat, which kept lifting aft to bow.

"But why doesn't he recognise you?"

"That's just it, I don't know."

"And Rook, is she really your sister?"

"Yes, why?"

"Well, wouldn't that mean the captain's her father too?"

"Naturally."

"The Giver told me some strange stuff about you two. She had some sort of recording device. On it, you were telling a story about yourself and Rook, how Rook got hurt . . ."

Quickly, almost violently, Erin pushed himself up and leant back against the mast, his legs bent, his forearms resting on his knees. Confused, Liam followed suit.

Erin glowered at his hands, which he clenched now. "She had no right. What's on that tape . . ." He squeezed his fingers together. "Back there, I thought I'd been given a second chance. But I could still remember everything. What are second chances for those who are haunted? Still, the people there seemed kind. That was until they discovered the tape-recorder. It was odd, I didn't even know I had it on me until the Giver found it. After she'd listened to it, she changed. She told me to drink the wine, that it would help me forget. But I realised, I didn't want to forget. Why should I get to begin again while others carry on paying the price? Even if it is in another world."

"Apparently you said removing the pain would've been like cutting out your heart."

Erin stared at his hands a moment longer and then sank back, placed his palms against his temples. "My sister, *Rook*," he said, with emphasis, "tried to help but I pushed her away. Now that she's pregnant, though," he said, rubbing his face, "I hoped we might start again."

Liam frowned. "Pregnant?"

Erin glanced up, a dark amusement on his face. "We were lying by that fire for some time. She told me everything. And who's the father, do you suppose?"

"If you're trying to say it's me, we'd only just . . ."

"Only just?" Erin actually burst out laughing. "If you hadn't noticed, she's from another species. It shocked me too but then I thought, why not? What is the average gestation cycle of a rook? A few weeks? A month at most? All I'm saying," he said, when Liam continued to stare, open-mouthed, "the rules here are different . . ."

iv.
———

"SHE LIKE GLASS!"

Woken by Enzo's cry, Liam dragged at the tarpaulin to see the man's tattooed back and curls arranged against an azure sky. He was leaning over the gunnel, staring at the sea. When Liam joined him, he saw that the water was completely flat. The boat seemed supported by a perfect rendition of itself.

Fredrickson and his men spent the day working the nets in almost total silence. Being becalmed was apparently bad luck. However, their truculence suited Liam, who had become more and more loathe to converse with anyone. He'd been given the task of mending the nets and though the needle was invariably uncooperative, its spiteful prickings were still preferable to the kind of glances the crew were still giving him. In contrast, the men had begun to treat Erin with much more equanimity. It was certainly impossible to ignore how hard he worked and how adept he was at everything he turned a hand to. Wires especially took to the redhead and the two often worked together, sorting the catch with Bloodhorn always nearby.

As morning drifted into afternoon, Liam tried to will clouds into existence but the sky remained stubbornly clear and no wind sprang up, despite his insistence. After days of pulling at the dry, stiff nets, his hands were cracked and bleeding but at least he was in the shade and up on deck. Erin and Wires were below deck where it was cooler but also much more malodorous. The others were sweating in the midday sun.

Late afternoon, Fredrickson told the men to head to the main cabin. Each trooped past Liam, who sat on the middle deck. Only the captain spoke to him and only to complain. "Fish swim deep when the sea's calm."

Before long, Liam heard shouts and laughter and saw clouds of smoke drifting from the cabin's portholes. Cards were being played. Not inclined to join in, he stared glumly at a sky and sea so seamless the boat and its reflection could have been reversed. He was wondering why Rook hadn't told him. Yet the answer was simple. He tried to remember what she looked like when she cut him loose but he'd been too intoxicated to notice.

Something else lay in his mind, a bothersome splinter that took him a long time to loosen. Only after the men had come up on deck to urinate into the sea numerous times and the sea itself had begun to catch fire did he manage to extract it. It was a feeling that had occurred during his reading of the fourth verse. Taking out the book, he located the slip of paper and then the line: "Clustered around by all her starry Fays . . ." But it was neither the verse nor the line that drew him, it was the word Fays, or rather, *Fay.* It filled his head like a sweet breath and he exhaled it now in a kind of fume so that it billowed across the boat: "*Fay . . .*"

It was such a slight sound, yet it sparkled in the air before settling on the water all about the boat in a kind of diamond dust. Moving to the gunwale, he watched it glitter and twist into the depths. By now only the sun's uppermost part was visible, gilding the sea with gold. The scene was the antithesis to that that had greeted him when he last stopped the world but, recognising the moment, he reached out and touched the fiery ball before him. The trick was instantaneous. Smoke hung suspended from the portholes. Birds decorated the sky. All was still.

Walking around the deck, his boots barking on the wood, he scanned the horizon. He was expecting a visitor but neither Eagle nor any other such appeared. He shouted but the sound was only greeted by a dull echo. No one came. From the ship's starboard side, he could see a tear-shaped shoal of fish fanned out a few feet ahead of a much larger creature, its mouth agape. Further down still, murky shapes stood out against the dark, turtles or some such suspended in amber.

Deciding to test the waters, he lowered himself from the side and dropped onto the glassy plane below. It was as slippery as ice and the moment he landed, his feet shot from under him. From that angle he saw that the boat was not the only object to cast a shadow. Between himself and the horizon, a black finger pointed at the sky.

With no other goal, he decided to head in that direction. Letting his feet slide a little, he realised he could actually skate across the surface and was soon moving faster than if he'd been walking. It was an exhilarating way to travel and what with the rosy light in his eyes and the cool air in his lungs, he was soon lost in pleasure. So lost in fact that he almost collided with a strange object mounted in the sea like an enormous tooth. Looking closer, he saw that it was connected to a torpedo-shaped body and a vertical tail. It was a shark, its flesh scarred, a grey lamprey spiralling from one of its gills.

As he neared the finger of rock, he realised it was actually a huge column of sparkling white stone, the base of which was surrounded by a series of boulders, their surfaces covered with barnacles. The White Rock, he thought. On the other side, he made out a sort of stairway cut into the tower's outer wall, a wide series of steps that spiralled around the outside of the column.

From far above him, he felt a faint tugs and he knew that he had to climb. The stairs were steep and he was soon sweating, though not as much as he would have been had the steps not been cut so deeply into the stone so that even on the western face, their inside edge still lay in gloom. With the outer edge exposed and the sea growing increasingly distant, he began to creep along this inner wall, keeping the drop at arm's length. Rounding the final spiral, he saw a block of blue sky and a flat, stone ledge. There wasn't a breath of wind. The ledge was only a few feet wide and hundreds of feet in circumference and ran in a circle around a mound of white stone, at the summit of which shone a bright light.

He stepped out to see, in the far distance, an island bristling with what looked like spears. Skirting the ledge, he saw the boat, far below. Beyond it, on the horizon opposite the sun, he recognised the Island of T'heel. On the other side, he spotted Sazani. The bristling island must therefore be the Island of Hats. The rock he was standing on lay at the centre of all three. He'd just worked this out when someone whispered his name.

Were he to slip, he'd fall hundreds of feet, his body smashed apart on the rocks below. Yet the voice did not faze him. It was as if he'd been expecting it. When he heard it again, he turned towards the central mound and began to climb. The rock's quartz-like surface was so smooth, the task was difficult and he kept imagining what might happen if he slipped. Still, he persevered.

As he neared the mound's zenith, he saw it was hollow. The stone stopped abruptly and he was struck by an overpowering aroma. He was perched on the edge of a huge, steep-sided bowl. From the centre of this hollow rose a tall, silver tree, its branches blazing in the constant light. Surrounding this were more trees, each one laden with flowers, the nearest of which was just a few feet below him. The accumulative scent was so heady, it was impossible to think straight. Trying to sit down, he misjudged his grip, slipped on the rock and then, in a complete daze, rolled over the edge.

Tumbling down through the branches, he was knocked this way and that before being arrested with a sudden jerk just a few feet from the ground. Breathlessly, angrily, he lowered himself into the bed of flowers below.

There, in the depths, the flora released a thick, tremulous perfume he had no choice but to inhale. It was so overpowering, it was a long time before he could even stand. Amid the velvet gloom, the trees were russet lines, garlanded with jade and pink and white. Again, the voice called to him, a word that sounded like 'Whim'. The silver tree glittered through the maze of branches ahead. Steadying himself against the aroma, he struck out for the middle of the basin.

As he stepped into the clearing that surrounded the tree, he saw that it was covered in foil, its branches angled in such a way that the sunlight was passed downwards. Beside the tree, bathed in a bright patch of peach-coloured light, sat a young woman, her legs crossed beneath her, her blue eyes regarding him as he moved across the clearing. The woman wore a white dress and a scarf the same shade as her eyes.

"How glad I am to see you," she said.

"You were expecting me?"

"Hoping, not expecting." When the woman smiled, lines formed around her eyes and mouth and she looked older.

"You know me?"

"We've met."

"Then who are you?"

"You may call me Rousseau." She moved her hand, which was resting on a small wooden box, to pat the grass. Then, when he sat down, she reached out and took hold of his hands. "Ah," she said, "rough hands feel good."

"I've been mending nets," he said.

"A fisherman are you now?" Her smile dropped and her skin became youthful again. "What are you doing here?"

"I'm not sure," he said. "Fleeing, though to or away, I don't know. I think we are at war, I feel a coming violence."

"But who are you at war with?"

He smiled. "I don't know, the whole world, maybe."

The woman called Rousseau squinted an eye. "Men have never been very good at waiting. They should be more like air or water. There are no two forces more passive or more powerful than the wind and the waves. Myself," she said, "I like to listen." She pointed at the tree. "This is an antenna. And this," she laid a hand on the box, "is a radio. I've been listening to your progress. You're getting closer."

He smiled doubtfully. "You know what I'm looking for?"

"I know what you think you're looking for." She held up the radio. "Would you like to listen?"

She led him through the clearing and along a path cut into the undergrowth. Mossy steps climbed all the way to the basin's lip, ending in a small platform.

"The reception's clearest up here," Rousseau said, sitting cross-legged again. The radio was wooden with push buttons like black teeth along its front. She turned a dial and the speakers gave a blizzardy hiss. Caught in that snowy wasteland, like two explorers who have drifted apart and are calling to each other, Liam heard words: "God's little foot . . . Worry is a misuse of . . ."

He told her to stop. "Go back," he said.

The woman laughed. "That's not how the radio works."

Meanwhile, she'd found the notes of a piano. For the first time, he saw the moon. It rested a little way above the setting sun, a ghostly fruit on a ghostly branch and his eyes were drawn to it as he listened. When the song finished he saw the woman was crying.

"My husband used to play this to me," she said. "I used to ask him, why play it when you know it makes me sad? Because, he said, when you cry you are even more beautiful."

Liam and Rousseau were looking at each other when a second song began. Again it was a classical piece, this time led by the flute. From the first note, Liam felt the world slide sideways, as if the sea all about them had become a screen full of holes through which other screens glinted. The sky grew unbearably bright and then just as quickly darkened, while the rock beneath them began to shake and the trees to whisper. Liam saw a white room, Rook kneeling beside a bed, a man in the bed, his eyes closed:

"Holy Mary, Mother of God," Rook was saying, her words barely audible, "pray for us sinners now and at the hour of death . . ."

When Liam opened his eyes, he was sitting in the clearing again. The light was dimmer, the silver tree bright only in its uppermost branches. Rousseau was beside him, her dress gossamer-like in the gloom. He told her he had to go and stood up. Rook was waiting for him.

"Stay," the woman said. She gave a bashful smile. "Be still with me a while."

Liam felt a rising panic. There was a kindness about this woman he wanted to burrow into. If he delayed any longer, he might never leave. "I can't. The world keeps turning. Even the still man is moving."

"Then hold me."

Liam imagined the sea churning like butter, the magic unstitching itself.

"Hold me until you must let me go," the woman said, holding out old hands.

"Why?"

She stood now, moved towards him. "Because it will fill my dreams until they float."

More as Samaritan than as friend he held her. But as he took her in his arms there rose from her a complex scent of clean sheets and the tall pink hyacinth that sprouts fresh and crisp in spring and before long he was overcome by a curious numbness so that he wondered where he ended and she began. The trees were separate winds in the dark and knew an unknown language.

Only Rousseau's voice felt separate. "Time is an unhappy seamstress. She always picks apart her work." She laughed, the exultation muffled. "Please don't let it worry you, all things fall apart, yet are forever connected." She pushed something into his hand and when she pulled away, she kissed his cheek. "Give your precious one this for me."

He followed the broken path until the silver tree was barely visible. Murmurous insects stitched the dark. He opened his hand, knowing what he would find there. The fifth verse. It was too dark among the undergrowth to read it but he didn't need to, for Rousseau was singing to him through the trees.

"I cannot see what flowers are at my feet . . . nor what soft incense hangs upon the boughs . . . but, in embalmed darkness, guess each sweet . . . wherewith the seasonable month endows . . . the grass, the thicket, and the fruit-tree wild . . . white hawthorn, and the pastoral eglantine, fast fading violets covered up in leaves . . . and mid-May's eldest child, the coming musk-rose, full of dewywine . . ."

Reaching the basin's lip, he was greeted by an incredible sight. The sun had almost set so that only its uppermost edge was visible, the flames from which had kindled deep-red fires in the lowest clouds and turned the sea into a field of slowly moving lava.

He fled down the steps and stumbled across the stones surrounding the White Rock, his panic increasing. The sea was melting, the boat just a speck. Worse, running was like sprinting through overgrown grass and he was soon out of breath. When he slowed down, his feet sank into the mush. Meanwhile, though the boat remained stubbornly distant, the world beneath the waves was changing. Directly below him, he spied a jellyfish opening its shawl. Further on, he saw a golden helix twist in ever-expanding coils. As for the fin, he was sure it was sitting lower in the water. He tried to run faster but it was all he could do to keep moving. As he neared the boat, he could see the Sixer's crew lining the starboard gunnel. All of them were shouting encouragement. Yet even as his hopes lifted, he saw the fin slither into the mush.

The boat was no more than thirty feet away. He told himself to run but his lungs felt punctured. The fin rose very slowly into view, puttered around him before disappearing again but though he searched below him, it was no use. He wanted to say sorry—to someone, to everyone but it was too late—for just then the surface beneath him ruptured, the sea parted with the sound of tearing leather and he was borne into the air by the creature's snout. At the same time, he heard a whistling, saw a spike sail through the air, felt a thud as it struck the shark. Erin had thrown a harpoon. Even as he and the shark tumbled into the pulp, he saw that Erin was wading towards him.

"Release it!" he heard him cry, before his head sank below the surface.

He was wrapped in sludge, yet he knew how to fight it. The sun. The shark presented row upon row of teeth but its efforts were hampered by starch. Then Liam glimpsed the sun's snaking red coils and reached out. The effect was instantaneous. All around him the water turned to liquid and he was able to thrash to the surface. Startled by the sudden change, the shark turned away but then Erin was there and it snatched at him, removing flesh from his arm and releasing a billow of blood. Despite his wound, Erin still managed to lean on the harpoon, pushing it deeper into the creature's gills and clouding the water with blood. Liam sought Erin's arm, felt Erin tug on something attached to the harpoon and before he knew it, he, Erin and the shark, were being dragged through the water.

v.

HE CAME TO WRAPPED in a blanket. A silhouette was winching the shark onto the deck beneath a spray of stars. He'd received only superficial wounds but, as he found out later, Erin's arm and shoulder had been opened to the bone and he'd lost a lot of blood.

Liam found him in a windowless cabin lit by candles. When he stooped inside, the room seemed to tremble. Fredrickson was applying a thick, evil-smelling unction to Erin's wounds and asked Liam to hold him down. Erin began to thrash about and moan but after the captain had finished, he calmed down. He was hardly conscious, yet after Fredrickson left, the slits of his eyes rarely strayed from Liam's face.

His words, when they came, were barely a murmur. "I was wrong. It's not me. None of this. It's you. What you did to the sea, the way

. . . it's obvious. I can't believe I didn't work it out before." A ripple of pain passed across his features. "But still," he said, after it had moved on, "the question remains. Why *this* world? You asked me before about your parents. Why are they so important . . ?"

Liam shook his head. "They're all I remember, I was with them, we were going somewhere . . ."

Erin frowned, as if to trap the pain. "Then while I can, I need to tell you who you are, where you come from."

Liam was shaking his head. "No. You've said enough. You're too weak. Save your energy."

But Erin was not to be deterred. He reached out, took hold of Liam's hand. "You have to know, you *have* to," he croaked. "Listen. Listen *care*fully. Where you come from, in that place, your name is William Zifla. You are married to a woman called Ruth. Ruth is my sister . . ."

But Liam wasn't listening, he couldn't listen. Instead, his ears were filled with a rushing sound and he saw that water was flooding the room, filling it up. He tried to warn Erin, saw the other look askance, felt his mouth fill with water.

"I'm *drown*ing!" he managed.

Darkness fizzed in his nostrils, slurped at his mouth. At the same time, something like electricity rushed up his nose and into his skull, setting light to everything he thought he knew—the Keeper, the lighthouse, Gale, Rook—and then he fell to the floor and began to convulse, the dog beside him, whining and pawing at the wood.

It was Wires who found him. The man must have thought him asleep, for after shaking him, he guided him to his usual resting place.

Over the next few days, Liam avoided Erin's company, yet the man was rarely alone, for not only did Bloodhorn spend almost every minute lying on the cabin floor staring up at him, the rest of the crew also set up a vigil. Occasionally, Liam would pass his cabin to see Chilli deep in prayer, or Wires playing a game of cards, alternately turning each hand to choose the best play.

Despite discovering that the men's newfound respect for Erin also extended to him, Liam felt more ostracised than ever, the sailors'

316

scrutiny seeming more reverential than sociable. He had turned the sea to glass, they had all seen it. Worse still were his dreams wherein he found himself hovering above the figure in the white room. Rook did not reappear. It was just himself and the broken man, a one-way contemplation punctuated by a steady bleeping.

Then one night, just before they reached the Island of Hats, he woke and knew he wasn't alone. He listened to the flap of tarpaulin, saw a previously unconsidered shape uncurl itself. His face was bathed in violet, kites and diamonds scattered the deck and then Ma'kin was there, crouching just beyond the tarpaulin's edge.

"So you've come for me," he said, fearfully, bitterly.

The creature worked its huge blue jaw into a smile. "You summoned me."

"Why would I summon my own death?"

Ma'kin sneered. "You needn't worry, you won't die tonight."

"Then why are you here?"

"Because you spoke my name."

"But why not kill me?"

"*Because you spoke my name*," the creature said again. "Though there's more than one way to kill a man."

Liam tried to sit up, pushed himself against the windlass. "Why do you hate me so?"

Ma'kin opened its mouth, lashed its tongue. "You gave dominion of yourself. And why? Because he told you what you wanted to hear. That you were the one, sent to save all the world. Oh, the vanity!"

"Dreams most vile," Liam said bitterly. "Not mine."

"Dreams, to *you*, perhaps," Ma'kin said. "But to me they are the length and breadth of my soul. They show me man's hatred of himself. But also his love. A woman loves her child in a way no one will ever love me."

Liam felt himself shiver. "When will you return?"

"When I am told. You're not the only one knows my name."

"The Keeper?"

Ma'kin bared its teeth.

"Then your enemy is mine. He is to blame for all this—"

317

"No, *you* are," Ma'kin hissed.

"But there's nothing I can do. What can I do?"

A sly expression stole over Makin's face. "If you want to take the war from my heart, you must replace it with love. The cavern in which I was born was full of books. In them I read of each creation's unerring desire for friendship. Why should I be any different? You saw the truth. My appearance reviles all those who lay eyes on me, including you, my creator. Yes," it said, more forcefully, "you *are* my creator, unwittingly or otherwise. It is *your* ignorance, *your* carelessness that pulled the genie from the bottle." Its tone became cajoling. "This desolation is too much. *Dream* for me, create a companion that I might not be lonely. We will fly away together and make a heaven in this hell." Ma'kin pushed its head inside the shelter, filling it with blue. "I too know the power of names, *Li*am. Next we meet, if you've not met my demands, I will take all you hold dear. You gave me a soul I do not want. Create for me a creature that will console me or I shall choose another."

And here Liam saw that the monster was not sexless for there stirred within its trunk a grub of enormous size.

"I cannot," he insisted. "I *will* not. With another of your kind you would be rampant. There would be no stopping your murderous rage."

"Murder?" Ma'kin spat. "You really do not know yourself at all. Or what you have done."

"I've killed *no* one!"

"Are you so sure?"

"What has he told you?"

"That you are looking for your dead parents."

"That is the Keeper's poison. Something that obviously runs freely in your veins."

"I have only *your* poison in my veins, father."

Incensed, Liam hissed, "And I will release it before my own run dry. This is war—"

Ma'kin's roar was a furnace. "You haven't the stomach for war! You who run from everything, seeking the womb, despite the fact that that cave is long *scourged!*"

Liam turned away, hid his face, a cowardly tremor shaking his whole body. How long he stayed that way—far longer than it took for his arms to grow numb and his eyelids to droop—he did not know but when he found a hand on his, he let out a wail.

Wires's face swam into view amid a weak, grey light. Above him, a halyard clanged against a mast. Lean, white birds wheeled through a pale sky.

"Ya' dree min 'gain, man," Wires said. "I come say, we reach lan'."

"It's here!" Liam pulled himself forwards, tore the tarpaulin aside. "Search the boat, it's found us!"

"Is delirium." Wires felt his forehead. "Jus' a ba' dream."

Liam shook the man off. "It'll kill us all. Search the boat."

Wires seized his jaw. "Dis tird time ya say. Twice ya scream da boat down, twice we search. Ting no find us!"

Liam stood up, looked about him. Undulating waves in every direction. Far off, an island shaped like a crown.

"Yur sole book needy take?"

Seeing Wires holding out the little red book, Liam tucked it into his trousers and went in search of Erin. Having avoided him for days, their last conversation had faded somewhat in his mind. Still he recalled the panic as he thought he might drown, the rush of light that seemed to eat the little that he knew. But if anyone would have an answer to the dilemma Ma'kin had presented to him, it would be Erin. Yet when he reached Erin's cabin, the captain was just leaving and shook his head.

"The sea is calling him home," he said.

The dog was lolling, its muzzle down, its eyebrows twitching mournfully. A single candle guttered and smoked. As Liam crouched beside the cot, he caught the salty scent of seaweed and the bitterness of ammonia, though were nothing beside the confection of decaying flesh.

"There'll be help soon," he said, looking down into his friend's swollen face. "We've reached land. Fredrickson says there're more people here than anywhere else in the world. Besides," he said, forcing a hopeful note into his voice, "what about Bloodhorn? You can't leave this mutt to me." He stared at the dog, which raised its head and gave a doleful yip. "And the captain? What of Fredrickson's pound of flesh?"

Erin's breath was weak and interspersed by long moments of silence. Yet at the sound of the captain's name, his eyes fluttered open and he mustered a few words. "Hold me . . . brother." He held out his hands and tried to smile, the movement cracking his parched lips. "I feel so cold. Do I feel cold?"

When Liam took his hands, they felt like ice. He bent down, tried to warm them with his cheek.

"It's too late, I'm going, I feel it." Erin's words were interrupted by a weak, rasping cough. He tried to squeeze Liam's hand. "Perhaps I will return. Who knows? If I can," he said, his voice but a thread, "I will. But if not . . ."

He closed his eyes and took one last, shallow breath. "It's off to pastures new . . ."

"No, no, no . . ." Liam took hold of Erin's face as if to kiss it. "Please, Erin, please, I need you, you're all I have, I'm sorry, I'm so sorry, I should never . . ."

But his pleading made no difference. Erin breathed out and then all was still. His eyes were open. His lips sagged. And though Liam continued to search his friend's face for signs of life, it was too late. He was gone.

PART TWO

*Sweeping from butcher's stalls, dung, guts, and
blood, drown'd puppies, stinking sprats, all
drench'd in mud, dead cats, and turnip-tops,
come tumbling down the flood.*

—JONATHAN SWIFT

Chapter 1

The Microwave

1

THE FACT THAT WILL had spoken and yet was not awake filled Ruth with an inexpressible horror. And though Keep tried, in his usual, excited way, to reassure her, it was no use.

She left Will's room in a daze, got into the lift and then out of it again without looking where she was going, only to collide with someone carrying a tray of cutlery. In a glitter of noise, knives and forks scattered everywhere, yet it was only when the chef touched her arm that Ruth realised who it was.

"I'm so sorry," she said, bending down to pick up the knives. "It's Will, he talked."

"He's awake?" The chef frowned. "And that's a problem?"

He steered Ruth towards the cafeteria, purchased two grey-looking coffees and insisted she tell him everything.

Yet when she'd finished, he only laughed. "He's in a coma. Imagine the kind of dreams you can have when you don't wake up?"

Ruth noticed an elderly couple watching them. Graham followed her eyes and then rattled the cutlery tray.

"Cutlery Convention, folks. It'd be knife if you'd fork off anytime spoon!" He laughed and then winked at Ruth. "You said he used the name Amena? And Allah? Do you know what happened in the car before the accident?" Ruth shook her head. "Well then, who knows what they were listening to? Some radio show, maybe . . . as for mentioning a body, that doesn't mean he dreamt about, well, you know? And even if he did, he's probably just worried. He was trying to get to the two of you when he crashed."

Again Ruth shook her head. "It wasn't like that. He sounded angry."

"Because he never made it! God, his parents drowned in the back of his car. This Dr Keep tells him about it and it sends his vitals sky high. Who knows what's going on in his brain? But at least something's happening, right? Where there's life—"

What Ruth hadn't told him was what had happened to the ceiling. It was Dr Keep who'd noticed it. One of the large polystyrene tiles above Will's bed had been damaged. It might have happened before. Perhaps she just hadn't noticed it. But what was really strange was the fact that the mark, a burn mark, if she wasn't mistaken, was in the shape of a wave.

Ruth stood up. She felt sick. "I've got to go."

Graham put out a hand but she moved back.

"It's not you," she insisted. "I know you mean well. It's just a lot to handle."

At home, she put Fay to bed and poured herself a glass of wine. She called Frank but didn't get an answer. He must have heard the phone though because he called her straight back. His voice sounded smoother than she remembered, as if he'd been to some previous engagement.

"And to what do I owe the pleasure?"

"Will spoke." She covered her mouth.

"He's awake?"

"No, in his, his . . ."

"Did you hear him?"

"No, well not at first. Dr Keep had a recording. He played it and then afterwards Will started saying all this stuff." She tried to explain but couldn't. "It was just so surreal."

"What exactly did he say?"

Ruth shrugged to no one. "He sounded angry . . ."

Frank's voice was warm in her ear. "Ruth, if he's dreaming, then that's great. And if he's having nightmares, they're only nightmares."

She gave a quick laugh. "That's what Graham said."

Frank paused. "Graham?"

"The chef, at the hospital, he bought me a coffee."

Frank went to speak, then said, "Well this can only be good news. As for Dr Keep, he seems legit. I looked him up. He's a neuro-something-or-other, specialises in head traumas. He's even written a couple of books." He laughed. "It wouldn't surprise me if Will's the subject of his next bestseller. You should be asking for royalties." His tone became warmer still. "But how are you? There was something else, wasn't there?"

Ruth rested her wineglass against her cheek. "Yes." She shut her eyes. "Will mentioned a daughter, his daughter's body . . ."

Frank's tut was kind yet dismissive. "If Will went into this coma knowing what happened to his parents, on top of what happened between you two, that's a lot to deal with. But if he's talking, there's light at the end of the tunnel."

Ruth smiled. "Eric used to say that the light at the end of the tunnel's probably an oncoming train." She drained her glass. "Listen . . . I've got to go. You've been a real tonic."

"Any time."

"Light at the end of the tunnel, right?"

"*Sun*light," Frank said, a smile in his voice. "Good night, Ruth."

ii.
——

WHEN SHE WAS NEXT at the hospital, Ruth went in search of the kitchens. She knew they were on the first floor somewhere but had to ask at reception for their exact location. When she finally found them, she was surprised how busy they were. At least ten men and women were working at various stations, some prepping food, others loading dishwashers. Graham was stirring a huge vat of pasta, his brow and tunic soaked in sweat. Even so, his face broke into an enormous smile when he saw her, though he did look worried for a moment.

"We're not allowed to have people back here," he said, guiding her towards a back corridor as cluttered as the kitchen.

"I just wanted to apologise for being rude the other day," Ruth said. "You were only trying to make me feel better. I brought you some fish from the market in Hove." She held up a plastic bag laden with mackerel. "This is fresh and kind of local . . ."

Just then, a man wearing a suit popped his head into the corridor. He looked as if he were about to say something but then decided against it.

"Taking a delivery," Graham said, pointing at the fish, his voice uncharacteristically timid.

The man said nothing and Ruth thought it best to leave, though not before giving Graham a brief hug.

They didn't see each other for another week. When they did, the chef was, as usual, in Will's room, reading to him, though not, Ruth noticed, from the menu. He looked up as she entered, an odd smile on his face. He hadn't shaved. His chin and cheeks were grey.

"I'm leaving," he said. "Thought I'd come and read him the funnies first though." He held up what she now saw was a folded newspaper.

She shook her head. "What do you mean?"

He told her he'd been fired. Apparently the couple in the cafeteria had complained about him.

"It wasn't really that though. Management knew it wasn't enough. There've been other complaints but this time they dug up my application form. I left two boxes unfilled. They said unless the form's been filled out correctly, the contract's null and void."

"But they can't do that."

"They know what they're doing," he said, a rueful smile on his lips. "This isn't about a complaint, it's about rubbing the right people up the wrong way."

Ruth thought about Will, what he'd been going through in the weeks leading up to the accident.

"I've worked in management, I know how they think. Didn't fit in there either." The chef grimaced good-naturedly. "That's why I retrained. Truth is, I love chefing but I'm the wrong side of forty. It's a slow slide into retirement from here."

Ruth imagined him in some pokey flat, a microwave meal on his lap. "Listen, why don't you come to mine tomorrow? I'll cook. Well, I'll try," she said, laughing.

Graham's mouth quivered and she realised his humour was a bluff. "Very generous of you," he said. "If you're sure?" He glanced at her, then looked down again. "Anyway, it'll give me a chance to talk to you about Dr Keep." He shook his head at her expression. "I'd rather not talk here, the walls have ears."

She wrote down her address. "Eight o'clock okay? Fay should be asleep by then so we'll have some peace."

"Thanks, Ruth." Graham offered a smile. "Red or white?"

"Whichever."

"It's a pity though," the man said, patting Will's bed. "I know he'd've loved my apple pie . . ."

Just then a face appeared at the observation window and Frank pushed open the door. He nodded to them both, asked if he was interrupting. Ruth shook her head.

He held up a book. "Thought I'd bring Will's homework. Wouldn't want him falling behind."

The two men smiled at each other and Ruth introduced them.

"I'd better go," Graham said, letting go of Frank's hand and looking at Ruth. "And thanks for the invite. I'll see you tomorrow at eight, one white, one red."

"The illustrious chef," Frank said after Graham had left. "And dinner to boot. I hope he's cooking."

Ruth resisted telling him Graham's bad news. "No, I am. I hope I don't kill him." She smiled. "He wants to talk about Dr Keep."

Frank's smile faltered. "Really, what about?"

"He wouldn't say. But why are you here? It's a long way to come for a one-sided conversation."

He raised the book. "I thought we could read a classic. It's about a teacher on a Mediterranean island who has to piece together clues left by the mysterious Mr Conchis."

"A Mediterranean island?" Ruth said, touching Will's hand briefly. "Reminds me of our honeymoon."

Frank smiled. "I also came with good news. For you both, actually. I spoke to the Head today. I wanted to check on this suspension thing. It seems the young lady in question has dropped the charges. When Simmons was going to tell you is anyone's guess but he's getting old, bless him."

"Dropped the charges?" Ruth felt her blood surge. Will's suspension was not a subject she'd talked about with Frank, or anyone, in fact. It had been rendered somewhat immaterial of late.

"Obviously the girl's got rather a wild imagination. John said if Will recovers, he's welcome back. Case closed and all that."

"That's fine," Ruth said sarcastically, "the guilty has been proven innocent. As far as I'm concerned, the school can go hang. Mr Simmons better find himself a good solicitor."

Frank clapped. "Bravo! Kids like Melissa Givens need to learn that with freedom comes responsibility. And schools need to be more loyal to their staff."

Ruth tried to relax. "What did she accuse him of, anyway?"

Frank shrugged. "Something about being alone with her at a party." He tutted. "Obviously a silly mistake. Will's just too trusting."

"Responsibility works both ways, though, doesn't it? Even so, I think I'll call the school."

"Good idea, hit them with both barrels. Though," Frank said, squinting at her, "if you'll take a little advice, I'd wait. People like Simmons make more than one mistake if you let them. My father used to say, give people enough rope and they'll hang themselves. Either way, you've the weekend to think about it and a meal to arrange. Graham's a lucky man."

"You haven't tasted my cooking."

They laughed for a moment but then Fay started snivelling. Ruth picked her up and rolled her eyes at Frank, who mouthed an apology.

"She needs feeding, that's all."

"You want me to go?"

"No. You've got a book to start."

He told her to call him if she needed anything. "Let me know if you decide to talk to Simmons. But . . ."

"I know," she said, flashing him a final smile, "enough rope. Thanks for the offer. And the advice."

Only on the drive home did Ruth think about the name Frank had mentioned. Melissa Givens. It was an odd coincidence that she just happened to share the same name with Shelley Givens. The thought struck her so suddenly, she almost hit the brakes. She'd mentioned the woman's name to Frank but he'd obviously not made the connection. Her brain however was lighting up like a Christmas tree. What if Melissa was Shelley's daughter? They would be about the right age. The day she'd caught Will, in some kid's bedroom of all places, she'd received a phone call warning her that he was meeting another woman. But she still didn't know who had made that call. The whole thing stank. It had obviously been a set-up, though why and by whom she had no idea. She thought about the little scrap of poetry she'd found, the one she'd later come to realise was a description (written by Will) of Shelley—and more precisely, of Shelley's eyes: *Her eyes are pools, grey pools into which one might slip, smooth grey rocks* . . . Grey eyes, she thought again, beautiful grey eyes. Eyes that had bedazzled her husband into climbing into bed with a witch.

iii.
—

THE NEXT DAY, SHE woke to find the window open, her breath like smoke. Fay lay in her cot, half-buried in a lilac bodysuit, oblivious to all but the furnace of her own heart. Ruth's thoughts returned to Melissa Givens. It was outrageous to say Will was welcome back just because Melissa had changed her statement. She thought about Frank's advice too, to give Simmons enough rope. As for Graham coming to dinner, she felt terrible that the man had been fired but she couldn't help wishing she'd not invited him. It was the last thing she needed.

In the meantime, she had to visit Avni and Elizabeth's solicitor. He'd sent another letter, reminding her that the Ziflas had chosen Will and her as executors of their estate. The letter was asking, in Will's absence, as it were, for her to go in and collect the will. Which was why, after showering and dressing and pulling her hair into a ponytail, Ruth bundled Fay into the car and drove over to Ashling.

The Zifla file had been inherited from a former partner by Louis Escher, a pale-faced young man with very fair hair. When Ruth gave him a copy of the death certificates and identification documents, he grinned at her through sugary eyelashes.

"The only bit of luck in all this," he said, "is that Mr Zifla kept his papers up-to-date. I haven't seen the details of the testament, so you'll have to call me if there's anything you're unsure about."

The solicitors' offices were housed in a Victorian building at the top of Kilwardby Hill. Mr Escher's office was small but tidy, though it seemed to have only recently been made so. The wastepaper bin was full and the room shimmered with air freshener.

Fay was in her car seat as usual and wide-awake. She kept staring at her fingers as if trying to do sums. Ruth sat with her own fingers linked in her lap. "So you didn't draw up the will?"

Mr Escher said, no, he only met Mr Zifla once but he'd been told the man was careful with his money. "He wrote his own testament."

As far as Ruth knew, Avni had never had to deal with any particularly large sums of money. The house had originally been priced in single figures and he'd never sold a car for more than a few thousand pounds. He and Elizabeth had rarely gone abroad or treated themselves to anything more than a Sunday roast at the pub. As Avni once said, even when he sold his stories, he only made enough to feed the chickens.

Escher nodded. "He did all the paperwork himself. However, we have duplicates, both of the original and of the new will."

Ruth opened her mouth. "He changed his will?"

"Yes, well, he delivered a new envelope. A few months after his sister died. I didn't work for the firm then but I would guess that he changed it as a direct result of his sister's passing."

It made sense. He told her Avni had named the two of them as executors, so in Will's absence he thought it prudent to ask Ruth to take delivery of the testament. "I like to tie up loose ends."

"If only everything were so simple," she said.

He surprised her by laughing. "Yes," he said. "If only."

332

He handed over a large Manilla envelope on which Avni had scrawled *Mr and Mrs William and Ruth Zifla* in his usual calligraphy and a second envelope with only Will's name on it. Ruth weighed them in her hand. A lifetime, she thought.

They sat on the passenger seat all the way home.

Back at the house, she made tea, curled up on the sofa and opened the first envelope. It contained Will's parents' last will and testament, signed by them both. They'd bestowed the house and all its contents, the contents of their joint bank account and their car to them both. It had been written prior to Ruth getting pregnant and made no mention of grandchildren. It also bestowed a sum of money, originally from Will's Mum's parents, to be used to pay Constance Baskerville's care home bill.

The second envelope she left on the coffee table. She knew it was personal. That it was not meant for her. But she had been entrusted with it and, furthermore, Will could not open it. What if it contained something important, something time sensitive? After lunch, she wandered into the living room and picked it up again. She figured it wouldn't hurt.

It contained a letter. As she began to read it, she felt as if she'd crept into someone's house and was going through their belongings.

My dearest Will,

I have never called you that but that is what you are. My darling child, my only son, my mountains and my moon. How strange it is to write like this when I was unable to say such things to you while I was alive. But I thought them continually. Maybe not in so many words but then words are overrated. More often than not they get in the way.

I instructed my solicitor not to give you this letter unless both myself and your mother had passed. I would like to begin then by saying mourn us if you must but know this, we had a good life, a full life. And you gave us such joy. We have always wondered why anyone would choose a childless life. We tried so long to have children and when you came along, it was like a miracle.

Unfortunately though this letter is not simply a goodbye from beyond the grave, as appealing as that idea is to my more morbid side. No. The reason I am writing this is to discuss the passing of someone I have hitherto been unable to mention. It is a confession concerning the man in Teto Karrina's kitchen. The night you called me, I drove to Shatterling to find myself facing an unenviable dilemma. As I entered Karrina's house, I saw the pair of you in the kitchen, standing there like two lost souls. This I am sure you remember all too well. But what you missed is the look on my sister's face as I joined you. I'd not seen the man lying on the floor for nearly forty years, neither of us had, but I recognised him straightaway.

I almost spoke to you about it the day of Karrina's funeral. Had I done that, I would not have needed to write this letter and, who knows, maybe Elizabeth and I would still be alive. What I am trying to say is that you and Ruth might be in some trouble. I understand that by writing this letter I will frighten you both but better that than you meet the same fate. The man who died that night was once a very sinister and very powerful figure. If I'd gone to the police and your actions were made public, despite your innocence, you would have been killed. I chose therefore to place as much distance between you and the body as possible. I lied to you knowing you wouldn't understand. I asked you to write a statement knowing I would never use it. But then I realised you were not happy with the arrangement; you smelled a rat as it were. So I arranged for a friend of a friend to come round dressed up as PC Plod. Unforgiveable really. But I had to convince you. And in the meantime, like a fool, I kept your statement. I don't know why, perhaps it was the hours you spent writing it, the honesty I saw there. I've known for years that you've been writing and I've been waiting for you to show me. But you never have so I kept those few pages instead.

The reason I said nothing after Teto Karrina's funeral is because I was hoping her death was the tragic accident it appeared to be. It didn't help that you and I had grown distant with each other. Perhaps this is because I raised you in the same unflinching way I was raised, without allowing room for the country in which you were born. England is far removed from the mountains and has changed immeasurably since I arrived on her shores. She has replaced her empire with an empirical approach. Yet at the same time, though these rain-sodden fell walkers lack the hardness and the clarity of a mountain people, they are morosely good-natured, they laugh at themselves, they celebrate modesty. All of this I saw in your mother and all of it made it impossible not to fall in love with her. Doing so was more frightening than coming down out of the mountains but I had little choice. There was no path behind me upon which to return. You are more your mother's child than mine. I do not mean by that that I love you less. I love you more for it. Like her, you see the best in people. You revel in possibility. Only I seem to bring out the Shqiptar in you. Only with me are you hard. But I deserve it, it is how I have been with you.

I've tried to talk to you about the events of that night and what happened afterwards several times since the funeral but it would not come. My mind betrayed me, continually flashing before me a vision, a look in your eyes, disbelief, or worse, rejection, so that I found myself saying nothing. I have only wanted to show you love but instead I have shown you weakness.

And now of course what has happened is what always happens. People die. Myself, your mother, Teto Karrina. After her death I was worried that she had been murdered as retribution. As you know, the Law of Lek demands a life for a life but too often one eye is not enough. I reasoned that if my sister's death were not accidental, someone would

*come for me. Then, just a few days after the funeral, as if I'd
somehow sensed what had happened, I decided to destroy
your statement. But when I looked for the safety deposit box
in which I kept it, I found it missing. There was no sign of a
break-in. Whoever came was very professional. For a while
I thought I might have misplaced it but even I am not that
scatter-brained.*

*I was anxious for months but nothing happened. That does
not mean however that our deaths, whatever their
appearance, were the result of an accident. What you do now
depends on that. If the circumstances do indeed seem
suspicious, you may wish to go to the police and if so you will
need to give them a name. The man in Teto Karrina's
kitchen was once called Feçor Loka. It is unlikely he was
using that name at the time of his death but at least it is a
start.*

*Finally, please know that your mother knew none of this.
Your memory of her must remain untarnished. As for
myself, I am sorry to relate these events in such a cowardly
way but I hope you can find it in your heart to forgive me
and to love me as I have loved you. Always and forever.*

Until we meet again, your father.

Ruth went through to the kitchen and leaned over the sink but
nothing came up. The mirror was full of broken sky. The events
described in the letter had occurred years ago. For all she knew there
was nothing to worry about. The police had never come calling and
neither had any strangers. No doubt Karrina's death was just as it had
seemed, an absent-minded accident. And certainly Will's parents
hadn't met a suspicious end.

She put her hand over her mouth, not knowing whether she was
stifling words or catching tears. To carry on, that was the key. For
now at least. Ring the office, follow her usual routine. However,
when she rang Harmondsworth, she was in for another shock. Joel
sounded embarrassed. He said he didn't think she'd call again so
soon. She told him every week, as agreed. He said, yes but things

have changed. She tried and failed to calculate his angle. "Such as?" she said.

"Such as you, Ruth."

It was another of Joel's games, she was sure of it. She asked him what he meant and he said that she'd rung him last week and asked to extend her maternity leave to six months. "We agreed," he said. "It made sense. But then, afterwards, you said . . . don't you remember?"

It took all she possessed to stay in control. She asked him what he was talking about.

"You said you'd been thinking that maybe you didn't want to come back at all. I asked you what you meant and you said . . . well, let's just say you told me what to do with the job in no uncertain terms."

She kept waiting for him to laugh. When he didn't, she grew angry. But before she could say anything, he said the company understood that she'd been through a lot but that he had to warn her, if she was abusive again, there may be consequences. Only with this innocuous threat did she remember. She'd called Joel the same afternoon she'd listened to Will speak of deserts and death. She'd gone to his room full of hope but Keep and his little black box had ended all that. When she got home, she'd called the office with the intention of extending her maternity leave but in the middle of the conversation she'd felt . . . she felt it now. A black wave. She didn't want to go back. She never wanted to let Fay out of her sight again. *Take your job.* She imagined Joel waiting on the other end of the line, his centre parting dotted with perspiration. *And stick it.* She had done that, sensible Ruth had done that.

She felt a kind of stomach-ache. When she finally apologised, Joel said something more but she was already putting the phone down.

She tried to phone Needlemire. A woman said he'd get back to her. She took several deep breaths and said she needed to speak to him now. The woman asked her to repeat herself and then said, "That's just not possible. If it's urgent," she said, "I can offer you a slot tomorrow."

Ruth kept staring at the letter. "I need today," she said.

337

"Mrs Zifla," the woman said, "you'll have to speak up."

She wanted to scream obscenities. Instead, she told the woman it had to be today.

"Sorry, Mrs Zifla," the woman said, "tomorrow is all I can manage."

Ruth ran Fay a bath, took a long time washing her and then dressed her in a jumpsuit patterned with tiny zebras. She ironed a red blouse with ruffled sleeves and a charcoal skirt. Then, while Fay watched, she made a cake. For Daddy, she said.

After placing the cake in the oven, she vacuumed the carpet in long, parallel lines, a smile stretching her cheeks. She imagined she looked resolute but when she finally saw herself in a mirror, she just looked mad. When the cake was ready, she put it on the side next to the knife block and removed the largest knife. The sponge had risen perfectly. She changed her grip on the knife, squeezed it very, very hard and then drove it down into the cake so violently, it sank into the chopping board. A sob dimpled her chin. With her left hand steadying the board, she pulled the knife out, held it in the air and then drove it down again. The impact was at once shocking and soothing, so that as she repeated it, chasing the slowly disintegrating mess out onto the kitchen side, thudding at it until her arm went numb, she felt better and better. Tears kept pushing their way outwards. Too thick to run down her cheeks, they blurred her vision.

When she finally stopped, the cake's guts were spread as far as the hob on one side and the toaster on the other. Crumbs littered the floor, chunks lay sprawled across the chopping board. Dozens of pockmarks scattered the chopping board and the laminate sideboard in random patterns. She pushed a hand into her eyes, smearing tears and makeup across her cheeks and then laid the knife on the side.

When Eric asked her what was wrong, she said, "I've always thought I was Dad. But I'm not, I'm Mum." Eric tried to say she was both, they both were. She said, "But I don't want to be her."

Fay began to cry.

Ruth was scaring the baby but she couldn't stop. "Joel, my, my superior," she said, "I wasn't really listening to him but I still heard."

Her voice was full of wonder. "I said I was quitting because I was afraid of flying. And it's true. I shake every time I think about it. It's been true ever since . . ." She tried to think when. "I said, do you know how many things can go wrong on a plane? I said if God meant us to fly, he'd have given us wings. That's not me speaking, that's Mum."

She carried Fay into the living room. With the lights off and the curtains closed, it felt like a mausoleum. The phone rang and a familiar voice asked if she'd requested an appointment. "I've managed to get you in today," the voice said.

A lifeline snaking out of the dark. "Yes," Ruth said, "seven o'clock."

iv.

—

SHE ONLY THOUGHT of the chef after getting Fay into the car. He was supposed to be coming at eight but after seeing Needlemire and visiting Will, she couldn't imagine she'd be in the mood. Annoyed at herself for not getting his number, she stood on the pavement, Fay's cries pawing at the glass. Finally she scribbled a note and left it hanging from the letterbox.

Needlemire's office lay on the ground floor at the opposite end of the building. The door was open and she went in without knocking. The room, which was both clean and modest, seemed designed specifically to draw attention to her windswept appearance. Needlemire sat behind an old pine desk, in front of which were arranged two chairs. Apart from a filing cabinet, a cheese plant and two silver frames, one containing a picture of a fair-haired woman with a turned-up collar and the other, a certificate, the rest of the room was empty. She set Fay's seat beside the desk and sat down.

Needlemire was writing but soon clicked his pen off. His smile was drawn. Though he didn't look it, he said he was surprised to see her. "How long has it been? I've been calling you."

She told him she must have missed his calls.

He clicked the pen on and off again. "Ruth," he said, "your husband's in a coma and I am his physician. Yet since you left the hospital, we've not spoken. Don't you think that odd?"

She said Dr Keep had been keeping her updated.

Needlemire stopped and then said, "Sorry, I'm not . . ?"

She told him he was a specialist.

Needlemire still looked confused. "Whatever doctors you've been consulting, their opinions are immaterial. I am Will's doctor, you speak to me." He dropped his pen on the desk. "Ruth, I've left a dozen messages."

She always checked her phone but now she thought about it, she couldn't remember the last time. "I wanted to talk to you," she said. She tried not to lean forwards or to rush what she was saying. She told him she'd handed her notice in at work but had forgotten doing so. She tingled with embarrassment.

"Apparently," she said, "I told them I was afraid to fly."

Needlemire asked her how she'd been sleeping.

"Not very well," she said. "I need something."

"I wished you'd come sooner," he said.

"I didn't realise how much I needed—"

"No." Needlemire squeezed the bridge of his nose. "Not for the pills, Ruth. For your husband."

She told him she'd been in nearly every day.

He told her he was worried. "I think we may be losing him. He's lost a lot of weight. It's an unusual case."

She shut her eyes and heard a hiss, imagined herself surrounded, by electricity, by layers of cable and insulation. "What about the tape?"

"We're trying, Ruth." Needlemire removed a writing pad from his desk, scribbled a few lines on it. "I'm sorry this was so brief. I thought you wanted to talk about Will. I've got to get back to my shift but we'll make a proper appointment, discuss Will's condition and yours of course and take it from there."

"I thought this was a proper appointment." Ruth stood up, the paper gripped in her fist. "Do you have any idea what I'm going through?"

He fixed her with a look. "Do any of us have any idea what *any* of us are going through, Ruth?"

She collected her prescription and took two pills, despite not having eaten. Once such niceties had seemed important but she knew now that the world and its steamroller did not care. The pharmacy was at the front of the hospital, tucked into a wing to the right of the main doors and she found herself staring at a tapestry dedicated to the hospital. With buttons and cloth, the piece captured a different Crawley, one with trees and parks and children. The only truth she recognised was the stream curling around the hospital. It looked so pretty, yet all she could picture was Will's parents carried along by its blue cloth current, their eyes stitched open, their mouths stuffed with silk.

Just before she left the house, she'd picked up the book of poetry. The idea that her voice might bring Will back had stuck with her. But she didn't know what to say to him. She recalled old memories, the day they met, their night in Birmingham, their first week in Hove. But she wanted something else, something deeper. The poem. Somehow it connected them all: the baby, Eric, Will, herself. She decided then, even as she was scribbling the note to Graham, that she would read him a verse each time she visited him. It would be something to look forward to.

Will was breathing so gently, his chest barely moved. It was easy to imagine he was simply sleeping. Ruth placed Fay's car seat on the floor beside the bed. The baby had her eyes closed and kept sighing from her nose. Moving round her, Ruth sat down and opened the book. Finding the page, she placed her hand on it, breathed in and let out a long sigh.

"I've brought the book," she said. "I'd like to read you the poem."

She didn't say which book or which poem. She was normally very practical but recent events had taken their toll and part of her hoped that simply hearing those first few lines would cause his eyes to flutter open.

She focussed on the page. "My heart aches . . ." Yes, she thought, "and a drowsy numbness pains my sense . . ."

He didn't even bat an eyelid. Yet something about reading to him felt right. On the drive home, Ruth was actually quite hopeful. She was aware that she had a mess to clean up when she got in and of the way her hand ached from gripping the knife so firmly. But at the same time, reading that first verse had made her feel connected to Will on a surprisingly intimate level and she enjoyed that feeling while it lasted.

It would, however, be another hour before she and the baby got in. It was past Fay's feeding time and they only managed to reach the stone pylons marking the city limits, before her cries became such that Ruth had to pull over. There were very few cars out that night, maybe due to the coming storm. Wind buffeted the car. Black road stretched behind and ahead of them. Vague, twisted spots danced among the trees. Yet the moment Ruth began Fay's feed, a wonderful calm settled over her. The inside of the car was warm and dry and though it was windy out and starting to spit, this only increased the sensation of safety and comfort. Ruth watched Fay's eyelids pulse as she suckled and felt her own lids grow heavier and heavier.

She woke with her head propped between the headrest and the window. The dashboard clock read 10:15, a fact she would forget for quite some time. The engine was still on, the car dark and warm. Fay lay asleep on her breast and after a brief pang, Ruth lifted her into the back. It was another one of those moments she would look back on with longing, for beyond it lay only hell.

She thought of the chef, a brief regret that they'd missed each other. Meanwhile the rain began to fall in huge glassy sheets so that as the car dropped down into Brighton, it was like they were slipping into water. Even though Ruth was able to park close to the house, the two of them were soaked by the time they got to the front door. Ruth noticed as she slammed it to that the note was gone.

After the noise of the downpour, the quietness of the hall was strangely dissonant. As was the unusual smell. It was as if she'd left something cooking. With the light on, she sniffed at the air again and was certain. It was definitely meat. She turned to place Fay's seat on the floor, only to kick something that skittered across the floor. When she bent to pick it up, she saw it was the silver rattle she and Will had bought in Lewes. It had been completely crushed. She stared down the hallway into the dining room, her heart thudding.

Walking slowly down the hall to the kitchen, she peered in and saw that the microwave was on. By its dim light she could see the edge of the kitchen side, the glint of a tap, her reflection trapped in the window. Her first impulse was to stop the microwave. However, as she stepped down into the kitchen, her foot connected with something soft and she tripped. Braced as her hands were for hard tiles, the soft clothing and cooling flesh that arrested her fall were difficult to process. She could see nothing. Her sense of smell, however, was almost supernatural. Beneath the scent of overcooked meat, she could smell the salty iron of blood and below that, Graham's aftershave. Green tracers of panic fired through the darkness, their frequency increasing as she tried to find purchase. Her left hand settled on tiles but her right found a hole big enough to push her hand into. Slipping again, her cheek and hair came into contact with cold, unshaven skin, while her hand registered the depth of the cavity. She tried to guard her brain from its calculations but it was too late. Then the microwave pinged and the room fell dark.

That simple sound, announcing the readiness of a meal, even more than that wet hole, severed something inside of her. She knew that it precluded other, fiercer sounds but she registered none of them for what they were. She screamed, so hard, each inhalation felt endless. She heard Fay's cry flood the hallway. She could see the chef's hair, the glass of his eye and could smell the meat waiting in its hot, dark box but she did not see and did not smell. There was rain against the backdoor, a light through the blinds from the neighbour's yard, an impression of a table at her back, a chair on its side, the table top above her, that hand, her hand, clinging wetly to her breast but there was nothing.

2

SHE WAS FOUND CURLED up under the table. From the noises she was making, their neighbour, Tom Addlestone, thought she was comforting a baby. Fay, however, was still in the hall, so close to the front door that when it was forced open, she was sprayed with splinters. Tom visited Ruth after she woke up and though she didn't respond, part of her must have been listening because she knew everything. He said an inspector had interviewed him, that he'd told the man, when he found her, it took him a moment to realise that she was actually holding a knife. In that deeply regretful way some older men have when sharing bad news, he told her that the body had been severely mutilated. "Severely," he repeated. Graham had been drugged and strangled. The attacker had then taken a knife from the knife block, sawed through his ribs and cut out his heart, before placing it in the microwave.

She was told later that her fingerprints were the only ones found on the murder weapon, their arrangement on the handle conducive to the kind of attack Graham had suffered, their clarity suggesting an extremely tenacious grip. The remains of a recently-baked cake were found spread over the kitchen side, the hob, the floor, even inside the victim's chest, along with fifty-three puncture marks ranging across the laminate top. It was assumed she had baked the cake and subsequently attacked it, though why she had done so could not be determined until she woke from the catatonic state the medics found her in. There were several theories, of course, none of which helped her case.

After interviewing Needlemire, Inspector Hart had more kindling for his fire. The doctor told him Ruth had been suffering from hallucinations and periods of forgetfulness. He said he'd not taken her claims seriously. She'd missed several appointments despite the fact that Will was in a coma. Then, the night of the attack, she'd visited his office without an appointment, only to spend the time talking about herself. He suspected postnatal depression or possibly posttraumatic stress and had prescribed antidepressants. When asked, Needlemire had believed it unlikely the pills could give her psychopathic urges or the kind of strength required to cut through a man's ribs but it was not impossible. As he later admitted, his conclusion was that, combined with other drugs, he could not be sure what the effect might be. When asked about her relationship with the victim, the doctor could only repeat hearsay, that they had known each other and that Mr Bull had been fired because of an incorrectly completed job application form. He'd been spending time in Will's room and had been seen in the cafeteria with Ruth.

She found out later, Hart also interviewed Graham Bull's daughter. The young woman had said, yes, he was going to see someone that night. No, he'd not said at what time. He'd said it was someone from the hospital, an ex-patient, and though the daughter had urged him not to go, he'd insisted, saying he was worried about Ruth. He hadn't elaborated further. Graham's ex-wife, who'd had no contact with him for several years, said that though he'd been a complete flop in the husband department, she couldn't think of any reason why anyone would want to murder him.

The investigation at Rutland Road revealed that neither of the doors had been forced. All the windows were undamaged. Hart reached the conclusion that Graham had been let into the house by somebody he knew, taken into the kitchen, given a drink containing barbiturates and then strangled. The post mortem revealed the time of death to be between nine and ten at night and hospital CCTV showed Ruth leaving the car park just after eight. That, Hart calculated, would put her at home just before nine.

Hart's team were left with two problems, the brutality of the crime and the motive. The first, given Ruth's state of mind and the drugs she'd taken, was explicable but the second was not. Why would she, a mother and a woman with no previous criminal record, who'd held down a responsible job for many years, commit such a crime? She was subjected to a thorough examination but they found no incriminating marks, though of course she was covered in the victim's blood. And of course, when Hart's team contacted her workplace, they found more evidence of erratic behaviour. Despite an unblemished record and exemplary conduct, she had, only the week before, handed in her notice, even though she was on maternity leave.

The police psychologist laid out a pattern of schizophrenic impulses, brought on, she suggested, by recent and crippling stresses. It was not, she said, unfeasible to believe the chef's murder to be the final act of a woman very much on the edge. All of this Ruth discovered in her subsequent dealings with Hart.

However, the man did not like fishing conclusions from muddied waters and had therefore decided to wait for her. Needlemire had suggested she be moved from the Royal Sussex County Hospital to Crawley, that his team look after Fay and her until Ruth responded to their care. He told Hart that her catatonia was a temporary response. He couldn't say what she would remember when she was finally able to speak but it would be good for her to know she was near Will. Hart agreed.

That is why, on the 3rd of February, Fay and Ruth were driven to Crawley and the family were all under one roof again.

ii.
⎯⎯

WHEN RUTH FINALLY returned, she was lying on a single bed next to a darkened window. A square of light, cast from a small window in the door opposite the bed, shone onto the wall above her head. Someone was peering at her, Dr Keep, she realised, his shadow over her face. He spoke without compunction, his eyes glittering like dark crystals.

"You are alone, Ruth. I don't think you've ever been more alone in your life. Needlemire moved you to Crawley to be near your husband. But make no mistake, it's you they are watching. They think you killed the chef. Think about it, Ruth," he said, "the mess you made of that cake? You were found holding the murder weapon, for God's sake. I wouldn't be here," he said, "if I didn't believe in you but you have to admit, it doesn't look good. They think you're a murderer. Unless you convince them otherwise, they're going to keep you in a room like this for the rest of your life."

Ruth tried to speak, heard a croak. "Who died?"

Keep looked surprised. "You invited the chef for dinner," he said. "But when you got home you found someone had ordered take out."

She felt lightheaded, saw his form waver and the door opening. Someone switched on the light.

"Can you hear me, Ruth?"

She blinked, realised her eyes were open, held open in fact by rubber-scented fingers. A face swam into view, a young man with green eyes was holding a torch and she had to look away. Against the wall beside the door stood a short man wearing a long coat and a red scarf. She couldn't say how she knew but she was immediately certain that this was the inspector, the man who would prove to be her most wily enemy.

The next time she saw Inspector Hart, he wasn't wearing the scarf but she still recognised him. He spoke to the nurse outside her door, patting his head as he talked, though his hair was already immaculately arranged. Then he was smiling in at her, one hand on the door, the other behind his back. He peered at Fay, bending slightly at the waist, his hand gripping his hat. Choreographed, she thought.

He smiled sideways at her. "Beautiful."

She did not like the little, grey-haired man. He'd made too much of an effort. The expensive camelhair, the button collar, the polished shoes, his coiffure, everything cried, 'Confide in me!' Only his red nose told the truth. He pulled up a chair and introduced himself without offering a hand. He said he was glad to see her awake, that he assumed she knew why he was there.

"Dr Needlemire told me you're rather delicate at the moment, so I'll be brief," he said. "Tell me what happened."

She tried but everything she said, Hart looked as if she'd dealt him a low card. He seemed interested in only two things—why she'd given in her notice—and what had happened to the cake. She said she'd decided to become a full-time mother. As for the cake, she'd baked it before going out. She'd left it on the side to cool. Considering the circumstances, she'd barely noticed its state upon her return.

"And the knife? Why were you holding it?"

Ruth's gaze solidified. "It was the first thing I found. What would you have done?"

Hart coughed at his hand before lacing his fingers across one knee. "How was your reasoning prior to discovering the body?"

Ruth felt something hard in her throat, pushed cold words around it. "I came home with my baby, got soaked to the bone, let myself in, left Fay in the hall and then murdered a man in my kitchen. Is that what you want to hear?"

Hart looked unperturbed. He tapped his lips with the tips of his forefingers. "We're just trying to follow all lines of enquiry, Mrs Zifla. I'm sorry if it is painful."

"You're sorry?" She looked at him.

Hart stood up. For a moment he seemed not to know what to do with his hands and she realised she'd been wrong. It wasn't that he managed them, quite the opposite, with each pose they caught him out, causing him to create various, improvised arrangements.

When they finally allowed her to see Will, Ruth was escorted to his room by a brusque, hard-eyed nurse who stood outside, occasionally peering in through the window. The last thing Ruth wanted was to read the poem. Instead she sat beside her husband, half-leaning on the bed, her hands clasped as if in prayer. Not that she was praying. Instead she was thinking of the memories Hart had stirred up. She'd wanted to tell him that her father used to fry cod livers. *That's* what it had smelled like.

"His heart." She covered her mouth, spoke into her fingers. "Something cut out his heart. What kind of animal does a thing like that?"

THE LONGER HART STAYED away, the sharper grew his insinuations. Often they were all Ruth thought about. Even to her bewildered brain, the message was clear. Hart had the murder weapon. All he needed was the motive.

She responded by throwing herself into motherhood, a rewarding distraction that revealed to her the loop observed in African art where mother and child are carved from the same wood. She devoured every baby book she could find and began teaching Fay yoga, as well as singing to her and reading her nursery rhymes. They spent hours bathing, or watching television. Some of Ruth's favourite moments though were when Fay fell asleep, her eyelids quivering like tiny pink scallops, her fingers slowly opening.

Though she didn't trust Needlemire, Ruth began to look forward to seeing his head appear at her window. The little dances they performed were a welcome test in the days prior to Hart's return. Every day she asked when she was being released and every day the doctor told her certain results were still pending, that she hadn't reacted to the medication as expected, that they were worried about Fay's weight. But they both knew the truth. They were watching her: her room and those rooms around it, for example, were more secure than any other part of the hospital she'd so far visited. But despite this knowledge, she kept her anger in check. If they wanted to play a waiting game, then she would wait.

It was another week before she visited Will again. It had been selfish of her to tell him about Graham's murder and as soon as she saw him, she wanted to kiss him, to hold him, to say sorry. But as she went in, her escort, an overweight nurse with big arms and a baby face, followed her into the room, sat by the window and opened a book. It was obviously another change Ruth would have to get used to. Unable to pour her heart out in front of a stranger, she decided instead to read Will the poem. Locating the book, she sat down, found the right page and began to whisper the words of the second verse straight into Will's ear, only occasionally glancing at the nurse who didn't once look up from her book.

"O, for a draught of vintage that hath been cooled a long age in the deep-delved earth . . ."

It was around that time that she also began reading to Eric, sometimes from Frank's book and sometimes from one of the rummage books she found at main reception. This distraction meant that she could keep her eyes and mind elsewhere. Fay was also a good antidote for the depression that stirred within her whenever she looked at her brother's face. She took the child to see both men, especially during the afternoons and would often lay her in her father's arms or on her uncle's tummy and watch her play there, perfectly happy on the precarious aerie in which she found herself.

Reading the third verse, however, made Ruth want to throw the book away. Its message was too bleak. She wondered if any of it was actually helping, or if, in fact, it might be making Will worse. She could see he'd lost weight and there were times when she'd come into his room to see a pair of nurses fussing round his bed, turning him or adjusting his pillows and wonder to herself, what was the point of *her*.

Had Penny not come to see her, such thoughts may have driven her back underground. But as it was, having returned to her room after reading the third verse, she found the nurse sitting in the chair under the television. Immediately, her spirits lifted. Penny had let her hair down, so that it draped over her shoulders in neat, caramel waves, but Ruth still recognised her. For a moment though, she couldn't recall her name.

"Penny," she said at last.

"I told them you knew me," Penny said, after talking to Ruth's escort. She opened a bag containing various magazines and chocolate bars. "I thought a familiar face might help."

Ruth felt giddy and had to sit down. She needed a friend so badly, she thought it must be written all over her face. She saw the trap, knew why Penny was really there but was so grateful, she felt sick.

Penny came every day after that so that before long, Ruth grew used to her presence, grew to rely on it, in fact. But though she was sure Penny had been planted by Hart, the woman never questioned Ruth about anything. She seemed to prefer playing with Fay to talking. She insisted on taking charge of the pram and would push Fay about the grounds, singing and cooing to her even as Ruth prattled on about the food or Needlemire or the hospital's need to cook its patients.

"I mean, surely the heating doesn't need to be on *all* the time!"

Penny also took Ruth to see Will and Eric. Apparently Needlemire had insisted. Ruth said she didn't mind one bit. When they next went to visit Will, she took advantage of their growing bond by asking if Penny would wait outside. It wasn't that she minded reading the poem in front of her, it was more the idea of exerting a little control again. When Penny agreed, if a little reluctantly, Ruth stepped into Will's room feeling almost liberated.

Winter sunlight blazed in the already warm air. A swatch of light lay across the bed, so that Will's face looked like it was glowing. Ruth read the next verse with great care. Realising it was one she was already familiar with, she also read it with a growing sense of hope, paying special attention to the last line, which she read several times in a row—

"Away! Away! For I will fly to thee . . . The Queen-Moon is on her throne, clustered around by all her starry Fays . . . by all her starry Fays; but here there is no light, save what from heaven is with the breezes blown . . ."

And then the next day, Inspector Hart came. After reading to Will a rather lovely verse in which the speaker was to be found wondering through a flower-scented darkness, Ruth returned to her room feeling similarly overcome. Deciding to rest, she lay down and just like that, fell asleep, only to wake to the sound of an all-too-familiar voice.

Hart was standing outside the door, exchanging a few words with the nurse. Ruth had time to sit up and to check on Fay, who was warbling away in her cot, her face just visible through the netting, before the man finally came in. He stood there patting down his hair, then pointed towards the end of the bed and sat down.

"Something you mentioned, Ruth," he said, before raising his fist to his mouth and giving a gentle cough, "last we spoke. You said you and your daughter . . ." he checked his notepad, "got 'soaked to the bone'?"

Of the drive home, Ruth recalled little more than the sweep of the wipers but she did remember arriving at the house. "It was pouring down," she said. "I managed to park near the house but Fay and I still got very wet."

"And what time was that?" he asked.

She said she couldn't remember.

He nodded. "The problem is," he said, "hospital CCTV shows you leaving the car park at half past eight. You say when you got home it was raining, yet it didn't rain until around ten."

"Then I must have arrived home at ten," she said.

"But if so, what were you doing the hour before that?"

She shrugged. "I don't know."

Hart sat there for a moment, his hands resting between his knees and then nodded. "My intuition," he said, "is that you're not our man as it were. What worries me is that, whoever it is, obviously intended for you to find that little present in your kitchen. But the question is, why? And, more importantly, what are they going to do next?"

For a moment clever games of cat and mouse evaporated and Ruth saw only a woman in a crumpled dressing gown and a man whose hands itched for a cigarette. Many of her thoughts were trapped in a kind of blinding brightness but to what degree was only just becoming apparent. The idea that the killer was still free had simply not occurred to her.

"I have an idea," she said. "But I need to talk to my mother." She tried to smile. "I've asked for a phone call but Dr Needlemire seems unsure exactly what class of prisoner I am."

The inspector sat staring at her. "You know who did it?"

"There's someone," she said. "He's been acting strangely. I'm sure he knows Graham too."

"Knew," Hart corrected. "And what's his name?"

Ruth thought of Avni's letter, the one he'd left with his solicitor. "First my phone call," she said. "Then the name."

Needlemire came just before lights out. Ruth remained quiet but he didn't seem to notice. He asked the usual questions and watched her with the usual squint. But there was something different about him. Finally he asked how long she'd known the killer's identity.

"I just need to talk to my mother," Ruth said.

"But you have an idea?"

"An idea," she said.

He looked at her very directly, then said he'd seen the photographs. He stood by the door, one hand keeping it open. "Hart showed me what happened to Graham. Flashbulbs don't miss much, you know?"

She asked if he was helping with the investigation.

"I liked him," he said, smiling at the door, "Graham, I mean. Unorthodox."

Ruth asked what Hart had shown him exactly. He said the Inspector had said she wanted to make a call, that he'd get them to bring in a phone.

As the nurse plugged in the phone, Ruth thought of Alison. She would come, she knew it. But then she recalled her children, her slightly overweight children, frowning up at her the last time they'd met. They'd all just come from church and one of them was wearing a badge that read: *All God needs is all you have*. No, she would call her mother. At least when her mother judged her, Ruth could laugh it off.

Except, the second she heard her mum's voice, she welled up.

"Ruthie?" the woman said. Then again, "Ruthie, is that you?"

When Ruth could finally speak, it was to apologise. "I'm sorry, it's just . . ." She tried to swallow. "I've been having a hard time."

Expecting Veronica to say, '*You've* been having a hard time?', when she asked instead what was wrong, the tears came for real.

Her mother must have heard it as well, because she said, "What is it, Ruthie? Is it Fay? Please, I'm your mother."

Mother. The word arrested Ruth. She opened her mouth but didn't know where to begin.

"I wasn't always a *good* mother," Veronica was saying, "or a good wife for that matter, but then you know that." Ruth heard her mother's throat quiver. "But things were different back then, people had arrangements, you know? And your father was always busy. Not that I'm blaming him but I felt neglected." An almost wistful tone. "There was this door-to-door salesman. He came by selling these plaster Madonnas. Beautiful little statues painted blue and gold. I wasn't like you in those days," she murmured, her tone maudlin now so that Ruth realised she'd been drinking. "I was big-hipped, big-breasted. Men expect a belly on a woman like that. He wore a tie, a *hat*, for God's sake, that's how easy I was. We used to lie in bed all morning and then he'd go out selling. He said the afternoon heat made people lazy. They couldn't be bothered to slam the door in his face." A thin, winsome sound. "At the end of the week my suitcase was packed, my Sunday hat, my dancing shoes . . ." She laughed like she was breaking an egg. "And then I just came out with it. Even now I don't know why. Me being married didn't bother him but when I said I was pregnant, I didn't see him for dust."

Ruth had always known her father to be wronged but he'd never talked about it. Still, it had hung over the family like a fume. "What is this, Mum? Why are you telling me this now?"

Veronica sounded desperate. "Because I need you to forgive me before it's too late. Because I don't want you making the same mistakes. Or maybe not the same, Ruthie," she said, hearing the derision on Ruth's breath, "but similar. Shutting yourself off from Will. You've been like it since you were a little girl. You must forgive. Do you remember what you were like before Eric's disappearance?"

"Do you?" Ruth asked coldly.

"So beautiful," Veronica said, missing the note in Ruth's voice. "You believed in everything, even me."

Ruth imagined her sitting up in bed, her candyfloss hair, her rings in the lamplight, the television screen full of muted news, mud and sticks sliding off the edge of the world.

"Did you ever love him, Mum?"

"I do now, Ruthie," she said softly. "But now is too late. All I can say is, my father wasn't like yours."

"Well. I forgive you," Ruth said, her tone expressionless.

"What?" Her mother sounded startled.

"I forgive you. That's what you asked for, so I forgive you."

Except there was anything but forgiveness in her voice. Her mother must have heard it too because a moment later, she disconnected the line.

iv.

PERHAPS HART WAS BUSY, or perhaps he was giving her more rope. Either way, he didn't come all that weekend. Then on Sunday something happened that made her forget all about him.

The first she knew someone was in the room, she felt their breath on her face.

"I'm awake," she said, her eyes still closed.

"So's he," a woman said.

Ruth opened her eyes to see a nurse with doughy skin and fine hairs, so short her belt buckle rode just below her breasts. She was leaning very close to the bed.

"I was checking on him," she said. "I thought I saw his eyes move, so I leaned over and then, just as I got close, he starts screaming. Gave me the fright of me life."

So he's awake," Ruth said.

The odd thing was she knew straightaway the nurse meant Eric. The woman said he was in a lot of pain, that they'd had to sedate him.

"I have to see him," Ruth said, struggling to sit up.

It felt as if she were throwing aside blankets of earth. But at the same time, she felt like, if she could just see Eric, if she could just speak to him, then all the weight she'd been carrying for so long, her whole life almost, all of it would just fall away and she would finally be free.

But of course it wasn't that simple. As the morning waned, Ruth began to feel more and more fractious. She'd asked to see Needlemire but he didn't come. Nor did anyone else. Finally, out of frustration, she pulled the cord to call for someone. She'd dressed Fay and had drunk three cups of strong black tea. Like underground water, the answer to her prayers was so close. She could hear it rushing, dripping, splashing but she could not drink. Around midday, she pulled the cord again and this time a nurse came straightaway, a baby-faced young man who had obviously decided beforehand that he was going to be taken seriously. He began to say something about how it wouldn't be possible, that Dr Needlemire had expressly something-or-other. Ruth didn't hear a word. Everything was suddenly bathed in a vivid red light and she lunged for the door before feeling the nurse's hands on her shoulders. When she shoved him off, he went sprawling. Faster than he looked, he sprang up and took a hold of her and this time they both went tumbling. Ruth's gown had ridden up but as she tried to push it down, she felt the nurse pin her hands.

There was no acceleration. One moment she felt relatively calm and the next she was using her heels like fists. She was dimly aware that there were others in the room but she didn't remember hitting anyone in particular. All she knew was what Penny told her later, that apparently she'd kicked a female orderly so hard in the crotch the woman had to have stitches.

v.

———

NIGHT-TIME. A METAL TASTE in her mouth. She tried to swallow, saw a glass of water and went to reach for it but couldn't. Her hands had been secured. A shape got out of a chair and came closer. Someone, Hart, held the glass to her lips and she drank. That was when she realised Fay's cot was gone.

"Did you know," the man said, replacing the glass, "if a child's placed with a foster family, even if the mother is cleared of any wrongdoing, she's not given the child's whereabouts. It's in the child's best interests."

Ruth asked what he wanted.

"I can't make my mind up about you. So few skeletons. The abortion, of course, your husband none the wiser, I'm guessing. Why else use the family doctor? An alcoholic mother. Raised your brother almost single-handedly, absent father issues. But that's it. Until recently. What's got you rattled?"

She repeated her question.

"You got your phone call," he said. "I want my name."

"But you think it's me," she said. "Why else show him the photographs?"

The inspector held up his hands.

She asked again. "Why did Needlemire need to see them? You wanted him to know what I'm capable of, right?"

"Of what are you capable, Ruth?"

"Not that."

He asked why she was so sure. "Under extreme stress," he said, "human beings forget the most extraordinary things. One of my men spoke to your manager, a Mr Jenkins? He was very helpful. He said you've forgotten several things lately."

She said that was hardly the same.

"Put yourself in my shoes. Look what happened here yesterday, the strength, the violence. What would you think?"

She said it'd been raining. That he'd said it didn't rain until ten, so how could she have done it.

"You want to use the rain as an alibi?"

She breathed in through her nose, trying to control her tears. "Check my coat, Fay's car seat. I thought forensics could do anything these days."

He said it didn't matter, that she might have stepped out into the rain afterwards. She heard herself say that she didn't do it, that he couldn't do this. Take away her daughter, destroy her life.

He moved closer. His words smelt of smoke. "Well let me make you another offer," he said. "You give me that name and I'll let you see Fay again. And Eric. The name, Ruth," he insisted, "give me my name."

She told him he couldn't stop her seeing Eric, that she had rights but he said not if Eric needed protecting. "Just give me the name."

She felt weak, saw spots. The door opened and someone told the inspector to move back but Hart was standing over her, his silhouette asking the same question over and over again. "Who did it? Who? What if Eric's next? Think of your brother! Who *did* it?"

She reached for his hand but he pulled away.

"The name Ruth, give me my name!"

She struggled up, felt hands hold her back, drew at the air but with less and less success. She kept saying, "I think, I think, I think—"

"The name!" he shouted. "*Give me my name!*"

"Keep!" she said. She kept gasping at the air. "Dr Keep. He works at the hospital, he must have known the chef. It must be him. It *must* be him."

vi.

WITH CLIFFS AS HIGH as those at Dover a jumper breaks every bone in their body. This is what she was thinking when she woke. It took her a while to work out why but then it came to her. They'd filled her with so many drugs, she couldn't move. She just lay on the bed as if waiting to be scooped up and put in a body bag.

At the same time, everything was imbued with a hopeful intimacy. It took the longest time just to turn her head. The view outside her window was of other windows and she became convinced that people were sitting behind each one and that each person was staring out at the rows of windows opposite. At her window. It reminded her of camping with her brother, the pair of them staring up at the stars, her wondering how many other little brothers and sisters were on other planets, each staring up, each imagining them.

After lunch, Penny came to ask if Ruth felt strong enough for a visitor. Unable to imagine who it might be, Ruth sat on her bed, almost excited, almost nervous. Finally, a woman peered round the door and Penny nodded.

"I'll be right outside."

It was as if the woman's eyes came into the room first, like she was searching for traps. She was holding a small bouquet of lilies. Ruth noticed that her hands were shaking. The woman placed the flowers on the table and sat down in the chair under the television. She was dressed in stilettos and a navy suit. Her blouse was so old, the collar was yellow. Her face was dotted with piercings, her bleached hair pulled back into a ponytail. Her lipstick didn't quite match the shape of her lips. She was brisk with nerves.

"Shit," she said, "they've got you drugged up to the eyeballs."

Ruth asked if she knew the woman but the woman shook her head. "We've never met," she said. She told Ruth they did speak once but only on the phone. "I'm Jane." She looked down at herself. "I can't believe I'm wearing a suit."

She said her dad had bought it for her for an interview she never went to. "Thought I'd better wear it or they might not let me see you."

Everything she said trailed off. "I told them in reception that I worked with you." She laughed nervously. "Loose lips."

Ruth said she didn't remember working with a Jane.

Jane spoke haltingly. "No, we don't work together, I just told them that. But I did call you. It was on the morning your husband went away for, for that trip, the weekend you caught him with that woman. I was the one who called you."

Ruth said, "I don't remember . . ." But then, quite unexpectedly, "Oh, yes, I think . . ."

As if in a peaceful white flash, she recalled the phone call, the day waiting. The caller told her to write down an address. She'd wondered about it all morning. She had a hundred emails to write but in the middle of some dull sentence, she'd find herself standing up and walking down the stairs to the bureau where she'd left the note. Don't go till late afternoon, the woman had said, they won't be in till then. Afterwards . . . after she'd driven all the way to Peacehaven and then home again, she kept wondering why the front door had been open.

359

Jane said, "I shouldn't have done it. Will's a good man."

Ruth asked her how she knew him.

"I would have come earlier," Jane said, "but he had photographs. If my parole officer saw them, I'd never see my daughter again. But Dad and me are leaving, so . . ."

Ruth told Jane she had a daughter too, that they wouldn't let her see her.

"Because of me," Jane said.

When she stood up, Ruth told her not to go. It was nice having her there. Jane drew a hand through her hair, took out a cigarette, crushed the packet. "Nice?" she said. "I'm the reason you're in here. And *him*."

"Who?"

"Frank," Jane said. "He made me call you. He knew Will was going to meet that woman and he wanted to cause trouble. I didn't know Will at the time. I just thought he must've had it coming. When Frank made me post that package, I didn't know it was to you. Then again I was so high at the time, I wouldn't have cared if I did. He never touched the envelope. He just said it was on the side, asked me to post it. Afterwards he told me, if anyone checked, they'd only find my fingerprints on it. Then it clicked. I asked him if it was for you, the woman I'd phoned. I only knew you as Ruth then. Did Will ever mention my dad?"

Ruth said no. Jane said he was the caretaker at Hellerbys, that it was because of Will that she got the room at Frank's. "When I got out of Holloway, I went straight back on the brown. But then I had a close call with my P.O. and it scared me shitless. So I got away from London, old friends, old habits, moved in with Dad." She kept waving the unlit cigarette in the air. "But we weren't meant to cohabit, so Dad asked your husband if Frank was all right."

Jane looked down and then, as if only just realising she was still standing, plopped back into the chair. "A teacher." She kept saying it, as if she couldn't believe it. "A teacher. There's something about that word you trust. I suppose it goes back to being at school. They seem so stuffy and so fake until you realise maybe some of them did care after all. Frank was nothing like that. Still, I fell for it," she said, "hook, line and sinker."

She said Will was one of the few teachers her dad trusted. He took Will's word that Frank was all right. She said it took her a while to realise he'd got it wrong. "Me though," she said. "Frank had me pegged from the start."

She described a party just after she moved in, said Frank was passing the booze round and she just thought he was being generous. Her dad had paid a month up front but she had no job, no money. "Even so, things were looking up. I'd been clean three months, longest stretch in years, even when I was inside, so why not have a drink?"

Ruth was listening to Jane like it was a bedtime story. She could tell by then that it wasn't the happily-ever-after kind but it showed how knocked out she was that she continued to nod and smile.

Jane said she didn't take any dope that night. Not downstairs anyway. Later she found herself in Frank's room. She thought they were going to do something and she didn't mind if they did but then she saw they weren't alone. One of the younger guys was already there, sitting on the bed. She said it was so daft, she laughed herself all the way over there. Frank kept chatting to her and touching her, saying things to this boy and she caught on pretty quick what he wanted, what the boy had been promised, in fact.

Ruth glanced at the observation window. She could see the back of someone's head. Penny was talking to someone. Jane said almost until it happened, she thought it was going to be Frank. Then she thought it was going to be both. Finally she realised it was just the boy. She found out afterwards he was only fifteen. She says she kept laughing at him. And then Frank passed her the pipe. She tried to push it away but then it just didn't seem to matter.

"Hit me like a cloud. I can still see each flash as Frank took the photos. The boy's chicken chest, his eyes, the smoke. I even posed. The boy got spooked, jumped up, started pulling on his trousers, the whole time with Frank laughing."

She said, "So you see why I couldn't come and tell you what I knew. It was a mess. I got in so deep, so fast, I didn't know what day it was. And then I saw what'd happened in the papers and grew too scared to go back to the house. The accident, that man dead. I left all my stuff. I was doing cold turkey at a friend's but I only knew him through Frank and became obsessed that Frank was coming for me. I made the guy swear not to say anything but I didn't trust him. Then I thought I heard Frank downstairs and climbed out of a third storey window. Thank God it had big enough drainpipes. Don't know how I made it down or how I got over to Renton. Next thing, Dad was waking me on his sofa, a bucket in his hand."

Ruth's smile had returned. "It sounds like you've been through a lot," she said, "but I don't see what any of it has to do with me."

Jane came and knelt down by the bed. Only then did Ruth see, what she'd taken for piercings were actually holes. Jane's face was adorned, not with jewellery but with scabs. "Frank's got everything to do with you," she said. "You see what he did? Ripped every single one out. My dad tried to pull him off. That crazy fuck just smacked him across the room. That's why we're leaving. First though, Dad said I had to warn Mrs Zifla. Redemption, he said. Took him three days to find out where you were. In the end he asked someone at the school. Apparently the police have been there asking all sorts of questions. They told Mr Simmons you had some kind of breakdown."

Ruth glanced at the window again but Penny was out of sight. She said Frank was a friend of Will's, that Jane couldn't possibly mean the same man.

"It *is*," Jane said. "He's responsible for everything. There's something between Will and him. I'm sure he killed that man, the one in the papers. You're not safe, Ruth. Not you or your baby."

"But it *couldn't* be Frank," Ruth insisted. "I told them someone else."

Jane took hold of her arm. "I warned your husband," she said, "but he didn't listen and now look at him. It's up to you, Ruth. You've got to wake *up*."

Ruth heard the door go, then Penny's voice, sharper than she'd ever heard it.

"Please take your hand off the patient. Visiting time's over."

Behind her hovered the man to whom she'd been talking, a grey-faced security guard, his hand on a half-holstered stick.

Jane looked at Ruth. "He won't stop until it's finished."

Penny pulled her away but Jane's eyes were on Ruth.

"Do it for Will, Ruth," she said, her tone quietly desperate. "Do it for your little girl."

Afterwards, Penny asked Ruth what she'd meant. "Who won't stop?" Ruth just said she needed to see Needlemire.

On her own again, she lay down on the bed. The woman was mad. The thought made her giggle but then she pictured her scarred face and imagined Frank's fingers at her mouth and cheeks. It was impossible. He couldn't do such things. He was a teacher. And her laughter rose again until the whole bed started shaking.

3
—

PENNY HAD OBVIOUSLY told Needlemire about the incident because when he arrived, he looked even more uncomfortable than usual. He said he was waiting for the inspector. Ruth's dinner cocktail of shepherd's pie, apricot yoghurt and diazepam was just beginning to kick in but she could still tell there was something bothering him.

"I asked to see *you*," she said.

The doctor had his hands behind his back. Ruth could hear a pen clicking on and off. He said it was good to see her so lucid today. She shook her head, the satin in her lungs expanding each time she breathed. She asked when she could see her brother. Needlemire said it wasn't that simple, that there'd been several episodes. It was his fault, he'd ignored the signs.

"I thought you were suffering from stress. Now though, I think I was wrong." He turned to the window. She could see his eyes reflected in the glass, the bridge of his nose. "You asked me, the day of the murder, if I had any idea what you were going through. I'm sorry I was flippant, I was under a lot of stress. I should have listened. I want to allow you to see Eric but if something else happens, the hospital will be held responsible."

She said Hart wanted to take Fay away from her.

"He said that?" He sounded surprised.

"He told me I was going to lose her," she said.

Finally the doctor said, "What can I say? His job is to solve this case."

The door opened and Hart entered. He held the door ajar, his arm slightly arched. "Sorry I'm late," he said. "I was just picking up DCI Lawrence."

Bending a little to pass under his arm, a woman wearing a linen suit and silk blouse stepped into the room. Aided by stilettoes, she was taller than the inspector and equal in height to the doctor. She was carrying a large shoulder bag.

Hart introduced them. No one shook hands. This was not, Ruth thought calmly, that kind of party. Hart said DCI Lawrence was there because he wanted another female present. Lawrence smiled at this, a neat pursing of the lips.

"Witch hunt," Ruth murmured. Before Hart could speak, she added, "I asked to see Dr Needlemire. I wanted to ask him something. I didn't want to see you." By this point the unwiring in her head was becoming more and more difficult to ignore. "So unless this is official," she said, "I'd like you to go."

Hart gave his neatly arranged head a rueful shake. "Ah, Mrs Zifla, unfortunately it is. We have some questions. I'd like to record the answers."

She asked him if he wanted to accuse her of something.

"No, nothing so dramatic," he said. "But if we record your answers, we won't bother you with the same questions."

The grey-faced security guard brought in three chairs, arranged them near the bed and left. Hart and Lawrence sat down. Needlemire turned back to the window. Hart took out a large recording device and placed it on the empty chair.

Ruth told him Dr Keep had a similar device, though his was smaller. Hart just glanced at Lawrence before pressing record. He stated the date and time, named all those present, said why they were there and then asked Needlemire to begin by relating the event that occurred on the evening of January --^th, __.

Needlemire had his hands behind his back and Ruth thought the pen was digging into his palm. "I asked why Ruth hadn't contacted me since her husband's accident," he said, "even though I'd left her several messages. She replied that a Dr Keep was keeping her updated."

Hart asked if she'd said anything else that evening. Needlemire said she'd told him she'd handed in her notice but had subsequently forgotten doing so. Hart asked if she'd said why she'd done so. Needlemire said the reason she'd given was because she was afraid to fly. Hart asked her what she meant by that. Ruth spoke slowly.

"I am," she said, "or *was*, a system safety and internal evaluation program specialist for a major airline. Part of my job was to take flights and check, check that *safety* procedures were being followed." She slowed down, tried to think more carefully. "All I can say is, perhaps knowing the details of every major air disaster over the last fifty years may have taken its toll."

"More recently," Hart said, "yesterday, in fact, you had to be subdued by several members of staff and in the process, a number of people were hurt." He looked at his partner. "Before I proceed, I would like DCI Lawrence to state her findings. She's been working on the case in the capacity of lead profiler and has made some pertinent discoveries."

Unlike Needlemire, Lawrence was not embarrassed to speak. Legs crossed so that her skirt split at the knee, she opened her bag and drew out several papers. "I've become particularly interested in your relationship with your brother, Mrs Zifla. I've been trying to establish state of mind in the months leading up to the incident. You were not in regular contact with Eric Fairweather, is that correct?"

"He moved to Portsmouth," Ruth said. "After my dad died. He's been working on one of Dad's trawlers. He was out to sea much of the time—"

"But when he wasn't out fishing, there was rarely any contact?"

"He's very independent," Ruth said.

"So there was no friction. Your husband, for example. Eric approved of the match?"

"The two of them were friends, *are* friends. That's how we met. But why are we talking about Eric?"

Lawrence said, "It was just a routine line of enquiry, Mrs Zifla. But then we found this."

As she opened the bag, Ruth could see two books, one of which was the book of poems, she was sure of it. She was about to say something but then saw that Lawrence had taken out the other book, Frank's, she realised. From inside it, she drew a copy of a doodle Ruth barely recognised. In the last week or two, when sitting with Will or Eric, she liked to draw. But she never left her drawings lying around. As silly as they were, they were personal and she always brought them back to her room. Lawrence passed her the piece of paper and asked her to read what was written on it.

Ruth peered at the words which she had surrounded by dozens of curlicues as if from miles away. "I am not my brother's keeper."

Lawrence asked if she was religious. Ruth shook her head.

"Unlike your mother?" Lawrence said.

When Ruth said nothing, the woman said, "Me neither. I had to look it up. It's from the Bible." She read aloud from another piece of paper. "'*After Cain murdered Abel, God asked him where his brother was. Cain answered, 'I know not. Am I my brother's keeper?'*'"

Ruth could have denied it, of course. But she didn't. She wasn't so sozzled that she didn't understand the implication. However its intention was much more innocent. After the time Eric ran away, their mother had taken it on herself to remind Ruth of it every time she drank. That she'd lied, that she'd let her down, that she'd let him down. Ruth had responded in a variety of ways. She was repentant, rebellious, she even went through a stage of reading the Bible. She became particularly fascinated by the story Lawrence had just related. In it God favours one brother's offering over another's, causing the scorned man to murder his brother. When Ruth was thirteen or so, those words—Am I my brother's keeper?—had struck a chord. She'd felt like her mother had cursed her and that if she wanted to be free of that curse, choosing to see Eric as her responsibility was just that, *hers*. She was not her brother's keeper, she was his sentinel. But unfortunately, that fateful afternoon, all she had written was 'I am not my brother's keeper' before surrounding it with a border of thorny branches, her idea of a joke, Eric being anything but a sleeping beauty.

She pointed out that the book, *The Magus*, belonged to Frank Stine, a colleague of Will's. "Which is why," she said to Needlemire, "I wanted to talk to you."

"And yet the only prints on it are yours, Ruth," Hart said.

The little cocktail they'd given her prevented any excessive emotions but Ruth was still able to feel dismay. She asked them how they'd got her prints but realised it was a stupid question. Her anger collected in her a brief reasoning. "Are you implying that I want to kill my brother? That's insane. This man," she said, pointing at Needlemire, "suggested I sign a form giving him authority to switch off Eric's life support machine. I said no and now he's awake."

Lawrence glanced at Hart then at Ruth. "Mrs Zifla, nearly two years ago, just after your father's death, your brother took out a life insurance policy, yourself and your mother being the beneficiaries. Several days before Graham Bull's murder, someone accessed your home computer to check that policy. Now let us suppose you found paperwork pertaining to this policy *after* you told Dr Needlemire you did not want your brother's life support machine turned off. It would put your note in a very different light."

Ruth felt herself smiling, knew it was the wrong response but couldn't help it. "I'd give my life for my brother."

Lawrence continued. "You've been experiencing blackouts, memory loss, unusual behaviour patterns." She looked down, composing her words. "Now let us suppose you did decide to kill your brother. Along with everything else, it would have put an enormous strain on you. Your symptoms, I believe, were brought about by a massive shock causing posttraumatic stress. Perhaps you didn't know what you were doing. Or perhaps you did. Perhaps you asked someone to help you, someone who liked you, someone who agreed to meet you that night."

Hart asked if Graham and Ruth had argued that night. "About money, perhaps?"

"All of you, you're trying to suggest . . . but it's *you*," she said. "How can you think like that?"

"Ruth." Needlemire was blushing. "We didn't, not until you mentioned your suspect, a man you referred to again this afternoon, Dr Keep."

"Yes!" she said, clutching at this final straw. "What did you find out?"

"That's just it, Ruth," Hart said slowly, perhaps savouring the words, "there *is* no Dr Keep here at the hospital. There's no doctor of that name in the whole of Sussex. How can he be a suspect when he doesn't exist?"

With her chin pushed downwards, Ruth felt her breath whisper across her skin. "He was here. He's been here several times. But it doesn't matter, that's what I wanted to talk to you about." She looked at Needlemire. "The lady who was here today, Jane, she told me who really killed Graham. It was the man who brought the book, Frank Stine."

Hart frowned. "The teacher? We've already spoken to him, Ruth. He was very concerned about you. Beyond your recent friendship, however, we found nothing. Certainly nothing to explain such a crime."

"Ask her, ask Jane," she said, desperately. "She told me. He hurt her and he's coming for my baby." She screwed up her fists. "Just fucking *ask* her."

The inspector glanced at Needlemire who said, "The woman who visited you today told reception her name was *Joan*. That she was a

368

work colleague of yours." He paused. "None of this is helping, Ruth. You tell us you think this Dr Keep killed Graham but the police can't find him. Now you're saying it's someone else."

"Then why not arrest me?" she said. "You seem to have it all worked out."

"Because we'd like to hear it from you," Hart said. "Give you the chance to do the right thing, Ruth, the sensible thing."

After they left, Ruth lay on her bed facing the door, shunning the twilight. All she could think about were corroded bolts, out-of-date seals, cracked fuselages.

When Penny came an hour later, she saw the lilies Jane had brought and asked if Ruth would like to arrange them. She fetched a plastic vase and water and only sat down when Ruth uncurled from her bed and knelt on the floor. The flowers were wrapped in two layers of cellophane and when the lilies finally sprang open, she discovered a knife amid the stems. She had her back to the nurse and it was only this that kept her discovery unnoticed. She felt her gown slide across her leg and pushed the knife into the hem.

That night, she couldn't sleep. She thought about the evening when Frank had come into the kitchen to help her make tea. The key had been in the backdoor as usual. But a few days later, when she went to hang out the washing, the key was gone. Then a few days after that, she found it buried in a pot of money on the kitchen windowsill.

As for the life insurance, she had no idea about any policy and had accessed nothing of the sort on the computer. But someone had. She imagined Frank letting himself into the house. She imagined him standing over Fay's cot. Suddenly the need to escape felt as sharp as the blade Jane had given her, the one that now lay under her mattress. All she knew was that she needed to find Fay and disappear. But first she needed clarity.

THE NEXT MORNING, she woke to the sound of a voice talking about snow. She was facing the window and saw white flakes pouring between the buildings so that sound and image were at once harmonious and disturbing. Had she really fallen asleep with the television on? She rolled over and switched it off, only to see a note on her pillow. Typed on a card similar to the kind people use to write out speeches, it read:

> *If he doesn't wake up*
> *soon, he never will.*
> *First you murder Eli,*
> *then you allow this?*

It was Frank, she was sure of it. But how had he gotten into her room? She pictured him looming over her sleeping form and shuddered. And how did he know about the abortion, or, better still, the name she'd given her unborn child? He and Keep were working together, it was all she could think. They may have approached from different directions but they'd done so with the same goal. To drive her mad. But they'd not reckoned on one thing. Fay. She was Ruth's light and all else lay in shadow. They were being hunted and the prey need not ask why, it need only flee. She imagined showing the note to Hart but knew Lawrence would only put her usual spin on it. She also knew that they would find only her fingerprints on the card. The last act of a desperate woman.

She remembered Frank saying he'd checked Keep's credentials— he'd been eager to verify them, in fact. Now she knew why. They were working together, it was the only conclusion. As for Hart, she also knew why he'd not yet arrested her. He needed a confession. For all his clever talk, his allegations were full of holes. She went over and over that night. Fay crying. Rain. That flash of blue. Why hadn't she asked Jane to go to the police?

It snowed all day. The following morning, cars, hedges, bushes, all had been turned into strange-looking cakes. Ruth peered through the glass. She could see a rectangular strip beyond the two buildings, cars scarred where young hands had scooped up snowballs.

At midday, a new nurse came. Gladys. She didn't introduce herself but every time she leaned over Ruth, her nametag loomed at her. Gladys watched her eat a croissant, stood over her while she swallowed her pills, examined her mouth.

Next came Needlemire. He didn't mention Hart directly but his words suggested that he disagreed with the man's methods. He said Ruth was in an unenviable position.

"You're not under arrest but neither are you free to go. There's sufficient evidence to suggest you may have had something to do with Graham's murder and also that you're . . . unstable. That's why I've agreed to keep you here under observation. Potentially, you're a risk to both yourself and Fay. But I see the way you look at her. And I hear your love for your brother when you talk about him. In my opinion it would do you good to see him. But, Ruth, if there is another incident, it'll my head on the chopping block."

Snowlight carved Eric's room into crooked lines. Ruth had been escorted by two nurses this time. One sat by the window, the second looked in from the corridor. Eric's eyes were open, his head at an odd angle so that it looked as if he were looking up and to the right. His smile was like a kick to the heart. Ruth crossed the room, hugged him, felt him nodding at her shoulder. He was paralysed from the chest down. He could move his head and arms but struggled to use his fingers. When she took his hand, he didn't return the grip.

Needlemire had said that Ruth needed to be gentle with him, that he could talk but was very weak. She pulled a chair up to the bed, sat there staring at Eric's face, the scar along his jaw, the way the bandages still hooded his left eye and told herself that whatever she did, she mustn't cry.

Normally, the hospital staff removed any personal effects but for some reason Eric was wearing his gold watch. Perhaps he had asked for it. He moved his hand over, slid it under his wrist, lifted it up.

"My watch," he said slowly. Hooded eyes stared at her from out of a shattered face. "Broken." His jaw rippled, stirring the scar there. "Like me."

She breathed in, trying to catch some calmer air. "You're not broken," she said finally.

"I'm *paralysed*. You don't get much . . ." He closed his eyes, took several slow breaths, his chest rising and falling as he did so.

"Are you comfortable, at least?"

When he nodded, she asked if he needed anything. He shook his head.

"Do you know what happened?" she said finally.

"Do I know what happened?" He gave a soft, derisive snort. "I used to think I knew everything but I know nothing." He looked at her. "It wasn't me, you know?" Tears filled his eyes and she felt herself well up in kind.

"I mean, do you know about . . ?"

He tutted, shook his head. "An inspector came. He told me about Will's parents. About you. That a man was murdered . . . But I can't help you," he said. "You need Will."

She looked at the nurse. "What do you mean?"

"You need him to return. He is . . . elsewhere. I was with him. I thought, I thought it was all me." He shook his head. "It doesn't matter what I thought. But I think maybe I can return. I think I can bring Will home. Now that I know his parents are dead, everything makes sense."

Ruth stared at her brother, convinced in that moment that he'd returned in body but not in mind. "What are you talking about?"

Eric breathed in, closed his eyes, opened them again. "You were there too. You could fly. My little Rook could fly."

She shook her head. "Did they tell you that? That I'm afraid to fly?"

He went to speak, swallowed, then said, "I am lost. Will too. Is it so mad that we found each other elsewhere?"

She felt hot, heavy tears break across her face. "Don't do this. Please, Eric."

"I can bring Will home but I've got to go back." He blinked and swallowed at the same time. "Will's looking for his parents. He doesn't know they're dead."

"And did you tell him?" she said, laughing.

"I didn't know," he said. He raised his head slightly as if to stress the importance of his next words. "Will's looking for a poem. He has the first few verses."

Ruth felt her knees give and sank into the chair. She'd been reading Will the poem and now Eric was telling her he'd found it. "How many?" she said quickly. "How many verses?"

"Four," he said, after a moment's thought.

She tasted bitterness. "Wrong, I've read *five*. Why are you doing this, Eric? Who told you I was reading to him?"

Hearing her tone, the nurse said, "She's not been well, Mr Fairweather."

He didn't look at her. "The inspector was asking about you." He tried to squeeze Ruth's hand. "You're in trouble. I'm broken. But if I bring Will home, he can help."

She was in a place so bright, everything was possible and therefore impossible. A place where no decision could be made, no path chosen, a place, for her at least, of madness. For that reason, for herself, but more importantly, for Fay, she could not follow where Eric was trying to lead her, despite a burning desire to do so.

She leaned in and hissed, "I can't do this. They're coming for me, *he's* coming for me. For *all* of us."

Eric made a great effort. "When I woke in that world, I thought it was delusion. I didn't want to believe the evidence of my own eyes. Then," he said, "I thought it was all me, all mine. *That* was my delusion. But still it is a place of great wonders. And it is Will's. Of his making. But even when I realised it, I knew there was something missing, some calculation . . . but I think I know what it is now."

"You're mad." Ruth held out a hand as if to ward off evil spirits. "No more."

But he was not to be deterred. "He met a chef, a man called Gribble." He looked at her, a grave light in his eyes. "He said he found him with his heart torn out. Just like . . ."

"Enough!" Ruth stood up but Eric carried on.

"I must return. And Ruth, you must carry on reading the poem. He hears you when you read to him. He's out there somewhere but he's searching for a way back."

"And what happens when he finds out his parents are dead?"

Eric shrugged. "I'll be with him. Just keep reading. You are his north. I'll be his rudder. We can bring him home, Ruth, I promise."

iii.

ALL HER LIFE, RUTH had been waiting for Eric to ask her for something. Now he finally had, she couldn't do it. Lawrence had the book. She tried to recall the next verse but it was useless. Had they not taken her phone, she could have looked it up but both Hart and Needlemire seemed determined to keep her in the dark.

And then, barely a day later, the doctor came to tell her that Eric had gone again.

"He had some kind of seizure," he said. "He's stable, which is something, but unresponsive."

Ruth closed her eyes. She felt unbearably light. Thinner than air. At the same time she saw Eric's words turning like a neon sign inside her head: *I must return. I must return.*

She imagined looking up some old school friend and disappearing. Yet the idea of leaving Will behind filled her with despair. Frank's note was very clear. If Will didn't wake up, he was going to kill him. The man wanted her to do something stupid, to start raving to Hart again, to try sleeping by Will's bed. But she wouldn't be pushed around, not by any of them. She would try and retrieve the book and read Will the poem. But ultimately, she had to think of Fay.

In order to help Fay, though, Ruth first had to get her head straight, which meant getting off the medication. Gladys though didn't miss a trick. The only way Ruth could get rid of the pills was to throw up after she'd eaten.

Her other problem was finding out where they were keeping Fay. They brought her to Ruth every day but Ruth wasn't allowed to visit her or leave her room without an escort. Still, she suspected they were keeping Fay on the postnatal ward, which was on the second floor. This, she thought, was at the end of the corridor parallel to the one below her own but she wasn't sure. Even if she were right, Fay might be elsewhere. Only when Ruth knew where Fay was could she work out an escape plan.

Everything relied on Penny. The woman still came to see her almost daily. Each time was like an oasis. She would bring a pack of cards and they would play for hours, or just watch television together, one or both of them commenting on some new quirk they'd noticed about Fay, the way she rocked back and forth in her highchair, or went cross-eyed when presented with a spoonful of food.

Normally Ruth awaited the nurse's visit with an excited impatience but that day, she felt only anxious. Penny noticed it straightaway. She drew the chair to the bed and took hold of Ruth's hands, asked her how she was. Ruth didn't know where to begin. The nurse was wearing a light, floral perfume, pale pink lipstick and nail varnish. Ruth was suddenly aware of her own bitten, unpainted nails.

She asked if Penny had any children.

The woman hesitated. "One day," she said. "I hope."

Ruth's smile made her aware of her tears. "They're trying to take Fay." When Penny asked who, she said, "The hospital, the police."

"They can't."

"They think I killed someone."

Ruth saw the truth in Penny's eyes. She already knew. Ruth had guessed as much. Penny had been sent to spy on her but ironically she was the only person Ruth felt she could trust. Occasionally she saw something in her face, a look she understood. She had known loss. She was a sister in her feelings, Ruth was certain of it.

"I know who did it," Ruth said. "They won't listen but—" She squeezed Penny's hands—"he's *dan*gerous."

375

"Is this the man your visitor was talking about?"

Ruth nodded. She told Penny she needed her to do something. "I need to know where they're keeping Fay."

Penny's innocence almost undid Ruth but she knew better than to tell the truth. "I just need to know where she is when she's not with me. I want to imagine her room. You can understand that, can't you? I just want to know where they're keeping her."

Penny had no time to respond. The door opened and another nurse came in, carrying Fay. Looking at her was like looking at the sun. Ruth carried her to the window, kissed her, whispered to her.

When the nurse announced that it was time to take Fay back, Penny said she didn't mind doing it. At the door, she turned and said, "I know how hard this must be for you."

Ruth tried to smile but her muscles betrayed her. "It's funny," she said but couldn't think what.

iv.
—

THE NEXT MORNING, she woke to more snow. Feeling something in her hand, she looked down. It was Penny's note. The previous afternoon she'd been eating lasagne and rhubarb custard and had just decided to eat only half of it and ask if she could save the rest for later when Penny came in. Gladys was sitting in the corner, doing her impression of a stonefish. After using the toilet, Ruth re-entered the room to find the two nurses sharing an uncomfortable silence. Penny said Fay had gained weight. She held out her hand and told Ruth she'd come back soon. Ruth felt the paper in Penny's palm and told herself not to look down.

Penny squeezed her hand. "Please don't thank me."

That evening, Gladys took Ruth to visit the Will and Eric. Her brother's bed hummed, turning him her way as if he had something to tell her. From Will's room, she stared out at a world of orange shapes and blue shadows. The window was ajar and she was grateful for the cold. Between the radiator and the orange reflections, the room felt like an oven.

Later, in bed, she lay there holding the knife. It was little bigger than a potato peeler but it was still comforting. With Eric gone again it was all she had against the howling.

In the morning she turned on the television to hear a newsreader speaking so seriously, she thought there'd been another terrorist attack. Apparently it was February's worst snowfall since records began.

Needlemire came at nine and made a fuss over her weight but she was in no mood to humour him. She asked about Hart. The man's absence was making her almost as nervous as the thought of his return. Needlemire rubbed his cheek and then turned his face as if to hide his words. Finally he told her that the enquiry had come under scrutiny.

When he left, Ruth studied the map Penny had drawn for her. She'd guessed correctly, Fay was being kept in the postnatal ward on the floor below hers but she'd been wrong about which side of the hospital it was situated. It was actually in the corridor directly below. The main lifts and stairs were situated at the centre of the building, meaning she would have to go along the corridor, down to the second floor, walk past several more wards, somehow get past the nurse's station, find Fay's cot and then retrace her steps back to the lifts before going downstairs. She had a good idea of the hospital's layout and its various exits. Once she reached the ground floor, she knew of two choices. Beyond that she could only imagine her flight. And what she would be leaving behind.

That evening the hospital suffered a power cut. On TV a news anchor was in the middle of saying they'd closed several airports when the screen winked off and all the lights went out. Ruth jumped up and tried the door. It was still locked. She banged on the window, saw herself from the other side, a wild-haired woman trapped in a box. She felt like her chance had come and gone, that she hadn't been in the right place at the right time. Her door was obviously powered by some kind of back-up unit so that sectioned patients couldn't escape during blackouts but had she been visiting Will or Eric, she might have been able to flee.

She lay in bed, staring out of the window, her terrors both weighty and insubstantial. She had to tell them. But if she involved Hart or Needlemire they'd think her mad and take Fay. And if she confronted Frank, he'd kill her. Either way, she'd fail to protect Fay. The radiator was belting hot. She imagined the hospital's heating system groaning away, while outside snow surmounted everything. They were trying to bury her too but she refused to lie still. She paced her room, walked everywhere quickly. She even did press-ups. But throwing up the pills had begun to take its toll. She was losing weight. Sometimes she felt faint. But at least she was clearer headed.

Whenever a nurse took her to see Will, Ruth tried to take in more of her surroundings. Emergency exits, fire hydrants, storage cupboards. One evening, she was drawn to a series of prints donated by someone or other and to one in particular, a scene of a city covered in snow. Through night-time air, some sort of light illuminated shops and houses.

That was the same evening she found the book. While Penny waiting outside, Ruth stepped into Will's room, only to be stopped by a strange feeling. Expectation. Like someone or something was waiting for her. She looked around but everything seemed normal. The window ajar, curtains gently billowing, blank-faced machines, their heads bowed, Will on the bed, his arms resting by his side.

Why she decided to pray, she couldn't say. She didn't even know she was going to do it until she'd removed her paper slippers and knelt down. She hadn't prayed since she was a teenager, when she'd so desperately hoped to get an answer. Now she didn't expect anything so obvious. Yet an answer is exactly what she got.

"Holy Mary," she said, clasping her hands and closing her eyes, "Mother of God, pray for us sinners now and at the hour of death."

When she was done, she felt at peace. Sitting back, she opened her eyes, focussed on the edge of Will's bed. Yet it was the shadowy space below it that caught her attention, its darkness veined by wires. Wires that used to be taped to the carpet. Wires that weren't taped anymore. Peering closer, she saw that someone had pulled them loose and shoved something underneath. A package wrapped in black plastic. Surely not? Yet it was the right shape and size. Reaching down, she pulled the package loose and unwrapped it to reveal a dark red cover. Her voice rang with disbelief.

"Someone put it under the wires. Who put it under the wires?"

She opened the book and found the page, her shoulders already shaking. "Darkling I listen . . ." Just those first few words were enough to cause tears to spring into her eyes. Swallowing them, she tried again. ". . . and for many a time I have been half in love with easeful death, called him soft names in many a rhyme, to take into the air my quiet breath . . ."

v.

_____

THE IDEA THAT SOMEONE, not Lawrence, obviously, but someone close to her, had retrieved the book and hidden it in Will's room, filled Ruth with a strange calm. How they knew it was important to her was of no consequence. Nor the fact that it meant that whoever it was, was spying on her. The next verse was all that mattered.

It was a long night. The feel of the mattress, the heat from her radiator, the ivory lines spilling in through her window, the tapping, humming, clanking sounds that came and went but never really stopped, the feel of her skin, which she hadn't bathed in weeks, just those awful, windowless showers and, above all, Fay's absence, stuffed her with so many sensations, she felt like a pincushion. Not to mention the fact that every time she turned on her side, the book kept pressing against her hip (the only place she could think to hide it being inside her pyjama trousers). It was a long night.

Nor did the next day bring good news. When a nurse came to take her to see Will, it wasn't Penny, it was Gladys. As graceful as an anvil, the nurse marched into her room, clattered her evening meal onto her bed tray and answered Ruth's tentative question as if talking to patients caused the woman actual, physical pain: apparently Penny couldn't make it in due to the snow.

The two made their way down to Will's room in complete silence. Ruth knew Gladys was going to follow her into the room but was still disappointed when it happened. She considered asking the nurse to wait in the corridor but knew that this was foolish. She hadn't yet plucked up the courage to tell Will she was leaving—she'd decided to do it today—but with Gladys there, she couldn't even imagine reading him the poem. But then came a minor miracle. Just as Ruth sat down in her usual chair, there was a knock at the door and a second nurse stuck her head in.

"Have you heard?" she said.

Gladys stepped out to talk to her.

As the door closed, Ruth surveyed the room. It was as if she and Will had agreed to do something intimate and she wanted everything to be just right. She straightened the newspaper she'd been reading to Will just yesterday, then smoothed down the sheet around his body. She knew he would have told her to take Fay and go. But as it was, only she could make that decision. A part of her believed her chance had already come and gone. During and after the blackout, panic had reigned. It might have been possible to slip in and out of Fay's ward then but not now. In truth, she almost hoped she was right, that her chances had evaporated. Then the decision would not be hers to make.

She touched Will's face, told him she was leaving, raised both her hands to her mouth, then said the words again as if she couldn't believe them. "I don't want to but I have to."

Only the book brought her back. She was here to read the next verse and this thought diluted her fear. Wiping her face, she sat back and looked at the shadows beneath Will's eyes, the stubble on his cheeks, watched the rise and fall of his chest and wondered if he really was in there somewhere, listening.

"Thou wast not born for death, immortal Bird."

She smoothed down the page, took a long, deep breath.

"No hungry generations tread thee down, the voice I hear this passing night was heard in ancient days by emperor and clown." She looked up, hoping to see some sort of change in Will's expression and that was when it happened.

"Perhaps the self-same song," she read, "that found a path through the sad heart of Ruth . . ."

Her chin trembled. The few times she'd scanned the poem, she hadn't seen her name. It was strange. But not as strange as what occurred next. As if speaking her own name had conjured some spell, she heard Will breathe in more deeply than usual, the kind of breath that foreshadows a yawn but instead of yawning, he spoke.

As she leaned forwards, she realised it was a name, *her* name: "Ruuuth . . ."

She felt breathless. "My God, he said my name." She said it again, then shouted it: "He *spoke*, he *spoke*! Quick, get a doctor!"

Only the darkness answered: "Too late, I'm already here."

Afternoon had turned to evening so that with the light off, all Ruth could see of the man standing beside the brightly lit observation window was a patch of sparsely-haired skin and a glint of glasses.

"No you're *not*," she said vehemently. "They searched the county records. There are no doctors registered under your name."

"Who told you that?" Keep asked calmly. When Ruth told him, he laughed. "The men I warned you about?"

"You were trying to make me paranoid," she said.

"And you weren't already? What I said before still stands. I'm your only friend in this whole business."

Ruth saw a hint of teeth as he pushed himself away from the wall. "What's it to be, Ruthie, fight or flight? A little bird tells me you're quite feisty when you want to be but, of course, flights are your real speciality, aren't they? Or at least they used to be. But I'd like you to know, there's no need to run. What's in your little black box," he said, "stays between you and me."

"You and me and Frank," she hissed. "You two have been playing games with me all along."

The doctor gave an amused frowned. "No, Rook," he said, "you're the one who likes playing games."

"My name is *Ruth*," she said.

Another step and the man's glasses became orange moons. "Perhaps your real fear is that you killed the chef. That for all your accusations, it was you all along. That Hart's right."

"He's not," she said. "I couldn't." The anger coursing through her made her feel faint. She tried to calm herself. "I just want to understand."

"That's not true either. Your greatest desire is to escape. But if you do, what will happen to him?"

Seeing his hand on Will's shoulder, Ruth felt sick. "I know what you're doing. You're trying to drive me mad. You want to take away my baby. This is some kind of sick game. But I won't let you," she said. "I won't *let* you."

Keep's whisper came from right behind her. "And your game is to play the little drowned girl."

She thrashed about her, found no purchase. All the same, she fought on, felt the bed thump against her side. Finding a curtain in her hand, she pulled it. The pole came away from the wall. When she felt hands seize her, she turned sharply, whipping the pole in a confusion of drapes, catching her attacker on the side of the head. She didn't see the doctor hit the floor but she heard it. When his hand seized her ankle, she hit downwards, jerking the pole towards her feet until his grip relented.

Her chest heaving, she stared at the space between the bed and the wall, pulled the curtains aside to see, not Dr Keep, but Gladys. She dropped to her knees, stared at what she'd done. However she'd imagined her escape, it had not been like this. She knew what would happen when she was found. She'd never see Fay again.

She took hold of Will, breathed her words right into his face. "You weren't there, they cut me open, they took her out of me. But I'm not letting them keep her." But even though he'd spoken her name, he remained unresponsive.

The observation window blazed with light. Knowing she had no choice, she leaned forwards, kissed Will and fled into the brightness.

Chapter 2.

The House of Pain

1

SLOW FOOTSTEPS, a hulking shape that only compacted the darkness. Finally, Enzo stepped into the cabin, doused the candle and, with a great gentleness, pulled Liam to his feet.

Up on deck, sea wind ruffled their hair. The shark hung from the lanyard, its long, meaty flank like a grey wall, its serrated mouth agape, its eyes black. Liam tried to push it and then struck out, first with his hands and then his fists. Enzo pushed at him, encouraging him towards the prow.

Fredrickson was watching the waves and spoke without turning, his voice tempered by genuine regret. "I'm sorry about your friend."

The sea was choppy, waves smacking against the hull like hungry lips. Liam leaned over the bowsprit, felt his stomach clench but nothing came up. He saw that his knuckles were bleeding. Half a mile away, bristling in the late morning light, a curved wall rose out of the water.

"Man's final stronghold," the captain said. "The Island of Hats. Joan hated the place. If it wasn't for her father, she'd never have returned. She believed the house couldn't educate those who didn't want it."

Liam shook his head dully. "What house?"

Fredrickson looked at him, his eyes glinting in the shadow of his cap. "Your father's. The House of Pain."

The man's words made Liam shiver. Something terrible awaited him there, he was sure of it. He'd wondered why the creature had not found him sooner. Now he knew. It was held on a leash. Its request was absurd. How could he dream of a mate? Even if he wanted to, the equipment the Keeper had used to bring Ma'kin to life lay hundreds of miles away, secreted in the cavern below the House of Visions. As for the Keeper himself, the man obviously needed Liam for something else. But what? He dreaded to find out. Without Erin, he felt even more exposed. He hadn't entirely trusted the man but there had been an authenticity about him that commanded loyalty.

Ironically, his only hope lay with Ma'kin. His first instinct had been right. It could be controlled by those who knew its name. Did that mean then he could have controlled it from the very start? Yet even as he thought this, he felt a great dread. It was a warning, this feeling, a premonition that left him shaking. Everything in him leaned away from this knowledge, yet he knew not why. It was as if his foot were poised above his own grave. He knew the creature's name, he had called it and it had obeyed. If all he had to do was wait for the opportune moment, surely that was cause for celebration? He'd mentioned Ma'kin's name to no one, uncertain as he had been in the moment he'd heard it. The knowledge then was his and his alone.

His first instinct was to find Rook and get her off the island. He wondered if his father might help him in this regard. If the man had established an important house here, he might be able to facilitate their escape. At the same time, the idea of finally meeting his father filled him with a lurching, hollow sensation, as if his tongue had just discovered a missing tooth. As for the captain, his remark suggested he knew more than previously mentioned. Erin's death had perhaps prompted him to reveal his hand.

As the island grew, so did Liam's feelings of oppression. The outer wall, a curved, tower-topped edifice, seemed to grow steadily taller until it was looming over the boat, which crawled into its shadow as might a beetle, the sound of its engine clapping back at them with a frail, nervous energy. Directly ahead lay a pair of gates, heralding a tunnel wide enough and tall enough to accommodate a boat twice the Sixer's size. Up in the deckhouse, Perry adjusted the throttle and the boat puttered into the opening, the noise from its engine suddenly magnified by the arch and the walls either side.

As the boat crept through the water, the light from the entranceway shrank, so that a cold, wet darkness soon pressed from all sides, its dominion made complete when the gates, which had been slowly closing, finally clanged to. Liam immediately felt his senses assailed, by the intensification of sound, the slop of water, by the sputter of the boat and the heady stench of diesel.

A few minutes later, Perry threw on the masthead light and reversed the engine, causing the boat to shudder to a halt, after which Liam saw Wires and Enzo, no more than silhouettes in the inky air, run along the boat's portside gunnel and jump onto a ledge. Reaching a deep recess, wherein glinted an enormous wheel, the two men slotted handles into the wheel's inner arch and began to heave at them until finally it cranked into action, its progress accompanied by a hungry rushing sound and a sudden lurching that caused Liam's knees to buckle. The water began to drain from beneath the boat. Meanwhile, Wires and Enzo jumped onto the poop deck, while Perry kept the boat steady with short bursts from the engine. As the craft descended, Liam wondered where they were going. Before long though, he saw a second pair of gates and realised the trick. They were being lowered to a level compatible with whatever lay inside the wall.

The captain put on his hat and drew another from inside his coat. "You'll be needin' this," he said. "It's not called the Island of Hats for nothing."

As light grew across the bow, a deep groaning resounded around them and then the gates began to open, churning the water into enormous swirls. Liam saw Fredrickson was holding a woollen hat and pulled it on.

"I once worked under a Captain Randel, a one-eyed bastard too fond of giving orders. Orders to be followed come hell or high water, he liked to say." The captain gazed coolly at his audience. "Those words ring true every time I see this place, only, I hear them the other way round, for here the second came first and the first second."

The sight beyond the gates was as extraordinary as it was bleak. The boat sat on the edge of a choppy circle of water, its surface interrupted by dozens of towers, all of them rising directly out of the sea and all of them full of holes. The rude walkways strung between them were teeming with people, their behatted heads bowed, their backs loaded with bundles, while below, ferries, junks, barges and rough-hewn gondolas, darted across the water, often passing so close to each other, it was a wonder they didn't collide. From at least a dozen windows, Liam could see people emptying buckets, unmindful of who might be below, while above all, concrete chimneys spumed clouds of smoke into the sky. Stringing all the buildings together were wire cords, their looped lines dangling with tin cans. Some kind of messenger service, Liam assumed.

"Like a bear trap," Fredrickson said, indicating the huge, circular wall, "ready to snap at the foot of God."

Liam was mesmerised. He was reminded of Karrin's dream of ants. Brown ants scurrying over a grey world. Here then was the detritus of man's greatness, the greatness the Keeper so desperately wanted to resurrect. He did not know which looked more broken, the ruin of what had once been civilised or the people picking their way through it.

"The higher they built them, the harder they fell," Fredrickson said grimly. "You'll realise by now, she's not really an island, not anymore. One story goes that the Mayor of Hats—or the 'Man-Hat-On' as his unofficial title went—was visited by a holy messenger, an angel who told him that the storm to end all storms was comin'. The more cynical prefer phrases like 'prior knowledge' to 'divine intervention' but, whichever, the Mayor responded by orderin' a wall to be built around the heart of the city, a great mass of concrete, painted a brilliant green."

Fredrickson leaned against the gunnel. "The only ways into the Emerald City, as it was dubbed, lay north and south, tunnels plugged at both ends by huge gates, predecessors of the canal system you've just witnessed, both guarded by men and dogs. When the waters rose, the city was under curfew but there were still those roamin' the streets, stowaways who'd ridden into the city coated in grease to avoid the dogs, holdin' on like limpets beneath station wagons or smuggled in for a fee. People who believed the wall was the only thing that could save them. People who were wrong.

"Most of them had no relatives livin' in the institutions that dominated the heart of the city, businesses that granted amnesty to many of their workers' families but turned away others, claimin' they had no space. So the few who got in here before the flood were forced to find other places to hide. Boarded-up shops, doorways, sewers, tunnels, abandoned vehicles. In the week before the deluge there were more people killed by trains in the underground than in its entire history. But they weren't suicides, they were refugees.

"However, it didn't really matter. Those who weren't killed underground, or crushed under the vehicles they rode beneath, or hunted down by the home-guard and their dogs, were culled in their thousands the first day of the flood."

The captain indicated the water behind them. "The ocean became a mountain range quarter of a mile high. When it struck, the wall acted more like a tomb than a shield. The water gutted much of the outer structure, turnin' this here into a whirlpool of brick and glass, devastatin' many of the buildin's in the interior.

"Just before The Last War, two of the city's most important buildin's were razed to the ground. When they were replaced, it was with one, apparently indestructible tower. The buildin' we're about to visit was constructed under guidelines that ensured it could withstand any impact."

Fredrickson, who'd rarely spoken more than a few words to Liam, was obviously in a sentimental mood that afternoon, for he continued with his history lesson all the way to their destination.

"People say God made the world a smaller place but for we fisherfolk, it became bigger. But we weren't the only ones whose horizons were expanded. Look up."

By now the boat was travelling between two beheaded structures still many storeys high. Above them, half-a-dozen shapes moved through an azure sky. Liam knew immediately they were not birds. They turned in dips and curves, directed, not by wings but by the inclination of a head or the twist of a hand.

"Birdmen," he said, imagining Rook among them.

"They prefer *Homo evolo*," Fredrickson said with a smile. "They're somethin' to look at, aren't they? There was a time I envied them their freedom but now there's another in the playground, I'm not so sure." He leant on the bowsprit, his face turned towards Liam's. "The seraphim you're so afraid of?"

Liam shook his head. "That's not what it is."

The captain squinted, crinkling the scar across his eye. "Perhaps. But perception's everythin'. You were certainly ravin' about it durin' your sleep. And," he said carefully, "about someone you called the Keeper . . ."

Liam was surprised. "I spoke of him?"

"The two are connected?"

Liam shrugged. "The Keeper both created and controls the creature. I believe he wants others to think it's an angel."

"Why?"

The boat was sweeping under a series of low walkways and Liam looked up as he spoke. "As you said, perception is everything. On T'heel the creature killed many people. I think that was the Keeper's intention." He neglected to mention his theory that he was still bait. "What do the *Homo evolo* want?"

"The same as anyone. To live. But all will become clear when we reach the House of Pain. You should know," the captain said, "the buildin' that houses it is surrounded by six others, known, since the flood, as the screamin' towers. Many of those inside took a long time to die. And though the central tower was protected, both because of its design and its position, the ghost stories that sprang up almost overnight ensured that it remained uninhabited. The *Homo evolo* were not so easily deterred. They began to nest there within weeks of the flood."

"Nest?"

"A figure of speech," Fredrickson said with a smile. "For all intents and purposes they look like you and me."

"I know," Liam said, deciding to divulge some of his own knowledge. "Erin's sister is one of them."

"Now why doesn't that surprise me?" the captain said. "A strange one, your friend. But heart in the right place."

Unable to trust himself on the subject, Liam asked where the captain was when the flood came.

"At sea. Even when we dock, I sleep on the Sixer. Did you know animals sense natural disasters before they occur? Fish are no different. They knew a change was comin'. So we knew too. Before the flood, most men had lost their appetite for instinct but fisherfolk are different. In that way we're closer to God."

"How do you know my father?"

"We started tradin' just after he set up the school."

Fredrickson smiled at Liam's expression. "Did I not mention that the House of Pain is a school? Aptly named, I believe. After I left Randel and acquired the Sixer, your father introduced me to a number of my original crew, includin' Joan."

"And how do you know I'm his son?"

"Because you used to live here. We never spoke but I saw you a few times. Besides, it's in your eyes."

"But why didn't you say anything after we boarded?"

The man glanced at him. "After your friend's rude introduction, I didn't feel inclined."

Motoring beneath two buildings, the Sixer slid out into a patch of water shimmering with oil, at the centre of which stood a circle of buildings, each taller than any previous. The screaming towers. At their centre, its nearside windows glowing in the morning light, stood a seventh tower a few floors taller than its neighbours. The only real damage looked purposeful. Far above them, almost at the very top of the tower, five consecutive storeys were entirely void of glass. Above this, vague shapes dipped and soared, their shadows moving across the higher panes.

"Our destination," the captain said, pointing, "those upper storeys, the House of Pain."

That was when they heard the voice neither of them had ever expected to hear again.

"Pain?" the voice said. "Now that I know something about."

Liam had been gaping upwards and turned with his mouth still open. It was an appropriate expression, for there, slumped on a pile of rope, naked from the waist up, his skin so pale it was almost translucent, sat Erin.

391

LIAM CAUGHT A SOUR whiff, the bitter odour of death. Yet Erin's shoulder and face were whole again.

The other's smile was sickly. "I told you I would return."

"From the dead?" Liam said.

Erin shook his head. "From somewhere much worse."

The captain was smiling. "Sly as ever."

Liam looked at him. "But he'd stopped breathing."

"Even so, here I am," Erin insisted.

"But everyone knew!" Liam said. "We all watched over you, you *died*, I *saw* it."

"I've taken him in hand," Fredrickson said. "Few fish have escaped me but him, he's a slippery one. Able to evade death's grasp, I'll bet."

"No," Liam persisted, "I know what I saw. His shoulder, look at it, it's unmarked. And his face!"

Erin shrugged. "The captain's juice obviously worked wonders." He looked up at the tower. "Is this where your poem leads? After the thicket and the fruit-tree wild?"

Liam opened his mouth but bit at nothing. The enormity of Erin in the flesh, alive and brimming with spite was too much. After his dreams of the last few days, his terror, his sorrow towards the man who was even now mocking him, it was a wonder he was still standing. But his mention of the fifth verse did not go unnoticed. As usual, Erin was ahead of him, even after resurrection.

Perry cut the engine and the other men gathered on the foredeck, their expressions grave and uncertain.

"Sea spat him back," Fredrickson said.

Enzo grinned. "Must've tasted like he looks."

"Li' bird shit," Wires said, clapping Erin on the back. "Good see you roun'."

As Liam listened to Chilli stutter similar sentiments, he couldn't help wondering if they were all in cahoots. It was either that or they'd accepted Erin's recovery as some kind of miracle, an idea he found even harder to swallow.

"Is nobody going to *say* something?" he said finally.

Everyone fell silent. There was no time for awkwardness, however, for just then Perry gave a shout and they all moved to the starboard gunnel and began casting buoys over the side. Not a moment too soon. The boat, which had been slowly turning through the low, choppy waves, squeezed one buoy after another as it settled against the stone separating the tower's lowest row of windows from the sea.

Erin got to his feet and stood there, one hand resting on Bloodhorn's head. He was staring at Liam, his gaze unblinking. Finally, he leaned forwards and whispered, "I now know why the good captain doesn't know me. Because the god of this postdiluvian cesspool has so decreed it. It's a little bit like the human eye. How everyone's really looking at things upside down. Some things work. Some things are important. Others can be discarded."

Tutting, he turned to the captain. "What now?"

"Now we go up," Fredrickson said.

"But don't you have a cargo to unload?"

"Our catch has always been bound for this house. The evolo will come down to fetch it once we've agreed a price."

Chilli appeared with Erin's shirt. Erin put it on, wincing as he did so. It was decided that Wires would watch over the boat with Bloodhorn. Still sulking, Liam said he would too but the captain shook his head.

"What you have to say will be of interest to the Caretaker."

It was with feelings of both presentiment and resentment then that Liam followed the others as they climbed through a hole in the tower's nearside wall and into a long space littered with florescent patches of sunlight, its floor scattered with lumps of concrete and rusted metal rods. The smell was of the sea, decomposition, the breathing out of life long dead.

Fredrickson led them through a doorway in the far corner, their footsteps quietening as they entered an enormous corridor choked with darkness and dust. The briny air was several degrees cooler.

The group groped their way forwards until the captain stopped at a door marked:

STAIR E 1 FLOOR 12

"There are holes, so watch your feet." He stared at Liam and Erin. "Remember, this is not our house, so it's shoes off at the door and best behaviour with the china."

The man shouldered the door open and disappeared. One by one, the crew followed, with Enzo and Liam bringing up the rear. The stairs were lit only wherever the outer wall had been breached and clogged with debris so that the group were forced to clamber over mounds of rubble and glass, often piled as high as the railing, a venture that became more and more precarious the higher they climbed.

"Like smoky quartz," Enzo said picking up a piece of glass and flashing his beautiful, dark-eyed reflection at Liam.

Catching sight of his own face, Liam took it from him. The young man he'd seen in the mirror in the House of Love had been replaced by someone older still, the hair on his head and chin longer, the skin about his mouth and eyes lined.

"Here we go."

They'd passed several doors on their climb but the stairwell beyond the final door was so choked, they had no choice but to exit. In red paint, someone had daubed *House of Pain* above the lintel.

Eying the party one by one, Fredrickson repeated his warning and opened the door. As Liam stepped into the chamber, he was able to appreciate the tower's dimensions. The space before them was five storeys high and completely open to the elements. All had been stripped away except for three-dozen struts supporting the building's infrastructure around which serrated cones had been welded, in order, or so Liam guessed, to prevent anyone from climbing them. Behind them, the blocked stairwell pointed like a severed finger into the open. The glassless spaces that had once been windows, cast a series of sunlit rectangles across the floor, becoming a single, golden parallelogram at the far end of the tower.

Set in the ceiling were half-a-dozen hatches lined with the same material as the rest of the ceiling so that they were all but invisible. Only when a number of men and women began dropping out of them did Liam see them.

"Birdmen," Enzo murmured, rather unnecessarily.

The evolo landed on fingertips and toes before rising to their feet, their movements more reminiscent of cats than of birds. A woman in black with hazel coloured eyes and short, ash blonde hair immediately began a discussion with the captain and then assigned her comrades to each of the Sixer's crew.

With no embarrassment or fuss, the men were lifted, one after the other, into the air. Liam heard a click as some kind of device was strapped under his arms and around his chest, felt hands lock across his stomach and then a lurch. They rose at such a speed, his eyes were battened shut. When he opened them, he was in a high, shadowy place and the hatchways were being slammed to, causing a series of clatters to ricochet off the walls around them.

They were standing in an arena half as high as the space below their feet, surrounded by seats and long, curved desks that travelled upwards in ever-increasing circles and was divided into quadrants by four aisles, each hosted by double doors. The arena was set within cylindrical walls so that the outside of the tower could not be seen, its only light pouring in from a colossal glass dome set into the roof, the curved surface of which made the sky look like a giant blue bubble.

While he was staring upwards, a voice called to them from one of the smaller doors circling the outer wall. Each section of seating was divided twice again, creating paths for which the doors provided access, all of which were closed but for one and it was from this doorway that the voice hailed them a second time.

"In a bowl to sea went wise men three, on a brilliant night in June. They carried a net and their hearts were set on fishing up the moon!"

"'Cept there's six of us, old bird," Fredrickson called up.

"But whom of you is wise?" the voice said.

From the doorway stepped an old man with thick, white eyebrows and bright blue eyes. He looked at Liam as he descended. "Welcome, dreamer. For you I have a special rhyme to add to your collection. Simple Simon went a-fishing for to catch a whale but all the water he had got was in his mother's pail." The man laughed, the sound thin and bronchial in that high room. "Or should the rhyme be shark and father's mark?"

Liam watched as the bald-headed man stepped onto the dais and shook each of their hands, starting with Erin and then himself. He patted Liam's hand appreciatively. "I am the Caretaker. I've been expecting you." Raising his huge white brow, he turned to the captain and said, "So like his father . . . Ah!" he said before Liam could enquire further. "Enzo, my boy, a new tattoo, I see. A phoenix, how appropriate. And Chillito, still a little hot under the collar, I'll warrant."

In this manner, the man made his way around the group before introducing them to the fair-haired evolo. "Star is our Chief of Operations. And as such," he said with what sounded like mock gravity, "she insisted on taking time out of her busy schedule to welcome you both."

Star appraised the guests without speaking, her hazel eyes lingering on Liam's face as if memorising his features.

The Caretaker bid the crew to follow him. "Your food awaits. Though," he said, glancing back at them with merry eyes, "the pescatarians among you will be sad to know we're out of fish!"

iii.
—

THE PARTY FOLLOWED the old man through a set of doors south of the arena and out into a corridor that quickly widened into a large kitchen area, at the far end of which figures could be seen moving through clouds of steam. The kitchen sat in the southwest corner of the tower and was surrounded on two sides by windows filled with glass, their view obscured by condensation.

Hats stowed, the group sat down just as a bell rang. Hundreds of youngsters began to stream into the hall, their noisy chatter echoing off the high ceiling. The table at which the Sixer's crew sat had obviously lived some previous life, for it was set on crates and consisted of a long strip of wood interrupted by a sink-shaped hole abridged by corrugated runnels. In this space sat a metal salver filled with jugs of lemon water, two of which the Caretaker now seized and commenced pouring into a cluster of receptacles, before passing them around. Meanwhile, youths wearing black aprons began bustling in and out of the kitchen carrying square plates laden with food, an operation Liam watched with some interest until he too was served, whereupon all such observations ceased, for the food smelt so good, he tucked in without another thought.

"Garlic, chicory and thyme," the Caretaker said, pointing at Liam's meal. "All from our gardens." He indicated the partially concealed view beyond the window. "Many of the towers hereabouts are uninhabitable but, luckily for us, they have perfectly useable roofs." He clattered the jugs back into the salver and sat down. "How's the pigeon, by the way?"

"Delicious," Liam said.

"Such hospitality is welcome to all," said the old man, cutting into a large potato, "but, sadly, only birds of a certain feather flock to us. Not," he said, turning his snowy brow in Liam's direction, "that we haven't plans." He soaked a wedge of potato in gravy, placed it in his mouth and began to chew in a meditative fashion. "Your father once said foes are merely untutored friends. The question is how to educate those who believe they've already found the answer."

"My father?" Liam said, swallowing.

"Ah, yes," the Caretaker said, grimacing gently. "Of him we will talk later."

"He's here?"

"I promise you," the man said, nodding his head and winking both his eyes, "I will try to answer all of your questions but not until you've a good meal inside you."

Star ate her meal away from the others, flanked by two darkly clad evolo. Yet as soon as the Caretaker's party rose from the table, so did she. As for the promised conversation, this did not occur after lunch, for the moment they finished eating, the Caretaker insisted on showing them around the house and introducing them to every teacher and student who crossed their path.

The tour began in the Mathematics Quadrant, a set of rooms layered in chalk dust reached via a narrow, steeply inclined set of steps at the back of the refectory that rang, not only with their boots but also with the Caretaker's oration.

"Sadly," he said, "at the moment, we can only staff four subjects, Mathematics here, Science in the northwest wing, Literature in the northeast and History in the southeast. Our students study all four and attend interdisciplinary lectures in the arena where you first arrived, an area that, being central to the house, ties all four disciplines together—hence our unofficial motto, 'Get Knotted!'"

Each wing consisted of several rooms joined by a maze of corridors and stairs and punctuated by dozens of windows, their various outlooks revealing the ruined city and the circular wall beyond it in all their glorious decrepitude.

"All has been constructed according to your father's principles," the Caretaker declared, "every book and cranny, rescued and restored from the ruins of before." He smiled for a moment. They had stopped in the Literature Quadrant where the old man was showing them a collection of books he called 'unbaptised literature.' "A rare commodity," he said, replacing a tome entitled *There and Back Again.*

The man floated down the brightly-lit corridor linking Literature to History on a tide of enthusiasm. "History! The ever changing mould into which we pour new and old, silver and gold, creating the ring that weds all other subjects!"

His chuckle blended with his words so that they too seemed buoyant. "Why is it people need to believe they invented the world, as if it didn't exist until the moment they arrived? Such is your friend, the Keeper." He turned to Liam. "Wouldn't you agree?"

Liam went to speak but again the old man raised his hand.

"All in good time?" Liam said, the frustration in his voice only half-masked by a quick smile.

The old man nodded. "Even though it's in such short supply."

2

FINALLY, THE CARETAKER took them to a large room on the second floor of the History Quadrant, a space dressed in maps and the pages of books, all of which had obviously been dismantled by the floodwaters before being mounted as wallpaper. Even the windows were covered, creating a maze of bright, criss-crossing lines. Many of the pages and most of the maps were drained of colour, their smudged type creating a kind of marble effect, a busyness that was further enhanced by the stacks of scrolls and piles of books that were placed in seemingly arbitrary locations, even upon the chairs and the table they surrounded, a large oval affair placed in the middle of the room.

"Sit, sit!" the old man said, waving a distracted hand.

Following Erin's lead, Liam cleared a chair and sat down, as did almost everyone else. Only Star chose to stand.

"Well," the Caretaker said, settling in a large, ribbon-back chair, "to business, as they say." He smiled at Fredrickson. "But first, Captain, why would you not tell me at lunch? How is my little Joan?"

Fredrickson, who sat opposite the Caretaker, lowered his eyes and said somewhat stiffly, "I haven't the words for it." He paused, then sniffed. "I'm afraid she's dead, sir."

The old man's eyes widened. "What? Are you sure? How?"

The captain nodded towards Liam. "Helpin' him."

The Caretaker leant on the table, all of his previous energy seemingly drained, before rising and turning to the bank of windows. When he asked how again, Liam knew the man was addressing him.

"I'd gone to T'heel looking for my parents," he said. "I was followed by a creature, the Keeper's creation. It killed many people, Joan among them. I'm sorry."

399

"He's shown great power," Fredrickson said. "Turned the sea to glass."

The old man frowned, wrinkling the furrows around his eyes. "So you can stop this creature?"

Liam shrugged. "I don't know. Maybe."

The Caretaker turned and gripped the back of his chair. "For each of us," he said, giving the wood a squeeze, "life is a cacophony of choices. But like that first decision, that first pebble, so there comes a time when the roar and fuss trickles down to one last stone. I chose to send Joan to that island, yes," he said to Fredrickson, "it was my idea, not hers. I told her to watch what happened there." He looked at Liam. "My decision not yours led to her death."

Recalling the brave way Joan had tried to distract the creature, Liam could not look at the old man, not even when he reached out and patted his arm.

"A crucial decision is coming for you too," he said. "But until then, all you can do is weigh each choice with as much clarity and compassion as possible. Starting," he said, "by telling me everything you know about this creature."

Liam wiped at his eyes. "I fell for every poisonous word that man spoke. He told me I'd killed my parents, that my coming was foretold. He showed me a passage in a book that seemed to confirm his prediction. When he finally took me to see Rook, I was convinced she was a monster."

"Ah, yes, Rook," the man said, glancing at Star. "She came to us. I think you'll be pleased to know she is here still. She told us of your friendship."

Liam bowed his head. "After agreeing to help," he said, "I gave the man my dreams, visions full of fire and death. He used them to wake that monster. When we were on T'heel, the Keeper called it and it . . . well, as I said."

The Caretaker was nodding. "That man's not the only one with spies. Through one such, we learnt how the Keeper had injected you with a serum designed to encourage certain, rather deleterious responses. You saw the world in the most cynical terms."

"I was a fool to trust him."

"Naïve, perhaps. And is that it, have you told us everything?" When Liam nodded, the Caretaker said, "Well then your honesty is appreciated and shall be reciprocated. We've known of the Keeper's ambitions for some time. Many who survived the flood were too young to remember the world before. But I can recall every blade of grass, every wooded knoll. But perhaps it's for the best. The heart does not miss what it's never loved. Still, the world was a troubled place, its habitats already terribly altered by our perverse greed. It was a time of secrets, guarded within ironclad walls. We have evidence that shows that at the height of the clandestine activities practised by the government, thousands of documents were being withdrawn from public view, on a daily basis. This was being done by dozens of agencies in every city, not just this one. Truth was ridiculed. Everything was seen as subjective, or even worse, hearsay. This is why the Keeper was able to get away with what he planned, what he did. Men like him, men who act out of raw self-interest, fear or expedience, have no regard for anything except their own narrow visions. And his vision was of flood."

"I know," Liam said. "Gribble, a man who worked on Sazani, he told me the flood was the Keeper's doing."

"Yes," the Caretaker said warmly, "it was Gribble who told us you'd been found. He works for us. He volunteered to keep an eye on the Keeper. So he revealed himself to you?"

"He did," Liam said flatly. "But now he's dead."

"From the poisoned chrysalis, a plague of butterflies," Erin said softly.

Liam went to rise but the old man weighed a hand on his shoulder. "We're not here to fight each other." He flashed a look at Erin. "This is not about a few lives, it's about *all* life. Do you two know what is at stake?"

When neither of them responded, the Caretaker stood up and walked over to the largest of the maps. "Then let me enlighten you. This is the world before the flood. Most of the world's surface covered in water. This—" the Caretaker pulled down a second sheet—"is the world now. As you can see, that percentage is much higher." His brow dropped as if weighed by snow. "The Keeper's real name is Adams. Adams was the founding member of an organisation who called themselves the New Adventists. It was their claim that science and religion asked the same fundamental questions and only together could they find the answers. But though the Keeper founded a society to draw these two disciplines together, he had very different plans to those he publicised. Indeed, he escalated what was, at the time, the world's most pressing issue, the ill-named 'global warming', by releasing a bacterium, completely depleting the polar icecaps. The result can be seen from any window."

The Caretaker tapped a finger at the map. "The question, of course, is why. I believe the answer is simple. He wanted to play God. The others in his group believed themselves God's creatures, bending to His will—"

"The Giver?" Erin said, his eyes on Liam.

"Yes, though her translation of certain scriptures is warped in its own special way. The Keeper's insanity, however, is of an altogether greater magnitude. But there is a fly in his somewhat watery ointment, or, to be precise, several." The Caretaker smiled. "Us. The birds. Though, in truth, we don't like to be called such. We have neither wings, nor tiny brains. Neither do we build nests, nor lay eggs. Though, as you may have guessed, the female of the species has been given one rather special, rather dangerous gift. Rook will be giving birth soon. Imagine how much fear such a gift strikes into the hearts of those who oppose us? Such makes our other talent little more than a party trick to them. They say we fly but we prefer to use the word transpose. It was one of your father's favourite lectures. We evolved the very first day the flood. He called it instant evolution. As the waters stole the land, so we stole the air."

His smile became droll. "Homo sapiens is Latin for wise-man, an oxymoron if ever I heard one. In contrast, your father coined the term Homo evolo, meaning flying-man. It was he who guessed that the Keeper's intention was to rouse what was left of mankind and raise himself upon a dais of his own making. Of the rest of his cabal, all but the Giver and Mayor Julian, the leader of this fair city, are dead and neither will stand in his way. Your father also theorised that the only reason Adams has not yet begun his new world order is because of us. And until now we were unsure what he planned to do about it."

Liam understood the man's unspoken suggestion. Until Ma'kin. A fact that would not exist but for him. Worse still, if his guess were correct, he was a magnet to the creature. Even now, Liam imagined the gap between them closing.

He stood up. "Then I must go."

"Sit down," the Caretaker said. "It is too late for that."

"I've too much blood on my hands already. This thing is coming and it's my fault. It can find me. You are all in danger." He looked at Erin. "*Rook* is in danger."

"As I said," the old man repeated, "it's too late."

"Then I will go, I *must*." Liam stepped towards the door, only for Star to block the way.

"We knew something was coming," the old man said, "though before today we knew not in what guise." For a moment his gaze was unguarded. "And we also knew it was you who would bring it. Please, sit down. *Sit*. My story," he said after Liam finally gave in, "centres on someone you've already met. My daughter, Joan."

The man laid his hand on an ornate looking box, his fingers troubled by a tremor. "This box," he said, "was given to me by her. It is very precious to me."

When he opened the box, Liam caught a glimpse of blue but the old man was too quick. He removed a sheet of paper and shut the box.

"When she was younger, my daughter used to be quite the night owl. Hence her nickname, Lazy Joan. After nights out on the tiles, quite literally," the man said, a mocking smile flitting across his face, "she slept all morning and was barely human by the afternoon. At night though she loved to hunt, though what she sought I never discovered. Sometimes when she came back, always with one flock or another, she would work her cards. She had quite the trick of them."

The old man fixed Liam with a look. "One night, a few years ago, she laid out a hand she thought your father should see. In those days, a number of us lived out there in the city, where we were welcome for a while."

"Until Julian worked his spell," Perry said quietly.

"Yes." The Caretaker lowered his snowy brow. "When Joan's mother died, the bridge between daughter and father collapsed. We lived in one of the towers atop the wall so I could keep watch over the sea but it was damp and wind-ridden and Joan hated it. She was too young to understand the meaning of duty. She wanted to live here, in this house, where many of her friends had already fled. Most nights I'd watch the sea while listening for her return. The night of her revelation, she didn't return at all. Instead, she came here to talk to your father. Though, apparently," he said, turning to the windows as if imagining what he described, "it took her several attempts to gain the parapet. Needless to say, when you're as high as a kite, you cannot fly as the crow. She told the watch she had an important message and when your father came, she laid the cards for him." The old man flapped the paper. "Joan said the prophecy described here wasn't set in stone but your father decided they couldn't take the risk. He had you sent away."

Liam shook his head. "Why? What did the cards say?"

The Caretaker opened the box, replaced the piece of paper, then closed the box again and placed his hand on it. "That like your father you would become a dreamer. But that one day your dreams would be used against you. That you would be rechristened and henceforth no one would know your name. Not even yourself. And finally," the man said, "the prophecy suggested that your dreams would destroy us all. In a tide of blood, no less. Though it broke his heart, your father felt he had no choice but to banish you."

Erin chuckled. "Be merciful," he said, "say 'death'."

It was too much. Liam leapt across the table, knocking scrolls and books aside in his efforts to reach Erin but Erin simply pushed his chair away, the look on his face one of amused consternation. Even as Liam sprawled to the floor, he felt Star's arm across his neck.

The Caretaker knelt down and spoke in grave tones. "I'm afraid, time is of the essence. Much of the prophecy has already come true but the worst still threatens. You said yourself, the creature is coming. We're all in danger. If it's coming for you, we need to keep you away from this house."

Liam tried to break free but the evolo's grip was irresistible. "What are you going to do with me?"

"Take you out to sea," Fredrickson said. "When the Keeper comes, we will meet him in my domain."

Liam's bitterness became laughter. "You're going to use me as bait?"

"We will protect you," the old man said. "But we must also protect ourselves."

"But if I pose such a threat, why bring me here?"

The Caretaker closed his eyes, causing his brow to bristle over his sockets. "We have many scouts. Provided we take enough supplies, some of us can fly great distances. We knew you were coming. We also know the location of this creature. It is resting on the Keeper's vessel half a day east. Captain Fredrickson brought you to me so I could find out what you know, which, as it turns out, is little more than we'd already surmised. And also, so I could tell you in person what was going to happen. I owe that much to you. And to your father."

"Let me at least see Rook."

"The decision's been made. We need to have you in place."

As Star drew Liam to his feet, he turned to Erin.

"Don't let them do this."

Erin shrugged. "I'm not letting them do anything. All this is on you."

The gathering stirred, then rose to their feet. As they traversed the corridors, Liam sensed Star walking just behind him. Erin had decided to stay on at the House of Pain but wanted first to check on Bloodhorn. The Caretaker walked them as far as the auditorium before bidding Liam goodbye.

"May we meet in more peaceful times."

Liam felt Star's hand on his shoulder and tried to restrain himself. "This is a mistake."

The man nodded. "Then let us hope it is the lesser evil."

"You said the prophecy talked about rechristening. If Liam is not my name, what is it?"

The old man softened for a moment. "I wondered when you might ask. Your mother was told she would never have a child, so when you arrived, she called you her little miracle baby. Perhaps that's why, even from a young age, you were so headstrong. And perhaps why she gave you the nickname she did. Either way, it stuck. Even your father used it. Whim. They called you Whim."

ii.
———

HEAD LOWERED, the Caretaker stopped walking, then nodded to Star, who urged Liam on. When he looked back, he saw that the man had already turned away. When Fredrickson caught up with him, he spoke with uncharacteristic reserve.

"I hope you're not going to be trouble."

"Trouble?" Liam said derisively. "Are you worried that you might not get to see the fish devour the treacherous bait?" He smiled coldly. "I'm sure you'll hold the rod steady, Captain. But who knows which of us will be gobbled up first?"

The captain shrugged. "Least I'll be where I'm meant to be. Out there, my blood will join the sea. Here, I'll just be another stain on the carpet."

The hatches were open. With their cargo strapped into place, the evolo dropped one-by-one to the concrete floor below, then returned whence they'd come, leaving only Star to escort the party onwards. With Fredrickson in the lead, they crossed the floor and began to troop down the stairs in single file. Evening sunlight crept into the building through numerous chinks, making a diminishing tableaux of the balustrade's warped casing and twisted balusters. Liam peered over the edge.

"It's a long way down," Star said, joining him.

Liam shot her a dark look. "Well spotted, eagle-eyes."

"No," Star said, a half-amused kink appearing between her brows, "I have not that honour. I am only Starling."

It was only as the party neared sea level that the evolo relaxed. With just a few flights to go, Liam could see water glinting at the bottom of the stairwell. With the rest of the group crossing a particularly precarious pile, Fredrickson called for Star and Liam to join them but as Star moved ahead, Erin pulled Liam aside.

"All of this is of your making," he said quietly. "Before I died—*yes*," he whispered, "you were right, so what? *Before I died*, you and I were talking and I told you who you were. Do you remember? Well, do you also remember having some kind of seizure? It was like the whole world started coming apart."

He gripped Liam's arm. "Of *your* making," he said again. "You are the author of your own fate. But how will the story end? Everything points to a great tragedy, does it not? And what then? On to pastures new? Well, I won't allow it. You're needed elsewhere. As for the poem, forget about it. If you reckon it's going to lead you back to your parents, think again. In the meantime, my sister is in great danger."

He nodded to where the balustrade was completely broken, the drop beyond it still considerable. "The best thing you can do for all concerned is to jump. If you end this now, I won't have to do it for you."

With that he let go of Liam's arm and marched on. Liam knelt down and peered over the edge, his stomach lurching. It was true, Rook was in danger. And the best thing for her was for him to stay away. Yet he wanted the chance to explain. Not to mention the fact that he was going to be a father. He'd grown more and more used to the idea. Erin obviously had some other motive that he was unwilling to divulge and until he did, Liam vowed to watch him very closely.

Traversing the last set of stairs, the group stepped out, one-by-one, into the lower corridor. As the door closed behind them, they were enveloped by complete darkness and had to feel their way along the wall. Upon reaching the room by which they'd entered the tower, however, they saw a light under the door.

Fredrickson cursed under his breath. "I said no lights."

But even as he spoke, the light went out and he opened the door into a room full of shadows. He crossed the space and called from the window for Wires to start the engine, before straddling the sill, stepping onto the Sixer's forward gunwale and jumping to the deck, followed by the others.

The air was a deep grey, the moon veiled by a scrim of cloud, the wind a soft moan among the rigging. The faint light, the movement of the boat, a clanking and creaking and the aromas of salt and diesel were all in that moment and then blinding lights sprang up from somewhere before them and a magnified voice boomed across the water:

"Do not move. You are all under arrest!"

As the voice boomed again, Chilli panicked and dropped to the deck, only for a whistling sound to come from somewhere beyond the lights, a low, burring shriek that materialised into an arrow even as it struck the boy's thigh. Chilli squealed and rolled onto his side, snapping the arrow in two.

"You can't do this, Julian!" Fredrickson yelled. "It's against the law!"

"Not our law it's not," the voice returned and a second arrow whistled out of the darkness, this time striking Chilli through the stomach, turning his howl into a frothy gasp.

Obviously torn between wanting to help the boy and the threat of more arrows, the captain yelled, "What've you done with Wires?"

With his eyes adjusted, Liam could see their greeting party more clearly. Moored just off the Sixer's portside, perhaps ten yards from where he stood, lay a long white cruiser. Twenty figures or so were lined up behind a series of spotlights, the fattest of whom wore a tall hat. Behind him stood a number of archers, their bows raised. Further out, the water looked oddly flat.

A shape made even thinner by the sodium glare stepped forwards. "I'm 'ere, cap'n," the shape shouted. "Dey came, I didn' know what to do."

Before Fredrickson could reply, the Mayor raised a conical device to his mouth. "Hear me, O Lord! Deliver us from evil!"

The captain's response was drowned out by a din that shook the walls:

"HEAR US, O LORD! DELIVER US FROM EVIL!"

Now Liam realised why the water behind the Mayor's boat looked odd. It was covered in boats. The way was so thick with them, he could almost have walked from the central tower to the outer wall without getting his feet wet. And every craft was packed with people, their bristling weapons grey against the deeper darkness, their featureless faces growing ever fainter as they dwindled into the distance.

Again the Mayor spoke and again the masses returned his cry, their timing punctuated by several bass drums: "HEAR US, O LORD! DELIVER US FROM EVIL!"

As the din died, Julian's voice echoed across the water. "Give us the dreamer. Do that and the rest of you may have safe passage."

Liam realised what he'd been missing, the vital link between the Keeper's plan and its execution. The hysteria of this moment. He'd felt it at the Giver's feast and then afterwards in the cavern below. If the Mayor stoked the fire any more, blood would be spilled, of that he was certain. A tide of blood.

He stepped forwards. "I am here!"

Fredrickson hissed for him to shut up.

Liam recalled the Giver's words: *The hooked fish has but one solace. It gets to gobble the bait.* That much he'd already worked out, that much the Caretaker had already known before he'd even arrived. The whole time the Keeper had been driving him forwards, first to T'heel and then here, to this island. To these people, to this crowd. The population of the Giver's island was nothing in

409

comparison, an outpost. Here then was mankind. And all of them disciples come to deliver the New Testament. Liam remembered the man who had been guarding the tunnel in the House of Love, the man who had asked if the seraphim were coming. He remembered Loverboy's cry as he burst into the cavern. *They're coming! The seraphim are coming!* That panic, that fervour, was here, caught in the throat of every man, woman and child as they cried for a third time: "HEAR US, O LORD! DELIVER US FROM EVIL!"

Finally, Liam recalled the captain's words about perception. The Keeper had not created Ma'kin so it could destroy the evolo, he'd created it to invoke fear. Fear of Nephilim, of being superseded, of being made obsolete. He'd created Ma'kin in order to unite mankind's remnants under his own banner, to turn them against the House of Pain, to tear apart his father's work and his father's people. It was not Ma'kin who would do the Keeper's work, it was man, for only he could produce a hell convincing enough to his own sensibilities that he would willingly be enslaved by it. As the staggering echo of ten thousand voices began to recede, Liam took another step forwards.

"Take *me*," he shouted. "The men and women in this tower are innocent. They only wish for peace, to *ed*ucate."

"Yes!" the Mayor responded. "To educate men in the rites of slavery, women in the rites of bondage. To change pure blood to mongrel, mankind to demon! For years I have preached of the rise of these fiends. It was they who caused the flood. And now they have come to take what is left. But we shall be delivered!"

"DELIVER US!" the crowd roared, the walls around them resounding their cry.

"Already they have murdered our kind on T'heel but they will not find it so easy here. Here we will fight until the seraphim are truly fallen. We will not stop until the water runs red!"

"DELIVER US!" the crowd roared and the dark grey of the wall silhouetted a thousand raised spears.

Erin stepped beside Liam. "Deliver us a pizza, now that'd be worth shouting about." He cupped his hands. "We'll exchange the dreamer for the dog!"

The captain murmured, "Erin, step down."

Erin ignored him. "Show me Bloodhorn!" Hearing its name, the dog's head appeared, silhouetted between Wires and Mayor Julian.

"Dog stayin' ri tear!" Wires shouted.

Erin nodded. To the captain, he said, "If you've got a plan, I suggest now is the time."

That said, he raised his fingers and whistled. The sound was barely audible but it had an immediate effect on Bloodhorn. The dog twisted its head, then growled, the sound loud enough to travel across the water. Wires bent down to see what was wrong. It was the last decision he ever made.

Liam was reminded of the first time he'd seen Wires with the dog. Bloodhorn had been standing on the Sixer's gangplank and Liam had thought the man was going to lose his nose but nothing had happened. That was then. Now, Bloodhorn twisted its thickly furred neck and snapped forwards, planting its jaws around the man's cheeks before shaking its head so hard, Wires was lifted off his feet, his flailing legs bowling over several archers.

While the mayor started screaming and waving his arms, men scrambled to get away from the seething ball in their midst and a number of archers tried to draw aim on the dog.

Before ascending the tower, the captain had returned Erin's knife to him. Drawing it now from his belt, Erin took several strides back and stood there rocking on the balls of his feet. He looked at Liam, his eyes savage with joy and then ran at the Sixer's far railing, striking it so hard, the boat lurched beneath them. The Mayor's boat was thirty feet away but Erin made it easily, landing with his hands on the deck. In a rabid panic, the Mayor lifted his leg to stomp at him but Erin simply caught the man's boot and swept his other from under him.

Fredrickson opened a trunk, drew out several sticks, passed one to Star. Then he turned his attention to his youngest shipmate. Chilli had painted the deck with his fingers. He looked up as the captain approached, his eyes wet with hope. Fredrickson nodded and spoke words of comfort, which only made sense in their sound. "Come now, little fishy, come now," he said as he took the boy in his arms, curling him into his lap, while at the same time removing his gutting knife from its sheath.

Unable to watch, Liam's eyes sought Erin. The young man was a black flash amid the lights. Though he was outmanned, when others came against him, it was they who fell. Bloodhorn attacked in a series of explosions, occasionally spraying the spotlights, which in turn projected an increasingly intricate nebulae across the Sixer's deck and the side of the tower.

"Time to go," Enzo said, pulling Liam away.

A projectile flew through the air and struck the Sixer's starboard side, where it quivered for a moment, its head driven into the metal. Liam saw it wasn't a spear, not a real one. It had probably been salvaged from the guts of some building. He looked out into the darkness. Whichever enterprising mind had grown restless and thrown the weapon, it was enough for the mob. The next missile to fly past Liam's head was an iron kettle, weighing enough to crush his skull.

Leaving Chilli curled up on the deck, Fredrickson started shoving at the rest of them: "Inside! Now!"

At the same time, Star brought the stick in her hands down onto her knee, causing a fizzing red light to burst across the deck. The third weapon, an enormous metal ball, was launched from a crude catapult aboard a nearby ship, its target inspired by the flare. Starling was too fast. A scarlet blur against the backdrop of the tower, she shot upwards, drawing, as a meteor might debris, a dozen or so projectiles, and then flew outwards, so that the weapons were soon splashing into the sea.

Not everyone was distracted by Star's display, however. Two more spears came flying through the air, the first passing over Liam's head, causing him to drop to the deck, the second slamming into the wood between his legs. Spluttering with fear and laughter, he looked round for someone to share this miracle with, only to see Enzo bearing down on him.

"I was, it almost . . ."

But before he could say more, the man had scooped him up and thrown him over the side of the boat.

3

THE SHOCK WAS ABSOLUTE. Water burned his nose, dragged at his clothing. For a moment he saw the tower, dark windows descending into gloom, the building's nearest corner resting many floors below at a crossroads of broad streets, their pavements and signs alive with rippling weeds and then Enzo, who had followed him into the water, was tugging at his jacket, trying to pull him away. He indicated for Liam to follow but before he could do so, he heard a muffled explosion and looked up. The Sixer's keel was a blue-black wedge. Further up, along an edge distorted by water, he saw a flickering line of red. The boat was on fire. Searching the gloom, he saw Enzo swimming towards the tower and began to follow.

By the time he reached the building, he was desperate for air. Enzo had disappeared into a hole in the tower's east side and when Liam followed, something passed his head, returned, probed his cheek, then seized his collar and dragged him up until his face was resting against a slippery, cold surface. He felt air, drew a loud, savage breath.

"Oh, my God, oh, my God!"

The space was completely dark and very narrow, their breathing deafening. Liam felt Enzo tug on his arm, then heard him splashing away. Tipping his head back, he began to follow, his nostrils sucking at the air-pocket. A minute later, the pocket ended and they were forced to swim underwater. Twice Liam was almost kicked in the face. The second time, he saw the foot coming and realised that the water was growing clearer. He looked down, saw they were swimming above a series of wide, green steps.

413

Finally they crawled out of the water and flopped together onto a dimly lit floor, sucking and spitting at the air, spraying droplets with each breath. They were lying near the centre of an enormous space tiered on all sides with balconies.

Enzo might have been grinning or grimacing. "We go up. We are needed."

He guided Liam towards the south wall, which lay behind the submerged steps, then along it to a door, which led into an outer corridor and finally to a stairwell. Through each window Liam caught glimpses of the city. The screaming towers were lit up, their balconies and windows flickering with flames. He kept expecting to be ambushed or at least to hear the sound of fighting but neither occurred.

After negotiating two sets of stairs and a doorway clogged with rubble, Enzo finally found the corridor he'd been looking for. At the far end, he started pulling plasterboard and girders away from another door until he and Liam could drag the door open. But then Enzo raised a warning finger. Liam listened, heard the distinct squeak of rubber on concrete. And then the sailor was poking an arm through the gap. Following Enzo, Liam saw a boy doubled over, one hand holding his gut, the other steadying himself on the landing floor. Seeing them, the boy tried to shout but Enzo quickly clamped his mouth.

Not a moment too soon. Footsteps came from the stairwell below. A second later, one of the boy's companions crept out onto the lower landing and looked up. Liam waited for him to react before realising that the darkness made them invisible, so long as they stayed still. Enzo, however, had other plans. Gathering the boy up, he threw him down the stairs.

Wasting no time, he shoved at Liam and the two of them began running up the stairs. It was an exhausting dash and it was only when Liam found himself confronted by a lintel daubed with the words *House of Pain* that he realised where they were. The red paint looked black in the dimness. He opened the door, unsure of what might greet them. A huge wedge of darkness highlighted by wide grey breaches, their filmy quality touched, indirectly, by a crawling orange light and, along the far wall, a few stars. Each shadow was thick enough to hide a dozen men but Enzo seemed unconcerned. He steered Liam to the nearest corner, where he fell against the low wall, his back to the concrete. Liam crouched beside him, catching, as he did so, a glimpse of the closest tower. It was alight on several floors. At the same time he tried to quieten his breath.

From the doorway they'd just exited, their pursuers came, spidering into the room on fingers and toes, splitting up as they entered. It was both admirably executed and of little use. Like bats, the evolo dropped, from the ceiling, from distant corners, from the wall above his head for all Liam knew, for they were virtually invisible. The only sound came from the men as they were picked up, one after the other, carried across the space and thrown out into the night. Thinning screams.

"The hard way," Enzo said as the last scream reached their ears. When a tattooed arm reached for him, Liam folded beneath it. Enzo spoke gently. "I always do things the hard way but it's not just me. The whole world."

Liam kept recalling those screams, though he was soon distracted by other, more prescient noises. Screeches and whoops coming from the screaming towers echoed against the concrete like clapping hands, some kind of klaxon and then a swelling roar like a wind-fanned fire. This last sound grew on his inner vision so that he saw it with his mind's eye before it appeared, a huge, hot shape that shot through one of the openings, struck a girder and sent a riddle of flames bursting in all directions, briefly lighting the chamber from end to end. From out of this brightness, a projectile careered off of several girders before tumbling towards Liam and Enzo, who scrambled away even as the wall on which they'd been leaning lit up.

Nor was it the last. The second fireball, though smaller than the first, was more deadly. When it disintegrated, its fiery innards caught two of the evolo and Liam watched in horror as they writhed on the ground, their cries soon overcome by the viscous liquid burning their skin. As a third missile came through an adjacent window, Liam found himself running and when it crashed in his direction, leapt out of its path. The rest happened very slowly.

He hit the wall, felt himself fall backwards, only to realise that he'd tumbled through one of the openings. Air screamed in his ears, his image flashed back at him in the glass. The jeers and screams were very loud, though not as loud as his clothes, which snapped about his body as he fell. He struck the wall, turned, saw a chaos of brightly lit boats rising towards him. Finally, as his lungs flattened, he knew he was going to die. Only then was he borne aloft.

The Caretaker shouted in his ear, "What happened?"

Liam could barely speak. "Ambushed!"

Their path took them past the eastern tower, its pitted surface shining like a block of ebony in the moonlight.

"Hold on." The Caretaker sped upwards at a rate that blurred Liam's vision. He gritted his teeth, trying not to think of the increasing drop beneath them.

Surging past the last floor, the central tower blazed into view. Flames gusted from several floors. Two of the screaming towers were also alight. He counted four rooftop gardens, though these plots were nothing to the allotment capping the House of Pain, a rippling field of corn cut into quadrants and cornered by watchtowers. From on high, the central dome looked like an onyx crown surrounded by a golden shawl.

"The blast of war blows in our ears," the Caretaker said as he dropped towards the field.

Wheat whipped at their legs. The old man strode to a stop, his chest heaving. What had seemed effortless in flight had reduced him to an almost cataplectic state. It was some time before he could speak but when at last he managed to do so, it was to try and comfort his guest.

"I wish you to know," he breathed, "your parents went looking for you. They would rather have lived out there, without friends, without comfort, than be without you . . ."

One hand pressing at his side, the man began to limp towards the nearest tower, where Liam could make out several figures. As they grew closer, he saw, to his amazement, that Enzo was among them.

The big man charged over and lifted him into the air. "Alive!" he cried, pointing at Star. "Snatched from the teeth of hell!"

"Not like this," the Caretaker said when Star stepped forwards. "We must sue for peace."

"We need iron, not water," the evolo said bluntly. "They've started a war you've no stomach for. It's time to let us finish what you cannot. We've tried your way, yet what has your beloved history taught us if it isn't that human beings are animals? Well it's time we animals became human beings."

"We are human in every way that matters," the Caretaker said indignantly. "And if history teaches us anything, it is that violence only begets violence."

"Well then, their violence bred ours. Julian killed Chilli. And why? For him?" She pointed at Liam.

"Julian was trying to prevent him from leaving and it worked. We must get him away before it's too late."

"The creature is as much a pawn as I am," Liam said coolly. "The Keeper wants to use it to fill these people with fear."

Star didn't deign to look at him. "Even if he is who you say, he could still be in league with them. Peregrine told us how he froze the sea."

Of course, Liam thought, Perry's name was Peregrine. The whole time they'd been travelling with a birdman on board.

Star turned and pointed. "Take him up."

Two evolo dragged Liam through a low stone doorway in the side of the watchtower, up a narrow set of stairs and pushed him into a room similar to his cell on T'heel, except that the window here was without bars. This was because the watchtower marked the corner of the tower proper and overlooked a drop of several hundred feet, a fact he discovered the moment he stepped onto the sill.

He stared down at the mist-enshrouded sea. To his right, lay one of the screaming towers, its many balconies lit by huge braziers around which indistinct figures warmed their hands or toasted food. He inhaled the moist evening air, smelt limestone, the wheat in the field behind the tower, the little weeds that grew between the runnels, their brief flowers. Those on the rooftop opposite were singing, the sound raucous and intermittent. Beneath this, from somewhere above him, he heard another voice, as projected inwards as the others were out. Whoever it was, was humming and singing under their breath, something about blackbirds in a pie.

He recognised it and even murmured the next line before leaning out and looking up. The lintel above him seemed carved of moonlight and shadow. He sang the next few words in a surprisingly pleasant baritone. As he did so, white fingers gripped the stone and a dimpled chin appeared. It was Rook, her eyes like coal-glass in the dark. They stared at each other for a moment and then she withdrew.

"Rook!" He leaned out. "How are you?" Gathering his nerves, he blurted, "How's the baby?"

There was a pause, followed by muted words: "Always kicking. It's like she wants to come early. But why are you here? Why've they locked you up? Are you in trouble?"

He felt tears blur his vision. "I just . . ." He tried to lean out. "Can't we at least talk face to face?"

A flash lit his peripheral vision and he looked down in time to see a flaming ball spiral across from the nearest tower. People had assembled along the edge of the roof to watch it fly. Further back, figures worked in near darkness, their outlines and that of some huge spiderlike shape thrown into relief by sparks. The projectile struck the House of Pain, spattering its windows and running in fiery lines across the stonework. Now when Rook's eyes appeared, they were coppery-coloured. Her words drifted down like petals.

"I've been worried that if I saw you again, that if I even spoke to you . . ." She spoke wistfully and when she frowned, she became no more than a furrow. "But I did *want* to see you again, if only to tell you that I miss you."

Her words made the scene before him swim.

"I'm in here because they don't trust me. But then again, why should they?" He looked up. "But you've done nothing wrong. Why are you here?"

"Apparently," she said, "this is how they treat those who are carrying a precious egg. As if we're too delicate to cope."

It was the last thing either of them said to each other, for just then there came the sound of footfall on the stairs, followed by a metallic jangle. A second later, Liam heard the creak of a door. Someone, their voice muffled, said something, after which Rook glanced downwards and then withdrew.

Liam called to her but when a face appeared, it was Erin's, his freckled skin swimming with orange light.

"My offer still stands, my friend," he said quietly. "There lies the precipice." He crouched down and leaned forwards. "Think about it. I died and yet here I am. This is not the end." So saying, he lowered his hand. "Take it. We'll fall together."

Instinctively, Liam backed away. "You're mad."

"Sometimes madness is our only sanctuary. But if you won't take me up on my offer, I'm going to have to take Rook away from here."

Liam reached up. "No. Please, Erin, help me."

"I *am* helping you," he said. "You're not meant to be here. But I believe it's up to you how and when you leave. If that means I too must go, then so be it. I think I understand now. The force that holds this world together is not imagination, it is e*mot*ion. You are being hunted, my friend. By love, by anger, by *guilt*. But you must turn and face your predators. Do it for her," he said, nodding towards his shoulder. "Do it for Fay."

And with that he was gone.

ii.

LIAM BANGED ON THE DOOR, shouted Rook's name, heard footsteps descend the stairs. "Don't trust him!"

He paced his cell, trying to think. He could wait, for Star, for Ma'kin, for the end of the world. Or he could try to escape. Dread

419

clotted his heart. It was coming, his dreamtime creation, his night-time terror. But as he ground his teeth, it was not Ma'kin's name he recalled but that of another. 'Fay.'

Again he smelt the cool dark earth in the field behind the watchtower, the ears of wheat, the nubs of gold within. He wondered why he'd not reacted when Erin had said the name but the answer was simple. He already knew it. It belonged to his unborn child. But if Rook hadn't yet named her, how was it possible that both he and Erin knew she was called Fay? He rested his head against the door, heard the din of another explosion, felt his breath hot on his collarbones. The name came from the poem. The book had been Erin's before it fell into the Keeper's hands. And it was no coincidence that Erin knew the poem so well. But how had the Keeper come to possess the book in the first place? He shut his eyes, let his mind dwell. Erin and the Keeper. The Keeper and Erin. And just like that, the mystery revealed itself. He'd been focusing on Erin and Rook when he should have been looking elsewhere. He'd found Erin's book in the Keeper's house. No doubt it had been placed there for that purpose. The fight with the Giver, the struggle for the knife, all staged in order to hoodwink him. Look how quickly he'd healed! Because the woman had inflicted no more than a flesh wound. He struck his head on the wood.

"Of course."

What better way to ensure he trusted Erin? And who had fought more than anyone, more than Liam himself, to ensure he reached the Island of Hats? The same person who had now left him trapped in a cell to await Ma'kin, the bait firmly skewered on the hook. The same who had taken Rook away from him, Rook and his unborn child. Liam's rage hissed until it highlighted the cracks and cobwebs around him. To think he had wept when he thought him dead. But he hadn't been dead, had he? In that moment, Liam's doubts and fears became one truth. He had to free himself and find Erin before he delivered Rook to the Keeper.

He was trapped without weapons or tools. He had nothing on his person except the book. Though this thought made him remember

420

something else Erin had said. He'd told him to forget the poem, that it wouldn't lead him back to his parents. Another trick, no doubt.

The idea was like a match in the dark. Aware of how desperate this hope was, he reached into his pocket and pulled out the book. The thing was still damp, the cover warped. He opened it, saw dim words, thumbed quickly through the pages, only to find the torn verses missing. He flicked back, began to search more carefully, moving towards the window as he did so. Page after page, he turned, until, finally, he could see the thread where the pages had been bound and knew he was looking at the book's middle. The central pages were intact. On closer inspection, he saw on them, not the words of a poem, but a list of supplies. Salt, medicine, brushes and so forth. Shutting the book, he scanned its cover. In letters so worn they were more indentation than ink, he read:

Supply Record
The Sixer
Isle of Hats

He inspected the book again, his anger growing until he thought his heart would explode. His skin softened, vibrated, swelled. The hair at the nape of his neck stood erect. This was not the book of poems, it was a supply catalogue belonging to the Sixer. Erin had not only taken Rook and Fay, he had taken the book. He had taken *every*thing.

There was no subtlety this time. No thought. His scream was that of an eagle, its breast impaled in flight. It was life raging at death, it was the horror of all he'd done, remembered and forgotten. A light pulsed from his head, a shimmering sheet that blinded him even as it severed the walls around him and shattered the structure above in an eruption of rubble and mortar. He drew breath and screamed again. Stones exploded outwards. But though he imagined them hurtling across the gulf, causing the men and women on the opposite roof to cry out, he neither saw nor heard, for he was listening to the tower. Erin's breath, constricted by a stairwell. Somewhere below. Leaping high into the air, he landed in the cornfield below with an explosive force, flattening crops, upending soil and roots, buckling the roof beneath. He jumped again, this time puncturing the roof's membrane. His body followed.

Between the roof's outer shell and the ceiling below was an assortment of struts, wires, insulation. He fell through it all and felt nothing, not as cables exploded, nor as beams warped. In this way, he plunged into the Literature Quadrant, crashed through a ceiling and dropped to the darkened concrete floor of a large study, accompanied by a rain of earth, stonework and dust. Pages landed like doves in the dark. He listened again. From the room below, he heard startled cries, a rush of voices, a clamour in the corridor outside.

Like some monstrous flea, he leapt up through the damaged ceiling before striking the study floor. Less resilient than the roof, it immediately caved, taking much of the floor, a large table and a bookcase with it. Amid this debris he fell, one dusty thing among others, a series of books, plasterwork, a drumming of fragments, a cloud of dust, all tumbling into a room full of students, each of them scrambling to the outer walls and windows, where the sun's imminence glimmered in the predawn darkness. Recognising none of this, Liam focussed on the table below him, spearing it with his feet, scattering cards and snapping the wood before punching through the foot of concrete that made up the house's lower floor. Thus, with one leap, he travelled through two floors, leaving behind him a vertical tunnel livid with dust.

Then he fell. For five storeys.

He struck the chamber floor in a clatter of wreckage and splintered concrete, peered at the space around him, recalling the fireball that had so narrowly missed him. The walls were scarred, the door to the stairwell missing, the space beyond choked. Preparing to leap again, Liam breathed the stink of burnt flesh and scalded iron, only for something to catch his eye. In one of the openings, a narrow gap perhaps fifty feet behind the collapsed stairwell, Liam saw a glowering shape. It exuded an all too familiar scent. With a fierce expulsion of air, Liam began to sprint through the gloom, his feet barely touching the concrete. *Three times*, he thought. *You will fall three times before you rise again.*

"Brother!"

Erin turned as Liam approached, his arms open, his grin a smear beside the brightness haloing his head, for just at that moment, the sun reached over the horizon and set fire to his hair.

As Liam leapt the last few feet, he wondered why Erin didn't turn aside. Even as Liam dropped upon him, the other waited with his arms open, his face beaming. The ledge was broad but Erin had chosen to perch on its outer edge so that the moment Liam struck, the two tumbled outwards. The change was immediate. A blur of surfaces. Wind tore at their clothing, their reflection flashing faster and faster against the glass. But nothing could distract Liam. He seized Erin's shirt, his neck, his throat.

"But how do I know?" Erin shouted, his hair rippling in the draft. "If she has no name, *how do I know it?*"

"In the book, the one you stole!"

"Oh, Will." Erin grasped the back of Liam's head and pulled him close. "Why would I steal it when it was I who gave it you in the first place?"

Liam felt his shirt whip against his ear, caught a glimpse of the Sixer through bright mist, saw the boat's charred deck like a burnt eye beneath them. A second later, they smashed through the engine room, tore through the keel and exploded into the sea in a tear-shaped cloud.

The dousing did nothing to cool Liam's rage. As his hand clasped Erin's neck, that slender tube through which the other's blood and nerves contrived to feed his brain, he felt such a sense of immediacy, it was several moments before he realised that Erin wasn't fighting back. Like a lover, he'd wrapped himself around Liam and it was in this manner that they settled, in a simmering haze, beside a half-buried signpost, its head decorated with four arrows and three barely discernible words: *West Street* and *Fulton*. Above them, the sun surmounted some obstacle and the water sparkled. The Sixer, a dark slice amid these bright flashes, was riding so low in the water, Liam

423

could see her starboard portholes. As he watched, her stern was overcome, her anchor snaked from its housing and she began to descend, accompanied by a low, animal groaning.

It seemed, at first, a slow process but as the air inside the boat slithered forth in quivering silver discs, her descent quickened, though Liam only realised this when he heard a dull clank and looked up to see that the anchor had reached its nadir. He tried to let go of Erin, to push himself away but still Erin held him fast. Only when the boat was so close that they were entirely within its shadow did he pull Liam aside. They slid through the water accompanied by a forceful undulation, turned to watch the Sixer land in the spot they'd so recently vacated, her mast crumpling beneath her so that, when the silt finally cleared, she looked like a dead shark, the actual shark, still attached to its chain, now seeming parasitic in size.

Still Erin held on.

Growing ever more frantic, Liam fought back but it was no use. Erin clung on with a gritty resolve. The need for air was like a black hole, a monstrous parasite that thrust tentacle after tentacle into every fibre of his being. Finally, given no choice, he took a breath. Once, twice, he breathed in, felt the water fill his lungs, waited for the inevitable pain—only to find that no pain came. Erin too was breathing the water and Liam saw him laugh, the expulsion more effervescence than sound.

As if suddenly grown bored, Erin let go and began to swim towards the surface. Liam followed. Ahead of him, he saw a long white keel, silver rungs, Erin slide upwards in a flurry of white, his own hand groping slowly forwards. Barely able to climb, Liam pulled himself from the water and collapsed onto the deck, his stomach knotting, water gushing across the teak. Through salt-sore eyes, the mint-green sky appeared distorted, the olive and pink clouds scattering it, vaporised.

Erin was similarly prostrate, the boards around him drenched and it was some time before he could sit up. Head bent to his knees, his hair hanging in jagged lines, he breathed as if winded. "We live to fight another day," he managed.

Liam lay on his back, his hands upturned on the deck. He turned his head, spat. "You tried to kill me."

"And yet I failed," Erin wheezed. "Why do you think that is? Because only you have the power to end this."

Liam coughed, felt his lungs expel more liquid. "Why should I believe a word you say?"

It was the Mayor's boat, he realised. Dead bodies lay everywhere. Beyond its starboard side, he could see three of the screaming towers, their broken reflections reaching across the water. "Where's Rook?"

Even as he dragged his shirt over his head, Erin was overcome by a coughing fit. "She's with the Caretaker," he managed at last. "I figured you might come after me." He began to wring out his shirt, water spattering the deck, then flashed Liam a grin. "I *wanted* you to."

Liam resisted the bait. "Why do you want me to die?"

Erin started to spread his top on the warm deck. "I told you, I'm just trying to point you in the right direction. Rook and Fay need you."

The taste of salt in his mouth made Liam want to retch. "How do you know that name?"

Erin gave a derisive snort. "Didn't I ask you the same thing?"

"This isn't a game. Where is my book?"

"I thought you had it."

"No," Liam said, "you *took* it. Just like you *took* Rook."

Yet though he was angry, something was distracting him. He felt eyes on him, dead eyes. More than that he felt a familiar tug. The Mayor's craft was long and narrow, the main deck graced by little more than a sleek white cabin and a metallic grab rail. The rail, however, was barely visible, covered as it was by the dead, themselves adorned with knife and teeth marks. Few had died with their hats on. Only one among them did he know.

Wires lay on a coil of rope, his back arched, his stomach exposed, his ribs painfully pronounced, his curled hands either side of his hips. His head grinned cheeklessly at the boat's bow. Even as Liam stared at the rib-splayed body, he recalled the last words Wires had ever spoken to him. *Yur sole book needy take*? There, jammed into the man's trousers, its uppermost edge just visible, was the very thing.

Erin watched, an amused expression on his face, as Liam picked his way between the corpses and bent to retrieve the book. Wires' body had swollen and he had to work the thing back and forth, a movement that forced a long, odorous sigh from the man's lungs. Seizing the book more firmly, he was able to pull it loose but when he opened it, the wind snatched at the verses. The nearest came to rest by a tripod supporting one of the spotlights, two more between the legs of a dead archer. Worried they would blow into the water, Liam gave chase. Only when he thought he had them all did he count them.

". . . three, four, five, *six*." Liam frowned, counted again. Again he got six. Identifying the odd one out, he held it up.

Stalking over, Erin peered down at the little slip. "Well what are you waiting for?" he said. "Read it."

Liam scanned the sixth verse, then began to read aloud. "Darkling I listen . . . and, for many a time I have been half in love with easeful Death, call'd him soft names in many a mused rhyme, to take into the air my quiet breath . . . now more than ever seems it rich to die."

The tremor in his voice was clearly discernible. "I knew it. It's about death. Death is coming."

But before he could say more, they both heard a leering call, its sound diffused by the vapour in the air:

"Where is your champion?"

A patch of mist high above them was tinged now with blue and red. Even as they stared, the lights seemed to writhe, one with the other, but they did not need such a display to know exactly who had issued the challenge, for it could only have come from one throat. Ma'kin's.

426

Chapter 3.

What Goes Up

1

LOOKING BACK THROUGH the observation window, Ruth saw a glitter of streetlight, the edge of Will's bed. Gladys's body was out of sight.

Two porters were walking down the corridor towards her, their uniforms a blur in the brightness. They seemed familiar but she'd seen so many staff by then, it was difficult to remember who was who. She turned and headed in the other direction. She didn't have Penny's map but it didn't matter. She knew if she kept going, she'd reach Fay's ward eventually.

Up ahead, a door opened. It was a nurse she knew. Removing an elastic band from her pocket, she began to pull her hair into a ponytail, keeping her elbows at such an angle that her arms covered her face as she passed the door. The nurse was speaking to someone inside the room. Daring a glance under her arm, Ruth saw an older man.

"It's been circling a while . . ." she heard him say.

Then she was pushing through double doors ahead.

The next part of the corridor was shorter and she realised she'd chosen the long way round. From what she remembered of Penny's map, the postnatal ward was in the opposite corner of the building, which meant going past waiting areas, a canteen, any number of hospital staff who might recognise her. Several doctors and pharmacologists and at least a dozen nurses knew her by sight. Even if she managed to reach the ward, it was a secure area, meaning she'd have to wait until someone went in or out before she could get through the doors. Not to mention the nurse's station. Without a sizeable distraction she didn't stand a chance.

A light buzz tingled the top of her scalp, adding a briskness to her step. From an abandoned gurney she picked up a clipboard and pencil and began studying the papers there, tapping the pencil as she did so. She felt a little of her old flame burning. It felt good despite the fumes. She saw a staff changing room and walked in, giving a bright, "Hello!" to a nurse she didn't recognise before opening a locker at the far end of the room. The nurse smiled and continued to heave a pair of trousers over her buttocks.

"Dying for a smoke," Ruth said. She didn't know where it came from. She needed to say something and she genuinely felt like a cigarette. She held the locker door, stared at vacant innards.

"Gave up, myself," the nurse said, her voice even louder than Ruth's. "Still miss it though."

"Like crazy," she said, "cr*aaaz*y." She sat down on the wooden bench behind her and began pulling off her shoes.

The nurse laughed. "Never seen so much snow," she said. "I had to walk." She adjusted her top, straightened the watch on her lapel. "Starting or finishing?"

"Sorry?" Ruth had her top halfway over her head. "Oh, starting."

"Me too. I've only been here a week. Transferred from St Bart's. It's so much quieter. Not for much longer though. Can you believe it? Three hours they've been up there." The nurse laughed and turned for the door. She was about to leave when Ruth asked if she had any makeup she could borrow.

"Sure." The nurse opened her locker and pulled out a bag.

Ruth said she'd only be a moment but the nurse said not to worry. "Use what you need and stick it back in there. I'll leave my locker open." She opened the door, waved and left.

Ruth was shaking. She tugged her top back on, moved around the room, pulling at locker doors, searching those she found unlocked. Within a minute she had dark trousers, a white coat, a cardigan and a blouse that smelt of Coco Chanel. A minute after that she was redressed and sitting in a toilet cubicle at the back of the locker room. She applied mascara, lipstick and foundation, tied her hair back and pulled several strands down round her face. Finally, she filed her nails.

As she put the makeup back in the nurse's locker, she spotted a pair of reading glasses and put them on. A very different Ruth stared back at her from the mirror near the door. She picked up the

430

clipboard and took another look. Then she re-entered the same cubicle, locked the door and settled down on the toilet to wait for midnight.

ii.

THE LOCKER ROOM HAD no windows and the light was on a timer. Ruth woke to total darkness. The building was much quieter. She'd not been aware of the voices and laughter, the rattle of wheels, the clatter of cutlery, until waking in that silence. She lifted her elbows from her knees, stood up and rocked back and forth, willing her legs back to life. Her plan was to find the postnatal ward, pose as a member of staff and get to Fay. After that she'd have to play it by ear. *Through the sad heart of Ruth, when, sick for home* . . . was that where she was going?

"First things first." But the first thing was a box containing many things and when it opened, the little slip of hope tucked inside the lid was soon overwhelmed.

When she re-entered the locker room, the hospital seemed more than silent, it seemed hushed. Ruth tried to tell herself it was her imagination but the feeling persisted. She crossed the room and stepped out into the corridor to find it empty in both directions. Two men in white coats walked around the corner and she walked towards them. Each room she passed, including a large open plan waiting area, its windows framing a snow-flecked darkness, was empty. The doctors disappeared through a side door.

The next intersection was softened by several armchairs and a display of crudely painted pictures labelled with children's names and ages. She turned right and walked past a bank of windows looking out over the town. The hospital was in an elevated position so that she could see dark, snow-covered buildings and streets stretching out almost to the horizon, beyond which were indistinct patches she took to be fields. This section of the building stepped inwards and was interspersed by several sets of double doors. It stretched for perhaps two hundred feet and was eerily empty. It was almost a relief then when she saw someone emerge from a stairwell and start in her direction. She recognised him as one of the porters from earlier. Instinctively, she turned and stared out of the window. Beyond the faint reflection of a strange woman wearing glasses, narrow streets stretched towards fields. Snow danced in front of the glass. A light came and went far out across the town. She watched the man's reflection approach and then turn and stand beside her.

"This is it," he said quietly.

She said nothing and then it happened. The light grew bright for a second and then erupted, briefly illuminating the streets and turning the grey specks nearest it orange. Even as the initial brilliance broke apart, a line of red and blue lights began to trickle across the lower part of the picture.

She sensed the porter shaking his head. "Jesus Christ."

Ruth's business had been aeroplanes for far longer than her qualifications stated, yet she did not recognise what had just happened. She opened her mouth and asked the question before she could stop herself.

"A *plane*," the porter said, like he was wondering where she'd been. "Been circling for hours. They told those driving the ploughs to clear a runway, except they cleared the wrong runway. Too short. And then it started snowing again. Most flights had been cancelled but there were a few who'd already set off, one of which was moved on from Heathrow. A commercial flight, hundred and fifty-six passengers."

The hospital had received a phone call asking them to free as many beds as possible. Only after the porter pointed out the fire and ambulance crews rushing along what Ruth now saw was a runway, did she finally realise how her prayers had been answered.

She started to say something to try and cover up her mistake but the man was listening to his radio. A loud voice on his hip was saying that the plane was in a whole lot of trouble. One wing was in pieces. "There are survivors," the voice said. "Shit and fan, Kenny. Shit and fan."

The porter apologised. "Al doesn't get out much."

Ruth asked Kenny how long until the first ambulance.

He calculated out loud. "Get in, cut 'em out, not much traffic, poor conditions . . . thirty to forty minutes?"

She held out a hand, introduced herself as Emma. She'd wanted to wait until midnight because the nurses worked shifts and those on the nightshift didn't know her face. She was aware that Gladys may have regained consciousness or may have been missed. Either way, they must have worked out by now that Ruth wasn't in her room. But she was gambling on the idea that they'd expect her to leave the building instead of waiting several hours before trying to kidnap Fay. They might still be on their guard though. She needed a way to catch them off it. She thought of the knife but was glad she didn't have it.

When the porter shook her hand, she told him she was a paediatrician. The hospital had called her in due to a staff shortage. She said she lived locally but it had still taken her nearly an hour to get in. She smiled and said she was there in case there were any children on the flight, could he perhaps direct her to the children's ward?

Kenny was nodding. He said, "So Broussard's not in?" She shook her head and he said, "Chief paediatrician, Esmé Broussard?"

"Oh, I don't know," Ruth said, "they just called me . . . reception was busy and I knew this was the floor . . ."

The old man said, "Typical. Of the Royal, I mean. *Dum spiro, spero.* While I breathe, I hope." He gave a sighing laugh. "Or in the case of many who leave here, while I don't. Anyway, my dear, follow me."

The bank of windows ended in a block of stairs labelled with a green and white fire escape sign, beyond which another corridor began at an acute angle to the last. If Ruth's bearings were correct, at the end of this corridor was the Enid Blyton Ward.

As they walked, Kenny made small talk, not seeming to notice her growing anxiety. "My wife died here last year," he said. "She was a little crazy at the end. Are you married, Emma?" He looked back at her.

She realised he was talking to her and shook her head. He asked if she had children and she hesitated. "Yes," she said, "a boy." When he asked his name, she said Elijah.

"A good name," he said, falling back to walk beside her.

As they approached the next set of doors, she saw a flash of red hair and realised it was Dr Needlemire. He pushed open a door, then held it for someone wearing a felt hat. Inspector Hart. Ruth reached out and touched the wall. Kenny asked if she was all right.

"Feel weak," she managed.

She felt his hand turn her and guide her to a door just behind them.

Hart's words drifted in her direction. ". . . hours but she might . . ."

The door was too heavy. Kenny reached over her shoulder, shoved it open and she stumbled inside. She kept waiting for the door to open again and it was only when the porter spoke that she realised he'd followed her.

"It's hit us all hard," he said. "Can I get you anything?"

His head was haloed by light. He was holding out a hip flask. She said she was all right.

"Listen, if you're really bad, you should go home," he said, "I'm sure this lot'll manage."

"No, it's just low blood sugar." She curled her fingers round his. "If you could take me to the ward, perhaps come in with me, we've still got time, haven't we? I need to acquaint myself with the ward but I might need a shoulder to lean on."

He patted her hand and told her he'd look after her. "At least until the fan cranks up."

She gave a faint smile. "Shit and fan, Kenny."

"That's right," he laughed. "Alfie's quite the poet."

"Alfie the poet," she said.

"Ay," Kenny laughed again, "that he is."

But Ruth wasn't laughing, she was thinking. Alfie the street poet. It was actually only one of the porters she'd recognised. Could it be that she knew him from somewhere other than the hospital? She'd

434

told no one about Eli, no one except a stranger on a beach. And she'd been certain Frank was using someone inside the hospital.

iii.

WHEN THEY STEPPED out into the corridor, Needlemire and Hart were gone. Less than a minute later, Kenny and Ruth were standing outside the Enid Blyton Ward. As he picked up the ward phone, she felt her face glow beneath her makeup. The shirt irritated her where it touched the back of her neck. Hart had been coming from this direction. She was sure he'd already been to the ward and warned the staff.

Kenny spoke, a buzzer sounded and he pulled open one of the doors. She followed him as he pushed through another set, saw a wide, low-lit space connecting several open-ended rooms, each lined with cots. The nurse's station was round to the right against the near wall. Sitting behind a desk curving beneath a second, higher desk, both cluttered with paperwork, were two people, a nurse Ruth did not recognise and a security guard she did. It was the grey-faced young man who'd escorted Jane from her room. He was sitting beside the nurse in a pool of light that ended just beyond the outer desk. The rest of the ward was in shadow. The guard was leaning back in his chair but Ruth caught the impression that he and his companion had been whispering together. She stopped just behind Kenny and focused on the young SRN. She felt weak.

Kenny moved round to the front of the desk, rested his hands on the wood. "I trust the hospital's as safe as ever beneath your keen gaze, Joe?"

The guard ruffled good-naturedly. "I've been asked to wait here, Kenneth," he said. "So less of the sarcasm." He smiled for a moment. "So she came down then?"

"Like a stone," Kenny said. "I watched from the north side. Emma and I were both there . . ." He turned to introduce Ruth but stopped when he saw her with her fingers steepling her brow. "You all right,

435

doc?" He glanced back at the two behind the desk. "Emergency paediatrician. Had a dizzy spell a moment ago."

She saw someone move round the desk, felt a hand on her shoulder. It was the nurse, her hair shining gold in the light. She told Ruth to come and sit down. Ruth said she was fine. She was looking at the nurse's face but out the corner of her eye, she was watching the guard. He was studying her, a look of concern on his face.

"It's just low blood sugar . . ."

The nurse reached under the shelf Kenny was leaning on and took out a Mars Bar. "Chef Donna to the rescue."

Ruth unwrapped the chocolate and took a bite. She hadn't had to exaggerate her symptoms. She was very hungry. And just being this close to Fay made her feel faint. She had no idea what to do next, just an urge to stay out of the light. Donna led her away from the desk, each step like a balm. They walked around a central plinth containing a water cooler and into a walk-through that ended in a room containing cots.

"I need to check on the girls," Ruth whispered, as Donna sat her in a chair, "*and* boys. I need to know they're all right. Before any new intakes." She swallowed the last of the chocolate. "Thanks. Work, rest and play, right?"

The nurse nodded. She looked too young to remember the advert.

"I need a phone." Ruth tried to look embarrassed. "My partner doesn't know I'm here. He was out when the hospital called. Sorry, mine's on the blink."

Donna told her to rest. "Work and play can wait," she added with a wink.

Ruth watched her walk away. The water cooler ran from the plinth almost to the ceiling so that she could see the nurse only as a vague distortion when she reached the desk. She heard voices and waited, her insides churning. They know. They must know.

When Donna came back, she was carrying a cordless phone and said she'd be back in a minute. "I'm going to get you another chocolate bar from the machine downstairs. Just in case. We've got two little ones in this section, there and there, so . . ." She raised a finger to her lips.

Ruth watched her walk away. A distorted white light shone through two large windows at the other end of the room, making the space a shade lighter but it was still difficult to make out which cots were occupied. She'd looked at Penny's note so many times but suddenly she was unsure of her phone number. She saw several digits in her mind, breathed in, held her breath and dialled. It took three guesses before she got a ring tone. An answer phone message simply repeated the number. When she dialled it again, Penny answered on the third ring.

"Hello?" She sounded very far away.

Ruth felt her insides tighten. "Penny, it's Ruth. I wouldn't ask this if I had a choice." She looked towards the nurse's station. Kenny and the guard were out of sight. "I need to leave the hospital."

Suddenly Penny sounded nearer, her voice sharper. "Why? Is it something to do with the crash?"

"Something bad is going to happen if I don't get Fay out of here. The man, he left me a note. He's coming. I need to leave. You have to trust me. I have to trust you." Ruth tried to whisper. "He's going to try and kill Will and I think he's going to try and take Fay."

"Why?" Penny asked again.

"I don't have time," Ruth said. "I'm taking Fay tonight, I need you to meet me." She told Penny to park on the road opposite the entrance. "I'll get to you," she said. "But please, tell no one."

2

DONNA WAS STILL NOT back. Ruth could hear the two men chatting. With a final glance towards the nurse's station, she advanced into the room. The cots were staggered left and right, a dozen in total. The first child lay on her back with her hands curled around her ears. It wasn't Fay. On the other side of the room, three cots in from the outer wall, a second child lay in a similar position, her arms also thrown above her head. Ruth's legs gave way and she

437

had to hold onto the top bar. It was Fay. The white from the window caught the cupid's bow of her lips, glazing her cheeks and eyelids as if with frosting.

"She's without her mother." Kenny was standing in the gloom just past the chairs.

He'd barely whispered but Ruth still jumped. He told her the baby's name was Fay. He stepped closer.

"I come in most days to check on them. Most of the other babies are incubated but these two are here because their mothers are elsewhere. One lady died, the other's away with the fairies." He shook his head. "Anyway, I came to tell you, Donna rang, she's been caught up in things downstairs. The first ambulances have arrived. Apparently faeces and fan are getting acquainted at quite a rate."

Ruth tried to smile. She told him she'd be done in a moment. "This one feels fine. The other one's a little flushed though and I haven't got my thermometer. Could you find me one?"

As the old man ambled away, Ruth saw a trolley against a nearby wall. When he returned two minutes later, she was leaning over the first baby's cot. He said he couldn't find a thermometer, that Donna had called again. She'd asked if Ruth could go down. Apparently Broussard wanted to talk to her.

Ruth stood up, not daring to look at the porter. "We'd better get some equipment together, just in case."

She grabbed the trolley and started giving him orders. "I'll need dressings, gloves, wipes, bandages, scissors—"

He asked her if a bag wouldn't be easier but she said she might need a flat surface, that she'd rather take one than rely on finding one. The trolley was obviously used around the ward. It had a thick plastic top with a concave edge and two drawers underneath, which slid into a metal frame. Both sides were draped with long blue curtains. As she pushed it, one of the wheels jammed and dragged along the floor. Hand to her chest, she corrected the wheel, before pushing the trolley up against the water cooler. There she opened all the drawers Kenny directed her to and began to load up the top tray.

When they were ready, she put a stethoscope around her neck, lowered her head and went to push the trolley out of the ward.

"Wait a minute, Emma." Kenny had stopped to speak to the guard. "All that turmoil down there, Joe," he said, "I thought it was your kind of gig?"

"Needlemire told me to stay here." Joe was still sitting in his chair but as he spoke, he was studying Ruth.

It was difficult to avoid his gaze so instead Ruth looked right at him, hoping the glasses and lack of light would be enough of a disguise.

"The doc says I gotta watch the babies tonight," Joe said, his eyes remaining steady. "There's a crazy on the loose."

"Which suits you and that chair right down to the ground, I bet?" Kenny chuckled. "Come on, doc, let's go do some work."

A second later, Ruth nodded. As she began to move away, the guard winked and just like that she understood why he'd been staring at her. Without responding, she turned and walked towards the exit, resisting the urge to look back.

The corridor had been transformed. It smelt of antiseptic and perspiration. A thickset matron with stern, worried eyes was marshalling a troop of staff, some of whom were pushing gurneys up and down the hall, while others were attending to patients wherever they'd been told to wait. One young lady lying on a gurney was trying to sit up even though she was being pushed along the corridor. She kept rolling her head and shouting 'Reggie.' A middle-aged man in a wheelchair was complaining about being manhandled to the obvious frustration of the nurse who was trying to wheel him into the toilets. They reached the lifts just as the doors opened. A group of women with dark, gentle eyes and headscarves stood in the gap, unsure perhaps if they had the right floor. Kenny said it was too busy and they walked on until they reached the stairwell.

"We'll have to carry the trolley," he said.

Ruth picked up her side and followed him down the stairs. Between them, they tried to keep the trolley level but with every step it tipped slightly and each time it did, Ruth caught her breath. When they reached the first landing, Kenny wheezed something about a bag being better but he still managed a wink. There were others on the stairs, a dark-haired nurse with wide nostrils who passed them without a word and further down, a fat old man coming up one step at a time. Then, just as she was wondering how they were going to get past him, the lights went out. There was a moment of dusty, breathless darkness and then they flickered back on again.

Alfie's voice was loud in the stairwell. "You there, Ken?"

The nurse glanced down at them and then carried on walking. The old man was staring up at Ruth with watery eyes.

Kenny said into his radio, "I'm kind of busy right now, Al."

Alfie asked where he was. Kenny said he was in the southeast stairwell, between second and first. Alfie said he was needed in the control room.

"You're the only one the boss trusts to kick the generator. If we get another power cut, its cat and pigeons time."

Kenny smiled indulgently. He said he was transporting someone to ground zero. Couldn't it wait?

That was when Alfie said, "I'll come up. Meet me on first."

And then the lights went out and stayed out. The gloom was punctuated by a vague light coming from somewhere below them. Ruth heard the nurse trip and curse in a foreign language. The old man stayed where he was for a moment and then began to retrace his steps. Kenny said they'd better go, that he needed to get to the generator room. Ruth took hold of the handle again.

As they began to shuffle downwards, she thought about the other porter. This time when he spoke, she'd listened very carefully. What she'd heard had made her shiver. She was certain it was Grey Master Flash. And he was coming to meet them.

At the bottom of the stairs they caught up with the elderly gentleman. Kenny leaned past, pushed the glass door open for him. As they followed, Ruth wondered if she should run but she was unsure which way to go. This corridor was even more populated than the last. Various patients were milling around or had stopped moving altogether. A few were sitting on the floor. There were no windows in the corridor but many of the doors along the outside wall stood open, each emitting a ghostly light. Almost opposite the stairs was a room that looked like an office. Through the open door and the window beyond, Ruth could see a snow-covered embankment, a darkened street lamp.

Kenny told her she needed to wait there. Alfie would take her down the last flight. "The generator's in the basement so I've got to head in that direction."

She told him to go but didn't get to finish, for just then another man materialised out of the dark.

"It's not looking good," he said, his eyes blinking on and off in the gloom. He took Kenny's arm. "The electricity company said it could be an hour. We need to get the back-up going. You better go, I'll take it from here."

In the half-light, Ruth saw Alfie turn to observe her.

Kenny introduced them. He said Broussard wanted her out front. To Ruth, he said, "Nice to meet you, Emma."

Realising Alfie had not yet recognised her, Ruth was reluctant to speak. She leaned forward and gave Kenny a hug. Then he was gone.

Alfie's teeth glowed greyly in the obscure hole that was his mouth, "So," he said, "welcome to the mad house."

He took hold of the trolley, pushed open the door to the stairs and stepped into the stairwell. Ruth didn't talk as they descended but luckily Alfie didn't stop. Only as they reached the bottom of the stairs did he shut up but only long enough to belch. "Sorry, Doc," he said, "the old belly's playing up tonight." His eyes bobbed eerily in the dark. "Must be all the excitement."

She said nothing. They were so close. The last corridor was filled with the smell of snow and was only busy around the lifts. The lifts weren't working but still the crowds waited, their heads tipped back, their throats glinting in the dark. Raised voices came and went from around the far corner and it was in this direction that Alfie pushed the trolley, Ruth trailing behind, the smell of cold tantalising her nostrils. Beyond the corner lay the main reception area, preceding a long, glass-covered walkway, leading, some way off, to a set of revolving doors, shouldered left and right by more doors, both propped open. The main entrance. Next to it, a group of people had gathered in a circle. To Ruth's left was a long, parquet-topped desk, to her right, the café area where she'd shared a coffee with Graham. Only the corridor and the revolving doors separated her from freedom.

And then the lights flickered, went out and came back on again. Reception, café, corridors, all became hard, bright realities. Alfie was speaking and she told herself not to look up but when his voice trailed away, she couldn't help herself. He was looking at her as if he couldn't believe what he was seeing. She felt trapped by light and lost in space and could only shut her eyes and wait for the inevitable.

So quietly, she barely caught it, Alfie said, "So you found me."

ii.

THE NOISE AT THE OTHER end of the corridor changed as those there stood up, some form in their midst rising with them.

Even as Ruth stared at Alfie, she felt her fingers reach for the trolley. "How long have you been working for him?"

Alfie wiped at his face. "You mean?" He couldn't even say Frank's name. "I didn't . . . that day at the beach . . . I didn't lie to you."

Ruth was glad she was holding onto something. In that moment, all of her doubt evaporated. It felt as if someone had thrown open a cage.

Alfie's eyes were shining. "I was homeless. No one gave a damn. Believe it or not, I used to work in finance. I got paid a fortune. Boozed it up with the best of them. Enjoyed a tipple a little too much." He sounded like he was reading an obituary. "Frank offered to take me in, said all I had to do was give up the drink. But that wasn't all," he said. "He got me running errands, passing messages. I never asked questions, I was too grateful. One of the first things he asked me to do was follow you, find out where you went, what you liked, what time you got in, what you did at the weekend. Truth was, I quite liked it, I felt like Philip Marlowe." He grimaced.

442

He said an old man was a great cover for Frank's kind of work. But Frank started getting frustrated. He wanted some dirt, something he could use. He told Alfie to approach Ruth when the time was right. He said to wait until she did something out of the ordinary.

Alfie's story was no surprise. Ruth should have been angry but she felt only gratitude. "You followed me to the beach?"

"I had my trunks in the car," he said. "I figured, old-man-out-swimming, how harmless can you get?"

Behind them, the lifts had begun working again and people were squeezing their way into them. The party coming up the corridor had stopped but as Alfie continued to talk, they started up again.

"I'm so sorry," he said. "You were grieving that day and I gave your secrets to that monster."

"So why are you here, Alfie?" she said, her voice cooler. If it were up to Grey Master Flash, she'd still be rotting upstairs.

He said after that, Frank cut all ties. "Likes to keep his nose clean. I've seen him at parties working a room full of junkies and unless you looked very closely, you'd swear he was as high as the next man but he never takes part. Frank only uses people."

"And you let him tear my family apart," she said, "which makes you no better. But that still doesn't explain why you're here."

His Adam's apple bobbed beneath his skin. "About a month ago," he said, "he found me again. I had a gig in the Laines but I was barely making enough to pay for a bedsit. He told me he didn't like to see me begging, said he'd found me a job in Crawley as a porter. I hadn't started drinking again but I was close. He said it was a no-brainer and it was. Twenty-six years out of regular employment, thirty as an alcoholic, Frank was offering an old man with no references, a job. I knew," he said, raising a finger, "I knew there was a big fat hook lying under the meat but I had to bite. If I'd started drinking again, the winter would've killed me."

Ruth watched as the group shuffled into reception carrying a man. She could see a limp wrist, a gold watch.

Alfie said Frank let him settle in, gave him just enough time to like what he had and then told him what to do. "Keep an eye on you. And the little one."

Ruth squeezed the handle.

Alfie looked more frightened than ever. "I'm sorry," he said, his grin skeletal. "I think all this has made me ill."

"But you did more than just watch us," she said. "What else did you do?"

Someone in the group nearby said, "*Doc*tor? We need help."

"It was you who placed the note," she said, "wasn't it?"

Alfie was nodding. He said he'd messed with the CCTV so no one would know. "By then I'd given up hope of ever being free. It was the darkest thing I've ever done. Afterwards, I heard one of the nurses say you liked reading your husband poetry but that one of the detectives had taken your book. I like poetry too, I even write it sometimes. Anyway, I got it back."

"You put the book under the wires?"

"That policewoman left her bag in the staffroom. I saw the book poking out. I didn't dare put it in plain sight in case she took it again so I hid it where you might find it."

She had to stop herself from thanking him. She asked instead when he'd last seen Frank. Alfie's forehead was glistening with sweat. He was trembling so badly, she could feel it through the trolley. "Here," he said, "today."

She looked around, convinced for a moment that Frank would be nearby. "Where?"

"In the car park," Alfie said. And then someone took hold of Ruth's elbow.

"Excuse me," a voice said, "we need a doctor."

She saw a man in his mid-fifties wearing glasses so large he looked like an owl. At the same time she heard a whimper from the gurney and looked at Alfie. She told the man she wasn't a doctor.

"Just take a look," the Owl said, pulling at her sleeve. "Please, I think he's dying."

Looking down, Ruth realised she was wearing a white coat. She looked back at Alfie, who was staring at the trolley and then the Owl was pulling her through the crowd until she was looking down at the man they'd been carrying.

"They pulled it out," one of the women said. "I told them not to."

The wounded man was looking up at Ruth. He tried to speak but his words turned to liquid. She heard Fay again. She'd placed her in the trolley's lower tray, cushioned by a fleece. She imagined Alfie pulling the curtain aside. The blood from the man's mouth shone in the light. Ruth went to speak but only laughed. "It would have been me," she said.

Looking up, she was overwhelmed by a ring of faces. Stained blouses, missing buttons, grey skin. Dr Keep was standing between two women, his balding head flashing a warning. It was there, with her hands on the wounded man's chest and her eyes on the doctor that she finally remembered where she knew him from.

He nodded. Ruth went to speak but that was when she heard the other doctor. Fay had stopped crying and when Ruth looked over, she saw Alfie kneeling beside the trolley. Needlemire spoke her name.

"What are you doing?" he said. And then he was reaching for her.

She only managed to avoid him by falling backwards. He would have had her had the wounded man not chosen that moment to come back to life. He seized Needlemire's leg.

"Help me," he said, blood frothing at his chin.

Ruth rose into a crouch, her eyes on Needlemire. "Help him," she said, "isn't that what you're supposed to do?"

"Yes," a woman said, seizing his lapel. "*Help* him."

Others in the group also began protesting and it was this that forced Needlemire to start tearing at the man's clothing. As he did so, he urged those around him: "Stop her—please!"

The Owl looked at him and then at her. Ruth reached the trolley and pulled it away from Alfie. Glancing behind her, she saw that Dr Keep was holding something up in the air. She followed his arm and realised it was Will's tin plane. The man's grin was like the edge of a

445

knife. She understood. Dr Keep was dead. He'd died just after she set eyes on him, several months before Will's accident. They'd been on the same flight, sitting in opposite rows. He'd kept his eyes closed most of the flight and it was only when she got up to use the bathroom that she realised why. He was praying.

She looked at Keep and nodded. With a silent whistle, he drove the plane downwards and her heart dropped with it. And then he was gone.

3

RUTH STARED AT ALFIE. "Help me."

His eyes swam in his face. "I can't."

"Then you'll live with our blood on your hands."

She heard the Owl's voice as he pushed towards her.

"Miss?"

With a final glance at Alfie, she seized the trolley and ran.

Needlemire shouted but she carried on, the trolley's wheels skipping and trundling across the floor. She heard a yelp and looked back. Alfie and the Owl were on the floor, Alfie on top, his arms wrapped around the Owl's middle. People hurried towards her but she didn't slow down. She ran the gurney along the wall, trying to miss the throng but it was impossible. A corner slammed into a nurse and she groaned at Ruth even as her face flooded with surprise. It was Donna.

"Emma?" she said. "Broussard's waiting—" But the rest was lost as Ruth rushed on.

Nothing was going to stop her, even the realisation that Keep was a figment of her imagination. By the time she reached the exit, she was out of breath. A number of people were coming through the doors and she searched for Hart's face but there were far too many to tell. With an icy wind ruffling her clothes, she lowered her head and pushed the trolley through the open doorway.

The forecourt was in chaos. Two ambulances arrived even as she stepped out, joining half a dozen others parked across the tarmac.

Most of the green and yellow chequered vans were host to several staff and civilians, some still inside the vehicles, others climbing out. A party from the last ambulance burst from its back doors and rushed towards Ruth. Spinning lights splashed red and blue across the front of the hospital, colouring each breath.

Here then was the answer to her prayers. For every up, a down. A party of medics hurried by with a patient. She avoided their eyes but couldn't resist looking back. Her glasses magnified the sway of arms and bodies, the rattling gurney, the body on it and a figure slouched against the wall to the right of the far door. He was wearing a camel hair coat and a trilby and was staring at the cigarette between his fingers. Then he looked right at her. She shoved the trolley towards a gap between two ambulances. Looking back, she could still see the spot where Hart had been standing. He was no longer there.

She sidestepped a stretcher, two paramedics and a nurse. The incline beyond was treacherously slippery. Red and blue snowflakes danced above her head and settled on the trolley, which was the only thing keeping her on her feet as she crossed the slope towards the bushes skirting the forecourt. Beyond the bushes lay a low wall and the road. Someone shouted her name but she didn't need to turn around. It was Hart.

With a final effort she forced the trolley between two bushes, reached down and slid the bottom drawer open. Fay stirred, a fist rubbing at her nose. A buzzing filled Ruth's head. She scooped Fay up, hugged her to her chest, turned towards the inspector. The man was running, despite the ice. Gripping the trolley, Ruth shoved it so hard that it shot across the frozen surface before toppling onto its side. Hart saw it and tried to slither out of the way but lost his footing and went down on one elbow. He barely had time to look up before the trolley caught him in the face. Ruth turned and forced her way to the wall, keeping her mouth in the crook of Fay's neck and her arm around her to protect her from the branches.

When they reached the wall, Ruth slipped. Pain shot across her pelvis. From her right, an ambulance swept towards her, before turning into the forecourt, a flurry of snow wheeling with it.

Clambering over the wall, she stumbled first one way, then the other, weeping in short gasps, Fay struggling in her arms. In a sudden despair, Ruth sank to a crouch.

Several vehicles away, a car flashed its lights. She rose with a groan and hobbled towards it. The windscreen was fogged over, hiding whoever was inside but then the passenger window slid down with a crackle of ice and Penny leaned over.

"Are you sure about this?" she said uncertainly.

Ruth didn't answer but instead pulled at the door. Warmth spilled out. She was so close. But then a thought rose up like a wall. The final verse. While they were in Ibiza, Will had proposed to her a second time. The first time, he'd been very nervous and had blurted it out after one too many drinks. In Ibiza, they were sitting in the garden behind Tommy's bar. A woman was strumming a few chords on an acoustic guitar and singing. Something about a broken-hearted fool, though Ruth's Spanish was a little rusty by then. The lights were low, the conversations around the other tables, intimate. Smoke drifted in the air. And then Will had gotten down on one knee and asked her for her ring, before breaking into song. He'd had a few drinks and something to smoke but was only a little merry. The guitarist accompanied Will's rather off-key singing with a few bars. It wasn't just Ruth who had finally been able to let go on their honeymoon, Will too had been different. Happier. More relaxed.

She had to go back. It was insane. She stared at Penny, a wild, desperate note caught between her teeth and then, with a groan of separation, handed over the baby.

"I can't leave him."

Penny was looking into her eyes. Ruth imagined her madness plainly writ.

The nurse paused, her jaw tense. Then she took hold of Fay and drew her to her chest. "When will I see you?"

Ruth told her in a few hours. She looked down at Fay. The fleece she'd found in the ward was hooded. The hood's fluffy edge framed the baby's fat little cheeks. Penny asked where they would meet and

Ruth shut the door and leaned in at the window. "I'll call you," she said. "Just keep her safe."

Penny gave a final, doubtful smile, put the car in gear and pulled away. Ruth watched as she drove up the street, saw her turn the corner. Then she was gone.

ii.

RUNNING TO THE ENTRANCE, Ruth made her way through the bushes and then skirted the car park, avoiding the light. When she reached the building's right-hand corner, she found the door there locked. Jogging down the side of the building, she tested the next door. The same. Trying to stay calm, she followed the back wall, skirted the delivery yard there and rattled the penultimate fire door. It was also locked. With only one door left, she slipped along the building between the wall and a chain-link fence. She had to wade through deep snowdrifts before finally reaching the door, where a fan-shaped outline, criss-crossed by several footprints and a scattering of cigarette butts, had been created in the snow. The door was ajar and opened to reveal a wide concrete stairwell.

The first floor landing was deserted, as was the landing on Will's floor. Ruth wanted to go straight to his room but she didn't know what she might find there. Or whom. She wanted the knife but that wasn't the only reason she carried on up the stairs. There was something else she needed too, something she hoped would help her face her fears once and for all.

She opened the door to the third floor. Seeing a nurse walking towards her, she shut it and waited. Once the nurse had gone, Ruth stepped out to find the way deserted. The hospital had assigned the passengers to rooms on the first three floors. Also, this part of the building was used for 'special' patients.

The doors that led to Ruth's room were both unlocked. The first, leading into the antechamber, caused an inner light to spring on, illuminating the door to her room which pushed inwards and clicked into place when it reached a right angle. She approached the bed, knelt down in the bright wedge of light cast from the anteroom and groped under the mattress until her fingers found what she was looking for. Both relieved and afraid, she slid the handbag free and held it up. She didn't say a prayer but she did send her thoughts ceilingward. Please show me mercy. Help me keep my shit together.

She popped the clasp, opened the bag's two wings and began to push the contents back and forth until she spotted what she was looking for. The mini-recorder recovered from Will's car. The day her mother left, the same day she first met Frank, she'd listened to the tape inside it. She could recall her brother's voice but not what he said. However, though she wanted to listen to his story again, it would have to wait. If she was right, the cassette contained another voice entirely.

She pressed rewind and halfway back, pressed play. Eric's voice jumped out at her and she shoved her thumb at the stop button. Too far. She pressed fast-forward and then hit play again. Still Eric. This time she held the button down, turning Eric's words into a squeal. When it stopped, she let go.

There was a hiss and then she heard a voice say, ". . . to death, alone, in the dark. I couldn't walk but I carried her—" Ruth pressed stop. It was a deep voice but even so, it belonged neither to Eric nor Will. She felt her shoulders trembling. She couldn't catch her breath. The whole time she'd lain here with this box underneath her, the one Dr Keep had played to her, except, of course, he hadn't. There was no Dr Keep. Nor was it Will's voice. Memories moved behind a kind of glaucoma. The day after listening to Eric's recording, there'd been a news report on the radio, violence in Palestine, a mortar attack in Gaza. The man interviewed was talking about his daughter, how she'd been killed, a little girl named Amena. The reporter said the day after the interview, the father had been killed in another bombing. Ruth had been in the car and had switched off the radio. She remembered switching it off and thinking about the little girl inside of her. Finally she'd taken out the mini-recorder and made the first recording.

A few days later she'd made the mistake of putting on the radio again. Unprecedented rainfall, floods in Kerala, hundreds dead. And again she'd made a recording.

So she was mad after all. She'd dreamt this dream and then played it to Will. It was her who'd told him his parents were dead, not Dr Keep. Dr Keep did not exist. Well, he had done, she thought, recalling the tin plane in the man's hand. She'd been on a 767 to Lisbon. She remembered seeing the man's lips twitching. It had been a particularly rough ride. A storm had swept the Atlantic but she'd barely noticed. She understood turbulence. But Dr Keep, a nametag still pinned to his lapel, was beside himself. As she returned from the bathroom, a particularly violent gust had shaken the plane and she'd heard him say, "Why are we up here?" Then he started clutching at his arm and a doctor was called for.

They lay him in the aisle and Ruth returned to her seat and put her earphones back in. He'd died and she'd flown into Lisbon, had a nice cold glass of *Reserva Branco* in the airport lounge and flown home again. She'd been six months pregnant and had not spoken to Will for almost two weeks. She'd had no one to talk to and no one at the office even mentioned it. People died on flights all the time. The event had obviously stayed with her though, because when she'd needed a doctor, Keep had come slipping through the cracks. She'd been so angry with Will. How dare he sleep while she went through hell? She'd wanted to tell him what he'd done. That his parents were dead. But it had been too much. So she'd found someone to do it for her.

She pressed fast-forward and then play. In a voice now recognisable as her own, she heard it again. Fire and flood. Her fears, her nightmares. All of the dead doctor's words wrung from her own soul . . . *You were found holding the murder weapon . . . and your game is to play the little drowned girl.* Fire and water. Fear and guilt. These were the feelings Keep had woken in her that night above Portugal but they'd always been there, with or without him.

She had only one thought. To finish the poem. Reading Will the last verse was all she had. Then, if he returned to her, they would face Frank together. If he comes, she thought. But of course he would come. He'd invested too much in this game of his.

At this thought, she began to feel under the mattress for the knife. But though she slid her fingers back and forth, she found nothing.

"Looking for this?"

The voice was full of a calm, cold humour. Ruth turned to see someone sitting in the chair beneath the television, a body swathed in shadow. Frank.

"I've been waiting here," he said, "wondering when you might notice me and turning that line over in my mind." He held up the knife. Ruth saw he was wearing leather gloves. "I'm just glad you didn't see me. It's been entertaining. That was your voice wasn't it, on the tape? But didn't you say Will had been dreaming? That he talked about Fay as if she were dead?"

"She's not though, she's gone," Ruth said. Despite her terror, she felt a momentary triumph.

Frank nodded. "I know. I was watching from Will's room. That was some trick you pulled. I was laughing so hard when you hit Hart with that trolley I nearly bust a kidney. And then I saw you come creeping back. I had a hunch you might come up here first." He waved the knife. "Jane told me all about it, how she'd added a little present to the flowers she brought you. Of course, I had to cut the truth out of her with something a bit bigger than this but it came."

She turned away but Frank's words followed her. "For in that sleep of death what dreams may come." He chuckled. "Is that why you made the tape? You couldn't live with your dreams, so you gave them to Will? Was it really you who wanted people to die? Fay?"

"You don't get to say her name." She turned on him. "Why make me believe Keep was real?"

Frank tapped the knife against his cheek. "When you told me a doctor came to see you, something didn't ring true. I looked into it and found there was no such person. I never look a gift horse in the mouth, Ruth."

"But why us?" she said. "And why Graham? He was a good man."

452

"You told me he had something to say concerning your imaginary friend. I suspected he was going to tell you about Keep, or rather, the lack of him." She heard Frank's skin crinkle into a smile. "I didn't want him ruining our friendship."

"You killed him because . . ?"

"I saw an opportunity to kill two birds with one stone. The chef had bitten off more than he could chew and I knew you were on the edge."

It was too much. Ruth screwed up her eyes, covered her ears. She was going to die. He was going to kill her. But Fay was safe. She'd done one thing right. She could hear Frank, despite covering her ears.

He touched her shoulder. "Are you okay, Ruth?"

She turned her head. The inspector was bending over her, concern wrinkling his red skin. He had a long, dark cut across his brow. "I've been looking everywhere for you," he said. "Lawrence said she saw you come round the back."

Ruth stared past him. Frank had risen and was standing just behind the door.

"What have you done with Fay?" Hart asked. "I'm just worried, that's all. I checked out your story. If it was raining when you got in that night that would mean you didn't get home until around ten. I checked the CCTV on the motorway. It took hours but I found your car. You pulled up just outside Brighton. You stayed there for over an hour. I know it wasn't you, Ruth."

It came to Ruth then, the blue flash. It was the digital clock on the Golf's dashboard. "I stopped to feed Fay," she said. "But it's too late."

"It's not," Hart said. "It's not. No one's going to take your baby."

"It *is* too late. He's here."

As Frank stepped past the door, his shadow cut across the light, causing Hart to turn his head but Frank had already slipped a hand around the man's forehead, the knife under his chin. Hart tried to jerk forwards but Frank simply followed him before pushing his hand into the flabby skin above the man's collar and sliding it sideways, spraying Ruth with blood. The inspector fell forwards, his mouth jerking blood onto her hip. Scrabbling backwards, Ruth hauled herself up onto the bed, tiny screams trembling in her throat and then Frank was on her, his hand over her mouth, the smell of leather filling her nostrils.

He pressed the knife into her hand. "The quick and the dead, Ruth," he hissed. "The quick and the dead."

Hart twitched several times, his shoulders jumping beneath his camel hair coat and then Frank was dragging her off the bed and out into the light.

Chapter 4.

Two Birds, One Stone

1

AN EVEN, SHIMMERING mist, the towers rendered ghostlike—and then they heard it again, a voice hollowed by distance, yet still somehow pleasant: "Where is he? Bring out your champion."

Liam felt himself shiver. If only he could rediscover his anger—with such he might scale the tower—yet his heart knew only fear.

"Where is she?"

Erin nodded upwards. "Up there."

They heard a murmur, as of a sporting crowd appreciating a good volley. The wind boiled the vapours, tore tunnels, Liam caught glimpses of balconies and balustrades, rooftops and walkways, all haunted. Higher still, he saw blue and red lights cutting through the milky air, a darting snarl of voltage made all but invisible by the wisps around it. And then the sun lanced down, burning the mist, and he saw Ma'kin, its hovering figure at such an angle that it might have been looking down.

"We need to get up there," he said, unable to look away.

"We'll go together," Erin said. "Whatever you may believe, I am on your side."

The unexpected words gave Liam's spirits a tremendous lift. They were both capable of extraordinary things. Why then could they not defeat the monster, especially together?

Yet even as he turned to thank Erin, he caught sight of something that caused his confidence to falter. The motley collection of boats around them had been joined by another craft, this one by far the oddest-looking. Poised beneath the collapsed buildings under which they'd first approached the central tower, sat a boat almost as long as the Mayor's and twice as wide and fronted by a broad black bow decorated with a wooden duck's head. Upon this unlikely platform stood a figure, its stooped shape recognisable, even from a distance, as that belonging to the Keeper. His hands gripping the wooden feathers rising from the duck's neck, a curved series of frills that formed a semi-circular railing, the man was staring across the water with invisible eyes. Nor could Liam see the man's mouth, yet when he spoke, his words were very clear: "It is time to fulfil your destiny."

Though Erin was speaking, Liam couldn't hear him. He wanted to respond, to point across the way but when he opened his mouth, nothing came out. He was aware of Erin's excitement, could see that he was pointing upwards, no doubt saying something about the scene above them but all Liam could hear was the gentle slosh of the waves and all he could see were the oars jutting from the Black Duck's lower deck. He could feel the creak too, the great pulling as the big black boat began to heave through the water towards them. He might have had time to warn Erin, except that every time he blinked, the boat grew closer, the man at its helm clearer.

By the time Erin turned, the two boats were side-by-side and a swarthy-looking man was reaching out with a thin, leathery loop protruding from a long pole. As it dropped over Erin's head, he threw himself backwards but to no avail. The cord tightened around his neck and though Erin tried to get his fingers under it, the man simply yanked him across the bodies piled against the railing and over the edge, where he hung with just a few fingers gripping the grab rail.

The boats swelled on oily waves. Up close, the Keeper looked even frailer than usual. He grasped the feather-shaped railing with thin white fingers, his head nodding in a kind of palsied fugue. Still his delight rose into the air as if it were heat.

"Cool him off," he said.

The man heaved on the pole, then twisted it downwards, causing Erin to slither into the water. Stumbling across the bodies, Liam peered over the edge to see Erin below the surface, his hands holding the pole, his green eyes seeming to shift as they stared up through the water.

Liam demanded they let him go. "If not, you'll regret it."

"A-*ha*!" said the Keeper, his voice full of a crowing delight. "The oracle wishes to bring his wrath to bear upon us. Well, I'm waiting, young man. Let's see of what you're made."

Provoked by the man's mockery, Liam did indeed search his heart, again hoping to reignite the anger he'd felt towards Erin but the truth was, that particular organ was still enfeebled.

The Keeper gave a high, whinnying laugh, interspersed by quick inhalations. "When he passes through the seas, he will not drown. When he passes through the rivers, they will not sweep over him. Ah, but when asked to perform a simple miracle, the oracle will froth at the mouth! But I'm only teasing." His gaze shifted to the shadows below him. "Your friend too has his part to play, isn't that right, Julian?"

Mayor Julian had been waiting inside the galley. Hearing his cue, he shuffled forth to frown up at the old man, his glasses and oversized teeth darkened by the angled shadow cast by the deck above, his rather battered-looking top hat sitting aslant on his bald head.

"That's right," he said, a confidence in his voice that belied his position and stature. "As brother to that birdling, our flame-haired assassin here might just be the lure we need. Though my vision is beyond the present," he added, setting his hat straight as he spoke, "and my instinct is that we should just let him drown."

"But first . . ?" the Keeper said, as if they were practising lines.

"But first," the Mayor added with a nod, "the fallen have held the high ground long enough. It's time we gave the meek their due." And with that, he coughed into his fist, a gesture that was obviously a sign, for one of his retinue now presented him with his amplifier. Raising the whining device to the sky, the little man took several jowl-quivering breaths, pursed his overly pink lips and then bellowed, "The deliverance of the Lord is upon us!"

His words echoed around the towers above them, yet the response was not as it had been, for the crowd seemed too distracted by the drama unfolding above.

"Revenge is *not*," the Mayor yelled, "a noble sentiment—but it is a human one! We must combat the spread of chaos and fear, we must, we . . ." It seemed though as if his tinder were not dry enough, yet even as he faltered, a man on a nearby balcony shouted, "Hear us, O Lord!"

459

It was enough. Like a trickling flame, his cry was taken up, catching as it rose until the voices of those on the highest balconies blazed with a zealous passion.

When the Mayor shouted it again, everyone joined in: "HEAR US, O LORD!"

Only then did the man cry, "*Release the cloudbusters!*"

ii.

WHILE ERIN WAS DRAGGED below, Liam was menaced into following the Keeper who had climbed to a deck almost level with the boat's prow. This platform was wider than that surrounding the figurehead and castellated so that all four sides could be defended by archers.

Looking up, Liam saw that the House of Pain and the towers surrounding it were no longer separate entities. Between them now lay dozens of silver lines, joining their summits into a steadily growing star shape. Even as Liam watched, more cords pulsed from each of the screaming towers—balls of cable that shot through the air, their ends weighted with hooks—before finding purchase and tightening into shimmering strands. Realising their enemy's intention, evolo darted back and forth, trying to cut the cords but it was a dangerous occupation, for several were struck in mid-air. And for every wire cut, ten more took its place.

"A single bridge," the Keeper said, "could easily be expelled but this way we tire them out with a hopeless task. When the bridges are ready to cross, the battle will already be half-won."

Liam was confused. "But surely the creature could clear the sky in minutes?"

"Many dogs will always beat a boar. I'm saving my creation for a special task. Besides," the Keeper said, pointing to those on the walkways and balconies, "I need *them* to do the dirty work. I must make this victory theirs. Only then will they be mine. If they kill for the dreams I've given them, as they own their dreams, so will I own

460

them. What would you have me use? Happiness?" The Keeper laughed. "Guilt and fear are life's primary pistons."

"So then it is you who are Satan?"

The Keeper looked amused. "To those of the wing, perhaps. Everything is its opposite somewhere. Let me assure you, before this day is through, I'll be sending them back to Abaddon. It is fear that guards the vineyard. They should be afraid of us and terribly afraid at that."

As the man spoke, the boat swept around the side of the nearest tower and in through a huge opening, created, it seemed, for just this purpose. At the last moment, the dripping tips of two-dozen oars rose up level with the main deck before being withdrawn. The craft slid into the shadows.

The vast space into which the boat swept reminded Liam of the expanse below the House of Pain, except that here the walls were all intact. The lowest floors had been hollowed out to form a manmade harbour bordered by a makeshift quay. Where the concrete flooring still stood, a long, wooden pier had been built, beyond which lay a number of shacks. The tower's outer windows were boarded up, the darkness punctuated by light from the entrance and from several oil drums, which burned along the quay's edge, their flames reflecting in long fitful lines on the sea's surface.

The Black Duck drifted in and came to rest beside the pier, beyond which behatted men and women strode in and out of open-fronted warehouses, fetching and carrying bundles and boxes of all shapes and sizes. Two women helped moor the boat, one of whom was then called to the Keeper's side. After the man had made some request, she went away, only to return with a large brass box on wheels.

The Keeper told Liam to follow him. "Don't worry," he said, seeing his eyes wander, "your friend will be coming too but I thought it best we travel without him. He has poor manners." The man pointed along a narrow thoroughfare with windowless, plasterboard walls. "Your carriage awaits."

Set into a huge pillar close to the outside wall lay a peculiar set of doors, flat and without handles. The Keeper pressed a button on the wall and the doors slid open, presenting Liam with a small, silver-walled cabin.

"Electronic," the Keeper explained, waving him in. "Luckily for these old feet, the back-up generators at the base of the tower still contain a little juice."

After being joined by the brass box and a rusting brazier, the doors closed and the cabin was drawn suddenly and smoothly upwards, causing Liam to grasp at the walls. Only when the neon numbers above the doors finally rolled past ninety, did the cabin slow to a stop.

As the doors opened, they were greeted by a pale light and a blustery wind heavy with the scent of roasting meat. Beyond the pitted surface in front of him, Liam could see the central tower, which lay perhaps a hundred yards away, its surface chequered with reflections. The two bridges visible from the lift glinted in the stormy light. As Liam watched, the body of a birdman enmeshed among the strands of the nearest bridge became further entwined.

Several men dragged the box and the brazier out of the cabin. The Keeper then led Liam around the lift-shaft and across the remains of a vegetable patch. Trampled leaves lay everywhere. Either side of them, similar patches were in the process of being destroyed as booted men opened and emptied wooden boxes filled with machinery. Others worked on the spider Liam had seen from his cell the previous night. This colossus crouched atop the roof, pulsing thread from its abdomen. A cloudbuster.

Liam listened to the wind moan through the wires. "None of this is God's work."

"As I said, God was dismantled. I am merely restoring Him to His former glory."

"In your own image?"

The Keeper smiled. "Close."

The air tasted of wet knives. To the west, a black-hearted storm was slowly sliding towards the sea. Nearer to, yellow tongues made brief outlines of the great wall.

Over on the next tower, Liam could make out the shapes of women and children. Here though there were only men, all of them either cooking or cleaning, building or stripping down, their efforts lubricated by lewd phrases swapped in loud, amicable voices.

The Keeper beckoned to an old soldier he called Gruffkin, a barrel-chested man with a thick brown neck and close-cropped, greying hair, who stood with his head bowed in order to bring his rather small ear closer to the old man's mouth. When the Keeper had finished speaking, Gruffkin began to pat at Liam's clothes, before shoving a hand under his waistband and pulling out the book. Too late, Liam tried to stop him, only to receive a stunning backhand. Reeling from the slap, he sensed rather than saw the Keeper pocket the book, felt Gruffkin take hold of his collar and was dragged over to a rat-faced soldier with a burn mark across his scalp. Through throbbing eyes, he saw the cloudbuster bolted near the centre of the roof. From it, hundreds of cords stretched across the floor and over the low concrete wall that ran along the tower's western edge. These cords, as tight as piano wires, ran past the left hand side of the lift block. By now the nearest bridge was almost traversable. Several feet above this slim walkway, other cables had been shot into place as handrails.

A fiery sting flared across the back of his legs. Rat Face, who had been holding a long baton out of sight, raised it again now, threatening another blow. He dragged Liam round the lift shaft and threw him down beside Erin, who lay on the ground, his hands tied, grit sticking to his swollen face, his long hair guttering like fire.

"He took your book?"

Liam nodded. Hearing a creak, they both turned to see Rat Face open the brass box and, one by one, lift out what looked like stone boots, each one clunking dully as it struck the concrete. Dragging one of the boots over to Liam, Rat Face raised his stick and brought it down with a quick, efficient stroke across Liam's stomach, causing him to curl up in pain. A scraping sensation as the man dragged the boot onto his foot. Nearby, another man had lit the brazier and was placing chunks of wax in a bowl.

"You have to get the book back," Erin hissed, as Rat Face began to drag a similar pair of boots onto his feet. "It might be the only answer."

But Liam didn't have the chance to respond, for Gruffkin and two other men pulled him up and started dragging him, boots and all, over to the edge of the building, where they heaved him up and placed him on the wall. The boots were so heavy, when he swayed forwards, he hung there as if stuck to flypaper. The House of Pain was less than a hundred yards away, yet it wasn't the school he was looking at but the many floors beneath it, their blue, stormlit windows descending down and down to the water below. Boats as dots, walkways as wires. He heard the men grunting over to the wall again and then sensed Erin.

"He took it because he recognises its power." Erin was eyeing the abyss as if peering into a drawer filled with bric-a-brac.

With the wax finally bubbling, the soldier manning the brazier pulled on a pair of gloves and carried the bowl over to the wall. Liam gritted his teeth as the scalding hot liquid was sloshed into his boots, where it quickly solidified.

Erin was smiling, bloody teeth screened by fluttering hair. "Remember, there is not enough darkness in all the world to put out the light of even one candle . . ." He spat over the precipice, a cobwebby trail of red saliva that broke apart on the wind. "But you don't remember, you don't remember anything. Only after I died did I learn the truth. We were *both* in that accident. That's why we're *both* here now. Look at the watch." He held it up. "It stopped the moment we collided. One minute past. Does that remind you of anything?"

A penetrating whine ripped through the air, followed by a voice, its echoing words reverberating around the towers. "RRooookk, wwee aawwaaiitt yyoouu!"

"The machines, all of them!" Eric shouted over the feedback. It was true, the voice was coming from the nearest cloudbuster but also, by the sound of it, from all of the machines.

2

"COME, ROOK," THE VOICE pulsed again, "join us! See here, your lover and brother—two brave souls come to lead those of the heel against those of the wing." The words pounded from the speakers in hard, metallic waves. "No *force*, no *tor*ture, no *in*trigue can eradicate the truth from the minds and hearts of men! Rook: your condition is not your doing. Come join your brothers and sisters!"

It was raining now and Erin's voice vied with the rain-spattered wind. "What is he doing? Why not just send in the creature?"

Liam too had to raise his voice. "He's keeping it in reserve. He wants them to believe it's one of the enemy. If the evolo look a little too human, then behold, the monster."

Again the Keeper's voice rang out. "Rook! Come! *Stand* with us!"

Beyond the bridge's furthest point, a number of evolo, Star among them, her hair shining in the twilight, were looking across the way, their heads close together as if talking. Liam scanned the field, looking for Rook, but with the distance, the failing light, and the rain, which had begun to fall in ragged, sheets, he wasn't quite sure what he was seeing. Yet even as he decided that he couldn't see her, a distant figure darted from the furthest turret and he knew immediately it was her.

"Here then is what you must see," the Keeper cried. "Behold!"

A ray of light sprang from each cloudbuster, six blazing beams that met just above the House of Pain. One second Rook was running and then another Rook was running, a supersized image that shone over the field, gilding the wheat and plating the rain. Seeing her magnified self, Rook whirled on her feet, the movement mirrored by the blazing image above her.

Finally the Keeper revealed his coup-de-grâce. "This is why we're here," he crooned, his voice at one with the electric rain. "Here is your wife, your mother, your *daught*er. Mankind must twist the neck of anyone who treats our women thus. This must end today. Unto death, if need be. Unto *death*!"

With the image of Rook's dazed, pregnant form staring up at herself staring up, men, women and children joined voices in a huge, howling choir. "*UNTOOO DEAAATH*!"

Yet as the first few shuffled forwards, there came a reply from the House of Pain that caused them to falter, for just then the evolo began to rise up in clouds so dense that from a distance they looked like black smoke. The soldiers though were not so daunted. As the evolo settled along the outer walls, Gruffkin's platoon assembled in single file behind their leader. With their spears angled, their bodies streaming with rain, their hair snaking down their foreheads, they began to cross the bridge, looking for all the world like a single creature.

Liam heard a high-pitched shout, saw a line of birdmen raise catapults. A moment later, the air was full of metallic balls, their flight all but invisible until they struck their targets. One tore at Gruffkin's ear, three more struck his men, one of whom was knocked from the bridge, his shield tossed like a coin into the abyss.

The bridges had been poorly designed, force as they did those crossing them to cling to the railing. What was more, they were slippery with rain and made precarious by the wind. The soldiers were able to raise their shields but could not keep them steady. In fact those strung out along the bridges looked to be in such a difficult position, Liam almost thought the battle over before it had begun. But just then, the sky filled with quivering sticks. Each of the screaming towers was lined with archers, their weapons raised. As the thickets began to rain down, the evolo darted to and fro but to little avail. Dozens were struck low.

Liam knew what Erin was thinking. That he should do something. Recalling Ma'kin's words—*You summoned me. You spoke my name*—he shouted, "I have a plan. It's a matter of timing."

466

"Timing?" Erin said, pointing to the image of Rook. "Doesn't it feel pressing enough already?"

Liam wondered why he didn't just tell Erin of his hopes but his secret thoughts possessed a disabling magnetism. There trembled within him the urge to be right, to be the one who knew what to do, to be the one who turned the tide just when all seemed lost. While they watched, those lining the House of Pain's walls fired again, causing more to tumble from the bridges but the evolo too were caught, thighs, shoulders and throats pierced. Even as a third wave took aim, their comrades lay dying at their feet.

Gruffkin had reached the far end of the bridge with half his men still with him. Evolo stood ready to fight but the grizzled soldier had other plans. Gaining the top of the wall, he drew a weapon from his belt and fired. A cord tipped with teeth shot out and attached itself to the nearest evolo, causing her to convulse before falling to the ground. With a flick of his wrist, Gruffkin retrieved the cord.

So mesmerised were they by the scene, neither man realised that Rat Face was standing behind them until the soldier spoke.

"Your work here is done." Small pink eyes leered up at them. "Which means," the man said, giving Liam's back a seemingly friendly pat, "that you two are no longer needed."

Just then, Rook's blazing image suddenly winked out. It seemed a terrible omen. Liam saw sticks floating on a black sea, winged motes wheeling on the wind. But even as Rat Face began to apply more pressure, there came a long, zipping sound and the tension ceased.

ii.
———

IT WAS THE CARETAKER who'd dealt with him. Landing beside them, the old evolo used the last of his strength to shove them backwards, causing them to sprawl to the rooftop in a heap, there to see Rat Face, his eyes staring, his bloodied throat pierced by a small, round hole.

The old man's ribs were heaving, his face gaunt. He spoke in little panting breaths. "We-managed to-disable one-of the-*bri*dges. Two-more still being defended but they've broken through on *three* fronts. Hundreds of *casual*ties al*ready*." The man nodded towards the wall. "What were you *do*ing?"

Liam slapped the boots, his anger finally surfacing now that the immediate danger had passed. "You're not the only one who wants to use me as bait."

The Caretaker spat blood-flecked phlegm. "You needed to be out there." He pointed out to sea.

"Just as Joan was where she needed to be? What would my father say to that, to sacrificing your own daughter? Oh, I forgot, he was only too willing to sacrifice his son."

It was the Caretaker's turn to snap. "Hard times call for hard decisions. What other choice did Eagle have?"

"Eagle?" The name ran through him like a thrill. "Then we did meet." But here Liam's voice grew bitter. "But that makes no difference. He left me to flee the Keeper, to fall victim to the Giver's plotting. I wasted my time looking for him. My mother too."

"You didn't find her?" The old man gave a rueful shrug. "Well, believe me, she would have done all she could to find you. Unfortunately her methods of travel are a little slower than your father's."

It took Liam a moment to catch his meaning. "You mean she's not evolo?"

The Caretaker shook his head.

"Then what am I?"

"You are *both*," the man insisted. "If Eagle found you but did not suggest a change of course, he must have deemed your course to be necessary."

You have others to think of now. By others, Liam had thought he meant Rook. He'd actually meant much more.

The Caretaker reached into his robe and removed the ornate box he'd last opened in his study. When he opened it this time, instead of hiding what it contained, he pulled out the slip of blue fabric Liam had only glimpsed before and held it up.

"This," he said, "once belonged to your mother."

468

Bringing the scarf to his nose, Liam breathed in jasmine and violets, a dark, peaty aroma. *Hold me until you must let me go . . .* in that moment his mother and father floated in his head like lights at the end of a long, dark tunnel. Both had known that when the time was right, he would begin to remember. He felt a great warmth grow inside his thoughts. He would see them again, he was sure of it. And in the meantime he would make a story worthy of the wait.

When he stood up, it was not the movement of a tired man, nor that of someone attired in stone boots, but rather that of someone who has woken to a bright morning, someone who has chosen to let in the light. Except he let it out. "I did meet my mother," he said. "She asked me to give my precious one a kiss."

With each word, shafts of light sprang from his mouth, silhouetting his teeth, opening the darkness about them. As if it were the most natural thing in the world, he pushed his fingers down into the boots, melting the wax. Extracting his feet, he stood with his footprints slowly solidifying on the concrete.

"Go to Rook," he told the Caretaker. "I will join you there."

Erin's eyes sparkled. "Is it home time, brother?"

After freeing him, Liam stepped towards the bridge. The thing shuddered in the wind but all he had to do was take hold of the handrail for the structure to steady. He stepped out, neither looking into nor caring for the abyss, his light glittering amid the bridge's many strands.

On the far side, he climbed onto the wall and surveyed the field. Running battles rose and fell. Individuals were locked in combat, their arms and legs, knees and teeth engaged in twists of cloth and flesh alike. Hundreds lay dead among the corn. Apart from their clothing and the occasional hat, in death, they looked the same.

The bridges heralded the greatest number of dead. Boys and girls lay beneath their elders, their limbs jutting as sticks might in a nest. Blood clotted beneath skin or coloured the wheat. Wrists, throats, temples, forever at rest. Both field and dome were host to hundreds of dead evolo, their bodies curled up or half-sitting, staring at

469

nothing. Many had been electrocuted, their skin blackened, their sockets dry.

"The ravishment of the many for the benefit of the few."

The voice came to Liam's left. He peered over the wall to see one of Gruffkin's soldiers propped against the stone, his lap and legs red. Liam's fingers, where they gripped the wall, had roused the man with light. He lay slumped, his neck twisted, his head to one side, his eyes raised to look at Liam. "The ravishment of the many," he said again, wet noises accompanying each word.

As Liam lowered himself from the wall, the light fell away. Beyond him were three evolo, all dead. Liam recognised the furthest from him as Peregrine, the Sixer's navigator. A man with whom he'd never spoken. Gruffkin had drawn a curved line of shields about the south-eastern watchtower. Noticing Liam, he ran along the line shouting at his men, picked up a shield and removed his weapon.

Erin, who had followed, stepped forwards but Liam said no. He walked through the broken stalks until he reached a young soldier. His light fell on the man's spear, causing him to lower it and speak.

"And you will hear of wars and rumours of wars."

Two more soldiers found themselves transfixed by rays, their spears limp in their hands.

The first man, grey about the temples, reached out to comfort his neighbour. "See that you are not troubled, for all these things must come to pass."

"But the end is not yet?" the other said.

Too late, Gruffkin shouted for his men to use their shields but Liam's light had already reached them and they stopped what they were doing.

"For nation will rise against nation," said the first.

"And kingdom against kingdom," said the next.

"And there will be famines, pestilences and earthquakes in various places."

"All these are the beginning of sorrows," finished the fourth.

Tears streaked their cheeks.

"We are the vessels of love and pain," said the fifth and youngest soldier, his knees still in the earth.

As Liam's light touched each man, he lowered his weapon and spoke and only the furthest managed to throw his spear, a long silver shaft that may have taken Liam through the chest had Erin not caught it.

Meanwhile, Gruffkin had ducked behind his shield and remained untouched by the light. Anger wormed at his face as he sidled forwards. "What've you done to my men?"

"Reminded them of their mothers," Liam said.

Gruffkin kept his shield high. "Well leave mine be. She tried to cut my throat last I saw her."

"And your father?"

"He art in heaven," Gruffkin growled. Lunging forwards, he brought his hand around the shield and fired. The coiled snake leapt out and bit into the flesh between Liam's thumb and forefinger, delivering a tremendous thump. But rather than knock him down, it only caused the light spilling from him to increase. Gruffkin was struck full in the face. For a moment his skin seemed to resist and then the battle was over.

"In your longing for your giant self lies your goodness." His chin wrinkled as if growing older. "And that longing is in all of you."

His men lay in the mud, their eyes closed but they heard him, for to a man they murmured, "Ay, sir."

Gruffkin's shield fell limp on his arm. "What have you done?"

"Removed the war from your heart," Liam said.

He walked on, pursued both by a glimmering circle of puddles and by Erin, who had taken to scouring the length and breadth of the field, a thin whistle on his lips. The shafts of light were working their wonders further afield too. As Liam walked, he heard bird say to man: "Like seeds dreaming beneath the snow, your heart dreams of spring." And man say to bird: "Trust the dreams, for in them is hidden the gate to eternity."

He raised his arms until light played across all four turrets, causing those there to stare in wonder at the eyes so close to their own. Faces blazed, shadows were thrown together. A young man slowly unlocked his fingers from a birdling's neck and spoke. "Save me from curious conscience that still lords its strength for darkness, burrowing like a mole."

Neck still vivid, the birdling said, "Turn the key deftly in the oiled wards and seal the hushed casket of my soul."

All, near and far, slowly untangled themselves, staring into the light as if from cellars long-sealed.

Just then, Erin, who had begun whistling again, made a growling noise and dropped to his knees, only to be struck by an obscure force that came hissing through the wheat before condensing into a huge ball of fur. Man and beast rolled together, splashing through the mud, kissing and nipping at each other, so that by the time they'd finished, it was difficult to tell them apart. "You little beauty," Erin kept saying. "You little beauty!"

As he approached the centre of the field, Liam saw the Caretaker and several others, their outfits blustering in the wind. Many of the House of Pain's dead had been lain around the dome's curved edge. He looked at the old man and then at Star. "Where is she?"

Star raised her chin. "Somewhere out there."

Liam thought for a second and then searched his pockets. Holding up the ring he'd made from Rook's hair, he asked Erin if maybe Bloodhorn could find her.

The redhead placed the ring under the dog's nose until it yipped and tried to pull away. Once freed, it trotted around the dome before veering off to nose at the bodies on the far side. All about, soldiers and citizens alike sat in dimly-lit huddles. Bodies were being carried away, the wounded attended to.

Liam's light was fading. The distant turrets and the broken pattern of stalks all around were becoming less and less distinct. The rain slicing through each beam still flashed but more and more faintly. He turned to observe Bloodhorn as it followed a trail between the dome and the northwest turret and realised that the light from his eyes had been entirely extinguished.

"We must find her," Liam said. "If we split up—"

But then two things occurred at once. Just as Bloodhorn started nudging at some distant shape, the cloudbusters sprang back to life, again projecting an image of Rook over the field, this time with a Bloodhorn nuzzling at its neck.

"Knight takes Rook," Erin said softly.

Liam immediately broke into a sprint, followed closely by the others, the speakers attached to the cloudbusters all whispering the same name as they ran: "Ma . . . *kin* . . ."

It was what he'd been expecting and though his light was fading, he felt ready. He'd listened carefully and was sure the Keeper had used the name 'Ma'kin', though the pronunciation sounded odd. Here then was the man's last move and Liam, who hoped he was one step ahead, threw all doubts aside even as he threw himself forwards.

3

ROOK'S LIKENESS ROCKED back and forth, its pale hands clutching its rounded belly. Only as Liam neared the real Rook did he glance up. The rain was sulphurous, the clouds like fiery waves. And there, dropping down through the spume, as if his fear had given it form, was Ma'kin, its wings drawing from that inverted sea a line so thin it could have been spider thread, its words drifting after it like some macabre mating call:

"Oh-wasn't-that-a-dainty-dish-to-set-before-the-king?"

Liam tasted iron. His legs were numb, his breath broken. But however fast he ran, Ma'kin's speed was far greater than his own. Now then was his chance, the moment of salvation, of triumph.

As its wings opened, he yelled, "Ma'kin, I order you, leave us!"

Wings sweeping downwards, Ma'kin slowed its descent, its gaze flickering between Rook and those running to protect her.

"I know your name," Liam shouted. "I speak it now and order you to go. Ma'kin, *be gone!*"

Ma'kin's words blasted the air and sank sword-like into Liam's flesh. "No, dreamer, I will not. *For that is not my name.*"

Everything after that was as of smoke, brightly lit but diaphanous. As the creature landed beside Rook, it was struck as if by a cannonball, Star's speeding form so quick, it was a blur. Rolling through the mud, the pair began to writhe together like two mismatched snakes, their struggle, though occasionally breaking out in violent motions, destined to produce only one victor. Ma'kin's blows fell with punishing force. Dazed and exhausted, Star would have been finished off were it not for her escort, two of whom landed on the creature's shoulders, while others began firing their weapons. Ma'kin simply drove the first two into the soil, then chased their companions into the air, there to dispatch them one after the other.

The air hummed with a familiar sound and Liam turned to see the Caretaker firing his catapult. Nor was he alone, for even as Liam looked their way, Fredrickson and Enzo both threw spears so that the two weapons flew in tandem through the air, causing Ma'kin to twist and turn mid-flight. But though the creature was fast, managing to avoid the first projectile and catch the second, one of the Caretaker's shots grazed its temple, spraying the air with blood.

Emitting a roar, Ma'kin returned the spear just as Enzo threw another. Both were perfectly aimed, Enzo's piercing Ma'kin's chest, Ma'kin's taking Fredrickson through the stomach.

Liam heard a groan and turned to see Erin, who'd been restraining Bloodhorn, scrambling over to the captain, catching him as he fell. The man's eyes were rolling, his skin grey, yet still he managed to draw his knife.

Erin pulled the man close. "I won't do it," he said, his words turning to tears. "I can't."

"You *must*," the man said, blood bubbling at his mouth.

And still the smoke rolled on and Liam was held in its thrall. These scenes were too close, too intimate, to be real. Ma'kin writhing in the mud, pulling at the spear in its chest, Erin and Enzo hauling a great chunk of rubble into the air.

Feeling Rook tug at his sleeve, Liam looked down to see her staring up at him with damp, slightly pink eyes, her mouth working at words, their silent shapes beyond his comprehension. "The streets," she whispered at last, "the underwater streets." She was panting and her next words came in snippets. "The *ba*-by, the *ba*-by's com-ing . . ."

He glanced up. The two men had raised the rock to their chests. But even as they struggled to lift it higher, the creature finally freed the spear and swept one of its wings through the mud, catching Enzo across the back of the legs and causing the rock to tumble after him.

Twice Ma'kin was struck by the Caretaker's pellets before it managed to roll forwards and raise its wings. Sweeping them downwards, it rose into the air, each thrust so powerful, it was soon out of reach. Perhaps sensing that it was vulnerable at last, the Caretaker darted after it, only for Ma'kin to turn and throw the spear. It was well aimed. Liam watched in horror as the old man fluttered to the ground, the spear protruding from his side.

Liam was holding Rook's hand too tightly. "What have I done?" he said. "What have I done?"

Yet somehow the Caretaker was still alive. He'd landed in a sprawl of mud and stems and looked for all the world like a stork sitting on a nest. He was mumbling something, his hand pawing at his tunic.

"The box," he said, speaking clearly at last. "The box."

He pushed the thing through the mud. Ignoring Rook's groan, Liam let go of her hand and struggled over to the old evolo. The ivory in the box's lid looked electric in the light. The thing opened easily and straightaway Liam saw, inside the lid, a tiny scrap of paper, its essence singing in a high, fearless voice.

Unfolding the paper, he mouthed the first line: "Thou wast not born for death, immortal Bird . . ."

But just then the puddles filled with purple fires and he looked up in time to see Ma'kin settle nearby, its wounds dark in the holographic light. For the first time, it seemed tired. Its one good eye drooped, its breath clicked and rattled in its throat. Yet the rage in its voice might have fuelled the kind of underground fires that burn for years.

"Where is my mate?" It staggered towards him, its breath clouding the air. "I but wanted to excite the sympathy of some existing thing. Yet I find myself alone."

"You killed my father." Erin had risen to his feet and was standing there, pale, swaying, as if the breeze might at any moment fell him. His jaw gurned. "*Twice* dead."

"Stop." Liam held up the shred of paper. "I have another verse." But his words fell on deaf ears.

Erin lurched forwards, Loverboy's knife in his fist, his eyes wild with grief. "You are a villain, a cold, remorseless villain."

"Villain?" Ma'kin snarled. "How so if I am only avenging myself? Who are you to take stock of my torment?"

"Leave him," Liam said, staggering to his feet. Then louder, "Take *me*."

But Ma'kin was too busy considering Erin. "Look at me," it said, touching its heart, its head. "Whose gifts are these? I was born without a soul. Do you know what that is like?"

"I know what it is like for a soul to die," Erin said. "To feel it wither up inside you." He pointed at the captain. "This man here is my father and you killed him."

The creature's sigh was almost human. "Well your father chose to fight in a war he cannot win. All is fair, as they say."

"Then it will be fair when I kill you," Erin laughed. And with that he leapt forwards, the knife raised.

It was Bloodhorn though that reached the creature first. A frothy snarl came running through the wheat and then, with an almighty bound, the dog sprang at Ma'kin, causing it to stumble backwards. At the same time, Erin leapt forwards and plunged the knife into its chest. An arachnid web of electricity engulfed dog, man and monster. A moment later the three were thrown to the ground in a smoking heap, filling the air with the stench of burning hair and warped plastic.

Liam stared in horror. Erin was lying very still, his skin patterned as if with lightning, Bloodhorn beside him, its body twitching. Ma'kin, however, was still conscious.

"Take you?" it said, turning its mud-spattered gaze Liam's way. "Take *you*? Then you still don't understand." Rolling over, it started to pull itself towards him. "I don't want you *dead.* I want you to feel and feel and go on feeling forever."

Rook was lying on a bed of broken wheat, her knees up, her head tucked. A groan broke from her lips. Liam knew he must try and lead the creature away but Ma'kin was rising now, its wings shivering into place.

"Where is *my* mate?" it said, following his gaze. "Why then do *you* deserve love?" And with that it bounded across the field and fell on him, its blood sloshing against the ramparts of its face, its breath sawing from its bloody mouth. "You believe yourself miserable now. Well, I will make you so wretched that even the light of day will be hateful to you."

So saying, it reached over, wrested a spear from the ground and thrust it downwards, pinning Liam where he knelt. Pain. Immediate. All-consuming. It hissed through his veins, pouring with such intensity down his legs, he fainted. Darkness. Bright spots. Water rushing through cracks. He opened his eyes to find himself upside down, a metal shaft pinning him to his seat. An angled piece of glass, veined by cracks, revealed an incline drumming with rain. Reflected in the mirror at the bottom of the window, he saw his mother's shoulders, floating wisps of hair.

And then he heard a scream. He was lying on his side, his face in the mud. Rook was panting, Ma'kin sniffing at her neck. He tried to sit up but the pain was too much. His parents were dead. He remembered them drowning. It was his fault. At the same time, he remembered meeting his father and mother so that these two truths were paradoxical. He saw something move and realised it was his hand. The slip of paper was stained but he could still read what was written there.

"Thou wast not born for death, immortal Bird." He raised his voice, spoke the line again. "Thou wast not born for death, immortal Bird! No hungry generations tread thee down, the voice I hear this passing night was heard in ancient days by emperor and clown—"

Ma'kin roared laughter. "Still trying to read me poetry? And still trying to remember my name, no doubt. The one you spoke in your sleep."

But despite the creature's seeming insouciance, Liam sensed doubt. "Perhaps the self-same song," he said loudly, "that found a path through the sad heart of Ruth." He paused. "When, sick for home, she stood in tears amid the alien corn."

The change was more profound than any caused by previous readings. All became grey—cracks zigzagged across the roof, through the air, over the bodies lying in the wheat, around those surrounding the scene. All were statues, even Ma'kin and Rook. Only Erin remained clear, the pink of his now scarless skin so fresh, he might have been a rare flower. Caught unawares by a rush of love that burst through him as a river bursts its banks after a flood, Liam stretched out a hand but before he could reach him, some spark, that name— *Ruth*—burned a hole in the grey and in that circle, he saw a woman wearing white, a sheaf of golden wheat laid across her arm. As she bent to gather more stalks, he recognised her, knew it was she who was sick for home, that her name was Roo . . .

"—*uth*?" he said, then louder and with more certainty, causing the word to tear across the field, making a dust-storm of the chaff. He shouted her name again and this time heard an answer.

"My God. He said my name."

The words were dulled as if by liquid but then the woman's voice rang clarion: "He *spoke*, he *spoke*! Quick, get a doctor!"

He heard the Keeper too. They were somewhere above him but pushing upwards was like trying to wade through wet mulch. His muscles began to rail, his eyes to sting. He heard Rook again, closer. What was the trick? All he need do was remember the trick but as he tried, he heard Ma'kin say something—*Two birds*—and everything around him suddenly shimmered. Indigo and violet and emerald, shivering inwards, crossing, vibrating outwards again. He could see Rook, her distended stomach glistening in the rain, Ma'kin's shadow spilling across her face.

478

But as everything rematerialised, Liam realised what he'd seen was more than a vision. The poem talked of a woman called Ruth and he'd heard her and before that he'd seen her but she'd not looked like Ruth, she'd looked like Rook

—*because Rook is a manifestation of Ruth*

—Ruth was not Rook. This Rook was lying on the ground, the mineral place between her legs twisting in the creature's shadow, for it had its knees either side of her head now. Next, the baby's head would appear, an enormous head with eyes as black as oil and then its body would slide out, followed by a torrent of blood and then Rook would die. But no, she would not die

—*because I am Liam but I am also Will*

It had all been so simple. All the Keeper had had to do was change his name.

"Two birds . . ." Ma'kin repeated, raising the rock in its hands.

But Liam was distracted and even called out, "Rook, it's all going to be okay . . ."

"Two birds with one stone," Ma'kin said again, throwing a final, murderous glance in his direction.

Only then did Liam see what it was holding and only then did the truth dawn—the baby's head was not going to appear as he'd imagined

—because the creature was lifting the rock, up and up, higher and higher, before bringing it down, not once but many times, a sound like friction squealing in its throat, its rage building to such a pitch that its whole body became a crimson flood, itself magnified by the effigy above it until every person watching it blazed red

—and then the monster was freeing the child from the wreckage of Rook's flesh, raising its stirring, bloody form into the air like some delicate morsel and swallowing it whole.

Chapter 5.

The End of the Rope

IN ALL THAT BRIGHTNESS Hart's blood seemed to blaze on Ruth's hand and trousers. She asked where they were going.

"Where else?" Frank leaned closer. "To the end of the rope."

"I'll scream."

He chuckled softly. "No you won't."

And he was right. She knew if she called out, he wouldn't hesitate, just as he hadn't with Hart. She wanted to run but she could barely walk. In the stairwell, she leant against the banister but Frank just dragged her. In the next corridor, she saw one of the doctors from earlier but before she could muster the nerve to shout, he turned and vanished.

"What have you got against Will? He's never hurt anyone."

Frank's jaw crinkled into a smile. "Tell that to his parents. And what about you? You said you never wanted to see him again. You set in motion the events that led to his parents' death. He must have hurt you a little, otherwise what was the point?"

She swung at him but he crushed her to his side.

"You flap your wings then deny the storm?"

They were passing a familiar picture, the city scene, houses and shops covered in snow, a bright light in the distance.

Ruth realised then that it wasn't the setting sun, it was a plane. Frank was talking about cause and effect. How complex systems, like the weather, like relationships, are difficult to predict and easy to alter. "It's not that simple," she said.

"It's complicated, certainly. I hate to think what you did to Will when you played him that tape. No wonder he doesn't want to wake up."

Suddenly the corridor seemed too short. A moment later, Frank was pushing her at Will's door, briefly filling his room with light. He steered her round the bed to the far chair. The curtain was still piled on the floor. Gladys was gone. Will lay with his arms exposed, his fingers almost touching, as if someone had just removed a bowl from his hands. Frank sat opposite, the light from the little window crescenting his head, his voice quiet, conspiratorial.

"The line between life and death is thin. Get too close to the edge, turn the steering wheel a little too far . . ."

He removed a clear plastic bag from his pocket, asked what Ruth had been reading to Will. She glanced at the table.

"Keats?" he said, picking up the book. "Why Keats?"

"Alfie knows you're here," she said.

"Way ahead of you there, Ruth. Our old pal took an overdose a few hours ago, he just doesn't know it yet."

I think all this has made me ill.

Frank tapped the table with a leathered knuckle. "Alfie has a table almost exactly like this, a sad little square of prefab upon which I laid, only this morning, a few photographs and a rather sad little poem." He leaned forwards. "You see, doctors consider poetry to be a sign of a deranged mind. They've too little imagination to understand the romantic. Looking at ruptured spleens and inflamed bowels all day, who can blame them? But me, I understand poetry." He curled his lip. "Having spent a good part of my youth reading illicit literature, I used to count poems among my friends. My father would bring me books and after I read them, he made me burn them. I used to sit in the garden watching the pages glow, the words merge." His smile was almost wistful. "By the time I was thirteen, I loved the burning almost as much as the reading." He made a creaking fist. "What were words compared to all that heat?"

The book of poems fell open and he caught the page and smoothed it out. "Well, well, well," he said, glancing in Ruth's direction. "*Ode to a Nightingale.* Hardly bedtime reading. The poet lamenting his own mortality . . ?" He scanned the page. "Ah, I thought so." He read the line with Ruth's name in it, his eyes sparkling. "You've actually been reading him poems about yourself." When she smarted, he broke into a grin. "Perilous seas and faery lands, is that where he's gone, to dream of you, his screwed-up little wife?"

"It's meant to bring him home," she said. She felt her lip tremble. "You wouldn't understand."

"Oh, believe me," he said, "I understand. But the truth is dreams and poetry are the stuff of delusion. Actions speak louder than words. Ask your friend the chef." He rubbed his jaw, settled back into the chair. "Your husband taught poetry. Look where it's got him. He teaches her story, I teach history. It was one of our little jokes. Will's been courting literature for a long time. So easy to slip between her sheets, so hard to impress her once you're there."

"What are we doing? What are we waiting for?"

"For the ladies. Isn't it always so?" He was watching her but she was too tired to hunt for his meaning. He waved the book and then put it down on the bed. "The first time my father handed me a package wrapped in several pages of the *Gazeta*, he told me to read it in my room." Frank smiled. "It was a third edition *Frankenstein*, published in 1831. I read it with my door locked, the book in one hand, a dictionary in the other. I can still picture Victor chasing the monster across the ice. The next book was a collection of short stories by Kafka, then a book by the British illustrator, Patrick Woodroffe. I read Orwell, Achebe, Faulkner . . ." For a moment Frank's smile was someone else's. "My father also brought home various historical texts and we would stay up late in order to discuss what he called *tani për tani*, 'right now'. To know history, he would say, right now is best, for right now you are closest to the truth. Which of course is a lie."

Frank leaned back, the light from the observation window jaundicing his eyes. He told Ruth his father used to take him to visit the city's churches and mosques. There, standing beneath ancient arches and listening to men talk of God, he said he saw history first-hand. Afterwards his father would pack him into an unmarked car and send him home. At the time he thought the man was trying to educate him. Only afterward did he learn that the lesson was not historical, it was political. A truth that was revealed to him by Aferdita, his mother.

"I AM ALBANIAN, or half, at least. This much I'm sure you've worked out. My father worked for the government. He was an intimate of Enver Hoxha. The first I knew of the change in Hoxha's fortunes was when my mother told me she was frightened. '*Për ju bir*,' she said. For you. And I knew this to be true for she was never afraid for herself. I'd seen my father knock her to the floor, her laugh in his face. But for us children, she would tear out her heart. That is why she told me what happened at those meetings after I was sent home, how my father closed the mosques and smashed up the churches like some kind of antichrist. Of those he arrested. Those he hurt.

"I listened to her tell me my father was not all I supposed him to be and that night, after I told him what she'd said, I listened to my mother's cries as she was beaten and knew she was right and hated her for it. In the morning, when I found my father gone, I hated her even more."

Frank raised a finger to his lips and shrugged. He said his father was gone for three weeks and returned smelling of strangers. "That night, we sat in the garden for the last time, the terrace soft with moss and honeysuckle. It was spring and the open windows were filled with the scent of lilies, the flowers my father always brought my mother after one of his absences. The housekeeper had arranged them in half-a-hundred vases, so that as we sat there, their smell spilled across the lawn in such profusion, I found it difficult to focus. Amid that sweet, rotting scent, my father told me what had happened. That Hoxha was on his deathbed. That my mother had spoken out of turn because she was scared. That he was not afraid for he had considered every eventuality. I remember the garden being extremely overgrown in its borders and full of dark-green, wet leaves where the sprinklers had soaked the plants, the enormous pampas grass in the centre of the lawn, its feathery spears bright against the back wall, itself black and invisible. By that wall, beneath an old yew hedge, my father kept a small incinerator. He handed me one last package and beckoned me to follow. 'It will be a first for you,' he said, 'to burn a book you've never read.'

"It was *The Magus* by John Fowles." Frank glanced at her. "I built a fire and when the book was alight, we retired to the chairs. My father told me that British writers were the best. That their understanding of absurdity was second-to-none. Not even the French or the Russians. '*Tani për tani*,' he said. 'Now you see everything collapse, now you watch the rats come pouring into our country, invading our cities in search of cheap liquor and even cheaper women. Study what happens, remember it. One day you will need that anger.'"

Father and son sat there for a long time, the smell of burning paper vying with the scent of dying flowers. And then, the next day, Frank's father was arrested. Frank knew what he was accused of, torture, extortion, rape. But he didn't care. He said his father was a great man. It was all he needed to know.

Yet Frank seemed unsettled. As if he did not completely believe this confession. But he believed it enough.

"My father was inside for less than a day," he said, "and left police headquarters untouched. To show his disdain for the new authorities, he took us to the cinema, where we watched the first western movie to play in the city for decades. He picked us up in his car, sat us in the front row. There, with the film creeping across the room, my mother and sister on one side, me on the other, he murmured his plans and smoked his cigar. When I asked why he'd been arrested, he told me all that had been taken care of. 'They want to make peace? We will sell guns.'

"And for a while that's what we did, everything ticking over like clockwork. Business boomed and money came in so fast, we had to buy another money counter. I was only fifteen and the things money can buy, the clothes and cars and girls, all were a balm oiling the troubled waters of my mind. We sold guns to gangsters who used them to kill young men with faces like mine. But still I followed my father, trusting his strength over my mother's, ignorant of what such devotion could give birth to. I did as I was bade, sold guns to murderers and racketeers, to wife-beaters and children, watched history rewrite itself in blood and found in my heart the anger my father had foreseen. But it was not always directed outwards. In the years between going into business and fleeing the country, there were many times when I doubted what we were doing. But when I questioned my father, he simply said, everyone we knew had a gun. Is it fair on those who do not?

"And then my mother died," Frank said, "and the change she wrought in me was complete."

iii.
—

FRANK PAUSED, STARTED nodding, spoke in time to this affirmation. "Aferdita Loka had thick black brows and wide dark eyes that she would flash around her like knives. She was Czech, tall, beautiful, always dancing, always somewhere between tears and laughter. But in the time after my father's arrest and before her death, my mother's playfulness caused only trouble. My father was filled with a violent spirit that inspired in my mother her brightest performances. She would ask his opinion on seemingly innocuous subjects and then laugh at his response, knowing full well he couldn't stand being laughed at. Then, after being thrown about the room, she would pick herself up and smile at my sister and me as if we were all playing a game.

"The day she died," Frank said, "her laughter, her smiles, her jokes, all became a book I'd rarely read but now would never open again. It was this as much as the sight of her body that drove me to do what I did. A week later, I left the country with blood on my hands and a mind never still enough to read again."

His voice was filled with disgust. "During my visits to both mosque and church, I heard any number of sermons. I learned that like the good Dr Frankenstein, God tried to destroy His creation, laying waste to cities and flooding the world. But only after my mother's death did I understand why, that all men are vile. It was a bitter pill, especially considering the fact that I now counted myself among their number. Unable to bear this reflection, I buried it in my heart.

"It was in this mood," he said, "that I fled Tirana and began a journey full of rattling carriages and tasteless meals, an aimless exodus only made bearable by my sister's presence. As if sensing my retreat, Rosafa adopted my mother's pose and would not let me alone. It was she who kept my head above water. Our father was too distracted. He had no time for either of us. Before our mother's death, Rosafa and I were separated by age and ideology, my sister being singularly devoted to our mother and me to our father. Nor was it our mother's death that brought us together. Indeed we never spoke of our separate loves. Instead it was little things, fields of flowers from train windows, the changing taste of water in hotel rooms, the sound of voices, accents, tones, each noticed and passed like love-notes as we lounged together, shoulder to shoulder, in one room or another, train after train, our father sitting nearby but never close. With these exchanges, we discovered a new love separate from the old."

Frank said they settled in Marseilles, helped run guns out of Africa. His father bought a vineyard and for several years they had some schooling, some security. Frank said he had a private tutor who taught him English. "Although," he sneered, "I was never quite able to remove the taint from my accent."

Then one day their father, without warning, told them to pack a bag and they were off again, this time to London.

"Not that we knew our destination for several weeks. My father never took the direct route."

Even when they reached London, it was only when their father told them to abandon their bags that Frank was certain. He'd slept much of the way from Lyon but even half-asleep he was aware of the meaning of his father's words and tutted when his sister tried to whisper to him, knowing that a life was beginning in which such murmurs had no place.

"We have money," his father said, "but we can't touch it. One day we will return to Shqipëria as kings. Until then, all we have is a clean

489

slate. England is the country of opportunity. We must watch and learn."

"He had contacts," Frank said. "People in Lazarat and Marseilles and before long we became familiar with various local networks. Everybody wanted a good time, they wanted to snort and smoke and inject themselves happy."

Frank started working the door at a club in Brixton, a one-room dive with cheap seats and watered-down drinks. Dressed in black, he said he felt like he was finally mourning his mother. He became acquainted with the kind of men who talk of violence but who have never known a truly violent day their whole life. "The women were worse. Nothing like the girls in Tirana. These bitches, they brayed like donkeys and fucked like pigs. My first Christmas, I remember watching the Queen's speech, a turkey dinner on my knee and smiling as she talked about life. As if being surrounded by well-advised advisors gives you some kind of wisdom." Frank looked at Ruth. "Such people do not live in the real world, Ruth. The real world is dirt under your nails and blood on your hands. It is burning buildings and husks on the lawn."

He squeezed his fist again and the plastic bag made a sound like crackling soap. "Still," he said, "I did not like my father's new direction. It hummed in me like a wire, a metallic quivering I heard whenever the world was still. I didn't dwell on it while I was awake but when I slept, I dreamt of the city, of running unclothed through its streets, my naked reflection running beside me. I studied every doorway, crossed bright carriageways, ran until my blood sang but there was no one. Everywhere I looked, the streets were empty. Beautifully empty. But again we made money, again I was distracted. Working the door, I was ideally placed to scout for dealers. Whenever I was approached, if the customer looked all right, if they were discrete enough to take me aside and didn't look half-cut, I made them repeat a number and pointed to the pay phone over the road. The number was for another pay phone manned by an associate of my father's. I never met the man, which was how my father liked to keep it. No one, not even his son, *especially* his son, got to see all the pieces. He said it was for my protection. But as it turned out, it almost got me killed."

Frank said the day his father disappeared, the man left him an answerphone message saying he was going out of town to look up an old girlfriend. Three days later, he still wasn't back. Frank listened to that message a hundred times to make sure he hadn't missed anything. He had no names, no numbers. Not even the keys to his father's office. He couldn't contact their supplier or find out anything concerning their distributors. His father believed mobile phones were a government plot. He carried everything in his head. The next shipment was due and without his father, it would be impossible to shift.

"What can I say? I'd let myself believe I could become greater than my nature allowed. The fear I felt over those next few days had an interesting effect. I became mute. At work, the others kept asking if I was sick. Then one night I woke up and thought we'd had a power cut. That was until someone switched on the light and I found myself looking at a guy so enormous he blocked the entire window. I never knew his real name. I called him Mr Eclipse. He asked two of his colleagues to take me through to the kitchen where he proceeded to give me a lesson in manners.

"You see this scar?" Frank showed Ruth a long white line running across the crook of his arm and round his elbow. "Done with one of my own knives. Next time Mr Eclipse said he'd take my arm."

2
———

THE NEXT DAY FRANK emptied his account to make up the debt. But without his father's contacts it was impossible to sell the bricks Mr Eclipse had left on his breadboard. He said he couldn't focus. He believed his father had abandoned him for a woman. He knew from experience, when his father disappeared it might be weeks before he resurfaced. Frank said he tried every way he could to find him but his enquiries came to nothing.

"We had several men working for us but after what happened in Tirana, Dad trusted none of them. I didn't even bother contacting them. My sister was studying medicine somewhere, though I never knew where. All I had was a phone number. When I finally called it, she said she'd not spoken to our father. She was worried but when I told her that our father's message mentioned a woman, I knew her thoughts mirrored my own. Out of desperation I broke into the office on the Burdett Road but found nothing useful.

"A few days later, having managed to shift less than half the product, the boss of the club where I worked, a skinny little pimp who liked to wear velvet, called me to his office. Sitting in his chair was Mr Eclipse. He told me he was disappointed, that if Feçor had disappeared, his son needed to step up. 'If you don't,' he said, 'my employers will receive satisfaction. They do not care about your problems. Pay up or lose an arm. *Krahu i djathtë i njeriut të duhur.* The right arm of the right man.'

"And then a contact from Brixton told me he'd seen my father's car. It had been abandoned in the middle of the Somerleyton Estate. Being too busy and having no one else I trusted, I asked my sister to pick it up. She collected the spare keys, caught a taxi, then drove the car back to London.

"We opened the boot together. Inside we found a roll of blue plastic. It covered all but the top of our father's face. His eyes . . . they were nothing like I'd ever seen. They stared but not at us. They were looking at something far beyond."

Frank's hazel eyes burned with a pale light. "Early the next morning, I dug a grave in Scadbury Park, placed his body among the roots of a chestnut tree. I stank of sweat and wet earth but it was nothing compared to my father. His body had been covered with salt to absorb the smell but still it stank. I poured lye, first onto his hands and feet, then his face, my eyes stinging from the vapours. When it was all gone, I filled in the grave and recited a prayer. Unlike my sister, I do not believe in God but still I prayed for my father. I then drove his car back to London."

Frank said he was left with a difficult decision. To save the business or find his father's murderer. He'd found a note in the man's pocket, an address in Kent but with Mr Eclipse's patience running out, he knew he had to be careful. He tried to choose both. He sent his sister away but continued to contact various dealers.

"But I was only ever really interested in finding who killed my father. My next night off, I went to the club, knowing I was being followed. I made a big show of getting drunk and then, when I saw some *zuskë* dancing with this man-mountain, I purposefully spilled vodka down her dress. After the meathead had given me a good hiding, two colleagues helped me into a taxi, the larger of the two accompanying me back to my apartment. After being helped up the stairs, I entered the place under my own steam, removed my coat to reveal the black clothes I'd been wearing all evening, cleaned up my face, applied some makeup, put on my jacket and paid the doorman who'd helped me. Finally, after pulling on a cap, I left the building with a sober swagger."

Frank said he'd told the taxi driver to go past the club and then on to the airport. He'd already purchased a ticket to Costa Rica. The plane was flying via New York but at JFK, he flew back to Europe using a ticket bought under a different name, though not yet that of Frank Štěpán. In Frankfurt, he shaved his head and drove through six different countries before finally arriving in Albania.

He said he stayed with a cousin who owned a stud farm, grew a beard and set about learning the horse trade. "It was months before I ventured into Tirana. I shouldn't have, not so soon but I couldn't resist." He said he had to know his father, really know the man he was planning to avenge. Luckily, he told Ruth, there was someone there he could trust, a relative who owned a little halal café, a fat *dështak* who let him sit in a booth at the back while he met with certain men. He already knew Feçor Loka had been a member of the Communist party, acting for the Central Committee as supervisor to the media, a role empowering him to close newspaper offices and television companies, to start companies of his own, even to change the weather forecast, this being the source of bitter amusement that had so confused Frank whenever his mother raised it. It was because of this that his father was able to bring home certain books.

"I learned that though many former party members were imprisoned or shot, my father was allowed to go free. He'd been gathering evidence against his associates long before Enver Hoxha died. It was this that bought him his freedom. He was banished from political office but allowed to become a man of business, the same business he described to me the night he was released. But unfortunately he was too greedy and despite precautions, his identity was purchased from one of his employees for a carton of cigarettes. That information I was also privy to, for it was that same young man I killed before fleeing Albania.

"I was told my father made many women happy. Perhaps it was this that drove me to visit the street where I grew up. The trees were still there but the house was new. I sat in my car and stared at where my life had once unfolded, amazed that one match could destroy so many memories. The day I came home to find the house burning, the orange trees out front were thick with pale blossoms and dark smoke. Already the stucco was turning grey. As I watched, one of the windows exploded, spraying glass across the porch. The front door was so hot I couldn't even get near it."

As the house was consumed, no human sound reached his ears. Not until the fire had been extinguished and he stood with his father and sister, waiting for the men searching inside, did he know. His mother was carried out and laid nearby. All but her shoes had been burnt from her body and of these, only the buckles maintained their shape, melted as they had been into the tops of her feet. "Her flesh was charcoal, most of her extremities, mere suggestions." Frank stared at his gloved hands and then at Ruth. "I walked away," he said, "with smoke in my chest and blood in my eyes and, at the age of twenty-two, killed a man for the first time. I remember a bank of trees, a shallow hill, a park bench, a girl with a balloon. She may have screamed but I did not hear it for there was a roaring in my ears as if someone had lit a furnace at the end of a long room. I didn't even hear the gun, or the other man's pleas."

Frank's time in the café was fruitful. After finding out all he needed to know about Feçor Loka, he told himself it was enough. His father was a man who decided how far another came into his house and which rooms he could explore. In truth, Frank admitted, he was really searching for himself but it was a waste of time. "I was nobody."

ii.

DURING THE NEXT FEW years he worked hard, saved money, prepared as thoroughly as he could. There were whole days when he did not think of his plans, even enjoyed himself. But he never forgot. Knowing what he knew, he'd decided to wait until his father's murderer had something precious to lose. Only then would he set his plans in motion.

"And then, Frank said, "I heard the news I'd been waiting to hear. William Zifla was married."

Ruth was exhausted and frightened, her mind racing. Oddly, until that moment, she'd thought Frank's story to be disconnected from them and their lives. But of course she'd read Avni's letter and had known the truth all along.

"I also heard round that time that Mr Eclipse had accidentally drowned in his own bath. A cousin from a certain horse farm succeeded him. After that I purchased the house in St James's Place and arranged the necessary papers so I'd arrive in the UK with a clean driving licence and a well-used passport in the name of Frank Štěpán. Do you know how much money is laundered through private schools in this country? Many millions. Hellerbys was open to donations and I brokered the deal. The stud farm was making good money, especially as it was fronting a little cocaine racket. My father's money was still tied up but my cousin knew I was good for it. Did Will mention the new labs? Nice clean lab equipment for nice dirty money."

Frank took out a phone, looked at the screen, then back at Ruth. He said Will had known nothing about it. If he had, he wouldn't have gone to Simmons. "He'd have known I was untouchable. How do you think a *shqiptar* like me got to teach at a school like that?

"We all have something that pries us loose, Ruth," he said, his tone philosophical. "Mine was my mother. Will's was Shelley Givens. When he mentioned her, it was like a thunderclap. I knew she'd been sent to me. Finding her, seducing her, all that was easy because it was meant to be. Using her I was able to put Will through the kind of hell he put me through. But I had too much fun. He ran away. And it is the law that a man cannot be killed in the family home."

"Killed?" Ruth said, the word sticking in her throat. "You still haven't told me why you would want to?"

Frank's next words were a sneer. "Because it was Will who murdered my father. Blood must be purged with blood."

"Must it?" Ruth said faintly.

"Yes," Frank said. "And it was Will's father who placed my father's body in the car, covered it in salt and drove it into London. Probably hoping that the car would be stolen and the trail muddied, if not erased. If only he'd checked my father's pockets."

He told Ruth he didn't know any of this when he visited Will's aunt. He suspected her involvement, Karrina being the woman his father had mentioned in his answerphone message but he didn't *know*.

"Before my father met my mother, Karrina was promised to him in marriage. In Albania, when a woman is promised in wedlock, that promise is law. But before they could be married, Will's father took her away. Eventually my father married my mother but he never forgot that promise and when we came to this country, he went looking for his betrothed.

"But it wasn't me who killed Karrina. When I got to her house, I found her front door locked. I knocked and waited, then walked round the back. Maybe she knew I was coming, maybe it was an accident but when I looked in at the kitchen window, she was smiling at me. Then she struck a match and the whole room erupted. I was lucky to escape with only a few cuts. But if she sacrificed herself, it was for nothing. Her family was easy to trace, Will's parent's house even easier to break into."

Ruth knew from Avni's letter what he'd found there too.

"A strongbox," Frank said, "containing a letter written by Will detailing exactly what had occurred."

Even as Ruth shook her head, he pulled the letter from a pocket and waved it at her.

"But why did he write it, Ruth? Why do such a stupid thing? It took me a long time to work out the answer. It's written in a certain way, don't you think? The detail, the tone, so different to the decoration found in his other writing. I believe it's not a confession but a statement. I know that Will called his father and that Avni took the body away. Did he then swear his son to secrecy? I think not. Will is too weak. So Avni pretended to call the police, told his son there was an investigation, that some harmless verdict had been reached.

"So finally," he said, "I knew everything. Who needed to die and why. I could have used others. I knew men in London and Brighton who would have killed for me. But it was too personal. I had to be the one. Shelley was just the beginning. I wanted to bring Will so low that when at last I stood over him, he would think me a giant. And not just him. His father too. But the law states that the home is inviolate. I had to wait until they both came out. I visited Ashling many times over those two weeks. Only once did they go out together. I followed them across town but they went to see another man. To my surprise, they drove back in separate cars.

"Then on Christmas Eve Will and his parents left the house together and I was sure that the time had come. The weather was awful. I followed Will's car very closely. It was because of this that I saw what happened. It was raining so hard, I didn't realise a car was coming from the other direction until the two cars collided. The second vehicle careered off the road and Will's crashed through the barrier. I pulled up and ran to the side of the road, saw his car on its roof, the boot submerged in a stream.

"I was . . . blown away. I didn't think the universe had anything left. But that, that was something else. I jumped back into my car and tried to decide what to do. Finally, I rang for an ambulance. Will and his father would die but only on my terms, only in the way prescribed by law."

There was still something Ruth didn't understand. "But what've I got to do with it?"

Frank stared at the ceiling, his body stiff. "Avni had blood on his hands, Ruth, he deserved to die. As does Will. Had it been that simple, I would've put a bullet in both their heads and been done with it. But there's one thing more. After settling in London, my father forbade me from seeing my sister. He said our business must go nowhere near her. Her purity would be our reward. A whole year I'd been working with my father, slowly rotting inside. My mother returned every day. But my sister I kept in the attic, beautiful, hidden. She knew nothing of what I'd become."

Frank's gaze was steady, his voice calm. They'd reached the eye of the storm. "As you know, when my father went missing, I asked my sister to bring his car back and when she did, we opened the boot together."

Frank's phone vibrated and he flipped it open. At the same time, Ruth moved her hand across Will's body, covered the book and drew it to her. Frank listened for a moment, then said, "Good. It is done."

His words made Ruth's scalp bristle. She pushed the book into her cardigan pocket.

"Then come." He snapped the phone shut. "You recall the note Hart found, I am not my brother's keeper?"

"I'm well aware of Alfie's little games," Ruth said coldly.

She might have said more but just then the observation window darkened and she realised someone was peering into the room.

"Except you're wrong," he said calmly. "It wasn't Alfie."

498

WHEN THE DOOR OPENED, Ruth opened her mouth to shout, before seeing who it was. Penny came in, quickly, quietly, pushed the door to and put a box on the floor. She'd dyed her hair dark brown. She slid down the wall, her knees reaching for her chin, her eyes not quite meeting Ruth's.

Realisation dawned like a black sun. "It was you."

Ruth choked on something that might have been laughter. "*You* left the note. But why are you working with him?"

"You were supposed to go, Ruth," Frank said, "to leave with Penny. It would have been easier. But unlike you, I've always been adaptable."

Penny was leaning forwards so that the light haloed her head. Ruth could see a slight tremor in her shoulders.

"You're his sister, aren't you? I *trusted* you." Ruth looked at the box. "What's in there?"

Frank leaned forwards. "Your belongings, Ruth, all that remains. Don't you feel lighter now, just one little bundle left?"

Tears pricked Ruth's eyes. "What are you talking about?"

"It's what he would've wanted, Ruth. After such a terrible accident, such awful injuries. Now you're both free."

He was talking about Eric. Imagining something awful, Ruth threw herself across Will, reaching for Frank's face. "It's not *true*. I'd *know* it!"

Frank caught her wrists, pulled her to him until her back lay against his chest, her arms locked across her breasts. He pushed his mouth into her hair.

"Finally you begin to understand the meaning of loss. Your brother's dead, Ruth. It wasn't my idea. My sister wanted to do it. What can I say? After we opened that boot, our father's expression . . ." She felt him tremble. "He was naked, Ruth. Avni stripped him. Can you imagine? I've seen death but my sister—"

Penny's words stirred from some lightless trench. "Your father died too. But when you shut your eyes, you can still see him, happy, whole. When I shut mine . . ."

Ruth's tongue felt thick with saliva. She tried to say they didn't have to do this, it wasn't too late. Frank ignored her.

"Penny was engaged to a doctor," he said. "Engaged and pregnant. But imagine seeing our father like that, it was too much. She lost the baby. It's called spontaneous abortion. Ironic, don't you think?" Ruth felt her hair catch on his lip. "Imagine then how she felt when she found out about your abortion? Until we knew that, you were never part of this."

His breath filled Ruth's head and she felt herself swaying. She remembered asking Penny if she had any children. Penny's words blazed in her mind. One day. I hope.

"Let me remind you of something else you said to Alfie on the beach that day. If we forsake one love, then is not all love forsaken? We, on the other hand, forsook nothing but still it was taken. Our mother, our father, my niece." Frank pulled Ruth tighter. "You're so wrapped up in yourself, you've lost sight of love's true nature. You have no idea what it means to fight for it. I wanted to show you that before love must come honour. You come from a country where compromise is seen as a good deal, as if sacrificing honour has no cost. You tell yourselves that this law or that law makes you just but it's not true, it just keeps your head above the shit. Will killed his father, he stole that from me. Blood can only be paid with blood, the offender's or any other male of his house. That's why your brother had to die." Frank seized her chin. "And now that he's dead, there's only one more debt to pay."

"I think the Devil doesn't exist." Ruth's voice sounded very far away. "But man has created him in his own likeness."

Frank looked at Penny. "Take her next door."

Ruth had imagined hurting Frank, she'd imagined persuading him. But now that the moment had arrived, she felt empty. Thinking that Eric might be dead, or more precisely, *allowing* herself to think it, swept everything away. Only one thing held the tide. She kinked her wrist, touched the book's spine. She considered asking if she could read from it but immediately dismissed the thought. At the same time, her finger brushed a thin metallic edge too small to belong to a knife. She explored its dimensions. It was a nail file. She'd filed her nails in the locker room. She must have slipped the file into her pocket. Frank stood up, keeping her pinned to him.

She twisted her neck, tried to look into his eyes. "I'd like to pray."

Frank barked laughter. But then to her surprise, he gripped the back of her neck and turned her to face the bed. "*One.*"

Keeping the book hidden, she knelt down, found the poem using only her fingers, opened the book and leaned in. The last time she'd read to him, Will had spoken her name. As she began to murmur the final verse, it was this thought that filled her with the wildest hope.

"Forlorn," she whispered. "The very word is like a bell to toll me back from thee to my sole self. Adieu. The fancy cannot cheat so well as she is famed to do, cheating elf. Adieu. Adieu. Thy plaintive anthem fades—"

But Frank must have guessed there was more than prayer on her lips, for he pulled her back, exposing the book.

He barked again, then hauled her to her feet. "Still trying to wake him with poesy? Don't you get it, Ruth? Nothing can save him now. Not even Dostoevsky. And especially not Keats."

Will's expression remained vacant. Ruth longed to finish the verse but Frank's patience was at an end. It was time to find out what lay at the end of the rope. Frank's grip on her neck was sure but she understood enough about anatomy to break against the thumb. As she stood up, she focused on the feel of it against her skin. He was holding her neck with his left hand. She needed to rotate to the right. He was speaking but she had her eyes closed and couldn't hear him.

She counted down, took a deep breath, then wrenched sideways, dislodging his grip. She heard a surprised snarl, turned as if dancing, half-leaning, half-rolling across his chest. He grabbed at her but only got her cardigan. Dragging Penny to her feet, she slid in behind her.

The file punctured Penny's skin. Ruth threw everything into her words. "I *will*, Frank." A thin line of blood ran into the hollow at the base of Penny's neck. "Frank, I will."

The light behind her filled her peripheral vision. The room appeared darker. Frank's face was made only of eyes.

The fury in his voice made it quiver. "Think carefully."

"Go near Will," she said, "I'll do it. If you want blood . . ."

"You?" Spittle flew into the light. Frank prowled at a distance. "That's all there is underneath, Ruth, *blood*." His voice broke and he ran a hand across his jaw. "Who are you fighting for? Him?" He pointed at Will. "I told him what would happen to Jane. Since they seemed so close I thought it only fair. But he didn't wake up and save her, just like he didn't save Melissa Givens." He paused, his demeanour taking on new weight. "But you've forgotten something, haven't you, Ruth?" He held up the plastic bag. "What is it?" As he spoke, he continued to pace, the light marbling his jacket. "What little something has slipped your mind?"

And with this last word, he dipped down, stretched out a hand. Ruth pulled Penny closer but Frank wasn't reaching for her, he was reaching for the box. She watched him pull it out of reach.

"My sister could have administered a sedative but I said no. The old ways, Ruth. A little gin."

As he opened the box, Ruth looked over Penny's shoulder, knowing what she would see before she saw it. Penny had lined the box with the fleece and Fay lay asleep in its folds, her knees spread-eagled, her arms as usual round her head. Only the point at Penny's throat held Ruth together.

"Please, Frank."

He laughed. A cold little chuckle. "You threaten my sister? *Blood*, you said. Did you think I'd be unprepared?" As he lifted Fay from the box, she frowned against the light. "Now you have to decide who pays the price, this little something here or that big nothing behind me?"

Without knowing she'd done it, Ruth pushed on the file, felt it dally in Penny's skin. Penny breathed in through her nostrils but made no other sound.

"An eye for an eye," Frank said calmly. "Both my father's eyes are rotting in the ground and for that I need a second. If you wish your husband to live, I will take your daughter." He took Fay by the neck. Her mouth pursed in a wail. "Now *drop* it!"

Ruth's voice trembled. "If I do, you'll kill my family."

"Her first, Ruth." Frank shook Fay so that her eyes shot open and her wail intensified. Ruth watched her wrap tiny fingers round Frank's hand.

He shook out the plastic bag, placed the opening over the top of Fay's head. His voice shook with emotion and his jaw rippled. "I am Ghaksur, the taker of blood, the *Lord* of Blood. This is your last chance." He rolled the bag down so that it covered Fay's eyes. "Just a few seconds to extinguish all those years, all those generations to come."

With a great cry, Ruth threw the file aside and slid down the door, her body wracked. "I only wanted to save him." She held out her hands. "Please," she said. "Give me my baby."

Frank stepped forwards, pulled Penny away. He picked up the file, put it to Fay's neck, pushing it into the fat there until the tip disappeared. "How does it feel?"

Ruth was shaking. She reached forwards, her hands and the child in front of her wavering. "I'm sorry." She said it again, to Fay, to Will, to Penny, even to Frank. She loved them all. "I'm so sorry."

In the splintering light, she watched Frank place Fay in Will's upturned hands. Oddly, she settled straightaway, closed her eyes and appeared to go to sleep.

"The price of love is always paid in blood, Ruth. And because you are learning this at last, I am willing to give you a choice." Frank lifted her jaw so that she met his eyes. "Will or Fay. They're both sleeping now. Neither can hear you."

"I love you." She looked across at Penny. "I love you both. I understand." She reached for Frank but he shied away, a look of

503

revulsion on his face. "You don't have to do this," she said. "I understand. I'm sorry."

"Choose!" Frank said, any trace of calmness deserting him. "Your husband or your child."

"*You* choose. Choose not to do it, choose to lay all this to rest. Tell him, Penny, help me."

Penny groaned and began to move but the ferocity of her brother's voice stopped her.

"*Choose*? The past is all most of us have. But after tonight, my sister and her daughter will have a future. Our blood will be cleansed." He stared at Penny. "I do this for you."

"Don't, *vëlla*," she said, shrinking back against the wall as if frightened by her own words. "The world is sick. What I . . . what just . . ." But she broke down and could not finish.

Ruth knew to what she was referring. Eric was dead. The person she'd tried to protect her whole life was dead. "I'm so sorry," she said again and this time she was speaking to Eric.

Frank said, "Choose, Ruth. Or I will kill them both."

She shook her head. "I can't."

"I will say a name," he said. "If you respond, that is who you wish to save." He waited for his words to sink in. "Do you want me to kill Fay?"

Imagining the bag around her daughter's face, Ruth could not stop the keening in her throat.

"Then it is done," Frank said firmly. "You've saved your daughter. But for now I will keep her." He stood up, business-like all of a sudden. "*Motër.*" He took hold of Penny's arm. "It's time. Take her next door."

Ruth tried to beg. "*Please.*"

Penny unfolded, drawn upwards by her brother's hand.

Frank kept hold of Fay. "I must know that you'll look after mine as I will yours." He opened the door, checked the corridor, pushed them both outside.

504

WHAT HAPPENED NEXT came in fragments. A glare, a hiss of viscose, the shudder of Eric's door as Penny shoved Ruth against it, a lurching as she tripped to the carpet. Unable to bring her hands round in time, Ruth caught most of the impact on her chin. She saw the base of Eric's bed, tubes, wires, a metallic cylinder, a white hand resting on the edge of the bed, then Penny was on top of her. Ruth felt her wrap some kind of cloth round her mouth, was too dazed to realise what she was trying to do. Even as she held her breath, a sweet, cloying scent filled her nostrils.

At the same time, words drifted through the air as quiet as ash. "Did you . . . read it?"

Ruth's eyes were streaming from whatever was on the cloth, she desperately needed to breathe but when she heard the voice a second time, a voice she knew as well as her own, the force that surged through her was more powerful than anything she'd ever known.

Instead of focussing on Penny's hand, she bucked her body upwards and rolled sideways, causing Penny to drop to the carpet. Pushing the woman's hands to the floor, Ruth collapsed on top of her so that their heads lay side-by-side, their mouths panting together. Penny was on her side, Ruth was straddling her hip, her left arm across Penny's neck, her right hand pinning her hands to the carpet. Even as Penny began to resist, Ruth slipped her shoulder behind the other woman's head, pushed her face towards the cloth. Ruth felt Penny's heel scrape her shin. The woman heaved against Ruth's weight, desperation strengthening her efforts but by then Ruth had pulled her knees into Penny's ribs and spine. She threw all she could spare, her shoulder, her head, her chest, into pressing Penny's face towards that vaporous material. Penny threw her body upwards, much as Ruth had done, but Ruth went with it, knowing that all that mattered was keeping what was in Penny's hand pressed to her mouth. Finally, the other woman's efforts weakened and she slumped to the carpet.

Ruth's chest heaved. She was aware of some mark, as if between water and air, rising and falling. It was a long time before the world regained shape. When it finally did, she slid sideways, gathered her hands and knees and pushed upwards. She was too weak to stand.

Eric's hand was so close, she could have kissed it. His face lay sideways. His eyes shone down. His mouth moved as if trying to create shapes. There was between them a kind of vapour, not the fumes that had debilitated Penny but something rarer, some pure spirit that shone from their eyes and infected their voices.

"Did you read the last verse?" Eric said hoarsely.

Ruth nodded. "Some of it." She tasted blood in her mouth. "I thought you were dead."

He licked his lips. "And Fay?"

"He has her." Ruth didn't say who. It didn't seem to matter.

"How's Will?"

"He has them both," she said.

"If you've read the poem, he will return."

Ruth held onto the side of the bed, pulled herself up, reached out and touched her brother's hand. He tried to smile.

She opened the door, looked back at Eric, then lurched into the corridor. Working her hand along the wall, she reeled towards Will's room, her teeth clenched. Yet when she reached his door, she hesitated, the promises beyond it too awful to contemplate. She felt the moment swell into something almost uncontainable, then threw herself forwards.

She was greeted by puffs of snow. The room was lit only by the light from the corridor. The first thing she saw was the window. It was completely broken from top to bottom. Jagged pieces of glass decorated the frame. She looked for Frank but he was gone. So was Fay. Will was lying on the bed, his face turned towards her, his eyes open.

Chapter 6.

The Last Verse

IN THE END THE MOB might have torn the creature apart had the Keeper not murmured its name. Awkwardly, fitfully, Ma'kin began to lift itself into the air, its body a neon stutter against the clouds. Soon it was no more than a fading star. Denied their aim, the crowd did not return to more bloodletting. Not only were they covered in so much mud, one creature did not know itself from the next, witnessing Rook's murder had dulled their appetites. The scene had blazed in the air above the House of Pain and every one of them had watched it. Now though, the cloudbusters had fallen dark and those who had survived the battle were left nursing their collective and private shames.

The earth was a delta of blood. Liam could not look at what was left of Rook. He stared at the red-marbled water, Erin beside him, his skin and hair bloodied and burnt, his cheek at a strange angle, his ear black.

"You said her name." Erin grinned madly. "Ruth, I mean. She needs you, Will. She is alive and she needs you."

Liam glanced at Rook, hated Erin for making him look, felt the other's fingers turn his face, a blaze of green.

"I was right, you do have to die. It makes sense. Occam's razor. It's the simplest explanation. You re*mem*bered Ruth," he insisted. "She's waiting for you, Will. Fay too. They need you."

Liam shook his head. "That is not my name."

Erin tottered to his feet and raised his hands. "Yes it is. Just as is this sentimental torture chamber. Our bodies exist in both worlds, the strands of which are woven together. We are brothers. We exchanged blood. Your watch, my book, remember? I would rather stay but for you I am willing to forgo this beautiful madness. You have another life, Will. With them, with Ruth, with *Fay*."

It was too much. With a savage cry, Liam rose up, only for Erin to leap forwards and push at the spear in his lap, eliciting a deep groan from his wounded friend.

"Don't you see?" Erin's eyes swam with tears. "This world of yours, it wishes to bind you in blood. It evolves with each choice you make. And you have only ever wanted destruction. You must choose life and to choose life, you must die."

"Well," Liam said in a great grinding of teeth, "if you want death so much then you shall have it."

And with that, he pulled the spear free, seized Erin as if in an embrace, spun in the soil and flung his friend far across the rooftop. Higher and higher he flew, further and further his dwindling form soared, until, far beyond the screaming towers and even the wall itself, it finally winked into nothingness.

The poem, his parents, all had been for nought. A conspiracy of delusions. And no one more complicit than the man in the shadows. Kneeling down, Liam swept Rook's hair from her lifeless eyes. He wanted nothing more than to lie down with her and never get up. But this was not what he deserved. He bent and kissed her, then staggered to his feet. This time, when he began to run, it was without haste, yet each step was faster than the last so that by the time he sprang from the roof's edge, he flew.

A shape grew on the opposite wall, an aquiline shadow that shrieked even as it landed amid the tangle of bodies on the opposite roof. The poem sang louder than ever before. Running across the roof, he saw a skittering moon scurry past the lift shaft. The Keeper.

Rather than follow him, Liam leapt into the air and dropped onto the roof so forcefully that the structure crashed inwards with a clatter of metal and plaster. The Keeper had already stabbed at the panel of buttons, causing the metal box to begin its lurching descent but Liam, unwilling to wait for such niceties, drove his foot through the floor, seized the old man by his collar and stuffed him through the hole. They plummeted through a cloying darkness, the scents of oil and dust clogging their nostrils until, with a great and invisible displacement, they struck the water at the bottom of the shaft and sank into the abyss.

They did not settle. Liam tore at the wall, before dragging the old man through several sunken rooms and out through a vast, paneless window into a subterranean street. Fish fled. Racing between gutted shells, he surged upwards, before breaking the surface in a roil of foam, causing the boats there to heave on their anchors.

He twisted the old man's collar in his fist. "Where is it!"

Despite choking and spitting and thrusting his chin, the man still managed a certain smugness. "I *knew* you'd come for it."

It did not matter. Groping at the man's sodden robe, Liam quickly discovered the book's hiding place and pulled it free.

"How does it feel?" the Keeper panted, his eyes full of a mad delight. "To watch them die and do nothing?"

Always this man had been able to find the best place to slip the knife but nothing could prepare Liam for the rage that coursed through him now. It exploded outwards, punching through the water and causing the boats to clatter and bang together. Intent on dashing the Keeper's brains out, Liam sank beneath the surface, got a better grip on the man's robe before surging towards the outer wall, churning a great chasm behind them. The speed and power with which they struck the wall shattered the blackened crust coating the concrete and the blocks beneath it and drove a fractured tunnel right though the structure itself. A moment later, they exploded into the sea beyond in a cloud of rubble.

Behind them, the fissure was immediately replaced by a rushing torrent that began to widen the hole, pulling at the pair with a sudden force. Sand, grit, rocks, all went whirling up from the seabed, a great tumult that would have taken them both if Liam hadn't been able to force himself forwards.

He imagined the flood now surging into the city, the towers crumbling, their floors folding, the whole house of cards tumbling down, the bodies, Rook's, Fredrickson's, Enzo's, spinning like insects into a drain. All had gone as planned, nothing was accidental. This then was the Keeper's final purpose.

It was a long time before the waters cleared and he could see again. Unlike the Keeper, he was able to breathe. For the longest time, the old man stared up at him before finally releasing the air in his lungs and taking a breath. His back arched, his hands clawed. He tried again, redoubling his agony. Even so, his eyes never left Liam's face.

When it was over, he weighed the Keeper's body down with stones. In death, the man looked little different than in life. The skin about his face and neck was grey, the hairs on his skull waved like dead weeds. Only his bulging eyes showed his true state. Dawn had broken across the sea and all was calm.

Liam rose from the water, neither amazed nor thrilled by his ability to do so. The horizon was a pale gold. The clouds were gone, revealing a few cold stars. Behind him the eddy was all but spent, the city beneath it a carousel of debris and bodies. Too little of him was left to care. He desired only one thing, to bury his daughter. After that he could finally send into the air his quiet breath.

ii.

FLYING TOWARDS THE RISING sun, his vision was taken by an inconsolable despair, for however fast he flew and however far, he could not escape himself.

He sped into the day, leaving behind him the darkness in which Rook had been ripped open, the darkness in which he had killed the Keeper. But the darkness was inside. He need only look.

Spying the White Rock, his throat burned with a fierce and unbearable love. Unsure what he would find, he descended the warming sky and drifted down between the silver tree's shining branches. Petals and the sweet, heady scent of jasmine floated in the air. On the grass, someone had laid out hundreds of photographs, each secured by a small, egg-shaped pebble. Whoever it was had also put out a jug of water and a glass. Even as he drank, the bower drew at his sorrow. If, as Rousseau had asked, he had stayed, Rook and Fay might still be alive.

"This is you," his mother said.

How long she'd been sitting there, he couldn't say. The sun was low now, the air full of dusk. Candles glimmered in the grass. Beside him lay a loaf of bread and a bowl of warm water, its vapours rising into the evening. His mother was holding a picture of him standing beside a man with a green splash in his eye. They were both holding fishing rods and Liam was wearing a hat.

"I remember," he said, taking the photograph. "We fished all day and caught nothing." He looked at her, his pain caught in the thinnest of nets. "I hoped you'd be here."

"You're not angry?"

"Not with you."

"Then," she said, "let me wash you."

He removed his clothes and she started with his feet, working her hands up and round his legs, the water steaming each time she broke the surface with her cloth. He kept his head bowed.

When he finally looked at her, the candlelight trembled in his tears. "I lost them."

She reached for him and he felt her head nodding against his shoulder, her voice murmur in his ear. "I promise you, it is not too late. Your precious one awaits."

When he was clean, she passed him his clothes and he pulled them on, a floral scent reaching for his senses. All across the basin, branches rose and fell, their underleaves burring white, their canopies alive with a gentle creaking. High above them, he heard a long, haunting screech and turned in time to see his father making his way down into the hollow, his face a dark mosaic in the candlelight. Liam's tears burst anew.

"All that time, I thought I was looking for you."

"When really," his father said, pulling him into a hug, "you were looking for yourself. It is not so different, I think."

"Have you the last verse?"

Stepping back, the man placed a hand on his cheek. "No. Your path does not end here."

"Then where? Where am I to find myself? The pain is too much."

His mother's top was decorated with bright flowers amid dark trees. As his father turned and helped her to her feet, Liam noted his shirt and jacket. Both wore the clothes they'd worn in his visions.

"Among books," his father said. "You are the reader, the writer, the dreamer. The three are inseparable."

But Liam was thinking about something else, another fork in the path. "Have I blood on my hands, father?"

The green in his father's eyes flashed a warning. "There are some things you must finish and some you must begin. This is neither." He spoke as if to a nervous horse. "You're finally on the path home, William. The last bridge awaits."

His mother held up the bread. "Eat. Please."

He could smell the warm hearth of it but though he told himself to step forwards, he found himself doing the opposite, so that soon the candles were a fallen halo at his feet.

His mother and father moved to the edge of the circle and spoke in unison: "At least take our gifts."

A scarf fluttered between his mother's fingers. The kite glowed in the candlelight. At the same time, a black shadow began to spread across the clearing and he looked up to see a roiling presence, heavier than cloud and denser than blood, creeping across the sky, a viscous thickening that began, one-by-one, to blot out the stars. The film is about to begin, he thought, the final solution. But no such thing happened. Instead a light flashed from one end of the sky to the other, a deluge so absolute that for a moment there was nothing: ". . . to dream of you, his screwed-up little wife?" The words were everywhere and faded away like the after-note of thunder.

When he looked down, the candles were out, the tree barely visible, his parents gone and suddenly he yearned to hold them and never let them go.

iii.
———

HE ROSE UP, THE HOLLOW slipping like silk from his skin, the night clothing his body in bright dust. All his longings were piled up in one great conflagration. He willed the cold to freeze his blood. To weigh in his veins and fell him from the sky. As he flew, his passage was paralleled by the reflection following him in the waves below.

Finally, he saw a light pass over the sea, a white line touching waves and distant rocks. As he neared the aerie, its details grew ever clearer but only when the lattice rang beneath his boots did he believe in it. Weakened by his journey and by his wound, he placed his hands and then his head on the cold, dark surface, dreams of revenge fleeing before his fatigue.

A fire burned in a box, a squat black incinerator placed at the end of a long, steeply-bordered garden. Behind blackened bars, burning books, the pages they contained roaring as if all their words were speaking at once.

He wrenched awake, heard the slow thunder of waves. Wind seasoned the air with salt. Penumbra was crouching beside him, her eyes wide with surprise.

"What a scare you gave me!" she said, her hand on her chest. "I was feeding the birds . . ."

Taking a moment to recover, she set about getting him up. "Come, you'll catch your death out here."

The lantern room was shielded by a dome consisting of oddly-angled panes of glass set into a rusting metal frame, making it impossible to see inside. Leading Liam to a low door, Penumbra ducked inside.

He followed, to see, on his right, a number of birdcages, their frames housing several cooing, fluttering forms, on his left, a low table and an open trapdoor. Directly in front of him, rising from floor to ceiling and surrounded by a ring of concentric lenses, stood a huge lamp, its light redirected through the lenses in evermore-concentrated beams. Across this crystalline landscape, lines ebbed and flowed as if independent of the structure, beautiful distortions cast, not only by the lenses themselves, but also by the dome and the aerie behind it. It was a mesmerising sight and though Liam told himself to look away, it held his gaze a moment too long and the turning beam fell full in his face. Even as he was blinded, he realised that two of the shapes ebbing and flowing across the glass were somehow familiar.

He called Penumbra's name. "Who's here with us?"

His nostrils filled with the scent of burning dust. He caught the rustle of wings and then a chuckle. He knew the sound and yet it was impossible. The dead do not laugh. He placed his hands against the panes behind him, closed his eyes. It made no difference. He saw only light.

"Penumbra, what is this?"

Her voice came from somewhere near the door. "The oldest beginning in the world."

He turned his head. "For you and—?"

"Us," a man said.

"All of us," said a second.

Liam shook his head. "It can't be. You're dead."

"As is everyone else," the first Keeper said.

"And now there is only here," the second Keeper added.

"But what of those on T'heel?"

The first Keeper spoke with a familiar smugness. "After you fled, the creature was difficult to control, even for those men who know its name."

The light pulsed past. His eyes averted, Liam began to recognise shapes. The two men stood on the other side of the lamp, their bodies visible as swelling, shrinking lines. He recalled the cave in which he'd first encountered Ma'kin, all those bodies strapped into wooden rigs.

"In every way identical," one of the men said, reading his thoughts. "What you did to the Keeper on the Island of T'heel? It was enough." A shape shrugged. "Did you not wonder that the man on the Isle of Hats was unmarked?"

Liam remembered hurting the Keeper. Yet the man's teeth on the third island had been unbroken. He could vaguely make out Pen's shape, a length of rope in her hands. "But why?"

"Paradise regained," she said.

"Adams," Liam said, recognising the irony of the Keeper's name. "With you as his Eve. What a fool I've been. All this time, I was the real Nephilim, a bastard child come to wipe man off the face of the Earth. Just so you can play Adam and Adam and Eve."

He looked at Penumbra. "What did you do to Gribble?"

"We visited the cave together," she said coldly. "He got too close. When the creature woke, it took his heart."

"So that's why you stopped speaking. You were preparing yourself for murder?"

"I was doing my *duty.*"

"We're going to start again," the nearest man said. "Here on this mountaintop we will rebuild mankind. But we want you with us, our oracle, our god. We needed you to feel the weight of that truth. This is your world."

Liam's smile felt brittle on his lips. "God, you say?"

"You must have realised your own uniqueness?"

As the man spoke, Liam found himself watching the light trail its golden petticoats across the glass. *Instead of darkness we get a light so bright we're blinded.* Who said that? He told himself to look away, that the light would blind him but that other voice—Erin's?— seemed to suggest otherwise. Instead, he did the opposite, he focussed on the revolving beams, forced himself to watch them sweep his way, waited to be blinded, while somehow, believing the contrary. One moment the reflections were like that of a train approaching along a curving tunnel, its beam growing ever brighter, ever more concentrated and then—just before they became a single burst—they winked out, plunging the aerie into gloom. Birds beat their wings against the bars. Between each burst, Liam heard footsteps. Moonlight glowed in the glass. *This world of yours, it wishes to bind you in blood.* But not just blood. They were going to imprison him here so he could never leave.

He heard one of the Keeper's mention the rope, caught a glint in the dark. They wanted to tie him to the light. They wanted to tie him to the light and make him watch what they did to the world. It was enough. With a groan, his clothing burst into flames, their cadmium light catching in the glass all around. He clasped at his head. Fire burst from his arms, rippling upwards, setting light to his hair. Seizing the moment, Liam leapt over the rope, landed beside the trapdoor and threw himself down the steps.

Someone shouted from above but with the fire roaring in his ears, he missed it. The man's next words were clear enough though: "Come to your father."

They were the same words the Keeper had uttered below the House of Love but now, instead of fear, he felt only joy. He heard a creaking. Dust shuddered from the ceiling.

"I'm coming," he said, beating at the stone. "I'm coming, my precious one."

Nothing would stop the flood in his head, nothing but blood for he had seen too much, been driven too low, been betrayed by too many to see anything but the pit. At the same time, he sensed, like grit in the corner of an eye, smearing it with each blink, recollections, his mother's hair floating in water, his father's stubbled cheek. He flew round each bend until finally flight wasn't enough. Throwing himself at the floor, he began to tear at the masonry before bursting through the chamber ceiling and dropping to the floor below. Rattling down the iron steps, he reached the cluttered antechamber just in time to see the library door judder, then lurch inwards with a shriek of hinges. Ma'kin's blazing body filled the doorway.

Words jerked from Liam's mouth as if each were hooked into flesh. "I've come for what's mine."

Its platelets clinking and glowing, Ma'kin leered at him. "You failed to bring me a bride, so I took my own. She becomes me, does she not?"

With a howl, Liam threw himself at the monster, sending it crashing down the steps and into the stacks beyond, splintering the wood and causing books to cascade in their hundreds. Imagining himself of stone, the creature's efforts skittered off his skin, while in contrast, he tore with stony teeth at its flesh, throwing aside each chunk so that walls and books were soon dripping.

Nothing would stop him from finding Fay but as his hand wormed at Ma'kin's guts, he found nothing. Shoving the creature aside, he scattered books left and right, spread his hands on the floor as if in supplication, then struck downwards with his fists, a resounding blow

518

that caused a huge crack to appear, a zigzagging rift wide enough and deep enough to all but swallow his last, agonising cry:

"What have you done with her!"

2

DESPITE EVERYTHING, the creature was still alive. It lay on the other side of the chasm, staring across at him, its body radiating a lilac hue. "Blood . . ." it said, in two, distinctly different voices, ". . . must be purged with blood."

Words. Words that could span worlds. Why, William, you do look handsome tonight. Who said that? He recalled a garden, terracotta pots, dusty plants, people laughing. He'd gone down on one knee. Why had he done that? Why did people do such things?

That was when she'd said it: Why, William . . . He'd asked her to marry him. Again. She'd said no and then laughed. "Of course I will. But you need to be careful. Giving a girl a second chance might make her have second thoughts."

There was life. Here was only death. Erin had said he only wanted destruction and it was true. But not anymore.

"My name is William," he said. "William Zifla."

Much of this concerned the power of names. He and the monster had been similarly bound. And by the same man, or rather, men. But something had changed. He recalled what the Keeper had said in the aerie: Here on this mountain, we will rebuild mankind. It was a strange phrase, almost scriptural. Yet his mind raced ahead. A certain possibility suggested itself, raised certain sounds to his lips. The buzz of the 'm', the way his throat vibrated, his tongue rising against his palette, the sharp 'k', the soft 'i', the same 'n', the final letter. Could it be that simple? Of course it could. He'd been so sure he knew it, had staked Rook's life on it but only now was he finally certain of the creature's name.

He saw a high darkness and a deep blue, spoke the name into both, saw it ripple across the surface like two snakes, heard the monster sigh, saw it settle, its armour clinking to the floor. It was looking across the gulf between them, its one good eye still burning with life.

He breathed in. "Close," he said. "So close."

ii.
———

WHEN HE WAS FINALLY able to walk up the stairs, he realised everything was vibrating, the iron steps, the lattice casing, even the walls. He heard the muttering of voices and stepped out into the chamber to see that it was full of old men, some sitting on the floor, others on the seats, their shadows thrown into oddly similar shapes by the lamplight. The Keepers turned as he appeared, the look in their eyes also similar. They were there to meet their god.

He told them he understood. "So long as I keep on believing, you will keep on living."

"You're ours." One of the Keepers stood up now, the wattle at his neck quivering as he spoke. "Made in our image. To worship as we choose."

Murmurs of assent bubbled across the room and when he tried to speak, another of the Keepers screamed for the creature, a cry that was taken up by the others until the sound all but drowned out even the metallic jangle coming from the staircase.

Will walked up several more steps and then turned round, intent on addressing them all, only for the old men nearest him to shuffle forwards. He could see them through the latticework, their skulls swaying like deadheads in the wind.

Afraid that he was leaving, several of them became prey to their own disease. "Only one need live!" Whoever this came from, it was taken up as a general cry but despite a room full of generals, no one seemed willing to lead the charge.

"You're nothing without us." This from the man standing nearest.

"Think of what we've done together," another said.

"Look around you. What were you before?"

"Just a reflection."

"A broken mirror."

"Here you are *God!*"

Will recalled Erin's words. *You are being hunted. By love, by anger, by guilt. But you must turn and face your predators.* Yet even though all those emotions were here, now, in the flesh, it was guilt that triumphed. "I must find the last verse."

He'd only hoped to soothe. Instead, a great moan rippled through the crowd. He took another few steps upwards and when he looked back, saw them squeezing onto the staircase two-abreast, their hands groping for him.

"He wants to take Gale."

"Eve, he wants Eve!"

No longer in need of leadership, they surged for the stairs, treading on each other in their eagerness to reach him. Jumping up the steps, he felt a hand clutch at his cuff and leapt for the landing. The whole staircase was swaying now, packed as it was with men fighting each other to make it to the top. He'd just gained the landing when his foot was seized and he would have been dragged back into the fray had the staircase not taken a sudden lurch sideways, so that one moment the old men were reaching for the landing and the next, the lattice was collapsing around them like claws. Pushing himself backwards, Will watched as the staircase, weakened by the hole he'd burrowed beside it, began to buckle and twist, wrapping ever tighter round those who had, only moments before, been surging up it. Finally, with a long, screeching groan and a ponderous cloud of dust, it was cleaved from its mooring and began to fold to the floor below, crushing those in its grasp as if with iron jaws.

iii.

WITH THE CRIES OF the dying trembling in his ears, he crawled across the landing, his heartbeat fluttering like a daemon. He'd lost a lot of blood. His jumper was stiff with it, the wool covered in purple swatches. His head ached and all around him little lights popped in and out of existence. Having reached his old landing, he rested, before pulling himself across the floor and up the next flight.

As he crawled up the last step, he saw a light, not from underneath Gale's door but from the room opposite. He pushed at the door, saw a sparsely decorated room and a metal-framed, rather high bed. The bed had bars, as if to prevent its occupant from falling out. The whole, somewhat cumbersome-looking contraption was highlighted by a diffuse glow, as was the figure lying on it. His pale skin and waxy orange hair were unmistakeable. It was Eric.

Will spoke his name, crept forwards and took hold of his hand. "Eric? They're alive, aren't they?" He trembled at the thought of his daughter's name. "You said Fay is alive. *Please*, Eric, tell me again."

He could hear the other breathe, a quiet whistle coming in and out of his nostrils but that was it. A shadow moved across the bed and then Penumbra was standing on the opposite side, her jaw set, her lips pursed. Seeing her stretch out her hands, he thought she was going to touch Eric's face. Only when she reached behind his head and took hold of his pillow did he realise that her intentions were far more sinister.

He tried to pull himself up. "Don't. Please. Not for him. He lied to you. You're not his Eve."

Penumbra had four eyes, two of which looked at him now. "No," she said, one pair of lips sounding out the words, the other, clearly visible beneath the first, inert. "I am Lilith, haunter of desert places, harbourer of young children."

As if woken by their voices, Eric frowned and then slowly opened his eyes. Seeing Will, he smiled, the effort crinkling the scar running across his jaw and causing his left eye to all but vanish into the purple swelling around his socket. His voice was a croak. "Not so beautiful as you once imagined?"

Despite the dizzying weakness coursing through him, Will understood that he'd never been more needed. "Eric—we're not alone."

Eric glanced up, saw Penumbra, her features once more reunited, her hands gripping each end of the pillow, her eyes closed, her lips moving as if in prayer. When he looked back at Will, doubt gleamed in his eyes.

"I am between."

Will was watching Penumbra. (No, not Penumbra, he thought. In that other place—where she used to read to him, of flood, of ark— she is Penny). Her pale skin was glistening with perspiration, her slender jaw rippling.

"Please don't."

But it was as if his words had the opposite effect, as if, in fact, they goaded her on. Penny opened her eyes, gripped the pillow more tightly, then lowered it over Eric's face.

Galvanised by a final, desperate strength, Will slid a hand under the pillow, raised a dome above Eric's lips and hissed into his ear:

"*Speak*! Tell her you're alive. Tell her you want to live."

Yet even as he spoke, Eric began to paw at the pillow.

Will pleaded. "You have to fight. You have to tell her that you want to live. We've come so far, seen so much . . ." Where his next words came from, he would never know but come they did: "What stories we might tell if only we live to fight another day."

He was a fool to think that he could reach across the void. But even as he despaired, the pillow fell away and Penny stumbled back, her eyes alive with fear. Removing his hand, Will saw that Eric's lips were moving and though he couldn't hear what he was saying, it was obvious that Penny could and that whatever it was, terrified her.

iv.
—

A ROARING DARKNESS, endless black waterfalls. He reached out but Eric was gone. Only the floor beneath him told of anything physical. Turning, he crawled away, sank to the landing outside and listened so that for a moment the world was but breath, a shapeless shifting that was both everywhere and intimate. His first day of freedom, he'd stood before Gale's door but had turned away, afraid of what lay beyond it, of what he might learn about himself. But new truths whispered to him now, seductive murmurings that promised other possibilities. He felt the book in his pocket. When he'd mentioned the final verse, the old men had assumed he was going to see Gale. Perhaps in their fear lay his salvation.

Feeling what might have been a door, he patted his hand upwards until he found a handle. The sensation was immediate. It was like being thrown out into the sky. Cold shoulders shrugged into the distance. A river drew ink through hills. Even as the wind twisted his feathers, a high shriek trembled in his mouth. It was true. Those seen alive were dead and those seen dead were alive. He released a final cry and turned the handle.

The room was quite ordinary. By a cone of light, he could see a bed, its half-tucked sheet dangling almost to the floor, the lower edge of which obscured a kite, its sail decorated with feathers, its spine attached to a long blue tail. His mother's scarf. Atop a low chest, a bulb glowed inside a linen shade, highlighting two dozen blocks, their sides emblazoned with letters. The bed was covered with a blanket, its creases hiding a small shape, an outline that shrugged and shifted beneath the cloth. He kept waiting for the door to slam and the light to go out but no such thing happened. The shape wriggled again and a mineral smell, as of mountain water newly thawed, filled the air. Still though he was afraid. If he reached down and pulled aside the blanket, something would take hold of his fingers and pull him into the abyss. Yet he knew enough of knowing to know he knew nothing and reached down regardless.

His efforts revealed a pinched, pink skull, a scalp covered with a mist of hair, the tufts of which sprang up like down as he pulled the blanket aside. Eyes squinted at the light. Against the baby's cream-coloured suit, her hands moved like pink anemones, underwater things that opened and closed at whim. She rubbed her nose, blinked and yawned, revealing bright pink gums. In one tight little fist she was holding a slip of paper and he realised why in his dreams he'd heard a rustling. It was the sound of paper. Here was Gale then, or rather, Fay.

At the same time, he heard Ruth say, "I'd like to pray."

The voice that replied possessed cruel claws. "*One.*"

He couldn't move his left arm. His right was weak. Still he was able to pick Fay up. After kissing her cheek, he lay down, the relief such that he almost fainted. The paper in Fay's fist was blank but as Ruth began to whisper—"Forlorn! The very word is like a bell . . ."—the words started scribbling across the page. And as each appeared, Will read it aloud until their voices were echoes: "To toll me back from thee to my sole self . . ."

But then he heard those claws slash at the air—"Still trying to wake him with poesy?"—and the words stopped.

Two lines, that was all. Worse still, those he'd read began to fade. He felt like throwing himself into that great white waste and wrestling those black sticks to the ground! Yet they were not the only things to disappear. The cone of light below the lamp was diminishing too and with it, the paper in his hand, the letters on the blocks, the blue scarf snaking across the floor, even the furniture and the floorboards. He could not see Fay, nor, when he moved his arms, could he feel her.

Instead he was standing on a curtained stage. Wooden boards gave beneath his feet, thick folds hung before his face. He saw a chink of light and reached out. As if a stone had been rolled aside, he was accosted by an alien landscape blasted by lights. A tiered auditorium petered into darkness, its egg box seats empty except for three stooges leaning their cheeks on their knuckles and staring at the stage. The fattest stooge leant forwards, his belly pressing against the seat in front.

"When you're ready, Mr Zifla."

Sniffler? He felt something tighten in his chest. No, I'm not ready, I'll never be ready and this thought emptied him so completely, no other dared trespass. He sensed a cloying closeness, an earthy darkness.

"And haply the Queen-Moon is on her throne . . ." His young voice trembled. "Clustered around by all her starry Fays." The words made no sense. "*Clustered around by all her starry Fays.*"

But Fay was gone. He fell to his knees. Where the boards had been lay only blunt ends. He was kneeling in a grave. A scattering of earth flew out of the light and fell across his legs, another into his lap.

He tried to move but more earth flew into the hole, weighing him down. Soil landed on his chest and neck. He lay with his head against sawn wood, heard his breath disturb the nuggets of earth piling against his chin and exhaled more fiercely. "One minute past."

Could it be that simple? That the cars collided at one minute past midnight? That somehow the accident, the poem, the watch, Eric, he, all were one?

He felt a great yearning, as if for one more shovelful, heavy, perfectly weighted, like the last wave that slaps you under. But the poem wouldn't leave him alone. *One minute past*, it sang, *leave the world unseen . . . and quite forget.*

"Forlorn," he murmured. "The very word, the very word, is like, is like a . . ."

And then he heard it, a bell—tiny, pure—and felt a stirring, followed by a delicate trickle of grains that caused him to open his eyes. Another movement and then he saw a thing half-buried, a tiny bird that shook itself loose and came hopping out of the soil as if fresh from diving for worms. After ruffling its wings and nodding its head, it took to the air, landing on a branch made all but invisible by the full moon behind it. There, perched on a high twig, the nightingale raised its head, opened its sharp little beak and began to sing. Pure euphoria! Ascending trills, crooning fiddles and pulsing hammers swelled across the stage, thumped at the curtains, punctured the walls, blasted the roof and, one-by-one, began to extinguish the lights until everything and everyone he'd ever known was tipped into a new kind of darkness, the darkness of times past, of aeons rolling by with the slow, unconscious curl of thunder. Secrets stolen by the light rewrapped themselves in velvet, frowning eyes widened, ears opened and all the time that song kept on drilling, drawing its rich dark oil up from the forgotten. Up in the aerie he'd extinguished the light so that he might better see and now he understood why. This shadow, so full of fear, this singing wonderland, was childhood, a treasure trove whose contents, sown together by the long curlicues of those lilting notes, a score that spoke of fear and at the same time, of the conquering of fear, could only be fingered by the imagination. The flame of youth, at its heart lay darkness, he understood that now. With such hands, one can grasp misfortune as one should, with a youthful confidence. Birds sing despite the predators their songs must attract. In youth, being afraid is natural, even to be embraced. Yet in adulthood, it is too often a vile thing, to be escaped down every bright tube.

He was terribly afraid, of what he'd done, of the consequences, but here in the universe of his own imagination he could finally turn and face it, turn and sing his own song in a voice shaking with joy: "Forlorn, the very word is like a bell to toll me back from thee to my sole self! Adieu! the fancy cannot cheat so well as she is famed to do, deceiving elf. Adieu! adieu! thy plaintive anthem fades, past the near meadows, over the still stream, up the hillside, and now 'tis buried deep in the next valley-glades: was it a vision, or a waking dream? Fled is that music—do I wake or sleep?"

He felt Fay yawn and mumble on his chest.

"The tower must fall," he said in the voice of story. "The tower must fall and I must die."

The last time he'd breathed anything so wonderful, he'd been poised above his mother's bower and now he was similarly toppled. He heard a low, masonic grumbling, followed by a great booming, a rolling, shuddering tumbling noise, then a vast shattering that shook the air. All around, the fractious sound of masonry splintering in huge, lustrous rifts, the outbursts springing, now singly, now several, then at longer intervals, then in rapid succession. Boom boom boom! With his stomach and throat singing, he fell as if through a tunnel, the rush of leaving humming in his skin. Eruptions thundered, rolled, melted together, sundered apart in long trails. In his mind's eye, he saw the ruin roll ever onwards, endless lines of dominos falling endlessly and every single one, the result of some choice. This then was death, connection, oblivion, an endless loop.

But then his descent slowed and he became aware of various sensations. Pain began to sniff at him, snuffling into his back, his joints, his buttocks. From these creatures, parasites swarmed, spreading about his body in dense patches, their jaws like probing needles. Teeth clenched, he opened his eyes just wide enough to sense a bright square of light high in the darkness, an indistinct patch to his left. Voices, a ranging vibration sweeping back and forth, followed by a higher note. He caught two words, ". . . kill Fay?"

More words, blotches of sound and then, for the first time, Frank's voice rang clear. "Then it is done."

3

SOMETHING WAS RESTING in his hands. A child. Fay. As his fingers curled around her neck and legs, he recalled his father's words. There are some things you must finish and some you must begin.

"It's time. Take her next door."

Light fell across the bed, then closed. His extremities teemed. Any movement made the sensation unbearable. But it was not for this reason that he stayed still. He didn't want Frank to know he had returned, though he had no idea what he was going to do. Even if he were well, he would have had little chance against the man but as it stood, he was useless. But he did have one hope. In the pit of his stomach, where his ribcage began, he felt a nauseous bloating. He felt very hot, his body prickled with sweat.

He could smell Frank's aftershave. The man was sitting nearby. When he spoke, he sounded as if he were pleading with someone.

"Help me, father. If we keep the child, history will only repeat itself. *Tani për tani.* His blood flows in her veins."

Will peered through his lashes. Frank was a black lump. Something crinkled in his fist.

Frank's voice became firmer. "But first things first. Blood must be purged with blood."

Again, Will heard the rustle of plastic, then felt Frank's breath against his face. "Any last words?"

Yes, one, he thought.

He felt Frank slide something over the top of his head and knew straightaway what the man was doing. He was going to suffocate him.

Frank forced the bag over Will's ears, his words reaching him as if through water. ". . . a sigh before and a sigh after . . ."

Will tried to open his eyes. The plastic flattened his lids, blurred his vision, but he could see Frank's face clearly enough. And Frank could see his. Realising what he was looking at, Frank's eyes widened but his resolve only seemed to harden, for he continued to pull the bag down over Will's face. When Will spoke, his words were muffled.

"Ann-kine, um' 'oo 'or 'ather."

Frank peered through the plastic. "What?"

Will felt the pressure relax, the plastic lift from his mouth. He moved his hand blindly, covered Fay's ears.

Frank's eyes were wide in the dark. The fingers splayed either side of Will's skull dug into his temples. "What did you say?"

Will's words buzzed at the plastic. "I said, *Mankind*, come to your father."

It was enough. His stomach ballooned against his ribs, as what was inside forced its way upwards. A solid mass that made it impossible to breathe, it oozed up his oesophagus, causing him to gag. Sounds popped, invisible flesh rearranging itself with sludgy half-turns and sudden-slips. It took a supreme effort of will to lie still. He wanted to turn and retch, to claw at his gullet but instead he lay with his mouth wide and his eyes streaming, hoping the birth would be quick.

Frank tried to retreat but as he did so, Will twisted the man's tie in his fist. Without warning, Will's head jerked sideways, his stomach convulsed. Spasms rippled up his body, contractions that encouraged the obstruction in his throat to expand upwards another few inches, enter his pharynx and slide onto his tongue before bunching against the back of his teeth, piling one fold upon another, almost unhinging his jaw. The skin about his face stretched, splitting around his mouth, squeezing his eyes.

Frank's eyes were bulging. He tried to escape but his efforts were weakened by shock. Realising Will had hold of his tie, he seized Will's fist, trying to wrestle it away. "What are you—?"

Will clung on, the thing inside him flattening his lungs and forcing his mouth ever wider, cramming it full before pushing out into the room, the wet sac of it slithering out and downwards where it began to pool on the floor.

Frank's mouth frothed shapeless thoughts. For all his strength, he could not shake Will's grip and danced on the end of the tie as if on a leash. He was a few feet from the door, his outstretched fingers nearly touching the square of light. The tie was so tight around his neck, his skin was crimson.

Will had trapped his feet beneath the bed. His right hand danced to and fro, his left covered the baby. Focussing on his solar plexus, he pushed down one last time and was rewarded with a great shifting as the creature he'd swallowed beneath the House of Visions, the monster who had succumbed to his will and allowed him to devour it, just as it had devoured his child, was born again, slipping with a final uncurdling to the floor.

Frank, trying to get his fingers under the knot of his tie, spoke in a strangled squeak. "*Motër.*"

His throat unconstricted, Will rasped at the air, his chest and stomach rising and falling in huge bursts, causing Fay to rise and fall with them. Frank was on the floor, his head turned away, one finger between his tie and his throat. He was as far from the bed as possible, which had in the course of the birth been pulled in his direction. Will's arm was stretched at a right angle to his body, his hand white, save the red ring where the tie bit into his skin. They both heard the thing beneath the bed but only Frank trembled. Will had already faced his demon. Mankind. How paradoxical a word, how facetious. We are born, Will thought, not as men but as possibility. But society must bind us, it must make us useful. But to whom? He'd guessed Frank might be waiting for him when he woke up and that the creature known as Mankind came from him. That Frank was its real father.

And here was the man himself, cowering on the floor. Frank took something from his jacket, began to work at his tie until the silk gave way with a rip. As Will's hand dropped, Frank heaved at the air and stared at the thing before him, which had swelled so much, its body now pressed at the base of the bed.

"Impossible." Rubbing his throat, Frank repeated the word and stared at Will. "What have you done?"

Will swallowed. "Returned."

"Im*pos*sible." Frank could have escaped but such would have necessitated rational thought and Frank seemed beyond it. From beneath Will came a wet sigh and Frank sank back. The bed juddered and his eyes widened in terror.

Will's voice was a croak. "I was guided home . . ." He raised a hand to tug at the bag crowning his head. ". . . by a poem."

Frank stared at the blade in his hand. "A poem?"

"Yes," Will said. "That ends with a question. 'Do I wake or sleep?' Do you know the difference?"

"That's it." Frank rubbed at his jaw. "I'm asleep."

Red and blue purpled the walls. From under the bed, the sound of a throat being cleared, wet slag through a funnel.

Will felt a smile creep into his lips. "Poetry brought me back from that other world. And as you can see, I didn't come alone. I returned with your child."

Frank tipped his head against the door. "This *slug*?"

The bed jerked then, jumping towards the door, pulling the lines in Will's side and arm. A machine made a loud bang as it crashed to the floor.

For a moment the bed reared up and then the creature was rising to its feet, its body swelling until its wings were pushing at the ceiling tiles, one of which was scarred by a strange, wavelike mark. Its red heart and aquamarine skull glowed as if made of ice. Frank was praying, his face almost touching the floor. Despite the channelling of light and energy, the wetness of Ma'kin's birth and the softness of its armour made it seem weaker. Still, it was magnificent and Will could only feel sorry for Frank as it bent as if to kiss him.

When it spoke, Will barely caught its words: "There are more things in heaven and earth, father."

Frank, visible as a smear through Ma'kin's chest, looked up, surprised perhaps to hear civilised words on its lips. That look, which sat uncomfortably on his skin, remained there, even as Ma'kin picked him up and even as Frank drove the nail file into the creature's half-formed flesh. Ma'kin appeared neither angry nor dismayed. Pulling Frank closer, it staggered back, caught the side of the bed, slid sideways.

In this way, they danced past the bed, back two more steps, followed by one final stumble. At the same time the shafts of light from Ma'kin's heart and head intensified, causing the room to glow. Frank turned his head as they passed, giving Will a look neither of fear nor desperation but only of wonder. Of Ma'kin, Will could not be sure. Its head was resting on Frank's, its arms wrapped around him, its eyes closed. They appeared to move slowly but as Ma'kin's leg caught the window ledge, time accelerated. The glass, hitherto invisible, became myriad and the creature's wings, suddenly rampant, reached through the falling glitter and scattering snow, flexed against the cold night air and then Frank Stine and his monster were gone.

Will stared at the window, then heard the door. Light poured in from the corridor. Clinging to the door, Ruth stared first at his face, then about the room. Fay had slipped between his legs and was shrouded by the sheet. It was obviously not to her liking though, for just then she began to mewl.

ii.
———

SUN LAY WARM AND STILL upon the room. Needlemire was peering at Ruth as if at some curious specimen, the rash of freckles across his face as pale as pollen in the morning light. Fay lay in the crook of her arm, the child's attention taken by the window where the melting snow dripped in bright, sunlit drops. Gladys was tending to Will with an uncharacteristic warmth.

Ruth felt like a survivor, as if she had pushed aside a twisted door and emerged from rubble, miraculously unscathed. Except, of course, it wasn't true. Each of them bore scars, soul wounds that only came to light over the coming weeks. It might have been easier were they not obliged to stay at the hospital. Will had to go through reconditioning as he called it and Eric was subjected to a series of tests to determine the extent of the damage to his spine. There was little point, therefore, in Ruth going back to Hove every evening, especially since she was offered a bed at the hospital. The problem with this was that it meant they were never far from gossip, for the hospital rumour mill ground on day and night, filled as it was, not only by reports of the air disaster but also by the shocking news that a member of staff had been assaulted and another was dead, that a police officer had been murdered and that a second man had mysteriously disappeared.

Ruth handled these various pressures by staying busy, seeing to Eric's needs, wheeling him to his various appointments, accompanying Will to rehab, taking quiet dinners with Fay and, of course, receiving visits from the police. It was a strangely lonely time, as if each of them were detained in adjacent bunkers. She desperately wanted to talk but it seemed she was the only one. Not that Will and Eric refused to answer her questions. It was just that their answers were so ambiguous, she was left dissatisfied and in the meantime they asked no questions in return. It felt as if they didn't need to. Having said that, with each other, they were even quieter and she would often find the two of them reading or dozing or watching television together, their shared silence frustratingly featureless.

Finally, on the day before they were due to go home, Ruth asked Will if he remembered dreaming. They were in the hospital common room, the remnants of a Chinese takeaway curdling in the bin. He shut his eyes for a moment, then said he remembered wanting to find his parents.

She'd told him some of what had happened, starting with the accident. But of what had followed, there was some yet to tell. She went to speak but he got there first and she could tell by his tone that he wished to say no more on the subject.

"I'll tell you what I do know," he said. "What is more important to me than anything else. It was your voice that brought me home."

Yet when they drove back to Hove, they found home not to be the place they remembered. They climbed out of the taxi, Will carrying their various belongings in a bin liner, Ruth with Fay's car seat clutched in both hands, both of them suffering a familiar sense of foreboding, as if this were some other house that just looked like theirs, a sensation that was heightened when Ruth opened the front door to be greeted by a smell reminiscent of the day they arrived home from their honeymoon, a faint, wet odour that caused her to clutch Fay to her side.

Will stood in the doorway as if dazed. "Home soggy home."

His attempt at humour fell on sour ground. Being in that house only reinforced the feeling that what they'd been through had wrought irrevocable changes. To Ruth the place felt haunted, a sensation that was heightened, both by Frank's disappearance, and by the fact that though the kitchen had been thoroughly cleaned, Graham was still there every time she crossed the threshold. Even Penny, who had, by the time Will and she were found, fled, lingered on in her imagination, so that whenever she opened a door, she kept expecting Penny's hand to wrap round her face.

At other times she imagined Penny letting Graham into the house, saw the chef's surprised expression, heard the pleasantries exchanged as they walked down the hall towards the kitchen. Her worst imaginings, though, involved Penny breaking in at night and taking Fay.

As for Will, though he agreed they could only carry on if they were completely honest with each other, Ruth knew that he wasn't telling her the truth about exactly what happened the night Frank disappeared. The idea that Will's waking had shocked the man into falling through a window was ridiculous. Despite conclusive proof that Frank had been at the hospital—a hospital porter, one Kenny James, had seen him talking to his associate, another porter called Alfred Moyles, later found dead—Frank's body remained undiscovered. The glass had indeed broken outwards as if he'd

534

jumped, or been pushed, as DCI Lawrence suggested, but there was no body. Indeed, there was no sign whatsoever that anyone had landed in the snow two storeys below Will's hospital window. Frank had simply disappeared.

It was thanks to Inspector Hart's foresight that Ruth herself was cleared of any suspicion. Before his murder, he'd placed a DVD in his safe containing the CCTV footage of her car parked beside the A23. Upon her insistence, a search had been made and the disc found. This evidence, along with the details of Frank's final hours, the discovery of his connection with the deceased, Alfred Moyles, and his historical connection with their family, ensured that she was cleared of any suspicion concerning Graham Bull's murder. But for her, it was not that simple. Frank's plan was obvious. He'd meant her to run away with Penny, taking Fay with her, a replacement for the child Penny had lost. Then when the authorities found Will and Eric dead, Ruth would have been blamed. Later, no doubt they would have found her dead too and Fay missing, or perhaps Frank would have let Ruth live. Who would have believed anything she said after they found Fay missing? But though she seemed to have regained all she'd lost, especially when she heard that Penny had finally been arrested, with Frank's body still missing, she had no closure. As for her feelings towards Will, his miraculous awakening and the unexplained way Frank had fallen through the window only made her feel he was a stranger to her, a feeling not helped by the changes she saw in him. Something had happened while he was sleeping. There was a calmness about him, a new resolution. She was no longer sure how they fit together. He no longer reached for life with nervous, excited fingers. The court case was approaching and he expected to be found guilty but he seemed to accept this without question.

There was then, in those first few weeks, only one bridge that brought them together. When they spent time with Fay, they were able to forget themselves and often caught a warmth in each other's eyes. It was perhaps this promise that, however slight, caused them both to look forward to seeing Eric again. In reality, though, Eric's presence did little to heal their wounds. After rejecting their offer to pick him up, no doubt knowing the last place they wanted to go was the hospital, Eric was driven to Hove in an ambulance and wheeled down a short ramp by a stocky paramedic wearing Mickey Mouse earmuffs.

The next day Ruth found Eric feeding Fay in the kitchen, Will laughing at something he'd said. Will was pouring coffee and offered her a cup. Ruth couldn't help feeling as if she were being invited to cross a ravine or shake the idea that, if she couldn't, neither of them would come back for her. With time, the impression only intensified. It was not that Will and Eric seemed to prefer each other's company, the three of them were almost always together, it was just that there was something between them so complete, Ruth couldn't bear being around it.

iii.

STILL, IT TOOK RUTH several more days to do the thing her mind kept returning to and only when the washing machine broke down and Will and Eric both offered to take Fay to the laundrette, did she dig out the cassette recorder.

As the tape rewound, reaching further and further into the past, she couldn't help feeling as if she were riding a time machine. She'd imprinted that long black slip with her own voice, dark tales played into Will's sleeping ear but as she sat there, she tried not to think about that. The spool stopped with a thwack. No, instead she was hunting another voice, another tale. She found the button with her thumb, felt a sickness in her gut, exhaled slowly. Pressed play.

She heard a sniff, then an eerie silence so that she became convinced she'd been wrong. Only then did Eric speak, his voice so immediate it was almost too much.

"I want to clear my head. Like, really clear it out . . ." A deep intake of breath and then Eric began once more to tell the story that in many ways had defined her life.

536

"Ruth'd hurt her foot. I told her I'd run up to the Granger place to get help. I remember feeling like it was a proper rescue mission. Real kid's stuff, you know?" Ruth could hear his breath against the microphone. "I had my dog with me, this little Collie pup, Toot. The two of us ran all the way up there. It was a big old house, very rundown. When we got there, the front door was choked up with ivy and stuff, so we had to go round the back. I remember all this old farm gear, harvester blades and pitchforks piled up in rusting heaps, a long, rundown greenhouse with a rusty frame. At the back of the house there was an old pagoda and a brick path bordering a small lawn. I knocked on the back door but no one answered. I tried peering through the window but the sun was too bright. Then when I knocked again, I hit the glass in the door a little too hard and cracked it. I just panicked. I thought I was going to be in a lot of trouble, so I turned and ran.

"But as I went to run past the greenhouse, I heard someone, a girl. She was saying something in French. It was weird. I remember slowing down and trying to listen. The inside of the greenhouse was covered with condensation but when I cupped my hands against the glass, I could make out the figure of a man and what might have been a girl. I don't know why but I decided to slide the door open. I remember just standing there trying to work out what was going on.

"Mr Granger was standing on a wooden walkway between two rows of tomato plants with his shirt open. The girl was sitting on an upside-down plant pot, her neck and shoulders obscured by a spray of leaves, the buttons of her blouse undone. They must have heard the door because they turned to look at me. I remember it being very humid. Putrefying tomatoes, all those hot, furry leaves filling the glass. The girl just sat there, her eyes like grey stones, but Mr Granger started walking towards me. The front of his shirt was completely soaked. When he took hold of my shoulder, his palm felt moist through my t-shirt. He reeked of paint stripper. That's when he said something about me coming to the house before. About the time, he told me, that his wallet went missing.

"He grabbed hold of me and started dragging me round the side of the house. Toot kept barking at him and I shouted for him to go home but it was too late. Mr Granger just scooped him up. I don't know what his intentions were but the moment he saw the broken windowpane, it didn't matter. He started shaking Toot and calling me a thief and a hooligan.

"I tried to stop him but he just pushed me away. That made me angry. I told him I didn't care if I broke it, that what he'd been doing was wrong and that he'd better let Toot go or I'd tell my dad. He just looked at me. He said, 'You're Freddie Fairweather's son, aren't you? Him that's always away? Him that's married to that trollop? Yeah, I know your family, especially that pretty, little sister of yours.' He grabbed the back of my neck. 'Just remember this,' he said. 'I know where you live. You won't be saying anything. But just in case you need proof of how serious I am . . .'" Eric stopped. The next few words were very difficult for him. "I can still see Toot trying to look at me, his head straining on his neck, his big, wet eyes . . . He killed him, Will. Right there in all that sunshine, he wrung his neck like he was wringing out a flannel and then threw him at me. I was so frightened, I couldn't even touch him."

Eric made an odd, choking sound. "I didn't even pick up the body. I just stumbled back round the corner. Only when I reached the greenhouse did I slow down. The girl was standing in the doorway, her collar half-tucked, her buttons done up wrong. She was looking at them but must have realised I was there because just then she looked up. I'll never forget that look. Never. It went beyond that day. It spoke of all the days to come."

Only now, at the end of his tale, did Eric's voice break. "I could have done things differently. I want to be *that* person who made *that* decision. But I'm not, I'm me. And because of that, I've been standing in that doorway ever since." Eric made a sound, something short and soft that quickly died. "Wherever I go, that's where I am."

The next day, Ruth had an appointment with Needlemire but couldn't bring herself to go. Will and Eric had gone out with Fay again and she figured she'd just run herself a bath.

538

An hour later, the doorbell rang and she opened the door to see Needlemire standing there. He was wearing a light denim jacket and dark jeans. With his pale skin and thin, red hair, he looked washed-out. His eyes, though, were as bright as ever. He hung up his coat and they walked down the hall to the kitchen. Ruth put the kettle on and they leaned on separate sides. He watched her, smiling whenever she looked at him but stopping when she looked away.

"Must be difficult," he said as she stirred the drinks.

"What must?" she said.

"Being here."

She offered him a cup. "What can I do?"

"Move?" Needlemire tapped the side of his cup with a fingernail. He asked how Will was.

"Coping," she said. "Admirably."

Needlemire said he'd spoken to Will's physiotherapist, that Will might just make the Guinness Book of Records.

"He's out walking now," Ruth said.

"With Eric?"

She nodded. "Did you go to the funeral?"

Needlemire grimaced. "Lots of policemen in well-pressed uniforms, the grieving ex-widow. Very becoming." He stared at her. "And how are you?"

She sipped her tea. "Managing."

"Are you?"

"Keep's not come back, if that's what you mean."

"But he might?" Needlemire shrugged. "You should talk to someone. What you've been through, have you told Will yet?"

"Some. I think both of us are holding out, you know?" She looked at him. She'd spoken to Will about Keep but hadn't yet mentioned his origins. She didn't know where to begin.

"And Frank?" Needlemire asked.

Of course Will had tried to convince her that the man was gone but nothing and nobody could make her feel safe until she knew. "He was in that room when I left and when I came back he was gone. It's all I know."

"Lawrence showed me the report. Fibres matching Frank's jacket were taken from the window."

"But the jacket hasn't been found. Neither has the body."

"The fibres were aligned in such a way as to almost certainly have been pulled loose as Frank went through the window." Seeing her doubt, Needlemire crossed the kitchen and reached out. His hand hovered beside her arm. "Ruth, those fibres were from Frank's jacket. He went through that window."

"Then where is he?" She held his gaze, then looked down. "Sorry. I don't know what to believe. Thanks for trying to convince me though, it's very noble."

When Needlemire's hand finally settled, it felt warm. "I wasn't trying to be noble—"

He didn't finish. Ruth leaned forwards and kissed him. They stayed that way for a moment, then pulled away. They looked at each other, aware of the sunshine between them.

"I'd better go."

Ruth said nothing.

Needlemire turned, then looked back. "You almost lost everything, Ruth. Don't give it away now it's been returned."

Ruth remembered thinking Frank had taken Fay, that he'd jumped through the window with her. She thought about Eric standing in that doorway. "Wherever I go, there I am," she said.

Edward Needlemire stepped towards her and touched her shoulder. "Then perhaps it's time you moved on."

iv.

———

THAT NIGHT, WHEN RUTH and Will went to bed, they lay apart as they had done every night since coming home, though when she spoke, he heard her well enough.

"I kissed Ed today."

Wind and streetlight made a shadow show of the cherry blossoms.

The next day Will packed his bags. He didn't tell Ruth he was doing so and she only found out when she saw him walking out of the bathroom with his toothbrush. He'd also packed a bag for Fay.

He told her he wasn't leaving her, that he was just going before she left him. "What we were is done but I hope what we will be is yet to come. I know we need to talk and we will," he said. "And after that we'll glue ourselves back together."

She asked where he was going.

"My parents' house. Eric's coming with me. I thought I'd take Fay too. It'll give you time to think. You've been looking after the three of us for long enough."

She looked so slight in the doorway. "Don't go."

"You need me to." He walked forwards, leaned over and kissed her.

"Then take my car. I'll go to Mum's. I can catch the train."

At the front door, with Eric and Fay in the car and Ruth on the step, he said, "We'll get through this."

The hedges along Foxglove Lane were full of young shoots. As they passed, Will glanced at Shelley's old house. The laurels were overgrown. He noticed Eric gazing that way too. Will got out and opened the gate.

The house was very cold. He turned on the heating, put the kettle on and set up Fay's highchair. Over the last few weeks, he'd watched the way she curled her fists and twisted her feet when excited, the way she laughed and the way her laughter quickly turned to tears. Recently she'd begun to smile when he held out his arms.

While Will set up the chair, Eric built a fire in the living room. By the time Will fed Fay, the room was warm.

Later, with Fay in bed and their bellies full, Will offered Eric a nightcap. They were watching some programme about a plane crash, survivors stumbling along a beach.

Eric switched off the television. "Why not?"

That was the only time either of them spoke of what had happened and it was only Eric who did so. He was drinking whisky and it had been a while so he was tipsy.

541

"I may not remember this in the morning," he said. "Which is why I'm saying it now. The way I see it is, if we don't believe in our own goodness, no good can come of anything. Maybe we lost sight of that. Maybe everybody does. But that doesn't mean we won't find it again. Maybe we already have. Reality springs from belief. What we believe in, we make true. If enough people believe in a good world, the world will be good."

Not long after that, Will carried Eric to bed. Strengthened by the booze, his legs were fine but on the landing Eric called him a hero and suddenly they were both laughing and shushing each other and then laughing some more. Will staggered through to the spare room, dropped Eric onto the bed, pulled the duvet from under him.

Afterwards, he pushed Fay's door open and stood in the half-darkness listening to her breathe. On the landing, he noticed his father's door ajar. No one had been upstairs since the night they left. Will was the last person to have gone in there.

He flicked on the light, looked around. His mother's samples were still against the wall, the kite on the table. Crossing the room, he turned on the computer and started reading his father's story again. He thought about what Eric had said. It was true, he'd lost sight of himself, he'd stopped believing. All his life he'd told everyone he was a writer, that one day he would write something great. But in truth he no longer believed it.

He spent the next three weeks writing and editing, letting up only to see to Fay or to share ideas with Eric. It felt as if he were pecking away at a cocoon. When, at last, he wrote the final sentence, he pressed save and switched off the computer, to be presented with a ghostlike face in the screen. He was aware of the kind of emptiness that used to fill him with fear. Now it filled him with peace.

A few days later he was accosted in the hallway by a furry ball that collided with his feet and began to needle at his trouser cuff. The creature plopped onto its backside and began panting so hard, its entire body shook. Ruth was in the kitchen, standing with her back against the side, holding a cup of tea.

"I got Eric a dog."

"So soon?"

"He hasn't had one for a while."

"No, I mean, you, here."

"I've been at Mum's but there's only so much Mum I can take." Her smile was slight but there was a new strength in her eyes. "That's my way of saying I missed you." She looked at the puppy. "The dog's for Eric. I've got something else for you."

"A cup of tea?"

"For now." She kissed him over Fay's head.

They spent the morning weeding the garden while Eric, Fay and the dog, immediately christened Nanook by a delighted Eric, played together on the grass.

Later, Will and Ruth went to look at the sycamore tree. The field at the back of the house was overgrown but they beat back the nettles with sticks. The gap in the wall was wider, the stones crumbling, the clearing beyond covered in low-growing vegetation, grasses, dandelion, dock leaves. The tree itself was bare.

They stopped just inside the wall, their arms around each other's waists. It was there he talked about Shelley again, their first meeting, their subsequent summer, the time his father caught them in the tree.

"Little secrets grow up with us." He looked down at his feet.

Ruth told him she'd listened to the tape. "The girl, the one Eric left behind . . ."

"Yes, one and the same. I've only recently worked it out myself. Something Shelley said about a greenhouse."

Ruth shut her eyes. Finally she said how sorry she was about the abortion. The tree dipped its branches before a wind that ran on through the undergrowth. "Where's Shelley now?"

He shrugged. "I don't know. It's funny though. I realised recently, if it weren't for her, I probably wouldn't be who I am. The day my father caught the two of us up in that tree, he sent me to bed early. He was always trying to get me to read but I was stubborn, you know? But that day, with nothing better to do, I started reading the book he'd placed by my bed and after that there was no stopping me. I used to read some and then put the book back in exactly the same position Dad left it. I thought he was fooled but he told me the night before he died that he'd always known. Why else would he keep replacing them?"

Ruth smiled. "You've always been fond of secrets."

"Secrets are fine, I guess, as long as they're the sort you can share with someone." He rubbed her side. "I've others I'd like to show you."

Back at the house, the garden yielded radishes and spring onions, which Will cleaned in the sink while Ruth boiled eggs and opened a tin of ham.

Afterwards, Eric built a fire and then offered to play with Fay on the rug. He knew that Will had something he wanted to show Ruth. When Will asked her, she wrapped her arm round her brother, who was ruffling Nanook's neck.

"He looks nothing like Toot, you know?"

Ruth kissed his temple. "Exactly."

In the study, Will switched on his father's lamp and shut the door.

"I told you I thought I was looking for my parents. Well, I found them." She allowed him to guide her into his father's chair. On the desk was a pile of paper. "Dad was writing a novel. He asked me to finish it."

"When?"

"It doesn't matter. I've been searching for myself in so many places when all the time I was here."

Ruth looked amused. "In this house?"

"No. Well, yes, maybe. I've come home, to my parents' house, to you, to Fay, to Eric." He looked at the flag on the wall. "I've been working on Dad's book for the last few weeks. I've changed some, added a lot. I'd like you to read it." He smiled. "Maybe afterwards we can fill in the gaps."

Ruth settled her eyes on the first sentence. "Cold water," she read, before flashing him a look, "a ceaseless roaring, a vast, eddying flow that dragged at his arms . . ."

But soon she was reading in silence and Will was sitting with his eyes closed and his head against the wall.

Thanks

To my first readers, Marcus Wroot and Luke Maddocks, your patience was barely dented, your advice invaluable.

Also to the literary dons at Granville School, Deborah Hollingworth, Sarah Rees, Sara Delaney, Katie Lewis and Andrew Hill. I have the fondest memories of you guys.

And of course to my mother, Heather Arthur, who has faithfully read everything I've ever written and to my mother-in-law, Patricia Major, who has done the same.

A special thank you to my brother, Paul Whitlam. My first rave review. Without you I might have given up years ago. Cheers, bro!

And finally to my latest reader, Kyesi Magalhães. The legend who pushed me over the line.

About the Author

Luke Bramley lives in Hastings in the UK and enjoys walks through Alexandra Park and drinks in the Old Town. He is the author of several works of fiction, *Other Worlds than These* being his first and in some ways the dearest to his heart as he has been working on it for quite some years!

His second novel, *Filthy Little Animals*, is much more pared back. One night, four characters, total darkness. Carl Farrow is having a quiet night in with his son when two teenage girls trick their way into his house and subject the pair to a night of terror. Trapped on separate floors, the Farrows are forced to pit their wits against the girls. But as the games of cat and canary escalate, it is Carl's nine-year-old son, Jason, who realises that only those with the sharpest claws will win.

To be released soon.

Finally, Luke's latest novel is called *Lights Out at the Electric*. Longlisted for both the Yeovil and the Bridport prizes, this novel focusses on a group of strangers who find themselves trapped in a cinema. No one knows why they are there or who locked them up. It is only a matter of time before they start to suspect each other.

To be released next year.

Printed in Great Britain
by Amazon